Homeplaces

Homeplaces

Stories of the South
by Women Writers

edited by Mary Ellis Gibson

University of South Carolina Press

Copyright © 1991 University of South Carolina

Published in Columbia, South Carolina, by the University of
South Carolina Press

"224" watercolor by Kip Gerard
Portfolio Gallery
Columbia, South Carolina

jacket and text by Rebecca Blakeney

Manufactured in the United States of America

Library of Congress Cataloging-in-Publication Data

Homeplaces : stories of the South by women writers / edited by Mary
Ellis Gibson.
    p. cm.
  Includes bibliographical references.
  ISBN 0–87249–784–4 (hard-cover : acid-free). — ISBN 0–87249–785–2
(paper : acid-free)
    1. Short stories, American—Southern States.   2. Short stories,
American—Women authors.   3. Women—Southern States—Fiction.
4. Southern States—Fiction.   5. Home—Fiction.   I. Gibson, Mary
Ellis, 1952–   .   II. Title: Homeplaces.
PS551.H65   1991
813'.01089287—dc20   91–4678

Contents

Contents

Acknowledgments

"First Dark," copyright © 1959 by Elizabeth Spencer. From *The Stories of Elizabeth Spencer* by Elizabeth Spencer. Used by permission of Doubleday, a division of Bantam Doubleday Dell Publishing Group, Inc.

"The Business Venture", Copyright © 1987 by Elizabeth Spencer, from *Jack of Diamonds* by Elizabeth Spencer. Reprinted by permission of the publisher, Dutton, an imprint of New American Library, a division of Penguin Books USA Inc.

"The Long Afternoon" from *The Wind Shifting West* by Shirley Ann Grau. First published by Alfred A. Knopf, Inc. Copyright © 1973 by Shirley Ann Grau. Reprinted by permission of Brandt and Brandt Literary Agents, Inc.

"One Summer" from *The Black Prince and Other Stories* by Shirley Ann Grau. First published by Alfred A. Knopf, Inc. Copyright, 1955 by Shirley Ann Grau. Copyright © renewed 1983 by Shirley Ann Grau. Reprinted by permission of Brandt and Brandt Literary Agents, Inc.

"Flight" from *Nine Women* by Shirley Ann Grau. Copyright © 1985 by Shirley Ann Grau. Reprinted by permission of Alfred A. Knopf, Inc.

"A Tender Man" from *The Sea Birds Are Still Alive* by Toni Cade Bambara. Copyright © 1974, 1976, 1977 by Toni Cade Bambara. Reprinted by permission of Random House Inc.

"Madame Bai and the Taking of Stone Mountain" (pp. 59–69) from *Confirmation: An Anthology of African American Women* by Amiri Baraka Ed. and author Toni Bambara. Copyright © 1983. By permission of William Morrow and Co., Inc.

"The Welcome Table" from *In Love & Trouble: Stories of Black Women*, copyright © 1970, 1967 by Alice Walker, reprinted by permission of Harcourt Brace Jovanovich, Inc.

Introduction

At the end of Elizabeth Spencer's early story "First Dark," a woman and a man walk away from an old house and a small southern town. The narrative voice has warned us already that the woman is escaping a trap. The problem with towns and houses like this, the narrator tells us, is that they make people into "bemused custodians" of the grave. In the end the woman gets her coat, walks out the door, puts the key under the mat, and doesn't look back. "First Dark," standing at the beginning of this collection, can be read as a farewell and a greeting in southern fiction. In the more than thirty years since it was first published in 1959 both southern writers and the characters they have created have walked away from homeplaces or have found their homes changed almost beyond recognition.

This collection focuses on homeplaces in all their many meanings, and it represents a variety of ways women writers have thought about home, estrangement from home, and the relationships between individuals and family traditions in the last twenty years. As the south has been redefined by urbanization, suburbanization, changes in women's roles, integration and the continuing struggle against racism, southern writers have taken the measure of these changes.

Women writers in particular, though by no means exclusively, have often approached these changes by exploring the illusory boundary between the public and the private. These stories show how redefinitions of home are caught in the larger web of relations between genders, races, classes, or regions. Many protagonists in these stories are women who have found their own places in home and culture shifting. The central characters in Opal Moore's "A Happy Story" and in Shirley Ann Grau's "Flight" live in a world where the anticipated life is not the one they actually experience. The patterns of the artist's storytelling and the stories people tell themselves to live by are always in flight.

The changing nature of home is reflected in these stories not only in the lives of women who are surprised by the new designs of their culture but also, and still more, in the lives of girls and young women who must try to find ways to grow up when the definitions of home are changing all around them. In Molly Best Tinsley's story "Zoe" a teenage girl attempts to find some stable point in the rootless world of the upscale condominium complex where her mother entertains a series of lovers. In the selection from Ntozake Shange's *Sassafrass, Cypress & Indigo* family solidarity is not in question, but the dangers of growing up black and female create fear that forges a bond between Indigo and her mother.

Of course the redefinitions of home and transformations of place in the South affect men as well as women. We can measure these changes as they affect men by contrasting Shirley Ann Grau's early story "One Summer" with Mary Hood's recent treatments of fathers and sons in her stories "Manly Conclusions" and "A Man Among Men." Grau's protagonist MacDonald Addams comes to terms with his grandfather's death and in the process creates for himself a picture of his own life taking the same course his father's has: he too will become a small-town doctor, marry, settle down into a life that he both mildly resents and ultimately accepts. In Hood's "Manly Conclusions" the definition of manhood is similarly passed from father to son, but now the very place called home is changing. Dennis Petty's house is encroached upon by the summer and weekend houses of rich people from Atlanta. All rural land is posted. Territorial disputes become violent. And the whole change—the suburbanization even of the country—is caught up in the larger legacy of war over territory. Dennis's father, a Vietnam vet, in spite of himself passes on to his son a legacy of violence, anger, and the struggle to control it.

What makes these stories so complex a representation of home is that they show home as the scene of mutual affection and protection against violence and as the place where the violence of racism or sexism is most intimately and immediately felt. This treatment of violence carries on the traditions of William Faulkner, Flannery O'Connor, and Margaret Walker; like O'Connor in particular, several of these writers show us how even global events play out in local communities. As in O'Connor's "The Displaced Person," an intense study of fascism, oppression, and moral responsibility, in Toni Cade Bambara's "Madame Bai and the Taking of Stone Mountain" and in Hood's stories the effects of distant conflict are brought immediately home and mirrored in local turmoil. Bambara's story, set during the time of the serial murders of black children in Atlanta, shows us the overtly violent side of a culture which, in the shadows of a Confederate monument carved in granite and its own racist ideology, is rapidly becoming cosmopolitan thanks to foreign trade and foreign war.

At the same time that they carry on this investigation of southern violence, community, and morality, these stories allow us to see the distance between current writers and previous generations of writers of southern fiction. No character in these stories, and virtually none in the many stories I read in putting this anthology together, acts from motives I would characterize as nostalgic: no one invokes memories of the Old South to justify their actions or to explain themselves to themselves. Motives for cruelty come from feelings of rage, or displacement, or the cultural reflexes of an unexamined and often unacknowledged racism. The knitting together of community comes from the recognition that community cannot now be made from geographic stability but must be made from the human capacity to remember and to regenerate significant ties of affection. Thus Sarah in Alice Walker's "A Sudden Trip Home in the Spring" and Cliffie in Hood's "Finding the Chain" return home, briefly, and leave, probably for good. Both have no continuing home to which they can return. Each takes with her the memories she values, and each is enabled to let go of the rest.

In the concern with home, with displacement and death, with the necessity of creating community, these stories have significant thematic connections. Many of them also examine the new dimensions of American race relations in the years following the Civil Rights movement.

As I chose these stories I felt that the changing sense of place in the American South could best be represented by including an equal number of African-American and white writers. I agree with Reynolds Price's observation that if any single characteristic distinguishes southern literature from the literature of other regions, it is the importance of race, in the fabric of southern culture and in its literary history. The suggestions for further reading and classroom use at the end of this anthology point out that African-American women writers outside the South are increasingly drawn to novels with southern settings or to novels exploring the history of slavery. Writers such as Toni Morrison, Gloria Naylor, Sherley Ann Williams, and Paule Marshall have in their recent novels written powerfully about slavery and southern culture in ways that will, I believe, have a lasting impact on the literary self-understanding of southerners. The stories I have collected here, though contemporary in their settings, have similarly the effect of redefining the meanings of "southern" and of home.

Most of the stories here that directly examine racism are by African-American writers; of the white writers in this anthology only Elizabeth Spencer is concerned directly with questions of race, though racial issues form important threads in the background of the stories by Shirely Ann Grau (much of Grau's other work is more explicitly about race). The settings of Molly Best Tinsley's stories and of those by Mary Hood involve, instead of a focus on racism, an examination of nationalism and of regional change.

In Spencer's "The Business Venture" we see the only direct examination by a white writer in this anthology of race in southern middle-class life since the Civil Rights movement. Spencer's "The Business Venture" presents us with a very uncomfortable picture of small-town southern life among relatively privileged young whites. She sees acutely the pressures of group solidarity among teenagers and young adults and subtly captures that mixture of enmity and attachment among people united by race, class, and old ties in a small town. These are the people who choose to stay home, though even they move to the new housing developments. They operate on the racist principles they have inherited, the principles assumed in segregated academies and less than elegant—but socially significant—small-town private clubs. When one of their number begins a business and perhaps a love affair with a black man, the outcome is not pretty. The business venture turns out to have dangerous consequences.

Several of the stories here by Opal Moore, Ntozake Shange, Alice Walker, and Toni Cade Bambara treat the consequences of racism still more fully than Spencer's powerful story does, though, as I have suggested, all of these writers are also concerned with other issues and themes. Alice Walker's "The Welcome Table" and Opal Moore's "A Pilgrim Notebook" make an especially interesting pair. The protagonist in Moore's story is dogged by the possibility of violence, by white society's expectation that as a black man he is himself violent. Ben's success in the corporate world makes possible both an affluent life and new sorts of discrimination to accompany older forms of fear. On a highway in the Middle West he feels suddenly surrounded by hostility, and it is an experience which makes geography irrelevant. Moore implies that the geography of racism is at once universal and has its own particular history: "Even safe inside his car, safe inside his era, he'd felt as if he were running—only steps ahead of some ancestor African—disoriented, afraid, rough feet clouded in red dust, running in circles. . . . He'd sworn that he would never return to Mississippi. But in the end, it didn't matter. The world was Mississippi."

Like Spencer's "The Business Venture," Alice Walker's "The Welcome Table" is a powerful presentation of the delusions and hypocrisy of racism; in this story the very South that haunts Moore's story comes to life and the defense of the group occurs at the expense of the excluded. In "The Welcome Table," as in "The Business Venture," the surface of white social convention would appear to be unruffled. Spencer's story leaves us at this point wondering about the futures of the business partners and their supposed friends, but Walker allows a triumph in death for the victim of racism. The old woman in Walker's story unconsciously tests white Christianity and finds it wanting, and it is she, not those who reject her, who goes on to her own spiritual reward.

Whether or not they are writing explicitly about relations between African-Americans and American whites, all the writers represented in this anthology find themselves attracted to stories of cultural clash, stories of the way otherness is constructed and confronted. Molly Best Tinsley's "Mother Tongue" is just such a story of familial and cultural estrangement which becomes, finally, self-estrangement.

Despite the changes and dislocations of home in the stories collected here, these stories also testify to the great variety that now characterizes southern culture and to the delight of exploring that variety. From Shange's Texas women's rodeo to the conclusion of Hood's "Finding the Chain," these stories do present their protagonists' joy in living. And the writers exhibit their own senses of the absurd and the ironic, their various delight in language and in art. Grau's "Flight," Shange's "Ridin' the Moon in Texas," and Moore's "A Pilgrim Notebook" achieve power in their daring forms and styles. Moore and Grau take us deeply inside the consciousness of characters in extreme situations. Shange's language itself, the particular texture and the energy of the speaking voice, is her principal source of power. At the very beginning of "Ridin' the Moon in Texas," which is excerpted from a series of writings to accompany images, Shange creates an individual language: "Houston Rodeo & Livestock Show ain't never seen the same since we come riding in from Arcola. All colored and correct. . . . and I'll say one thing. That flock of niggahs on them gorgeous horses and them wagons, now that was something to look at! Must be why ain't none of us forget it. The trailride and all. And the rodeos. The black ones, of course, white folks don't quite have the hang of it. I mean, how you sposed to look, your image, on your horse. It takes a colored point of view." Elizabeth Spencer achieves a different power, capturing the speech and thoughts of a very different character in "The Business Venture," while Mary Hood relies on a central carefully crafted symbol to bring home the point of her story.

The stories included in this volume, then, were chosen for this power of language and of craft and for their astuteness about place and cultural change in the contemporary South. In order to emphasize the historical coherence of this group of stories, I have arranged the writers chronologically in the order of their birth. I include early stories by Shirley Ann Grau and Elizabeth Spencer to reflect the range of their writings and the scope of the changes in Southern place, family, and culture that their works measure. Although no collection of only eight writers can fully represent the variety of fine writing now being produced by southern women writers and by women writers outside the South who treat southern history and culture, this collection does provide an introduction to the work of these writers; by selecting two or three stories by each, I have tried to represent something of the depth and variety of their work and to indicate the changing concerns of recent southern fiction.

While this anthology does focus on the writing of southern women and on writing about the South, gathering stories into such a collection necessarily raises the unanswerable question of what is southern. At this point, anthologists customarily insert their disclaimers, defining "southern" tautologically to encompass whatever they wish to include. Any definition of southernness, my own included, is in some respects arbitrary. Of the writers here, Elizabeth Spencer could be considered both an important force in southern fiction and one of the most widely respected of southern writers, yet she lived in Europe and in Canada for many years and many of her fine stories are set in Canada. Toni Cade Bambara, who lived in Georgia for eighteen years, was born and reared in the northeast and recently moved to Philadelphia. Opal Moore has lived in Virginia for a number of years, but most of her published work is set in the Middle West, and she is now working on a group of stories about displacement and dislocation which is set in Las Vegas. Molly Best Tinsley has lived most of her adult life in the area around Washington, D.C., and she teaches at the Naval Academy; whether this qualifies as "southern" is an interesting question. Yet Tinsley's stories are particularly appropriate for this volume because they so carefully examine cultural displacement and the relatively homogeneous anonymity of contemporary suburban life. In sum, these writers and their stories can tell us about our own lives in the South an in regions beyond, for each writer is attuned to the ways place and community and cultural change are connected.

When I began thinking about this anthology and a title to encompass these themes, I was drawn to the southern expression "homeplace." Echoing in my memory was the voice of my mother during most of my childhood speaking of going "down home." And those trips themselves provoked many stories about so-and-so's "homeplace"— always stories in the past tense, reflecting on the distance the speaker had come from home or the destruction of the world as she or he had known it. As anyone who rides through the rural South can see, homeplace is now, often enough, a bare chimney in a field or, more likely, a weathered farmhouse with a house trailer or a brick ranch on the highway side of the yard. Outside many southern cities and towns homeplaces grand enough to be saved may be seen surrounded by subdivisions, their old trees reminding us by their age of the farm that once was there. Less grand homeplaces have disappeared so completely that the landscape itself, reshaped by graders, pavement, or landscaping, may be unrecognizable; the former inhabitants are elsewhere— driving cars and eating foods with names unheard of in 1960. These transformations of home and its meanings are a new source for southern fiction, and the eight writers I have included here have explored old and new ways of imagining what a homeplace might be. Their writing can tell us much about the ways work, places, and families create one another in the contemporary South.

Mary Ellis Gibson
University of North Carolina at Greensboro

Homeplaces

Elizabeth Spencer

First Dark

When Tom Beavers started coming back to Richton, Mississippi, on weekends, after the war was over, everybody in town was surprised and pleased. They had never noticed him much before he paid them this compliment; now they could not say enough nice things. There was not much left in Richton for him to call family—just his aunt who had raised him, Miss Rita Beavers, old as God, ugly as sin, deaf as a post. So he must be fond of the town, they reasoned; certainly it was a pretty old place. Far too many young men had left it and never come back at all.

He would drive in every Friday night from Jackson, where he worked. All weekend, his Ford, dusty of flank, like a hard-ridden horse, would sit parked down the hill near Miss Rita's old wire front gate, which sagged from the top hinge and had worn a span in the ground. On Saturday morning, he would head for the drugstore, then the post office; then he would be observed walking here and there around the streets under the shade trees. It was as though he were looking for something.

He wore steel taps on his heels, and in the still the click of them on the sidewalks would sound across the big front lawns and all the way up to the porches of the houses, where two ladies might be sitting behind a row of ferns. They would identify him to one another, murmuring in their fine little voices, and say it was just too bad there was nothing here for young people. It was just a shame they didn't have one or two more old houses, here, for a Pilgrimage—look how Natchez had waked up.

One Saturday morning in early October, Tom Beavers sat at the counter in the drugstore and reminded Totsie Poteet, the drugstore clerk, of a ghost story. Did he remember the strange old man who used to appear to people who were coming into Richton along the Jackson road at twilight—what they called "first dark"?

"Sure I remember," said Totsie. "Old Cud'n Jimmy Wiltshire used to tell us about him every time we went 'possum hunting. I could see him plain as I can see you, the way he used to tell it. Tall, with a top hat on, yeah, and waiting in the weeds alongside the road ditch, so'n you couldn't tell if he was standing down in the ditch or not. It would look like he just grew up out of the weeds. Then he'd signal to you."

"Them that stopped never saw anybody," said Tom Beavers, stirring his coffee. "There were lots of folks besides Mr. Jimmy that saw him."

"There was, let me see . . ." Totsie enumerated others—some men, some women, some known to drink, others who never touched a drop. There was no way to explain it. "There was that story the road gang told. Do you remember, or were you off at school? It was while they were straightening the road out to the highway—taking the curves out and building a new bridge. Anyway, they said that one night at quitting time, along in the winter and just about dark, this old guy signaled to some of 'em. They said they went over and he asked them to move a bulldozer they had left across the road, because he had a wagon back behind on a little dirt road, with a sick nigger girl in it. Had to get to the doctor and this was the only way. They claimed they knew didn't nobody live back there on that little old road, but niggers can come from anywhere. So they moved the bulldozer and cleared back a whole lot of other stuff, and waited and waited. Not only didn't no wagon ever come, but the man that had stopped them, he was gone, too. They was right shook up over it. You never heard that one?"

"No, I never did." Tom Beavers said this with his eyes looking up over his coffee cup, as though he sat behind a hand of cards. His lashes and brows were heavier than was ordinary, and worked as a veil might, to keep you away from knowing exactly what he was thinking.

"They said he was tall and had a hat on." The screen door flapped to announce a customer, but Totsie kept on talking. "But whether he was a white man or a real light-colored nigger they couldn't say. Some said one and some said another. I figured they'd been pulling on the jug a little earlier than usual. You know why? I never heard of *our* ghost *saying* nothing. Did you, Tom?"

He moved away on the last words, the way a clerk will, talking back over his shoulder and ahead of him to his new customer at the same time, as though he had two voices and two heads. "And what'll it be today, Miss Frances?"

The young woman standing at the counter had a prescription already out of her bag. She stood with it poised between her fingers, but her attention was drawn toward Tom Beavers, his coffee cup, and the conversation she had interrupted. She was a girl whom no ordinary description would fit. One would have to know first of all who she was: Frances Harvey. After that, it was all right for her to be a little odd-looking, with her reddish hair that curled back from her brow, her light eyes, and her high, pale temples. This is not the material for being pretty, but in Frances Harvey it was what could sometimes be beauty. Her family home was laden with history that nobody but the Harveys could remember. It would have been on a Pilgrimage if Richton had had one. Frances still lived in it, looking after an invalid mother.

"What were you-all talking about?" she wanted to know.

"About that ghost they used to tell about," said Totsie, holding out his hand for the prescription. "The one people used to see just outside of town, on the Jackson road."

"But why?" she demanded. "Why were you talking about him?"

"Tom, here—" the clerk began, but Tom Beavers interrupted him.

"I was asking because I was curious," he said. He had been studying her from the corner of his eye. Her face was beginning to show the wear of her mother's long illness, but that couldn't be called change. Changing was something she didn't seem to have done, her own style being the only one natural to her.

"I was asking," he went on, "because I saw him." He turned away from her somewhat too direct gaze and said to Totsie Poteet, whose mouth had fallen open, "It was where the new road runs close to the old road, and as far as I could tell he was right on the part of the old road where people always used to see him."

"But when?" Frances Harvey demanded. "Last night," he told her. "Just around first dark. Driving home."

A wealth of quick feeling came up in her face. "So did I! Driving home from Jackson! I saw him, too!"

For some people, a liking for the same phonograph record or for Mayan archaeology is enough of an excuse to get together. Possibly, seeing the same ghost was no more than that. Anyway, a week later, on Saturday at first dark, Frances Harvey and Tom Beavers were sitting together in a car parked just off the highway, near the spot where they agreed the ghost had appeared. The season was that long, peculiar one between summer and fall, and there were so many crickets and tree frogs going full tilt in their periphery that their voices could hardly be distinguished from the background noises, though they both would have heard a single footfall in the grass. An edge of autumn was in the air at night, and Frances had put on a tweed jacket at the last minute, so the smell of moth balls was in the car, brisk and most unghostlike.

But Tom Beavers was not going to forget the value of the ghost, whether it put in an appearance or not. His questions led Frances into reminiscence.

"No, I never saw him before the other night," she admitted. "The Negroes used to talk in the kitchen, and Regina and I—you know my sister Regina—would sit there listening, scared to go and scared to stay. Then finally going to bed upstairs was no relief, either, because sometimes Aunt Henrietta was visiting us, and *she'd* seen it. Or if she wasn't visiting us, the front room next to us, where she stayed, would be empty, which was worse. There was no way to lock ourselves in, and besides, what was there to lock out? We'd lie all night like two sticks in bed, and shiver. Papa finally had to take a hand. He called us in and sat us down and said that the whole thing was easy to explain—it was all automobiles. What their headlights did with the dust and shadows out on the Jackson road. 'Oh, but Sammie and Jerry!' we said, with great big eyes, sitting side by side on the sofa, with our tennis shoes flat on the floor."

"Who were Sammie and Jerry?" asked Tom Beavers.

"Sammie was our cook. Jerry was her son, or husband, or something. Anyway, they certainly didn't have cars. Papa called them in. They were standing side by side by the bookcase, and Regina and I were on the sofa—four pairs of big eyes, and Papa pointing his finger. Papa said, 'Now you made up these stories about ghosts, didn't you?' 'Yes, sir,' said Sammie. 'We made them up.' 'Yes, sir,' said Jerry. 'We sho did.' 'Well, then, you can just stop it,' Papa said. 'See how peaked these children look?' Sammie and Jerry were terribly polite to us for a week, and we got in the car and rode up and down the Jackson road at first dark to see if the headlights really did it. But we never saw anything. We didn't tell Papa, but headlights had nothing whatever to do with it."

"You had your own *car* then?" He couldn't believe it.

"Oh no!" She was emphatic. "We were too young for that. Too young to drive, really, but we did anyway." She leaned over to let him give her cigarette a light, and saw his hand tremble. Was he afraid of the ghost or of her? She would have to stay away from talking family.

Frances remembered Tommy Beavers from her childhood—a small boy going home from school down a muddy side road alone, walking right down the middle of the road. His old aunt's house was at the bottom of a hill. It was damp there, and the yard was always muddy, with big fat chicken tracks all over it, like Egyptian writing. How did Frances know? She could not remember going there, ever. Miss Rita Beavers was said to order cold ham, mustard, bread, and condensed milk from the grocery store. "I doubt if that child ever has anything hot," Frances's mother had said once. He was always neatly dressed in the same knee pants, high socks, and checked shirt, and sat several rows ahead of Frances in study hall, right in the middle of his seat. He was three grades behind her; in those days, that much younger seemed very young indeed. What had happened to his parents? There was some story, but it was not terribly interesting, and, his people being of no importance, she had forgotten.

"I think it's past time for our ghost," she said. "He's never out so late at night."

"He gets hungry, like me," said Tom Beavers. "Are you hungry, Frances?"

They agreed on a highway restaurant where an orchestra played on weekends. Everyone went there now.

From the moment they drew up on the graveled entrance, cheerful lights and a blare of music chased the spooks from their heads. Tom Beavers ordered well and danced well, as it turned out. Wasn't there something she had heard about his being "smart"? By "smart," Southerners mean intellectual, and they say it in an almost condescending way, smart being what you are when you can't be anything else, but it is better, at least, than being nothing. Frances Harvey had been away enough not to look at things from a completely Southern point of view, and she was encouraged to discover that she and Tom had other things in common besides a ghost, though all stemming, perhaps, from the imagination it took to see one.

They agreed about books and favorite movies and longing to see more plays. She sighed that life in Richton was so confining, but he assured her that Jackson could be just as bad; *it* was getting to be like any Middle Western city, he said, while Richton at least had a sense of the past. This was the main reason, he went on, gaining confidence in the jumble of commonplace noises—dishes, music, and a couple of drinkers chattering behind them—that he had started coming back to Richton so often. He wanted to keep a connection with the past. He lived in a modern apartment, worked in a soundproof office—he could be in any city. But Richton was where he had been born and raised, and nothing could be more old-fashioned. Too many people seemed to have their lives cut in two. He was earnest in desiring that this should not happen to him.

"You'd better be careful," Frances said lightly. Her mood did not incline her to profound conversation. "There's more than one ghost in Richton. You may turn into one yourself, like the rest of us."

"It's the last thing I'd think of you," he was quick to assure her.

Had Tommy Beavers really said such a thing, in such a natural, charming way? Was Frances Harvey really so pleased? Not only was she pleased but, feeling warmly alive amid the music and small lights, she agreed with him. She could not have agreed with him more.

"I hear that Thomas Beavers has gotten to be a very attractive man," Frances Harvey's mother said unexpectedly one afternoon.

Frances had been reading aloud—Jane Austen this time. Theirs was one house where the leather-bound sets were actually read. In Jane Austen, men and women seesawed back and forth for two or three hundred pages until they struck a point of balance; then they got married. She had just put aside the book, at the end of a chapter, and risen to lower the shade against the slant of the afternoon sun. "Or so Cud'n Jennie and Mrs. Giles Antley and Miss Fannie Stapleton have been coming and telling you," she said.

"People talk, of course, but the consensus is favorable," Mrs. Harvey said. "Wonders never cease; his mother ran away with a brush salesman. But nobody can make out what he's up to, coming back to Richton."

"Does he have to be 'up to' anything?" Frances asked.

"Men are always up to something," said the old lady at once. She added, more slowly, "In Thomas's case, maybe it isn't anything it oughtn't to be. They say he reads a lot. He may just have taken up with some sort of idea."

Frances stole a long glance at her mother's face on the pillow. Age and illness had reduced the image of Mrs. Harvey to a kind of caricature, centered on a mouth that Frances could not help comparing to that of a fish. There was a tension around its rim, as though it were outlined in bone, and the underlip even stuck out a little. The mouth ate, it took medicine, it asked for things, it gasped when breath was short, it commented. But when it commented, it ceased to be just a mouth and became part of Mrs. Harvey, that witty tyrant with the infallible memory for the right detail, who was at her terrible best about men.

"And what could he be thinking of?" she was wont to inquire when some man had acted foolishly. No one could ever defend accurately the man in question, and the only conclusion was Mrs. Harvey's; namely, that he wasn't thinking, if, indeed, he could. Although she had never been a belle, never a flirt, her popularity with men was always formidable. She would be observed talking marathons with one in a corner, and could you ever be sure, when they both burst into laughter, that they had not just exchanged the most shocking stories? "Of course, *he*—" she would begin later, back with the family, and the masculinity that had just been encouraged to strut and preen a little was quickly shown up as idiotic. Perhaps Mrs. Harvey hoped by this method to train her daughters away from a lot of sentimental nonsense that was their birthright as pretty Southern girls in a house with a lawn that moonlight fell on and that was often lit also by Japanese lanterns hung for parties. "Oh, he's not like that, Mama!" the little girls would cry. They were already alert for heroes who would ride up and cart them off. "Well, then, you watch," she would say. Sure enough, if you watched, she would be right.

Mrs. Harvey's younger daughter, Regina, was a credit to her mother's long campaign; she married well. The old lady, however, never tired of pointing out behind her son-in-law's back that his fondness for money was ill-concealed, that he had the longest feet she'd ever seen, and that he sometimes made grammatical errors.

Her elder daughter, Frances, on a trip to Europe, fell in love, alas! The gentleman was of French extraction but Swiss citizenship, and Frances did not marry him, because he was already married—that much filtered back to Richton. In response to a cable, she had returned home one hot July in time to witness her father's wasted face and last weeks of life. That same September, the war began. When peace came, Richton wanted to know if Frances Harvey would go back to Europe. Certain subtly complicated European matters, little understood in Richton, seemed to be obstructing Romance; one of them was probably named Money. Meanwhile, Frances's mother took to bed, in what was generally known to be her last illness.

So no one crossed the ocean, but eventually Tom Beavers came up to Mrs. Harvey's room one afternoon, to tea.

Though almost all her other faculties were seriously impaired, in ear and tongue Mrs. Harvey was as sound as a young beagle, and she could still weave a more interesting conversation than most people who go about every day and look at the world. She was of the old school of Southern lady talkers; she vexed you with no ideas, she tried to protect you from even a moment of silence. In the old days, when a bright company filled the downstairs rooms, she could keep the ball rolling amongst a crowd. Everyone—all the men especially—got their word in, but the flow of things came back to her. If one of those twenty-minutes-to-or-after silences fell—and even with her they did occur—people would turn and look at her daughter Frances. "And what do you think?" some kind-eyed gentleman would ask. Frances did not credit that she had the sort of face people would turn to, and so did not know how to take advantage of it. What did she think? Well, to answer that honestly took a moment of reflection—a fatal moment, it always turned out. Her mother would be up instructing the maid, offering someone an ashtray or another goody, or remarking outright, "Frances is so timid. She never says a word."

Tom Beavers stayed not only past teatime that day but for a drink as well. Mrs. Harvey was induced to take a glass of sherry, and now her bed became her enormous throne. Her keenest suffering as an invalid was occasioned by the absence of men. "What is a house without a man in it?" she would often cry. From her eagerness to be charming to Frances's guest that afternoon, it seemed that she would have married Tom Beavers herself if he had asked her. The amber liquid set in her small four-sided glass glowed like a jewel, and her diamond flashed; she had put on her best ring for the company. What a pity no longer to show her ankle, that delicious bone, so remarkably slender for so ample a frame.

Since the time had flown so, they all agreed enthusiastically that Tom should wait downstairs while Frances got ready to go out to dinner with him. He was hardly past the stair landing before the old lady was seized by such a fit of coughing that she could hardly speak. "It's been— it's been too much—too *much* for me!" she gasped out.

But after Frances had found the proper sedative for her, she was calmed, and insisted on having her say.

"Thomas Beavers has a good job with an insurance company in Jackson," she informed her daughter, as though Frances were incapable of finding out anything for herself. "He makes a good appearance. He is the kind of man"—she paused—"who would value a wife of good family." She stopped, panting for breath. It was this complimenting a man behind his back that was too much for her—as much out of character, and hence as much of a strain, as if she had got out of bed and tried to tap-dance.

"Heavens, Mama," Frances said, and almost giggled.

At this, the old lady, thinking the girl had made light of her suitor, half screamed at her, "Don't be so critical, Frances! You can't be so critical of men!" and fell into an even more terrible spasm of coughing. Frances had to lift her from the pillow and hold her straight until the fit passed and her breath returned. Then Mrs. Harvey's old, dry, crooked, ineradicably feminine hand was laid on her daughter's arm, and when she spoke again she shook the arm to emphasize her words.

"When your father knew he didn't have long to live," she whispered, "we discussed whether to send for you or not. You know you were his favorite, Frances. 'Suppose our girl is happy over there,' he said. 'I wouldn't want to bring her back on my account.' I said you had to have the right to choose whether to come back or not. You'd never forgive us, I said, if you didn't have the right to choose."

Frances could visualize this very conversation taking place between her parents; she could see them, decorous and serious, talking over the fact of his approaching death as though it were a piece of property for agreeable disposition in the family. She could never remember him without thinking, with a smile, how he used to come home on Sunday from church (he being the only one of them who went) and how, immediately after hanging his hat and cane in the hall, he would say, "Let all things proceed in orderly progression to their final confusion. How long before dinner?" No, she had had to come home. Some humor had always existed between them—her father and her—and humor, of all things, cannot be betrayed.

"I meant to go back," said Frances now. "But there was the war. At first I kept waiting for it to be over. I still wake up at night sometimes thinking, I wonder how much longer before the war will be over. And then—" She stopped short. For the fact was that her lover had been married to somebody else, and her mother was the very person capable of pointing that out to her. Even in the old lady's present silence she heard the unspoken thought, and got up nervously from the bed, loosing herself from the hand on her arm, smoothing her reddish hair where it was inclined to straggle. "And then he wrote me that he had gone back to his wife. Her family and his had always been close, and the war brought them back together. This was in Switzerland—naturally, he couldn't stay on in Paris during the war. There were the children, too—all of them were Catholic. Oh, I do understand how it happened."

Mrs. Harvey turned her head impatiently on the pillow. She dabbed at her moist upper lip with a crumpled linen handkerchief; her diamond flashed once in motion. "War, religion, wife, children—yes. But men do what they want to."

Could anyone make Frances as angry as her mother could? "Believe what you like then! You always know so much better than I do. *You* would have managed things somehow. Oh, you would have had your way!"

"Frances," said Mrs. Harvey, "I'm an old woman." The hand holding the handkerchief fell wearily, and her eyelids dropped shut. "If you should want to marry Thomas Beavers and bring him here, I will accept it. There will be no distinctions. Next, I suppose, we will be having his old deaf aunt for tea. I hope she has a hearing aid. I haven't got the strength to holler at her."

"I don't think any of these plans are necessary, Mama."

The eyelids slowly lifted. "None?"

"None."

Mrs. Harvey's breathing was as audible as a voice. She spoke, at last, without scorn, honestly. "I cannot bear the thought of leaving you alone. You, nor the house, nor your place in it—alone. I foresaw Tom Beavers here! What has he got that's better than you and this place? I knew he would come!"

Terrible as her mother's meanness was, it was not half so terrible as her love. Answering nothing, explaining nothing, Frances stood without giving in. She trembled, and tears ran down her cheeks. The two women looked at each other helplessly across the darkening room.

In the car, later that night, Tom Beavers asked, "Is your mother trying to get rid of me?" They had passed an unsatisfactory evening, and he was not going away without knowing why.

"No, it's just the other way around," said Frances, in her candid way. "She wants you so much she'd like to eat you up. She wants you in the house. Couldn't you tell?"

"She once chased me out of the yard," he recalled.

"Not really!"

They turned into Harvey Street (that was actually the name of it), and when he had drawn the car up before the dark front steps, he related the incident. He told her that Mrs. Harvey had been standing just there in the yard, talking to some visitor who was leaving by inches, the way ladies used to—ten minutes' more talk for every forward step. He, a boy not more than nine, had been crossing a corner of the lawn where a faint path had already been worn; he had had nothing to do with wearing the path and had taken it quite innocently and openly. "You, boy!" Mrs. Harvey's fan was an enormous painted thing. She had furled it with a clack so loud he could still hear it. "You don't cut through my yard again! Now, you stop where you are and you go all the way back around by the walk, and don't you ever do that again." He went back and all the way around. She was fanning comfortably as he passed. "Old Miss Rita Beavers' nephew," he heard her say, and though he did not speak of it now to Frances, Mrs. Harvey's rich tone had been as stuffed with wickedness as a fruitcake with goodies. In it you could have found so many things: that, of course, he didn't know any better, that he was poor, that she knew his first name but would not deign to mention it, that she meant him to understand all this and more. Her fan was probably still somewhere in the house, he reflected. If he ever opened the wrong door, it might fall from above and brain him. It seemed impossible that nowadays he could even have the chance to open the wrong door in the Harvey house. With its graceful rooms and big lawn, its camellias and magnolia trees, the house had been one of the enchanted castles of his childhood, and Frances and Regina Harvey had been two princesses running about the lawn one Saturday morning drying their hair with big white towels and not noticing when he passed.

There was a strong wind that evening. On the way home, Frances and Tom had noticed how the night was streaming, but whether with mist or dust or the smoke from some far-off fire in the dry winter woods they could not tell. As they stood on the sidewalk, the clouds raced over them, and moonlight now and again came through. A limb rubbed against a high cornice. Frances's coat blew about her, and her hair blew. She felt herself to be no different from anything there that the wind was blowing on, her happiness of no relevance in the dark torrent of nature.

"I can't leave her, Tom. But I can't ask you to live with her, either. Of all the horrible ideas! She'd make demands, take all my time, laugh at you behind your back—she has to run everything. You'd hate me in a week."

He did not try to pretty up the picture, because he had a feeling that it was all too accurate. Now, obviously, was the time she should go on to say there was no good his waiting around through the years for her. But hearts are not noted for practicality, and Frances stood with her hair blowing, her hands stuck in her coat pockets, and did not go on to say anything. Tom pulled her close to him—in, as it were, out of the wind.

"I'll be coming by next weekend, just like I've been doing. And the next one, too," he said. "We'll just leave it that way, if it's O.K. with you."

"Oh yes, it is, Tom!" Never so satisfied to be weak, she kissed him and ran inside.

He stood watching on the walk until her light flashed on. Well, he had got what he was looking for; a connection with the past, he had said. It was right upstairs, a splendid old mass of dictatorial female flesh, thinking about him. Well, they could go on, he and Frances, sitting on either side of a sickbed, drinking tea and sipping sherry with streaks of gray broadening on their brows, while the familiar seasons came and went. So he thought. Like Frances, he believed that the old lady had a stranglehold on life.

Suddenly, in March, Mrs. Harvey died.

A heavy spring funeral, with lots of roses and other scented flowers in the house, is the worst kind of all. There is something so recklessly fecund about a south Mississippi spring that death becomes just another word in the dictionary, along with swarms of others, and even so pure and white a thing as a gardenia has too heavy a scent and may suggest decay. Mrs. Harvey, amid such odors, sank to rest with a determined pomp, surrounded by admiring eyes.

While Tom Beavers did not "sit with the family" at this time, he was often observed with the Harveys, and there was whispered speculation among those who were at the church and the cemetery that the Harvey house might soon come into new hands, "after a decent interval." No one would undertake to judge for a Harvey how long an interval was decent.

Frances suffered from insomnia in the weeks that followed, and at night she wandered about the spring-swollen air of the old house, smelling now spring and now death. "Let all things proceed in orderly progression to their final confusion." She had always thought that the final confusion referred to death, but now she began to think that it could happen any time; that final confusion, having found the door ajar, could come into a house and show no inclination to leave. The worrisome thing, the thing it all came back to, was her mother's clothes. They were numerous, expensive, and famous, and Mrs. Harvey had never discarded any of them. If you opened a closet door, hatboxes as big as crates towered above your head. The shiny black trim of a great shawl stuck out of a wardrobe door just below the lock. Beneath the lid of a cedar chest, the bright eyes of a tippet were ready to twinkle at you. And the jewels! Frances's sister had restrained her from burying them all on their mother, and had even gone off with a wad of them tangled up like fishing tackle in an envelope, on the ground of promises made now and again in the course of the years.

("Regina," said Frances, "what else were you two talking about besides jewelry?" "I don't remember," said Regina, getting mad.

"Frances makes me so mad," said Regina to her husband as they were driving home. "I guess I can love Mama and jewelry, too. Mama certainly loved *us* and jewelry, too.")

One afternoon, Frances went out to the cemetery to take two wreaths sent by somebody who had "just heard." She drove out along the winding cemetery road, stopping the car a good distance before she reached the gate, in order to walk through the woods. The dogwood was beautiful that year. She saw a field where a house used to stand but had burned down; its cedar trees remained, and two bushes of bridal wreath marked where the front gate had swung. She stopped to admire the clusters of white bloom massing up through the young, feathery leaf and stronger now than the leaf itself. In the woods, the redbud was a smoke along shadowy ridges, and the dogwood drifted in layers, like snow suspended to give you all the time you needed to wonder at it. But why, she wondered, do they call it bridal *wreath*? It's not a wreath but a little bouquet. Wreaths are for funerals, anyway. As if to prove it, she looked down at the two she held, one in each hand. She walked on, and such complete desolation came over her that it was more of a wonder than anything in the woods—more, even, than death.

As she returned to the car from the two parallel graves, she met a thin, elderly, very light-skinned Negro man in the road. He inquired if she would mind moving her car so that he could pass. He said that there was a sick colored girl in his wagon, whom he was driving in to the doctor. He pointed out politely that she had left her car right in the middle of the road. "Oh, I'm terribly sorry," said Frances, and hurried off toward the car.

That night, reading late in bed, she thought, I could have given her a ride into town. No wonder they talk about us up North. A mile into town in a wagon! She might have been having a baby. She became conscience-stricken about it—foolishly so, she realized, but if you start worrying about something in a house like the one Frances Harvey lived in, in the dead of night, alone, you will go on worrying about it until dawn. She was out of sleeping pills.

She remembered having bought a fresh box of sedatives for her mother the day before she died. She got up and went into her mother's closed room, where the bed had been dismantled for airing, its wooden parts propped along the walls. On tne closet shelf she found the shoe box into which she had packed away the familiar articles of the bedside table. Inside she found the small enameled-cardboard box, with the date and prescription inked on the cover in Totsie Poteet's somewhat prissy handwriting, but the box was empty. She was surprised, for she realized that her mother could have used only one or two of the pills. Frances was so determined to get some sleep that she searched the entire little store of things in the shoe box quite heartlessly, but there were no pills. She returned to her room and tried to read, but could not, and so smoked instead and stared out at the dawn-blackening sky. The house sighed. She could not take her mind off the Negro girl. If she died . . . When it was light, she dressed and got into the car.

In town, the postman was unlocking the post office to sort the early mail. "I declare," he said to the rural mail carrier who arrived a few minutes later, "Miss Frances Harvey is driving herself crazy. Going back out yonder to the cemetery, and it not seven o'clock in the morning."

"Aw," said the rural deliveryman skeptically, looking at the empty road.

"That's right. I was here and seen her. You wait there, you'll see her come back. She'll drive herself nuts. Them old maids like that, left in them old houses—crazy and sweet, or crazy and mean, or just plain crazy. They just ain't locked up like them that's down in the asylum. That's the only difference."

"Miss Frances Harvey ain't no more than thirty-two, -three years old."

"Then she's just got more time to get crazier in. You'll see."

That day was Friday, and Tom Beavers, back from Jackson, came up Frances Harvey's sidewalk, as usual, at exactly a quarter past seven in the evening. Frances was not "going out" yet, and Regina had telephoned her long distance to say that "in all probability" she should not be receiving gentlemen "in." "What would Mama say?" Regina asked. Frances said she didn't know, which was not true, and went right on cooking dinners for Tom every weekend.

In the dining room that night, she sat across one corner of the long table from Tom. The useless length of polished cherry stretched away from them into the shadows as sadly as a road. Her plate pushed back, her chin resting on one palm, Frances stirred her coffee and said, "I don't know what on earth to do with all of Mama's clothes. I can't give them away, I can't sell them, I can't burn them, and the attic is full already. What can I do?"

"You look better tonight," said Tom.

"I slept," said Frances. "I slept and slept. From early this morning until just 'while ago. I never slept so well."

Then she told him about the Negro near the cemetery the previous afternoon, and how she had driven back out there as soon as dawn came, and found him again. He had been walking across the open field near the remains of the house that had burned down. There was no path to him from her, and she had hurried across ground uneven from old plowing and covered with the kind of small, tender grass it takes a very skillful mule to crop. "Wait!" she had cried. "Please wait!" The Negro had stopped and waited for her to reach him. "Your daughter?" she asked, out of breath.

"Daughter?" he repeated.

"The colored girl that was in the wagon yesterday. She was sick, you said, so I wondered. I could have taken her to town in the car, but I just didn't think. I wanted to know, how is she? Is she very sick?"

He had removed his old felt nigger hat as she approached him. "She a whole lot better, Miss Frances. She going to be all right now." Then he smiled at her. He did not say thank you, or anything more. Frances turned and walked back to the road and the car. And exactly as though the recovery of the Negro girl in the wagon had been her own recovery, she felt the return of a quiet breath and a steady pulse, and sensed the blessed stirring of a morning breeze. Up in her room, she had barely time to draw an old quilt over her before she fell asleep.

"When I woke, I knew about Mama," she said now to Tom. By the deepened intensity of her voice and eyes, it was plain that this was the important part. "It isn't right to say I *knew*," she went on, "because I had known all the time—ever since last night. I just realized it, that's all. I realized she had killed herself. It had to be that."

He listened soberly through the story about the box of sedatives. "But why?" he asked her. "It maybe looks that way, but what would be her reason for doing it?"

"Well, you see—" Frances said, and stopped.

Tom Beavers talked quietly on. "She didn't suffer. With what she had, she could have lived five, ten, who knows how many years. She was well cared for. Not hard up, I wouldn't say. Why?"

The pressure of his questioning could be insistent, and her trust in him, even if he was nobody but old Miss Rita Beavers' nephew, was well-nigh complete. "Because of you and me," she said, finally. "I'm certain of it, Tom. She didn't want to stand in our way. She never knew how to express love, you see." Frances controlled herself with an effort.

He did not reply, but sat industriously balancing a match folder on the tines of an unused serving fork. Anyone who has passed a lonely childhood in the company of an old deaf aunt is not inclined to doubt things hastily, and Tom Beavers would not have said he disbelieved anything Frances had told him. In fact, it seemed only too real to him. Almost before his eyes, that imperial, practical old hand went fumbling for the pills in the dark. But there had been much more to it than just love, he reflected. Bitterness, too, and pride, and control. And humor, perhaps, and the memory of a frightened little boy chased out of the yard by a twitch of her fan. Being invited to tea was one thing; suicide was quite another. Times had certainly changed, he thought.

But, of course, he could not say that he believed it, either. There was only Frances to go by. The match folder came to balance and rested on the tines. He glanced up at her, and a chill walked up his spine, for she was too serene. Cheek on palm, a lock of reddish hair fallen forward, she was staring at nothing with the absorbed silence of a child, or of a sweet, silver-haired old lady engaged in memory. Soon he might find that more and more of her was vanishing beneath this placid surface.

He himself did not know what he had seen that Friday evening so many months ago—what the figure had been that stood forward from the roadside at the tilt of the curve and urgently waved an arm to him. By the time he had braked and backed, the man had disappeared. Maybe it had been somebody drunk (for Richton had plenty of those to offer), walking it off in the cool of the woods at first dark. No such doubts had occurred to Frances. And what if he told her now the story Totsie had related of the road gang and the sick Negro girl in the wagon? Another labyrinth would open before her; she would never get out.

In Richton, the door to the past was always wide open, and what came in through it and went out of it had made people "different." But it scarcely ever happens, even in Richton, that one is able to see the precise moment when fact becomes faith, when life turns into legend, and people start to bend their finest loyalties to make themselves bemused custodians of the grave. Tom Beavers saw that moment now, in the profile of this dreaming girl, and he knew there was no time to lose.

He dropped the match folder into his coat pocket. "I think we should be leaving, Frances."

"Oh well, I don't know about going out yet," she said. "People criticize you so. Regina even had the nerve to telephone. Word had got all the way to her that you came here to have supper with me and we were alone in the house. When I tell the maid I want biscuits made up for two people, she looks like 'What would yo' mama say?' "

"I mean," he said, "I think it's time we left for good."

"And never came back?" It was exactly like Frances to balk at going to a movie but seriously consider an elopement.

"Well, never is a long time. I like to see about Aunt Rita once every once in a great while. She can't remember from one time to the next whether it's two days or two years since I last came."

She glanced about the walls and at the furniture, the pictures, and the silver. "But I thought you would want to live here, Tom. It never occurred to me. I know it never occurred to Mama . . . This house . . . It can't be just left."

"It's a fine old house," he agreed. "But what would you do with all your mother's clothes?"

Her freckled hand remained beside the porcelain cup for what seemed a long time. He waited and made no move toward her; he felt her uncertainty keenly, but he believed that some people should not be startled out of a spell.

"It's just as you said," he went on, finally. "You can't give them away, you can't sell them, you can't burn them, and you can't put them in the attic, because the attic is full already. So what are you going to do?"

Between them, the single candle flame achieved a silent altitude. Then, politely, as on any other night, though shaking back her hair in a decided way, she said, "Just let me get my coat, Tom."

She locked the door when they left, and put the key under the mat—a last obsequy to the house. Their hearts were bounding ahead faster than they could walk down the sidewalk or drive off in the car, and, mindful, perhaps, of what happened to people who did, they did not look back.

Had they done so, they would have seen that the Harvey house was more beautiful than ever. All unconscious of its rejection by so mere a person as Tom Beavers, it seemed, instead, to have got rid of what did not suit it, to be free, at last, to enter with abandon the land of mourning and shadows and memory.

The Business
Venture

We were down at the river that night. Pete Owens was there with his young wife, Hope (his name for her was Jezzie, after Jezebel in the Bible), and Charlie and me, and both the Houston boys, one with his wife and the other with the latest in a string of new girlfriends. But Nelle Townshend, his steady girl, wasn't there.

We talked and watched the river flow. It was different from those nights we used to go up to the club and dance, because we were older and hadn't bothered to dress, just wore slacks and shorts. It was a clear night but no moon.

Even five years married to him, I was in love with Charlie more than ever, and took his hand to rub the reddish hairs around his wrist. I held his hand under water and watched the flow around it, and later when the others went up to the highway for more whiskey, we kissed like two high school kids and then waded out laughing and splashed water on each other.

The next day Pete Owens looked me up at the office when my boss, Mr. McGinnis, was gone to lunch. "Charlie's never quit, you know, Eileen. He's still passing favors out."

My heart dropped. I could guess it, but wasn't letting myself know I really knew it. I put my hard mask on. "What's the matter? Isn't Hope getting enough from you?"

"Oh, I'm the one for Jezzie. You're the main one for Charlie. I just mean, don't kid yourself he's ever stopped."

"When did any of us ever stop?"

"You have. You like him that much. But don't think you're home free. The funny thing is, nobody's ever took a shotgun to Charlie. So far's I know, nobody's ever even punched him in the jaw."

"It is odd," I said, sarcastic, but he didn't notice.

"It's downright peculiar," said Pete. "But then I guess we're a special sort of bunch, Eileen."

I went back to typing and wished he'd go. He'd be asking me next. We'd dated and done a few things, but that was so long ago, it didn't count now. It never really mattered. I never thought much about it.

"What I wonder is, Eileen. Is everybody else like us, or so different from us they don't know what we're like at all?"

"The world's changing," I said. "They're all getting like us."

"You mean it?"

I nodded. "The word got out," I said. "You told somebody, and they told somebody else, and now everybody is like us."

"Or soon will be," he said.

"That's right," I said.

I kept on typing letters, reeling them on and off the platen and working on my electric machine the whole time he was talking, turning his hat over and picking at a straw or two off the synthetic weave. I had a headache that got worse after he was gone.

Also at the picnic that night was Grey Houston, one of the Houston brothers, who was always with a different girl. His former steady girlfriend, Nelle Townshend, kept a cleaning and pressing shop on her own premises. Her mother had been a stay-at-home lady for years. They had one of those beautiful old Victorian-type houses—it just missed being a photographer's and tourist attraction, being about twenty years too late and having the wooden trim too ornate for the connoisseurs to call it the real classical style. Nelle had been enterprising enough to turn one wing of the house where nobody went anymore into a cleaning shop, because she needed to make some money and felt she had to be near her mother. She had working for them off and on a Negro back from the Vietnam war who had used his veterans' educational benefits to train as a dry cleaner. She picked up the idea when her mother happened to remark one night after she had paid him for some carpenter work, "Ain't that a dumb nigger, learning dry cleaning with nothing to dry-clean."

Now, when Mrs. Townshend said "nigger," it wasn't as if one of us had said it. She went back through the centuries for her words, back to when "ain't" was good grammar. "Nigger" for her just meant "black." But it was assuming Robin had done something dumb that was the mistake. Because he wasn't dumb, and Nelle knew it. He told her he'd applied for jobs all around, but they didn't offer much and he might have to go to Biloxi or Hattiesburg or Gulfport to get one. The trouble was, he owned a house here. Nelle said, "Maybe you could work for me."

He told her about a whole dry cleaning plant up in Magee that had folded up recently due to the old man who ran it dying on his feet one day. They drove up there together and she bought it. Her mother didn't like it much when she moved the equipment in, but Nelle did it anyway. "I never get the smell out of my hair," she would say, "but if it can just make money I'll get used to it." She was dating Grey at the time, and I thought that's what gave her that much nerve.

Grey was a darling man. He was divorced from a New Orleans woman, somebody with a lot of class and money. She'd been crazy about Grey, as who wouldn't be, but he didn't "fit in," was her complaint. "Why do I have to fit in with her?" he kept asking. "Why shouldn't she fit in with us?" "She was O.K. with us," I said. "Not quite," he said. "Y'all never did relax. You never felt easy. That's why Charlie kept working at her, flirting and all. Then she'd have been one of us. But she acted serious about it. I said, 'Whatever you decide about Charlie, just don't tell me.' She was too serious."

"Anybody takes it seriously ought to be me," I said.

"Oh-oh," said Grey, breaking out with fun, the way he could do— in the depths one minute, up and laughing the next. "You can't afford that, Eileen."

That time I raised a storm at Charlie. "What did you want to get married for? You're nothing but a goddamn stud!"

"What's news about it?" Charlie wanted to know. "You're just getting worked up over nothing."

"Nothing! Is what we do just nothing?"

"That's right. When it's done with, it's nothing. What I think of you—now, that's something." He had had some problem with a new car at the garage—he had the GM agency then—and he smelled of clean lubricating products and new upholstery and the rough soap where the mechanics cleaned up. He was big and gleaming, the all-over male. Oh, hell, I thought, what can I do? Then, suddenly curious, I asked: "*Did you make out with Grey's wife?*"

He laughed out loud and gave me a sidelong kiss. "Now that's more like it."

Because he'd never tell me. He'd never tell me who he made out with. "Honey," he'd say, late at night in the dark, lying straight out beside me, occasionally tangling his toes in mine or reaching for his cigarettes, "if I'd say I never had another woman outside you, would you believe it?"

I couldn't say No from sheer astonishment.

"Because it just might be true," he went on in the dark, serious as a judge. Then I would start laughing, couldn't help it. Because there are few things in the world which you know are true. You don't know (not anymore: our mamas knew) if there's a God or not, much less if He so loved the world. You don't know what your own native land is up to, or the true meaning of freedom, or the real cost of gasoline and cigarettes, or whether your insurance company will pay up. But one thing I personally know that is *not* true is that Charlie Waybridge has had only one woman. Looked at that way, it can be a comfort, one thing to be sure of.

It was soon after the picnic on the river that Grey Houston came by to see me at the office. You'd think I had nothing to do but stop and talk. What he came about was Nelle.

"She won't date me anymore," he complained. "I thought we were doing fine, but she quit me just like that. Hell, I can't tell what's the trouble with her. I want to call up and say, 'Just tell me, Nelle. What's going on?'"

"Why don't you?" I asked.

Grey is always a little worried about things to do with people, especially since his divorce. We were glad when he started dating Nelle. She was hovering around thirty and didn't have anybody, and Grey was only a year or two younger.

"If I come right out and ask her, then she might just say, 'Let's decide to be good friends,' or something like that. Hell, I got enough friends."

"It's to be thought of," I agreed.

"What would you do?" he persisted.

"I'd rather know where I stand," I said, "but in this case I think I'd wait awhile. Nelle's worrying over that business. Maybe she doesn't know herself."

"I might push her too soon. I thought that, too."

"I ought to go around and see old Mrs. Townshend," I said. "She hardly gets out at all anymore. I mean to stop in and say hello."

"You're not going to repeat anything?"

See how he is? Skittery. "Of course not," I said. "But there's such a thing as keeping my eyes and ears open."

I went over to call on old Mrs. Townshend one Thursday afternoon when Mr. McGinnis's law office was closed anyway. The Townshend house is on a big lawn, a brick walk running up from the street to the front step and a large round plot of elephant ears in the front yard. When away and thinking of home, I see right off the Townshend yard and the elephant ears.

I wasn't even to the steps before I smelled clothes just dry-cleaned. I don't guess it's so bad, though hardly what you'd think of living with. Nor would you particularly like to see the sign outside the porte-cochere, though way to the left of the walk and not visible from the front porch. Still, it was out there clearly, saying "Townshend Dry Cleaning: Rapid Service." Better than a funeral parlor, but not much.

The Townshend house is stuffed with things. All these little Victorian tables on tall legs bowed outward, a small lower shelf, and the top covered katy-corner with a clean starched linen doily, tatting around the edge. All these chairs of various shapes, especially one that rocked squeaking on a walnut stand, and for every chair a doily at the head. Mrs. Townshend kept two birdcages, but no birds were in them. There never had been any so far as I knew. It wasn't a dark house, though. Nelle had taken out the stained glass way back when she graduated from college. That was soon after her older sister married, and her mama needed her. "If I'm going to live here," she had said, "that's got to go." So it went.

Mrs. Townshend never raised much of a fuss at Nelle. She was low to the ground because of a humpback, a rather placid old lady. The

Townshends were the sort to keep everything just the way it was. Mrs. Townshend was a LeMoyne from over toward Natchez. She was an Episcopalian and had brought her daughters up in that church.

"I'm sorry about this smell," she said in her forthright way, coming in and offering me a Coke on a little tray with a folded linen napkin beside it. "Nelle told me I'd get used to it and she was right: I have. But at first I had headaches all the time. If you get one I'll get some aspirin for you."

"How's the business going?" I asked.

"Nelle will be in in a minute. She knows you're here. You can ask her." She never raised her voice. She had a soft little face and gray eyes back of her little gold-rimmed glasses. She hadn't got to the hearing-aid stage yet, but you had to speak up. We went through the whole rigmarole of mine and Charlie's families. I had a feeling she was never much interested in all that, but around home you have to do it. Then I asked her what she was reading and she woke up. We got off the ground right away, and went strong about the President and foreign affairs, the picture not being so bright but of great interest, and about her books from the library always running out, and all the things she had against book clubs—then Nelle walked in.

Nelle Townshend doesn't look like anybody else but herself. her face is like something done on purpose to use up all the fine skin, drawing it evenly over the bones beneath, so that no matter at what age, she always would look the same. But that day she had this pinched look I'd never seen before, and her arms were splotched with what must have been a reaction to the cleaning fluids. She rolled down the sleeves of her blouse and sat in an old wicker rocker.

"I saw Grey the other day, Nelle," I said. "I think he misses you."

She didn't say anything outside of remarking she hadn't much time to go out. Then she mentioned some sort of decorating at the church she wanted to borrow some ferns for, from the florist. He's got some he rents, in washtubs. "You can't get all those ferns in our little church," Mrs. Townshend said, and Nelle said she thought two would do. She'd send Robin, she said. Then the bell rang to announce another customer. Nelle had to go because Robin was at the "plant"—actually the old cook's house in back of the property where they'd set the machinery up.

I hadn't said all I had to say to Nelle, so when I got up to go, I said to Mrs. Townshend that I'd go in the office a minute on the way out.

But Mrs. Townshend got to her feet, a surprise in itself. Her usual words were, You'll excuse me if I don't get up. Of course, you would excuse her and be too polite to ask why. Like a lot of old ladies, she might have arthritis. But this time she stood.

"I wish you'd let Nelle alone. Nelle is all right now. She's the way she wants to be. She'd not the way you people are. She's just not a bit that way!"

It may have been sheer surprise that kept me from telling Charlie all this till the weekend. We were hurrying to get to Pete and Hope Owens's place for a dinner they were having for some people down from the Delta, visitors.

"What did you say to that?" Charlie asked me.

"I was too surprised to open my mouth. I wouldn't have thought Mrs. Townshend would express such a low opinion as that. And why does she have it in the first place? Nelle's always been part of our crowd. She grew up with us. I thought they liked us."

"Old ladies get notions. They talk on the phone too much."

To our surprise, Nelle was at the Owenses dinner, too. Hope told me in the kitchen that she'd asked her, and then asked Grey. But Grey had a date with the little Springer girl he'd brought to the picnic, Carole Springer. "If this keeps up," Hope said to me while I was helping her with a dip, "we're going to have a Springer in our crowd. I'm just not right ready for that." "Me either," I said. The Springers were from McComb, in lumber. They had money but they never were much fun.

"Did Nelle accept knowing you were going to ask Grey?" I asked.

"I couldn't tell that. She just said she'd love to and would come about seven."

It must have been seven, because Nelle walked in. "Can I help?"

"Your mama," I said, when Hope went out with the tray, "she sort of got upset with me the other day. I don't know why. If I said anything wrong, just tell her I'm sorry."

Nelle looked at her fresh nail polish. "Mama's a little peculiar now and then. Like everybody." So she wasn't about to open up.

"I've been feeling bad about Grey is all," I said. "You can think I'm meddling if you want to."

"Grey's all right," she said. "He's been going around with Carole Springer from McComb."

"All the more reason for feeling bad. Did you know they're coming tonight?" She smiled a little distantly, and we went out to join the party. Charlie was already sitting up too close to the wife of the guest couple. I'd met them before. They have an antique shop. He is tall and nice, and she is short (wears spike heels) and nice. They are the sort you can't ever remember what their names are. If you get the first names right you're doing well. Shirley and Bob.

"Honey, you're just a doll," Charlie was saying (if he couldn't think of Shirley, Honey would do), and Pete said, "Watch out, Shirley, the next thing you know you'll be sitting on his lap."

"I almost went in for antiques myself," Nelle was saying to Bob, the husband. "I would have liked that better, of course, than a cleaning business, but I thought the turnover here would be too small. I do need to feel like I'm making money if I'm going to work at it. For a while, though, it was fun to go wandering around New Orleans and pick up good things cheap."

"I'd say they'd all been combed over down there," Bob objected.

"It's true about the best things," Nelle said. "I could hardly afford those anyway. But sometimes you see some pieces with really good design and you can see you might realize something on them. Real appreciation goes a long way."

"Bob has a jobber up in St. Louis," Shirley said. "We had enough of all this going around shaking the bushes. A few lucky finds was what got us started."

Nelle said, "I started thinking about it because I went in the living room a year or so back and there were some ladies I never saw before. They'd found the door open and walked in. They wanted to know the price of Mama's furniture. I said it wasn't for sale, but Mama was just coming in from the kitchen and heard them. You wouldn't believe how mad she got. 'I'm going straight and get out my pistol,' she said."

"You ought to just see her mama," said Hope. "This tiny little old lady."

"So what happened?" Shirley asked when she got through laughing.

"Nothing real bad," said Nelle. "They just got out the door as quick as they could."

"Yo' mama got a pistol?" Charlie asked, after a silence. We started to laugh again, the implication being plain that a Charlie Waybridge *needs* to know if a woman's mother has a pistol in the house.

"She does have one," said Nelle.

"So watch out, Charlie," said Pete.

Bob remarked, "Y'all certainly don't change much over here."

"Crazy as ever," Hope said proudly. It crossed my mind that Hope was always protecting herself, one way or the other.

Shirley said she thought it was just grand to be back, she wouldn't take anything for it, and after that Grey and Carole arrived. He had another drink and then went in to dinner. Everybody acted like everything was okay. After dinner, I went back in the kitchen for some water, and there was Charlie, kissing Shirley. She was so strained up on tiptoe, Charlie being over six feet, that I thought, in addition to being embarrassed, mad, and backing out before they saw me, What they need is a stepladder to do it right.

On the way home, I told Charlie about catching them. "I didn't know she was within a country mile," he said, ready with excuses. "She just plain grabbed me."

"I've been disgusted once too often," I said. "Tell it to Bob."

"If she wanted to do it right," he said, "she ought to get a stepladder." So then I had to laugh. Even if our marriage wasn't ideal, we still had the same thoughts.

It sometimes seemed to me, in considering the crowd we were always part of, from even before we went to school, straight on through, that we were all like one person, walking around different ways, but in some permanent way breathing together, feeling the same reactions, thinking each other's thoughts. What do you call that if not love? If asked, we'd all cry Yes! with one voice, but then it's not our habit to ask anything serious. We're close to religious about keeping everything light and gay. Nelle Townshend knew that, all the above, but she was drawing back. A betrayer was what she was turning into. We felt weakened because of her. What did she think she was doing?

I had to drive Mr. McGinnis way back in the woods one day to serve a subpoena on a witness. He hadn't liked to drive since his heart attack, and his usual colored man was busy with Mrs. McGinnis's garden. In the course of that little trip, coming back into town, I saw Nelle Townshend's station wagon turn off onto a side road. I couldn't see who was with her, but somebody was, definitely.

I must add that this was spring and there were drifts of dogwood all mingled in the woods at different levels. Through those same woods, along the winding roads, the redbud, simultaneous, was spreading its wonderful pink haze. Mr. McGinnis sat beside me without saying much, his old knobby hands folded over a briefcase he held upright on his lap. "A trip like this just makes me think, Eileen, that everybody owes it to himself to get out in the woods this time of year. It's just God's own garden," he said. We had just crossed a wooden bridge over a pretty little creek about a mile back. That same creek, shallower, was crossed by a ford along the road that Nelle's car had taken. I know that little road, too, maybe the prettiest one of all.

Serpents have a taste for Eden, and in a small town, if they are busy elsewhere, lots of people are glad to fill in for them. It still upsets me to think of all the gossip that went on that year, and at the same time I have to blame Nelle Townshend for it, not so much for starting it, but for being so unconscious about it. She had stepped out of line and she didn't even bother to notice.

Once the business got going, the next thing she did was enroll in a class—a "seminar," she said—over at the university at Hattiesburg. It was something to do with art theory, she said, and she was thinking of going on from there to a degree, eventually, and get hold of a subject she could teach at the junior college right up the road. So settling in to be an old maid.

I said this last rather gloomily to Pete's wife, Hope, and Pete overheard and said, "There's all kinds of those." "You stop that," said Hope. "What's supposed to be going on?" I asked. (Some say don't ask, it's better not to, but I think you have to know if only to keep on guard.)

"Just that they're saying things about Nelle and that black Robin works for her."

"Well, they're in the same business," I said.

"Whatever it is, people don't like it. They say she goes out to his house after dark. That they spend too much time over the books."

"Somebody ought to warn her," I said. "If Robin gets into trouble she won't find anybody to do that kind of work. He's the only one."

"Nelle's gotten too independent is the thing," said Pete. "She thinks she can live her own life."

"Maybe she can," said Hope.

Charlie was away that week. He had gone over to the Delta on business, and Hope and Pete had dropped in to keep me company. Hope is ten years younger than Pete. (Pete used to date her sister, Mary Ruth, one of these beauty-queen types, who had gone up to the Miss America pageant to represent Mississippi and come back first runner-up. For the talent contest part of it, she had recited passages from the Bible, and Pete always said her trouble was she was too religious but he hoped to get her over it. She used to try in a nice way to get him into church work, and that embarrassed him. It's our common habit, as Mary Ruth well knew, to go to morning service, but anything outside that is out. Anyway, around Mary Ruth's he used to keep seeing the little sister Hope, and he'd say, "Mary Ruth, you better start on that girl about church, she's growing up dynamite." Mary Ruth got involved in a promotion trip, something about getting right with America, and met a man on a plane trip to Dallas, and before the seat-belt sign went off they were in love. For Mary Ruth that meant marriage. She was strict, a woman of faith, and I don't think Pete would have been happy with her. But he had got the habit of the house by then, and Mary Ruth's parents had got fond of him and didn't want him drinking too much: they made him welcome. So one day Hope turned seventeen and came out in a new flouncy dress with heels on, and Pete saw the light.)

We had a saying by now that Pete had always been younger than Hope, that she was older than any of us. Only twenty, she worked at making their house look good and won gardening prizes. She gave grand parties, with attention to details.

"I stuck my neck out," I told Hope, "to keep Nelle dating Grey. You remember her mama took a set at me like I never dreamed possible. Nelle's been doing us all funny, but she may have to come back someday. We can't stop caring for her."

Hope thought it over. "Robin knows what it's like here, even if Nelle may have temporarily forgotten. He's not going to tempt fate. Anyway, somebody already spoke to Nelle."

"Who?"

"Grey, of course. He'll use any excuse to speak to her. She got mad as a firecracker. She said, 'Don't you know this is nineteen seventy-*six*? I've got a business to run. I've got a living to make!' But she quit going out to his house at night. And Robin quit so much as answering the phone, up at her office."

"You mean he's keeping one of those low profiles?" said Pete.

Soon after, I ran into Robin uptown in the grocery, and he said, "How do you do, Mrs. Waybridge," like a schoolteacher or a foreigner, and I figured just from that, that he was on to everything and taking no chances. Nelle must have told him. I personally knew what not many people did, that he was a real partner with Nelle, not just her hired help. They had got Mr. McGinnis to draw up the papers. And they had plans for moving the plant uptown, to an empty store building, with some investment in more equipment. So maybe they'd get by till then. I felt a mellowness in my heart about Nelle's effort and all—a Townshend (LeMoyne on her mother's side) opening a dry cleaning business. I thought of Robin's effort, too—he had a sincere, intelligent look, reserved. What I hoped for them was something like a prayer.

Busying my thoughts about all this, I had been forgetting Charlie. That will never do.

For one thing, leaving aside women, Charlie's present way of life was very nearly wild. He'd got into oil leases two years before, and when something was going on, he'd drive like a demon over to East Texas by way of Shreveport and back through Pike and Amite counties. At one time he had to sit over Mr. McGinnis for a month getting him to study up on laws governing oil rights. In the end, Charlie got to know as much or more than Mr. McGinnis. He's in and out. The in-between times are when he gets restless. Drinks too much and starts simmering up about some new woman. Once tried, soon dropped. Or so I like to believe. Then, truth to tell, there is really part of me that not only wants to believe but at unstated times does believe that I've been the only one for Charlie Waybridge. Not that I'd begrudge him a few times of having it off down in the back of the gym with some girl who came in from the country, nor would I think anything about flings in New Orleans while he was in Tulane. But as for the outlandish reputation he's acquired now, sometimes I just want to say out loud to all and sundry, "There's not a word of truth in it. He's a big, attractive, friendly guy, O.K.! But he's not the town stud. He belongs to *me*."

All this before the evening along about first dark when Charlie was seen on the Townshend property by Nelle's mother, who went and got the pistol and shot at him.

"Christ, she could have killed me," Charlie said. He was too surprised about it even to shake. He was just dazed. Fixed a stiff drink and didn't want any supper. "She's gone off her rocker," he said. "That's all I could think."

I knew I had to ask it, sooner or later. "What were you doing up there, Charlie?"

"Nothing," he said. "I'd left the car at Wharton's garage to check why I'm burning too much oil. He's getting to it in the morning. It was a nice evening and I cut through the back alley and that led to a stroll through the Townshend pasture. That's all. I saw the little lady out on the back porch. I was too far off to holler at her. She scuttled off into the house and I was going past, when here she came out again with something black weighting her hand. You know what I thought? I thought she had a kitten by the neck. Next thing I knew there was a bullet smashing through the leaves not that far off." He put his hand out.

"Wonder if Nelle was home."

I was nervous as a monkey after I heard this, and nothing would do me but to call up Nelle.

She answered right away. "Nelle," I said, "is your little mama going in for target practice these days?"

She started laughing. "Did you hear that all the way to your place? She's mad 'cause the Johnson's old cow keeps breaking down our fence. She took a shot in the air because she's tired complaining."

"Since when was Charlie Waybridge a cow?" I asked.

"Mercy, Eileen. You don't mean Charlie was back there?"

"You better load that thing with blanks," I said, "or hide it."

"Blanks is all it's got in it," said Nelle. "Mama doesn't tell that because she feels more protected not to."

"You certainly better check it out," I said. "Charlie says it was a bullet."

There was a pause. "You're not mad or anything, are you, Eileen?"

"Oh, no," I warbled. "We've been friends too long for that."

"Come over and see us," said Nelle. "Real soon."

I don't know who told it, but knowing this town like the back of my hand, I know *how* they told it. Charlie Waybridge was up at Nelle Townshend's and old Mrs. Townshend shot at him. Enough said. At the Garden Club Auxiliary tea, I came in and heard them giggling, and how they got quiet when I passed a plate of sandwiches. I went straight to the subject, which is the way I do. "Y'all off on Mrs. Townshend?" I asked. There was a silence, and then some little cross-eyed bride, new in town, piped up that there was just always something funny going on here, and Maud Varner, an old friend, said she thought Nelle ought to watch out for Mrs. Townshend, she was showing her age. "It's not such a funny goings-on when it almost kills somebody," I said. "Charlie came straight home and told me. He was glad to be alive, but I went and called Nelle. So she does know." There was another silence during which I could tell what everybody thought. The thing is not to get too distant or above it all. If you do, your friends will pull back, too, and you won't know anything. Gradually, you'll just turn into, Poor Eileen, what does she think of all Charlie's carryings-on?

Next, the injunction. Who brought it and why? I got the answer to the first before I guessed the second.

It was against the Townshend Cleaners because the chemicals used were a hazard to health and the smell they exuded a public nuisance. But the real reason wasn't this at all.

In order to speed up the deliveries, Nelle had taken to driving the station wagon herself, so that Robin could run in with the cleaning. Some people had begun to remark on this. Would it have been different if Nelle was married or had a brother, a father, a steady boyfriend? I don't know. I used to hold my breath when they went by in the late afternoon together. Because sometimes when the back of the stationwagon was full, Robin would be up on the front seat with her, and she with her head stuck in the air, driving carefully, her mind on nothing at all to do with other people. Once the cleaning load got lighter, Robin would usually sit on the back seat, as expected to do. But sometimes, busy talking to her, he wouldn't. He'd be up beside her, discussing business.

Then, suddenly, the business closed.

Nelle was beside herself. She came running to Mr. McGinnis. Her hair was every which way around her head and she was wearing an old checked shirt and no makeup.

She could hardly make herself sit still and visit with me while Mr. McGinnis got through with a client. "Now, Miss Nelle," he said, steering her through the door.

"Just when we were making a go of it!" I heard her say; then he closed the door.

I heard by way of the grapevine that very night that the person who had done it was John Houston, Grey's brother, whose wife's family lived on a property just below the Townshends. They claimed they couldn't sleep for the dry-cleaning fumes and were getting violent attacks of nausea.

"Aren't they supposed to give warnings?" I asked.

We were all at John and Rose Houston's home, a real gathering of the bunch, only Nelle being absent, though she was the most present one of all. There was a silence after every statement, in itself unusual. Finally John Houston said, "Not in cases of extreme health hazard."

"That's a lot of you-know-what," I said. "Rose, your family's not dying."

Rose said: "They never claimed to be dying." And Pete said: "Eileen, can't you sit right quiet and try to use your head?"

"In preference to running off at the mouth," said Charlie, which made me mad. I was refusing, I well knew, to see the point they all had in mind. But it seemed to me that was my privilege.

The thing to know about our crowd is that we never did go in for talking about the "Negro question." We talked about Negroes the way we always had, like people, one at a time. They were all around us, had always been, living around us, waiting on us, sharing our lives, brought up with us, nursing us, cooking for us, mourning and rejoicing with us, making us laugh, stealing from us, digging our graves. But when all the troubles started coming in on us after the Freedom Riders and the Ole Miss riots, we decided not to talk about it. I don't know but what we weren't afraid of getting nervous. We couldn't jump out of our own skins, or those of our parents, grandparents, and those before them. "Nothing you can do about it" was Charlie's view. "Whatever you decide, you're going to act the same way tomorrow as you did today. Hoping you can get Alma to cook for you, and Peabody to clean the windows, and Bayman to cut the grass." "I'm not keeping anybody from voting—yellow, blue, or pink," said Hope, who had got her "ideas" straight from the first, she said. "I don't guess any of us is," said Pete, "them days is gone forever." "But wouldn't it just be wonderful," said Rose Houston, "to have a little colored gal to pick up your hand-kerchief and sew on your buttons and bring you cold lemonade and fan you when you're hot, and just love you to death?"

Rose was joking, of course, the way we all liked to do. But there are always one or two of them that we seriously insist we know—really *know*—that they love us. Would do anything for us, as we would for them. Otherwise, without that feeling, I guess we couldn't rest easy. You never can really know what they think, what they feel, so there's always the one chance it might be love.

So we—the we I'm always speaking of—decided not to talk about race relations because it spoiled things too much. We didn't like to consider anyone of us really involved in some part of it. Then, in my mind's eye, I saw Nelle's car, that dogwood-laden day in the woods, headed off the road with somebody inside. Or such was my impression. I'd never mentioned it to anybody, and Mr. McGinnis hadn't, I think, seen. Was it Robin? Or maybe, I suddenly asked myself, Charlie? Mysteries multiplied.

"Nelle's got to make a living is the whole thing," said Pete, getting practical. "We can't not let her do that."

"Why doesn't somebody find her a job she'd like?" asked Grey.

"Why the hell," Charlie burst out, "don't you marry her, Grey? Women ought to get married," he announced in general. "You see what happens when they don't."

"Hell, I can't get near her," said Grey. "We dated for six months. I guess I wasn't the one," he added.

"She ought to relocate the plant uptown, then she could run the office in her house, one remove from it, acting like a lady."

"What about Robin?" said Hope.

"He could run back and forth," I said. "They do want to do that," I added, "but can't afford it yet."

"You'd think old Mrs. Townshend would have stopped it all."

"That lady's a mystery."

"If Nelle just had a brother."

"Or even an uncle."

Then the talk dwindled down to silence.

"John," said Pete, after a time, turning around to face him, "we all know it was you—not Rose's folks. Did you have to?"

John Houston was sitting quietly in his chair. He was a little older than the rest of us, turning gray, a little more settled and methodical, more like our uncle than an equal and friend. (Or was it just that he and Rose were the only ones so far to have children—what all our parents said we all ought to do, but couldn't quit having our good times.) He was sipping bourbon. He nodded slowly. "I had to." We didn't ask any more.

"Let's just go quiet," John finally added. "Wait and see."

Now, all my life I'd been hearing first one person then another (and these, it would seem, appointed by silent consensus) say that things were to be taken care of in a certain way and no other. The person in this case who had this kind of appointment was evidently John Houston, from in our midst. But when did he get it? How did he get it? Where did it come from? There seemed to be no need to discuss it.

Rose Houston, who wore her long light hair in a sort of loose bun at the nape and who sat straight up in her chair, adjusted a fallen strand, and Grey went off to fix another drink for himself and Pete and Hope. He sang on the way out, more or less to himself, "For the times they are a-changing . . ." and that, too, found reference in all our minds. Except I couldn't help but wonder whether anything had changed at all.

The hearing on the dry cleaning injunction was due to be held in two weeks. Nelle went off to the coast. She couldn't stand the tension, she told me, having come over to Mr. McGinnis's office to see him alone. "Thinking how we've worked and all," she said, "and how just before this came up the auditor was in and told us what good shape we were in. We were just about to buy a new condenser."

"What's that?" I asked.

"Takes the smell out of the fumes," she said. "The very thing they're mad about. I could kill John Houston. Why couldn't he have come to me?"

I decided to be forthright. "Nelle, there's something you ought to evaluate . . . consider, I mean. Whatever word you want." I was shaking, surprising myself.

Nobody was around. Mr. McGinnis was in the next county.

Once when I was visiting a school friend up north, out from Philadelphia, a man at a party asked me if I would have sexual relations with a black. He wasn't black himself, so why was he curious? I said I'd never even thought about it. "It's a taboo, I think you call it," I said. "Girls like me get brainwashed early on. It's not that I'm against them," I added, feeling awkward. "Contrary to what you may think or may even believe," he told me, "you've probably thought a lot about it. You've suppressed your impulses, that's all." "Nobody can prove that," I said, "not even you," I added, thinking I was being amusing. But he only looked superior and walked away.

"It's you and Robin," I said. I could hear myself explaining to Charlie, Somebody had to, sooner or later. "You won't find anybody really believing anything, I don't guess, but it's making people speculate."

Nelle Townshend never reacted the way you'd think she would. She didn't even get annoyed, much less hit the ceiling. She just gave a little sigh. "You start a business, you'll see. I've got no time for anything but worrying about customers and money."

I was wondering whether to tell her the latest. A woman named McCorkle from out in the country, who resembled Nelle so much from the back you'd think they were the same, got pushed off the sidewalk last Saturday and fell in the concrete gutter up near the drugstore. The person who did it, somebody from outside town, must have said something nobody heard but Mrs. McCorkle, because she jumped up with her skirt muddy and stockings torn and yelled out, "I ain't no nigger lover!"

But I didn't tell her. If she was anybody but a Townshend, I might have. Odd to think that, when the only Townshends left there were Nelle and her mother. In cases such as this, the absent are present and the dead are, too. Mr. Townshend had died so long ago you had to ask your parents what he was like. The answer was always the same. "Sid Townshend was a mighty good man." Nelle had had two sisters: one died in her twenties, the victim of a rare disease, and the other got married and went to live on a place out from Helena, Arkansas. She had about six children and could be of no real help to the home branch.

"Come over to dinner," I coaxed. "You want me to ask Grey, I will. If you don't, I won't."

"Grey," she said, just blank, like that. He might have been somebody she met once a long time back. "She's a perpetual virgin," I heard Charlie say once. "Just because she won't cotton up to you," I said. But maybe he was right. Nelle and her mother lived up near the Episcopal church. Since our little town could not support a full-time rector, it was they who kept the church linens and the chalice and saw that the robes were always cleaned and hung in their proper place in the little room off the chancel. Come to think of it, keeping those robes and surplices in order may have been one thing that started Nelle into dry cleaning.

Nelle got up suddenly, her face catching the light from our old window with the wobbly glass in the panes, and I thought, She's a grand-looking woman, sort of girlish and womanish both.

"I'm going to the coast," she said. "I'm taking some books and a sketch pad. I may look into some art courses. You have to have training to teach anything, that's the trouble."

"Look, Nelle, if it's money— Well, you do have friends, you know."

"Friends," she said, just the way she had said "Grey." I wondered just what Nelle was really like. None of us seemed to know.

"Have a good time," I said. After she left, I thought I heard the echo of that blank, soft voice saying, "Good time."

It was a week after Nelle had gone that old Mrs. Townshend rang up Mr. McGinnis at the office. Mr. McGinnis came out to tell me what it was all about.

"Mrs. Townshend says that last night somebody tore down the dry cleaning sign Nelle had put up out at the side. Some colored woman is staying with her at night, but neither one of them saw anybody. Now she can't find Robin to put it back. She's called his house but he's not there."

"Do they say he'll be back soon?"

"They say he's out of town."

"I'd get Charlie to go up and fix it, but you know what happened."

"I heard about it. Maybe in daylight the old lady won't shoot. I'll go around with our yardman after dinner." What we still mean by dinner is lunch. So they put the sign up and I sat in the empty office wondering about this and that, but mainly, Where was Robin Byers?

It's time to say that Robin Byers was not any Harry Belafonte calypso-singing sex symbol of a "black." He was strong and thoughtful-looking, not very tall, definitely chocolate, but not ebony. He wore his hair cropped short in an almost military fashion so that, being thick, it stuck straight up more often than not. From one side he could look positively frightening, as he had a long white scar running down the side of his cheek. It was said that he got it in the army, in Vietnam, but the story of just how was not known. So maybe he had not gotten it in the war, but somewhere else. His folks had been in the county forever, his own house being not far out from town. He had a wife, two teenaged children, a telephone, and a TV set. The other side of Robin Byers's face was regular, smooth, and while not especially handsome it was good-humored and likable. All in all, he looked intelligent and conscientious, and that must have been how Nelle Townshend saw him, as he was.

I went to the hearing. I'd have had to, to keep Mr. McGinnis's notes straight, but I would have anyway, as all our crowd showed up, except Rose and John Houston. Rose's parents were there, having brought the complaint, and Rose's mama's doctor from over at Hattiesburg, to swear she'd had no end of allergies and migraines, and attacks of nausea, all brought on by the cleaning fumes. Sitting way in the back was Robin Byers, in a suit (a really nice suit) with a blue-and-white-striped "city" shirt and a knit tie. He looked like an assistant university dean, except for the white scar. He also had the look of a spectator, very calm, I thought, not wanting to keep turning around and staring at him, but keeping the image in my mind like an all-day sucker, letting it slowly melt out its meaning. He was holding a certain surface. But he was scared. Half across the courtroom you could see his temple throbbing, and the sweat beads. He was that tense. The whole effect was amazing.

The complaint was read out and Mrs. Hammond, Rose's mother, testified and the doctor testified, and Mr. Hammond said they were both right. The way the Hammonds talk—big Presbyterians—you would think they had the Bible on their side every minute, so naturally everybody else had to be mistaken. Friends and neighbors of the Townshends all these years, they now seemed to be speaking of people they knew only slightly. That is until Mrs. Hammond, a sort of dumpling-like woman with a practiced way of sounding accurate about whatever she said (she was a good gossip because she got all the details of everything), suddenly came down to a personal level and said, "Nelle, I just don't see why if you want to run that thing you don't move it into town," and Nelle said back right away just like they were in a living room instead of a courthouse, "Well, that's because of Mama, Miss Addie. This way I'm in and out with her." At that, everybody laughed, couldn't help it.

Then Mr. McGinnis got up and challenged that very much about Mrs. Hammond's headaches and allergies (he established her age, fifty-two, which she didn't want to tell) had to do with the cleaning plant. If they had, somebody else would have such complaints, but in case we needed to go further into it, he would ask Miss Nelle to explain what he meant.

Nelle got up front and went about as far as she could concerning the type of equipment she used and how it was guaranteed against the very thing now being complained of, that it let very few vapors escape, but then she said she would rather call on Robin Byers to come and explain because he had had special training in the chemical processes and knew all their possible negative effects.

And he came. He walked down the aisle and sat in the chair and nobody had ever seen such composure. I think he was petrified, but so might an actor be who was doing a role to high perfection. And when he started to talk you'd think that dry cleaning was a text and that his God-appointed task was to preach a sermon on it. But it wasn't quite like that, either. More modern. A professor giving a lecture to extremely ignorant students, with a good professor's accuracy, to the last degree. In the first place, he said, the cleaning fluid used was not varsol or carbon tetrachloride, which were known not only to give off harmful fumes but to damage fabrics, but something called "Perluxe" or perchlorethylene (he paused to give the chemical composition), which was approved for commercial cleaning purposes in such and such a solution by federal and state bylaws, of certain numbers and codes, which Mr. McGinnis had listed in his records and would be glad to read aloud upon request. If an operator worked closely with Perluxe for a certain number of hours a day, he might have headaches, it was true, but escaping vapor could scarcely be smelled at all more than a few feet from the exhaust pipes, and caused no harmful effects whatsoever, even to shrubs or "the leaves upon the trees." He said this last in such a lofty, rhythmic way that somebody giggled (I think it was Hope), and he stopped talking altogether.

"There might be smells down in those hollows back there," Nelle filled in from where she was sitting, "but it's not from my one little exhaust pipe."

"Then why," asked Mrs. Hammond right out, "do you keep on saying you need new equipment so you won't have any exhaust? Just answer me that."

"I'll let Robin explain," said Nelle.

"The fact is that Perluxe is an expensive product," Robin said. "At four dollars and twenty-five cents a gallon, using nearly thirty gallons each time the accumulation of the garments is put through the process, she can count on it that the overheads with two cleanings a week will run in the neighborhood of between two and three hundred dollars. So having the condenser machine would mean that the exhaust runs into it, and so converts the vapors back to the liquid, in order to use it once again."

"It's not for the neighbors," Nelle put in. "It's for us."

Everybody had spoken out of order by then, but what with the atmosphere having either declined or improved (depending on how you looked at it) to one of friendly inquiry among neighbors rather than a squabble in a court of law, the silence that finally descended was more meditative than not, having as its most impressive features, like high points in a landscape, Nelle, at some little distance down a front bench, but turned around so as to take everything in, her back straight and her Townshend head both superior and interested; and Robin Byers, who still had the chair by Judge Purvis's desk, collected and severe (he had forgotten the giggle), with testimony faultlessly delivered and nothing more he needed to say. (Would things have been different if Charlie had been there? He was out of town.)

The judge cleared his throat and said he guessed the smells in the gullies around Tyler might be a nuisance, sure enough, but couldn't be said to be caused by dry cleaning, and he thought Miss Townshend could go on with her business. For a while, the white face and the black one seemed just the same, to be rising up quiet and superior above us all.

The judge asked, just out of curiosity, when Nelle planned to buy the condenser that was mentioned. She said whenever she could find one secondhand in good condition—they cost nearly two thousand dollars new—and Robin Byers put in that he had just been looking into one down in Biloxi, so it might not be too long. Biloxi is on the coast.

Judge Purvis said we'd adjourn now, and everybody stood up of one accord, except Mr. McGinnis, who had dozed off and was almost snoring.

Nelle, who was feeling friendly to the world, or seeming to (we all had clothes that got dirty, after all), said to all and sundry not to worry, "we plan to move the plant uptown one of these days before too long," and it was the "we" that came through again, a slip: she usually referred to the business as hers. It was just a reminder of what everybody wanted not to have to think about, and she probably hadn't intended to speak of it that way.

As if to smooth it well into the past, Judge Purvis remarked that these little towns ought to have zoning laws, but I sat there thinking there wouldn't be much support for that, not with the Gulf Oil station and garage right up on South Street between the Whitmans' and the Binghams', and the small-appliance shop on the vacant lot where the old Marshall mansion had stood, and the Tackett house, still elegant as you please, doing steady business as a funeral home. You can separate black from white but not business from nonbusiness. Not in our town.

Nelle came down and shook hands with Mr. McGinnis. "I don't know when I can afford to pay you." "Court costs go to them," he said. "Don't worry about the rest."

Back at the office, Mr. McGinnis closed the street door and said to me, "The fumes in this case have got nothing to do with dry cleaning. Has anybody talked to Miss Nelle?"

"They have," I said, "but she doesn't seem to pay any attention."

He said I could go home for the day and much obliged for my help at the courthouse. I powdered my nose and went out into the street. It wasn't but eleven-thirty.

Everything was still, and nobody around. The blue jays were having a good time on the courthouse yard, squalling and swooping from the lowest oak limbs, close to the ground, then mounting back up. There were some sparrows out near the old horse trough, which still ran water. They were splashing around. But except for somebody driving up for the mail at the post office, there wasn't a soul around. I started walking, and just automatically I went by for the mail because as a rule Charlie didn't stop in for it till noon, even when in town. On the way I was mulling over the hearing and how Mrs. Hammond had said at the door of the courtroom to Nelle, "Aw right, Miss Nellie, you just wait." It wasn't said in any unpleasant way; in fact, it sounded right friendly. Except that she wasn't looking at Nelle, but past her, and except that being older, it wasn't the ordinary thing to call her "Miss," and except that Nelle is a pretty name but Nellie isn't. But Nelle in reply had suddenly laughed in that unexpected but delightful way she has, because something has struck her as really funny. "What am I supposed to wait *for*, Miss Addie?" Whatever else, Nelle wasn't scared. I looked for Robin Byers, but he had got sensible and gone off in that old little blue German car he drives. I saw Nelle drive home alone.

Then, because the lay of my home direction was a shortcut from the post office, and because the spring had been dry and the back lanes nice to walk in, I went through the same way Charlie had that time Mrs. Townshend had about killed him, and enjoyed, the way I had from childhood on, the soft fragrances of springtime, the forsythia turned from yellow to green fronds, but the spirea still white as a bride's veil worked in blossoms, and the climbing roses, mainly wild, just opening a delicate, simple pink bloom all along the back fences. I was crossing down that way when what I saw was a blue car.

It was stopped way back down the Townshend property on a little connecting road that made an entrance through to a lower town road, one that nobody used anymore. I stopped in the clump of bowdarc trees on the next property from the Townshends'. Then I saw Nelle, running down the hill. She still had that same laugh, honest and joyous, that she had shown the first of to Mrs. Hammond. And there coming to meet her was Robin, his teeth white as his scar. They grabbed each other's hands, black on white and white on black. They started whirling each other around, like two schoolchildren in a game, and I saw Nelle's mouth forming the words I could scarcely hear: "We won! We won!" And his, the same, a baritone underneath. It was pure joy. Washing the color out, saying that the dye didn't, this time, hold, they could have been brother and sister, happy at some good family news, or old lovers (Charlie and I sometimes meet like that, too happy at some piece of luck to really stop to talk about it, just dancing out our joy). But, my God, I thought, don't they know they're black and white and this is Tyler, Mississippi? Well, of course they do, I thought next—that's more than half the joy—getting away with it! Dare and double-dare! Dumbfounded, I just stood, hidden, never seen by them at all, and let the image of black on white and white on black—those pale, aristocratic Townshend hands and his strong, square-cut black ones—linked perpetually now in my mind's eye—soak in. It's going to stay with me forever, I thought, but what does it mean? I never told. I didn't think they were lovers. But they were into a triumph of the sort that lovers feel. They had acted as they pleased. They were above everything. They lived in another world because of a dry cleaning business. They had proved it when they had to. They knew it.

But nobody could be counted on to see it the way I did. It was too complicated for any two people to know about it.

Soon after this we got a call from Hope, Pete's wife. "I've got tired of all this foolishness," she said. "How did we ever get hung up on dry cleaning, of all things? Can you feature it? I'm going to give a party. Mary Foote Williams is coming home to see her folks and bringing Keith, so that's good enough for me. And don't kid yourself. I'm personally going to get Nelle Townshend to come, and Grey Houston is going to bring her. I'm getting good and ready for everybody to start acting normal again. I don't know what's been the matter with everybody, and furthermore I don't want to know."

Well, this is a kettle of fish, I thought: Hope, the youngest, taking us over. Of course, she did have the perspective to see everything whole.

I no sooner put down the phone than Pete called up from his office. "Jezzie's on the warpath," he said. (He calls her Jezzie because she used to tell all kinds of lies to some little high school boy she had crazy about her—her own age—just so she could go out with Pete and the older crowd. It was easy to see through that. She thought she might just be getting a short run with us and would have to fall back on her own bunch when we shoved her out, so she was keeping a foothold. Pete caught her at it, but all it did was make him like her better. Hope was pert. She had a sharp little chin she liked to stick up in the air, and a turned-up nose. "Both signs of meanness," said Mr. Owens, Pete's father, "especially the nose," and buried his own in the newspaper.)

"Well," I said doubtfully, "if you think it's a good idea . . ."

"No stopping her," said Pete, with the voice of a spectator at the game. "If anybody can swing it, she can."

So we finally said yes.

The morning of Hope's party there was some ugly weather, one nasty little black cloud after another and a host of restless crosswinds. There was a tornado watch out for our county and two others, making you know it was a widespread weather system. I had promised to bring a platter of shrimp for the buffet table, and that meant a whole morning shucking them after driving out to pick up the order at the Fish Shack. At times the lightning was popping so close I had to get out of the kitchen. I would go sit in the living room with the thunder blamming so hard I couldn't even read the paper. Looking out at my backyard through the picture window, the colors of the marigolds and pansies seemed to be electric bright, blazing, then shuddering in the wind.

I was bound to connect all this with the anxiety that had got into things about that party. Charlie's being over in Louisiana didn't help. Maybe all was calm and bright over there, but I doubted it.

However, along about two the sky did clear, and the sun came out. When I drove out to Hope and Pete's place with the shrimp—it's a little way north of town, reached by its own side road, on a hill—everything was wonderful. There was a warm buoyancy in the air that made you feel young and remember what it was like to skip home from school.

"It's cleared off," said Hope, as though in personal triumph over Nature.

Pete was behind her at the door, enveloped in a huge apron. "I feel like playing softball," he said.

"Me, too," I agreed. "If I could just hear from Charlie."

"Oh, he'll be back," said Pete. "Charlie miss a party? Never!"

Well, it was quite an affair. The effort was to get us all launched in a new and happy period and the method was the tried and true one of drinking and feasting, dancing, pranking, laughing, flirting, and having fun. I had a new knife-pleated silk skirt, ankle length, dark blue shot with green and cyclamen, and a new off-the-shoulder blouse, and Mary Foote Williams, the visitor, wore a slit skirt, but Hope took the cake in her hoop skirts from her senior-high-school days, and her hair in a coarse gold net.

"The shrimp are gorgeous," she said. "Come look. I called Mama and requested prayer for good weather. It never fails."

"Charlie called," I said. "He said he'd be maybe thirty minutes late and would come on his own."

A car pulled up in the drive and there was Grey circling around and holding the door for Nelle herself. She had on a simple silk dress with her fine hair brushed loose and a pari of sexy new high-heeled sandals. It looked natural to see them together and I breathed easier without knowing I hadn't been doing it for quite a while. Hope was right, we'd had enough of this foolishness.

"That just leaves John and Rose," said Hope, "and I have my own ideas about them."

"What?" I asked.

"Well, I shouldn't say. It's y'alls' crowd." She was quick in her kitchen, clicking around with her skirts swaying. She had got a nice little colored girl, Perline, dressed up in black with a white ruffled apron. "I just think John's halfway to a stuffed shirt and Rose is going to get him all the way there."

So, our crowd or not, she was going right ahead.

"I think this has to do with you-know-what," I said.

"We aren't going to mention you-know-what," said Hope. "From now on, honey, my only four-letter words are 'dry' and 'cleaning.' "

John and Rose didn't show up, but two new couples did, a pair from Hattiesburg and the Kellmans, new in town but promising. Hope had let them in. Pete exercised himself at the bar and there was a strong punch as well. We strolled out to the pool and sat on white-painted iron chairs with cushions in green flowered plastic. Nelle sat with her pretty legs crossed, talking to Mary Foote. Grey was at her elbow. The little maid passed out canapés and shrimp. Light was still lingering in a clear sky barely pink at the edges. Pete skimmed leaves from the pool surface with a long-handled net. Lightning bugs winked and drifted, and the new little wife from Hattiesburg caught one or two in her palm and watched them crawl away, then take wing. "I used to do that," said Nelle. Then she shivered and Grey went for a shawl. It grew suddenly darker and one or two pale stars could be seen, then dozens. Pete, vanished inside, had started some records. Some people began to trail back in. And with another drink (the third, maybe?), it wasn't clear how much time had passed, when there came the harsh roar of a motor from the private road, growing stronger the nearer it got, a slashing of gravel in the drive out front, and a door slamming. And the first thing you knew there was Charlie Waybridge, filling the whole doorframe before Pete or Hope could even go to open it. He put his arms out to everybody. "Well, whaddaya know!" he said.

His tie was loose two buttons down and his light seersucker dress coat was crumpled and open but at least he had it on. I went right to him. He'd been drinking, of course, I'd known it from the first sound of the car—but who wasn't drinking? "Hi ya, baby!" he said, and grabbed me.

Then Pete and Hope were getting their greetings and were leading him up to meet the new people, till he got to the bar, where he dropped off to help himself.

It was that minute that Perline, the little maid, came in with a plate in her hand. Charlie swaggered up to her and said, "Well, if it ain't Mayola's daughter." He caught her chin in his hand. "Ain't that so?" "Yes, sir," said Perline. "I am." "Used to know yo' mama," said Charlie. Perline looked confused for a minute; then she lowered her eyes and giggled like she knew she was supposed to. "Gosh sakes, Charlie," I said, "quit horsing around and let's dance." It was hard to get him out of these moods. But I'd managed it more than once, dancing.

Charlie was a good strong leader and the way he danced, one hand firm to my waist, he would take my free hand in his and knuckle it tight against his chest. I could follow him better than I could anybody. Sometimes everybody would stop just to watch us, but the prize that night was going to Pete and Hope, they were shining around with some new steps that made the hoop skirts jounce. Charlie was half drunk, too, and bad on the turns.

"Try to remember what's important about this evening," I said. "You know what Hope and Pete are trying for, don't you?"

"I know I'm always coming home to a lecture," said Charlie and swung me out, spinning. "What a woman for sounding like a wife." He got me back and I couldn't tell if he was mad or not, I guess it was half and half; but right then he almost knocked over one of Hope's floral arrangements, so I said, "Why don't you go upstairs and catch your forty winks? Then you can come down fresh and start over." The music stopped. He blinked, looked tired all of a sudden, and, for a miracle, like a dog that never once chose to hear you, he minded.

I breathed a sigh when I saw him going up the stairs. But now I know I never once mentioned Nelle to him or reminded him right out, him with his head full of oil leases, bourbon, and the road, that she was the real cause of the party. Nelle was somewhere else, off in the back sitting room on a couch, to be exact, swapping family news with Mary Foote, who was her cousin.

Dancing with Charlie like that had put me in a romantic mood, and I fell to remembering the time we had first got serious, down on the coast where one summer we had all rented a fishing schooner. We had come into port at Mobile for more provisions and I had showered and dressed and was standing on deck in some leather sandals that tied around the ankle, a fresh white T-shirt, and some clean navy shorts. I had washed my hair, which was short then, and clustered in dark damp curls at the forehead. I say this about myself because when Charlie was coming on board with a six-pack in either hand, he stopped dead still. It was like the first time he'd ever seen me. He actually said that very thing later on after we'd finished with the boat and stayed on an extra day or so with all the crowd, to eat shrimp and gumbo and dance every night. We'd had our flare-ups before, but nothing had ever caught like that one. "I can't forget seeing you on the boat that day," he would say. "Don't be crazy, you'd seen me on that boat every day for a week." "Not like that," he'd rave, "like something fresh from the sea." "A catfish," I said. "Stop it, Eileen," he'd say, and dance me off the floor to the dark outside, and kiss me. "I can't get enough of you," he'd say, and take me in so close I'd get dizzy.

I kept thinking through all this in a warm frame of mind while making the rounds and talking to everybody, and maybe an hour, more or less, passed that way, when I heard a voice from the stairwell (Charlie) say: "God Almighty, if it isn't Nelle," and I turned around and saw all there was to see.

Charlie was fresh from his nap, the red faded from his face and his tie in place (he'd even buzzed off his five-o'clock shadow with Pete's electric razor). He was about five steps up from the bottom of the stairs. And Nelle, just coming back into the living room to join everybody, had on a Chinese-red silk shawl with a fringe. Her hair, so simple and shining, wasn't dark or blond either, just the color of hair, and she had on the plain dove-gray silk dress and the elegant sandals. She was framed in the door. Then I saw Charlie's face, how he was drinking her in, and I remembered the day on the boat.

"God damn, Nelle," said Charlie. He came down the steps and straight to her. "Where you been?"

"Oh, hello, Charlie," said Nelle in her friendly way. "Where have *you* been?"

"Honey, that's not even a question," said Charlie. "The point is, I'm *here*."

Then he fixed them both a drink and led her over to a couch in the far corner of the room. There was a side porch at the Owenses', spacious, with a tile floor—that's where we'd all been dancing. The living room was a little off center to the party. I kept on with my partying, but I had eyes in the back of my head where Charlie was concerned. I knew they were there on the couch and that he was crowding her toward one end. I hoped he was talking to her about Grey. I danced with Grey.

"Why don't you go and break that up?" I said.

"Why don't you?" said Grey.

"Marriage is different," I said.

"She can break it up herself if she wants to," he said.

I'd made a blunder and knew it was too late. Charlie was holding both Nelle's hands, talking over something. I fixed myself a stiff drink. It had begun to rain, quietly, with no advance warning. The couple from Hattiesburg had started doing some kind of talking blues number on the piano. Then we were singing. The couch was empty. Nelle and Charlie weren't there. . . .

It was Grey who came to see me the next afternoon. I was hung over but working anyway. Mr. McGinnis didn't recognize hangovers.

"I'm not asking her anywhere again," said Grey. "I'm through and she's through. I've had it. She kept saying in the car, 'Sure, I did like Charlie Waybridge, we all liked Charlie Waybridge. Maybe I was in love with Charlie Waybridge. But why start it up all over again? Why?' 'Why did you?' I said. 'That's more the question.' 'I never meant to, just there he was, making me feel that way.' 'You won't let me make you feel any way,' I said. 'My foot hurts,' she said, like a little girl. She looked a mess. Mud all over her dress and her hair gone to pieces. She had sprained her ankle. It had swelled up. That big."

"Oh, Lord," I said. "All Pete and Hope wanted was for you all— Look, can't you see Nelle was just drunk? Maybe somebody slugged her drink."

"She didn't have to drink it."

I was hearing Charlie: "All she did was get too much. Hadn't partied anywhere in months. Said she wanted some fresh air. First thing I knew she goes tearing out in the rain and whoops! in those high-heeled shoes—sprawling."

"Charlie and her," Grey went on. Okay, so he was hurt. Was that any reason to hurt me? But on he went. "Her and Charlie, that summer you went away up north, they were dating every night. Then her sister got sick, the one that died? She couldn't go on the coast trip with us."

"You think I don't know all that?" Then I said: "Oh, Grey!" and he left.

Yes, I sat thinking, unable to type anything: it was the summer her sister died and she'd had to stay home. I was facing up to Charlie Waybridge. I didn't want to, but there it was. If Nelle had been standing that day where I had stood, if Nelle had been wearing those sandals, that shirt, those shorts— Why pretend not to know Charlie Waybridge, through and through? What was he really doing on the Townshend property that night?

Pete, led by Hope, refused to believe anything but that the party had been a big success. "Like old times," said Pete. "What's wrong with new times?" said Hope. In our weakness and disarray, she was moving on in. (Damn Nelle Townshend.) Hope loved the new people; she was working everybody in together. "The thing for you to do about *that* . . ." she was now fond of saying on the phone, taking on problems of every sort.

When Hope heard that Nelle had sprained her ankle and hadn't been seen out in a day or so, she even got Pete one afternoon and went to call. She had telephoned but nobody answered. They walked up the long front walk between the elephant ears and up the front porch steps and rang the old turning bell half a dozen times. Hope had a plate of cake and Pete was carrying a bunch of flowers.

Finally Mrs. Townshend came shuffling to the door. Humpbacked, she had to look way up to see them, at a mole's angle. "Oh, it's you," she said.

"We just came to see Nelle," Hope chirped. "I understand she hurt her ankle at our party. We'd just like to commiserate."

"She's in bed," said Mrs. Townshend; and made no further move, either to open the door or take the flowers. Then she said, "I just wish you all would leave Nelle alone. You're no good for her. You're no good I know of for anybody. She went through all those years with you. She doesn't want you anymore. I'm of the same opinion." Then she leaned over and from an old-fashioned umbrella stand she drew up and out what could only be called a shotgun. "I keep myself prepared," she said. She cautiously lowered the gun into the umbrella stand. Then she looked up once again at them, touching the rims of her little oval glasses. "When I say you all, I mean all of you. You're drinking and you're doing all sorts of things that waste time, and you call that having fun. It's not my business unless you come here and make me say so, but Nelle's too nice to say so. Nelle never would—" She paused a long time, considering in the mildest sort of way. "Nelle can't shoot," she concluded, like this fact had for the first time occurred to her. She closed the door, softly and firmly.

I heard all this from Hope a few days later. Charlie was off again and I was feeling lower than low. This time we hadn't even quarreled. It seemed more serious than that. A total reevaluation. All I could come to was a question: Why doesn't he reassure me? All I could answer was that he must be in love with Nelle. He tried to call her when I wasn't near. He sneaked off to do it, time and again.

Alone, I tried getting drunk to drown out my thoughts, but couldn't, and alone for a day too long, I called up Grey. Grey and I used to date, pretty heavy. "Hell," said Grey, "I'm fed up to here and so are you. Let's blow it." I was tight enough to say yes and we met out at the intersection. I left my car at the shopping-center parking lot. I remember the sway of his Buick Century, turning onto the Interstate. We went up to Jackson.

The world is spinning now and I am spinning along with it. It doesn't stand still anymore to the stillness inside that murmurs to me, I know my love and I belong to my love when all is said and done, down through foreverness and into eternity. No, when I got back I was just part of it all, ordinary, a twenty-eight-year-old attractive married woman with family and friends and a nice house in Tyler, Mississippi. But with nothing absolute.

When I had a drink too many now, I would drive out to the woods and stop the car and walk around among places always known. One day, not even thinking about them, I saw Nelle drive by and this time there was no doubt who was with her—Robin Byers. They were talking. Well, Robin's wife mended the clothes when they were ripped or torn, and she sewed buttons on. Maybe they were going there. I went home.

At some point the phone rang. I had seen to it that it was "out of order" when I went up to Jackson with Grey, but now it was "repaired," so I answered it. It was Nelle.

"Eileen, I guess you heard Mama turned Pete and Hope out the other day. She was in the mood for telling everybody off." Nelle laughed her clear, pure laugh. You can't have a laugh like that unless you've got a right to it, I thought.

"How's your ankle?" I asked.

"I'm still hobbling around. What I called for, Mama wanted me to tell you something. She said, 'I didn't mean quite everybody. Eileen can still come. You tell her that.'"

Singled out. If she only knew, I thought. I shook when I put down the phone.

But I did go. I climbed up to Nelle's bedroom with Mrs. Townshend toiling behind me, and sat in one of those old rocking chairs near a bay window with oak paneling and cane plant, green and purple, in a window box. I stayed quite a while. Nelle kept her ankle propped up and Mrs. Townshend sat in a tiny chair about the size of a twelve-year-old's, which was about the size she was. They told stories and laughed with that innocence that seemed like all clear things—a spring in the woods, a dogwood bloom, a carpet of pine needles along a sun-dappled road. Like Nelle's ankle, I felt myself getting well. It was a new kind of wellness, hard to describe. It didn't have much to do with Charlie and me.

"Niggers used to come to our church," Mrs. Townshend recalled. "They had benches in the back. I don't know why they quit. Maybe they all died out—the ones we had, I mean."

"Maybe they didn't like the back," said Nelle.

"It was better than nothing at all. The other churches didn't even have that. There was one girl going to have a baby. I was scared she would have it right in the church. Your father said, 'What's wrong with that? Dr. Erskine could deliver it, and we could baptize it on the spot.'"

I saw a picture on one of those little tables they had by the dozen, with the starched linen doilies and the bowed-out legs. It was of two gentlemen, one taller than the other, standing side by side in shirt-sleeves and bow ties and each with elastic bands around their upper arms, the kind that used to hold the sleeves to a correct length of cuff. They were smiling in a fine natural way, out of friendship. One must have been Nelle's father, dead so long ago. I asked about the other. "Child," said Mrs. Townshend, "don't you know your own grandfather? He and Sid thought the world of one another." I had a better feeling when I left. Would it last? Could I get it past the elephant ears?

I didn't tell Charlie about going there. Charlie got it from some horse's mouth that Grey and I were up in Jackson that time, and he pushed me off the back steps. An accident, he said; he didn't see me when he came whamming out the door. For a minute I thought I, too, had sprained or broken something, but a skinned knee was all it was. He watched me clean the knee, watched the bandage go on. He wouldn't go out—not to Pete and Hope's, not to Rose and John's, not to anywhere—and the whiskey went down in the bottle.

I dreamed one night of Robin Byers, that I ran into him uptown but didn't see a scar on his face. I followed him, asking, Where is it? What happened? Where's it gone? But he walked straight on, not seeming to hear. But it was no dream that his house caught fire, soon after the cleaning shop opened again. Both Robin and Nelle said it was only lightning struck the back wing and burned out a shed room before Robin could stop the blaze. Robin's daughter got jumped on at school by some other black children who yelled about her daddy being a "Tom." They kept her at home for a while to do her schoolwork there. What's next?

Next for me was going to an old lady's apartment for Mr. McGinnis, so she could sign her will, and on the long steps to her door, running into Robin Byers, fresh from one of his deliveries.

"Robin," I said, at once, out of nowhere, surprising myself, "you got to leave here, Robin. You're tempting fate, every day."

And he, just as quick, replied: "I got to stay here. I got to help Miss Nelle."

Where had it come from, what we said? Mine wasn't a bit like me; I might have been my mother or grandmother talking. Certainly not the fun girl who danced on piers in whirling miniskirts and dove off a fishing boat to reach a beach, swimming, they said, between the fishhooks and the sharks. And Robin's? From a thousand years back, maybe, superior and firm, speaking out of sworn duty, his honored trust. He was standing above me on the steps. It was just at dark, and in the first streetlight I could see the white scar, running riverlike down the flesh, like the mark lightning leaves on a smooth tree. When we passed each other, it was like erasing what we'd said and that we'd ever met.

But one day I am walking in the house and picking up the telephone, only to find Charlie talking on the extension. "Nelle . . ." I hear. "Listen, Nelle. If you really are foolin' around with that black bastard, he's answering to *me.*" And *blam!* goes the phone from her end, loud as any gun of her mother's.

I think we are all hanging on a golden thread, but who has got the other end? Dreaming or awake, I'm praying it will hold us all suspended.

Yes, praying—for the first time in years.

Shirley Ann Grau

The Long Afternoon

Like the weeks that had preceded it, the day was hot. There wasn't a speck of dust or a breath of air moving. Under the burning white light of the sun, things seemed closer than they were really. Hilda Marie Merrick, who was called Patsy, sat on the edge of the front porch and dangled her bare legs. She had been home from the hospital a week, and there was nothing to do. She lifted her right leg to stare attentively at the red polish on her toenails. She'd been up since eight, when the morning got too hot for sleeping. She'd washed her hair and set it too tightly; her head was beginning to ache. "When I woke up this morning, I wanted to die," she called over her shoulder.

In the living room, by the open window, her mother sealed the letter she had just finished and began writing the address. "Did you, dear?"

"Yes, I did." Patsy reached one finger to loosen the tightest of the curls. "Mother, do you know that there is not a single person left in this town that I would care to talk to. They have gone to camp, every single one of them."

Mrs. Merrick's voice took on a faint warning color. "The doctor told you no."

"I don't care what he said. I just don't care."

"Now you're being silly."

"I wouldn't hurt myself. I could be so careful."

"No."

There was the soft rubbing sound of pen on paper, and over by the hedge the ragged sound of a cricket.

"Do you know something?" Patsy said. "You would think that with the way they all came down to the hospital and stood around, looking all worried and wanting to do every little thing for me—a person would think that they wouldn't go off to camp and leave me where I haven't got a single person I know in town."

"Oh, Patsy."

"It is not often that eleven-year-old people have their appendix out, and as serious as mine."

"It wasn't serious."

"It was. I could feel it. You just don't know what it was like."

"Baby, how spoiled you got."

"You don't know." Patsy's hand felt lightly for the scar. "It's still sore."

Across the street a power mower started noisily, and from farther away still came the empty sound of a horse's hoofs and the singsong chant of a fruit vendor.

The street was paved on one side only. The city council had started to surface it months before, only to discover that they had overestimated the available funds. They had then announced that unless the people who lived on the street paid for it themselves, it would stay that way. It had stayed that way.

A small girl, not more than eight or so, came up the center of the half-paved road and in through the Merricks' gate, walking with the measured, scuffing tread of her age. Her hair was pulled back freshly into two pigtails, which stuck out from the nape of her neck; from each one dropped a ribbon. The starchiness of her dress was already beginning to wilt in the heat. One hand was stuck into the skirt pocket. The other hand held a brown roll—an old-fashioned leather music case. She climbed the steps, smiled shyly at Patsy and Mrs. Merrick, and, with a sidling glide, slipped in the front door. Between her thin, nubby shoulders her dress was already stained by perspiration.

"I didn't look like that," Patsy said, "at her age."

"Yes, you did," her mother said.

"No."

Mrs. Merrick began putting the note paper back in the box. "Why are you so trying, dear?"

"I was born that way." Patsy pointed her nose at the white, hot sky. "Mother, I itch all over."

"The heat powder is in the downstairs bathroom."

"It's not that kind of thing. I feel just like I could shake myself once or twice and my skin would fall right off. Like I'm not attached to it at all."

"The heat is bad," Mrs. Merrick said. Her gray eyes had a misty look as they stared out at the lawn. And her pencil was busy making little doodling marks.

From inside the house came the first hesitant chords of the scale.

"Here we go." Patsy gave a long, whistling sigh. "Why does Claude have to take pupils here?"

"Because there isn't any other place."

"Oh, hells bells!"

Inside, fumbling fingers began striking G-major chords. Patsy closed her eyes and tried seeing how long she could hold her breath. Her eyes popped open when a truck stopped, but she was so intent on holding her breath that she didn't wonder about the large crate two men unloaded. She went on counting.

The men balanced the crate on the edge of the steps and wiped the perspiration from their chins. "Where you reckon you want this?" one asked. He had bright china-blue eyes behind the tight folds of lids squinched up against the glare.

Patsy shrugged and went on with her silent counting. Fifty-one, fifty-two, fifty-three . . . She heard the door bell and then her mother's surprised murmur. She always manages to sound surprised, Patsy thought. And at that exact moment, without thinking, without deciding, she took a long breath of air. Fifty-eight.

"Patsy, honey," her mother called. "Come see—the new television's here."

She got up and ambled into the hall. Her mother was signing the receipt, on the top of the packing case. In the little room on the left that they called the music room she could see the bent small back of the pigtailed girl and the bent long back of her brother Claude. His finger moved directingly up and down, keeping time.

Patsy sat down in the hall, in one of the round-backed chairs that had belonged to her grandmother, and waited until the men had just passed her and were at the front door. "Mama," she said, "I'm growing again. I got to get a bigger bra."

The men coughed with laughter, and her mother closed the front door sharply after them. To Patsy, she said, "Just what are you trying to do?"

"Nothing." Patsy stared after the men, puzzled. She had not expected the laugh—a look maybe, or a wink. "I hate people."

"Young lady, you'd better find something to do," her mother said, and left her.

The little pigtailed musician departed, grinning broadly this time. Her dress was soaked with perspiration, her glasses were blurred and smeary, too, but she did not seem to notice. She had put her music away so hastily that the white edges showed ragged at the ends of the rolled case. Only one of the leather straps was fastened; the other dragged in the dirt. She skipped out the front gate and began to run back the way she had come, following the exact center of the street, so that one foot ran on concrete, the other on mud. It gave her a kind of lopsided, jack-rabbit pace.

"If there was any traffic, she'd get killed," Patsy said with satisfaction. She had returned to the porch.

"But there isn't," Claude said. He swung his long leg over a chair and sat astride it. The Coke bottle in his hand dripped bits of ice to the porch floor.

"You didn't bring me one," Patsy said.

"This is the last."

"Now, that's not true. I saw a whole case."

"They're all warm." He held out the bottle. "You want the rest of this?"

"No." She threw back her head and stared at the bright blue ceiling. Wasps were building their round mud nests up against one corner. "You've got all sorts of germs I don't want to catch."

"Okay."

"You drink noisier than anybody I ever knew."

"More noisily," he corrected.

"Why do you have to wear those silly-looking shorts?"

He tipped his head back and finished the Coke with a gurgle. "And those long socks are the silliest things I ever did see."

"Quit it."

"You're too thin to wear things like that—that's what Mama told you."

"One day," Claude said, "I'm going to strangle you."

"Mama did tell you you were too thin for shorts. I heard her."

He yawned.

"You got the biggest teeth I ever saw," she said. "Like a horse."

"Do you want to fight?" He pulled out his handkerchief and dried his hands. "I haven't got time now. Later this evening, huh?"

Patsy turned away. "I don't want to be here this evening. I won't be here this evening at all."

Mrs. Merrick appeared. She was one of those women who never step outside without a hat—in winter because it is cold and in summer because it is sunny. Now she wore a light-green straw with a wide, flopping brim.

"You're always wearing green," Patsy said accusingly.

"Idiot child, shut up." Claude balanced the bottle on one finger.

"Really, Claude," Mrs. Merrick said. "Don't be nasty to her."

"You heard her," Patsy said. "You heard what she told you."

Claude shrugged, and blew through loose lips: "Ruuuuup."

"I wish I had eyes pretty as yours, Mama," Patsy said.

"Honey, you have lovely eyes."

"Brown." Patsy crinkled up the corners of her mouth in disgust. "Everybody's got brown eyes. And anyhow it makes me look like Claude."

"God forbid," Claude said softly, and his mother threw him a warning glance.

"Patsy, honey, don't you want to come along with me?" she said.

"Where?"

"I'm going to pick up the laundry."

"Nuh-uh."

"It would give you something to do," Mrs. Merrick said. "We'll be right back."

A ride across the little town to the Negro section, which was called Bridge City. Then a talk with the laundress while her oldest son brought out the bundle and put it in the back seat of the car and her other kids swung from an old tire hung from the branches of the big chinaberry tree.

"No," she said.

"Did Mary Beth finish her lesson, Claude?" Mrs. Merrick asked.

"Yep. Lucille won't be along until three-thirty."

"Why do I have to have a brother who gives music lessons?" Patsy demanded.

"Now, dear," her mother said.

"Why can't it ever be quiet around here."

"Hilda Marie, you are being mean, plain and simple mean, to your only brother," her mother said.

"I want to be mean. I want to."

Mrs. Merrick only waved as she headed for the garage.

"You *are* crazy," Claude told Patsy pleasantly and went inside to put back the Coke bottle.

Patsy threw her head far back over her chair, pressing until the wood cut into the back of her neck and little lights danced in front of her eyes.

"Fool jackass!" she cried at the top of her voice. "Crazy fool jackass!"

At lunch, Mr. Merrick, a short, very heavy man, looked longingly at the other plates and then began his own low-calorie fare.

"I don't see how you eat that without salt," Patsy said. "And so dreadful to begin with."

"I don't either, kitten," her father said.

"You'd think Claude would put on some weight, instead of being a bean pole like he is," Patsy said.

"Like is not a conjunction," Claude said.

"Now don't begin that," her mother said.

"What grades did you get in English?" Claude asked.

"I got a B-plus, Mr. Jackass."

"That's enough," her father said.

Patsy moved her fork in circles around her plate, following the gold bands. "I reckon I am not hungry. I would like to be excused."

"You're not sick, dear?" her mother asked.

Patsy turned at the door, with one hand holding the frame. "I am dying," she said. "I am dying of loneliness with everyone away."

"What an act," Claude said.

Patsy retreated to a porch chair and propped her feet up on the railing. She was trying with all her might to see if she could pop the back hook of her bra by hunching her shoulders when her father came out and sat beside her.

"Dessert?" He offered her a plate.

She shook her head sadly. "Like I said, I am not hungry." She regretted the first word the minute it was out of her mouth, but he did not correct her.

He still held out the plate. "Chocolate cake."

She took it. "Mama said it wasn't polite to offer things with your left hand."

"She's absolutely right," Mr. Merrick said, "but I am not going to fight, kitten, so stop trying."

"I wish you would stop calling me that name. I hate that name more than anything."

"Hilda Marie?" he suggested.

She made a face.

"What, then?"

She did not answer.

"Don't forget to take the plate in with you, kitten, when you go," Mr. Merrick said, getting up.

"Daddy," she said. He turned.

"Can't I come to town with you?"

He put one foot on the step and leaned his elbow on his knee. "Kitten, you'd be in the office half an hour and you'd get tired and want to come home. And I'd have to stop and bring you."

"No," she said. "No, I wouldn't." But he shook his head and was gone.

In the shade of the big red honeysuckle, an orange-striped cat stretched lazily, and then it sauntered over to the deeper shade of the butterfly bush. The long, hot afternoon was beginning.

Claude came out and started down the steps.

"Everybody's leaving," Patsy said. He didn't answer or turn, so she followed him, scuffing her heels on the gravel of the walk. "Where are you going?" she asked.

His car was at the curb. "I'm going to see Joyce."

"Like that?" She pointed to his shorts. "I didn't think you'd want anybody outside the family to see you like that."

"Look, twerp . . . Why don't you find something to do? Anything."

"That's what everybody tells me. You going to play bridge?"

"Yes, I *am*."

"I could play with you."

"If you could play."

"You could teach me."

"No," Claude said.

"It wouldn't take long."

"Not on your life." He got in the car and pulled the door to.

She stuck her head in the window. "If I had a car, I could drive around and visit people way over in Jackson, if I had a car."

He switched on the ignition and started the motor. "Well, you haven't. Now move before you get hurt."

The car drove away. She stood and watched, swinging her right leg back and forth so that her sandal scuffed along the gutter edge. After the car disappeared, she stared down at her moving foot. Then, carefully, she bent her sandal back against the cement. Pressing with all her weight, she snapped the sole so that it flapped loosely as she walked.

In the side yard a mulberry tree was dropping its full purple berries into the grass. She heard them squish under her feet. From a branch just over her head she pulled one of the nubby berries, and put it in her mouth. It prickled for an instant and tasted of dust. Then the heavy, overripe juice flooded out on her tongue. She reached up for a cluster of berries this time. They crushed between her grasping fingers. She whistled softly between her teeth and wiped her hand across the front of her skirt.

Claude had left one of his hunting knives on the back porch. She picked it up and began tossing it idly into the ground, trying without success to spear a small fragment of wood. Tiring of this, she left the knife sticking in the ground and wandered over to the sunny end of the porch to inspect her geraniums—four little pots of earth, each with a couple of scraggly stems reaching up into the air. Only one had a leaf, a shriveled brown bit that wrapped itself around the dead stalk.

Patsy filled the watering can and poured a little water on each one. Then she went into the kitchen.

"Fanny."

The short, stocky black woman turned around. "Yeah?"

"We got any coffee grounds?" Even as she asked, Patsy was making for the coffeepot.

"What you want that for?"

"My geraniums." They had been on her bedside table at the hospital, and she had loved each single one. "Mama says coffee grounds are good for plants."

"Ain't nothing gonna help them plants. Watch out my floor!" Fanny said as Patsy carried a handful of dripping grounds. "They is dead."

Patsy sprinkled the grounds around the bare twigs, watered them again, and went back in the kitchen. She got herself a glass of water and leaned on the refrigerator, drinking and swinging her leg so that the broken sandal flapped slowly.

Fanny turned. She was perched on a high red stool at the sink, polishing demitasse spoons. "What I hearing?"

Patsy held up her foot.

"Might just as well throw them out. They ain't no more good than those plants of yours," Fanny said.

Patsy rubbed the back of her thighs against the cool enamel of the refrigerator. "This is the longest day."

"Iffen you want things to do, you could get that big silver pitcher from out the dining room and polish it up."

"Did Estes come yet?" He was Fanny's boy, a couple of years older than Patsy. He came sometimes to keep his mother company, if he didn't have anything else to do. "Did he?" Patsy demanded.

"No, he ain't, yet."

Patsy stood on one leg and curled the lifted foot around the other ankle. She watched Fanny's movements, narrowing her left eye with the effort of her perception. "Lord, but you sure are slow."

The hand stopped its motion. "You come all the way back here to pester me?"

"Nuh-uh. Fanny, why don't you give them to him?"

Fanny reached her rag into the jar of pink silver polish. "Give who to who?"

"You just don't listen to me. Give those spoons, the ones right there, to Estes."

"Now, why I want to do that?"

"He could sell them for a lot of money." Patsy squatted down on the floor.

"You mama say for you not to sit like that. She say it ain't becoming for a young lady."

Patsy pretended not to hear. "Don't you want to make a lot of money?"

Fanny turned around again. "And what you mama going to say to that?"

"She wouldn't know."

"And what the police gonna say when they see you mama's initials all over the tops of them spoons?"

"We could take the initials off," Patsy said, "or take them over to Atlanta, where nobody'd know."

"You been looking too much at that television. I told you mama that."

"That's got nothing to do with it."

"You looking at it all day in the hospital there, I told her it ain't good."

"You talk so much. Yack, yack, yack."

Fanny swung back to her work, so violently that she had to catch hold of the counter for balance. "I ain't even begun to talk."

Chewing her lip, Patsy gazed up at the crosspiece of the doorway. After a minute, she said, "I bet you anything I could chin myself on that."

Fanny whistled—"Euuuuuuu."

"Well, I could."

"And bust all that stitching the doctor put in your stomach. And pour your insides all out over the floor."

Patsy stood up, her arms moving nervously. That was a nightmare she had sometimes: the hole in her stomach opening up. Sometimes, when she woke up, she would reach inside her pajamas and run her fingers along the new scar, just to be sure that it still held together.

"Fanny, what would you do if I was sick right here?"

"Iffen you gonna get sick, you just plain better go out in the back yard, where it don't matter none," Fanny said calmly.

Patsy pounded her fist against the door. "You are just so mean that I am going to make my mama fire you, and then I'm gonna tell everybody about you, and you won't be able to get another job, and you'll starve to death. That's what I'll do."

"Man, man," Fanny said to the chrome-plated faucet of the sink. "She sure is changed. They must put something else in her when they took that appendix out."

Before she thought, Patsy said, "You reckon they did?"

"You reckon they did?" Fanny mimicked in a high-pitched voice. "You reckon they did?"

"Crazy fool jackass!" Patsy exploded as she banged out the door. "Crazy fool jackass!"

Fanny shouted after her, "They done fill you up with all sorts of garbage to make you act so ugly! That what they done!"

Tucking her hands in the back belt of her shorts, Patsy sauntered around the corner of the house, still whispering to herself, "Fool jackass, crazy fool jackass."

She spotted Jo Dillard's rumpled black head, almost hidden by one of the big old hydrangea bushes. The Dillards lived next door. "What are you doing by my house?" Patsy asked.

Jo turned her head slowly, and the clear, blue, five-year-old gaze focused first on Patsy's feet, then climbed her body, coming almost indifferently to her face.

"I asked you what you doing by my house."

The eyes climbed down the body again. "Digging," Jo said. She pointed with her left hand. "See?" Behind the hydrangea bush was a little hole she was making with an old wavy-bladed bread knife.

"What you doing that for?"

"Nothing. Digging."

"You're lying."

Jo did not answer.

"Tell me."

"Huh?"

"You tell me."

Jo turned back to her work. Two thin sinews stood out on the back of her neck, beneath the ragged fringe of her clipped hair.

"You are the ugliest-looking kid I have ever seen," Patsy told her. "You are positively the ugliest thing. And you get uglier every day. You do."

The eyes lifted, circled her face, and wandered off.

"And the way you do everything with your left hand—that's the silliest thing, too."

The child went on digging, her head bent.

"Tell me." Patsy's voice dropped, and she crouched down by the smaller figure.

The child watched the ground intently, fascinated by each small load of mud. A round white marble came to the surface. Two small, squarish fingers went down and picked it up; the hand closed over it.

"What you find?"

The knife continued to lift small pats of dirt.

"What did you find in my garden? Give it here."

The blade fell to the ground. Jo clenched both hands around the marble. Her fingers wove tightly together.

Patsy picked up the knife. She scraped it against the brick foundation and ran her finger over the wavy edge of the blade. "I am going to kill you," she said. "And a dozen policemen will come to take you away."

With a small whinny of fear, Jo scuttled home, her hands still clenched.

Patsy jumped up and, waving the knife over her head, shouted, "Don't come back! Don't ever come back!"

She tossed the knife up against the trunk of the hydrangea bush and walked away, wiping her dirty hands on her bare thighs. A window flew up, and Mrs. Dillard called, "Patsy, what are you doing! Patsy . . ." She pretended not to hear as she strolled to the back of the yard, rolling her hips under the tight white shorts.

In the quiet of the hot afternoon, she could hear the clicking of the dial phone. "Maybe she is calling the police," she told herself aloud. "And they will come and get me in one of the white cars with the chrome siren on top. And my scar will pop, and I'll bleed all over everything." She fingered her side; it was sore to the touch.

Inside her own house, the phone began to ring. She cocked her head, listening. She could almost hear Mrs. Dillard's angry words.

"She is old and ugly," Patsy said aloud. From a low branch a fat swallow beat a clumsy retreat. "She is old and fat and ugly and I hate her."

Dragging her feet so that the tips of her toes brushed the crispy edges of the grass, she went around the two chinaberry trees, grown close together and circled by an old wisteria vine with ragged shreds of flowers still among its leaves. She was hidden from the house.

Her mother appeared on the side porch and called, "Patsy!"

"She is old and ugly and I hate *her*, too," Patsy whispered.

"Patsy, come her this instant. This very instant."

Patsy reached out and took hold of the sharp rough bark of the tree. "No," she whispered.

Fanny popped out the kitchen door. Through the vines Patsy saw the sun glint on her black skin.

"What she did this time?"

Mrs. Merrick opened the screen and came down into the yard; her heels made a sharp clatter on each step. "This is just too much."

"What she did?"

"Patsy!" Her mother folded her hands and rested her chin on them. She was really angry; that was a sure sign.

"Ugly," Patsy whispered.

Right in front of her were crosspieces of wood nailed to the trunk of one of the chinaberry trees—the steps leading up to the tree house. She tilted back her head. Vaguely, through the dense foliage, she could see the brown, weathered boards. Slowly and carefully, so as not to hurt her scar, she began to climb.

"Patsy! . . . Look in the back yard, Fanny." Mrs. Merrick started across the grass.

Patsy reached the platform, railless and tiny: only four boards wide. She sat down cross-legged on the wood that had been warped by winter rains and stained almost black by the falling berries.

"I won't ever come down," she whispered. The sound startled her, so she went on talking to herself silently. I'll live up here. Until I get old and die. I'll stay until I get old and older and die.

Below, hidden by the feathery leaves, her mother demanded, "Patsy, come here immediately."

I won't ever come down. I won't.

She clenched her fists and closed her eyes in determination. But already, under the lids, the tears were beginning.

One Summer

You forget most things, don't you? It's even hard to remember in the hurry and bustle of spring what the slow unwinding of fall was like. And summer vacations all blur one into the other when you try to look back at them. At least, it's that way for me: a year is a long time.

But there's one summer I remember, clear as anything; the day, a Thursday in August.

It had been a terrific summer, the way it always is here. There was dust an inch thick on everything. The streams were mostly all dry. Down in the flaky red dust of the beds—where the flood in spring was so fast you couldn't cross it and where now there was just a foot or two of slimy smelling water—you could find the skeletons of fishes so brittle that they crumbled when your foot touched them. The wells were always dug extra deep just for summers like this: there's always water if you go down deep enough for it. There was plenty of water for drinking and washing and even maybe enough to keep the gardens watered, but nobody did; most of the plants withered and crumbled away. By August, cracks were beginning to show in the ground, too, crisscross lines maybe half an inch wide showing under the brown dead grass.

So that when this big pile of thunderheads came lifting out of the south everybody watched them, wondering and hoping.

I was sitting on Eunice Herbert's porch, over in the coolest part, behind the wooden jalousies. There was a swing there, and an electric fan on a little black iron table, and two or three black iron stands of ferns, all different kinds—her mother was crazy about them. Maybe it wasn't cooler there, but with the darkness from the closed jalousies and the smell of wet mud from the fern pots, it seemed comfortable.

Eunice was the prettiest girl in town, there wasn't any doubt of that. She had hair so blond that it looked almost silver white. All summer long she kept it piled up on top of her head with a flower stuck right on top; she got the idea from the cover of *Seventeen*, she said. Whenever she was at a party, there was nearly always a fight between some boys. It was just sure to happen, that's all; I was in enough to know. I almost had got thrown out of school because of one of them: at the spring party in the gym of the big yellow-brick high school. I don't remember how it started. I was just dancing with some girl when over at the table where Eunice was sitting two fellows started to fight. I remember dropping the girl's arm and walking over. Not wanting to fight, not really, but somehow I did; and somehow I got a Coke bottle in my hand and started swinging. It was the bottle that nearly got me expelled. My father had to do an awful lot of talking so I could go on and finish the year with the rest of my class.

One thing though—it set things up fine between Eunice and me. In those two months she hadn't had a date with another fellow.

That hot Thursday afternoon in August we were sitting on her porch swing, holding hands under the wide skirt of her dress, which she had spread out so that her mother wouldn't see anything but two people sitting and talking. Her mother was inside, doing something, I never found out what, but every ten minutes or so she'd stick her head out the door and ask: "You children want something?" And Eunice would say: "Oh, Mamma, no," with her voice going up a little on the last word.

We were just sitting there swinging back and forth, staring at the green little leaves of the ferns. I was feeling her soft thin fingers. There was a kind of shivering going up and down my back that wasn't just the electric fan blowing on my wet shirt.

Then her mother stuck her head out the front door to the porch for maybe the fifteenth time that afternoon—she was a little woman with a tiny face that reminded me of a squirrel somehow, with a nervous twitching nose. "Children," she said (and I could feel Eunice's fingers stiffen at the word), "just you look out there—" she pointed to the south; "here's a big pile of rain clouds, coming right this way."

"Yes, ma'am," I said. We'd noticed the clouds come up half an hour past.

And then because she kept staring at us we had to get up and walk over and peer out through the little open squares in the jalousies and look at the sky.

"It looks like rain," I said, because somebody had to say something.

Without turning around I heard Mrs. Herbert take a seat in one of the wicker chairs. I heard the cane creak and then the rockers begin to move softly back and forth on the wood flooring. Alongside me I could feel Eunice stiffen like a cat that's been hit by something. But there wasn't anything she could do: her mother was going to sit and talk to us for the rest of the afternoon. I might just as well go sit in one of the single chairs.

The afternoon was so quiet that from my house—just across the street and one house down—you could hear our cook, Mayline, singing at the top of her voice:

> *"Didn't it rain, little children,*
> *Didn't it rain, little children,*
> *Didn't it rain?"*

So she'd noticed that big mass of clouds too.

"Is that Mayline I hear?" Mrs. Herbert said. The words came out slowly, one for each creak of her rocker.

"Yes, ma'am," I said and sat down in the red-painted straight chair.

Eunice dropped down in the middle of the swing and folded her hands on her lap and didn't say anything.

"Well," her mother said with just an edge of annoyance, "if you children are doing anything you don't want me to see . . ."

"Oh, Mamma," Eunice said, staring down at her hands.

"Yes, ma'am," I said, and then changed it to "No, ma'am," and all the while I was thinking of a way to get us out of there.

From the corner of my eye I saw that Eunice's mother was getting that hurt bewildered look all mothers use.

And then—just at the right minute—we heard Morris Henry come running down the street. He was a poppy-eyed little black monkey

Negro, no taller than a twelve-year-old, but strong as a man and twice as quick. He had little hands, like a child's or a girl's maybe, with nails that he always chewed down to the quick. Even when there wasn't anything more to bite on, he'd keep chewing away at the fingers with his wide flaring yellow teeth.

He came running down the road—you could hear the sound of his bare feet on the dirt road quite a ways in front of him. He took a short cut through the empty lot at the corner and came bursting through the high dry grass that went up like a puff of smoke all around him.

With the dust in his nose he started sneezing, but he didn't stop. He tore down the middle of our street at top speed, both hands holding to his trousers so they wouldn't fall off. He took our fence with a one-hand jump, made a straight line through the yard to the kitchen door, and was up the steps two at a time. The door slammed after him.

It was quiet then with him inside my house. All you could see was the path he'd broken for himself through the dry stalks of the zinnias in the front yard.

"My goodness," Mrs. Herbert said. "Hadn't you better go see what's wrong?"

"Yes, ma'am," I said.

"I'll come with you," Eunice said quickly.

We yanked open the screen door and we were all the way down the steps and halfway to the front gate before we heard it slam, we were running that fast.

"The front way," I said. And we rushed up the front steps and in the front door.

We had to stop for a minute: the parlor was always kept with the blinds drawn, and coming out of the sun we couldn't see a thing. I could hear Eunice breathing heavily alongside me. She was so close it was the easiest thing in the world to put my arm around her. I kissed her hard, and for as long as I dared with people so close—the voices in the kitchen sounded excited.

"You hurt," she said.

And I just grinned at her; it was the sort of hurt she liked.

And then we went into the kitchen to see what had happened.

Little Morris Henry was sitting in a red-painted kitchen chair and my mother was holding his thin little shoulder, that was all bulged and lumpy with muscle. Over in a corner Mayline stood with her mouth open and a streak of flour on her black face.

Next to my shoulder I could hear Eunice let her breath out with a quick hissing whisper. No one seemed to have noticed that we had come in. Mayline was looking over in our direction and her eyes rested right on us, but there wasn't any recognition in them. They were just empty brown eyes; only they weren't brown any more, but bright live metal. They were eyes like flat pieces of silver.

Because we didn't know what to do, we stood very still and waited.

In a minute my mother looked around. She seemed to feel that we were there; she couldn't have seen us, we were behind her. But she looked over. Keeping her hand on Morris Henry's shoulder she twisted her head around and looked at us.

"He says there's something wrong with the old gentleman. . . ." Her voice wandered off. She had spoken in such a whisper and the words had slipped so gradually that you couldn't quite tell when she stopped. I wondered if I had really heard anything at all.

She seemed to realize this, because she repeated louder this time, in a way that you couldn't mistake: "He says there's something wrong with the old gentleman."

That would be my grandfather. Everybody called him that. They never did use his name. When they were talking about him it was "the old gentleman" and to his face they always said "sir."

"The old gentleman's gone fishing on the Scanos River," they'd say. And that would mean he'd taken his little power boat out into the middle of the muddy red yellow river and stopped the motor and thrown over his line and was sitting there waiting for the fish to bite; and they always did; he was a fine fisherman.

Or maybe Luce Rogers, who was Mayline's husband—of a sort and not a legal sort—would stick his head in the kitchen door and wipe his shiny face with his broad hand and look at Mayline and shake his head and say sadly: "Baby, I can't set with you this morning. I got to go to work." And Mayline would look at him from under her lids, not quite believing him because he didn't like to work and he sure had a wandering eye. So she would suck in one corner of her mouth and hold it between her teeth and stare at him, nodding her head just a little. And he would open his eyes very wide and shake his head and say: "You ain't got no cause to suspicion me, baby. I was just plain walking past the place when the old gentleman yells at me from the porch."

And Mayline would relax for a little while anyhow, because that would mean that my grandfather had found some work for him to do, like mowing the grass maybe or washing the windows, or doing some other work that the regular girl, whose name was Wilda Olive, couldn't do. It was just about the only time Luce Rogers worked—when my grandfather caught him.

That Thursday afternoon in the kitchen, it was Eunice who moved first. She slipped around me—she was standing almost half behind me in the doorway—and went up to my mother and put her arms around her.

"You better sit down, Mrs. Addams," she said. She had the chair all pulled out from the table and ready. "You look a little pale."

That wasn't true; my mother looked perfectly all right. But that was Eunice's way—she'd used that line in the high-school play a couple of months before and she didn't see any reason not to use it again. Or maybe it was because she didn't really know what to say either.

Anyhow, my mother did sit down. And she leaned one arm against the table and beat a little tattoo on it with her fingers.

The minute she sat down, Morris Henry bounced up and went over and stood by the window, chewing his little knuckles. Eunice stood next to my mother and looked over at me. And I looked down at the ground.

My mother began tapping the heel of her shoe against the floor. That was a sure sign she was thinking. Finally she said to me: "Mac-Donald—"

"Yes, ma'am," I said.

She was the only one who ever used my full name like that. To most people I was just Mac. But she liked that full name, maybe because it had belonged to her family. Or maybe she just liked the sound of it.

"Go see if there's a car in the neighborhood we can borrow. . . . Go outside and look.

"Eunice," she was giving orders now, "put in a call for Dr. Addams. . . . I've got to put on a regular dress." She only wore a kind of smock-like affair around the house, because of the heat.

I went out in the yard and looked up and down the block. There wasn't a single car in any driveway. It wasn't surprising, because most people either took the car down to the business section with them if they were going to work, or if they left them at home their wives took them to the market or the movies. I had known that I wasn't going to find anything when I went out.

I went back up the stairs into the hall. Eunice had finished calling and had put the phone back on the little black wood table that teetered if you touched it too hard. She was leaning against the wall, at an angle with it, and her legs were crossed. The way she had hunched her shoulders her peasant blouse was slipping way down on one side.

Eunice waved at me to come back. She had just called my father's office. He wasn't there. Nobody had expected that he would be. He was out making his calls. He had a big practice—he was probably the most popular doctor in the county or maybe even in this part of the state—and there was no telling exactly where he was.

Eunice put down the phone for a minute. "Isn't it just dreadful, Mac?" she said in a whisper; "about your grandfather, I mean."

"Yeah," I said. I was looking at the smooth stretch of her shoulder.

She saw my gaze and pulled up the cloth.

"You the prettiest girl in this town," I said, "bar none." I had told her that before, and she always answered the same way.

She gave a little giggle and said: "Men . . ."

My mother came out into the hall. She just looked at us and walked over and took the phone off the hook. There was somebody on the party line. She broke through that in a minute and had the operator. "Can you find Dr. Addams?" she said. "Tell him it's his father."

That was the way you located either of the two doctors in this town, if you needed them fast. You just called up Shirley Williams, who was the operator, and told her. And sooner or later my father would make a call and she'd recognize his voice and give him the message. It worked fast that way; much faster than you'd think. I was sure that in about half an hour my father would know about it wherever he was.

She hung up the phone and looked at us. "This is just no time for you to behave like children. . . . MacDonald, is there a car we can borrow?"

"No, ma'am," I said.

"I'll just have to walk then." She took a sunshade out of the closet and slammed the door. She was halfway down the walk before she turned to look at me.

"I reckon you better come along," she said slowly. "I might need you to take a message."

My grandfather wouldn't ever have a telephone in his house. There was always somebody passing by soon enough to take a message for him, he said.

She pointed me back into the house. "Go get a hat," she said. "It's killing out here."

On the way out I said to Eunice: "I'll see you tonight."

It was an agreement we had. During the last two months, almost every night I'd slip out of my room and throw one small piece of gravel against her window screen. And then when she'd looked out I'd blink my flashlight real quick, just once. And she would slip down. . . . If her folks ever found out, there'd really be a row. Though they didn't have to worry. Eunice wasn't that sort of a girl. We'd just stand out in the dark, not even talking, so no one would notice us. Until the mosquitoes got too bad; and then I'd kiss her good-night.

"I'll see you tonight," I told her as I grabbed my hat and rushed out after my mother.

The sun was so hot you could feel it tingling your skin right through the clothes. It was so hot you didn't sweat any more. My mother went right on walking very fast, so that we covered the five blocks to my grandfather's house in maybe two minutes. And all the while I had my eyes on the big pile of thunderheads, the ones that had just come up and were hanging there in the sky promising rain. The people we passed, sitting on their shaded porches, who nodded or waved to us, were watching them too and they called out to ask us if we had seen them.

My mother answered them, hardly politely sometimes, we were walking so fast.

As it turned out we needn't have been in such a hurry after all.

My grandfather had died that hot afternoon in August, while everybody for miles around was watching the big pile of thunderheads. And nobody was paying much attention to an old man.

He had tumbled out of his chair in the living-room and died there on the floor with his mouth full of summer dust from the green flowered carpet. Wilda Olive, the colored woman who kept house for him, found him there about an hour later. She'd been puttering around in the back yard, making like she was sweeping off the walk, but really, just like everybody else, keeping an eye on those clouds.

She came in to tell him about the rain that might be coming and found him where he'd done a jackknife dive into the carpet. For a while she just stood looking at him, with his seersucker coat rumpled up in back and his bald head buried under his arm, bald head that was getting just a little dusty on the floor. She took a couple of steps backwards (she didn't even go near or touch him) and she lifted up her apron and put it over her head and began to cry. It was one of those long aprons that wrap all around and it was big enough to cover up her head. She just stood there, bent over in the dark from the heavy linen folds, and wailing. Not high, the way a white woman would cry, but a kind of flat low tone that you could almost see curling its way up through the layers of heat in the day.

Morris Henry, who happened to be passing by in the street, had heard it and gone in to look. After one look his poppy eyes stuck out even more than usual; and he headed straight for our house, at a run. And my mother and I came rushing over in the full heat of the afternoon sun. . . .

Minute we stepped through the front gate we began to hear Wilda Olive's moaning. My mother nodded toward the pecan tree in the north corner of the yard. "You just sit down there and wait for me," she said.

Of course, I didn't do anything of the sort. I followed her right inside.

She pushed past Wilda Olive and bent over the old man and stretched out her hand but didn't quite touch him and pulled back her hand and straightened up and just stood there. Finally she reached over and pulled the apron from Wilda Olive's head. "Stop that," she said sharply.

Wilda Olive didn't seem to hear her. My mother held up her own hand, with fingers outspread, and looked at it carefully. Then slapped Wilda Olive hard as she could. That hushed her.

"We'll need some ice water," my mother told her. "It's perishing hot out, walking." Wilda Olive went to the kitchen. And my mother came and stood on the porch. "MacDonald," she said when she saw me, "I thought I told you to stay out in the yard under the tree."

She wasn't really paying any attention to me; I could tell that from her tone; so I didn't move. She took one of the cane rockers from where it was leaning backwards against the porch wall and turned it around and sat down, very slowly. Very slowly, with one hand she rubbed the left side of her face, the two skins rubbing together smoothly and squeaking just a little from the wet of the perspiration.

Wilda Olive brought the ice water and disappeared. "Let's hope she doesn't start that racket again," my mother said, and listened carefully. But everything was quiet. "We'll just wait for your father," she said.

I sat down on the edge of the porch, my feet stuck through the railing and hanging down. It was so hot it was hard to breathe.

There was a little bead of sweat collected very slowly on my neck, right over the little hump of bone there. I hunched my shoulders so that the shirt would not touch and break it. I felt it getting bigger and bigger until it had enough force to cross the bone and begin to wiggle slowly down my back. It was all the way down to within an inch of my belt when my father came driving up.

My mother jumped up and went out to meet him. Her feet in their white sandals went by me very fast and I noticed for the first time how small they were and how brown and smooth the turn of her ankle. I'd never thought of my mother as having nice legs before. . . .

My mother stood against the side of the car leaning in through the window, the sun full and hard on her white print dress. I saw the line of her thighs and her narrow hips. It was funny for me to be thinking of my mother that way now, with my grandfather lying all doubled up on the floor inside and dead. I saw something I'd never seen before: she had as good a figure as Eunice Herbert.

When my father went inside, she sat down, not saying anything to me, rocking herself slowly, her foot beating out the time. There was a fuzz of yellow hair all up her leg; I saw that out of the corner of my eye.

Then my father came out and sat on the arm of her chair. I looked up and saw how she sat there with her eyes tight closed. My father was writing out the death certificate, the way he had to; I recognized the form. I'd seen them lying around his office enough.

And I thought how he was writing his father's name: Cecil Percival

Addams. I could see his hand printing out the name, slow and steady. He was writing out his father's name on a death certificate.

Just the way it would be for me someday. What he was doing now, I would be doing for him someday. I would sit where he was now; and there would be my wife alongside me, crying a little bit and trying now to show it. I would be a doctor, too, writing just the way he was now. And he would be lying dead inside.

And then we'd all move up one step again. And it would be my son who'd be looking down at me, lying still and dusty. I'd never thought of that before.

The trickle of sweat reached to my belt, broke, and spread, cold on my hot skin. I shivered. The thunderheads were still piled up in the south, shining gray-bright in the sun. They struck me as being very lonesome.

My father signed the paper and laid it out on the railing. "Jeff'll need that," he said quietly. Jeff was the undertaker, a little man, quick and nervous and bald, who wore black suits in the winter and white linen ones in the summer. His wife had run off with a railroad engineer and disappeared. He had a married daughter over to the north in Birmingham and he visited her twice a year.

My mother bent her head over in her lap with a quick sharp movement. My father slipped his arm around her.

"Honey," he said, "don't. Let's go home."

He lifted her up and they walked to the car. I could tell from the way he braced himself that he was almost carrying her. And even a small woman like my mother is a heavy load in one arm. I hadn't thought my father was that strong.

My mother slipped in the front seat and made room for me alongside her.

"No," my father said. "Let him stay here."

My mother shook her head doubtfully.

"Somebody's got to," my father said as he got behind the wheel. "He's almost a man. And there isn't going to be anything for him to do."

My mother didn't look convinced.

"Look," my father said shortly, "he's staying."

"There's a phone next door in the Raymond place," my mother said faintly, "MacDonald, if you want to call."

"Yes, ma'am," I said.

"Stay on the porch, son, if you want to," my father said. "Just see that Jeff gets the certificate. And keep an eye on Wilda Olive."

"Yes, sir," I said.

As they drove off, my mother rubbed her face deep down in my father's shoulder, the way a girl does sometimes on a date coming home.

And just for a second I could really feel Eunice's cheek rubbing against my shoulder and hear the soft sound it made on the cloth. And there was the tickle of her hair on my chin. And the far faint odor that wasn't really perfume—though that was part of it—but was the smell of her hair and her skin.

Then all of a sudden I didn't have that picture any more. I was back on my grandfather's porch, watching my father drive off with my mother. She had her face buried deep down in his shoulder. My father's arm went up and around to pull her closer to him. Then I couldn't see any more, the dust on the road was so thick.

I looked around. In the whole afternoon there wasn't a thing moving, except me. Except my breathing, up and down. And that seemed sort of out of place.

For a while I sat on the porch. Then I thought that maybe I ought to have a look at Wilda Olive. I didn't want to go through the house, so I walked all the way around it, outside, around to the kitchen door. "Wilda Olive." I thought I called loud but my voice softened in the heat until it was just ordinary speaking tone.

She was in the kitchen, scouring out the sink, quietly, like nothing had happened. She looked up and saw me. "Yes, sir," she said.

She'd never said "sir" to me before. The old man's death had changed that. I had moved up one step. I was in my father's place. It was funny how quick it all happened.

"Yes, sir," she said.

"You all right?" That sounded silly. But I'd said it, so I stuck my hands down deep in my pockets and lifted up my jaw and waited for her to answer.

"Yes, sir." She dropped her eyes. Ordinarily she would have gone back to her work and let me stand there to do what I wanted. But that had changed, too. Now she stood waiting for me. Not going on with her work because of me.

"You were cutting up pretty bad when we came," I told her.

"Yes, sir," she said. There wasn't the slightest bit of expression in her face now.

"Well," I said, "I'll be out front if you want me—on the porch, because it's too hot inside." That wasn't the reason. I didn't want to stay inside with the old man. But she mustn't know that. I wanted to go around, the way I'd come—through the garden—but I knew she was expecting me to go straight through the house. And so I did, walking fast as I could without seeming to hurry.

I had hardly got out on the porch before I saw Eunice coming. She had a red ruffled parasol held high against the sun and she was carrying something wrapped in a checked kitchen towel in her other hand. I watched her open the gate and come up to the porch.

"I thought you'd be steaming hot," she said, "so I brought you over a Coke." She unwrapped the towel and there it was, the open bottle, still with ice all over the outside.

"Thanks," I said. I drank the Coke, but I couldn't think of anything else to say. Somehow she didn't belong here. Somehow I just didn't want her here.

She took the bottle from me when I had finished. "I got to get back," she said. "I promised Mamma to help with dinner."

"Thanks," I said again.

At the foot of the steps she turned. "I'm awful sorry."

The sun was shining on her just the way it had on my mother.

"It's okay," I said. "It's okay."

She was gone then. And there was only the Coke taste in my mouth to remind me that she had been there. And that was gone soon, and there was just the dust taste. And there wasn't a trace of her. I just couldn't believe that she had been there . . . it was funny, the way things were beginning not to seem real.

That evening they came, the little old people who had been my grandfather's friends . . . or maybe his enemies. Time sort of evened out all those things.

Jeff, the undertaker, had come and gone and the house was really and truly empty now; I found I could breathe better. (That was another strange thing: I had never feared my grandfather, living and moving; but dead, he made me afraid. . . .)

Matthew Conners was the first. I saw him way off down the road, coming slowly, picking his way carefully between the ruts, testing the deepest ones with his cane, lifting himself carefully over them.

The sun had gone down but the sky was still full of its light, hard and bright. The rain clouds hadn't moved.

Matthew came up the walk and stood at the foot of the steps. "He come back yet?"

"No, sir," I said. "Jeff'll have him along soon."

Matthew Conners nodded. His head bobbed quickly up and down on the sinewy cords of his neck. He'd been a handsome man once, they said; the bad boy of the southern counties. There was a picture of him in an album of my grandfather's; very tall, very thin, with hair carefully pompadoured in front. Even in the picture you could see how bright the stripes of his tie were. He'd never married. He'd gone on living in the two rooms behind his hardware store (which was on the busiest corner in town, next to the post office). Until one day he sold the business to a nephew. He kept the rooms, though, and lived there. He spent most of his days there, sitting on the doorstep, not saying much to people who were passing, just sitting there, as if he were waiting.

Matthew Conners climbed slowly up the porch steps and sat down on the chair where my mother had sat and put the cane down between his knees and crossed his hands on it and waited.

I saw those hands, blue spots and heavy-veined, crossed and folded together, and I thought how maybe at that very minute Jeff was pressing my grandfather's hands together. . . .

They came all evening, the old people. After Matthew Conners came Vance Bonfield and the short, very fat woman who was his wife, Dorothy, her double chins dripping with perspiration.

I said: "Good evening." They nodded but didn't answer.

And then Henry Carmichael, walking because he didn't live far at all. By this time the porch chairs were all filled—there were only three of them. I started to bring out another chair, but the old man just shook his bald shiny head in my direction and went in the house. Slowly and with great care he began bringing out a dining-room chair, his old hands trembling with its weight. He brought two chairs out, stopped and counted them carefully with one finger. Then he took a handkerchief out of his coat pocket, wiped his face carefully, and with a tired sigh sat down with the others.

They didn't seem to talk to each other at all, beyond the first hello, just sat there waiting, with their hands folded.

So I sat down on the steps and waited, too. Only thing is, I was careful not to fold my hands. I put them out flat, one on each knee.

The long summer twilight had just about worn out when Jeff and his four Negro helpers brought my grandfather back, in a shining wood coffin this time, and put him in the living-room. I heard Wilda Olive begin to cry, softer this time; so I didn't bother to stop her. I don't think I could have anyway. The old men didn't seem to notice; they didn't turn their heads or say anything. They just sat staring out at the front lawn.

I moved out into the side yard and sat down under the locust tree. The dry ground had cracked up, pulling apart the tangled grass roots. In one of the cracks there was a lily bulb, shriveled and dry. I tried to think what kind it must have been, but I couldn't ever remember seeing a flower in that spot.

My father came back. He parked his car, came in the gate, and walked straight up to me. He held out his hand. I wasn't sure whether he wanted to shake mine or give me a pull to my feet. I reckon he did both.

"Go ahead home, son," he said, still holding my hand.

I found myself saying very softly and slow and sure, as if I wasn't in a bit of a hurry: "Don't you reckon you going to need me here?"

"That's all right," my father said.

"You be all right?"

"Sure," my father said, and turned away, walking toward the house. "You just hurry. Your mother's waiting supper on you."

I couldn't help feeling that my father wanted me to stay, that he wanted company somehow, but couldn't have it. So I left, walking as fast as I could.

When I caught sight of our house, even if it was so hot, I began to run.

My mother was sitting very quietly in the parlor waiting for me. She had a copy of the *Ladies' Home Journal* in her hands, but she wasn't reading it. She was just using it for something to hold on to. She was wearing the same light print dress she had on before, but now the fresh starchness was gone. The lace on the organdy collar wasn't standing out stiff any more and there were perspiration spots on the shoulders.

She didn't look up from the book when I came in. "Just wash your hands down here, MacDonald. Mayline won't mind if you use the kitchen sink this once."

"Yes'm," I said.

"And we'll eat dinner right away—and then get dressed."

"Yes'm," I said.

"We can keep fresher that way—for the evening." She hesitated over the last words. It was one thing about my mother; wakes always scared her a lot; she'd said so once.

"You hungry, MacDonald?" she asked finally, standing up and putting the magazine back on the table under the lamp.

"No'm," I said. "Not much, just sort of."

After supper my mother and I walked back over to the house. She was wearing a black chiffon dress; and the dye gave off a peculiar smell in the heat: not sour like perspiration, nor sweet like some flowers, nor bitter like Indian grass, but a mixture of all three. I had got dressed too, because I had to: a white suit and a tie, a black tie that had been part of my father's navy uniform. Under the coat I could feel the cotton of the shirt get wet and stick to my body.

Mrs. Herbert was out in the front yard cutting zinnias with a big shiny pair of scissors. She was the only woman I ever knew who kept her house filled with zinnias, and the strong woody odor of them was in all the rooms. Standing there in the half dark she looked like one of those flowers, with her thin body and her frizzy ragged-looking red-brown hair. (Eunice said her mother never had her hair just cut, but singed; she thought it was good for it.)

Eunice was sitting on the top step of the porch. When my mother stopped to say a word to Mrs. Herbert, she came down and stood a little way farther down the fence, leaning on the top rail, her fingers crumbling the dry heads of cornflowers.

"You look nice, all dressed up like that," Eunice said to me softly.

"It's plenty hot," I said. "With a tie and all."

"It makes you look different."

"How?"

"I don't know," she said. "Just different."

My mother had turned around now and was standing waiting for me.

"I got to go," I said. "I got to be there. . . ."

Eunice nodded. It was funny how, being a blonde like she was, her eyelashes were almost black. And when she stood looking down the way she did now, they were just a black semicircle on her cheeks. Usually I would have spent the evening on her porch or at a movie with her. And now I couldn't because my grandfather had to have a wake.

"Look," I said. "I won't be all that late tonight. . . . I'll let you know when I get home."

She nodded, still looking down, the eyelashes still making that dark mark on her cheeks.

I turned around and walked off quick as I could after my mother. And all the way over—in the first dark, which was dusty and uncertain to the eye—I was angry. I kept asking myself why I had to be a part of the old man's dying.

My mother took my arm, formally, and I wondered suddenly if I did look different or something.

The windows of the house were all wide open, it was so hot, and there was a light in every room. Very dim light, from a single bulb that was either small or shaded over with brown paper. The rooms were crowded and full of talk, buzzing whispers that didn't seem to say anything, and vague nodding heads. There were people here who'd come from all parts of the county and some from Montgomery, even. All people I knew, but I had a hard time recognizing them, their faces were so different in the half light.

Out in the kitchen there were two new colored women, working under Wilda Olive's direction. They were cooking everything, emptying out the cupboards. There wasn't any reason to watch the larder any more; the stuff had to be used up. Wilda Olive had never had anyone to help her before; she'd never had anyone to boss about—the way she did now. And she was really fixing a supper, for all the people who'd come. Not even the white women stopped or interfered with her. The smell of cooking was all over the house, making the air so heavy I couldn't catch my breath. I had to go outside.

There was only one light globe burning with all its brightness, full away—the one out in the yard. The summer moths were flying around in big swooping circles, and two little kids—a boy and a girl—were standing in the circle of light, swatting them down with pieces of folded newspaper. Each time they hit one, it would disappear with a tiny popping sound and a puff of something like smoke.

The whole yard was full of kids, the youngest ones who were not allowed in the house. They were wandering around, making up games to play or fighting or just sitting, or calling for their mothers in hushed uncertain voices. Mamma Lou Davis, a big fat colored woman, had posted herself at the front gate, to make sure that they didn't wander away.

In the far corner of the garden, next to the row of leathery old live-forever bushes, a bunch of kids had begun to play funeral. They'd found a trowel somewhere and they dug a little hole. Then very carefully they filled it and heaped it so that the mud came to a mound on top. The sticks they'd tied together like a cross wouldn't stand up in the loose dry ground, so they pulled off the silvery leaves from bushes and stuck them all over the mound, like feathers. Then they stood in a circle, solemn all of them, with their hands folded behind their backs, and sang:

> "We will gather by the river,
> The beautiful, beautiful river,
> We will gather by the river . . ."

There were more verses, dozens of them, but they only seemed to know those three lines. So they sang them over and over again.

There was one—a girl with a fat round face—who was sitting on the ground a foot or two away from the group. Her fresh starched pinafore dress was getting all dusty and rumpled, and every time the group paused for breath, in that second or two of quiet, she'd ask: "Which river? Which river? Where?" Not paying any attention to her, they'd go on singing:

> "Gather by the beautiful river."

Their voices together were thin and high-pitched and ragged.

Eunice and her mother came (her father was the druggist and had to stay at the store until it closed at eleven); they didn't see me. I could tell from the polite and cautious way Eunice was looking around that she was searching for me as she followed her mother inside.

I just stood there in the far corner of the yard, not thinking much of anything, just sort of letting my mind float out on the heavy waves of jasmine odor. It couldn't have been long—not much more than a half-hour—when I saw Eunice come out on the porch again. She walked right straight over to the railing this time and stood there, with her right hand rubbing up and down her throat. You could see that she wasn't steady on her feet. Almost immediately her mother came rushing out of the door and put her arm around her and whispered in her ear, and then the two of them came down the steps and got in their car and drove away.

Mamma Lou Davis spoke to me from her stand near the gate: "That little girl sure got plenty sick, green sick. . . ."

"Yeah," I said.

"It plain affect some people that way, dying does." One of the kids, a little boy, made a dash for the gate and the street beyond. Mamma Lou's broad black hand caught him neatly on the top of the head and turned him back into the yard.

"She weren't in there long," Mamma Lou said. "But she got plenty sick."

"Yes," I said, "I could tell that."

I looked over on the porch and saw the extra chairs had been filled. Asa Stevenson had come, a short man, almost a midget. (They said he had killed three wives with his children. He had ten or eleven kids, all told, and every one of them was big and strapping; every one of them was exactly his image.) And Mrs. Martha Watkins Wood, a big woman with yellow wrinkled skin stretched tight across her heavy bones, and with the long sad face of a tired old horse, had come out from Montgomery.

Now in the circle on the porch, all the chairs were filled. Old Carmichael had known just who was coming, had expected them. With the arrival of Mrs. Wood the circle was complete. You could almost see it draw up on itself and close—a solid circle of wooden chairs. And at that precise moment I noticed that the silence was gone. They began talking, their voices light and rustling in the hot night air. Nobody went near them.

Over in the corner of the yard one of the kids was still singing:

> *"We will gather at the river,*
> *Gather at the beautiful river. . . ."*

By ten o'clock it had turned very quiet. The kids had fallen asleep—most of them—on the porch steps or out on the grass. A couple of them were using the little grave they had dug for a pillow. Mamma Lou was still at the gate, but she was sitting now, on a camp stool somebody had brought her from the house. I recognized the stool—it was the one my grandfather used when he went fishing.

Inside, the people seemed to have no more to say. They sat in the chairs that had been brought from all parts of the house for them, and looked at each other, and occasionally one of the women managed a smile, a kind of hesitant one, that seemed even littler in the half light.

From her position on the lowest step little Trudy Wilson shivered with a nightmare and began to cry. Her mother's heels made a kind of running clatter on the straw matting of the hall. They were the first to leave, the Wilsons, even though Trudy had waked up from her dream and was smiling again. The people with the children left first, and then the people who had a distance to drive. And then the people who had a business day coming with tomorrow. Until there were only my parents and me and the old people on the porch.

"Do you suppose they'll stay all night?" my mother asked.

"How could I know?" my father said. "They'll leave when they get ready and not before."

That was true enough. Hoyt Stevenson, who'd driven over with his wife and their three daughters and his father, had tried to get the old man to drive back with them. He tried for at least ten minutes, talking to the man in a low voice. And the old man just didn't answer, just kept shaking his head.

That's the way it was with all of them. So their families got together and figured out a way that they could get home to bed and not worry about the old people's getting home. Jim Butts, who owned the sawmill and who could afford a big car and a chauffeur, offered to ride home with somebody and leave his car and the colored driver. That's the way they did it. Finally there was just Butts's big light-yellow-colored Cadillac parked out front with the fuzzy-haired Negro asleep at the wheel, his arms wrapped all around it. And our car, which was parked up the drive, next to the house.

"Ruby, honey," my father said, "why don't you go to bed?"

My mother smiled at him limply. "I reckon I will. . . ."

Wilda Olive came in softly, carrying a round wicker tray with small cups of coffee.

My father took two. "I'll need them to stay awake."

"Thank you," my mother said. "I nearly forgot you were here, Wilda Olive."

"Yes'm," she said softly, gave me my cup of coffee, and went out on the porch to bring the rest to the old me.

I tasted the coffee. It had brandy in it.

"Say," my father said, "she sure made this a stiff dose."

"I'm so tired," my mother said. "It'll make me light-headed as anything."

"You can be in bed by that time," my father told her; "go ahead."

She stood up. "Come on, MacDonald," she said to me.

"I'm staying."

She appealed to my father. "I couldn't ever walk home alone at this time of night."

"MacDonald," my father said.

"Okay." I got up.

My father put his coffee cup down slowly. "What did you say?"

"Yes, sir."

My mother was tugging at my arm.

"Can I come back?"

My father shook his head.

"Don't you want company?"

"Go home," my father said.

My mother pulled my arm. "MacDonald, please—" And outside she gave a sigh of annoyance. "I'd think you'd have some sense. Can't you see your father's all upset without you pestering him?"

"Yes, ma'am," I said.

When we were almost home I asked her: "Why do you suppose he didn't want company?"

"Sometimes you want to be alone, MacDonald."

"I wouldn't," I said. I saw her staring at me with a funny kind of look. I rubbed my hand quick all over my face to wipe off whatever expression she was worried about.

On our porch I stopped and took off my coat and tie. I dropped them on a chair. Meanwhile she had opened the door.

"Come on in, son."

I shook my head. "I reckon I need a walk." I started down the steps.

"MacDonald," my mother said, "you aren't coming to bed?"

"No'm."

"Your father said—"

"I don't care—" and because I didn't want to hear her answer to that, I bolted around the corner of the house. I didn't quite know where I wanted to go, so I just stood for a minute, just looking around. There was a thin flat hard sliver of moon pasted up in the west. The sky was almost bright blue and there were piles of thunderheads all over it now, shining clear in the light. There wasn't a bit of air. The dust wasn't even blowing. Everything was still and moldy and hot in the moonlight.

It was the sort of night when you breathe as shallow as you can, hoping to keep the heat out of your body that way, because your body is hot enough already. And you feel like you have a fever and maybe you do—on a thermometer—but you know it's just summer, burning.

I began to walk, not going anywhere, just wading through the dark and the heat. There were mockingbirds singing, like it was day. In the houses all the windows were wide open, and even out in the streets you could hear the hum of electric fans.

I passed a couple of colored boys walking, in step down the sidewalk. They rolled big white eyes at me as they went past. They were wearing sneakers; you couldn't hear their steps at all even in the quiet.

I wasn't thinking of anything. I was just moving around feeling how good the little breeze that made was. I walked through the town, through the business section, the closed stores and the grocery and the movie house; and the railroad station, open, but empty; and the rails shining white in the light, but empty too. I kept on walking until I had swung back through town in a circle and started back toward home. And the first thing I knew I was passing my grandfather's house. I saw the big jasmine bush at the corner of the lot—dusty but full of yellow flowers.

I went around to the side yard out of the reach of the street light and climbed over the fence. It was just a wire and wood fence and I had to swing over quick before my weight brought it down.

I was right by the kitchen window, so I looked in. Wilda Olive was standing there, at the kitchen table. She was dressed in a black linen dress so starched that it stood out all around her like stiff paper. And her hair was just combed and pulled straight on top her head and shining with lacquer. She wasn't asleep; her eyes were open.

Out in the yard, so close that I could almost put my hand down and touch it, a mockingbird was singing. I looked around carefully trying to see him. I saw a spot of gray close by the back porch that could have been the bird, but I wasn't sure.

My father was in the dining-room—I slipped over and looked through that window. He was sitting in one of the armchairs, all hunched down in it so that his head rested against the back. He was facing toward the living-room doors. My grandfather was in the first room, the one with the curtains drawn and the light shining dull brown through them.

And the old people were still on the porch. I could hear their voices, light and rustling.

I walked around the house and stood on the front steps, listening to them.

"There was plenty of timber for a house," Vance Bonfield was saying. He was a little wrinkled man, with a full head of clear black hair, which he dyed carefully every week. "But Cecil Addams wouldn't have any of plain pine. He had to have that cypress brought out from Louisiana."

"Wasn't him," Matthew Conners said. "His wife wanted it. Wanted a house just like she used to have. That's what it was."

Vance looked at him, blinking his pale-blue eyes slowly.

"Her name's plain gone from my memory," he said. "Do you happen to recall it?"

"Linda," Mrs. Wood said.

"Louise." Mrs. Bonfield's double chin quivered with the word.

"It was Lizette," Matthew Conners said.

"Ask him," Vance said, and lifted his thin old hand to point to me. (I jumped; I hadn't really thought they'd noticed me.)

"Ask him," Henry Carmichael said; "young people always remember better."

"Not so," Matthew Conners said, and banged with his cane on the porch boards. "They just got less to remember."

And then I said as loud as I could, because some of them were deaf: "Her name was Eulalie."

They looked at me and slowly shook their heads.

And I added quickly "Lalia for short."

They sighed together: "Aahh"; they looked relieved.

"That's a bright young boy," Matthew Conners said. "A bright young fellow."

They looked at me. "He's a fine young fellow."

"Looks like his grandpa," Vance said. "A man's looks goes on in his sons."

Wilda Olive brought out a round of whiskies.

Looking at her, Vance said: "I can remember when she was the prettiest high-brown girl in this part of the state."

Matthew Conners cackled to himself, remembering. "And wasn't it a hell of a to-do when he brought her home after his wife died."

"I remember," they said.

I stood looking at them, wondering what it was they remembered, all of them together. Something I didn't know, something I couldn't know. Nor my father. Something my grandfather had known, who was dead.

Wilda Olive served them the drinks as if she never heard.

Vance held the glass in his hand, which shook so that the ice tingled. "Yes, sir," he said. "She was the prettiest thing you ever laid eyes on. Skin all yellow and burning."

Wilda Olive went inside. I looked after her and tried to see how she had looked years ago, when she had been pretty, so pretty that she'd caught my grandfather's eye. But all I saw was a colored woman, middle-aged and getting sort of heavy, with grieving lines down her cheeks.

"Prettiest thing," Vance said. "Sort of thing a young man can have, if he wants it."

"Man can't have anything long," Matthew Conners said.

They were looking at me. I began backing away.

"He's got a girl already," Asa Stevenson said, and hunched his dwarfed shoulders. "He got in a fight over her and near got thrown out of school."

"Who?" Mrs. Bonfield's fat chin lifted up and stared at me.

And Vance put in: "The Herbert girl, what's her name?"

I was backing off. They called to me: "Wait."

I had to stop.

"What's her name?" Matthew Conners leaned forward and rested his thin wrinkled chin on his cane. "What's her name?"

"I don't know," I said. The words sounded stupid and I knew they heard that too, but the only thing I could do was repeat: "I don't know."

"Not know your girl's name," Carmichael said, shaking his head. "Not know your girl's name . . ." His voice trailed off. "How do you call her to come out to you?"

Matthew Conners cackled softly. "You plain got it twisted, man. He's the one that come out. . . ."

"She's a pretty girl," Mrs. Wood said, her voice high and shrill in her solemn long face.

"You're right to pick a pretty girl," Vance said. "While you can."

I saw the hate in their eyes and I began to be sick. I backed away, down the steps and around the corner of the porch. This time they didn't seem to notice and let me go.

"It isn't long a man has anything," Matthew Conners was saying, and the ice cubes in his glass rattled. "It isn't long."

I climbed back over the fence, and the wire squeaked with my weight. I walked along the other side, slowly, curling my toes in the hard dry grass at each step.

Finally I sat down under the big locust tree near the street; I knew they couldn't see me there.

There was a funny sort of quivering in my stomach. I leaned back against the rough bark of the tree and looked up through the leaves at the sky that was almost bright blue. Out of the corner of my eye I could catch the sheen of the moon on the car waiting in the street. And that same moon made little blobs of light all around me. It was hot; I just sat there with my arms wrapped around my knees, feeling the sweat run down my back. I noticed a movement over on the porch. I looked more carefully. One of the old men, my grandfather's friends, was wiping his face slowly on a white handkerchief.

I sat under the locust tree and stared up at the sky that was so bright the stars looked uncertain and dim. I don't know how long I sat there before I began to notice something different. The rustling of voices was changing. I shifted my eyes from the sky to the porch.

Their talk was drying up quickly. The words got fewer and farther apart. They began watching each other with a quick sidewise slanting of eyes. And mouths came to a stiff closed line. They began to fidget nervously in their chairs.

Then one by one, with an imperceptible murmur, they slipped away. Singly, each singly, they left. I watched them leave, quiet and alone, and I thought: that's how they came.

The road ended here. They had to walk one way. And soon there were five of them, scattered down the length of the road, poking their way along, feeling the way with their sticks, black on a bright road.

I got up and went over and woke Claude, the chauffeur. He pushed his cap back on his head and rubbed his face with one hand.

"Claude," I said, "there they go."

"Huh?" He held his hand pressed to his face so that his stub nose was all pushed to one side.

"There they go," I repeated. "You better catch them."

He opened his eyes and looked down the road. "Christ Almighty," he said, starting the engine, "they plain near got away."

He swung the car around and went after them. I stood leaning on the gatepost watching. He drove up to the last man, drove a little past him and stopped, got out, opened the door quick. The old man never stopped walking, just kept walking until he was right abreast of the car, and then Claude stepped up and took his arm and almost lifted him into the car. Then he closed the door, quietly (I couldn't hear a sound), and went on after the next one. He did that until they were all safely in the car.

I started home then, and all the way I kept thinking of the picture of the old people moving down the road.

And suddenly I remembered the last time I had seen my grandfather—two days ago. We had both gone to the same place fishing. In deep summer there was only one place around here that you could fish in, only one place where the water stood deep and cool. He'd showed it to me himself the summer past—in an old gravel pit, way back behind the worn-out holes and the sandy ridges. It was quite a trick getting into it; it's hard climbing in loose gravel. I got to the top of the ridge and stood looking down at the line of aspens and willows and red honeysuckle bushes that grew around the pool. Then I noticed that my grandfather was already there, sitting on his camp stool, his rod in his hand. And at first I grinned and thought how surprised he would be to see me; and how much better it was to fish with company, even though you never say a word.

I started to climb down to him, and some loose gravel rolled away under my feet. He looked up and saw me. And he got up and grabbed his stool and his bait box and hurried away up the other side of the ridge. And I noticed a funny thing: his line wasn't out. He'd been sitting there, holding his rod, and waiting, but he hadn't cast out his line. He'd just been sitting there, waiting. . . .

And I understood then. . . . Why Matthew Conners had sold his store and didn't seem to notice the people passing by who talked to him. Why Mrs. Martha Watkins Wood wouldn't keep a servant full time in the big old empty house of hers in Montgomery, just day help. Why Vance Bonfield and his wife suddenly took separate rooms after sleeping in the same bed for forty-six years. Why Henry Carmichael shouted at the noisy grandchildren who climbed the wisteria vines to peer into the windows of his room. Why old people wanted to be left alone. . . .

There was the fear in my grandfather's eyes the day at the gravel pool. Even from a distance I had seen it. The fear that had made the old man pick up his bait basket and scurry off as fast as his stiffening legs could go.

The fear of dying . . . the fear that grows until at last it separates you from the people you know: the dusty-eyed old people who want to be left alone, who go off alone and wait. Who fish without a line.

One day I'll be that afraid. . . . All of a sudden I knew that. Knew that for the first time, I'll be old and afraid.

I'll be old and restless in company and want to be alone. Because loneliness is more bearable than company, when you are waiting; because it's a kind of preparation for that coming final loneliness.

I could feel it starting, just the beginning of fear.

I'll be old and sit on porches and talk in dry rattling whispers and remember the past and the things that I had when I was able to have them. And in the shaded parlors, in the faces of dead friends, see the image of my fear. The fear that will live with me: will follow me through the day and lie down with me at night and join me again in the morning, until there isn't any more morning and I don't get up at all. . . .

I began to run, not knowing where I was going, not caring. And there was the fear running with me, just with me.

It was so hot, I was running through a blank solid wall. I had to breathe and I kept trying, but there wasn't any air, just heat.

From far away there was the pounding of my own feet on the ground. I looked down at them, moving. I could hear the strangling sound of my own breathing, but that was far away too.

Only, the mockingbird was singing louder and louder and there was a spot of gray flying alongside me. Like it was laughing at me, trying to run away from it.

I was getting tired, so tired; I tried but I couldn't keep up the pace. It was hard too to keep my balance; I kept falling forward. I stretched out my arms; they touched something and I held on to it tightly. I stood shaking my head until my eyes cleared. It was a fence, a picket fence. And just beyond was our house. I had come home. Not thinking about it, I had come home. All the hot noisy outside had come down to this: our green-painted clapboard house with the olive-colored shutters and the big black screen porch all around it. But somehow I couldn't go inside.

I lifted my eyes. And there were the thunderheads. They were right behind the house, right in line with it, but miles up in the sky. Just where they'd been all day. They'd turned red with the sunset and disappeared with the first dark and then reappeared silver-white with the moon. And there they were, hanging cool-looking and distant.

I looked away from them, down and across the street, to the light in the side window of the Herberts' house. That would be Eunice, waiting for me. For just a minute I saw her face and her eyes that crinkled at the corners and the way her hair was piled up on top of her head with a flower stuck in it.

I thought of all these things and I just turned away from the yellow square of light. And I took a couple of steps backward until I pressed up against the big thick barberry hedge. One of the crooked thorns scratched my hand; I looked at it, bleeding slightly; it didn't hurt. Somehow nothing much seemed real—not Eunice, nor my house, nor the hedge that had cut me. Nothing but the pile of thunderheads up in the sky and the fear that had caught up with me, was running circles around me.

Circles and circles around me. Like the mockingbird that was singing louder and louder. The brown-gray bird.

Very slowly I sat down, leaning my back against the sharp thorns of the hedge. And listened.

Flight

"There's nothing you can do?"

"We are fairly sure now that the primary site is the liver. That's somewhat unusual."

"But you can't help her?"

"I am sorry. There is nothing at all we can do."

"I'll go home now, Michael. It's time."

"Mother, why not wait a bit longer?"

"Tomorrow, I think. I'll go tomorrow."

"It's a long flight."

"It was just as long when I flew here to visit you, Michael."

"You were stronger then, Mother."

"There was more time then, too. Or I thought there was. Will you see to the tickets? I'll go back the way I came, that flight through Dallas."

"Mother, please wait until you are stronger."

"I will not get stronger. You have talked to the doctors. And I know they are right."

"You could stay here. We are all here."

"I will take the plane home tomorrow, Michael. . . . Now I am sleepy. . . . Is it raining outside? I hear rain very clearly." Water: whispering, giggling.

She, the small child, waited for rain, watched across Mr. Beauchardrais's pasture as the clouds gathered, black and silver. Heavy clouds with ball and chain lightning dancing between them, silently. The spiky clumps of pasture grass faded to pale yellow, glimmering, reflecting like water to the sky.

She sat in the porch corner, wedged comfortably against peeling boards which were corded like the veins in her mother's hands, her father's arms. Sometimes she even imagined that the house's blood flowed through those raised twisting networks in the wood.

Mouse, people called her for her habit of sitting silent and still in corners. And Doodle Bug for the hours she spent under the house, crawling between the low brick foundation pillars, creeping cautiously through broken glass and slate to settle comfortably, flat on her back, at the center of the house, where the damp air smelled of mildew and tomcats and a heavy sweet stickiness that was the breath of the ground itself. . . .

While her mother's feet thudded up and down across the boards overhead, she lay on her back and watched the spiders weaving the thick gray webs around the water pipes. Watching for the Black Widow, small with a single red dot on its stomach. . . . When it rained, neighborhood dogs and cats sheltered under the house, politely, deliberately ignoring each other. Huddled against the underside of the front steps, a calico fed her latest litter while two dogs slept, twitching and yelping in their dreams. . . .

She sat cross-legged on the porch where the sun-bleached wood was so hard her small pocketknife could barely scratch a mark. She had to be very careful; if her parents caught her testing the strength of the boards, she would get a paddling for sure. As if the boards were something to be guarded, as if they were worth anything at all. . . .

She watched the rain. It began with a yellowish kind of darkness in the air, then a shiver while leaves rushed into the neatly swept hard clay yard and spun in rising circles. Just like the cartoons she saw on Saturday afternoons, when her mother had extra money to send her to the movies. (On good days her father walked to work and saved his carfare in a jelly glass on the kitchen counter. For her.) When those cartoon characters ran, they left swirls of motion behind them like the wind and the dead leaves.

Rain meant her father rode the streetcar and no extra coins went into the kitchen glass.

She settled back—no movie this week, that was for sure—and waited for the rain.

On the tin roof, drops tapped, then knocked, then rattled like hailstones. A whispering, a hissing ran along the roof gutters to the cistern at the corner of the house.

Her mother called loudly, "Willie May, come quick. Come help me."

In the backyard her mother was putting chicks and ducklings into the poultry shed. Willie May hated to touch them—the small bony bodies felt skeletal and evil in her hands. She held her breath as she hurriedly put the small blobs safely under shelter. They were so stupid that they would stand in the rain, gawking in curious confusion, and drown.

Afterwards, back in the porch corner again, wet clothes plastered tight to shoulders, nostrils filled with the scent of her own dripping hair, she watched the air turn smoky gray. She sniffed the sweet moisture-laden dust and occasionally, after a close crash of thunder, she could smell the sharp, nose-tickling odor of ozone.

Another time her mother called her. That once in September during the hurricane season. "Willie May," her mother cried, voice shaking with fear and pain, "Willie May, help me." The child she was carrying was born too soon, a small hairy boy who gasped a couple of times and was perfectly still.

Willie May ran off into the rain, hiding in the heavy tangle of titi bushes and myrtle trees on the other side of the street. She shivered all over—not with cold, because it was September and very warm, and not with fear of the weather, because though the winds were high they were not nearly hurricane strength. She huddled against the trunk of a big wax myrtle, and rain and leaves and bark pelted down on her. Her arms and hands twitched, like a puppet, her body shook so hard that she could scarcely breathe. Perhaps she'd even stopped breathing for a while, because she found herself lying full length on the ground, one ear and eye pasted shut by soft oozing mud.

It was still raining hard and the sky was darker, not with the greenish dark of a hurricane, but the gray dark of night. Looking out carefully from her shelter, across the empty ground, she could see that all the lights in her house were on.

She went home then, because she had no other place to go. The deep gutters on each side of the dirt street were filled to the top (crawfish would like that, she thought), the water was ankle deep on the three loose boards that served as a bridge to her house. She inched her way across, carefully. The boards shivered and quaked, about to wash away. In the morning she would have to go hunting for them and put them back in their place. She'd most probably find them near the Duquesnay house where the ground rose just a bit. An Indian mound, people said, and children frightened each other with stories of walking ghosts.

Out of the darkness her father said, "Willie May."

She hadn't known he was there. His voice came from the dark corner of the porch by the living room window. She stared, dazzled by the bright square of light, saw nothing. Mosquitoes, attracted to the moisture of her eyes, swarmed on her, and she blinked rapidly.

"You ran off," her father said, "when your mama called you. You left her and the baby died."

She wanted to say: I didn't kill him.

But no sound came out.

"Your mama knew you were afraid when you saw the baby, but she thought you'd know enough to run to Rosie's house."

No, she hadn't thought of that. Never once thought of running the three blocks to her Aunt Rosie's house and telling her. She'd thought of nothing but digging under the weeds and bushes, hiding. Like a mouse gone back to earth.

I'm sorry, she wanted to say.

But again no words.

The water-washed boards suddenly shifted sideways and she fell into the muddy night-black rushing water, coming up coughing and choking, crying with fear, scrambling up the bank of the ditch to the firm hard-swept mud of the front yard.

Her father did not move. She would not have known he was there, except in the quiet night she could hear his breathing.

"Mother, please stay. You're comfortable here and the doctors are so good."

"I do not need doctors now."

"Mother, listen. We only want to take care of you. Don't you understand. We love you."

Oh, I understand. The trap. The trap that caught my father and my mother and even me. But that was years ago, not now. No more love.

She would run away again. Only, when she went to earth this time, it would be for good. And she would choose her own spot.

"The baby didn't die because of you," her mother said.

But Willie May knew better. She knew.

"He died because he was born too soon. If I hadn't strained and fought with that window because the rain was pouring in, and if the window hadn't been stuck . . . He wasn't your fault. But you shouldn't have run away."

She hung her head and the old guilt and disgust settled in her stomach while her chest ached so much that she thought she too would die.

"Your duty," her mother said, "you don't ever run away from your duty to your family. Not ever. Not until you die."

Willie May thought wearily, and with horror: You aren't ever free. Something always holds you, stops you, brings you back.

"Good evening, Mrs. Denham. Will you have your sleeping pill now?" The night nurse: round black face under a round white cap.

"You still wear your cap, Nurse. None of the others do."

"The hospital doesn't require it any more, Mrs. Denham." She had a habit of repeating the patient's name over and over again. Perhaps she had been taught to do that. "But I worked hard for this bit of organdy and I intend to keep on wearing it."

"I know what it is to work hard for something."

"Yes," the nurse said.

Then there were the usual little night sounds: rubber-shod feet thudding ever so softly, and the soft silky whispering of nylon-clad thighs moving up and down the halls.

I did not come for this, she thought dully, I came to see my son, my only son who lives a continent away in a house with green lawns and dogwood blooming outside the windows, who has two sons, his images. I came to visit and I broke down on the road like an old car.

She could smell the sickly sweet stench of her own skin. Her whole body had an aura of decay.

The smell reminds me of something. Something years ago. I was young, but my skin still carried this smell.

I have only to live until the morning. It is time.

Time had so many different patterns. After her father died, when they were very poor with only his small pension to support them, Willie May went off to work at the Convent of the Holy Angels. Thirteen, tall and strong, and afraid. For three years she lived in a maze of echoing halls that smelled of floor wax and furniture polish and a laundry that smelled of steam and bleach and starch for the stiff white coifs and wimples the nuns wore. Three years of small hard beds in tiny rooms. Of weariness and sick exhaustion. Of prayers and echoing Gregorian chant. And a great emptiness. Occasionally in the garden as she swept the covered walkways, she could hear children shouting as they walked to school. She envied them and their living fathers whose hard-earned money sent them laughing along the sidewalks.

Eventually her mother remarried, a police sergeant named Joseph Reilly, a widower nearly sixty. "Hello, Willie May," he said, when she came back from the convent. "I married your mother." "Okay," she said. He smiled then, and it was settled.

He liked to cook, and despite his name he cooked Italian style. Her mother was beginning to grow fat on spaghetti and sausage and peppers, all glistening with olive oil.

He was a quiet man who spent every evening at home listening to the radio, sitting in his special chair (one he had brought with him to her mother's house) with his feet propped on a stool. He was a kind man and treated her like his own child. Each birthday he bought her a pair of white gloves to wear to church, and every Christmas he gave her a box of Evening in Paris cosmetics, blue bottles held in shining white satin.

There was no talk of her returning to school, the time for that had passed. On her sixteenth birthday she went to work at Woolworth's, at the big store on Decatur Street. She sold potted plants and stood all day behind the counter near the front window, and when she wasn't busy she watched the street outside. The cars and the big delivery vans and the green streetcars rocking unsteadily past on their small clacking iron wheels. Women in print dresses and hats, breathless and harried from the excitement of shopping. Office messengers with brown envelopes and packages and long cardboard tubes. Girls in navy blue school uniforms, arm in arm, and boys gathered at the corner by the traffic light. Bookies and numbers runners whose territory this was; she grew to recognize them and smile, and they lifted their hats to her in passing.

As she watched she felt her quietness and her loneliness slipping away. She felt herself become a part of things, no longer a child looking in, but an adult and part of the busyness and bustle that was life. Her hands, broadened and thickened by the convent work, their nails clipped very short and square across, grew soft and slender, and she filed her nails into careful ovals. She buffed them too, until they had a high shine; she might have worn nail polish of a color to match her lipstick (they sold those sets at the cosmetic counter at the back of the store), but the management did not allow that.

She had money of her own now, and the delicious expectation of each week's pay. (Dutifully she gave half to her mother, the rest was hers.) Sometimes she would stand for long minutes, half-smiling, half-dozing, smoothing the bills between her manicured fingers, pressing the coins against her palms until they left their imprint on her skin.

Every evening on the streetcar home, she stared through the dirty finger-smeared window, lulled by the steady rocking, and dreamed half-visions of the future. She had never done that before. She had met only one day at a time, fearful. Now she was the future, a series of busy days. Beyond grimy windows the littered crowded streets were mysteriously inviting. She lived now in a state of great excitement, with a fluttering in her stomach, a feeling of endless energy, a sense that flowers were beautiful and rain was lovely, that colors were brighter than they had ever been before, that something wonderful was about to happen. She had no experience of it, but she thought this must mean that she was happy.

One day John Denham walked past Woolworth's big front window. They stared and blinked and then laughed at the sight of each other grown up. They had been children together; he'd lived two blocks away. In those half-remembered days before her father's death, they had played and adventured together. "When you get off work," he said, "I'll be waiting for you." He rode home with her on the streetcar, but he wouldn't come near her house. "Your mama wouldn't like me."

"Why not?"

"She won't like any boy hanging around you. I'll see you after work tomorrow."

He did, every evening. They talked the whole way home, nervously, rapidly summarizing the years. He told her that years ago his family had moved across town to share a house with his aunt. "Way out," he said. "Nothing but swamps behind us. We used to go crawfishing a lot." Once, he told her, he'd gone back to their old neighborhood and people said she'd gone off to the convent.

"I thought you were going to be a nun," he said.

"Not me." She held up her soft manicured hands, admiring them against the scratched varnish of the car seats. "Mama went to work but she couldn't make enough to keep me and the house both, and then Father Lauderman heard that the convent needed somebody, and that somebody turned out to be me."

"They teach you anything?"

"Sure. Cooking—would you believe they've got thirty-seven nuns there. And embroidery and crochet. And a lot of prayers."

"Okay," he said, "say me a prayer."

"I get plenty enough prayers in church on Sunday," she said. "Anyway, the next stop is mine."

He got off with her and they stood talking until a car came going the other way. He swung on, she walked home.

And so she saw him six days a week. She learned that he still lived at home with his parents and his orphaned cousins and his grandmother. That he'd finished Jesuit High School and right away was lucky enough to get a job with the post office, delivering mail. "I like it," he said. "I couldn't ever stand being inside at a desk all day long."

"I like my job too," she said.

"What do you do on Sundays?"

"Go to mass. Do my laundry and my ironing and be sure my clothes are ready for the week. And I help my mother with her garden, and in the evenings there's always the radio programs."

"You don't work much in the garden, not with hands like that."

"I didn't know you noticed my hands."

"Sure I notice. I notice everything about you."

She felt pleased and shy.

"But your Sundays don't sound like any fun to me."

"I like it just the way it is," she said. But in truth she didn't like it as much as she had.

"Where do you go to church? St. Rita's?"

"Mama and I go to the eleven o'clock every Sunday, rain or shine. She wouldn't miss it."

"What would you say if I told you I'd be there? That'd surprise you, wouldn't it? Well, I used to go to that church when I was a kid living just down the street from you, and I might just take myself back there again. Oh, I wouldn't talk to you, just spy on you. I know they get a big crowd for mass, so you see if you find me. And I bet you can't."

On Monday he said triumphantly, "You had a blue skirt and a white blouse and a tie like a man's, and you had to sit in the middle of a pew because you got there late, and you dropped your purse because you were so busy looking for me."

"I don't think that is a funny game," she said.

"I'm tired of it too." He popped a match against his thumbnail and lit a cigarette. "Let's not go to church next Sunday. Let's go out to the lake and walk along the seawall and have a look at all the big boats. I'll meet you at the streetcar stop at the end of Prentiss Street."

She did not meet him. She felt tired and out of sorts that Sunday, but she worked very hard in the garden, spraying the tomato plants with tobacco water to control aphids, staking and tying the beans.

"You are such a big help," her mother said. "You've got such a lot of energy."

The following day John Denham said, "You sure did miss a good time yesterday."

"I told you I was busy."

"Sure you were," he said. "I'll believe anything."

Day after day he waited for her. "Who's your boyfriend?" the other girls at Woolworth's asked. "He's not a boyfriend, he's just somebody used to live in my neighborhood."

The September rains began and he carried a big gray post office umbrella. The interior of the streetcars smelled of wet mud and musty sawdust, but the windows were washed clean by the pounding rain.

"You can't work in that precious garden now," he said.

"Not much any more," she said.

"So let's go out this Sunday."

"I am busy on Sundays," she said. "I have very important things to do."

"What's more important than me?"

She hesitated, not wanting to tell him, not really, but telling him anyway. "I crochet."

"All day? You're crazy."

"No." This time she didn't try to explain how pleasant Sundays were—with the street quiet and empty except for a few wandering dogs. Even kids' games sounded muted on Sundays, without so much screaming. She'd sit on the front porch with her mother, while Joseph read the newspaper and then, finished, slept soundly in his special rocking chair. Sometimes they were so silent and still that mourning doves perched on the railing and watched them. In chilly weather they sat in the parlor. Joseph dozed in the chair that he had brought in from the porch, the bright red patterned cushions almost hidden by his bulk. Her mother read aloud from the *State Times* or the *Diocesan Chronicle*, news of weddings and births and deaths. She herself sat surrounded by baskets of yarn, all colors, pale sea green her favorite. Her crochet hook flashed faster and faster, in and out, catching, dragging, snaring. The soft wool nets slipped away from her hands, completed.

"Okay," John said, "so what do you crochet that takes all day, every Sunday."

"They're called fascinators," she said. "You saw me wearing one the other day."

"That head scarf thing?"

"Not a scarf," she said. "They're pretty and they're warm. I always used to wear mine to church, I made them in two or three different colors to match the altar vestments."

"What?"

"It seemed respectful," she said. "Well, ladies began stopping me, wanting to know where I got them, because the department stores don't have anything nearly so nice. I made some for them, and I found I could do it very fast. So I put a notice in the *Chronicle*. Now I take orders, any color if you bring me the wool and any stitch if you show me what it is. I've got lots of orders for Christmas. People don't mind what they spend at Christmas."

"Money," he laughed, "is that all you ever think about? You got a job and you still want more."

"I've been poor," she said slowly, trying to explain, "and the convent took me in and the nuns taught me needlework, all kinds of needlework. It was like they were making me a present of it. And I can use it now."

"You are plain crazy," he said.

Still, every day after work he waited at the streetcar stop. It was December now, with cold winter rain. The early azaleas showed their buds and the sasanquas opened their flat pink and white flowers.

"Something likes this weather," she said to him, pointing to the gardens as they passed.

"Not me," he said. "Look," he said, "make one of those fascinators for me and I'll give it to my mother for Christmas. She'll be expecting something."

"Okay," she said.

"They look kind of pretty on you, so maybe they'll do something for her too."

She felt herself flushing, as pleased as if it had been a proper compliment.

After Christmas the rain stopped. In the parks camellias bloomed and all the big purple azaleas.

"Come to the park with me this Sunday," he said. "We'll look at those flowers you're so crazy about and then we'll go to the aquarium and watch them feed the seals."

"I work on Sunday," she said primly.

"You're not still making those stupid scarfs," he said. "Christmas is over."

"I'm making baby dresses."

"Don't tell me the nuns taught you that."

"They taught me to smock," she said. "People want real smocking on their baby clothes and I add little embroidered rosebuds too."

"And people buy that?"

"All I can make," she said.

"Okay," he said. "I'm going to walk by your house this Sunday and I am going to see."

"You're checking up on me," she said, and was flattered by the thought. "If you walk past I am going to pretend I don't know you."

"What makes you think I'm going to talk to you?" he said. "I just want to look."

He did. He walked by slowly, looking at the houses on both sides. She did not lift her head from her work, not even when he walked back again.

"I hope you are satisfied," she said.

"You are crazy, I knew it."

"No."

"You don't ever think of me, I bet. You won't even miss me when I'm gone."

She stared at him. "Where are you going?"

"Got your attention that time, didn't I? You heard about this little thing called the draft, and yours truly is 1A. They're going to haul me off any day now."

"I forgot."

"Well, old Uncle Sam ain't going to let me forget. Hey, look, next stop is yours. You better ring the bell."

They stood talking longer than usual that day, leaning against the rough trunk of one of the young oak trees at the corner.

"I bet you won't even miss me when I'm out there getting shot at."

"There ain't any war," she said, "not unless you know something I don't."

"They're drafting an army," he said. "You don't make an army if you don't plan to use it."

The last azaleas faded, purple wisteria ran wild along the fences, lost its flowers and put out its leaves; high up on the old buildings the Rose of Montana vine began to show its small pink flowers. Then one day he wasn't waiting at the streetcar stop, and she rode home alone. He wasn't there the next day, or the next. The weather turned stormy, fishing boats scurried back into port. It rained so heavily that the streets flooded and she waded home in waist-deep water. By morning the water was down; children were fishing for crawfish in the ditches, all of them playing hooky from school.

Finally he was back, thin and tired-looking. "I got my induction notice," he said, "four or five other guys too. We all took annual leave and got drunk. Then we took the train to Chicago just for the ride."

She wasn't too sure exactly where Chicago was, though she did remember learning about it in geography class. So he had just gone off like that, to a spot on the map. . . .

"We decided we didn't much like Chicago so we came back. Here's your streetcar, didn't you notice?"

Again he disappeared without a word.

"What happened to your boyfriend?" Norma, who sold cosmetics, asked.

"The army," she said. "And he's not my boyfriend."

Norma lifted her eyebrows. "Too bad."

Evenings Willie May rode home alone, feeling strange and a little hurt that he had not said good-bye. He shouldn't have just disappeared, she thought.

Joseph retired from the police force, complaining of pains in his chest. The doctor told him to stop drinking beer and lose weight; her mother fussed over him, fixing special meals which Joseph wouldn't eat. She hid his beer. He started spending afternoons at the Paradise Bar, two blocks away. He liked their draft, he said, a lot better than bottles.

Willie May herself had so many orders for children's dresses that her mother had to help with the cutting and some of the simple sewing and the ironing and the folding in tissue paper. And she still worked at Woolworth's. In the summer heat, the air in the store turned musty and sweaty and heavy. The tall fans barely pushed it along the aisles. The floorwalkers complained all day long about dust on the counters, and the clerks polished and rearranged them constantly. Aphids appeared like white frosting on all the potted coleus. Two stock boys took them to the back loading platform and dabbed at the bugs with rubbing alcohol.

In August Willie May got her first order for a christening dress, a peau de soie robe over a long lawn shift. She worked on it for a month, carefully dusting her hands with talcum powder so that her sweating fingers left no mark on the white material.

One Sunday as she and her mother sat on the porch and Joseph dozed in the hammock he had slung between two mulberry trees in the yard, John Denham sauntered up the walk and stood with one foot on the steps, grinning. His hair was so short that he seemed quite bald and he was in uniform. "I got leave," he said. "You want to take a ride out to the lake and get an ice cream?"

"I've got to finish the dress," she said.

Her mother took the material from her hands and carried it carefully inside.

He laughed. "Your ma says yes."

"I suppose so," she said. She was very confused and she did not like the feeling at all. "You surprised me," she said. "I don't like being surprised."

"Look, don't blame me," he said; "the army owns me now."

Her mother said from inside the screen door, "It will take her just a few minutes to freshen up. Would you like some iced tea, what did you say your name was?"

So they caught the streetcar to the lake and ate ice cream cones and walked along the seawall and looked at the muddy water and sat on benches under small pine trees and listened to a band play marches and waltzes and opera overtures. Children skated on the concrete walks and chalked the outlines of hopscotch games. The young women were there in their summer dresses, full skirted and starched crisp against the summer heat. The young men were in uniform.

"What's the matter with you," he said. "You're scowling."

She answered truthfully, "I felt afraid, all of a sudden."

He grinned and put his arm around her. "Baby, you got nothing to be afraid of when I'm with you."

"Oh," she said. And didn't tell him she knew he was wrong about that.

They settled finally on a shady bench near a fountain. They could hear the water trickling and bubbling in the wide basin.

"Look," he said. "You ever think about yourself? Like what you're going to do next? And why you want to do it?"

"No," she said.

"Well, you should. Now, you're a good-looking gal. A real pretty face and a nice figure even if you are too thin. But then, you can be pretty disagreeable and grumpy and you can set that mouth of yours tight like a nun."

She stared at him, anger beginning in a flush.

"But I still think we ought to get married."

She stopped, realized her mouth was open, and shut it with a click of teeth.

"It kind of makes sense. We get married, and you stay at your mother's house, and I come back when they give me leave. You keep working and if I get killed you get the insurance. I'm sure as hell worth more dead than alive."

Two children were running across the open field, their dresses bright multicolored spots on the green. Water dribbled from the bronze urn held high by a fat bronze boy on the edge of the fountain.

It isn't real, she thought.

"We go meet my family tonight. I already met yours. Tomorrow I see the priest and it'll all be arranged when I pick you up after work tomorrow. What do you say to that?"

"All right," she said. "Fine with me."

The banns were announced at three masses the next Sunday, and they were married that evening. It was just about the only free time the priest had, there were so many weddings on such short notice.

He came back twice on leave before war started and he was sent to England. Willie May left Woolworth's for a job at the shipyards. It was hard and dirty work—but she saved her money carefully and watched the total grow slowly month after month. In the second April of the war, her mother died in her sleep. Then Joseph remembered his children in Texas and grew lonesome for them and his grandchildren, and went to spend his last days with them. He did not write, so she never knew exactly how many last days he had.

There were few letters from John, but she did not worry. He was a headquarters clerk and they never got shot at, he told her. "I'm still handling the mail, only now I'm getting paid a lot less for doing it." He was a corporal, then a sergeant. "If you don't hear from me," he said, "you know I'm all right."

In a way she was glad he didn't write, nor expect her to write very often. She was just too tired. She worked the graveyard shift at the shipyards—the pay was better—and she never quite got used to sleeping in the daytime with children shouting just outside the window. Once she had her picture in the shipyards' paper: a group of four women, waving to a newly completed PT boat. She clipped that out and sent it to John. She did not sew or knit or crochet any more; her hands were too stiff and heavy. Occasionally, holding a pencil awkwardly, she would sketch a child's dress. She always felt better then, when she could dream about the clothes she would make one day for other people's children, lovely things she herself had never had.

When the war was over, she got a long letter from John, the only one ever. He'd been drinking, he said, and he'd been thinking. . . . There'd been some talk about them having to go into occupation forces, but the captain said that was just stupid, maybe the unit would go, but any guy with nearly five years' service could get out if he wanted to. . . . And he wanted to. "So one of these days you'll see me come walking up to the yard and maybe I'll have one of those big FOR SALE signs on my shoulder and we'll go for a paddle in the canal. Like we used to. You remember?"

She did. It was the best game of the long rainy summers of that faraway childhood.

First the oldest and the boldest and the strongest children gathered the large wood and metal signs one particular realtor installed at his buildings. C ME FOR SALE C. BELL the signs said in red and black letters. The children stole them from walls and lawns and hid them away until heavy rains filled all the drainage ditches and canals. Then each large sign became a raft for two children, their paddles the curved fronds of the tall palm trees.

Willie May smelled the freshness of rain-cleared air and the nutty odor of her own sweat. She was aware also of the presence of another child. (Had that been John? She didn't know.) She saw her arms (long and thin and spotted with mosquito bites) and she saw the brush-burns on her knees (large dark scabs always bleeding). She was shivering with pride and excitement: the smell of drainage water, the smell of sweet decay, was the smell of freedom.

She was never afraid, though they all knew it was dangerous. Childhood sheathed her, protected her.

The children slid down the grass-spotted mud banks of open drainage ditches to launch their rafts on the slow-moving water. Buoyed by its wood frame, the sheet of tin floated a fraction of an inch above the surface. Each stroke of the paddle sent a thin sheet of water across it.

Because the city was built on perfectly flat land, it was drained after every heavy rain by huge pumps concealed in brick buildings. (Keep out of the canals, all the mothers screamed, you'll drown, they'll pick you out of the screens at the pumping station with the drowned dogs and the drunks, and the runaways from the state hospital. . . . None of the children paid attention, though they once did see a body floating. The police were already there, grappling for it.)

The grassy ditches led into wider concrete-lined canals where rusting iron pipes high over their heads dripped small streams of water. Here the surface was slack and oily, showing only the faintest pull of the distant pumps.

Soon they passed under High Street Bridge. A man named Duke, who worked in the gas station on that corner, had made himself guardian of that stretch of canal and watched it all day long. He'd rescued so many children from the water that newspapers often did stories about him. Willie May had seen pictures of him, beaming, dripping wet, holding a child in his arms. Sometimes he was too late; the children were drowned. He snagged their bodies with a long hooked pole and dragged them out. Then the newspaper picture showed him holding a small wrapped bundle.

Willie May remembered him clearly, shouting, leaning over the side of the bridge, one arm reaching down to catch them, a thick hairy arm with a hand so huge it filled the sky.

The children crouched down, swinging their palm frond paddles like bats against him. Sometimes they felt the air from his grasping arm against the backs of their necks. (If he caught you, he took your raft and sent you home.) "You'll kill yourself, you damn fool kids," he shouted. They shouted back at him in their high reedy voices, "No, no, no."

Farther down the canal there was a dark-haired woman who sat in her backyard under a medlar tree. She waved to them, silently.

Even farther along there was an old man, a very old man, who always wore a grayish bathrobe and held a glass of red liquid in his hand. He called to them, using the same words every time: "You pass on my canal, and you never stop to talk to me. Come talk to me and I will give you some cream soda." And he held up the red-filled glass and rattled the ice against its sides.

Though he was much too old and frail to chase them, they were afraid, and never looked directly at him as they passed. He might have the evil eye.

Now, listening carefully, they heard the sucking, gurgling sound of fast-moving water. They were nearing the point where their canal emptied into a still larger one, where the water was very swift and the pumps less than a mile away through a great brick-lined underground culvert.

Already ripples surged across the tin surface of their raft. They dug in their paddles, turned the raft into the side. They landed with a thump and a splash. Quickly, they scrambled up the slope and stood on the concrete parapet to watch.

The empty raft, freed of their weight, floated off. It slipped into the main canal, its prow bobbing, nodding to itself, as trickles of water splashed across its tin deck. The raft shifted from side to side, anxiously, nervously, then began spinning in circles, traveling faster and faster. Until it vanished into the darkness of the brick tunnel.

Willie May and the other child watched it disappear, their adventure half over, only the trip home left. Stretching and whistling, arms out, they pranced like acrobats along the narrow concrete edge. Tiring of that, they wandered through strange yards, teasing dogs, stealing medlars or pomegranates or figs, according to the season. At Calhoun Street, at the traffic light, they hitched rides on the backs of trucks, hunched down carefully out of the drivers' sight. If they were very lucky, they might catch an iceman's truck and find a handful of ice flakes under the dark canvas.

Among those children had been John Denham, her husband. He remembered, even if she didn't. But then she always had trouble remembering John. When he walked into her living room that November day in 1945, still in uniform, duffel bag on his shoulder, she blinked with surprise. He'd never seemed quite real to her.

He went back to work in the post office. She was pregnant three months later with a boy, their only child, named Michael.

While she waited for his birth, while her body grew thick and full and her work-stiffened hands became soft and pliable again, she began setting up her own business: children's dresses. She got out the designs that she had drawn so awkwardly during the war years, and she selected the best, carefully, lovingly. Her designs were always ornate, the colors always unusual—her clothes would be easy to recognize. A year later she sold the first of her special christening dresses, one with a cape of seed pearls to be used later in a wedding veil. For that, because she did it herself alone, there was a waiting period of five months.

"Those women are crazy enough to order that far in advance?" John said. "My God, Willie May, they've got to call you as soon as they find out they're pregnant."

"Yes," she said smugly, "they do."

"But our kid didn't have a fancy dress when he got baptized."

"I didn't have the time," she said with a smile.

She hired three women, then five, and that was all.

John said, "If you advertised, you could sell a hell of a lot more. You could have a real factory, not just five people, you could be growing."

She shook her head. "I don't want to advertise, I want the mothers and the grandmothers to hear about me. I want them to see my dresses and then want to buy them. Sure, I could hire more people right now, but I want the customers to wait. They will. The Mary Lynne Shop gave me an order yesterday, even when I told them it would be four months before delivery."

"Crazy," John said.

"No," she said, "they know my clothes are hard to get and expensive."

"And they like that?"

"Yes," she said, "that's exactly what they want."

Their son, Michael, was healthy and strong, polite in his catechism class and good in school. The three of them lived quietly, well-organized and orderly. Every Sunday after ten o'clock mass they went to John's family for midday dinner. Sunday afternoons they went for drives in their new Plymouth, stopping in the park to watch the child play. They went to a downtown movie on Saturday night and Bingo on Thursday. John went out with the boys on Friday night. Sometimes he did not come back to the house at all, but went directly to work on Saturday morning. He kept his post office uniform neatly folded in the trunk of his car.

Eventually those Friday evenings became whole weekends. Willie May scarcely noticed. She still took their son downtown on Saturday evenings to the big movie house with its curving stairs and crystal chandelier and velvet curtains. And she went to John's family for Sunday dinner, saying only, "John won't be here." His parents never asked about him.

She decided on a name for her company. Until then her dress labels carried only three gold fleurs-de-lis (she'd seen them on the banner of St. Louis King of France). Now she added *Beatrix Designs*, named for the author of Michael's favorite book, *Peter Rabbit*.

Somewhere in those years, once, John asked, "You want to take a vacation? I got all this annual leave coming to me. I got to use it or lose it."

"I don't know of any place I want to go," she said slowly.

"A couple of the boys are talking about driving over to Morrisport for some fishing. We can rent a camp there. And I might just go."

"Fine," she said.

Quicker than she thought possible, Michael was finishing high school, and John took fishing vacations several times a year. It took her a couple of days to notice that he had not returned from one of them. Only then did she discover that his clothes were gone.

Feeling oddly embarrassed, as if she were peeping into an uncurtained window, she asked his family about him. He had retired, they said; he had twenty years' service.

She supposed he still lived in town, but it did not occur to her to look for him. The boy she had played with, sailing the drainage ditches after a heavy rain, the young man who had appeared at the counter in Woolworth's, the soldier who had walked into her house—they were all different, detached, set apart by time. They were none of them connected to the balding, middle-aged husband and father.

These things, they were all of them beyond her reach. Forces changing her life, and beyond her control. Impersonal, like wind and rain. Unquestioned.

Why should she be thinking of John now . . . She had not taken a

Seconal last night and so she'd been up very early, long before day showed the other side of the drawn hospital blinds.

"Good morning, Mrs. Denham. Your son's already called to tell us that he's on his way."

"I will be glad to leave."

She let her eyes wander lazily around the room, across the pictures—soft landscapes and seascapes—the two large chairs, the flowers.

A better room to die in, she thought, than ever I was born in. But I don't die here today. Today I go home.

Whispering rubber voices of wheelchairs across polished corridor floors. Into cars. Into other corridors and other cars. Endless whispering.

Long before she boarded the plane, she was so tired she could scarcely hold her head upright.

It will be too much for me, she thought, I should not have tried. It will be too much for me. I shall die on the way. But no, I didn't drown on the raft all those years ago. I balanced and paddled and reached the end and got home safely.

Propped against the vibrating plane wall she dozed, woke to pain. Michael was there. "Here, Mother." White pills and a fuzziness that did not change the pain, only pushed it farther away. As if it were happening to somebody else. In another place, another time.

Michael said, "Mother, this is Dallas. We'll be here for a little while. Would you like a change of scene? Would you like to see the new airport?"

Look at something I will never see again? No. I have seen enough. I carry enough images inside my head to need no more. My world grows smaller, the edges peel back, an orange shedding its skin.

But who would think an hour could be so long . . . Time doesn't rush toward its end. It groans and creaks and creeps along. Like the beat and the wheeze of the heart, its clock. Each tick like a slow hammer stroke, a gong sounding to mark something or other. Whatever.

She opened her eyes and saw people in the plane as skeletons, she saw right through their flesh, saw their bones, saw their blood running through its appointed channels.

She thought: Were I ever so small, a microbe, a molecule, I would ride my raft along those red courses, I would follow those warm canals, exploring.

She floated on the warm canals, she saw the flaws in the bone, inspected them carefully: the chips and the old breaks and the dusty grit of arthritis. She noted them all, and also the swirls and the eddies and the cumbersome debris all along the warm red courses,.

Long before the plane left Dallas, she herself left the ground, flying. The air was soft, silvery birds flew so close to her that their feathers tickled her cheeks. She brushed them away.

Michael said, "Mother?"

But he was not with her, he was far away, held in the plane, and his voice was faint.

She was flying, alone, complete. She saw rushing toward her, rushing past her, everything. Leaves uncurled, people rose from their beds. Cats crouched, claws tearing fur across backs. Copulation: a jumble of arms and legs. She saw hospitals and bodies lying open and bloody until they were sewed back together missing some part or other. She saw rain falling and snow falling and flowers opening their buds like ticking clocks. She saw people brushing their teeth and people weeping in corners. She saw police dozing in squad cars. She saw bitches strain in birth and puppies born like chains of pearls. She saw suns rise and stars dance in their paths across the seasons. She saw ants and oceans and curving endless space. She saw her house, the one she had lived in all her life. She saw a leaf fallen in the gutter. And swamp water bubbling with its own gases, shivering with the swarms of life beneath.

Secure in her power and boastful of her strength, she raced the plane home. And won.

She was waiting at the airport when Michael pushed her wheelchair through the gates. She sniffed at the thin figure sagging sideways, dribble of saliva draining from the mouth, eyes half open but unseeing.

Filled with distaste, she joined them for one more, the last, passage in this trip. Another trailing hiss of rubber wheels across shiny machine-polished floors, another car, another ride.

She grew impatient with their progress and tried to lift herself from the car to float on the layers and levels of the wind. This time she could not. Her power drained, she was trapped inside the tin shell, inside her shattered body.

Michael was there and Michael would let her out. Michael would open the door as soon as they reached home. Until then the endless pale concrete highways, looping rises and the turnoffs, dark night and day all one and the same. Sun and shade. Highways like ribbons, streams of concrete.

They stopped finally and Michael opened the doors and lifted her out.

She was too tired now to rise and soar and find the wind. She would need help. In the sky there seemed to be something . . . a kite. She could ride a kite.

"Is that a kite, Michael? Over there in the sky?"

"No, Mother," he said, "there isn't anything there."

There were other people, but she did not bother noticing them. She stayed hidden behind her eyelids, thinking about all the roads she had traveled that day, the twists and turns that had brought her home. And this was her house, she knew it by its smell. She was home. She smiled to herself, ignoring the distant voices. Was that Michael calling? Well, she would not answer.

She discovered that she was floating, lightly, delicately, on water flickering and iridescent with oil film. Was somebody with her? John? But John was dead years ago. She was alone. Her body was small and light and when she dabbled her fingers in the water, her hand was a sunburned child's hand. The day was sunny and there was a very slight breeze. In the sky there were fluffy white clouds that people called bishops, they were so fat and smug and self-important looking. The water flowed swiftly, carrying her past familiar trees: fig and medlar branches drooping with out-of-season fruit. The bridge now, the High Street Bridge. There was no one on it today, no hand stretched down to bring children home safe from danger. The water made little cooing, coaxing sounds. . . . past the spot where the old man sat, the old man who offered them cream soda to stop and talk to him. No one tempted her today. The raft was moving very fast now, streams of water like banners on each side.

Here was the end of the familiar journey, here was where they always paddled to the side and scrambled away home. But now she had no paddle. And the current was swifter than she ever remembered. No stopping. The raft moved lightly, steadily, floating like a leaf, turning gently, seeming to know its way.

She had never been here, where the water was wide and the sun sparkled on tiny surface waves. She had never dared come this far before and she was astonished at how easy it was, how smooth and how silent.

The raft began to spin in circles, the sun and the clouds flickered across the sky. On both sides was the cream color of hospital walls, and there was nothing to see on them, only rising emptiness.

Then, as she knew she must, she saw the tunnel ahead. Just as she had seen it from the banks of childhood. She looked at it wonderingly, unsurprised. It waited. The raft sailed directly into it, into the dark.

Toni Cade Bambara

A Tender Man

The girl was sitting in the booth, one leg wrapped around the other cartoon-like. Knee socks drooping, panties peeping from her handbag, ears straining from her head for the soft crepe footfalls, straining less Aisha silent and sudden catch her unawares with the dirty news.

She hadn't caught Cliff's attention. His eyes were simply at rest in that direction. And nothing better to do, he had designed a drama of her. His eyes resting on that booth, on that swivel chair, waiting for Aisha to return and fill it. When the chatty woman in the raincoat had been sitting where the nervous girl sat now, Aisha had flashed him a five-minute sign. That was fifteen minutes ago.

He hadn't known he'd mind the waiting. But he'd been feeling preoccupied of late, off-center, anxious even. Thought he could shrug it off, whatever it was. But sitting on the narrow folding chair waiting, nothing to arrest his attention and focus him, he felt crowded by something too heavy to shrug off. He decided he was simply nervous about the impending student takeover.

He flipped through a tattered *Ebony*, pausing at pictures of children, mothers and children, couples and children, grandparents and children. But no father and child. It was a conspiracy, he chuckled to himself, to keep fathers—he searched for a word—outside. He flipped through the eligible bachelors of the year, halting for a long time at the photo of Carl Davis, his ole army mate who'd nearly deserted in the spring of '61. He was now with RCA making $20,000 a year. Cliff wondered doing what.

The girl was picking her face, now close to panic. In a moment she would bolt for the door. He could imagine heads lifting, swiveling, perfect strangers providing each other with hairy explanations. He could hear the women tsk-tsking, certain that their daughters would never. Aisha came through the swinging doors and he relaxed, not realizing till that moment how far he had slipped into the girl's drama. Aisha shot three fingers in his direction and he nodded. The girl was curled up tight now, Cliff felt her tension, staring at the glass slide Aisha slid onto the table. She leaned over the manila folder Aisha opened, hand screening the side of her face as though to block the people out. She was crying. The sobbing audible, though muffled now that the screening hand was doubled up in her mouth. Cliff was uncomfortable amongst so many women and this young one crying. Cliff got up to look for the water fountain.

Up and down the corridors folks walked distractedly, clutching slips of colored papers. A few looked terror-struck, like models for the covers of the books he often found his students buried in. Glancing at the slips of green or white, checking them against the signs on the doors, each had a particular style with the entrance, he noted. Knocking timidly, shivering, Judgment Day. Turning knobs stealthily and looking about, second-story types. Brisk entrances with caps yanked low, yawl deal with me, shit. Cliff moved in and out among the paper-slip clutchers, doorway handlers, teen-agers pulling younger brothers and sisters along, older folk pausing to read the posters. The walls were lined with posters urging VD tests, Pap smears, examinations painless and confidential. In less strident Technicolor, others argued the joys of planned parenthood.

Cliff approached the information desk, for the sister on the switchboard seemed to be wearing two wigs at once and he had to see that. The guard leaned way back before considering his question about the water fountain, stepped away from a woman leaning over the desk inquiring after a clinic, gave wide berth to all the folk who entered and headed in that direction, then pointed out the water fountain, backed up against the desk in a dramatic recoil. Cliff smiled at first and considered fucking with the dude, touching him, maybe drooling a bit on his uniform. But he moved off, feeling unclean.

At the water fountain a young father hoisted his daughter too far into the spout. Cliff held the button down and the brother smiled relief, a two-handed grip centering now the little girl, who gurgled and horsed around in the water, then held a jaw full even after she was put down on the floor again.

"This place is a bitch, ain't it?" The brother nodding vigorous agreement to his own remark.

"My wife's visiting her folks and I'm about to lose my mind with these kids." He smiled proudly, though, jutting his chin in the direction of the rest of his family. Two husky boys around eight and ten were doing base slides in the upper corridor.

"Man, if I had the clap, I sure as hell wouldn't come here for no treatments." His frown made Cliff look around. In that moment the lights seem to dim, the paint job age, the posters slump. A young girl played hopscotch in the litter, her mother pushing her along impatiently.

Yeh, a bitch, Cliff had meant to say, but all that came out was a wheezy mumble.

"My ole lady says to me 'go to the clinic and pick up my pills.' Even calls me long distance to remind me she's running out. 'Don't forget to get the pills, B.J.' So I come to get the damn pills, right?" He ran his hand through his bush, gripping a fistful and tossing his head back and forth. "Man oh man," he groaned, shaking his head by the hair. The gesture had started out as a simple self-caress, had moved swiftly into an I-don't-believe-this-shit nod, and before Cliff knew it, the brother'd become some precinct victim, his head bam-bam against the walls. "Man oh man, this crazy-ass place! Can't even get a word in for the 'What's your clinic number?' 'Where's your card?' 'Have you seen the cashier?' 'Have you got insurance?' 'Are you on the welfare?' 'Do you have a yellow slip?' 'Where's your card?' 'Who's ya mama?' Phwweeoo! I'm goin straight to the drugstore and get me a crate of rubbers right on. I ain't putting my woman through this shit."

"Daddy." The little girl was yanking on his pants leg for attention. When she got it, she made a big X in the air.

"Oh, right. I forgot. Sorry, baby." He turned to Cliff and shrugged in mock sheepishness. "Gotta watch ya mouth round these kids these days, they get on ya. Stay on my case bout the smoking, can't even bring a poke chop in the house, gotta sneak a can of beer and step

out on the fire escape to smoke the dope. Man, these kids sompthin!"
He was starting that vigorous nodding again, watching his sons approach. Cliff couldn't keep his eyes off the brother's bobbing head. It
reminded him of Granddaddy Mobley so long ago, playing horsy,
whinnying down the hallway of Miss Hazel's boardinghouse, that head
going a mile a minute and his sister Alma riding high, whipping her
horse around the head and shoulders and laughing so hard Miss Hazel
threatened to put them out.

"Yeh," he was sighing, nudging Cliff lest he miss the chance to dig
on the two young dudes coming, punching invisible catcher's mitts,
diddyboppin like their daddy must've done it years before. "Later for
them pills, anyway. It's back to good ole reliable Trojans."

"Pills dangerous," Cliff said.

"Man, just living is a danger. And every day. Every day, man."

"We going to the poolroom now?" the older boy was asking,
nodding first to Cliff.

"I want some Chinese food." The younger seemed to be addressing
this to Cliff, shifting his gaze to his father long after he'd finished
speaking.

"Hold it, youngbloods. Hold on a damn minute. I gotta catch me
some sleep and get to work in a coupla hours. Yawl bout to wear my ass
out."

"Daddy."

"Oh damn, I'm sorry. Sorry." The brother made two huge X's in
the air and dropped his head shamefaced till his daughter laughed.

"Man, you got kids?"

"Yeah" was all Cliff said, not sure what else he could offer. It had
been pleasant up to then, the brother easy to be easy with. But now he
seemed to be waiting for Cliff to share what Cliff wasn't sure he had to
share. He bent to take a drink. "Daughter," he offered, trying to
calculate her age. He'd always used the Bay of Pigs invasion as a guide.

"They sompthin, ain't they?" the brother broke in, his children
dragging him off to the door. "Take it slow, my man."

Cliff nodded and bent for another drink. Bay of Pigs was the
spring of '61. His daughter had been born that summer. He bit his lip.
Hell, how many fathers could just tick off the ages of their children,
right off the bat? Not many. But then if the brother had put the

question to him, as Aisha had the day before—What sort of person is your daughter?—Cliff would not have known how to answer. He let the water bubble up against closed lips for a while, not sure what that fact said about the man he was, or at least had thought he was, hoped he was, had planned to be for so long, was convinced when still a boy he could be once he got out of that house of worrisome women.

Aisha had come quietly up behind him and linked arms. "Hey, mister," she cooed, "how bout taking a po' colored gal to dinner." She pulled him away from the water fountain. "I'm starving."

Starving. Cliff looked at her quickly, but she did not react. Starving. He stared at her, but she was checking the buttons on her blouse, then stepping back for him to catch the door. She moved out swiftly and down the stairs ahead of him, not so much eager to get away, for she'd said how much she liked her job at the clinic. But eager to be done with it for the day and be with him. She waited at the foot of the stairs and linked arms again.

Cliff smiled. He dug her. Had known her less than a week, but felt he knew her. A chick who dealt straight up. No funny changes to go through. He liked the way she made it clear that she dug him.

"Whatcha grinnin about?" she asked, adjusting her pace to his. She was a brisk walker—he had remarked on it the day before—Northern urban brisk. I bet you like to lead too when you dance, he had teased her.

"Thinking about the first time I called you," he said.

"Oh? Oh." She nodded and was done, as though in that split second she had retrieved the tape from storage, played it, analyzed his version of what went down, and knew exactly what he had grinned about and that was that. He had kidded her about that habit too. "You mean the way I push for clarity, honesty?"

That was what he had meant, but he didn't like the cocky way she said it with the phony question mark on the end. She was a chick who'd been told she was too hard, too sure, too swift, and had made adjustments here and there, softening the edges. He wasn't sure that was honest of her, though he'd never liked women with hard edges.

"No," he half-lied. "Your sensitivity. I like the way you said, after turning me down for a drink, 'Hey, Brother—'"

"I called you Cliff. I'm not interested in being your sister."

He hugged her arm. "Okay, 'Hey, Cliff,' you said, 'I ain't rejecting you, but I don't drink, plus I got to get up at the crack of dawn tomorrow to prepare for a workshop. How about dinner instead?'"

"And that tickles you?"

"It refreshes me," he said, laughing, feeling good. It wasn't so easy being a dude, always putting yourself out there to be rejected. He'd never much cared for aggressive women; on the other hand, he appreciated those who met him halfway. He slowed her down some more. "Hey, city girl," he drawled. "This here a country boy you walkin wid, ain't used to shoes yet. The restaurant'll be there. Don't close till late."

"I'm starving, fool. Come on and feed me. You can take off them shoes. I'll carry em."

He hugged her arm again and picked up his pace. It was silly, he told himself, these endless control games he liked to play with assertive types. He was feeling too good. But then he wasn't. Starving. She had raised that question: Can you swear no child of yours is starving to death? Not confronting him or even asking him, softening the edges, but addressing the workshop, reading off a list of questions that might get the discussion started. The brother next to him had slapped his knees with his cap and muttered, "Here we go again with some women lib shit." But a sister across the aisle had been more vocal, jumping up to say, "Run it down to the brothers. Let's just put them other questions on hold and stay with this one a while," she demanded. "Yeah, can you swear?" Her hot eyes sweeping the room. "Can you deal with that, you men in here? Can you deal with that one?"

The discussion got sidetracked, it'd seemed to Cliff at the time. Everybody talking at once, all up in each other's face. Paternity, birth control, genocide, responsibility, fathering, mothering, children, child support, warrants, the courts, prison. One brother had maintained with much heat that half the bloods behind the walls were put there by some vengeful bitch. Warriors for the revolution wasting away in the joint for nonsupport or some other domestic bullshit. "Well, that should point something out!" a sister in the rear had yelled, trying to be heard over a bunch of brothers who stood up to say big-mouth sisters like herself were responsible for Black misery.

Starving. Cliff had spaced on much of the discussion, thinking about his daughter Rhea. Going over in his mind what he might have said had he been there to hear Donna murmur, "Hey, Cliff, I think I missed my period." But he had been in the army. And later when the pregnancy was a certainty, he was in Norfolk, Virginia, on his way overseas, he thought. And all the way out of port he lay in his bunk, Donna's letter under his head, crinkly in the pillowcase, gassing with Carl Davis about that ever-breathtaking announcement that could wreck a perfectly fine relationship—Hey, baby, I think I'm pregnant.

He had not quite kept track of the workshop debate the night before, for he was thinking about parenthood, thinking too of his own parents, his mother ever on the move to someplace else his father'd been rumored to be but never was, dragging him and his little sister Alma all over the South till the relatives in Charlotte said whoa, sister, park em here. And he had grown up in a household of women only, women always. Crowded, fussed over, intruded upon, continually compared to and warned not to turn out like the dirty dog who'd abandoned Aunt Mavis or that no-good nigger who'd done Cousin Dorcas dirty or some other low-down bastard that didn't mean no woman no good.

"You're unusually preoccupied, Cliff," Aisha was saying gently, as if reluctant to intrude, but hesitant about leaving him alone to wrassle with the pain he was sure was readable in his face. "Not that I know you well enough to know what's usual." He followed her gaze toward the park. "You feel like walking a while? Talking? Or maybe just being quiet?"

"Thought you were starving?" He heard an edge to his voice, but she didn't seem to notice.

"I am. I am." She waited at the curb, ready to cross over to the park or straight ahead to the Indian restaurant. Cliff disengaged his arm and fished out a cigarette, letting the light change. Had he been alone, he would have crossed over to the park. He had put off taking inventory for too long, his life was in a drift, unmonitored. Just that morning shaving, trying to fix in his mind what role he'd been called on to play in the impending student takeover, he'd scanned the calendar over the sink. The student demands would hit the campus paper on the anniversary of the Bay of Pigs.

He'd made certain promises that day, that spring day in '61 when the boat shipped out for Vietnam they'd thought, but headed directly for the Caribbean. He'd made certain promises about what his life would be like in five years, ten years, ever after if he lived. Had made certain promises to himself, to the unborn child, to God, he couldn't remember to whom, as the ship of Puerto Ricans, Chicanos and Bloods were cold-bloodedly transported without their knowing from Norfolk to Cuba to kill for all the wrong reasons. Then the knowledge of where they were and what they were expected to do, reminded of the penalty for disobeying orders, he'd made promises through clenched teeth, not that he was any clearer about the Cuban Revolution than he was about the Vietnamese struggle, but he knew enough about Afro-Cuban music to make some connections and conclude that the secret mission was low-down. Knew too that if they died, no one at home'd be told the truth. Missing in action overseas. Taken by the Vietcong. Killed in Nam in the service of God and country.

"Worries?" Aisha asked, "or just reminiscing?"

He put his arm around her shoulders and hugged her close. His life was not at all the way he'd promised. "I was just thinking," he said slowly, crossing them toward the restaurant, "about the first time I came North as a kid." He wasn't sure that was a lie. The early days came crowding in on him every time he thought of his daughter and the future. And his daughter filled his mind on every mention of starving.

He hadn't even known as a boy that he was or for what, till that Sunday his aunts had hustled him and Alma to the train depot. But Granddaddy Mobley didn't even get off the train when it slowed. Just leaned down and hauled them up by the wrists, first Alma, then him.

"Hop aboard, son," he'd said, bouncing the cigar to the back of his jaw. "This what you call a rescue job."

Son. He had been sugar dumpling, sweetie pie, honey darling for so long, as though the horror of Southern living in general, the bitterness of being in particular some poor fatherless child could be sweetened with a sugar tit, and if large enough could fill him up, fill those drafty places somewhere inside. So long hugged and honey-bunched, he didn't know he was starving or for what till "son" was offered him and the grip on his wrist became a handshake man to man.

Dumfounded, the women were trotting along after the still-moving train, Cousin Dorcas calling his name, Aunt Evelyn calling Granddaddy Mobley a bunch of names.

"Train, iz you crazy?!" Aunt Mavis had demanded when she

realized that was all the train intended to do, slow up for hopping off or kidnapping. "Have you lost your mind?" Cliff could never figure to whom this last remark was said. But he remembered he laughed like hell.

Granddaddy Mobley chuckled too, watching Cousin Dorcas through the gritty windows, trotting along the landing, shaking her fist, dodging the puffs of steam and the chunks of gravel thrown up by the wheels, the ribbons of her hat flying in and out of her shouting mouth.

Leaning out of an open window over his sister's head, Cliff could make out the women on the landing getting smaller, staring pop-eyed and pop-mouthed too. And when he glanced down, li'l Alma was looking straight up into his face the way she did from the bunk beds when the sun came up, the look asking was everything okay and could the day begin. He grinned back out the window, and grinned too at his sister cause yeah, everything would be all right. He couldn't blame the women, though, for carrying on like that, having taken all morning to get the chicken fried and the rugs swept and the sheets boiled and dough beat up. Then come to find old Mobley, highstepping, fun-loving, outrageous, drinking, rambler, gambler and everything else necessary to thoroughly scandalize the family name, upset the household with his annual visits, giving them something to talk about as the lamps glowed at night till next visiting time, ole Mobley wasn't even thinking about a visit at all this time. Wasn't even stopping long enough to say hello to his daughter, not that she was there. Just came to snatch the darling little girl and the once perfect little gentleman now grown rusty and hardheaded just like his daddy for the world.

"We going North with you?" Alma had asked, not believing she could go anywhere without her flouncy dresses, her ribbons, and their mother's silver hairbrush from the world's fair.

"That's right."

"We going to live with you?" young Cliff had pressed, eager to get things straight. "To live with you till we grown or just for summer or what?"

Instead of answering, the old man whipped out a wad of large, white handkerchiefs and began to unfold them with very large gestures. The children settled in their seats waiting for the magic show to commence. But the old man just spread them out on the seats, three for sitting on and one for his hat. Cliff and Alma exchanged a look, lost for words. And in that moment, the old man leaned forward, snatched Alma's little yellow-haired doll and pitched it out the window.

"And you'd better not cry," he said.

"No, ma'am."

Cliff laughed and the old man frowned. "Unless you in training to take care of white folks' babies when you grown."

"No, ma'am."

Cliff had smiled smugly, certain that Alma had no idea what this rescue man was saying. He did. And he looked forward to growing up with a man like this. Alma slid her small hand into his and Cliff squeezed it. And not once did she look back after her doll, or he at the town.

"I met your wife in the bus terminal—"

"Ex-wife," Cliff said, jolted out of his reverie.

Aisha poured the tea. "Ex-wife. Met her last Monday and—"

"You told me."

"I didn't tell you the whole thing."

Cliff looked up from his plate of meat patties. He wasn't sure he wanted to hear about it. Every time he had tried to think of his daughter, he discovered he couldn't detach her from the woman he'd married. Thinking about Donna made him mad. Thinking about his daughter Rhea just made him breathless. Rising, he jingled change in his pocket and stalled for time at the jukebox. That was the first thing Aisha had said to him when they were introduced just four days ago on campus. "Hemphill? I think I know your wife, Donna Hemphill. Ran into her at the bus terminal less than an hour ago."

After his own class of the day and a quick meeting with the Black student union, he'd sought her out in the faculty dining room, convinced that his chairman would at least give her the semi-deluxe treatment, particularly considering his taste for black meat (or so the rumor went, though he rarely did more toward orienting new faculty members than pointing out their cubicle, shoving a faculty handbook at them, and warning them about the "Mau Mau," his not-so-affectionate name for the Black student union). She had pursued the topic the minute Cliff had seated himself next to her, remarking quietly that his wife had seemed on the verge of collapse. He welcomed the mention of Donna only for the opportunity it offered to point out that one, she was very much an ex, two he was single, three he found her, Aisha, attractive. Beyond that, he could care less about Donna or her mental state. Aisha had remarked then—too sarcastically for his taste—that this very ex-wife with the mental state was the woman who was raising his daughter. He had eaten the dry roast beef sullenly, grateful for the appearance of his colleague Robinson, who swung the conversation toward the students and the massive coronaries they were causing in administrative circles.

Some Indian movie music blared out at Cliff's back as he picked out one of the umpteen rhythms to stroll back to the table doing, slapping out the beat on his thigh.

"I didn't say this before"—Aisha was reaching for the drumming hand—"cause you cut me short last Tuesday. I'm sorry I didn't press it then on campus, cause it's harder now . . . that I know you . . . and all."

"Then forget it."

She slid her hand back to her side of the table and busied herself with the meat patties. He drummed on the table with both hands, trying to read her mood. He felt he owed her some explanation, wanted even to talk this thing out, his feelings about his daughter. Then resented Aisha for that. He drummed away. The last thing he would have wanted for this evening, the first time they'd been together with no other appointments to cut into their time, the last thing he wanted, feeling already a little off-center, crowded, was a return to that part of his history that seemed so other, over with, some dim drama starring a Cliff long since discarded. Cliff the soldier, Cliff the young father, Cliff the sociology instructor—there was clarity if not continuity. But Cliff the husband . . . blank.

He had pronounced the marriage null and void in the spring of '61. On the troop ship speeding to who knew where, or at least none of the dudes in that battalion knew yet, but to die most probably. He'd read the letter over and over, and was convinced Donna was lying about being pregnant and so far advanced. He was due home for good soon, and this was her way to have him postpone thinking of a split. He and Carl Davis had gassed the whole time out of port about what they were going to do with their lives if they still had them in five months' time. Then some of the soldiers were saying the fleet was in the Caribbean. And all hell broke loose, the men mistakenly assuming—assuming, then readying up for shore leave in Trinidad. The CO told them different, though not much. First there was a sheaf of papers that had to be signed, or court-martial, papers saying they never would divulge to press, to family, to friends, even to each other, anything at all regarding the secret mission they were about to embark upon. Then they got their duties. Most work detail the same—painting over the ship's numbers, masking all U.S. identification, readying up the equipment for the gunners, checking their packs and getting new issues of ammunition.

"We're headed for Cuba," Carl Davis had said.

"That's crazy. The action's in Vietnam."

"Mate, I'm telling you, we're off to Cuba. T. J. was upside and got the word. The first invasionary battalions are Cuban exiles. They'll hook up with the forces there on the island to overthrow Fidel Castro."

"You got to be kidding."

Carl had sneered at Cliff's naïveté. "Mate, they got air coverage that'd made the Luftwaffe look silly. We rendezvous with a carrier and a whole fleet of marines moving in from Nicaragua. I'm telling you, this is it."

T. J. had skidded down the stair rail and whispered. "They got Kennedy on a direct line. Kennedy! Jim, this operation is being directed from the top."

"Holy shit." Cliff had collapsed on his bunk, back pack and all, the letter crumpling under his ear. A child was being born soon, the letter said. He was going to be a father. And if he died, what would happen to his child? His marriage had been in shreds before he'd left, a mere patchwork job on the last leave, and she'd been talking of going back home. His child. Her parents. That world. Those people.

"I never knew Donna well," Aisha was saying. "We worked at Family Services and I used to see her around, jazz concerts, the clubs. I pretty much wrote her off as a type. One of those gray girls who liked to follow behind Black musicians, hang out and act funky."

Cliff looked at Aisha quickly. Was she the type to go for blood? He'd had enough of the white girl–brother thing. Had been sick of it all, of hearing, of reading about it, of arguing, of defending himself, even back then on the tail end of the Bohemian era, much less in the Black and Proud times since.

"Use to run into her a lot when I lived downtown. The baby didn't surprise me—hell, half of Chelsea traffic was white girls pushing mulatto babies in strollers. We used to chat. You two seemed to be always on the verge of breakup, and she was forever going down in flames. I got the impression the baby was something of . . . a hostage?" She seemed to wait for his response. He blanked his face out. "A hostage," she continued, seeming to relish the word, "as per usual."

The waiter slid a dish of chutney at Cliff's elbow, then leaned in to replace the teapot with a larger, steamier one. Cliff leaned back as the plates and bowls were taken from the tray in some definite, mysterious order and placed just so on the table. Cliff rearranged the plate of roti and the cabbage. The waiter looked at him and placed them in their original spots. Cliff sneaked a look at Aisha and they shared a stone-faced grin.

"Cliff?" She seemed to call to him, the him behind his poker face. He leaned forward. Whatever she had to say, it'd be over with soon and they could get on with the Friday evening he had in mind.

"I asked Donna on Tuesday to give up the child. To give your daughter to me. I'm prepared to raise—"

Cliff stared, not sure he heard that right.

"Look. She's standing in the bus terminal having a crying jag, listing fifty-leven different brands of humiliations and bump-offs from the Black community. She's been trying to enroll your daughter in an independent Black school, at a Yoruba cultural center, at the Bedford-Stuyvesant—"

"Bedford-Stuyvesant?"

"Yeah, your wife lives in Brooklyn."

"Ex-wife."

Aisha spread her napkin and asked very pointedly, "You were not aware that your daughter's been living in Brooklyn for two years?" Cliff tried to remember the last address he had sent money to, recalled he had always given it to Alma. But then Alma had moved to the coast last spring . . .

"Hey, look, Cliff, I've noticed the way you keep leaning on this 'ex' business. I'm sure you're sick to death of people jumping on you, especially sisters, about the white-woman thing. Quite frankly I don't

give a shit who you married or who you are . . . not now . . . I only
thought I did," she said, spacing her words out in a deliberate challenge. "What does interest me is the kid. I'll tell you just what I told her,
I'm prepared to take the girl—"

"Hold it. Hold it." Cliff shoved his plate away and tried to sort out
what he was hearing. If only he could have a tape of this, he was
thinking, to play at his leisure, not have to respond or be read. "Back up,
you're moving too fast for me. I'm just a country boy." He smiled, not
surprised that she did smile back. She looked tired.

"Okay. She's been trying to move your daughter into cultural
activities and whatnot. Very concerned about the kid's racial identity.
For years she's always been asking me to suggest places to take her and
how to handle things and so forth. So I'm standing in the bus terminal
while this white woman falls apart on me, asking to be forgiven her
incompetence, her racism, her hysteria. And I'm pissed. So I ask her—"

"Where's the nigger daddy who should be taking the weight."

Aisha studied her fork and resumed eating. Cliff clenched his jaws.
She was eating now as though she'd been concentrating on that chicken
curry for hours, had not even spoken, did not even know he was there.
Was that the point of it all, to trigger that outburst? And it had been an
outburst, his face was still burning. Was she out for blood? It was a
drag. Cliff reached for the chutney and sensed her tense up. She looked
coiled on her side of the table, mouth full of poisonous fangs. She was a
type, he decided, a type he didn't like. She had seemed a groovy
woman, but she was just another bitch. She had looked good to him less
than half an hour ago, bouncing around in the white space shoes. Had
looked good in that slippery white uniform wrinkling at her hips. And
all he thought he wanted to do was take her to his place and tell her so,
show her. He thought he still might like to take her home to make love
to her—no, to fuck her. The atmosphere kept changing, the tone, the
whole quality of his feelings for her kept shifting. She kept him off
balance. Yeh, he'd like to fuck her, but not cause she looked good. Cliff
tore off a piece of roti, then decided he didn't want it. Looked at her and
decided he was being absurd. What had she said she was pissed about?
Donna, an unhinged white woman raising a Black child. Why had he
been so defensive?

"This was a bad time to meet," he heard himself saying. "I wish he had met at some other time when—"

"Look, sugar," she spat out with a malice that didn't match the words, "no matter when or where or how we met, the father question would've come up. And I'd have had to judge what kind of man you are behind your whole sense of what it means to bring a child into the world. I'm funny that way, mister."

"What I was thinking was," he pressed on, shoving aside the anger brewing, clamping down hard on the urge to bust her in the jaw, not sure the urge to hold her close wasn't just as strong, "in a year or so you might have met me with my daughter. I've been considering for a long time fighting for custody of Rhea."

"How long?"

"Off and on for years. But here lately, last few weeks . . ." It occurred to him that that was exactly what he'd been trying to pull together in his mind, a plan. That was what had been crowding him.

"Donna said she'd talk to you about it, Cliff, then get back to me. It was a serious proposal I was making."

"She hasn't called me. Matter of fact, we haven't talked in years."

"Uh-hunh." She delivered this with the jauntiness of a gum-cracking sister from Lenox Avenue. Cliff read on her face total disbelief of all he'd said, as though he couldn't have been really considering it and not talk with the child's mother. He was pissed off. How did it get to be her business, any of it?

"Anyway, Brother," she said, shifting into still another tone, "I'm prepared to take the child. I've got this job at the clinic, it'll hold me till summer when the teaching thing comes through. My aunt runs a school up on Edgecombe. She's not the most progressive sister in the world, but the curriculum's strong academically. And there're several couples on my block who get together and take the kids around. I'm good with children. Raised my nephews and my sisters. I'd do right by the little girl, Cliff. What do you want to ask me?"

Her voice had faded away to a whisper. She sipped her tea now, and for a minute he thought she was about to cry. He wasn't sure for what, but felt he was being unjustly blamed for something. She hadn't believed him. That made him feel unsure about himself. He watched her, drifting in and out among the fragments of sensations, questions that wouldn't stay formed long enough for him to get a hold of. He studied her until his food got cold.

She wasn't going to sleep with him, that was clear. He knew from past experiences that the moment had passed, that moment when women resolved the tension by deciding yes they would, then relaxed one way, or no they wouldn't, and eased into another rhythm. Often at the critical point, especially with younger women, he'd step into their timing and with one remark or a caress of the neck could turn the moment in his favor. He hadn't even considered it with Aisha. There had seemed time enough to move leisurely, no rush. They'd had dinner that first night, then he'd had a Black faculty meeting. He'd picked her up last night to get to the workshop, and after they'd had coffee with Acoli and Essa and talked way into the night about the students' demands. He hadn't even considered that this evening, which just a half-hour ago seemed stretched out so casual and unrushed, would turn out as anything but right.

Hell, they weren't children. They had established right from the jump that this would be a relationship, a relationship of meaning. And he'd looked forward to it, had even thought of calling Alma long distance and working Aisha somehow into the conversation. He knew it would please his sister, for he knew well how it pained her whenever he launched into his dissertation on Black women, the bitterness for those Black women who had raised him surfacing always, and for the others so much like them—though Alma argued it wasn't so—who'd stepped into his life with such explosions, leaving ashes in their wake. And Alma argued that wasn't so either, just his own blindness contracted from poisons he should have pumped out somehow long ago cause they weren't reasonably come by either. He was sick of his dissertation, the arguing, the venom, even thinking about it.

"You can imagine, Cliff . . . well, the irony of it all, meeting you right after seeing Donna after all these years of running into her, hearing about you . . . Look, it's very complicated—my feelings about . . . the whole thing."

"How so?" He poured the last of the hot tea into her cup and waited. She seemed to study the cup for a long time as though considering whether to reject it, wait for it to cool, drink it, or maybe fling it in his face. He couldn't imagine why that last seemed such a possibility.

His sister Alma would have argued that he simply expected the worst always and usually got it, provoked it.

"On the one hand, I'm very attracted to you, Cliff. You care about the students. I mean . . . well, you have a reputation on campus for being—" She was blushing and that surprised the hell out of him. He decided he didn't know women at all. They were too weird, all of them. "Well, for being one of the good guys. Plus you so sharp, ya know, and a great sense of humor. Not to mention you fine." She was looking suddenly girlish. He wanted to laugh, but he didn't want to interrupt her. He was liking this. "And I dig being with you. You're comfortable, even when you're drifting off, you're comfortable to be with." He bowed in his seat. They were smiling again.

"On the other hand"—she cocked her head to signal she hoped to get through this part with the same chumminess—"well . . ." She drank the tea now, two fingers pressed on each side of the Oriental cup, her face moving into the steam, lips pursing to blow. If they ever got around to the pillow talk, he'd ask her about her gesture and whether or not it had been designed to get him. He found all this blowing and sipping very arousing, for no reason he could think of.

"On the other hand," she said again, "while you seem to be a principled person . . . I mean, clearly you're not a bastard or a coward . . . not handling the shit on campus like you been doing . . . but—" She put the cup down.

"Hey look. It's like this, Cliff. I don't understand brothers who marry white girls, I really don't. And I really don't see how you can just walk away from the kid, let your child just . . . Well, damn, what is your daughter, a souvenir?" It was clear to Cliff that his reaction was undisguised and that she was having no trouble reading his face. "Perhaps"—she was looking hopeful now, his cue to rise to the occasion—"perhaps you really have been trying to figure out how to do it, how to get custody?"

"I considered it long before we even broke up. When I first heard that the child was an actual fact, was about to be born, I was in the army. As a matter of fact, I was up to my neck in the Bay of Pigs shit." He had never discussed it before, was amazed he could do it now, could relate it all in five or six quick sentences, when times earlier he hadn't even been able to pull it together coherently in a whole night, staring at the ceiling, wondering how many brothers had been rerouted to the

Philippines to put down the resistance to Marcos and the corporate bosses, how many to Ethiopia to vamp on the Eritrean Front, and how many would wind up in southern Africa all too soon, thinking they were going who knew where. How many more caught in the trick bag of colored on colored death if all who knew remained silent on the score, chumps afraid of change?

Cliff had always maintained he despised people who saw and heard but would not move on what they knew. His colleagues who could wax lyric analyzing the hidden agenda of SEEK and other OEO circuses engineered to fail, but did nothing about it. Bloods in his department grooming the students for caretaker positions, all the while screaming on the system, the oppression, hawking revolution, but carefully cultivating caretakers to negotiate a separate peace for a separate piece of the corrupt pie, claiming the next generation would surely do it. And even Cousin Dorcas and Aunt Mavis years before, going through a pan of biscuits and a pot of coffee laying out with crystal clarity the madness of his mother's life, chronically on hold till she could just get to that one more place to find the man never where folks said he'd be. But never once wrassling the woman, their sister, their kin, to the floor, demanding she at least put the children on her agenda, if not herself. And Cliff himself, heroic in spots, impotent in others, he had postponed for too long an inventory of his self, his life.

"The Cuban people were ready. They kicked our ass. That first landing troop ran smack into an alligator farm in Playa Girón and got wiped out. The second got wasted fore they even got off the beach. And all the while our ship was getting hit. Cannonballs sailing right between the smoke stacks of the ship. And Kennedy on the line saying, 'Pull back,' realizing them balls were a warning, a reminder of what could happen in the world if the U.S. persisted."

Aisha poured him a glass of ginger beer and waited for him to continue. Cliff felt opened up like he hadn't been in years.

"The idea that I might be killed, that my wife Donna would move back to her parents, my child growing up in an all-white environment . . . I use to run the my-wife-is-an-individual-white-person number . . . I dunno . . . it all scared the shit out of me," he was saying, not able to find the bridge, the connection, the transition from those thoughts, those promises made in Cuban waters and what in fact he lived out later and called his life.

"When we broke up, I turned my back, I guess," he said, finding his place again, but not the bridge. "I use to see my daughter a lot when my sister Alma lived in the city. And if I could just figure out how to manage it all, have time for my work and—"

"Your work?" she said, clutching the tablecloth. "Your work?" she sneered. "You one of those dudes who thinks his 'real' work is always outside of—separate from—oh, shit."

He felt her withdraw. He would make an effort to draw her out again, even if she came out blazing in a hot tirade about "women's work" and "men's work" and "what a load of horseshit." He would do it for himself. Later for the them that might have been.

"We were discussing all this recently in class—'The Black Family in the Twentieth Century,' my new course."

"Yeah, I know," she said.

"You know?"

"My niece is in your class. She tapes your lectures. Big fan of yours, my niece."

"Oh." Cliff couldn't remember now just what he had wanted to say, had lost the thread. Aisha had motioned the waiter over and was scanning the dessert list. He shook his head. Dessert was not what he wanted at this point.

He had handed back the students' research papers on their own families when the vet who sat in the back got up to say how odd it was that their generation, meaning the sophomores or juniors, despite the persistent tradition in their own families of folks raising children not their own, odd that this younger generation felt exempt. How many here, someone in the front of the room had asked then, can see themselves adopting children or taking in a kid from the streets, or from a strung-out neighbor, as their own? Cliff had expected a split down the middle, the brothers opting for pure lineage, the sisters charging ego and making a case for "the children" rather than "my child." But it didn't go down that way. The discussion never got off the ground. And after class, the vet had criticized Cliff for short-circuiting the discussion. Cliff hadn't seen his point then. But now, watching Aisha coax the recipe for some dessert or other from the waiter, he could admit that he had probably spaced.

Naturally he'd been thinking of his daughter Rhea, wondering how many others in the class had children and whether it would be fruitful to ask that first. The problem was, he could never think of Rhea without also thinking of Donna. Even after he refused to visit the child on his wife's turf, preferring the serenity of Alma's home for the visits, Rhea was still daughter to the woman who'd been his wife. And he was outside.

He'd been so proud when as a baby she had learned to say "Daddy" first. That had knocked him out. His sister had offered some psycholinguistic-somethinorother explanation, completely unsolicited and halfway unheard, about a baby's physical capacity to produce *d* sounds long before *m* sounds. Cliff paid Alma no mind.

But as the baby grew more independent, more exploratory of the world beyond her skin, he realized why she could say "Daddy" so much sooner. Cause Mommy was not separate, Mommy was part of the baby's world, attached to her own ego. He was distinctly different. Outside. It was some time before Mommy was seen as other. And still later that Rhea could step back from herself and manage "Rhea," then "me." Meanwhile he was outside. Way before that even he was outside—pregnancy, labor, delivery, breastfeeding. Women and babies, mothers and children, mother and child. Him outside. If only she had looked more like him, though in fact she resembled Alma more than Donna. But still there was distance. He knew no terms for negotiating a relationship with her that did not also include her mother. How had Donna managed that? Hostage, Aisha had said.

He chuckled to himself and stared at Aisha. He started up a nutty film in his head. All over the country, sisters crouching behind bushes with croaker sacks ready to pounce and spirit away little mulatto babies. Mulatto babies were dearer, prizer. Or sisters shouting from the podiums, the rooftops, the bedrooms, telling warriors dirty diapers was revolutionary work. Sisters coiled in red leather booths mesmerizing fathers into a package deal. He clamped down hard on fantasies leaching poisons into his brain. Package deal—me and the kid.

"Were you proposing to me by any chance?" he asked just for the hell of it.

"Say what?" She first looked bewildered, then angry, then amazed. She burst out laughing, catching him off-guard when she asked in icy tones, "Is that basically your attitude? Big joke?"

He shrugged in innocence and decided to leave it alone. She was bristly. Let her eat her pastry and drink her mint tea, he instructed himself. Put her in a cab and send her home. He wanted time to himself, time to take a good look at the yellow chair Alma had bequeathed to him when she moved to the coast. Its unfolding capacity never failed to amaze him. It would make a better bed than the Disney pen he'd spied in a children's store that morning. He was feeling good again.

He leaned forward and Aisha slid a forkful of crumbly pastry into his mouth. She was looking good to him once more. He grinned. She jerked her chin as if to ask what was he about to say. He wasn't about to say anything. But he was thinking that no, they hadn't met at the wrong time. It'd been the right time for him. The wrong time for them maybe. But what the hell.

"What did you want to be when you grew up?" she asked. He leaned in for another forkful of pastry. "Just don't be like your daddy" rang in his ears. "A tender man," he said and watched her lashes flutter lower.

The question he would put to himself when he got home and stretched out in that yellow chair was what had he promised his daughter in the spring of '61. He smiled at Aisha and leaned up out of his chair to kiss her on the forehead. She blushed. He was sure he could come true for the Cliff he'd been.

Madame Bai and the Taking of Stone Mountain

1

Headachy from the double feature, she tells Tram and Mustafa that she'll take a rain check on dinner. The rest of the household, after all, expect her back by ten o'clock for an English conversation lesson.

"A coffee?" Mustafa suggests. He answers himself with a groan. The only decent cup of coffee to be had in Atlanta is at the house. "Home, then," he shrugs and saunters across the street for a paper.

She views it all as a bit of footage. That is what seeing her neighborhood, the city constantly on the news has done to her perception. Figures moving out of the Rialto into the wind. Man and woman wait on curb. Third figure crossing street. Mustafa's coat, elegantly draped around his shoulders, falls in soft, straight folds, his sleeves swinging like regal robes. From the back he could be her father. All he needs, she's thinking, is a horn case and his beret set a bit more ace deuce.

"Rain check?" Tram gazes at the wintry sky perplexed, wrinkles scarring his broad-boned cheeks. She mumbles an explanation of the figure of speech, standing at the curb hipshot as her mother would. But she does not tap her foot. She can't chance it with the wind beating at her back and her still wobbly from that particular loss. It's a new way to be in the world, she's discovering—unmothered.

"Rain check." Tram nods, dipping his chin down to his arms crossed against his chest, and shoves up his quilted sleeves. He stands against the wind an untippable figure, a pyramid. She shifts her weight to match his stance.

Two young bloods, in defiance of the curfew, shoot out of Luckie Street and race between cars bouncing over the parking lot braker. She takes this in as though through a viewer, widening the lens to incorporate a blind man tapping along the pavement toward them. There is, she decides as Mustafa rejoins them, too lively a curiosity behind the dark glasses. She watches warily as the blind man stops behind the boys inspecting the *kung fu* posters outside the Rialto, his chin stuck out as if to sniff the wind, as if to catch the aromas from the restaurant farther on, as if to smell out his prey. To her list of suspects—Klan, cops, fiend in clerical cloth, little old ladies with poisoned cookies, monsters in Boy Scout gear, young kids in distress used to lure older ones to their death—she now adds blind people.

Mustafa reads the headlines. She does not correct his pronunciation. She's watching the blind man who has hooked his cane in the crook of his arm and is following the boys down Forsyth.

"Oh God," she mutters, bracing herself against her companions and ready to call out a warning. But the boys scoot down a side street toward Central City Park and the blind man continues straight ahead toward Marietta Street. She exhales.

"Yes?" Mustafa is studying her, his eyebrows arched so hard in query, his narrow forehead all but disappears under his beret.

"What?" Tram, hunched and shivery, growls.

She flops her hands around by way of explanation. Her companions exchange a look. Their landlady/friend/English instructor bears watching, the look says. Tram lifts an elbow for her to catch on. Mustafa tucks the paper away and sweeps his coat open. But he doesn't pull his sweater cuffs down. She hesitates. His wrists are deformed. They move up Forsyth, heads ducked, bodies huddled. She's grateful, wedged between the two, for the warmth and support. And grateful too that Mustafa has not offered his latest theory on the missing and murdered children of Atlanta. He doesn't usually talk freely in the streets, reserving his passionate tirades against global fascism for the late-night talk fests in the kitchens, having learned a hard lesson.

They hung him from the barracks ceiling by the wrists. The Israelis whose parents had had them baptized in '36 then sent to the convent school in Mustafa's district to save them from the Nazis. The same convent school Coptic Christians of the district sent their children to save them from the backwardness of Jordanian society. The same district whose faithful evicted the French nuns to save Islam from the infidels. Mustafa, a brash young student, had been relating the take-over of the old convent school by the Israelis, who'd converted it into an army barracks "to save the city from terrorists." Too much irony in too loud a recitation, Mustafa was hustled in for interrogation.

"Whatcha got up your sleeve, Chinaman?"
selfsame line delivered in badly dubbed stereophonic sound, followed by a whistling knife spun from a tobacco-brown silk sleeve that pinned the speaker's shoulder blade to a beam in the rice shop. Courtesy of Hong Kong Eternal Flame Films, Limited.

"I'm talking to you."

Four white punks in gray, hooded sweatsuits have slipped up alongside and cut them off. They carry what looks like a three-foot grappling hook, something you'd drag the river with. She freezes.

"Whatsa matter?" the leader leers, jiggling the pole. "No speaky de English?" The Confederate flag snaps down at the sharpened end.

Mustafa slides his arm away and quickly rolls his paper into a bat. She fingers the pick comb in one pocket, her key ring in the other. Tram is in a crouch, staring hard at the belt buckle insignia of the big-bellied punk. In the East it would be the reassuring Shorinji *kempo* figure, but in the West the interlocking *z*'s have been corrupted into the swastika. They're jabbing the pole straight at Tram's midsection, the flag snapping like a whip, like teeth.

"Chinky Chinaman no speaky de English." The leader nudges Big Belly with his hobnailed wristband, grinning to his cohorts. "Speak gook then," he prods Tram, no grin.

She does not see the lunge or the spin, only Tram's fists, pulled out of sleeves, striking as he lands. Two of the punks slam hard against the donut shop window. The others stumble between the two newspaper boxes near the curb. Mustafa gets off a few good whacks before his weapon buckles. The clang of the pole against cement propels her. She's leaning hard on the skinniest punk flung against the donut shop window, her pick in his gut, her keys grating across the bridge of his nose. Brothers in the shop have left the counter to rush to the window.

"The cruel and lively Thai boxer legs," Mustafa is announcing to the crowd at the glass, bouncing Big Belly off the *Wall Street Journal* box. She hears glass shatter and half expects to see the donut shop window break away in slow motion, falling. She brings her knee up into the groin as she rams both elbows down hard between collarbones.

Tram's final kick-spin ends with one foot catching the leader on the side of the head, the other foot shoving Big Belly into the street. She and Mustafa rush the two who are scrambling backward over a spatter of glass into the gutter. Brakes screech, tires squeal as the hooded ones race across toward a construction site where the Loews Grand used to be. They leap hurdles of haystacks and sandbags and disappear.

"Well, all right." A brother in seaman's cap and sweater, his body moving in sportscaster replay, retrieves Mustafa's coat and slaps it on. "Welcome to Margaret Mitchell Square," he laughs and hands her her keys.

"That was some set-to," an elderly gent with jelly on his front tooth says, hand raised high to give five but not sure who to give it to. She extends her hand. The brothers size her up—twentyish, redbone, whatcha doin' with these foreign jokers, whatcha story? She knows that look. The gent gives a stingy five as though she, skin-privileged, doesn't need it. And then the two rush back into the warmth of the shop, leaving her with a bad feeling.

Mustafa is brushing off his coat and adjusting the beret. Tram is standing back hard on his heels, the wind plastering his sweater against his chest so that eight separate segments of abdominal muscles lift like bas-relief. He looks like sculpture, she's thinking, the raised scar on his rib cage a length of packing twine, his quilted jacket a packing mat—statuary ready for shipping.

"Let's go home," Tram says squinting when his examination of the construction site shadows fails to produce a sneak attack of rock and rubble.

Once again they hook arms and, huddled, move to the bus stop, saluted by raised coffee mugs and soup spoons.

She hopes the bus will be overheated. Though her companions shelter her from the wind, she is chilled through, brittle, on the brink of cracking. They talk in French, Mustafa recounting each blow in the battle, being droll, inviting her to join in, Tram complaining that breaking bones is not why he studies the arts, not why he's come to Atlanta to await the arrival of the celebrated Madame Bai.

"With these two fingers," he explains, shoving two blunt-nailed fingers near her nose, "I can go home and help heal the wounds of war."

"The first to create the phrase 'What is up the sleeve, Chinaman?' did not meet this *kung fu* fighter," Mustafa chuckles. She ghosts a smile, clamping her jaws tight.

"I'm Vietnamese," Tram says flatly, ignoring the compliment and wagging his two fingers against Mustafa's lapels. "They go in so quick to snatch out disease, no scar tissue forms," he says, snipping off a button.

"Fine hands," Mustafa says, eyebrows arched.

Tram drops the button in Mustafa's palm and shoves his arms up his sleeves once more. "Not Chinese," he adds with a warning grunt. She closes her eyes for a moment, hoping Mustafa will not offer the usual taunts that provoke Tram into a diatribe against Bruce Lee and all things Chinese and launch the rest of the household into endless debate over whether Mao makes it a Gang of Five. Tram leans over to peer for the bus. Mustafa attempts to fit a cigarette into an ivory holder. His hands are shaking, she notices, ruining what might have been an elegant portrait: Jordanian poet, ivory tusk smoldering, coat collar blown against chin. Tobacco shreds down his coat. She looks away and thinks of the figures in Madame Tussaud's, of her mother waxy and spent.

"There will be news on the television," Mustafa says, tossing the broken butt away. "Another child found murdered."

Tram catches her from behind under the armpits before she knows she is falling. Mustafa leads her to the curb waving an oversized hanky. She dumps lunch into the gutter.

2

Madame Bai arrives on a dismal day the week of inauguration. There are two *kung fu* movies playing at the Rialto. There are always two *kung fu* movies playing at the Rialto. The bill is not in honor of the warrior-healer woman revered in *shaolins* and *ashrams* around the globe, honored by masters of the arts, quoted in the reliable texts. The Tai Chi Association silk-screens a batch of T-shirts. But the *yin-yang* figure is not bordered by the trigrams that signal the flag of Korea. Madame's presence in the city is not the occasion for the artwork. Not a line of copy is devoted to Madame's arrival in Atlanta, magnet city for every amateur sleuth, bounty hunter, right-wing provocateur, left-wing adventurer, do-gooder, soothsayer, porno-film maker, scoop journalist, crack shot, crackpot, or cool-out leader not born from the fires of struggle.

The Reagans moving in, Carter moving out, and the hostages coming home from Iran hog the news. The best of medical and psychological help is mobilized for the hostages. Less than little is available for Vietnam vets suffering from shell shock, stress, and Agent Orange genetic tampering. Gifts of things, of cash, of promising jobs await the returnees. But a minister on TV tells people not to send a dime to the parents of Atlanta: "They were getting along without our help before their children got killed. They can get along without our help now." Speeches are made about the hostages, about Carter, about the new President Reagan. Phrases like "not racially motivated" and "no connection between the children's murders and violence in other places" are fed to Atlantans. "The parents are not above suspicion," the FBI poison pen leaks. And as solidarity groups move to mount a movement, "The parents did it," say the authorities.

Yellow ribbons flap from flagpoles, trees, door knockers, wrists in the northeast section of the city. In the southwest green ribbons and black armbands are worn solemnly. The red, white, and blue is waved in *The Thunderbolt* and *Soldier of Fortune*, as articles urge good patriots to beat back the colored hordes rising to take over God's country.

Tram runs a vacuum over the dining room floor, lifting the skirt of the tablecloth pointedly to rout the household from its round-table discussion over the latest National States Rights Party rag. It features faces of African Americans superimposed on apes' bodies. Mustafa, wearing an elaborate headdress of pillowcases and carrying a hammer, goes to tack a sign of welcome on the door for Madame Bai. Panos, at the top of his lungs, sings anti-junta songs and restrings his *oud*. Jean-Paul at the ironing board composes aloud angry op-eds on the refugee situation. Maaza, the Ethiopian film maker, and Madas, the Chilean novelist, fold sheets and discuss a collaborative project built around the visiting Madame with English narration to be supplied by their landlady/English instructor/friend.

She's in the kitchen inching out saffron into the rice and grumbling. The couple from Bahia are mincing peppers and listening.

"Democratic action can be taken too far," she complains. A collective vote was made to postpone lessons—and with it, her salary—until Madame is settled in her studio school. Tram yells over complaints, singing, and hammering to review once more the self-defense system Madame Bai had designed especially for women, a sleight-of-hand technique in which one masters critically quick placement on critical organs while maintaining an ingratiating mien and nonaggressive stance. So quick a placement, it bypasses the notice of the aggressor. So deft a placement, the violent mind is discouraged.

"In days to follow," Mustafa on cue calls from the doorway, "the rogue is coughing blood and urinating red."

"But he continues to think he's tough and won," croons Panos.

"Yeh, yeh," says Maaza, bored.

"All one needs," she mumbles to the Bahians, "is seven years of anatomy and fifteen degrees in one or more arts."

They assemble in the living room to wait like schoolchildren, the house aromatic with rosemary, curry, *ouzo*, and stinking with *nuoc nam* that couldn't be voted down. She is prepared for a light-filled eminence to grace them like song, for an amazon to perform strike-rock-fist on the door, for Madame to pole-vault like dragon fire through the window, or to materialize *ninja*-style in the shadows of the fireplace. Madame Bai arrives like an ordinary person, steps in behind Tram on soft cloth shoes. Bows, sits, eats, fusses with her hair, pinning her grayed topknot with two golden carved fibulae from her grandmother's chest as she explains. With Tram as translator, Madame jokes, converses, and proves herself to be the sagelike wonder he'd promised all along. And by 9 P.M. Madame has stolen away all of her students. A collective decision is made to redistribute the usual thirty dollars a week for room, board, and English lessons into fifteen dollars for her and fifteen dollars for Madame.

"There's such a thing as taking democratic action too far," she complains for months at Madame's studio. They begin with a roster of thirty—adepts from the Oracle of Maat, instructor from the *tai chi* group near Lonox Plaza, two medicine men and a clan mother from Seminole County in Florida, herbalists from Logos, *shiatsu* therapists and rolfers from the massage school, Fruit of the Nation from the Bankhead mosque, two ex-bodyguards from Mayor Jackson's elite corps, and her erstwhile students of English grammar and conversation. By Easter she is experiencing a body-mind-spirit connection she'd imagined possible only for disciples in the nether mountain ranges of Nepal. Attendance drops off steadily as the weather turns warm, her boarder/students returning to the fold and restoring the good health of her budget. Most of her nights are spent plowing through *Gray's Anatomy* and sticking pins in the red dots of her pressure point chart. Her days are spent working with defense teams, bat squads, and root watchers. She's made a marshal of the citizen search team for her calm and logical way in the woods.

By late May, when the media converges on Wayne Williams' drive across the Chattahoochee Bridge, complaints are rife at the studio. No mats, no *ka-li* charts to study. No striking bags or apparatus for stretching the legs. No *shurikens*, iron fans, *nunchaku* sticks for practice. Not even an emblem to patch on a sweater, transfer to a shirt, solder on a key ring. Wholesale defection begins in June when headlines around the country announce the fiend has been nabbed. One man charged with two counts of murder, the case hanging literally by a thread, a bit of carpet fiber that changes color as the days advance but no journalist seems to notice. One man, two counts, leaving twenty-six "official" deaths still on the books and an additional thirty-eight or more not being discussed. Eight hundred police are withdrawn from the neighborhoods. One hundred state patrolmen returned to the highways. Roadblocks vanish. Helicopters disappear. Neighborhood security groups disperse. Search teams disband. Safety posters come down. Bumper stickers tatter. Amnesia drifts into the city like fog. "Let the Community Heal Itself," say the sermons. She grunts and continues training. The Medfly in California, a tsetse epidemic in Atlanta, she masters butterfly metamorphosis and requires only five hours of sleep at night.

Madame smiles and wishes the departing students well on their journey. Madame smiles and intensifies training for those that remain. At the studio, at the house, throughout the neighborhood, she is learning to be still as her mother used to counsel, to silence the relentless chatter inside in favor of the small-voiced guide she is experiencing as a warm hand steering at the base of her spine. The cadres of the neighborhood call her the Alarm Clock. She keeps the block security tight and keeps watch over the children.

3

They are sitting in a sauna with a name she cannot even pronounce. Nerves frayed, mind seared, muscles screaming for release, she sits beyond endurance till she is the sauna, focused. Madame dismounts from the only cushion in the room and glides to the center of the circle and sits. She looks at Madame's back and traces the carver's journey along the golden fibulae to the points. She senses a summoning, as though her mother had set a space heater down before her, then dragged it slowly away by its cord for her to follow. Madame sending out her power, she concludes, rising to walk round into the light. She sits back on her heels before Madame, palms on her thighs, poised, ready. Madame's face turns from skin to old parchment, an ancient text she's being invited to read.

"One question, daughter." Madame says it in English after a long while. She waits, as if all her life this question has been forming. Not a favor to tax her friendship, nor a task to test commitment, but a question coming together, taking shape, her shape. Daughter. It drives deep within to jimmy open a door long closed, padlocked, boarded over. She leans against the boards, feels the grain of the wood as it swings wide to a brilliant and breezy place she's not visited since the days when she was held dear and cherished simply because she was she and not a pot to mend or dress to hem or chair leg to join.

She smiles at Madame by way of signaling, Let the test begin. Then panic gathers behind the door to shove it to. She gathers the weight of her years into a doorstop. Test. She's heard of disciples who roam the earth unkempt and crazed by a *koan* a master has posed for solution: Where does the dark go when the light is switched on? Why does the arrow never reach the mark despite the illusion of the bowman? The door pushes against her back. She heaves against it, listing. The warm hand at the power base rights her. The door swings wide again.

"Stone Mountain," Madame says finally.

Stone Mountain. A rock to prop a door with. A rock dropped into the pool of the mind. For a moment, she's in a muddle. Rocks rear up out of the ocean. She scrambles across the rock ledge braille-reading the fossils embedded deep within. Stone Mountain. It tumbles down into the waters. She surfaces, crawling across the wet rubble in a quarry. Stone. From ledge to peak to cliff she follows the goat trail, shreds of fleece caught on briars and shrubs. She gathers it all within the pouch of her shirt. Mountain. Could it be a Red Army libretto in the repertoire of the Peking Opera? Someone near beats out a tattoo on a knuckle drum. Her mother used to pummel her, knuckles against both temples, when she was too impatient to be still and receptive.

She exhales and lets it flow to her. Stone Mountain. Of course. A mere thirty-minute ride out by U.S. 78. Stone monster carved tribute to the confederacy Mountain. Tourist-trap entrapment of visiting schoolchildren lured under the spell of the enslavers of Africans, killers of Amerinds. Lewdly exposed mammoth granite rock of ages the good ole boys hide in from history. Eight hundred and sixty-five feet high, the guide books say. Five hundred and eighty-three acres. The sacred grove of grand dragons, wizards, greater and lesser demons who crank out crank notes in the name of Robert E. Lee, Jefferson Davis, and Stonewall Jackson riding across the monument on horseback. She smirks.

Madame lifts her brows. Everything above Madame's eyes slides up and back, taking her hair line out of view as though someone is standing behind, tugging at mask and wig, about to reveal the woman as a person she has known always, who has been there all along, just beyond peripheral vision, guiding her through the various rites of passage.

"What is it for, Stone Mountain?" Madame asks with her face in place.

For? To rally the raunchy, Madame, to celebrate the. She clutches the ropes as the scaffolding swings against the side of the mountain scraping her knuckles. For this you summon me? You could have called the Chamber of Commerce, asked any schoolboy at the Peachtree Academy, checked the nearest public li. Balanced, she leans against the cool, damp rock and traces the sculptor's line across hind parts, boot stirrups, folds in the uniforms. For? Any almanac, encyclopedia, atlas could have told you what. Wind and rain have eroded the line of the nose here, a ripple of hair there. An ice pocket just below Stonewall's hand, holding the reins loosely, proves just deep enough to drive the chisel point in. Eighth Wonder of the World, some say, Madame, and. The hammering enlarges a hairline fissure running from the brim of one hat to the forelegs of the first horse. Five sticks of dynamite shoved in just so can bring the whole thing tumbling down. They say, Madame, that staunch materialists who favor symbols over reality can be thoroughly demoralized if. A people's army should focus on.

"Teacher." The word blows through her chest cavity, a breeze amplified in that resonating chamber. The words to be spoken already reverberating around the room, releasing the circle from the sauna. She hears the slap of flesh against wood, a signal, an army awaiting direction.

"Stone Mountain is for taking, Madame."

Alice Walker

The Welcome Table

for sister Clara Ward

I'm going to sit at the Welcome table
Shout my troubles over
Walk and talk with Jesus
Tell God how you treat me
One of these days!
                    —Spiritual

The old woman stood with eyes uplifted in her Sunday-go-to-meeting clothes: high shoes polished about the tops and toes, a long rusty dress adorned with an old corsage, long withered, and the remnants of an elegant silk scarf as headrag stained with grease from the many oily pigtails underneath. Perhaps she had know suffering. There was a dazed and sleepy look in her aged blue-brown eyes. But for those who searched hastily for "reasons" in that old tight face, shut now like an ancient door, there was nothing to be read. and so they gazed nakedly upon their own fear transferred; a fear of the black and the old, a terror of the unknown as well as of the deeply known. Some of those who saw her there on the church steps spoke words about her that were hardly fit to be heard, others held their pious peace; and some felt vague stirrings of pity, small and persistent and hazy, as if she were an old collie turned out to die.

She was angular and lean and the color of poor gray Georgia earth, beaten by king cotton and the extreme weather. Her elbows were wrinkled and thick, the skin ashen but durable, like the bark of old pines. On her face centuries were folded into the circles around one eye, while around the other, etched and mapped as if for print, ages more threatened again to live. Some of them there at the church saw the age, the dotage, the missing buttons down the front of her mildewed black dress. Others saw cooks, chauffeurs, maids, mistresses, children denied or smothered in the deferential way she held her cheek to the side, toward the ground. Many of them saw jungle orgies in an evil place, while others were reminded of riotous anarchists looting and raping in the streets. Those who knew the hesitant creeping up on them of the law, saw the beginning of the end of the sanctuary of Christian worship, saw the desecration of Holy Church, and saw an invasion of privacy, which they struggled to believe they still kept.

Still she had come down the road toward the big white church alone. Just herself, an old forgetful woman, nearly blind with age. Just her and her eyes raised dully to the glittering cross that crowned the sheer silver steeple. She had walked along the road in a stagger from her house a half mile away: Perspiration, cold and clammy, stood on her brow and along the creases by her thin wasted nose. She stopped to calm herself on the wide front steps, not looking about her as they might have expected her to do, but simply standing quite still, except for a slight quivering of her throat and tremors that shook her cotton-stockinged legs.

The reverend of the church stopped her pleasantly as she stepped into the vestibule. Did he say, as they thought he did, kindly, "Auntie, you know this is not your church?" As if one could choose the wrong one. But no one remembers, for they never spoke of it afterward, and she brushed past him anyway, as if she had been brushing past him all her life, except this time she was in a hurry. Inside the church she sat on the very first bench from the back, gazing with concentration at the stained-glass window over her head. It was cold, even inside the church, and she was shivering. Everybody could see. They stared at her as they came in and sat down near the front. It was cold, very cold to them, too; outside the church it was below freezing and not much above inside. But the sight of her, sitting there somehow passionately ignoring them, brought them up short, burning.

The young usher, never having turned anyone out of his church before, but not even considering this job as *that* (after all, she had no right to be there, certainly), went up to her and whispered that she should leave. Did he call her "Grandma," as later he seemed to recall he had? But for those who actually hear such traditional pleasantries and to whom they actually mean something, "Grandma" was not one, for she did not pay him any attention, just muttered, "Go 'way," in a weak sharp *bothered* voice, waving his frozen blond hair and eyes from near her face.

It was the ladies who finally did what to them had to be done. Daring their burly indecisive husbands to throw the old colored woman out they made their point. God, mother, country, earth, church. It involved all that, and well they knew it. Leather bagged and shoed, with good calfskin gloves to keep out the cold, they looked with contempt at the bloodless gray arthritic hands of the old woman, clenched loosely, restlessly in her lap. Could their husbands expect them to sit up in church with *that?* No, no, the husbands were quick to answer and even quicker to do their duty.

Under the old woman's arms they placed their hard fists (which afterward smelled of decay and musk—the fermenting scent of onionskins and rotting greens). Under the old woman's arms they raised their fists, flexed their muscular shoulders, and out she flew through the door, back under the cold blue sky. This done, the wives folded their healthy arms across their trim middles and felt at once justified and scornful. But none of them said so, for none of them ever spoke of the incident again. Inside the church it was warmer. They sang, they prayed. The protection and promise of God's impartial love grew more not less desirable as the sermon gathered fury and lashed itself out above their penitent heads.

The old woman stood at the top of the steps looking about in bewilderment. She had been singing in her head. They had interrupted her. Promptly she began to sing again, though this time a sad song. Suddenly, however, she looked down the long gray highway and saw something interesting and delightful coming. She started to grin, toothlessly, with short giggles of joy, jumping about and slapping her hands on her knees. And soon it became apparent why she was so happy. For coming down the highway at a firm though leisurely pace was Jesus. He was wearing an immaculate white, long dress trimmed in gold around the neck and hem, and a red, a bright red, cape. Over his left arm he carried a brilliant blue blanket. He was wearing sandals and a beard and he had long brown hair parted on the right side. His eyes, brown, had wrinkles around them as if he smiled or looked at the sun a lot. She would have known him, recognized him, anywhere. There was a sad but joyful look to his face, like a candle was glowing behind it, and he walked with sure even steps in her direction, as if he were walking on the sea. Except that he was not carrying in his arms a baby sheep, he looked exactly like the picture of him that she had hanging over her bed at home. She had taken it out of a white lady's Bible while she was working for her. She had looked at that picture for more years than she could remember, but never once had she really expected to see him. She squinted her eyes to be sure he wasn't carrying a little sheep in one arm, but he was not. Ecstatically she began to wave her arms for fear he would miss seeing her, for he walked looking straight ahead on the shoulder of the highway, and from time to time looking upward at the sky.

All he said when he got up close to her was "Follow me," and she bounded down to his side with all the bob and speed of one so old. For every one of his long determined steps she made two quick ones. They walked along in deep silence for a long time. Finally she started telling him about how many years she had cooked for them, cleaned for them, nursed them. He looked at her kindly but in silence. She told him indignantly about how they had grabbed her when she was singing in her head and not looking, and how they had tossed her out of his church. A old heifer like me, she said, straightening up next to Jesus, breathing hard. But he smiled down at her and she felt better instantly and time just seemed to fly by. When they passed her house, forlorn and sagging, weatherbeaten and patched, by the side of the road, she did not even notice it, she was so happy to be out walking along the highway with Jesus.

She broke the silence once more to tell Jesus how glad she was that he had come, how she had often looked at his picture hanging on her wall (she hoped he didn't know she had stolen it) over her bed, and how she had never expected to see him down here in person. Jesus gave her one of his beautiful smiles and they walked on. She did not know where they were going; someplace wonderful, she suspected. The ground was like clouds under their feet, and she felt she could walk forever without becoming the least bit tired. She even began to sing out loud some of the old spirituals she loved, but she didn't want to annoy Jesus, who looked so thoughtful, so she quieted down. They walked on, looking straight over the treetops into the sky, and the smiles that played over her dry wind-cracked face were like first clean ripples across a stagnant pond. On they walked without stopping.

The people in church never knew what happened to the old woman; they never mentioned her to one another or to anybody else. Most of them heard sometime later that an old colored woman fell dead along the highway. Silly as it seemed, it appeared she had walked herself to death. Many of the black families along the road said they had seen the old lady high-stepping down the highway; sometimes jabbering in a low insistent voice, sometimes singing, sometimes merely gesturing excitedly with her hands. Other times silent and smiling, looking at the sky. She had been alone, they said. Some of them wondered aloud where the old woman had been going so stoutly that it had worn her heart out. They guessed maybe she had relatives across the river, some miles away, but none of them really knew.

A Sudden Trip
Home in the Spring

For the Wellesley Class

1

Sarah walked slowly off the tennis court, fingering the back of her head, feeling the sturdy dark hair that grew there. She was popular. As she walked along the path toward Talfinger Hall her friends fell into place around her. They formed a warm jostling group of six. Sarah, because she was taller than the rest, saw the messenger first.

"Miss Davis," he said, standing still until the group came abreast of him, "I've got a telegram for ye." Brian was Irish and always quite respectful. He stood with his cap in his hand until Sarah took the telegram. Then he gave a nod that included all the young ladies before he turned away. He was young and good-looking, though annoyingly servile, and Sarah's friends twittered.

"Well, open it!" someone cried, for Sarah stood staring at the yellow envelope, turning it over and over in her hand.

"Look at her," said one of the girls, "isn't she beautiful! Such eyes, and hair, and *skin!*"

Sarah's tall, caplike hair framed a face of soft brown angles, high cheekbones and large dark eyes. Her eyes enchanted her friends because they always seemed to know more, and to find more of life amusing, or sad, than Sarah cared to tell.

Her friends often teased Sarah about her beauty; they loved dragging her out of her room so that their boyfriends, naive and worldly young men from Princeton and Yale, could see her. They never guessed she found this distasteful. She was gentle with her friends, and her outrage at their tactlessness did not show. She was most often inclined to pity them, though embarrassment sometimes drove her to fraudulent expressions. Now she smiled and raised eyes and arms to heaven. She acknowledged their unearned curiosity as a mother endures the prying impatience of a child. Her friends beamed love and envy upon her as she tore open the telegram.

"He's dead," she said.

Her friends reached out for the telegram, their eyes on Sarah.

"It's her father," one of them said softly. "He died yesterday. Oh, Sarah," the girl whimpered, "I'm so sorry!"

"Me too." "So am I." "Is there anything we can do?"

But Sarah had walked away, head high and neck stiff.

"So graceful!" one of her friends said.

"Like a proud gazelle" said another. Then they all trooped to their dormitories to change for supper.

Talfinger Hall was a pleasant dorm. The common room just off the entrance had been made into a small modern art gallery with some very good original paintings, lithographs and collages. Pieces were constantly being stolen. Some of the girls could not resist an honest-to-God Chagall, signed (in the plate) by his own hand, though they could have afforded to purchase one from the gallery in town. Sarah Davis's room was next door to the gallery, but her walls were covered with inexpensive Gaugin reproductions, a Rubens ("The Head of a Negro"), a Modigliani and a Picasso. There was a full wall of her own drawings, all of black women. She found black men impossible to draw or to paint; she could not bear to trace defeat onto blank pages. Her women figures were matronly, massive of arm, with a weary victory showing in their eyes. Surrounded by Sarah's drawings was a red SNCC poster of a man holding a small girl whose face nestled in his shoulder. Sarah often felt she was the little girl whose face no one could see.

To leave Talfinger even for a few days filled Sarah with fear. Talfinger was her home now; it suited her better than any home she'd ever known. Perhaps she loved it because in winter there was a fragrant fireplace and snow outside her window. When hadn't she dreamed of fireplaces that really warmed, snow that almost pleasantly froze? Georgia seemed far away as she packed; she did not want to leave New York, where, her grandfather had liked to say, "the devil hung out and caught young gals by the front of their dresses." He had always believed the South the best place to live on earth (never mind that certain people invariably marred the landscape), and swore he expected to die no more than a few miles from where he had been born. There was tenacity even in the gray frame house he lived in, and in scrawny animals on his farm who regularly reproduced. He was the first person Sarah wanted to see when she got home.

There was a knock on the door of the adjoining bathroom, and Sarah's suite mate entered, a loud Bach concerto just finishing behind her. At first she stuck just her head into the room, but seeing Sarah fully dressed she trudged in and plopped down on the bed. She was a heavy blonde girl with large milk-white legs. Her eyes were small and her neck usually gray with grime.

"My, don't you look gorgeous," she said.

"Ah, Pam," said Sarah, waving her hand in disgust. In Georgia she knew that even to Pam she would be just another ordinarily attractive *colored* girl. In Georgia there were a million girls better looking. Pam wouldn't know that, of course; she'd never been to Georgia; she'd never even seen a black person to speak to, that is, before she met Sarah. One of her first poetic observations about Sarah was that she was "a poppy in a field of winter roses." She had found it weird that Sarah did not own more than one coat.

"Say listen, Sarah," said Pam, "I heard about your father. I'm sorry. I really am."

"Thanks," said Sarah.

"Is there anything we can do? I thought, well, maybe you'd want my father to get somebody to fly you down. He'd go himself but he's taking Mother to Madeira this week. You wouldn't have to worry about trains and things."

Pamela's father was one of the richest men in the world, though no one ever mentioned it. Pam only alluded to it at times of crisis, when a friend might benefit from the use of a private plane, train, or ship; or, if someone wanted to study the characteristics of a totally secluded village, island or mountain, she might offer one of theirs. Sarah could not comprehend such wealth, and was always annoyed because Pam didn't look more like a billionaire's daughter. A billionaire's daughter, Sarah thought, should really be less horsey and brush her teeth more often.

"Gonna tell me what you're brooding about?" asked Pam.

Sarah stood in front of the radiator, her fingers resting on the window seat. Down below girls were coming up the hill from supper.

"I'm thinking," she said, "of the child's duty to his parents after they are dead."

"Is that all?"

"Do you know," asked Sarah, "about Richard Wright and his father?"

Pamela frowned. Sarah looked down at her.

"Oh, I forgot," she said with a sigh, "they don't teach Wright here. The poshest school in the U.S., and the girls come out ignorant." She looked at her watch, saw she had twenty minutes before her train. "Really," she said almost inaudibly, "why Tears Eliot, Ezratic Pound, and even Sara Teacake, and no Wright?" She and Pamela thought e.e. cummings very clever with his perceptive spelling of great literary names.

"Is he a poet then?" asked Pam. She adored poetry, all poetry. Half of America's poetry she had, of course, not read, for the simple reason that she had never heard of it.

"No," said Sarah, "he wasn't a poet." She felt weary. "He was a man who wrote, a man who had trouble with his father." She began to walk about the room, and came to stand below the picture of the old man and the little girl.

"When he was a child," she continued, "his father ran off with another woman, and one day when Richard and his mother went to ask him for money to buy food he laughingly rejected them. Richard, being very young, thought his father Godlike. Big, omnipotent, unpredictable, undependable and cruel. Entirely in control of his universe. Just like a god. But, many years later, after Wright had become a famous writer, he went down to Mississippi to visit his father. He found instead of God, just an old watery-eyed field hand, bent from plowing, his teeth gone, smelling of manure. Richard realized that the most daring thing his 'God' had done was run off with that other woman."

"So?" asked Pam. "What 'duty' did he feel he owed the old man?"

"So," said Sarah, "that's what Wright wondered as he peered into that old shifty-eyed Mississippi Negro face. What was the duty of the son of a destroyed man? The son of a man whose vision had stopped at the edge of fields that weren't even his. Who was Wright without his father? Was he Wright the great writer? Wright the Communist? Wright the French farmer? Wright whose white wife could never accompany him to Mississippi? Was he, in fact, still his father's son? Or was he freed by his father's desertion to be nobody's son, to be his own father? Could he disavow his father and live? And if so, live as what? As whom? And for what purpose?"

"Well," said Pam, swinging her hair over her shoulders and squinting her small eyes, "if his father rejected him I don't see why Wright even bothered to go see him again. From what you've said, Wright earned the freedom to be whoever he wanted to be. To a strong man a father is not essential."

"Maybe not," said Sarah, "but Wright's father was one faulty door in a house of many ancient rooms. Was that one faulty door to shut him off forever from the rest of the house? That was the question. And though he answered this question eloquently in his work, where it really counted, one can only wonder if he was able to answer it satisfactorily—or at all—in his life."

"You're thinking of his father more as a symbol of something, aren't you?" asked Pam.

"I suppose," said Sarah, taking a last look around her room. "I see him as a door that refused to open, a hand that was always closed. A fist."

Pamela walked with her to one of the college limousines, and in a few minutes she was at the station. The train to the city was just arriving.

"Have a nice trip," said the middle-aged driver courteously, as she took her suitcase from him. But for about the thousandth time since she'd seen him, he winked at her.

Once away from her friends she did not miss them. The school was all they had in common. How could they ever know her if they were not allowed to know Wright, she wondered. She was interesting, "beautiful," only because they had no idea what made her, charming only because they had no idea from where she came. And where they came from, though she glimpsed it—in themselves and in F. Scott Fitzgerald—she was never to enter. She hadn't the inclination or the proper ticket.

2

Her father's body was in Sarah's old room. The bed had been taken down to make room for the flowers and chairs and casket. Sarah looked for a long time into the face, as if to find some answer to her questions written there. It was the same face, a dark Shakespearean head framed by gray, woolly hair and split almost in half by a short, gray mustache. It was a completely silent face, a shut face. But her father's face also looked fat, stuffed, and ready to burst. He wore a navy-blue suit, white shirt and black tie. Sarah bent and loosened the tie. Tears started behind her shoulder blades but did not reach her eyes.

"There's a rat here under the casket," she called to her brother, who apparently did not hear her, for he did not come in. She was alone with her father, as she had rarely been when he was alive. When he was alive she had avoided him.

"Where's that girl at?" her father would ask. "Done closed herself up in her room again," he would answer himself.

For Sarah's mother had died in her sleep one night. Just gone to bed tired and never got up. And Sarah had blamed her father.

Stare the rat down, though Sarah, surely that will help. *Perhaps it doesn't matter whether I misunderstood or never understood.*

"We moved so much looking for crops, a place to *live*," her father had moaned, accompanied by Sarah's stony silence. "The moving killed her. And now we have a real house, with *four* rooms, and a mailbox on the *porch*, and it's too late. She gone. *She* ain't here to see it." On very bad days her father would not eat at all. At night he did not sleep.

Whatever had made her think she knew what love was or was not?

Here she was, Sarah Davis, immersed in Camusian philosophy, versed in many languages, a poppy, of all things, among winter roses. But before she became a poppy she was a native Georgian sunflower, but still had not spoken the language they both knew. Not to him.

Stare the rat down, she thought, and did. The rascal dropped his bold eyes and slunk away. Sarah felt she had, at least, accomplished something.

Why did she have to see the picture of her mother, the one on the mantel among all the religious doodads, come to life? Her mother had stood stout against the years, clean gray braids shining across the top of her head, her eyes snapping, protective. Talking to her father.

"He called you out your name, we'll leave this place today. Not tomorrow. That be too late. Today!" Her mother was magnificent in her quick decisions.

"But what about your garden, the children, the change of schools?" Her father would be holding, most likely, the wide brim of his hat in nervously twisting fingers.

"He called you out your name, we go!"

And go they would. Who knew exactly where, before they moved? Another soundless place, walls falling down, roofing gone; another face to please without leaving too much of her father's pride at his feet. But to Sarah then, no matter with what alacrity her father moved, foot-dragging alone was visible.

The moving killed her, her father had said, *but the moving was also love.*

Did it matter now that often he had threatened their lives with the rage of his despair? That once he had spanked the crying baby violently, who later died of something else altogether . . . and that the next day they moved?

"No," said Sarah aloud, "I don't think it does."

"Huh?" It was her brother, tall, wiry, black, deceptively calm. As a child he'd had an irrepressible temper. As a grown man he was tensely smooth, like a river that any day will overflow its bed.

He had chosen a dull gray casket. Sarah wished for red. Was it Dylan Thomas who had said something grand about the dead offering "deep, dark defiance"? It didn't matter; there were more ways to offer defiance than with a red casket.

"I was just thinking," said Sarah, "that with us Mama and Daddy were saying NO with capital letters."

"I don't follow you," said her brother. He had always been the activist in the family. He simply directed his calm rage against any obstacle that might exist, and awaited the consequences with the same serenity he awaited his sister's answer. Not for him the philosophical confusions and poetic observations that hung his sister up.

"That's because you're a radical preacher," said Sarah, smiling up at him. "You deliver your messages in person with your own body." It excited her that her brother had at last imbued their childhood Sunday sermons with the reality of fighting for change. And saddened her that no matter how she looked at it this seemed more important than Medieval Art, Course 201.

3

"Yes, Grandma," Sarah replied. "Cresselton is for girls only, and *no*, Grandma, I am not pregnant."

Her grandmother stood clutching the broad wooden handle of her black bag, which she held, with elbows bent, in front of her stomach. Her eyes glinted through round wire-framed glasses. She spat into the grass outside the privy. She had insisted that Sarah accompany her to the toilet while the body was being taken into the church. She had leaned heavily on Sarah's arm, her own arm thin and the flesh like crepe.

"I guess they teach you how to really handle the world," she said. "And who knows, the Lord is everywhere. I would like a whole lot to see a Great-Grand. You don't specially have to be married, you know. That's why I felt free to ask." She reached into her bag and took out a Three Sixes bottle, which she proceeded to drink from, taking deep swift swallows with her head thrown back.

"There are very few black boys near Cresselton," Sarah explained, watching the corn liquor leave the bottle in spurts and bubbles. "Besides, I'm really caught up now in my painting and sculpting. . . ." Should she mention how much she admired Giacometti's work? No, she decided. Even if her grandmother had heard of him, and Sarah was positive she had not, she would surely think his statues much too thin. This made Sarah smile and remember how difficult it had been to convince her grandmother that even if Cresselton had not given her a scholarship she would have managed to go there anyway. Why? Because she wanted somebody to teach her to paint and to sculpt, and Cresselton had the best teachers. Her grandmother's notion of a successful granddaughter was a married one, pregnant the first year.

"Well," said her grandmother, placing the bottle with dignity back into her purse and gazing pleadingly into Sarah's face, "I sure would 'preshate a Great-Grand." Seeing her granddaughter's smile, she heaved a great sigh, and, walking rather haughtily over the stones and grass, made her way to the church steps.

As they walked down the aisle, Sarah's eyes rested on the back of her grandfather's head. He was sitting on the front middle bench in front of the casket, his hair extravagantly long and white and softly kinked. When she sat down beside him, her grandmother sitting next to him on the other side, he turned toward her and gently took her hand in his. Sarah briefly leaned her cheek against his shoulder and felt like a child again.

4

They had come twenty miles from town, on a dirt road, and the hot spring sun had drawn a steady rich scent from the honeysuckle vines along the way. The church was a bare, weather-beaten ghost of a building with hollow windows and a sagging door. Arsonists had once burned it to the ground, lighting the dry wood of the walls with the flames from the crosses they carried. The tall spreading red oak tree under which Sarah had played as a child still dominated the church-yard, stretching its branches widely from the roof of the church to the other side of the road.

After a short and eminently dignified service, during which Sarah and her grandfather alone did not cry, her father's casket was slid into the waiting hearse and taken the short distance to the cemetery, an overgrown wilderness whose stark white stones appeared to be the small ruins of an ancient civilization. There Sarah watched her grand-father from the corner of her eye. He did not seem to bend under the grief of burying a son. His back was straight, his eyes dry and clear. He was simply and solemnly heroic; a man who kept with pride his family's trust and his own grief. *It is strange,* Sarah thought, *that I never thought to paint him like this, simply as he stands; without anonymous meaningless people hovering beyond his profile; his face turned proud and brownly against the light.* The defeat that had frightened her in the faces of black men was the defeat of black forever defined by white. But that defeat was nowhere on her grandfather's face. He stood like a rock, outwardly calm, the comfort and support of the Davis family. The family alone defined him, and he was not about to let them down.

"One day I will paint you, Grandpa," she said, as they turned to go. "Just as you stand her now, with just"—she moved closer and touched his face with her hand—"just the right stubborn tenseness of your cheek. Just that look of Yes and No in your eyes."

"You wouldn't want to paint an old man like me," he said, looking deep into her eyes from wherever his mind had been. "If you want to make me, make me up in stone."

The completed grave was plump and red. The wreaths of flowers were arranged all on one side so that from the road there appeared to be only a large mass of flowers. But already the wind was tugging at the rose petals and the rain was making dabs of faded color all over the green foam frames. In a week the displaced honeysuckle vines, the wild roses, the grapevines, the grass, would be back. Nothing would seem to have changed.

5

"What do you mean, come *home?*" Her brother seemed genuinely amused. "We're all proud of you. How many black girls are at that school? Just *you?* Well, just one more besides you, and she's from the North. That's really something!"

"I'm glad you're pleased," said Sarah.

"Pleased! Why, it's what Mama would have wanted, a good education for little Sarah; and what Dad would have wanted too, if he could have wanted anything after Mama died. You were always smart. When you were two and I was five you showed me how to eat ice cream without getting it all over me. First, you said, nip off the bottom of the cone with your teeth, and suck the ice cream down. I never knew *how* you were supposed to eat the stuff once it began to melt."

"I don't know," she said, "sometimes you can want something a whole lot, only to find out later that it wasn't what you *needed* at all."

Sarah shook her head, a frown coming between her eyes. "I sometimes spend *weeks*," she said, "trying to sketch or paint a face that is unlike every other face around me, except, vaguely, for one. Can I help but wonder if I'm in the right place?"

Her brother smiled. "You mean to tell me you spend *weeks* trying to draw one face, and you still wonder whether you're in the right place? You must be kidding!" He chucked her under the chin and laughed out loud. "You learn how to draw the face," he said, "then you learn how to paint me and how to make Grandpa up in stone. Then you can come home or go live in Paris, France. It'll be the same thing."

It was the unpreacherlike gaiety of his affection that made her cry. She leaned peacefully into her brother's arms. She wondered if Richard Wright had had a brother.

"You are my door to all the rooms," she said. "Don't ever close."

And he said, "I won't," as if he understood what she meant.

6

"When will we see you again, young woman?" he asked later, as he drove her to the bus stop.

"I'll sneak up one day and surprise you," she said.

At the bus stop, in front of a tiny service station, Sarah hugged her brother with all her strength. The white station attendant stopped his work to leer at them, his eyes bold and careless.

"Did you ever think," said Sarah, "that we are a very old people in a very young place?"

She watched her brother from a window of the bus; her eyes did not leave his face until the little station was out of sight and the big Greyhound lurched on its way toward Atlanta. She would fly from there to New York.

7

She took the train to campus.

"My," said one of her friends, "you look wonderful! Home sure must agree with you!"

"Sarah was home?" Someone who didn't know asked. "Oh, *great,* how was it?"

"Well, how was it?" went an echo in Sarah's head. The noise of the echo almost made her dizzy.

"How was it?" she asked aloud, searching for, and regaining, her balance.

"How was it?" She watched her reflection in a pair of smiling hazel eyes.

"It was fine," she said slowly, returning the smile, thinking of her grandfather. "Just fine."

The girl's smile deepened. Sarah watched her swinging along toward the back tennis courts, hair blowing in the wind.

Stare the rat down, thought Sarah; *and whether it disappears or not, I am a woman in the world. I have buried my father, and shall soon know how to make my grandpa up in stone.*

Molly Best Tinsley

Mother Tongue

More than time had passed since summer, the evening my father
sat my mother down opposite him in the kitchenette and promised her
things would get better. In a restrained voice he read out loud his orders
for Sweden, a choice assignment to the Naval Attaché in the American
Embassy. He reminded her that he had dreamt of such a chance.
Stockholm was a beautiful city, he said. "Clean. Picturesque." He
watched for the effect of his words on my mother's downcast face. She
twirled a fingernail in the sweat on her glass of iced tea. There was no
sound except the window fan in the living room vainly sucking at the
muggy Norfolk heat. "We'd all be together," he said finally, knowing
that was no clincher. "For a year."

As though drifting in and out of sleep, she had registered objections. There was mention of me—"Cynthia's happy here. She's got her
feet on the ground in junior high." I supposed that was true. I had
heard her ask often enough, what did my father know about us children
anyway that she didn't have to tell him?

"Over there," he had countered, "she goes to a fancy private school
and the Embassy picks up the tab." And I supposed from his tone that
was something to be desired. My welfare was as rhetorical an issue to
me as it was to them. On my seventh school in as many grades, I'd
learned not to care where I was. My mother was partly right, I did tend
to confuse the stability of indifference with being happy.

She had finally conceded as she always did, with a stiff correction
of her posture, as if she knew some other, more important private

victory had been sealed. And now here we were, aliens camped in a village outside Stockholm, in a house of shabby yellow stucco, facing an early winter. I say *camped* because our household goods had been shipped by accident to England. My father and mother, Charles and I each had a cot and one worn blanket, courtesy of our landlord. Georgie, the baby, slept in the biggest suitcase on his own bunched clothes. Our father fixed the hinges so that no matter how much Georgie wiggled in his sleep the lid couldn't drop and smother him.

As foreseen, I was enrolled in *L'Ecole Française Internationale*, a four-story facade of reddish stone in the middle of the city, in a special class for children of diplomats. It must have been clear to the Sisters from the start that my knowledge of French was limited to what I had learned in Norfolk from a Miss Lafave during a brief exposure to ballet. But they were unfathomable women, the Sisters, in their dark skirts and heavy black stockings, their faces drawn like long grey masks. No matter how poignantly I tried to dramatize my ignorance, I could not move them to either compassion or anger. They simply expected me, from my first day and every night thereafter, to memorize whole pages in their language on the subject of *Mesopotamie, l'Esquimaux*, or *la famille Lebrun*. My failure also to memorize the correct pronunciation was simply a matter of fact, to be brought to the attention of the rest of the class almost daily and met with a terrible silence. Time after time, I tried with humble eyes and posture to plead my good faith before old Madame Sibouet, who simply stared up at me over her spectacles and nibbled the inside of her lips while the room slowly filled with sounds of derision.

I soon learned not to mention these humiliations at home, for the certainty of living together for a full year was making my parents edgy and temperamental. Actually, none of us was used to it. I loved my father desperately. Very tall and thin, he had a narrow, bronze moustache at a time when such adornments were daring. He could be deployed on the other side of the world but he would see to it that bouquets of flowers were delivered to my mother and me on our birthdays: *Always, Frank*, promised the neatly printed card. *Always, Father*. Home on brief leaves, he was a limitless source of practical wisdom—how to bluff a large dog; how to extinguish different kinds of fires. During his weeks on shore, I used to stand behind his chair while he watched "The Cisco Kid" or "Dragnet" and scratch his head. Later when he was back on cruise I tried to remember the smell of his scalp.

But his steady presence now was like living a story you know will not end well. It meant always performing and waiting to hear the one thing you did wrong. "It's only a little thing," he'd say, "but those little things pile up." What about the mistakes piling up, burying me at school? He could never accept my mother's need to keep to herself. "Relax," he instructed her. "If you would just relax," and I could feel her silence get brittle and unsafe. I had to work to protect it, fussing at Charles and Georgie lest their mischief and blind demands become the last straw, cause it to buckle, casting us all down into something worse than silence, the bitter currents of blame.

Yet no matter how careful we children were, out mother could always stare suddenly off over our heads and wonder, "How in God's name did I ever fall for this one?" We could be about to take our places on the floor, at the corners of a sheet spread with Saturday's lunch—hardbreads and *lingon* jelly, sweet butter and cheeses, her favorite strong-smelling Port-Salut among them. The sunlight could be streaming through the wide window and warming the bare wood around us. Georgie could manage not to kick over his jar of milk. And still she asked, "What in God's name am I doing here?" and drained the taste from everything.

Our father sat cross-legged, a knife in one hand, a wedge of Gouda in the other. "Caesar's armies marched on bread and cheese," he would announce, passing slabs around on the blade.

"The more I think about it," she went on, still with a distant, speculative look, "the more I think things were fine in Norfolk."

"You mean, without me," Father said.

I broke the corner off a piece of hardbread, tossed it in the air, and caught in on my tongue.

"I mean, where it wasn't impossible to cook a decent meal for the children. Where we had a table to eat at. Where they had beds to sleep in."

I threw another piece of bread over my head, arched and fell backwards trying to capture it in my mouth.

"Where I had a place to sit."

"If you took an interest in something besides those frigging books,"

Father said. She was staying up late every night, propped in a corner of the living room, rereading, by the light of its tarnished fixture overhead, the historical novels she had hand-carried onto the ship.

"I had plenty of interests in Norfolk," she said, wrenching me upright by one arm. We had lived there a long time for us—two years in the same grey-shingled house. She had established rosebushes against its sunny south side, and in back, she'd unrolled a wire fence around a playhouse left by a much earlier tenant and filled it with six Rhode Island Red hens. Every day she poked around in their odorous feathery litter for the bright surprise of an egg, free of cost. But she could never get them to settle down enough to lay.

Charles was throwing crumbs of hardbread all over the sheet.

She smacked his arm and then turned to me. "Is this how you set an example?"

On weekend afternoons, my father went off on long walks, along the residential lanes of the village and down to the horseshoe of shops on the shore of Lake Malaren. He invited me to go with him. He said we should meet our Swedish neighbors, but our Swedish neighbors did not believe in gratuitous meetings and preferred to watch us from behind delicately parted curtains. For the return route we bought a bag of macaroons or, my father's favorite, a few pieces of marzipan. Now and then we passed a knot of girls my age. "*Hej,*" they cried in unison, their knees flexing in the quick curtseys my father's age demanded. "*Hej,*" he called back, to my embarrassment, his mouth full of sweet, scooping up air with his hand. "Come here a sec. *Komm.*" He held out our open bag as bait. But they giggled and shied off. "The Swedes are a cold people," he told me.

One Saturday as we approached our house, each bracing in silence to reenter, a girl was standing on one of the stone posts that flanked the steps up into the yard. The sun low and at her back, she loomed above us, then spread her arms and jumped, scooting to where we stood in the road. "Welcome to Sweden," she said, as though we had just arrived. She was too intent on pronouncing the *w*'s correctly to smile.

"*Tack,*" my father said, the word for *Thank you*. He could barely control his delight. "*Tack so mycket.*" Without taking his eyes off her, he ordered me, "Quick, go get the book," as though she were about to run away.

She was smaller than I, though her face made her two or three years older. It was thin and cheekless, with a wide thin mouth and teeth a discomfiting grey. The upper lip dipped very long at the center, like a flap over the lower, and gave her a wry expression, the expression of someone not about to escape, someone appraising the situation with an eye to moving in. What I wanted to do was disappear inside with my mother; but I dawdled back with my father's book.

He riffled through it and put a question together syllable by syllable.

The girl's face pinched and wrinkled with the effort to understand. "May I have a look?" she asked. Then her face slackened. "Oh, it is Pia Brandberg. My-name-is-Pia."

"Tack," he said emphatically. *"Tack so mycket."* He eked out another sentence from the book with "Cynthia" at the end.

"Cynthia," said Pia. The *th* drew her tongue out and back over her upper lip.

I glanced at her and made my mouth smile. I didn't like the way her straight hair separated to show the rims of her ears.

"So much for the language barrier," my father boasted to me sidelong.

"In the future," Pia said, "you must ask like so: *Vad heter du?* What-are-you-called. It is the Swedish idiom." She guessed I had no idea what an idiom was. "I shall teach you," she said. Her small eyes glittered with purpose.

On a good day at school, no one paid any attention to me. Bad days left me in such despair I hardly knew who I was. What had happened to the opportunities my father had touted, to make friends from other lands? There was the Egyptian, Ada, a single black braid down her back as thick as my wrist, with an aloof beauty beyond her years; there was Tulla from Finland, whose round face and rough red cheeks seemed to promise friendliness; and Geeta from India, dark and thin, with a gooey red spot between her eyes. They had in common a language I could not seem to learn.

And then there was Wendy, the daughter of the American ambassador, who according to school legend, had mastered French overnight, who found my struggle to remember which consonants not to pronounce entertaining. Mornings in the cloakroom before we donned the school smock, she showed off her frilled blouses and furry sweaters, each monogrammed with her initials. She wore a gold pin etched with *Wendy* and tortoiseshell barrettes shaped like *W's*. For larger political reasons which I could never have grasped, the Sisters allowed her free and capricious play in the class. She was the one who shot my attempts at recitation with snickering rounds, until I gave in myself to spasms of anxious laughter. Sometimes these spilled into incontinence—*accidents*, my mother called them with Georgie—and all I could do was to pray the knee-length smock would hide their traces. At home in secret I washed them out.

Perhaps it was Wendy's ridicule at school that fueled the contempt I felt for Pia Brandberg. Afternoons and Saturdays, I dreaded the scratching at our door, and when I dragged it open, the elfin, unsmiling face announcing, "It is Pia."

Did she think I couldn't see that?

"The persistent Pia," my father called her affectionately. It was fine for him—to try out a few Swedish idioms and then pawn her off on me.

"What shall we do now?" she always asked, as if we had just accomplished something mutually satisfying, as if we faced an array of choices.

Nothing, I wanted to shout. *Just leave me alone*. She never showed up with anyone else; she'd never been among the girls Father and I passed on our walks, girls who now and then strolled by our house, chatting in steamy bursts, darting sidelong looks around the yard, stirring my hopes. Their faces brightened by the cold, they seemed to exude gregarious well being. Might they be trying to make contact? Would they speak English? Wasn't the inevitable presence of Pia, spidery thin, homely Pia, scaring them away?

"I can't come out now," I might say diplomatically.

"Quite fine," said Pia. "I shall wait." Then while I watched from the kitchen window, she scrambled up onto one of the stone pillars on which she'd first appeared to us and, arms spread to perfect her balance, leaped back and forth between the two like an angel guarding the gates.

She worked on teaching me a game that involved juggling balls off the wall of our garage—she was an expert juggler and could keep four going, interspersed with handclaps, knee slaps, and full turns. Half-hearted, I fumbled around with two balls, and even though she allowed me extra misses per turn, she did most of the juggling while I watched.

As darkness crept into the afternoons, she invented a form of hide-and-seek that didn't permit you actually to hide your entire body, but rather position it in such a way that in the deepening twilight it could be mistaken for something else—a shrub, a mound of rock. It was another game that guaranteed her advantage, for she could melt into the dusk with me standing practically beside her. I finally let my brother Charles play with us, so I wouldn't always be *it*. Often as I held myself still and breathless, arms angled from my body, perhaps, like the branches of the hemlock beside me, I could hear the cries of other players, other games, carrying on the cold air from other yards, and I wondered at life's unfairness, that it offered me nothing more than one weird friend, my own kid brother, and the challenge of trying to pass for a tree.

By November, it was dark at three o'clock and still there came the scratching on the door and the announcement, "It is Pia."

"What shall we do now?" I sighed.

"A bloose," she said one afternoon. "We shall sew for you a bloose."

"A bloose?"

"I shall teach you. With a collar, like so. And a pocket, perhaps. Do you wish for pockets?"

"A blouse," I said. It had never occurred to me to wish for pockets or blouses, much less to imagine the creation of either to be within my power. In fact, I didn't care about clothes. My mother discouraged it; she was in charge of figuring out what I needed, and more important, what we could afford. I had never expected this to include furry sweaters or monograms. Now when packages of coarsely woven long underwear showed up on my dresser, through no wishes of mine, I assumed I was going to need them, and grotesque or not they would have to be worn.

"Quite right, a blouse," Pia said. "Shall you come, have a try?"

Her proposition was mildly disquieting—*wish for something*, it said, and what's more, that something might be gotten for nothing. I could hear my mother's reproach. Trying to act as though my following her was a duty to friendship, no more, no less. I entered Pia's house for the first time. It was down a block toward the village center, a large cottage whose faded blue paint hung from the wooden siding in shreds. Inside, a single lamp gilded the layer of dust on a grand piano in the living room. Cobwebs filled in the legs of a carved wooden horse on the hearth in the kitchen and threaded the blue and white plates on a shelf above. A pure white cat rubbed my ankles. Pia's mother bustled aimlessly in a dark dress and baggy apron. Her hair was pulled back in a bun to display the same pointed face as Pia.'s She seemed terribly grateful to see me with her daughter and insisted on serving us hot chocolate, with a dollop of whipped cream. The way my mother's set expression was an unfocussed scowl, Pia's mother's was a smile, twitched into place several times a minute, turned almost to a simper by protruding eyeteeth.

But Pia was fresh with her mother. I didn't need to know Swedish to understand, *None of your business*, or *See what I care*. It made me very uneasy to hear her rudeness and ingratitude echo unpunished, and I felt obliged to counter them by meeting Fru Brandberg's bleached blue eyes as often as I could and returning her smiles, twitch for twitch. When she left the kitchen for a moment, Pia dragged me away from the table, into the hall and up a narrow staircase. "That was a revolting perform-ance," she hissed over her shoulder. I didn't understand. To which of us three was she referring? To what?

The next thing I knew I was flung into the elaborate, demanding world of Pia's room under the eaves. It seemed to contain everything, packed in with compulsive efficiency. There were no empty spaces. The sloping ceiling and walls were covered with maps, over which were tacked photos, postcards, labels, envelopes, signs. Feathers and dried flowers and pieces of colored glass dangled from threads at the one window. Rugs overlapped on the floor; dolls and stuffed animals lay heaped on the bed. Dresser and desktop held stacks of assorted boxes and books. A bookcase on one wall had been converted by upright dividers into an elegant mansion for the smaller dolls. Pia had made all the furniture herself, from more boxes, papier mâché, scraps of wood and fabric and yarn. There were wire chandeliers, crocheted rugs, framed pictures, bowls of fruit, tiny down pillows and quilts on each bed.

"So this is your room," I said emptily, when it seemed I had to say something. The last thing I wanted was for her to think I was compar-ing it to the one I had been assigned at home, a servant's cubicle on the first floor off the kitchen, while the rest of the family slept upstairs.

Pia went right to the kneehole of her desk and pulled out a basket and from it a pile of neatly folded remnants of cloth. "These are for you to choose," she said.

It was too much. "I should go home," I said.

"For the *blouse*," she said.

"I don't really need a blouse," I said. "Why don't we make *you* a blouse?" She always wore the same dull sweaters, the same rumpled grey ski pants.

"Do you wish flowers or no flowers?" She stared at me blankly. I let out a sigh. "Flowers."

"Like so?" She pulled a doll from the crowd on the bed, tidied it up, then held it in front of me. It was wearing a blouse of flowered print, with tiny buttons, a collar trimmed with lace, and pockets.

"Did you make this one?" I asked.

"I make everything," she said.

She lifted my arms away from my sides and began measuring me with her tape. Her quick, light touch caused me to flinch, but that she ignored. Soon she was unfolding the cloth on the floor and cutting through it with long, crunching shears. Then she sat down at the old machine on her desk and began rhythmically pressing the pedal with her foot while she tugged at the cloth above, her pursed face rapidly aging with concentration. I continued to stand there until I realized there was nothing else for me to do. With tentative relief, I sat and slowly let myself loll back on the bed among the dolls. I had had my fill at school of being taught the impossible. It also seemed to me that the less I had to do with the blouse, the greater its chances would be of becoming one, and my chances of deserving it. So she worked by the light of a green-shaded lamp, and I watched from the shadows, and sometimes her foot pumped slowly and other times it broke into a convulsive race, faster than the eye could see.

After a very short time, she stood up and pointed to the floor in front of her. I rose and let her spread out my arms again. She draped me with flowered fabric, smoothed it across the back, pulled it down in front, and straightened the shoulders. It was a shapeless tunic at this stage.

"It's nice," I said politely, actually pleased to find its appeal no stronger. She slipped it off and showed me the side seam, the special way she had double-sewn it to enclose the rough edges. "That's nice too," I said, and I was feeling more relaxed, enough to kneel beside the bookcase and study the decoration of each compartment. Pia invited me to touch things, as I wished, but I kept my hands folded in my lap.

After another stint of pedaling she stopped, reached over, grabbed a handful of my sweater and said, Take it off." I obeyed her the way my mother taught me to obey the doctor. Then Pia helped me slip the blouse on over my undershirt.

There was no mirror in that room, but from what I could see of my arms and front, I thought I must look very stylish. Two puffy sleeves had attached themselves to the tunic, sleeves that gathered in a ruffle at each cuff. I studied Pia's face for a confirmation, but could learn nothing from the way she fussed at the fabric, lapping it closed in the front, a fan of silver pins pressed between her lips. It was a little tight some-where—across the back, or at the armholes—but this was a constraint I could live with. When she reached into her pants pocket and disclosed a handful of red plastic buttons shaped like hearts, another sigh escaped me. I saw myself in the cloakroom at school, and Wendy silent with envy. Pia's stern expression never changed.

She snapped her fingers twice. "Give it me," she mumbled through pressed lips.

I peeled the blouse off and handed it to her. She sat down at the machine. Oddly contented, I lay back on the bed and drew a crocheted afghan around my bare shoulders. "Did you make this too?" I asked her, hugging it around myself. I felt oddly, blandly sociable.

"I make everything," she reminded me.

Again her foot rose and fell on the pedal, her deft hands guided the fabric under the pulsing needle, the machine chattered hypnotically. On the train home that afternoon, I had been working to memorize another passage from *Une Jolie Maison à la Campagne*, home of the family Lebrun, and for some reason it returned now to my mind in perfectly pronounced cadences—the roof touched in all seasons by the sun, the balcony adorned by the red pompons of a climbing rose, Madame Lebrun happily knitting on the *rez-de-chausée*, while beside her a canary sang in its cage.

There came a pause in the rhythm of the machine. "Pia," I said, "do you know how hard it is to speak French? I don't think I'm ever going to learn."

"I suppose not," she replied without looking up.

"You don't?" I hadn't expected her to agree with me.

"It is not your mother tongue."

"I don't care what it is," I said. "It's a dumb tongue."

"Because you are at home in English." She began pumping at the pedal.

I thought about this for a while, found her certainty reassuring. "But you learned to speak English," I reminded her above the noise of the machine.

Her foot stopped. "But I am not at home," she said. "I try for many years, but I am not at home." She began pedaling again and fiddling with my blouse, and as I watched, I seemed to feel every tug and stroke of her hands on the cloth, as though it were part of my body, threaded with my nerves. She pinned and basted and clipped the collar, and my neck bristled at the touch. It was a sensation too unfamiliar to understand, but I wished it might never stop. Until Pia announced that it was time for me to go, I watched those hands avidly, but it was still not enough. As I walked back to our house in the dark, I thought that it would be just like Pia to come calling for me tomorrow with her mind set on doing something else.

I never did see my blouse again. I asked after it once or twice, knowing that it must exist somewhere, lacking only its heart-shaped buttons—I could have sewn them on myself. "That isn't necessary," Pia told me. "I must fix it," she said vaguely. I didn't really pursue the matter; in fact, giving up the blouse was easy. After months of adjustments and resignations, losses in translation, what was one more?

The next day after school, I went straight from the train station in the village to Pia's and knocked on the door. No one answered. The window upstairs glowed dully. I was about to knock again when Pia's voice spoke up from the shadows, "I do not wish to be in that house." There was a woodstack at the far end of the porch and she was perched, chin to knees, upon it. She wore nothing over her usual sweater and pants. "It is quite intolerable," she said.

"You'll catch cold," I said.

"It's nothing." She slid down and stamped her feet.

"We could go to my house." I hoped she could see as clearly as I did what an empty prospect that was.

She shivered. "It is always nothing." She shouldered open the door. In the kitchen Fru Brandberg glanced up from where she stood clutching the sink. Her eyes and nose were swollen and red. I made myself look away, kept moving behind Pia, until the dim intricate warmth of her room surrounded me. I threw down my books, dropped my jacket, sank onto the foot of the bed with the relief of someone arriving, after long absence, home.

Something was bothering Pia. She paced the channel between bed and bookcase, stopped at the window, pulled on her long upper lip.

"What shall we do?" I asked.

She began to draw in the steam on the glass—a square inside a circle, a circle inside that square, and so on, until things all ran together. As if this had given her an idea, she asked, "Do you wish to play with the dolls?" She was teasing me, I thought, for she reached over and picked from the pile behind me the one wearing the miniature of my blouse.

"Sure," I said, and accepted the others she tossed in my lap—a mother with cottony hair and an apron, a father in felt trousers, then like an afterthought, the male twin of the girl in the blouse. I carried them to the bookcase, knelt, and began amenably to arrange them in the living room. Meanwhile, I assumed, Pia would begin working on my blouse. The mother doll, having acquired a tiny book from a basket, was bent into a striped satin chair to read. The father, who didn't bend, lay on the matching sofa, leaving the boy to play some boy's game on the floor along the back wall. I was deciding what room, what activity to assign the girl when Pia began pounding on the bookcase with her fist and shouting in Swedish.

It was a strange creature she clutched around the middle and shoved headfirst into my comfortable scene—a bald baby doll painted black, swaddled in black cloth, and under its chubby rubber arm, the one prop Pia had not made, a miniature lead gun.

From its little mouth hole where the toy nipple went were coming those loud incomprehensible commands.

"Pia," I said.

She snatched the girl from my hands and threw her into the living room, toppling the spool lamp and the mother in her chair. She snarled again in Swedish, then turned to me and said calmly, "Put up their hands."

I began to understand. I reached into the room for the father, half the size of the black baby, and adjusted his arms. I was working on the mother when Pia's Swedish became soft and sibilant She jerked her head in my direction, then made the same sounds, by which I understand they were my lines—rather, the mother's lines—so I tried to reproduce them. Then flatly, out of the side of her mouth, Pia translated: "Please, I have done nothing. Please, don't shoot me right through the heart."

As the scene went on, the intruder forced mother, father, daughter to take off the meticulous clothes Pia had made for them and assume embarrassing positions on the round doily rug in the middle of the room. And I continued to repeat the lines Pia fed me in Swedish, mimicking every melodramatic inflection, curious to hear the English translations that came afterwards in quick neutral asides. "Would you like to see a trick?" the girl asked. "I will do anything you wish, but please don't kill me." The father began to rage at the mother for not locking the door, until the black baby threatened to cut his fingers off. The mother tried at first to be polite, offering the baby food, and was pitched again onto the floor. "What have I done," she cried, her legs thrust straight into the air. "Oh what have I done?"

Before long I wasn't pretending the emotion; it rose up to meet the Swedish Pia pronounced for me as though I knew just what it meant. The more I understood the showdown in the bookcase, the more I forgot everything else. There came a point, and I could not say when, when the script became bilingual, though the parts in original English still came to me by surprise, like translations from another tongue. The girl muttered nasty insults behind the baby's back. The father threatened the baby impressively with the full power of the U.S. Embassy, but was butted aside. From where he landed facedown beside the couch, he demanded that his own life be taken to spare the rest. My eyes filled at the nobility of his intention. But the mother had other ideas. She sidled up to the baby and whispered in my voice, "Why don't you just take the girl instead? We don't need her. Take her and leave the rest of us alone."

It was a terrible thing to hear. For a few seconds I was stunned silent, waiting, I think, for some objection from the father, but he was not moved to speak. Then more to escape what I felt than to give it expression, I started to whimper. I was still holding the mother doll, and I pressed her to my chest like a hurt child. "Oh Pia," I cried, "no mother would ever say that." I rocked back and forth in distress. "No mother could."

My tears seemed to elate her. Her eyes grew bright and her chin jutted sharp as a trowel. She picked up the father doll and threw the girl down in his place, then poked at her with his foot, exploding with a string of Swedish. Breathing as if she had just come running from far away, she blurted the translation: "It doesn't matter what happens to this one. I shall never think of her as mine."

She looked at me expectantly. I studied the mother doll in my hand as though its shape and construction would tell me what to say. There was nothing left. When I glanced up, Pia was still looking at me. I felt slightly dizzy, seemed to be staring out of a deep cave. I returned to whimpering.

All this time the boy doll sat neglected against the back wall. Now I heard fumbling amid the furniture and looked up to see the black baby point the gun at the boy's head, and fire it throatily. The boy fell sideways and expired without a word.

Walking home in the dark, I felt sick to my stomach. What had happened? I thought of Pia's own words, "a revolting performance." I had spoken forbidden words, thoughts, I had cried, sunk to some unspeakable depth. Hoping to avert discovery and punishment, I made a promise to the starless sky never to visit Pia's room again.

For three days I kept it, assuming all the while persistent Pia would come to call for me and manage cleverly to break me down. When she never did, the promise faded into the shadowy irrelevance of other guilty reflexes, like smiles for Fru Brandberg. By the end of the week, I was trudging to Pia's house, trying to look less like a sinner defying hell than a martyr approaching the stake. Her front door opened before I could knock, and there she stood like fate, that sharp, needy face, the pallid skin, urgent eyes. She raced up the stairs by twos, I went after with attempted dignity. She greeted me on her threshold with the dolls. Hating her, and myself, I accepted them from her trembling hands.

Where was the flowered blouse, with the lace trim and heart-shaped buttons? It seldom entered my mind, caught up as I was in the black baby's hypotheses of sensual violence. At school, when Madame Sibouet was her most impassive or Wendy her most supercilious, I imagined the most satisfying reprisals in which they were stripped of their power and pretense, along with their clothes. Then one day in real life, I scored a victory over Wendy, who hung over my desk and whispered, "You don't even know what *pee* is," grinning to expose the gap between her upper front teeth.

My breath caught: I thought she had somehow discovered the dreadful secret of my accidents.

She shifted her weight from one patent-leather shoe to the other, shook her curls, and tapped on my desk. "Knock, knock. Who's there. Stupid. Cynthia doesn't even know about *pee.*"

"Pia's a name," I gasped. "I have a friend called Pia."

Wendy doubled over with a fake laugh. "She says it's a *name.*" Geeta chuckled and rolled her bulging eyes.

Maybe I saw *Pia* spelled in my mind, maybe it was just that I had to say something, anything, to deny the old truth, that I deserved their contempt many times over. A desperate answer came to me, something I'd forgotten I knew from seventh grade in Norfolk. "You mean *pi.*" I tried to sound contemptuous myself. "Pea is a green vegetable. Pi is equal to three point one four."

Wendy's cute features went blank, and I realized, in disbelief, that my answer was the right one. "You should learn to pronounce English better," I said hoarsely before she flounced off.

After school in Pia's room meanwhile, we worked to embellish our basic scene. We set matchstick fires in a glass ashtray and, threatening the family with the same fate, threw their smaller furnishings into the flames. There was open warfare now among family members, as each offered to strike a different bargain with the baby. In the end, Pia always took over and brought off the recurring finale when the baby announced to the boy doll, "Now you're going to get it," and he did.

It must have been my father, the sailor, who once told me that the farthest stars have burned themselves out by the time their beams prick out night sky. It may be the same with shared secrets—no matter how dazzling, how outrageous their shine, it is phantom light, its source exhausted once shown. As the weeks passed, the scenes Pia and I staged began to lose energy. There was a limit to the delinquent novelties our minds could come up with. As the passion subsided, the black baby seemed silly. We began watching, hearing ourselves, and each other. That first revulsion I had felt toward Pia and what we were doing returned unchecked.

I think Pia was having a similar reaction to me. Her lines grew stilted, began presenting themselves in carefully composed but listless English. One afternoon when I arrived at her house after school, Fru Brandberg opened the door and gave me to understand that Pia had gone to the Milk Central on an errand, and I felt relieved. The next two days I went straight home and, as if for penance, memorized more attentively than ever before a long passage about winter *chez la famille Lebrun*—how the snow covered the earth and wove a light lace on the branches of the trees, how the boy named Maurice made balls of it, and his sister Jeanne slid happily on the ice, while the blackbirds, which were called crows, flew about the house seeking something to eat, but found nothing.

My partnership with Pia might have ended then, I think, with the dwindling of novelty and need. French was no longer impossible, Wendy no longer invincible, and our household goods arrived, no worse for their detour to Liverpool. But then one night, just as we were sitting down to dinner at our long-lost-chrome-legged kitchen table, my mother happened to mention what she'd learned from the woman who lived behind us: two years before we arrived in Sweden, Pia's brother had killed himself—put a gun to his head, pulled the trigger, very messy. It was information passed from woman to woman by pantomime and sheer resolve, for neither spoke the other's language. Apparently Pia's mother had dreamt of a career as a concert pianist for her gifted son, while Pia's father, who sold vacuum cleaners, wanted his boy to become an engineer. The boy didn't want to become an engineer. Or a concert pianist. He wanted to go to America and play jazz. His mother cried, his father laughed. So. My mother pointed at her temple. "Please pass the meat loaf," she said.

My stomach was churning. Spread in front of me were our familiar Melmac plates, the matching aluminum glasses, the hen saltshaker, the rooster pepper mill. Georgie was where he belonged, in the old wooden high chair, scrubbed almost paintless. The rooms beyond had filled up with more familiar things, unpacked, arranged in order. As though he were the expert, my father said the place had begun to look like home. How could this, what my mother said, be true?

"Apparently Mr. Brandberg went north after it happened. He chops down trees. His wife gets a little money every month."

There was a tinted sepia portrait of Pia's brother sitting on a square of yellow lace on the Brandberg's grand piano. I remembered the close-set eyes, their brown stare mocked by too-pink lips and cheeks. Pia had said he didn't live with them any more. Her mother had nodded, twitching smiles. There had been no sign of a father anywhere.

"We should all of us try to be nice to Pia," my mother said.

I could feel myself flush under her gaze. Why was she looking at me? I didn't shoot Pia's brother. How could she dare pretend to look sad over this death of someone she didn't know? "Two hands," I reminded Georgie, who was raising his cup of milk.

"Cynthia," my mother said, as though she had an inkling of the games Pia had taught me.

"I *am* nice to her," I said. The fact was Pia was too imperious and preoccupied to notice whether you were nice to her or not. But what did my mother know? This wasn't one of her books. This wasn't picturesque.

"Does she ever mention?" my mother asked.

"Angie," my father said.

"I'm only curious," she said.

"I don't think it's any of your business," I said haughtily. I would defend my friend Pia, the juggler, the hider, the maker, from her easy words.

"Cynthia," my father said.

"You would think that poor child would have mentioned it." My mother's tone implied I was withholding information. "The poor child has lost more than a brother, after all."

In my mind I saw Pia in her kitchen, picking at her dinner, separated from her inconsolable mother by two empty chairs. I looked across at Georgie, who had gone red-faced and Buddha-like the way he did when he was doing his business; then over at Charles, chewing potatoes and beets with his mouth open. The fact was I *had* known for some time the story my mother had just reported with such self-importance. Maybe not the gaudy details, but the same dark, furious core. Tomorrow afternoon, I would call for Pia, we would turn our backs on these tables, these intolerable houses, we would walk the dark road out of the village arm and arm.

"Still waters run deep," my mother said. If that was supposed to be some wise reference to Pia, who talked and moved incessantly, she couldn't have been more impertinent.

"Dow," said Charles, pretending to shoot himself in the head with his finger. "Dow, dow, dow."

She turned on him ferociously. "Don't ever let me see you," she said, slapping his hand out of the air. Charles tucked his fist in his armpit and laughed.

Zoe

She liked to be the first to speak. It wasn't that she wanted to be nice, or put them at ease; it was her way of warning them not to be, of setting the tone she liked best: bemused, even ironic, but formal. She didn't want any of them thinking she was someone to cultivate. Whenever those voices, low and strained, interrupted her life downstairs, whether they came late at night from the front hall or mornings from the kitchen, she slipped into the one-piece camouflage suit she used as a bathrobe, wrapped the belt twice around her slim waist, and ascended to meet her mother's latest. She liked to catch him with breakfast in his mouth, or romance on his mind, and then before he could compose himself, announce, "I am Zoe, her daughter," offering a little bow and a graceful hand, limp as a spray of japonica.

It usually left him stammering, fumbling—this blend of childlike respect and self-possession. If he'd already begun to imagine her mother recharging his life with pleasure and purpose, Zoe's winsome presence made such visions more intense, then tipped them into unsettling. Though he'd never gone in for kids before, he might find himself thinking at first how agreeable it would be to have a delicate creature like her around, slender, long-legged, with pale freckles across her nose. These days she has her auburn hair bobbed at the ears so it curls up shorter in back above a softly fringed nape. But if he thought for a moment how much the child must know, her poise could seem ominous—all the things *he* didn't know, was hungry to find out, but might not want to hear.

"So what's it like, living with her?" one of them asked Zoe once, as if he expected soon to be sharing the experience, to be given exclusive credit for recognizing that her mother was an extraordinary woman. He reminded Zoe of a large rabbit—a confusion of timidity and helpless lust.

"There's never a dull moment," Zoe answered, sweet but nonchalant. "I meet a lot of interesting men." That was stretching things. Most were rabbits.

Often they felt called upon to tell Zoe, "Your mom's a great lady." Did they think Zoe was responsible for raising her mother and not the other way around? Or that she had a choice of mothers? Or that she couldn't guess what they meant, that her mother was something else in bed, that they'd never done it to a Sibelius symphony before?

Since the age of five when her parents split up, Zoe Cameron and her mother, Phyllis Rush, have lived beyond the D.C. Beltway in The Colonies of Virginia, clusters of townhouses subtly tucked into one hundred acres of rolling woods, whose inhabitants readily paid a little more to get aesthetic design and proximity to nature. Set against the ridge of a hill, with cathedral ceilings and an expanse of glass to the south, Zoe's mother's unit welcomes light, draws it in to challenge her work—heavy terra cotta, here and there a dull giant bronze—set off by white walls. Each piece has been given a woman's name, yet they are only parts of women, global buttocks and thighs, pairs of breasts larger than the heads mounted upon them—Leda, Electra, Helen, truncated. They are one reason Zoe stopped bringing home friends, who tended to stare about in stunned silence or whisper words like *gross* and *perverted*. Zoe has learned contempt for kids her own age, who cannot understand true art. Yet she hates her mother's women: fat, naked blobs. The bald definition of nipple or vulva makes her sick. There are more of them on exhibit in the local gallery her mother manages in The Commons. The public tends not to buy them, but Phyllis does enter them in shows and they have won awards, including a purchase prize at the Corcoran. After that, a man from the *Washington Post* came out to photograph Phyllis at home in her skylit studio. Zoe declined to be in any of his shots. He took her mother to dinner in Great Falls. When Zoe came up the next morning to leave for school, he was in the kitchen alone making raisin toast. He offered her a slice, trying to act as if he owned the place, but she drank her sixteen ounces of water as if he weren't there. It was easier than ever to resist that sweet yeasty aroma, tainted as it was by his male pride.

As far as Lucas is concerned, Zoe would give anything to go back and start over again with the moment she arrived home in the early afternoon to find his body sticking out from under the sink. Thinking her mother had finally called someone to fix the dishwasher, Zoe set her wide-brimmed hat down on the table and looked on absently as the body twisted and grunted with its efforts. Her hunger had been stubborn that day, conjuring extravagant food fantasies that almost sabotaged a test in pre-calculus. But she had conquered temptation, and now what she wanted was plenty of water and maybe a carrot to get through until dinner.

"Let me out of here," came a roar, all of a sudden, followed by bumping sounds and *great god*'s, and the upper part of the man extricated itself from the cabinet. His knuckles were smudged with black, his once-starched shirt was sharply wrinkled, and he rubbed the top of his head ruefully, but when he saw Zoe, his expression flexed in a smile. "Well, look at you," he said. "Don't you look out of this world!" And not expecting such a remark from a repairman, Zoe, who was known to become transfixed by her own image whenever she found it reflected, who that day was wearing one of her favorite suits—broadly padded shoulders over a short slim skirt, a blue that turned her eyes blue—could not bring herself to disagree, nor think of anything to say back. She did try her ironic geisha bow, but in the same instant noticed the roaches hurrying over the sill of the sink cabinet and out across the kitchen floor in a dark stream.

Before she knew it she had emitted a soft scream, more out of embarrassment than fear. She had certainly seen roaches in the kitchen before, those nights when she gave in to temptation and felt her way up the stairs in the dark. Thinking it was almost like sleepwalking, she was almost not responsible for what she was about to do: forage for food, cookies, bagels, leftover pasta, cinnamon raisin toast drenched in butter. When she turned on the light, there they always were collected on some vertical surface in clusters of imperceptible activity, and she caught her breath in disgust, but went on to get what she had come for. "They must have a nest under there," the man said, a little out of breath. He was somehow hopping and stooping at the same time, slapping at the creatures with one of his moccasins. "How about giving me a hand here?"

Zoe looked down helplessly at her clothes, her inch-high patent heels.

"How about insecticide, a spray or something?"

"If we have any, it's in there." She pointed to the cabinet from which they kept coming. The floor around him was awash with brown spots. Some had been hit and were finished moving. "Close the door," Zoe cried. When she realized the sense of her suggestion, she repeated it more calmly.

He smacked the door shut, and the stream was cut off. "Good thinking," he said.

She pursed her lips to hide her pleasure. Producing a fly swatter from the closet in the front hall, she commenced ceremoniously to slap at the remaining roaches from the comfortable distance its handle allowed. "Mother," she called.

"She went to the store," the man said, rubbing his bare foot along his pants leg, then replacing his shoe. "I thought I'd keep myself busy until she got back."

That was when Zoe realized he wasn't a plumber and that she had been inexplicably foolish. Her mother, who scorned home maintenance, who refused to spend any time on fixing things when she could be making something new—why would her mother suddenly hire a plumber? "I am Zoe, her daughter," she said, with a final stroke of the swatter, but it was too late.

"I assumed as much," the man said. "From the side you're a dead ringer." He introduced himself: Lucas Washburn. He had light, almost frizzy hair and eyebrows, no cheekbones to speak of, and his nose must have been broken once and never set straight. His skin was fissured from past acne, and his eyes were a flat, changeless gray. He was not handsome, Zoe decided, but there was something about him. His hair was cropped short, his skin evenly tanned, his khaki pants creased. Clean—in spite of his disarray, he seemed oddly, utterly clean.

"I assumed you were the plumber." Zoe pulled the broom out from beside the refrigerator and began with dignity to sweep roach hulls into a pile.

"I can see why. I hear you're down to one bathtub."

Zoe stiffened at the forced intimacy, the hint of sympathy. She normally did not interfere in her mother's affairs, patiently allowing what Phyllis would call nature to take its course. But this man, with his long cheekless face, who had poked around under their sink, discovered their roaches—he was not at all her mother's type, and the sooner he was history, the better. "And it happens to be my bathtub downstairs, which gets pretty inconvenient if you think about it. One of her quote friends pulled the soap holder off the wall in *her* tub and half the tiles came with it, and the guest tub has a leak that drips into the front hall. Actually, the whole house is a total wreck." She finished, and made herself laugh, but in the silence that was his reply, she heard her words echo like a blurted confession, false notes, as if something were playing in the background in a different key. Blasé wasn't working.

"If I had my tools," Lucas said, "we could get this sink to drain, and I could take a look at those tubs. Next time I'll bring my tools."

That is a lot to assume, next time, Zoe thought, and to her surprise, that was what she said.

Lucas nodded solemnly, then turned his back on her and began washing his hands. Should she explain that her mother had very liberal views, that if men and women were allowed to live naturally, without the inhibitions imposed by society, they would choose to spend their nights in each other's beds all the time, different other's beds as the impulse moved them, mornings parting, more often than not, forever? And that was all right with her, Zoe, for it was much worse when a man of her mother's showed up a second time, all twitchey and trembly, and suggested doing something that included her, and her mother, seduced by some transient vision of family, agreed.

"I appreciate the warning," Lucas said, drying his long hands finger by finger. Then he added, "Maybe I've got something in common with those guys in there"—he jerked his head toward the roach settlement—"I'm pretty hard to get rid of."

That night her mother and Lucas fixed strip steaks, steamed artichokes, wild rice. As she often did, Phyllis set up small folding tables on the balcony off the living room in view of the sunset, but Lucas moved the hibachi to the backyard below to comply with the county fire code. ("What fire code?" Phyllis asked. She had never heard of any fire code.) Zoe went downstairs to change into a faded denim jumpsuit, espadrilles. She rolled a fuchsia bandana into a headband and tied her curls down, Indian-style. She freshened the strip of pale blue shadow on her lower lids, all the while aware that Lucas was right beyond the glass door, the drapes that don't quite meet, calling arguments up to her mother in favor of well-done. Phyllis stuck to rare. Her face blank and impersonal, Zoe made a last appraisal in the full-length mirror. She pushed a fist into her sucked-in abdomen. *I hate my stomach,* she thought. You couldn't trust mirrors; they could be designed to make people look thinner. All the ones in stores were deceptive that way.

Lucas sawed off huge blocks of meat and swallowed them almost whole. Her mother plucked her artichoke, petal by petal, dragged each one through her lips slowly, her subtly silvered eyelids drooping with the pleasure. She had a strong jaw, and a wide mouth, with large teeth—but she knew how to recontour her face with light and shade, to make her eyes seem bigger, mysterious. Yes, Zoe had her nose, rising fine and straight from the brow, nostrils flared back, so that if you happened to have a cold or be cold, their moisture was open to view. Zoe had learned to carry her head tilted slightly forward, to make it hard for anyone to see into her nose.

To Lucas' credit he seemed not to be noticing Phyllis' sensual performance. He was expressing his suspicion that her clogged dishwasher and drain stemmed from a failure to scrape dirty dishes thoroughly; a small chicken bone in the trap, for example, was all it took to start an obstruction.

Phyllis threw her head back and laughed. "You sound like my mother," she said.

Lucas wasn't fazed. "You're talking to someone who's trained to eliminate human error." Lucas flew for Pan Am; Phyllis had picked him out of the happy-hour crowd in the lounge at Dulles Airport after dropping off a friend.

Phyllis stroked his closest arm. "That's Mother all over again."

"Another word for it is *accident*."

"It's only a dishwasher," Phyllis said, sullenly, and the fatalist in Zoe settled back with the vaguest sense of loss to watch this man ruin things with her mother long before he could get the bathtubs fixed.

In a steady, almost uninflected voice, he was talking improvements. He could see a brick patio in their backyard, and redwood planters and a hexagonal redwood picnic table. Zoe saw clumsy strategy, tinged with pathos. He frankly admitted he was tired of living on the tenth floor of a condo in Hunting Towers. Between his job and the apartments he unpacked in, he never had his feet on the ground. "It's about time I got my feet on the ground," he said. Phyllis suggested he sprinkle dirt in his socks.

She was being strangely tolerant; maybe he had touched off an attack of what she called her *passion for reality*, when practical dailiness, what everyone else did, became the exotic object of curiosity and desire. Lucas was neither suave nor witty. If you sanded his face, he might be handsome. Zoe guessed he had what her mother would call a good body, though she, Zoe, had trouble looking at a male body long enough to form a complete picture of one. She tended to focus on them piece by piece, and they stayed like that in her mind, a jumble of parts. Her mother often said it was an insult to women the way men let themselves go after a certain age, after they had good incomes. Phyllis herself kept her weight down by smoking and thought women should band together and hold men to the same physical standards everyone held women to.

"Why me?" Phyllis asked Lucas, and seemed genuinely to wonder. "For how many years you've been tied to no place particular and been perfectly happy? Why pick on my place? Maybe I like it this way."

"Look at that," Lucas said, pointing above them at a strip of white streaks and blotches on the cedar stain. "Look at the mess those birds have made of your siding. Starlings. They must have a roost in the eaves. I'd have to take care of that before I'd put in a patio right under their flight lines!"

Phyllis pulled forward a lock of her thick dark hair. "I don't begrudge them that. It's nature." She gave a quick yank, then let the breeze lift an offending gray strand from her fingers.

"Like roaches under the sink."

Zoe held her breath as her mother lit a cigarette. Was he joking or criticizing? Either way he had no right; either way her mother would finally put him in his place. Then why was she stretching, smiling languidly at his rudeness? "Everyone has them," she said, blowing a plume of smoke. "They're a fact of life."

"You don't have to give in totally," Lucas persisted.

"It isn't in me to go around poisoning things."

Her mother's reasonableness was a puzzle to Zoe. *Why him?* she kept asking herself, until the answer came to her, all at once: it made her a little queasy. It was obviously something to do with sex that gave Lucas this power, this license. Wasn't her mother always declaring that everything came down to that? It must be something sexual he did to her mother or for her, which she, Zoe, for all her determined precocity, had not yet figured out. Then she felt very empty—empty as though she had failed an exam, empty because she didn't want to think of Lucas that way. In the back of her mind, she had been hoping he was different, and she didn't even know she was hoping until he turned out to be the same—just another male, who in the irresistible flux of life must soon disappear. Well, she could care less.

That night Zoe ate. Once dead silence told her Lucas and her mother had settled down, she stole upstairs in the dark, removed from the freezer a half gallon of vanilla ice cream and went back down to her room. She sat on the bed, and gazing at the photos of lithe models she had cut from her magazines, began to spoon ice cream into her mouth. Each mouthful hit her empty stomach like a cold stone. It made her feel a little crazy; she couldn't think straight anymore. She swung between defiance—when she agreed with herself that this was incomparable pleasure, no matter how high the price, this cool, bland sweetness, this private solitude—defiance, and despair. "Eat up," she heard her mother encouraging, as she had all evening, though never showing concern when Zoe didn't. "She eats like the proverbial bird," her mother told Lucas. And then Lucas had said, "Do you know how much a bird eats? One of those starlings, for example? They eat something like four times their body weight in one day."

Ah Lucas, the way he looked at Zoe then, as if he knew that sometimes she forgot she must be thinner. She forgot the terrible burden of stomach and hateful thighs, which kept you from ever being wonderful, and she ate, and having forgotten, she ate more, to forget she forgot. One hand around the damp, softening box of ice cream, in the other the spoon, hands like bird claws, eating like a bird. Her stomach danced madly as it filled with birds. Her whole body felt in motion. She strutted across her own mind, plump-chested, preening; she opened her wings and took off, soared and swooped above the balcony where Lucas, the flier, watched captivated. And then the ice cream was gone, and all that motion froze, like someone caught in the act. She looked down at her denim thighs spreading against the bed; she could barely get both hands around one. Her stomach was monstrous, almost pregnant. She was losing her shape. She would turn into one of those crude female blobs of her mother's. The thought alone was all it took to convulse her, as, eyes closed above the toilet, she imagined all the birds escaping from the cage of her ribs.

Afterwards she would not allow herself to sleep. Awake burned more calories, burned flesh from bones. She held one hand to the hollow of her throat and felt her heart beating fast and hot as a bird's.

This afternoon Zoe found her mother nestled in the wine velvet cushions of the sofa, her legs drawn up under a long Indian cotton skirt, smoking with one hand, sipping maté tea with the other. From the dull puffiness of her mother's eyes, Zoe could tell she had been crying. *It is all right to cry,* Phyllis has always said. *It is a natural response of the body. Holding it back is harmful.* Zoe hates it when her mother cries, hates to see the pain, the rivulets of mascara, the surrender.

"The bus was a little late today," Zoe says, hitching the knees of her linen pants and perching on the chair opposite.

Her mother pulled herself upright, bare soles on the floor, began carefully to shift the position of everything around her—the huge pillows, ashtray, teapot, the extra cup, which she filled and handed to Zoe. "You're not happy," she told her daughter.

"I'm not?" Zoe asked, with a careful laugh.

"Oh, Zoe, you don't have to pretend. But why, when two people love each other, can't at least one of them be happy? You'd think they could pool their resources and work on one of them. Tell me something you want, Zoe, okay?"

"Kids my age just aren't very happy." Her mother was in one of her moods. "We grow out of it. It's no big deal."

"But what would make you happy? We could manage it."

"You must have had a bad day," Zoe said.

Phyllis took a long pull on her cigarette. "For six hours I have tried to work." She didn't exhale but let the smoke seep out as she talked. "I felt like any minute my hands were going to do something no one has ever done before, but they never did. Nothing. I might as well have been kneading bread. At least I'd have something to show for my time."

"Let's go to the mall," Zoe suggested. She and her mother have always had a good time shopping for Zoe's clothes. When Zoe was small, her mother said, it was like having a doll. Now Zoe has her own ideas, and Phyllis, rather than objecting, seems able to guess almost infallibly what they are—sophisticated angular lines, in pastels or white and black, plenty of defining black; Phyllis combs the racks, and brings a steady supply of possibilities into the fitting room for Zoe to try. Phyllis has always shopped for herself alone and piecemeal, at craft fairs, antique markets, Episcopal church rummage sales in Leesburg, Fairfax. She's owned her favorite jacket for over twenty years—brown leather with a sunrise appliquéd in faded patches and strips on the back.

"I'm going back to pots," Phyllis said dramatically. "Tomorrow I'm hooking up the wheel."

"Let's go to the mall." Zoe bounced twice in the chair to demonstrate eagerness. "I need summer things. That would make me happy."

Her mother paused, searched Zoe's face. "Lucas gets in at five," she said finally. "I think he'll be coming right over."

"Lucas?" Why the flare of panic? Zoe had not seen him since the afternoon of the roaches, assumed that, like one of her mother's moods, he had passed.

"That's what he said last week before he left. He had back-to-back European runs. He said he'd be carrying his tools in the trunk of his car." Her mother's voice quavered, as if she were afraid of something, too.

"What did *you* say?"

Her mother went into a prolonged shrug. "I said all right."

"Well, you must like him then," Zoe said dismissively, deciding it was all right with her, at least one of them would be happy.

"I don't know. I don't understand him. I don't know what he's after." She laughed nervously.

"Mother," Zoe said, stressing each syllable. This was no time for either one of them to act innocent.

"Do you know what he said to me? He said, 'Why do you women assume that's all you've got to offer?'" Phyllis shook her hair violently. "We shouldn't be talking like this."

"We always talk like this."

"I know, but . . ."

"Don't be weird, okay? You've got to tell me what's going on." That has been, after all, Zoe's main fare—knowing. "I can handle things."

"I was asking him to spend the night."

"So?" Zoe had handled that countless times. Then all at once question and answer came together in her mind. "He didn't spend the night?" A rush of feeling, worse than any amount of fear, washed away her strength. She fell back into the chair, crushing her linen blazer.

"He said, number one, it wasn't safe anymore and I should know better, and number two, that it didn't matter because he'd promised himself the next time he met a woman he liked he would wait to sleep with her for six months." Her mother spoke haltingly, as though his reasoning mortified her.

"He said he liked you anyway?"

"He said he'd been through enough relationships that began with great sex. He can't afford another."

Zoe pulled herself up straight again. "Did you tell him what you think, about tapping into the flow of nature, and creating the sensuous present?"

"I can't remember," her mother said faintly, then all at once roared angrily through her teeth. "Forget him," she said, bounding up, jabbing each foot into a thong. "Let's go. He's too damned controlled. Forget him."

"I don't mind staying here and waiting to see if he shows up." Zoe's voice was playing tricks on her, first whispering and then suddenly wanting to shout. "It would be nice to have the plumbing work."

Lucas arrived around seven, looking as if he'd never thought for a moment that he wouldn't. He was wearing fresh khakis and a white knit shirt, with the last of four neck buttons open. He had stopped somewhere to rent a giant ladder, which he had tied onto the ski rack of his perfectly restored Karman Ghia. If there was awkwardness in the rather formal greetings he received from mother and daughter in the front hall, he didn't seem to notice; he was more interested in introducing the two of them to his plumber's pliers, assorted wrenches, a drain snake, a staple gun, and a roll of six-inch-wide screening. He was ready to work.

"You must be hungry," Phyllis said. "I've got pastrami, Swiss cheese. A wonderful melon. Aren't you too tired for this? I mean, what time is it for you? It must be after midnight. You ought to sleep. I can make up the couch," she added quickly.

He wasn't ready to sleep. He'd spent all that time in the air dreaming of feet-on-the-ground work, making mental lists of things to do. He had promised to return the ladder the next morning, and the sun was already dropping into the trees in back. "First things first," he said, unlashing the ladder from his car. He took one end, Phyllis and Zoe the other, and he led them back into the house, down the front hall, miraculously through the living room, without bumping a life-sized bronze of staunchly planted legs and hips—the Arch of Triumph, he had dubbed it last week. Out on the balcony, he pressed his end over the rail and took over theirs.

He dug the ladder firmly into the grass below, then produced a shoelace from his pocket and tied one end around the staple gun, the other around a belt loop. He slipped the roll of screen up his arm, swung a leg onto the ladder, and descended. When he reached the ground, he stamped his feet a few times as if to get used to it. "Come on down," he called back to them. Zoe had never been on a ladder before—the whole thing made her think of burning buildings, great escapes—she scrambled over the edge, linen pants, Capezios and all, and breathing deep against the slight sway, carefully eased herself from rung to rung. She was afraid of losing it if she looked down, so turned her eyes on her mother's face, where she found the blank patient expression of someone lying low.

"I think I'll use the stairs," her mother said, and disappeared. By the time she slid open the glass door, Lucas had extended the ladder twice to the impossible height of three stories. "It's simply physics," he had told Zoe, waving away her offer to steady the bottom. "It can't go anywhere." He had one foot on the first rung.

"Wait a minute, wait a minute," Phyllis said.

Lucas froze, eyes front, hands in midair.

"What are you going to do?"

"I am going to staple this stuff over the vents in the soffit, to keep the birds from getting up under your eaves and building nests and shitting on your siding." It took great control for him to speak that slowly, clearly.

"And you have to do it right now? I mean, it must be two in the morning."

Lucas looked at his watch and then back at Phyllis, stared at her as if he were having trouble translating her language. He didn't want to sleep, he didn't want to stop and wait for sleep to overtake him, he wanted to push himself until he dropped—at least that was what Zoe recognized.

Phyllis clenched her jaw, swallowed visibly. "I don't know whether I'm being pushed around or cared for."

"Give it a while," Lucas said, "and you ought to be able to tell the difference." Unblinking, he watched her, as she appeared to consider this. Then her shoulders fell forward.

"I'll be inside," she said.

Lucas was on the ladder, his feet over Zoe's head, when she realized that she must love him. She wasn't sure why—maybe because he didn't belong to her mother, maybe because there was something so definite about him, but it wasn't a boyfriend sort of love. He didn't have to return it; in fact she would rather he didn't. He just had to stay there, in her life, and let her watch him while he fixed things, and she would privately love him. The ladder flexed in toward the house.

"You sure this will hold you?" she called up to him. "What if the three pieces come apart?"

"I checked everything out," he called from the higher rungs. "But thanks for your concern."

She pursed her mouth. He was pressing the strip of screen against the eaves with the fingertips of one hand. With the other he tried to bring the staple gun into range, but he couldn't get it there: the shoelace was too short. He cursed and then tugged again, but only managed to hike his pants up on the right side where he'd tied it. The ladder shuddered, and Zoe clutched it for all she was worth.

Then resolutely, Lucas climbed up a rung, and then another, until his head and shoulders ran out of ladder, the tips of which had come to rest just below the gutters. He wrapped his legs around the top rungs, twisted his right hip toward the house, and blindly felt the screen into place, firing the staple gun along its edges, clunk, clunk. He wavered precariously at each recoil. She gaped up at him in wonder, and not just his body at the odd foreshortening angle, but his whole heroic being seemed clear to her, shining. She was still afraid he would fall, but just as sure that there was a way to fall, a way to land so you didn't get hurt, and Lucas would know what it was.

In a few minutes he was down, and without pausing to comment or change the arrangement with the inadequate shoelace, had moved the ladder and mounted it again. He did this three times, four. And Zoe remained dutifully at its foot, face upturned, holding him in place with her eyes.

At first she thought her ears had begun to ring from craning her neck so long. She covered and uncovered them—the noise was outside, she had never heard it start, and now it had grown in volume to something shrill and unpleasant. Beyond the cluster of townhouses to the south, a long cloud of black birds hung in the pale violet sky. They were their own fixed path, funneling in from the invisible distance, spreading to rest in the saved trees at the base of the back slope. The shrieking came from the trees; when you looked closely among the leaves, it was as if each branch was thick with black fruit. Zoe had never seen anything like it.

When Lucas came down to move the ladder for the last time, she said, "They don't like what we're doing." It did seem their shrieking was directed at the two of them. "Maybe they think you've caught one of their friends up there behind the screen," Zoe said, to be amusing, but Lucas said it was just what starlings did, gather for the night in communal roosts. They had probably been there every night since early spring, carrying on, making a mess. She had just never noticed it.

"I guess I'd rather sleep up under our eaves where I could get comfortable than have to balance all night on a tree branch," said Zoe.

"Starlings are the roaches of the bird world," Lucas called down meaningfully as he climbed one last time. A few minutes later he was finished, sliding the ladder back to carrying size with loud clanks.

"Could you see whether they've built any nests yet up there?" Zoe asked.

"Didn't look," Lucas said.

"Probably they haven't yet." She gazed skeptically at the streaks and blotches on the siding.

"Hard to say. It is that time of year. You know," Lucas went on, "being a pilot, there's no love lost between myself and birds. I could tell you a story or two about the accidents they've caused, hitting propellers, getting sucked into jet engines, gumming up the works. A couple months ago out of Kennedy a bunch of gulls sailed right up into one of my engines two minutes after takeoff."

"That's weird. What happened to them?"

"The point isn't what happened to them. The way a jet turbine works, it's got these finely balanced blades. A bird carcass gets in there and the engine chokes up." Zoe made a little gagging sound of revulsion. "Look," Lucas said, "that engine was ruined. I had to fly out over the Atlantic and dump 100,000 pounds of fuel before that jumbo was light enough to land minus an engine. That's good money down the drain, not to mention the danger. When you look at it that way, it's them or us."

Zoe could tell that she was being tested. She wasn't supposed to waste sympathy on the gulls, act squeamish at their fate. That was all right. She could see that a jumbo jet was more important than a handful of birds. Lucas was realistic. How much he knew about certain things—clear, definite knowledge. She searched her mind for something comparably definite to say, something to suggest she was in agreement with him on the issue of birds. But all that came to mind in that driving clamor of bird screams was a jumble of her mother's pronouncements, bitter and nebulous as a mouthful of smoke.

Lucas has showered in Zoe's tub and crashed on the sofa, which Phyllis fixed up for him. There was nothing for mother and daughter to do then but retire early to their own rooms upstairs and downstairs, leaving him the middle. Was it because Lucas was watching that Zoe hugged her mother before they parted, something she never did willingly, unless for a camera? And why her mother's body seemed so sadly appealing to her arms—her mother's odd scorched smell, so suddenly sweet—Zoe didn't know.

Zoe won't be able to eat tonight because she doesn't dare try to sneak by Lucas. That is all right. She would much rather know he is stationed there at the center of the house, a guardian of order. Stomach clenched around its treasured pain, she lies awake thinking about this man—his determination on the ladder, when he thanked her for her concern. She goes over and over these moments in her mind, savoring them. She imagines that she has emptied herself in order to be filled more purely and perfectly by his image. When she closes her eyes, he is all she sees, poised at the foot of the ladder, then at different stages of his ascent. *Give it a while*, he keeps telling her, and she knows that he does what he does because he cares.

He has climbed far above her now, and the ladder keeps lengthening. He is climbing far beyond the roof of the house, so far she can hardly see him. Her stomach begins to ache with worry. Then the dreadful noise begins—she knows even while it is dim and distant, it is dreadful. She tries to call a warning to Lucas, but he is too high to hear, and soon the noise is deafening, and the sky darkens with enemy starlings. Lucas is engulfed by a black cloud of them; Zoe screams as loud as she can, but nothing can be heard over that noise. Then as she looks up, something comes sliding down the ladder, something shapeless, shrunken lands at her feet. She wakes up in terror, the noise still in her ears.

She must calm herself. She is awake now. She is safe inside. There are no birds, they are all asleep in the trees, balancing somehow on their branches without falling.

But that noise still shrieks in her ears, and she must make sure. She turns on the light and stumbles to the window, pulls the drape aside, tries to peer beyond the glass, through the reflection of her own room, her own body, all arms and legs, wrapped in a large men's T-shirt. She is awake now, yet it seems the noise has filled her room, and she drags open the glass door to let it out. The night air flows in, chills her into alertness. The noise inside dissipates, met as it is by another sound from above, beyond the screen, softer, but as shrill and relentless, the sort of sound, like crickets, or running water, you could confuse with silence unless you had been warned it was there.

Ntozake Shange

From *Sassafrass, Cypress & Indigo*

"Indigo, I don't want to hear another word about it, do you understand me. I'm not setting the table with my Sunday china for fifteen dolls who got their period today!"

"But, Mama, I promised everybody we'd have a party because we were growing up and could be more like women. That's what Sister Mary Louise said. She said that we should feast and celebrate with our very best dresses and our very favorite foods."

"Sister Mary Louise needs to get herself married 'fore she's lost what little of her mind she's got left. I don't want you going round that simple woman's house. You take my good velvet from 'tween those dolls' legs. Go to the store and buy yourself some Kotex. Then you come back here and pack those creatures up. Put them in the attic. Bring yourself back here and I'm going to tell you the truth of what you should be worrying about now you sucha grown woman."

"Mama, I can't do that. I can't put them away. I'll have nobody to talk to. Nobody at all."

"Indigo, you're too big for this nonsense. Do like I say, now."

"Mama. What if I stopped carrying Miranda in the street with me, and left my other friends upstairs all the time, could I leave 'em out then, could I? Please Mama, I know they're dollies. I really do.

Sassafrass and Cypress kept all the things they made when they were little, didn't they?"

"That's a lie. Don't you have all their dolls? I can't believe a girl as big as you, wearing a training bra and stockings to school, can't think of nothing but make-believe. But if you promise me that you going to leave them in your room and stop asking me to sing to 'em, feed 'em, and talk with 'em, you can leave them out. Now go on to the store."

Indigo left her lesson book on the kitchen table, went to her mother tearing collards by the sink, and gave her a big hug. Her mother's apron always smelled like cinnamon and garlic no matter how many times it was washed. It smelled of times like this when her mother felt a surge in her bosom like her nipples were exploding with milk again, leaving her damp and sweet, but now it was Indigo's tears that softened her spirit.

"Indigo, you're my littlest baby, but you make it hard for me sometimes, you know that."

"Mama, I can make it easier today 'cause I awready know what it is you were gonna tell me when I came back from the store."

"You do, do you?"

"Yeah, you were going to tell me that since I became a woman, boys were gonna come round more often, 'cause they could follow the trail of stars that fall from between my legs after dark."

"What?"

"The stars that fall from 'tween my legs can only be seen by boys who are pure of mind and strong of body."

"Indigo, listen to me very seriously. This is Charleston, South Carolina. Stars don't fall from little colored girls' legs. Little boys don't come chasing after you for nothing good. White men roam these parts with evil in their blood, and every single thought they have about a colored woman is dangerous. You have gotta stop living this make-believe. Please, do that for your mother."

"Every time I tell you something, you tell me about white folks. 'White folks say you can't go here—white folks say you can't do this— you can't do that.' I didn't make up white folks, what they got to do with me? I ain't white. My dolls ain't white. I don't go round bothering white folks!"

"That's right, they come round bothering us, that's what I'm trying to tell you . . ."

"Well if they bothering you so much, you do something about 'em."

"Is that some sass coming' out your mouth?"

"No, M'am. It's just I don't understand why any ol' white person from outta nowhere would want to hurt us. That's all."

Indigo moved to her mother, with a seriousness about her that left the kitchen emptied of all its fullness and aroma.

"I love you so much, Mama. & you are a grown colored woman. Some white man could just come hurt you, any time he wants, too? Oh I could just kill 'em, if they hurt you, Mama. I would. I would just kill anybody who hurt you."

Holding her child as tight as she could, as close into herself as she could, the mother whispered as softly as she could, as lovingly as she could: "Well, then we'll both be careful & look after each. Won't we?"

Indigo sort of nodded her head, but all she remembered was that even her mother was scared of white folks, and that she still wrote out the word Kotex on a piece of torn paper wrapped up in a dollar bill to give to Mr. Lucas round to the pharmacy. This, though Indigo insisted Mr. Lucas must know what it is, 'cause he ordered it for his store so all the other colored women could have it when they needed it. After all, even her mother said, this bleeding comes without fail to every good girl once a month. Sometimes her mother made no sense at all, Indigo thought with great consternation. On the other hand, as a gesture of goodwill & in hopes that her littlest girl would heed her warnings, the mother allowed Indigo one more public jaunt with Miranda, who was, according to Indigo, fraught with grief that their outings were to be curtailed.

Weeping willows curled up from the earth, reaching over Indigo & Miranda on this their last walk in a long friendship, a simple, laughing friendship. Miranda thought the weeping willows were trying to hug them, to pull them up to the skies where whether you were real or not didn't matter. Indigo, in her most grown-up voice, said, "No, they want us to feel real special on this day, that's all." Miranda wasn't convinced, and neither was Indigo, who managed to take the longest walk to the drugstore that her family had ever known.

After following the willows' trellises till there were no more, Indigo reverently passed by Mrs. Yancey's, back round to Sister Mary Louise's, down to the wharf where she & Miranda waved to her father who was living in the sea with mermaids, & then 'cross to the railroad tracks looking for Uncle John. Indigo liked colored folks who worked with things that took 'em some place: colored folks on ships, trains, trolley, & horses. Yoki was a horse. Uncle John did go places, and after that night with Mrs. Yancey in the street, Indigo figured him mighty powerful.

In between two lone railroad cars was Uncle John's wagon. Sequestered from ill-wishers & the wind, there he was chatting away with the air, the cars, or Yoki. Sometimes men of Color disappear into the beauty of the light, especially toward day's end. It's like clouds take on color & get down on the ground & talk to you, or the stars jump in some black man's body & shine all over you. Uncle John was looking like that to Indigo's mind, just brushing away, leaving Yoki's coat glimmering like dusk.

"Good evening, Uncle John."

"Humph." Mr. Henderson turned round knowing full well who'd come calling, but not wanting to let on. "Oh. If it ain't my girl Indigo. & who's that ya got witcha?"

"This is Miranda. We're going to Mr. Lucas' to pick up something." Indigo was quite careful not to say what she was going to the drugstore for, 'cause her mother had said not to say anything to anybody.

"Indigo, Mr. Lucas' place way off from heah, don't ya think?"

"Well, Uncle John, that's some of it, but not all of it."

Laying down his brush, pulling a stool from the other side of a fire where he was cooking either a chicken or a pigeon, Uncle John motioned for Indigo to take a seat.

"Some of it, but t'aint all of it, ya say? Well, I would be guessin' the rest of it be a matter for discussion."

"Yes, Uncle John. I want you to tell me something. I'm asking you 'cause you been doin' what suits your own mind since I was born."

"No, long fo' that, chile."

"Well, anyway, I want to keep on talkin' with all my dolls. You know they my very best friends." Indigo was talking so fast now, Uncle John started walking in a circle around her so as to understand better. "& Mama wants to put 'em way 'cause now I am a woman & who will I talk to? I can't seem to get on with the chirren in the school I go ta. I don't like real folks near as much." Indigo had jumped off the stool with

Miranda in her arms, much like a woman daring someone to touch her child. Uncle John stood still for a minute, looking at the shadows of the rail cars on Yoki's back.

"Indigo, times catch up on everybody. Me & Yoki heah been catched up by trains & grocery stores. Now you bein' catched up by ya growin' up. That's what ya mama's tryin' to say to ya. Ya gotta try to be mo' in this world. I know, it don't suit me either."

Miranda was crying, nestled in Indigo's elbow. Uncle John mumbled to himself, & climbed in his wagon. Indigo stayed put. Folks said that sometimes, when Uncle John had said all he had to say, he got in his wagon & that was that. Other times folks said Uncle John would get in his wagon & come back out with something to keep your life moving along sweeter. So Indigo didn't move a muscle. Miranda prayed some good would come of all this. They still hadn't gone to Mr. Lucas'. Indigo could hear Uncle John humming to himself, fumbling in that wagon. He was looking for something for her so she could keep talkin' & not have to be with them real folks & all their evil complicated ways of doing. The last of the day's sun settled on Indigo's back, warmed the taut worry out of her limbs, & sat her back down on the stool, jabbering away to Miranda.

"See, you thought that I was gonna just go on & do what Mama said & never play witya no more or go explore & make believe. See, see, ya didn't have no faith. What's that Sister Mary Louise is all the time sayin'?"

"Oh ye of lil faith . . ." Miranda rejoined.

Uncle John didn't come out of his wagon first. A fiddle did. Uncle John was holding it, of course, but he poked the fiddle out, then one leg, his backside, and the other leg, his precious greying head, and the last arm with a bow in his grasp. Indigo & Miranda were suspicious.

"What we need a violin for?" Miranda sniggled.

"Hush, Miranda, Uncle John knows what he's doin'. Just wait a minute, will ya?"

Uncle John sure nuf had intentions to give this fiddle to Indigo. His face was beaming, arms wide open, with the fiddle & bow tracing the horizons, moving toward Indigo who was smiling with no reason why.

"Indigo, this heah is yo' new talkin' friend."

"A fiddle, Uncle John?" Indigo tried to hide her disappointment, but Miranda hit her in her stomach. "Uh, that's not what I need, Uncle John." She sat back on the stool like she'd lost her backbone. Uncle John was a bit taken back, but not swayed.

"Listen now, girl. I'ma tell ya some matters of the reality of the unreal. In times blacker than these," Uncle John waved the violin & the bow toward the deepening night, "when them slaves was ourselves & we couldn't talk free, or walk free, who ya think be doin' our talkin' for us?"

"White folks, of course," snapped Indigo.

Uncle John's face drew up on his bones like a small furious fire. His back shot up from his legs like a mahogany log.

"Whatchu say gal?? I caint believe ya tol' me some white folks was doin' our talkin'. Now, if ya want me to help ya, don't say nary another word to me till I'm tellin' ya I'm finished. Now, listen. Them whites what owned slaves took everythin' was ourselves & didn't even keep it fo' they own selves. Just threw it on away, ya heah. Took them drums what they could, but they couldn't take our feet. Took them languages what we speak. Took off wit our spirits & left us wit they Son. But the fiddle was the talkin' one. The fiddle be callin' our gods what left us/be givin' back some devilment & hope in our bodies worn down & lonely over these fields & kitchens. Why white folks so dumb, they was thinkin' that if we didn't have nothin' of our own, they could come controllin', meddlin', whippin' our sense on outta us. But the Colored smart, ya see. The Colored got some wits to em, you & me, we ain't the onliest ones be talkin' wit the unreal. What ya think music is, whatchu think the blues be, & them get happy church musics is about, but talkin' wit the unreal what's mo' real than most folks ever gonna know."

With that Uncle John placed the fiddle in the middle of his left arm & began to make some conversations with Miranda & Indigo. Yes, conversations. Talkin' to em. Movin' to an understandin' of other worlds. Puttin' the rhythm in a good sit down & visit. Bringin' the light out a good cry. Chasing the night back round yonder. Uncle John pulled that bow, he bounced that bow, let the bow flirt with those strings till both Miranda & Indigo were most talkin' in tongues. Like the slaves who were ourselves had so much to say, they all went on at once in the voices of the children: this child, Indigo.

When Indigo first tried to hold the fiddle under her neck like the children in the orchestra at school, Uncle John just chuckled, looked away. When she had it placed nearer her armpit & closer to her heart, with the bow tucked indelicately in her palm, he said, "Now talk to us, girl." Indigo hesitated, pulled the bow toward the A string, took a breath, & stopped. "I don't know how to play a violin, Uncle John."

"Yeah, ya do. Tell Miranda somethin' on that fiddle. 'Cause after today, ya won't be able to reach out to her like ya do now. Ya gonna haveta call her out, wit that fiddle."

Indigo looked at Miranda lying on the stool & then back at Uncle John whose eyes were all over her face, the fiddle, the bow. & in a moment like a fever, Indigo carried that bow cross those fiddle strings till Miranda knew how much her friend loved her, till the slaves who were ourselves made a chorus round the fire, till Indigo was satisfied she wasn't silenced. She had many tongues, many spirits who loved her, real & unreal.

The South in her.

It was already so late Mr. Lucas had started to lock up his shop. Only the lights in the very back were still on. Indigo held onto her violin with its musty case religiously, & she beat on the door of the pharmacy like somebody possessed. "Please open up, Mr. Lucas. It's a emergency," she shouted. Mr. Lucas, portly & honey brown, peered out the door thru the lettering: Lucas' Pharmacy, Oldest Negro Drugstore in Charleston, S.C. Between the "S" & the "C" there was Indigo's face, churning & shouting. Mr. Lucas opened up remarking, "An emergency is somebody dyin' or a woman who needs some Kotex." Indigo was stunned. "Hi, Mr. Lucas, how'd you know that?"

"Oh, I been in this business a long time, Indigo. Tell your mother she almost missed me this time."

"Oh, it's not for Mama, it's for me." All of a sudden Indigo blushed & shrank. She'd gone & done what her mother had asked her please not to do. Mr. Lucas took a step toward Indigo, like he was looking for the woman in her. He'd seen younger girls than Indigo who were busy having babies. He'd even seen girls more comely in a grown-woman manner than she who didn't bleed at all. But here was this girl with this child body & woman in her all at once. It was difficult for Mr. Lucas to just go & get the Kotex. He wanted to keep looking at this girl, this woman. He wanted to know what she felt like.

Indigo heard somebody talking to her. She saw Mr. Lucas coming toward her & somebody talking to her. Telling her to get the Kotex &

get home quick. Get the Kotex & get home quick. Indigo ran to the back of the store, grabbed the blue box, stuffed it under her arm with Miranda & whipped thru the aisles with Mr. Lucas behind her, lumbering, quiet. The fiddle was knocking all kinds of personal hygiene products off shelves: toothpaste, deodorant, shaving cream. Indigo almost dropped it, but she held tighter, moved faster, heard somebody telling her to get home quick. She got to the doors, started to look back & didn't. She just opened the door as best she could without letting go of anything & ran out.

Mr. Lucas stood in the back of his pharmacy, looking at his S.C. Certification, his diploma from Atlanta University. He knew he might be in some trouble. Didn't know what had got hold to him. Every once in a while, he saw a woman with something he wanted. Something she shouldn't have. He didn't know what it was, an irreverence, an insolence, like the bitch thought she owned the moon.

"Yeah, that's right." Mr. Lucas relaxed. "The whole town knows that child's crazed. If she says a thing, won't a soul put no store in it."

The South in her.

Ridin' the
Moon in Texas

Houston Rodeo & Livestock Show ain't never seen the same since we come riding in from Arcola. All colored and correct. Long-sleeved shirts, cowboy hats, chaps, spurs, covered wagons, and a place all our own in Memorial Park. Ain't never seen that many niggahs in Memorial Park no way, least not at 4:30 in the morning. Perking coffee over open fires and warming each other with bourbon and one rodeo yarn after another. Ain't nothing white folks can do bout it, even Sam Houston enlisted this black fella could talk five Indian languages—five and English, of course. Even Sam Houston had enough sense to ask this niggah to go talk some sense to them Cherokees, so's they wouldn't fight gainst Texas independence. Well, we independent now and riding proud right down Hwy. 59 to Texas Avenue. Don't understand why that woman didn't buy those boys some hats. She knows cain't no man be in a trailride or a rodeo without a hat. Shame, too. They came all the way from Abilene to sit by the wayside with them other folks. Just looking. And I'll say one thing. That flock of niggahs on them gorgeous horses and them wagons, now that was something to look at! Must be why ain't none of us forget it. The trailride and all. And the rodeos. The black ones, of course, white folks don't quite have the hang of it. I mean, how you sposed to look, your image, on your horse, It takes a colored point of view.

"Twanda, whatcha gone do tonight? Louisiana Red is up for everything from bronc-busting to steel-dogging!"

"Oh go on gal, you know I cain't do nothing but barrel racing. Sides, I've got some business out yonder."

"Whatchu mean, you got some business out yonder? You ain't plannin' on messin' with me or them hard-head cowboys come to laugh at us tonight. You know this is our night, the All-Women's Rodeo, Navasota, Texas, honey. We the stars this evening, girl, even if you do gotta itch in your twat—them races come first—you got some business out yonder—huh!—you better check Dallas—you really gonna let that Jamaican chick use your horse for calf-roping?"

"Her horse is sick. She's an allright broad. You know she was champion two years in a row."

"But not with your horse."

"You know you can be one petty bitch when you wanna."

"I spose that's why you gonna investigate your business out yonder?"

"Listen, honey, I'ma see about Dallas. He misses me if I'm gone more than a hour and before a race he just gets beside himself and I gotta sweet talk him and snuggle up to him, specially fore I put that bridle thru his mouth—he don't like that thing at all—-I sure do like them Oak Ridge Boys. Listen, can't ya hear it?"

"Hell, no. Why don't cha just ride bare back."

"I might—"

"Sure."

"No, I might saunter thru the night bare back on Dallas; naked as a jay bird."

"Oh yeah, where?"

"Out yonder, I told ya."

"Girl, you know you don't make no sense sometimes. Did you pay up for the bronc-busting and barrel racing?"

"Course I did. Cost me seventy dollars. That's why I gotta get Dallas feeling high and sweet. We gotta win alla that money back and then some."

"You signed up for the breakaway?"

"Hell, no. That ain't no rodeo. That's some real bullshit. Can you rope a runaway calf?"

"Some folks cain't."

"Well, that ain't shit to me. Rope the damn thing and tie it in eight seconds. That I can understand. Breakaways just some other way for the 'pro-mo-tors' to make some more dough."

"So what? There's money in it."

"And a lotta fools, too."

"Go on now. See bout Dallas. I'ma get me a beer and some barbecue. Thank God, they finally playing Charlie Pride. I just love how that man can sing. Love me some Charlie Pride."

The night was fresh, more like morning should be. The grass and brush beyond the rodeo arena were moist and seductive, begging to be touched or lain on. The moon sat up in the sky like a hussy in red with her legs wide open. So what if all the women riders from Muskogee to Lubbock, Marshall to Lafayette, showed for the All-Women's Rodeo? Just last year, Susie Louise won bronc-busting and she was four months pregnant. Her momma won calf-roping and her daughter ran away with the steel-dogging. Shit. What a night that was. Take a look at those men come to look at us. I can't believe Lee Andrew had the nerve to tell me he came out here cuz he likes to see the expression on my face: see me change from pretty to ugly. Talk about nerve. I'ma bring me one of my pretty cowboys right on back here. It's so quiet. Most like there wasn't no rodeo going on. Maybe I'll ride Dallas by that rhiney boy with those dogging arms, the one in the black and red satin shirt with white fringe and red suede chaps dangling silver coins. He's the one whispered "I'm a black man who wants to ride off on a filly." Yeah, mister. I got something for your ass. God, I wonder how James is doing? I forgot to call the hospital once the ambulance carried him off. That bull stamped all over his ass and he ain't but so big. Big as a minute actually. Not much bigger than a minute. Jesus. That gore was more than I could handle. And that fool Joe-Man had the gall to say I didn't have no heart cuz I was paying up for calf-roping instead of seeing to James. Shit. James finished his event. How was I gonna calf-rope and see to James. Humph. that's awright, Dallas. We're just warming up, that's all. Getting a feel for the wind and the ground round here. Come on, I'ma kick it up! See if we can get neath these tree limbs and over that stream without hurtin' ourselves. Watchu say, baby? That's a boy. Do like momma say and she'll give you a bright shiny apple. That's a boy. Let's get it. Go for it. There ain't nothing out here but prairie and me and you and the wind. So that makes it the moon, the wind and a little satisfaction. Those folks crazy now, they playing Otis Redding. Come on, now. Show momma whatcha can do. She needs some satisfaction too. Right, baby? Do it for momma.

"Breakaway:
"Nancy Bourdan—Houston—Score 57.
"Sally Johnson—Midnight, Mississippi—Score 55.
"Molly Hanks—Conroe, Texas—Score 52."

"No, man, just give me a beer from that cooler in your truck. I ain't out here to compete tonight. How can I do that? This is All-Women's Rodeo—ain't it? Well, ain't it?"

"Yeah, that why I'm out here, cain't really tell if a woman's a woman til you see how she could ride a horse."

"You right bout that, bro!"

"Gimme that beer and a joint."

"I'ma get some more barbecue but I'ma say one thing. Just one thing. The ladies is the horses. If you get my meaning. But the way my lady friend ride is fantastic. All that tension and excitement from the Diamond L all the way out here to Navasota to Madisonville. Now they got some great rodeo in Madisonville, but you know I got three daughters and I'ma black man and I'd rather have my girls here than anywhere else."

"Oh, man, go and get the barbecue."

"Whatever you say, Bubba. Watch the horses all right. These gals ain't got no more scruples than that white bitch, whatcha call it, Belle Starr?"

"Yeah, man. I got it covered. Just get the beer, man, and let me know if you see that sassy gal what races barrels."

"There's Bo-Peep with those damned armadillos in a pond of draft beer. When these guys gonna learn armadillos get drunk. They chasing beer. They ain't racing. That's all right, Dallas. We'll just ignore that. Okay, baby."

"Hey, Twanda."

"Huh?"

"Ain't that what they call you, Twanda?"

"Some do, some don't. What it to you?"

"That's a nice-looking animal you got there."
"I know that. You got a nice-looking face too."
"It's just a cowboy's face."
"I know that. Come on, Dallas."
"Hey, don't ride off like that."
"Whatcha think I'm on a horse for, to stay still somewhere? Let's go, Dallas."

"All right, everybody clear the arena—it's time for the Cotton-eyed Joe."

"Well, cain't you dance, gal?"
"Whatchu mean? Of course I can!"
"Twan, let's me and you gone and do the Cotton-eyed Joe."
"Shit yeah. If you can keep up with me."
"Watch me, baby. Careful how you do that horse and you'll see what all I could do. What all I could do for you, baby."
"Sure, hot stuff."

"Calf-Roping:
"Agnes Moralez—San Antonio, Texas—Score 7.6.
"Sally Johnson—Midnight, Mississippi—Score 8.1.
"Louisiana Red—Lafayette, Louisiana—Score 7.2"

I cain't exactly explain how it happened, but out there somewhere how the prairie snapped up the last bits of night. Bubba and Twanda raced free as sepia roses on their horses' bare back. Holding the manes and each other the way you'd have to when you're dealing with a steer and you come out grinning and then be screaming. They fell out near a smooth mossy cloud neath a cypress tree. "Guantanamera" blasting from the arena.
Guantanamera, Gaujiro, Guantanamera.

Twanda was murmuring, "I'm in the rodeo cuz my momma was and my first night out I won ninety dollars just for running round barrels. You cain't beat that, for running round barrels." Bubba somehow quieted her. He was unsettled by her drive. She had to win. She was one with her horse. She had no sense of anything sides speed and her animal, but that was when she was racing. She said. She liked he was a champion. She said, "Look a heah, I'm a champion too," when she wrapped that huge silver buckle round her slight waist. The hairs from her thighs creeping like ferns from her navel. Women and horses. Black women and horses. An all-women's rodeo. What next? Bubba slapped his thigh and reached for that joint and Bud.

Twanda pulled him to her and let him play with a piece of grass she slipped tween his lips. Then she lay back on his shoulder. Let the sky celebrate her victory: Twanda Rochelle Johnson—Barrel-racing— 17.5—First Place—$532.

She smiled, contented; remembered that business she'd had out yonder. Out on the prairie where black folks have always felt at home. She pulled the straw outta Bubba's mouth. He didn't know what was happening til she sang a cowgirl's song / sweet & tough / soft and rough:

let me be a chorus of a thousand / tongues
and your lips dance on a new moon / while
Daddy Cool imagines synchopated
niggahfied erotica on Griggs Road

We'll have skimmed the cream off the milky way / made a permanent ellipse by the yet uncharted tail of Halley's Comet / these tongues and lips make a time step of Bojangles in fast forward / merely slow motion in a sultry dusk / so natural / is the tone of your chest under the gaze of the wild stallions by the waterfalls, enveloped by scarlet blossoms like a woman's heart / your sweat seeps into my mouth / we sleep / deep / deep / like in Texas."

"Hey, ain't that the Judds—ain't that something."

"We gone sleep / deep / deep like in Texas."

Opal Moore

A Pilgrim Notebook

Part I: The Odyssey

The man. he
sped bold across the landscape
broke barriers of time   space
He was   simultaneous
He was yesterday   today   tomorrow . . .
—*The Pilgrim Diary* (1)

Country music is good company if you're alone, if it's a quarter to dawn, if it's all you can get in the middle of Missouri, middle of nowhere. The words of an old song ran through Ben's head, *luv the one ya with . . . ya got-ta . . .* Ben leaned into fifth gear *luv the one ya with* as he watched the changing sky, as he only half watched the winding road, as he squealed into a sudden curve, as the sky bloomed pink.

He wanted Jazz. A little Miles. Trumpet mellow into morning. Or saxophone—the moaning sax . . . oh yes. How-ever, in the absence of Jazz, he had been known to settle for The Chi-Lites, The Delphonics. The Moments talkin about: I found Luv on a 2-way street . . . Wanted Jazz. Motown would do. But if you're alone on the road at a quarter to morning in the absence of Jazz and with no possi*bili*ty of soul, country music can grow on you. Ben tapped a finger to the rhythm. The sky was a bruised pink.

He sped out of another curve, foot heavy on the accelerator. The little sports car's tail end wagged.

"Like a frisky woman itchin' to get loose," the rental guy had said, "she's just a little dangerous if you don't keep her in a firm hand," They had both laughed.

Her name was *Arroyo II*. Just on the market. She was cute but no BMW. She was flashy. She was candy-red outside with a creme interior. Ben had smiled as he slipped into the creme.

Luv on a 2-way street . . . Ben stretched out, in his mind, in *Arroyo II*, his She-machine. Inside, he was borderless, infinite. Anything was possible in this car, in this picture postcard landscape complete with pretty cows on endless fields and quaintly crumbling haybarns. And the space—wide fresh-air country sky—was a welcome relief from the elbow-to-elbow anonymity, crush and secrecy of the city. He raced boldly across his picture of a landscape. He was complete. He felt like yesterday, today *and* tomorrow. *you are ev'rything, and ev'rything is you, ooh ooh ooh* . . . Ben smiled a smile like horizon. The chilly half-circle of sun dangled before him like a gold coin slipped in a pocket.

Ben twisted the rearview to an odd angle to check the knot of his tie. Perfect, as expected. Everything was perfect (except for the music, of course). But even that was ok. Today he could love what he didn't love: a backwoods view, a country tune. Even Saundra's bad mouth, the way she always managed to say what he didn't need to hear when he least needed to hear it. Like this morning, could have been a stellar beginning. Like a saxophone solo: her warm sighs, her tapering back-side sliding across new linen, his lyrics. But no. She has to roll over and put her mouth on this trip—in that voice, like satin ripping:

"You drivin 400 miles to witness a football pat on the ass? You could watch that on TV all day *and* save gas." Saundra could be depended upon *not* to understand. Sometimes the girl was ok. She was certainly the make and model he preferred in women: recent year, low wind resistance, . . . but then her mouth would open and reveal such *serious* flaws in workmanship. What he was doing today was not play. It was business—it was, it was like an odyssey.

Ben touched his tie, readjusted his rearview to watch his progress, watch the road lay down behind him in submission. Everything was "go"—smooth road newly laid leading from here to . . . well, to wherever he chose to go. Who could say what the future held? Except for Saundra, who knew?

Green signs, white and blue signs leaped up to tally his progress, point the way, take him past all the wrong exits to the right ones. Ben just had this *feeling* that this ceremony for his friend Billy was a signpost of the 90's, that the day would mark the decade clear as any of these man-made signs posted along the roadside.

Ben flipped the station dial (a little country goes a long way). He listened to news reports—hog futures and weather, Bushwhacking and the oil war, evangelists begging, car salesmen pitching. He twisted the dial, barely listening, hearing only the rumble of his thoughts:

"As of today," he'd announced to Saundra, "Billy Mills, I mean, William Randolph Mills, is no longer just a man. He's a landmark. A signpost in the pageant of history."

"He's unemployed," said Saundra. "What kind of signpost is that?"

"This is history in the making," said Ben.

"Um," she'd said and watched him prepare.

Ben had decided his closet was too drab. He'd bought everything from the skin out, brand new. At Fields, he'd gone through suits, ties, shoes, everything. He'd inquired about a manicure, shampoo and haircut at a salon. And finally, he'd decided to rent the car. His old 1970 Chrysler was steady—a classic really—but it just wouldn't do for the occasion. It just did not make *quite* the right . . . statement. He needed a chariot—the *Arroyo II*. Throughout his preparations, Saundra's eyes had worn an expression of bored ridicule.

"It's not like it's the *real* Hall of Fame," she said. "It's just some small town, small college homecoming-halftime filler stuff."

Women. They simply did not understand men—a man's style is to play the game all the way through to the end. Even if the stakes seem small. Even if it looks like you can't win. Even if it takes a lifetime to tally the score. Even if nobody but you ever knows the game has been played. The college's Hall of Fame might seem like nothing, but no black player had ever been named. Billy had played like a champion on an unknown team, and had gotten nothing for it. Couldn't she *see* that no victory was insignificant? This was one more capitulation, a psychological Berlin Wall falling, quietly, with no fanfare, but it had been a long time falling and so it was still victory. Still sweet. A small victory for 1959 was better than none. Fifty-nine had been a bruiser. Nobody talked about '59. Everybody talked about THE SIXTIES. But they couldn't have had a 60's without 1959. In 1959, he and Billy and a few other brothers had been imported to this small nowhere town for purposes of football and not a damn thing else. Townies'd never seen black folks before—not in the flesh. He remembered the pale stares of wide-eyed girls, hard and vulnerable—and dangerous, to a handful of black men mailordered to the middle of nowhere. In 1959 he and Billy had made a vanguard—a front line. *They* had stood pissing into the headwind; *they* had faced the backsplash. *They* had survived. And sometimes a ceremony 31 years late was all you got. He'd explained all this to Saundra, with her mouth turned down, looking at him out of the tops of her eyes.

To Saundra, born in the year of The King's death, 1959 was pre-history—biblical at best. Even the people who'd been there were trying to forget. Billy himself had said of the nomination, "Man, it's nothing. It's no big deal." Ben had had to explain to him the importance of it—that the record of his excellence, of his perseverance, his *games*manship, his courage when the chips were down—*that*, not football, was his contribution. It was a life lesson that he, Ben, personally would *never* abandon. Billy had shook his head. 'Man,' he said, 'you always *been* deep.'

Ben smiled to himself.

> he sped bold
> across the landscape
> a warrior
> black and determined
> veteran of Time
> fearless
> on his way to be overcome.
>
> —*The Pilgrim Diary* (27)

Ben flicked at a speck of lint on his trouser leg. Tested the razor crease in the subtle tweed. Caressed the perfectly tied silk blend burgundy tie. He leaned over to glimpse himself in the mirror. He was the same now as then. No. He was better. Definitely better. He'd kept his football weight. His hair. Most often, he could go without his glasses, even though women told him his glasses made him look more distinguished. He was among the top salesmen in his region. And, he was wiser. His motto: put the past in the past. He told every young black executive he met, past is passed. Today is today.

Ben rearranged himself in his cockpit. He was streamlined for forward motion. Today was the blossoming of a seed planted long ago and forgotten. *Well, but I mean, is this little Hall of Fame lollipop parade likely to turn into some sort of job? Cause, I mean, it's a job the man needs—not another ball game plaque. Is it any money in it?* Saundra. Famous last words. Ben twisted the radio dial as if her voice were a stray telecast. He cracked the window an inch. The cold blade of morning air was a relief. Brisk country morning air can clear a man's head of debris. The road curved sharp and sudden.

It was not easy living with a woman who did not understand reality. Billy was not just some guy out of a job. He was a symbol. Ben put the accelerator to the floor, cocked his jaw. The little car's tail end lashed decidedly.

Except for Saundra, who knew? Someday Billy's story might be told. A transcendent tale, a modern *Iliad* and *Odyssey*. New heroes and magical conquests. Like the ancient tales of the griots, the entire history of a man and his kind read from the inward eye. Too bad how the great epics were now interred in books, how the stories no longer resided in the hearts of men. Ben straightened his tie. Twisted the radio dial. Nothing but static and country music. *What if you drive all the way down to that god-forsaken place and nobody else shows up? I mean, if the man is out of work, he can't really afford to waste the time. Can't afford to waste the gas!* Like the static in the radio, Saundra's voice could not be fine-tuned out of his head.

> a pilgrim soul
> in a foreign landscape.
> it is an epic tale
> of the overcome.
>
> —*The Pilgrim Diary* (495)

Doggedly, Ben tried every frequency along the radio dial. A man could only stand so much of this backwoods banjo shit. He settled for news finally. A woman newscaster, her voice smooth and practiced, fought through the static:

"Early last evening a county woman was forced into the back seat of her own car where she was repeatedly assaulted."

"Jesus!" said Ben, his eyes scanning the crisp clean panorama of country. What a horrible thing. A violation really. Out here. Didn't fit. He winced a little as he imagined a helpless woman stumbling across the hard cold ground. . . . "The woman's assailant was unknown to her," the newsvoice said. Ben's finger hovered at the dial.

"The assailant was described (don't let him be black) as a black man . . . (What else?) . . . 5'11", 160 pounds, wearing dirty jeans and a dirty green shirt. He was last seen walking along the highway."

The "assailant" was also a fool.

"The woman managed to drive her own car to a nearby farmhouse where she received assistance. Police were summoned . . ." The newscast wavered and fluttered. Ben leaned into a curve. The broadcast ceased abruptly in a rage of static. The newslady voice succumbed with a struggle.

Ben breathed out slowly. "Damn," he said.

The sky ahead seemed to be darkening. The sun, so promising earlier, seemed to fade as it climbed higher into the sky.

They're after you man

Ben checked his watch. Longines. Second anniversary—third wife. Shifting out of a curve, he put a heavy foot on the accelerator. She probably picked him up. A hitchhiker. When would these white girls learn anything? Not that he didn't feel bad for the girl. . . . *they're after you man, after you for sure.*

He shut the window—the invigorating country air had become numbing. The landscape slid by grey and threatening. Ben loosened his tie a bit, checked the rearview mirror frequently. He wondered if he could make it to the auditorium by noon.

glancing over one shoulder, he ran.
hands palms forward
like a blind man's hands
touching the future first
before he stumbles in.
feet in a furrow, plowed out, he
ran. agonizing forward like a dream,
aching slow awkward in the ditch
green Arrow shirt
plastered in cold sweat.

—*The Pilgrim Diary* (999)

Rough farmland stretched infinite on either side of a strip of highway. Somewhere out there was The Assailant, identified Black. In the silence of no radio, Ben entertained the thought of him, The Assailant, on foot. The report had to be wrong. Couldn't have been a Black man. On no. Black man would've put her ass out, made *her* walk to the nearby farmhouse (where she received assistance . . .) while he put a few strategic miles between him and the jailhouse. The car, being identifiable, presented its own problems of course. But he could have eventually ditched the car and hopped a bus or train. Park a car in a mall parking lot and it's not likely to be found for a month. Of course that would add a charge of grand theft auto to the assault, but what did it matter if you did not intend to get caught? Then again, there were probably no reputable malls in Hicksville. Still there were fields. Miles and miles of unsupervised space. Was it possible for a man to walk a country unnoticed?

A large dark bird flapped into view interrupting the smooth yellow centerline of Ben's thoughts. The bird stood still, seemed to watch him approach in his speeding rent-a-sports-car. The bird watched with only a casual interest. Or was it arrogance? Ben put the nose of the racing car right down the dividing line—CHICKEN! he yelled. The bird flapped leisurely to the shoulder, cocked one wing and stared. Ben watched the bird diminish to a black speck in the quick distance of the rearview mirror, but oddly, he felt himself shrinking in the bird's cold black eye.

Ben's eyes lingered on the makeshift lean-tos and rotting sheds that sprinkled the passing fields. He noted how the harvested cornstalks were shaved to cruel spikes making his toes curl involuntarily inside their soft Italian leather casings. He discovered a new tightness in the pit of his stomach. It reminded him of the day before yesterday. The ink could not have been dry on her contract before the new "boss" had come in announcing, like it didn't make a difference, that "they" should not expect any bonus this year.

"The profit margin just doesn't warrant it," she'd said.

she

Not that he had anything against women. But who would have believed that one would be put over his division? Ben tapped a steady rhythm on the steering wheel.

She didn't dress like an executive. Briefcase full of nothing but Kleenex, probably. Full of lip gloss, electric haircurler, fingernail polish to dot the runs in her pantyhose probably. Who would have thought . . .? Ben shook his head. Thumped the steering wheel sharply. The little car swerved dangerously into the opposite lane. It didn't matter. He had her in a firm hand. And he was alone in this middle of nowhere—no Jazz, no soul, no sound. It was the same sound he'd felt in that room full of salesmen when she looked dead at Ben and said, "You men had better get off your laurels, they're spreading." She'd looked dead in *his* face when she said no bonuses as if he were responsible somehow. And everyone's eyes had followed hers, looking at him. It was then that he had heard his aloneness. It was as if they expected him to provide an explanation, or apologize. The down profit margin wasn't *his* fault. He was the best in his division. His numbers were at the top, up there with the best in the region. Maybe she didn't know that? Her eyes had singled him out. It was not paranoia. He had not imagined that the very next day his best account—he'd spit blood to build that account—had been taken from him—handed over like an ice cream come to their "boy," the division runt. She *had* known. "We need *team* players," she'd said to Ben. "Sometimes you've got to *pass* the ball to win the game."

Ben swallowed. The insides of his mouth stuck like gummy paper. Team players! He was a man, alone—The Assailant, scaling a wall one narrow foothold at a time. He could hear "them" holding their breath, waiting for a misstep. What damn laurels?

she

Didn't even dress like an executive.

Road signs flashed past overhead but Ben did not need signs. He had seen his future murdered in their eyes, in the eyes of the men who would like to see him eat filthy humble pie.

she's after you hotshot

He didn't need signs. He'd seen the writing on the wall. He was no fool. He'd smiled in her face, invited her to lunch and put in for a transfer all in the same day.

Team play. That was the line they bought your soul with. The line they used on Billy. Billy Mills could've dusted them all. He'd been *star* material. He could've broken every record in the book that year. But he went for that "team player" bullshit. Could've been NFL, but he'd nodded and grinned while they nailed him to the bench, "team player" plastered across his chest. The hell with the team. Ben would play "the game," but by a winner's rules. He was no Billy Mills. Billy was a good guy, but he hadn't used his head. He'd gambled his future against a cheap trophy and a few grins. Life was no sport. A smart man knew when to concede defeat. Cut and run. What is honor when your pockets are picked clean?

The sun pulled clear of the treeline just to disappear behind a cloud. Ben glanced in his rearview. The black bird was, of course, long gone. Its cold indifferent stare remained.

No FM, no tape deck, no sounds. That was the trouble with these rental deals. You paid through the nose for a set of fancy bare bones— AM, four wheels and a gas tank. The Chrysler was old, but at least it had insides. It had character. It had a tape deck. Why had he left it behind? He couldn't remember. Ben felt stripped as he raced breakneck through a bass-ackwards state full of black tar, one long yellow line, and dead cornfields everywhere. . . .

Ben bitched. Flipped the radio on for another try but nothing had changed and so he turned it off again. Silence. Barren fields. Blunt, cruel. Infinite visibility. No alleyways to duck down, no supermarkets to dodge through and out the back way, no holes to disappear into. He thought of the first and last time he'd driven through the South, Mississippi that is. Dense foliage buttressing broad stretches of bald land. The Beautiful, laced with a horrible feeling of dread. The passing trees, close and deep. They had seemed to threaten him with their green, secretive silence. And the dust—the dust really was red. It had occurred to him then that one step, one misstep, would be enough to cast him backwards into a history he did not care to relive. *the past is passed*. The past is never past. The past was like one of those big redwoods. You cut off the top and leave what you can't get at. Even safe inside his car, safe inside his era, he'd felt as if he were running—only steps ahead of some ancestor African—disoriented, afraid, rough feet clouded in red dust, running in circles. . . . He'd sworn that he would never return to Mississippi. But in the end, it didn't matter. The world was Mississippi. Ben thought of the bird and felt unlucky.

hauling ass
pedal to the metal
plan in his pocket
for to overcome.
he will round the bend
see too late
too late
the flaw in the picture
pit in the peach
see the man run
crash into fate.

—*The Pilgrim Diary* (9,999,999)

The sporty little car was surrounded by implacable fields of harvested crop squeezing in on the black two-lane stitch. The fancy red toy shot forward escaping out of the pinch. Every blind curve tugged at Ben's stomach, every billboard was concealment, every car stalled on the side of the road, an ambush.

The sky was darkening at the edges, something gathering ahead. Maybe rain. Ben tugged at his tie, fatigued. A man with a fundamental resemblance to himself was being sought in America. In the country. In the neighborhood. There was something mercurial about the air, heavy and falling to the bottom, weighing at the bottom of this bland rural picture, like a tickertape disaster bulletin rolling silently at the foot of a TV screen. *The Assailant was described as . . .*

It was instinct that eased Ben's foot from the accelerator slowing the sleek car to well below the limit. He swallowed the bitter juice that kept squeezing into his mouth. Billboards hung against the grey sky. STUCKY'S, next exit. Bright markers popped red and white and green against the pallid sky: JOHN'S PIT STOP 2 mi. Bright-faced, pink-faced people, too happy to eat, smiled all the way to their back teeth because of MARY ANNE'S HOME COOKED FOOD, 4 mi. The road was exhausting.

He ought to stop for a breather. A quick bite, some bad coffee, a little grim-faced sullen-faced waitressing, smudgy fingerprints on the john door might cheer him up. MARY ANNE'S—that was the ticket. A short detour. A quick bite.

MARY ANNE'S. Fly-specked, dust-dark window glass. Shantytown eatery. A hand-lettered sign propped in the window declared the establishment OPEN FOR BUSINESS. But it was not OPEN. Why not? It just wasn't.

OPEN. The word seemed to hang there like a smirk because, on the back side of every OPEN there is always the hidden CLOSED. Ben knew that it did not really matter which side of the sign was showing, only what was hidden made any difference.

The wind was a high whine. Dead leaves clung to their tree limbs as if winter had not already claimed them, rattling, vibrating like fingers on open hands. Thousands of hands. He looked at the door of Mary Anne's, locked and bolted, looking like it had never been open, never would open; looked at the OPEN sign so misleading. He wanted to take the door full throttle, *make* it OPEN, feel it opening, feel the scream of glass breaking. The reined power of the car's idling engine surged up through Ben's legs like an electrical current, quick, like zero to sixty in six; perilous, like a fast car leaping, fishtailing on loose rock, out of control, snatching a slender reflector pole, bending dragging it to the ground before skidding to a shuddering stop. *Arroyo II*, and Ben, hung on the downside of a ditch.

Ben flung himself out of the car and crawled, scrambled up the embankment, his thin shoes snagging and turning in the hard, pitted ground. Water came, cold, into his eyes as he stood, toes at the line where asphalt crumbled into country dust, stood looking back in the direction from which he had come, expecting nothing, anything. After a moment, he knelt, rubbed the chalk from his shoes, wondering how far he could run in them.

he
be hauling ass
awkward in them ditches
singin "in a *coooold* sweat"
by John Brown
or H. Rap
or James of the same name.

I seent 'im yesterday
say he be 'round today,
'less he don't get here
til tomorrow. . .

—*The Pilgrim Diary* (Prologue)

A Happy Story

"What's this story about?" Everett leans over my shoulder. He really wants to ask "when will dinner be ready?" But he will not have it spread about that he is a traditionalist.

"It's about a woman," I say as he inspects the contents of pots with an air of disapproval. I continue. "Intelligent. Attractive. Educated. A career is possible if she plays her cards right." Everett has thrown open the refrigerator door, is standing, feet apart, fists on hips, as if silently demanding that certain foods present themselves for his until-dinner-gets-ready snacking. I continue. "But one morning she wakes up to realize that despite her efforts, she is living the same life her mother led. She feels desperate at this idea—"

Everett is desperately opening up foil wrappers. Finds one cold pork chop.

"—and in that moment, she begins to plan her own suicide."

"Why?" mumbles Everett around a mouthful of pork chop. "I thought she was so intelligent."

"Maybe she's intelligent enough—" I say to his back as he returns to his armchair enclave, "—intelligent enough to wonder if surviving is worth the trouble."

Everett rattles his newspaper. The TV drones. I sweep up crumbs from the table and deposit the abandoned pork chop foil wrapper in the trash can. Slowly I recover my thoughts, make a few scribbles on my yellow pad.

"Why don't you ever write a *happy* story?" Everett says, moments later, newspaper crumpling in his lap. I pretend I don't hear him, wish that I hadn't.

"Angel? Didja hear me? Why can't you write a *happy* story for a change?" I don't even look up.

"You know one?" I say. "Tell me a happy story and I'll use it," I say. When I do look up, his eyes are waiting. We look at each other. I smile, feeling some triumph. "Tell me," I say, "and I'll write it."

Everett is a determined optimist; I call it self-delusion. I am a realist; he calls it "bad disposition." I say that he pretties up life with pretense. He says that I don't consider the cloud's silver lining. I say you're liable to be struck by lightning standing in a thunderstorm looking for a silver lining. He says I live for bad news. "Tell me a happy story," I persist. "I can't wait to write it."

His tongue is working inside of one cheek; maybe he's thinking . . . or maybe he's just after a sliver of pork chop caught between his teeth. He seems to regard me with infinite patience and pity. But now, his unflagging optimism comes to rescue his face from furrows of doubt. I see firm determination light his eyes. He will, now as ever, rescue me from myself. I am caught off guard by my own laughter; it comes snorting unladylike from my nose.

"Come on," I say, "Lay this fairy tale on me."

It has to be a fairy tale. All stories with nice happy endings are—either that, or gothic romance. But I prefer fairy tales. At least they don't pretend to be in any way real—just morality tales cloaked in an entertainment. Snow White bites the poison apple but does not die—she lives happily ever after (and the bad queen dies a horrible death). An ancient wish for moral justice, but certainly no reflection of life, where victims don't sleep but die, and bad queens suffer fame and millions made on the Vegas circuit.

The problem with fairy tales is that they end just where true stories begin. What if the story of Snow White continued beyond the grand wedding, and her prince carried her to a land called Newark, to a tenement castle subdivided for multiple family dwelling? And what if his princely income waned, and his ardor, as her body sagged with childbearing, and the mirror chanted a different tune, and Prince Charming—whipping up his trusty steed—stumbled across a younger damsel in distress upon the urban glade? And the matronly Snow White became the poison-toting neglected wife. . . .

It would not take much to convince me that happiness *is* the darker side of life: suburban housewife pushing husband and kiddies off to work and day care just to crawl back into illicit daydreaming; the unrequited lover tasting the most profound ecstasy at the lip of the poison cup. . . . I try to return to my *own* thoughts, abandon this tired academic problem of art vs. life. But Everett has been pondering.

"You could write a story about my mother," he says.

"Your mother's story is not happy," I say.

"My mother is a saint," he says.

"Saints do not happy stories make. Saints are tragic," I point out. "In order to even qualify for sainthood, one must suffer inordinately and die pathetically for the purpose of inspiring pity, guilt, and other behavior inhibiting emotions. Not a prescription for a truly happy story."

"But it's their triumph over suffering," he says, "That's the happy part."

"The happy part is that it was *their* suffering and not *yours.*" I think this, but I don't say it. Everett can't stand being *al*ways wrong. So I nod at his last protest even if I don't agree. Because nobody overcomes hardships: we merely survive them, like car wrecks, to haul the scars around with us until we die. But I nod as if the saintly mother story is a possibility to consider. Heartened by this, Everett continues:

". . . And mama has spent her whole life trying to help other people. As hard as her life has been, she could always find something to give. Isn't that happy?" Everett pauses. Studies my face which I make sure is giving away nothing. He waits for my acquiescence on his last point; I can't give it. So I tell him flat out, "That's the saddest story there is. Along with being the oldest." Everett's face tightens. The words sound harsh. Maybe the truth will go better with a musical accompaniment. So I toss aside my writing, flip through albums for something mellow—something sad.

I wouldn't object to writing his mother's story if, in her old age, she had put hard times behind her and was now enjoying some ease and peace of mind. But Everett's mother is living in the same two-story walkup of her childhood—the same, but different, because it's older, more decrepit. The beams are termite riddled, the front porch is a hazard, and her new neighbors are young acid heads who don't know the difference between sleep and death. It is not triumph but the height of tragedy—the final kick: sacrifice rewarded with pain. Maybe it is irreverent to say that her story is the oldest story on record, but it is: a mother sacrificing body and mind for children who will eventually spurn her (or idealize her) but never recognize what was traded for their lives. It is old. It is sad. . . . It is true. It is not happy. And now I hope that Everett can realize the magnitude of the thing he has so frivolously proposed. It's easy to *say* "write a happy story," but when you get down to the brass tacks of it, the task is formidable.

Of course I could manufacture happy tales unending if I made them out of wish instead of life: flawlessly beautiful men and women living lives full of satisfaction; modern episodes of Ozzie and Harriet; heroic tales of John Wayne justice, Right prevailing over Wrong; evil creatures disarmed with a fortuitous bucket of water—

The stove hisses vehemently.

"Your pot is boiled over," says Everett cocking one eye to the stove, then to me. I cross the kitchen, deliberately sly, watching the foaming white water smear down the sides of the saucepan, sizzle into the hot recesses of the stove where it will congeal into an impossible to remove glue.

"What about Alice?" says Everett.

I think about my friend Alice, now a very big costume jewelry magnate on the East coast. She *is* a success story.

"Is Alice happy?"

"She made more money last year than most people ever see— outside a Monopoly game," Everett says.

I swab the stove top with a soppy dishcloth. "Is she happy, you think?" Everett doesn't answer. I stir pots.

"What's *this* story about?"

"Alice's happy story fragment. It's not finished."

"How much've you got?"

"I've got:

"At seven, Alice was a pretty girl. Everyone always said so. Especially her uncle, her mother's step-brother, who had Sunday dinner with them every week without fail.

"But they were poor, so Alice's mother had no chicken for Sunday pots, but depended on her step-brother to bring fish that he caught at the lake. He always brought an extra fish for Alice who hated fish but was always made to thank her uncle for her extra portion with a kiss.

" 'You see Alice, a pretty girl will always get more,' he whispered to her every Sunday without fail, and endlessly, like the smell of fish that she came to associate, not with a meal, but with her uncle. With his breath, his shirt, his fingers that squeezed her quick and rough whenever she had to kiss him.

"Men told Alice she was pretty. Alice's mother said, 'You must think you're cute, or somethin',' and slapped her when she was angry. But Alice loved her mother. She knew the slaps were not from lack of love, but because her mother hated fish also. So Alice gathered pretty trash, lost buttons, bright chips of glass, and strung them for her mother who wore them on 'chicken days'—Christmases and Easters—to make Alice smile."

"That's happy?" Everett asks incredulous.

"Well . . .," I say, "She never went hungry."

"The uncle is a lech."

"She overcomes that hardship," I say. But Everett has heard enough.

"Alice never had any uncles like that," he says.

"How do you know?"

"And she was never poor."

"This is fiction, not biography," I say. "Besides, a story should be universal. Every girl has an uncle, or *some*body, like that."

"Did you?"

"This is fiction, not autobiography," I say.

Everett takes a deep exaggerated breath. "Alice's family was well-off, she went to college, majored in Business Administration. She married, had two sons, and in her spare time, she blasted her way into the costume jewelry market and made a killing." The world according to Everett.

I amend. "Alice was a neglected child who hung around college campuses, married a rich man's son, had two sons right quick, divorced the rich man's son, sued for humongous alimony, bought herself a nanny, and a costume jewelry business," and reality reigns once again.

"You don't have to put it like that. You could emphasize the success part," says Everett.

I sweep gleaming vegetables from the chopping board into the skillet. The hot butter gives a long sigh. "So," I say. "A happy story is a story with the sad parts snipped away. And writing is an aberrant form of—cosmetology?"

I don't agree with this dishonesty, but I have to admire Everett's clear vision, a man for whom happiness is attainable through good sound planning—or a good pearl eraser. Later, as I clear and wash up from dinner, I wonder if he isn't right about Alice. With one son in jail, the other a part-time hairdresser and her series of interesting but impermanent men, she was surely, I had thought, in pure agony. I scrub pots. Ironic that Everett would be the one to suggest that a woman's happiness could exist despite the failure of children and men.

Everett seems to have lost interest in this quest for the happy story, but I am tortured by it. The problem is the thing itself—happiness. What is it? The attainment of what I *think* I want, or just the absence of grief? Who has it? How did they get hold of it? Hang onto it? Or is it just mind control—looking for the bright side while constantly living in the dark? Is it the predictable routine of Everett's mother's last years, whose whole life was spent in flux? Is her happiness the mere absence of the awful unexpected, the knowledge that there are no new disasters? That her own death is no longer frightening—that it is a not altogether unpleasant prospect? The idea that every eventuality can be met? The reason that she can refuse to be rescued from the dilapidation of life, finally insist upon having some things her own way and not worry about the consequences? There might be a certain satisfaction in this.

Still, how sad if happiness boiled down to a kind of good-natured fatalism. I wanted my happiness to be more perfect, even if that made it impossible to obtain. Even if it had to remain the property of childhood ignorance, or of memory.

"Are you trying to say you've never been happy?" says Everett.

"I would never say that."

"What was the happiest time of your life?"

"Happiest?" I repeat, balancing a stack of plates to a high shelf. "It's so hard to speak in degrees. . . ."

"Give me one time," he says. "When?"

"When?" I repeat.

When. Everett's voice is like the crossed arms of my old piano teacher. Mrs. Poindexter. One hand always gripping a ruler. "Give me the time," she would say, smacking the ruler against her narrow backside for the tempo. And I played, struggling to meet the demand. Everett waits. I rifle through my life, days, and years, in search of a single convincing moment. I think it must be something wholly selfish and completely satisfying—

Like the time two nickels bought me two whole Big Time candy bars to eat all by myself and *not* share. It had taken me all day to shake little sisters and supervision. The city air had smelled sweet to me as I ran, full tilt, without stopping, to the basement store. The agony, sweet, of impossible choices: candy necklaces or candy mint juleps or "wine" candy sours. But I had already known I wanted the Big Times that were hurt-yourself good and never enough when you had to split one two ways, or three, or four. But I had two nickels and a little bit of time. . . . Except I remember the candy didn't taste as good as I had expected. Maybe they were stale. Or maybe it was because I ate them so fast, afraid of being discovered, afraid of the sudden cry of: "dibs dibs!" our unrefusable demand to share. Or worse, some unexpected adult demanding to know "—and where'd you get the money for that?" Because a nickel for candy was unusual, and two was rare if not completely unheard of. And the nickels were "borrowed" from my grandmother's mantel. No, this was not a happy memory. The selfish moment is always spoiled by guilt.

A happy moment would, evidently, have to be some occasion of selfless generosity or sacrifice. When I was oh, maybe ten years old, my sisters and I had saved a wool sock full of money. A collection of nickels, quarters and even some dollar bills. We counted it constantly, thoroughly excited at our thrift. We discussed what to do with the money, but could think of no purchase exciting or satisfying enough to justify spending all of that money, close to thirteen dollars. It must have been Palm Sunday, or some other special occasion. It could not have been an ordinary Sunday when we carried our treasure in its black wool "bank" to Sunday school, and we decided to give a whole dollar in offering. Our Sunday School master must have smelled our excitement, or our money, because she kept on begging and prodding, saying: "Oh, our class has never won the distinction of best offering. A little bit more, and we might earn a special blessing." (One more dollar). And: "Oh!

wouldn't it be something if the children of the Sunday School out-shined the adults in their offering to God?" (*Two* more dollars). And: "I just checked and we're still five dollars lower than the Elders' collection plate." In defeat, we emptied the entire remains of our sock savings into the plate. . . . And, in a moment, a great cry rose up in the church. Three daughters had given thirteen dollars to the collection plate. Wasn't that a wonderment! Wasn't that the spirit of God at work! But there was jealousy in the House of God because a rally cry went up. The adults reached into their deep pockets and came forth with dollar after dollar. Even so, we almost earned our special blessing, which was little enough reward I thought, when my own father came forward with five dollars in his hand. The adults grinned. I wept. No. Selfless generosity was, and always had been, for the birds. How could I have forgotten that even joyful giving *must* offer *some* small reward.

The last possibility: happiness must be some simple uncompli-cated moment when your purposes—no matter how unambitious—go unthwarted.

Like I had my own house once. And once, I had a certain recogni-tion for particular kinds of Saturday afternoons, early dusk, mild uneventful days. Yes, summer Saturdays, early dusk, just as the worst of the midday heat has dissipated, and every window is thrown open to the deepening air, the beginning breeze; rooms stretch out infinite in growing shadows. I am part of the shadows, sweaty, rank. But every surface is scrubbed, rubbed to gleaming. Leisurely, slow, I lean in to every doorway and everything is perfect order: perfumed linen, gleam-ing glass, dark scent of wax and incense burning into dusk. And jazz saxophone mellow on the box—Standing sour and damp, old clothes sticking to me, scalp pricking sweat, lifting my shirtfront to the breath of a breeze, knowing I am the only imperfection within this small perfection made by me. And I, for the moment, am my own creation. It is not the weekly grind of housework that satisfies, but purposes being met without interference. Completion. The signature on the painting. The flourish at the end of the performance.

"Climbing into the wonderful world of Calgon is bliss," I say to Everett. "I have been happy."

"Taking a bath is happiness for you?" he says, voice cracking. His look is scorching. I guess I have missed a beat somewhere. I suppose I ought to include *him* in it somehow.

I return to myself in an incredibly hot bath, so hot I am floating up like the mist, so perfect my thoughts burst open like the bubbles I nudge with my toe. I can dissolve into the sweat of mirrors that multiply me, disappear into the yellow brilliance of saxophone straining toward the treble—a single superb note the horn blower discovers at the top of the riff. He blows, bending at the knees until his chest caves—holding it . . . holding on. . . . It is the uncertainty of the moment that inspires absorption: knowing the sweetness of the bath can't last, knowing how hot dissipates to tepid, knowing that the record will end. That the silence will be broken . . . by a faint sound—the deadbolt sliding back under the key. Joy is the prior regret for the sweet ending of an irretrievable moment. I tell Everett that his returning home from an absence and I'm brand new in the bathtub is an intensely exquisite experience.

Everett considers this—tongue busy. But I'm dissatisfied. What is this feeling I'm looking for, so fleet, like a bubble I burst with my toe? Why should it be that I can recall injuries and slights to no end, have at my disposal infinite evidence of the world's injustice, malice, and casual cruelty. And disappointments: like discovering that there *is* no magic—no benevolent and timely fairy godmother to rescue us from the daily cinders and rubble; that the bread crumbs strewn to show us the way are *al*ways food for birds, or the hustling industrious ants, leaving us all standing, faces tipped, staring up into a knit of blankness. Where are the matching memories of joy so powerful, so engulfing, enough to muffle the continuous pummeling of life?

This is a happy story with a dole of sadness, like the surplus bread handed out to the poor. Like the rich man whose joy in his richness is tainted with a worry that the poor might get too much. . . .

My neighborhood church is a dispensary to the poor. I volunteer to hand out surplus food to the needy. Sometimes cheese, sometimes bread. The Reverend Lester hands out religion. "Jesus fed the multitude with five loaves and two fish," he preaches a popular sermon.

"You givin' out fish too, Rev'rend?" a young woman asks.

"They given out fish," someone passes it on.

"*Some* folks got fish," another says, dissatisfied. "They ran out."

The people stand in lines. I think of fish dinners, back yard fish fries, slapping mosquitoes on summer nights, pungent hot sauces, cold beer and lemonade. Mountains of catfish, perch, fried golden crisp, the hot steam trapped inside the skin. How it would take all day to get ready with errands and cleaning the fish, and sweeping stray children from underfoot. The air full of expectation and no one too impatient.

A woman stands in front of me, her hands held forth for her portion. Her expression is sour. She looks at the smooth blocks of cheese thinking of fish. She takes the cheese, hands the large weight of it to her small child standing beside her. The child wobbles with the burden.

"There never was any fish," I say to her.

"Sure," she says.

"It was just a rumor," I say, but she stalks off. She wants to know who is in charge. My eyes are met by the direct stare of the woman standing behind her. She is elderly; her skin in smooth like rubbed, cured wood. After a moment, she smiles.

"The good Lord didn't need fish nor bread to do what he done. Don't never call *that* no rumor," she tells me, mocking-stern. "God bless," she says, receiving the cheese into her arms carefully. "I gives some of this to my nephew," she says. "He don't qualify. He earn $10.00 over the limit." Her smile is full of yellow gold, a bright chip drawing the vague light of the dim room to a single brilliant mite. She leaves me with my own smile.

"The happiest day of my life was the day we were married," Everett confesses to me, then waits. Then he says, "What about you?"

"I'm still working on it," I say.

"You weren't happy on our wedding day?" he says.

"Well," I say, "I didn't want to take *your* happiest day."

"But it *was* the happiest? So far? Right?"

Everett no longer asks me about my stories. Now I *make* him listen.

"This is a story about happiness," I say. "It's not finished." Everett says nothing. "This is what I have so far," I say.

"Alice always loved weddings. So, as a young girl, she resolved to have several. Each one would be more beautiful than the last, each husband more beautiful than his predecessor. Therefore, the spareness of her first wedding and the sparsity of beauty in the face and form of her first husband did not disturb her excessively. When the aged preacher misread a few of the vows, it was not devastating to Alice who, later, had to console her new husband's anger regarding the matter.

"'You didn't plan to keep all those promises anyway,' she chided him, laughing, teasing. The accusation shocked him at first, as he did not expect her to know this, and he protested the fidelity of his heart. But, a day later, when Alice found her husband's eyes wandering behind an unfamiliar woman, he smiled, licked his lips and resolved to be more careful.

"His name was Cheever. Cheever did not have good looks but knew 'how to make him some money.' He said this often and Alice, who was always agreeable, agreed.

"But Alice did not despise Cheever for his lack of handsomeness. She felt genuinely grateful to him—he's been her escape route from home, from her uncle's fish smell. She was satisfied with her marriage and learned how to keep house out of magazines, cooked out of books, and drew designs with colored pencils which she pinned all over her walls until they lived inside a montage of faint scribbly color. She even pinned the light designs to the bedboard above their heads. And sunny mornings when she woke to Cheever thrusting love at her from behind, matter-of-factly like a drowsy bear rubbing an itch against a slender bark, she had only to lift her eyes to study the outlines of dreams, outside the sudden odor of private lust.

"One day, when Cheever had gone, Alice crawled back into the spoiled sheets that held her daydreams. And behind her lids grew a tree supple and bending beneath the jewels that budded on the tips of its branches. She plucked one red fruit and made it disappear inside the warm dark of her palm."

"She's living in a dream world," says Everett. "Her husband is selfish and inconsiderate. *And* ugly. Where does the happy part come in?"

"It's coming," I say.

I am still writing the story of the woman—intelligent, ambitious, attractive, educated. Did I say intelligent? Because she is no longer planning suicide, realizing it was a waste of her time since death is already scripted and requires no additional preparation. Realizing that her mother's life contained some moments of joy because she was a woman who worked towards the completion of tasks small and large and always spoke of her life without excluding any of its parts.

Mary Hood

A Man
Among Men

1

His old man lay in Grady Miller's best steel casket with the same determined-to-die look on his face that he had worn throughout his final two months of decline, from the night Olene had run red-eyed back through the Labor Day rain with his uneaten supper on its wilting picnic plate to report, "He's gone in that camper and put on his nightshirt and gone to bed. For keeps." She had shaken the rain from her jacket and scarf, using one of the green-checked napkins to dry her face. "He's talking funny. I don't like the way he's talking. Made me lay out his dark suit where he could see it and told me, 'No shoes, no use burying good leather, just see my socks are clean,' all because of a dog. A dog!"

"Daddy thought the world of Smokey Dawn," Thomas pointed out.

He and the old man had spent their entire holiday looking for the hound, as far south as Buck's Creek, all around the public hunting lands, calling, calling from the windows of the truck. She had never stayed out so long. She had never trashed in her life. From time to time the old man raised his arm and hissed, "Listen," his bladey hand like an ax. Once it was the waul of a blue-tailed rooster, strutting in a dried cornfield; it almost sounded like the dog. The cock stepped toward them, icy eye taking it all in. "Shoot!" The old man fell back against the seat, disappointed. They drove on.

There was a strange feel to the weather; the sky was so overcast the morning glories in the corn were still open wide. "Weatherbreeder," the old man said, staring at the clouds, but he wasn't looking for rain. In a few miles he spotted them—three buzzards—freckles on the flannel belly of the afternoon. The old man tensed up and leaned forward, still hoping, and peered down the dirt lane to where she lay in the gold-enrod. Before Thomas got the truck full-stopped, his daddy was scrabbling out. He thrashed his hat all around to keep the birds aloft. He still had that sense he was rescuing her. His tough old shoes barely cleared the dust as he hastened toward the corpse, stumbling over pebbles and lurching on, stiff-footed.

Thomas lagged back, letting him handle it. He lit his cheroot on the third match; there was an east wind, mean and cold, shaking the young pines. Handfuls of sparrows sifted themselves out of the blow, deeper and deeper into the thickets.

His daddy was shivering.

Thomas shed his jacket and offered it to the old man, who wasn't dressed for the knifing wind. He took it, knelt, and wrapped the dog in it. "I reckon it was her heart," he said, beating his parchment fist against his chest. "No bigger than a fiddle when I got me my first redbone pup, Billy Boy it was." He looked away as Thomas lifted the dog and carried her back to the truck. The old man walked alone, counting up his losses: "After Billy it was Babe . . . and Ginger Tom out of Babe and French Lou—she had the straightest legs of them all—and Red Pearl and Rabbit Joe, one-eyed but it never cost him a coon, heart like a tiger . . . did I say Racing Joe? And Joe's Honey and Honey's Nan . . ." He flinched when Thomas slammed the tailgate: a solemn closing, the end of an era. They headed home. "And Jolly, and Honey's Nan, I mention her yet? And Prince Ego and Skiff. And Smokey," he said, "Smokey Dawn." He stared toward the darkening west, his eyes cold and gray as a dead-man's nickels. "Well, that's about it." They rode in silence then.

By the time Thomas parked, at home, the old man's interest had waned to a single, final point. "Dig it deep" was how he put it. "I don't want a plow turning her up some day." He headed for his mobile home and went in and closed the door.

When Olene saw the windbreaker over the dog's body, she said, "I'm not washing that in my machine."

"Dean's not home yet?"

"I'm not worried." She laughed. "When you're seventeen you run on nerve and Dr. Pepper, not Daylight Saving. You'll have to bury her yourself."

It was already raining—the first huge cold drops—when he went to get the mattock.

Olene had never had much patience with the old man's sulks. "Do something," she said, after supper, just as the phone rang. She went scraping the old man's untouched food into the garbage. "Turned his head to the wall, not one bite would he taste, and me on my feet chopping and cooking since noon." All the time Thomas was on the phone she kept reciting her welling grievances at his back. She broke off when he reached for his uniform jacket on its hook.

"Now what?

He zipped the jacket to his chin, then unzipped it halfway; he dug out his truck keys and clipped his beeper to his belt. "A car hit a deer on the quarry road."

"Couldn't someone else?"

He unlocked the cabinet and took down his service revolver. "I had last weekend off, remember?"

"We didn't do anything."

He loaded the gun and clicked it shut. "I'll just step on across and check on Daddy before I go." Lightning showed the walk to be running like a brook. "And it's not a camper," he said as he plunged out into the deluge.

He splashed across the flagstones to the mobile home. The windows were open; it was cave-damp and dark inside. The wet curtains dragged at his hands as he cranked the jalousies shut. He turned on the lights and ran the thermostat up. At the bedroom door he hesitated. "It's Thomas," he announced softly.

"Come on."

Thomas took the old man's hand and clasped it; it was cold. His daddy puzzled him out a feature at a time from his pillows. He shook his head; they were strangers. "I recollect you now," he bluffed. "We were running Blue Jolly and Nan . . ." He trailed off, uncertain. "That old coon—tail shot off four years back—no fight left in her, no fight. So fat she dropped into the dogs and just let 'em rip. No play in the pack

for that. Funny . . ." He yawned for breath. "Funny . . ." He opened
his eyes and stared all the way through Thomas, clear out the other side
into the young century when someone, someone . . .

"*Who?*" he asked irascibly. He focused again, present tense. "My
memory's shot to chow," he confessed. He glanced indifferently around
the room, recognizing nothing but his suit on the chair. "I'm checking
out of here," he announced abruptly, flailing himself upright, then
falling back, exhausted. "You help me, mister?"

Thomas nodded.

"You notify my son, Little Earl—Earl Teague, Jr.—on the Star
Route . . ." He gestured with his thumb, south.

Thomas watched the pulse wriggle in the old man's temple. Was he
just sulking, like Olene said? Or was it another of the little strokes that
left him more and more a stranger?

"Daddy?" Thomas said, sharp, calling the cloudy eyes back into
focus.

Frowning, he examined Thomas' face and resumed, "Highly
thought of . . . in the book . . . look him up . . . Earl Teague, Jr. He'll
come take care of me."

"But what about Thomas?" Thomas asked, for the record.

The old man seemed to have dozed off.

"Daddy?"

He blinked awake. "Who is it?"

"Thomas."

"Not him," he said, irritated. He had never suffered fools gladly.
"He's dead." He looked at Thomas and yawned.

You son of a bitch, Thomas thought. He wanted to shake the old
man, wake him, make claims. But what was the use of that now? Or
ever? When Little Earl was killed by the train, hadn't his daddy stared
at Thomas standing by the closed coffin and asked, "Why couldn't it
have been you?"

That was when Thomas knew.

2

His old man lay in Grady Miller's front parlor between the adjusta-
ble lamps casting their discreet 40-watt pink-of-health upon him head
and foot. He was dressed in his Sunday best. Olene had tucked a rose
into his lapel. She came up to Thomas standing there and ran her arm

through his. "Isn't he sweet?" she said, giving the little bouquet of buds and baby's breath a pat, smoothing the streamers across the old man's chest. GRANDDADDY was spelled out in press-on gold letters on the satin ribbon. She had ordered that, in Dean's name. The boy hadn't seen the old man. since the last week of the hospital stay, when life-support was all that tethered him to the world. He hadn't seen him dying, and he hadn't seen him dead. Thomas' simmering resentment of that finally boiled over on Saturday night when Dean came in late for supper, said he wasn't hungry, and announced that the clutch had torn out of his Chevy again.

"Ten days!" Thomas said. "This time it lasted ten days!"

"Three weeks," Olene corrected. She looked it up in the check-book. "He can drive mine."

"He won't need it; he's coming with us," Thomas said.

"I can fix it myself in three hours if I get the parts."

"Not tonight." Thomas finished his coffee, standing. He set the cup in the sink.

"I'm not going down there."

"Your granddaddy—"

"Is dead and I'm not. I'm sure as hell not," Dean said. He laughed. He drank what was left of the quart of milk right from the carton. When Thomas backhanded him, it knocked his sunglasses and the empty milk carton across the kitchen. One of the lenses rolled over by the trash.

"No!" Olene stepped between.

"I'd beat his ass till it turned green if I thought it would do any good," Thomas said, over her head. Still he couldn't see into the boy's eyes. How long had it been since they *saw* each other? He turned away, shrugged off Olene's restraining hand. In the silence, which prolonged, the boy wiped the milk mustache off with his fist.

When Olene saw the look on his face, she said, "He's just trying to raise you."

"All he raises is objections," Dean said.

Thomas headed up the stairs, two at a time, to shave and dress for the wake. "Don't wait up," Dean bragged as he left. He took Olene's car.

It was the first time he had stayed out all night that they didn't know where to find him.

On Sunday morning (the old man's funeral would be that afternoon) the beeper summoned Thomas on a dead-body call. He left Olene and the men's Bible class on honor guard at Miller's and headed across town to Doc Daniels' pharmacy. Doc was the one who had spotted the body in the weeds, followed the footprints from his broken-in back door out through the frost and down the gullied fill-dirt specked with soda cans and gum wrappers. Doc had called, "Hey! HEY!", a wake-up call in case it was sleep and not death he had been stalking, but when he got close enough to be fairly sure he hurried back to the phone to spread the news. The EMS driver got there first and made a tentative diagnosis—overdose—but now they were waiting on the coroner and Thomas to arrive.

When Thomas got there, Doc led the way again, down the clay bank, his white bucks getting pinker with every dusty step. Thomas was in a hurry; Doc caught at his sleeve to stay apace. He was panting to keep up. Together they leaped the last gully. All the way Doc was telling, telling, fixing his magnified gaze on Thomas' profile.

"Look at him," Doc accused, as they came to the corpse.

A boy, curling a bit toward the fetal pose, lay on his left side. For a moment Thomas thought he knew him—a trick of the mind after a sleepless night—dirty sneakers, faded jeans, blue windbreaker, watch cap. He swayed, rubbed his eyes, then knelt for a closer look, resting his hand on the boy's stiff, angled knees.

Behind him Doc was saying, "This makes the sixth time I've been robbed. I've got payments to make like anyone else—"

Thomas searched the boy's pockets for ID. He flipped through the haggard wallet. Doc leaned forward, squinting. "So who gets the bad news?" he wondered.

Thomas stood up. "I'll tell them," he said, and started up the bank to his truck. He took the time to smoke one of his little cigars. He answered no questions. The crowd moved back to let his truck pass. He drove fast though there was no hurry.

He crossed the tracks at midtown and turned right onto a forgotten road hardly more than an alley paralleling the rails. He headed south till the paving turned to gravel; it peppered the underside of his truck as he negotiated the lane's washboard heaves and hollows. He rolled his window up against the dust rather than slow down.

The road dead-ended in a grove of blighted elms beyond a bare yard, clean-swept with a broom in that country way of deterring snakes. Mazes of rabbit fence held back the frost-nipped remains of faded petunias. On the staggering mailbox, in decrescendo, red paint not a season old announced ELSiE BLaND beneath the former tenant's name, shoeblacked out. A dingy cat leaped up onto the truck hood, settled on the cab roof, and held aloof from Thomas' hand. From the grayed house came the sound of fast sad blues, decades old, scratchy— an ancient, sturdy record salvaged from attic or rummage sale. Before Thomas crossed the porch the music sped up to 78 rpm; people were laughing. They didn't hear him.

He knocked again. Louder.

A laughing woman materialized behind the rusty rump-sprung screen door, wiping her eyes with her fingers and shaking the tears away. "Sounds like mice in them cartoons," she explained. She leaned into the dark to call, "Jude? Jude! You shut that down now, *shut* it." To Thomas she said, "It's Sunday, I know, but I didn't reckon it'd hurt anything for him to listen. We been to church this morning, early." She guessed he was a preacher.

Because they did not know each other, because he had come in his pickup truck instead of the cruiser, because she did not notice the blue light on the dashboard behind the windshield reflecting October, because he was dressed for his daddy's funeral and wasn't in uniform, he could see she had no idea at all who or what he was. He held up his badge and said, "It's the Law, ma'am. I'm Tom Teague. Are you Mrs. Bland?" And because he had come on official business and there was more than courtesy conveyed in his manners—some additional intimation of apology for bad news, perhaps the worst news—the solemnity communicated itself through the rusty screen and into her heart instantly and flamed up into remorse, as though the fires of regret and grief had long been laid and awaited but the glint of Thomas' badge to kindle them.

"My boy Ben! Killed oversea in the service!" she screamed, voicing her oldest premonition, her dreams that woke her, brought her to her knees in the nightwatch. She had a map of the world with Lebanon marked on it in ballpoint, circled and circled, to help her focus her prayers.

"No," Thomas said. He tried the door. It was latched. "Mrs. Bland . . ." he appealed. Something in his tone arrested her wild attention.

The needle scratched loudly across the old record and resumed playing again, at proper speed, the fast sad blues. She settled her eyes on Thomas'.

Quieter, she said, "Then it's about Ray." She unhooked the screen and admitted trouble into her scrub-worn rooms. Every windowsill had its beard of green plants in foil-covered pots. Above the mantel with its clutter of photographs hung a lithograph of radiant Christ.

"Jude, honey," his mama suggested, "about time for your train."

Jude came in from the kitchen, a man who would be a boy all his life.

"We got to discuss," she told him. "You go on out." No introductions.

Passing by, the boy stuck out his hand to Thomas. "Please to," he said. The old ladies that Elsie cleaned for praised his manners and his willingness to climb ladders; they let him unclog their gutters for cookies and dimes.

The train at the town limits sounded its whistle. The boy hurried out to admire the pink Albert City Farmers grain cars rolling past on tracks not a city block away.

"Just a little something went wrong when he was borned, a good boy, no trouble, not like Ray." Elsie breathed faster. She aimed her sharp nose at Thomas and angrily asked, "What about him? Tell me what he done."

"I'm afraid it's bad news, Mrs. Bland."

She thought it over. "Bound to be." She pushed herself up out of the chair and fetched one of the photographs from the mantel. She handed it to Thomas. Its cheap metal frame was cold and sharp as a knife. There was the face of the boy Doc had found in the weeds. Thomas cleared his throat. He handed the picture back; for a moment they both held it, then he let it go.

"He's dead," he told her. There was nothing to tell but the truth, and it only took two words. Thomas thought that was how he would want to hear it, if he ever had to. Elsie heard it, Thomas thought, without surprise. She seemed stupefied, though, and it was a minute before she repeated, "Dead." She sat staring at the photograph in her lap.

"He's the one like his pappy," she specified. She just sat there. Silent.

"You'll want to ask me some questions," Thomas suggested.

Elsie looked out the window at Jude. "He purely loves them trains. Don't miss a one. Always try to locate near the tracks for him."

Georgia, Clinchfield, and West Point stock rolled past, slowing, and the British Columbia car with its magnolia logo stopped directly in view as the L&N engines switched back and forth uptown, shunting a feed car aside.

"He's the good one," Elsie said. Canny, she studied Thomas' face, reading there her familiar, bitter lesson. "Ray done bad?" she guessed. She set the photograph back in its place on the mantel. "You don't love them for it, but you love them. There's good in between the bad times." She smoothed a wrinkle in the mantel runner, chased the fold ahead of her fingers to the fringed end, then chased it again.

The train, readying itself for the run north through the deep cuts and poplar hills, revved its engines until the whole house rumbled, making itself felt in every bone.

"The Lloyd Jesus knows I love all my boys!" she cried, her face lifted to the calendar Christ as she wept. When she was calmer she wiped her face on her apron and took her seat again, her tear-shining hands inert on the arms of her chair, her swollen feet in their strutted oxfords braced heel by heel for the truth. "All right," she consented. She sniffed deeply, inhaling the last of her tears. "You tell me what it is. What'll be in them newspapers. Tell me in so many words. I don't want to read about it." Her voice was worn down with speaking up for herself and her sons, husky from making itself heard over mill racket, muffled by sorrows. "I hate to read about it," she explained, then cleared her throat with a sigh and waited.

That was when Thomas, though it wasn't his intention, admitted, "It could have been my own son. I thought it was."

3

His old man lay in Grady Miller's lifetime-guaranteed burial vault, and the mourners—those windblown few who waited for the closing and the anchoring of their wreaths in the raw clay—drifted like dark leaves against the whited wall of Soul's Harbor Church. Olene's sinuses were acting up; she couldn't wear a hat over that hairdo and she had left her scarf in her other coat. She withdrew to the sanctuary of the darkened church itself. Miller's assistants were already folding the chairs, rolling up the fake grass, loading the pulleys and frame and plush seat covers into their van. The pastor gave Thomas a little tap with his Bible as he went by, saying, "We'll keep in touch," and headed briskly for his car. His wife was already buckled in, ready.

There came that general, genteel exodus, with no backward glances, as life went on. The road and margins cleared of traffic and then it was so quiet; there was only the flutter of the canopy's scalloped canvas as the wind rocked it on its moorings. The grave-diggers' words were blown far afield, toward the kneeling cattle, fawn-colored jerseys, on the distant hill. They looked legless; they reminded Thomas of that deer on the quarry road Labor Day night, her front legs sheared in the accident, yet somehow she was still alive.

He had knelt beside her. Her doe eye, widely dilated, stared vacantly up at the sky, her nostrils flaring with each quick breath. She was dying, and it was taking too long.

"Where the hell is the Ranger?"

The inevitable crowd had begun to gather. G. W Laney, first responder, stamped and snorted like a dray beast. He was a volunteer, whose wife had given him an emergency light for his birthday. Its intermittent red sweep refreshed his sunburn and turned the rain to blood. His scanner spat static. Thomas had a headache. He and G. W. laid a tarp over the deer.

"Back 'em up," Thomas told him, and G. W. herded the bystanders deeper into the dark. "Appreciate y'all coming, folks, but how about clearing on off for home now?" They mostly went. Thomas couldn't see how the deer was still alive. He checked her again, ran his hand down her neck.

"I'm not waiting," he decided.

At the gunshot, the door of the ditched car ratcheted open and a young man climbed uphill out into the downpour. Thomas stared. They hadn't told him it was Dean! The boy had a bloody handkerchief tied around his left palm. They stood in the rainy circle of flashlight and Thomas asked, first off, "Whose car have you wrecked this time?"

"Ginnie let me drive. You know Ginnie—Doc Daniels' daughter."

The kind you find dead in a ditch some day, Thomas thought, watching her get out now, her jacket held over her head to keep the rain off her bright hair. Her T-shirt advertised Squeeze Me, I'm Fresh. She sided with Dean, facing Thomas down, two against one.

"It's totaled," Thomas said, surveying the wrecked sedan.

"I'm insured," Ginnie said. "but still I bet Daddy'll shit a brick." She laughed. Dean started to laugh, then didn't. Then did. Ginnie flicked a few tiny cubes of safety glass off his shoulder.

"You been drinking?" Thomas asked, officially. And unofficially.

"Naw, uh, just beer. Just one." Dean shut his eyes, stood on tiptoe, and began touching first one index finger, then the other, to his nose. "See?"

"You need a doctor?" Thomas kept his voice casual as he eyed that blood-blackened bandage.

"It's just a cut." Dean was exhilarated by the adrenalin. "Damn deer bust right out on me! Like a bomb. Clean through the windshield." He avoided looking at that mound under the rain-glittering tarp.

"How fast were you going?" Thomas shone the flashlight along the pavement. "Where'd you brake?"

"You saying it's my fault?" The boy's raw fist in its bandage tightened.

"I'm saying what I'd say to anyone."

Dean crossed his arms over his chest when he heard that and bent a hot, hurt look on his father—part anger, part disappointment—as though he had been handed a stone instead of bread.

Thomas knew that look well enough. "Sue me," he told the boy. The wrecker was backing up to Ginnie's car and the Ranger had arrived, with a notebook to fill with facts. He began asking Dean and Ginnie the hard questions. When he finished and had no charges to file, Thomas offered, "Y'all need a lift?"

Ginnie said, that quick, "We're going with G. W.," and G. W. grinned, because he hadn't asked them and because Ginnie was like that, fixing things to suit her. (She had a way of daring him that sent Dean diving off the rocky cliff over the reservoir at least once a summer, risking his neck for one moment of her laughter, and before the peony of spray had settled around him, before he had surfaced, she was bored, thinking up something else. Thomas had warned them off those rocks, but Ginnie was worth the risk, worth the slow climb back up the cliff to her lacquered toes.) She swung herself up into G. W.'s front seat and Dean got in the back.

"Keep it between the ditches," Thomas had called as they rolled off, white water fluming up from beneath the wide tires of the Jeep.

"How much longer?" Thomas wondered. He had objected to the machine, backfilling, so the men were shoveling by hand.

One of the mourners, with an estimating glance over toward the undertaker's canopy, said "*Now*, I think. They're about done." The grave was covered and the wreaths were being laid. The ribbons rattled in the wind.

Thomas led the way, alone. Friends who had stayed set out in a broken rank behind him, by twos and threes, across the intervening graves, picking their way around the minimal obstacles of granite and marble, not talking. The throaty mufflers of Dean's orange Chevy caught their attention from the moment he rounded the curve by Foster's store. He burned a week's worth of rubber off its tires and stopped in a scour of gravel at the foot of the hill. Thomas turned to watch. They all did.

Dean had a bucket of bronze mums. He came on fast, loping across the field, hurdling the cemetery wall, catching up. They made way for him, but still he hung back, only stepping up to set the flowers at the headstone, between his grandparents' graves. Then he rested on Little Earl's footstone, catching his breath. He had nothing to say when they greeted him. Sullen, he raised the hood of his jogging suit and tied it snug, but they could still see his black eye. He stood suddenly and stamped his foot. "Cramp," he explained, doing some exercises to stretch the kink from his calf. "Gotta work it out." He jogged off east across the field, over unclaimed ground, then down toward the gravel pit, and around again.

As they watched him go, one of the men said, "Give him time, Tom, he's just a kid." That was what Olene was always saying. But wasn't that what everyone had said about Little Earl? Wild as sunspots and dead at twenty-four after losing a race with a locomotive, and not a day in that whole wasted life had he ever thought of anyone but himself.

The others paid their last respects to the old man, calling him a man among men, shaking Thomas's hand, and heading on down the hill to their cars. The diggers, behind the church, loaded their backhoe onto its trailer, threw in their handtools, and drove off.

When they had gone, Dean trotted back. "I wasn't going to come," he said. He pulled up his left sock, then stood not quite facing his daddy. They were alone now.

"You just about missed it," Thomas agreed. Why had he bothered to come? Thomas couldn't look at him, at that bruised eye. Had he hit him *that* hard? Where the hell had he been all night?

"Your mother was worried sick," Thomas said. He fumbled with his matches. Dean didn't say anything, as usual, just looked around. "She's in the church," Thomas told him. The boy shrugged.

"You're the ones who let the air out of the cruiser's tires, aren't you? You and Ginnie." He'd figured that out in fifteen seconds. Did they think he was a fool?

"Sue me," Dean said. Thomas blinked when he heard himself quoted. The boy stepped up to the curb of the plot and balanced on his toes, taller than his daddy, then stepped back down. "I was pissed," he said.

Before Thomas could decide if that was an apology, the door of the church skreeked open, then slammed. Olene stood on the steps, her eyes shaded by her upheld hands as she stared their way. She waved and shouted something, but the wind scattered her words. She gave up, but stayed out, as though she wanted to keep an eye on them. She sat on the top step in what was left of the sun, hugging her cold knees.

"And leave Ginnie out of it," Dean added.

"I figured it was you." Thomas unpocketed his fists to stoop and right a spray of carnations the wind had tipped over. The shoulders of his suit were white from leaning against the chalky shingles of the church. The scent of dying flowers choked him. Just that mere whiff made him remember all the other times, but he didn't want to remember. A phoebe settled hard, rocking a little on the rusty gate, feebly singing. Thomas concentrated on the bird.

When he caught Dean looking at him, he nodded toward the boy's car and said, "You fixed the clutch." He was getting hoarse.

"Yeah." Dean almost smiled.

The wind was strong enough to lean on, like it would never die. Dean glanced at his watch and sighed. He held out his hand, signaling *five minutes more* to Olene, waiting.

Thomas crossed his arms. "Don't let me keep you."

One by one Dean popped the knuckles of both hands, taking his time. Thomas hated that. "You going to stay out here all night?" Dean asked.

"Look who's talking."

"At least I was warm," Dean said.

Thomas checked the sky. "This time it didn't rain. It always rains." He watched the blue pickup truck bump across Langford's far pasture, and the cows begin walking toward the hay in back. One of the calves bawled and ran to catch up with its mother.

Olene came across the cemetery, making careful steps in her high heels, holding her coat shut. "Thomas?" she called. She lurched, stopped, and removed her shoes, then came on, faster, over the grass. "I'd rather have pneumonia than broken bones," she said. She looked from Thomas to Dean and back again. Thomas took her shoes and put them in the pockets of his suitcoat. She reached up to touch Dean's bruised eye, but he pulled away.

Olene knelt to gather up the remains of the everlasting and lilies she had planted. "Look what they did," she said. The careless mower in his zeal had laid them low. The diggers had chipped the granite corner monogram and snubbed the rose, the only volunteer. Thomas toed a stray clod from his daddy's footstone, which was already in place, part of the package deal when they buried his mother.

"All they've got to do is cut the date of death," Olene said, bending to tap the cold stone. "Its been a while, but they can match Mama Teague's numbers exactly." Olene dusted her hands and hugged her coat tighter to her. "I'm freezing to death," she said. "I'll be next."

"We'll go," Thomas said. Olene ran on and got into Thomas' truck and shut the door, but Dean stayed. Thomas was shivering. He made a giveaway gesture at the ground: farewell. "Maybe Mama can do something with him," he said. "I sure as hell never could."

The phoebe on the iron gate flew out and back, out and back, preying and preening. The wind had finally let up, and for a moment there was no other motion in the world but the lone bird, weakly singing. Then Dean stepped across Little Earl's grave and brushed the chalk dust off Thomas' shoulders, brushed and brushed.

That was when Thomas began to cry.

Manly Conclusions

His wife, Valjean, admitted that Carpenter Petty had a tree-topping temper, but he was slow to lose it; that was in his favor. Still, he had a long memory, and that way of saving things up, until by process of accumulation he had enough evidence to convict. "I don't get mad, I get even," his bumper sticker vaunted. Fair warning. When he was angry he burned like frost, not flame.

Now Valjean stood on the trodden path in the year's first growth of grass, her tablecloth in her arms, and acknowledged an undercurrent in her husband, spoke of it to the greening forsythia with its yellow flowers rain-fallen beneath it, confided it to God and nature. Let God and nature judge. A crow passed between her and the sun, dragging its slow shadow. She glanced up. On Carpenter's behalf she said, "He's always been intense. It wasn't just the war. If you're born a certain way, where's the mending?"

She shook the tablecloth free of the crumbs of breakfast and pinned it to the line. Carpenter liked her biscuits—praised them to all their acquaintances—as well as her old-fashioned willingness to rise before good day and bake for him. Sometimes he woke early too; then he would join her in the kitchen. They would visit as she worked the shortening into the flour, left-handed (as was her mother, whose recipe it was), and pinch off the rounds, laying them as gently in the blackened pan as though she was laying a baby down for its nap. The dough was very quick, very tender. It took a light hand. Valjean knew the value of a light hand.

This morning Carpenter had slept late, beyond his time, and catching up he ate in a rush, his hair damp from the shower, his shirt unbuttoned. He raised neither his eyes nor his voice to praise or complain.

"You'll be better at telling Dennis than I would," he said, finally, leaving it to her.

She had known for a long time that there was more to loving a man than marrying him, and more to marriage than love. When they were newly wed, there had been that sudden quarrel, quick and furious as a summer squall, between Carpenter and a neighbor over the property line. A vivid memory and a lesson—the two men silhouetted against the setting sun, defending the territory and honor of rental property. Valjean stood by his side, silent, sensing even then that to speak out, to beg, or order, to quake would be to shame him. Nor would it avail. Better to shout "Stay!" to Niagara. Prayer and prevention was the course she decided on, learning how to laugh things off, to make jokes and diversions. If a car cut ahead of them in the parking lot and took the space he had been headed for, before Carpenter could get his window down to berate women drivers, Valjean would say, "I can see why she's in a hurry, just look at her!" as the offender trotted determinedly up the sidewalk and into a beauty salon.

She was subtle enough most times, but maybe he caught on after a while. At any rate, his emotional weather began to moderate. Folks said he had changed, and not for the worse. They gave proper credit to his wife, but the war had a hand in it too. When he got back, most of what he thought and felt had gone underground, and it was his quietness and shrewd good nature that you noticed now. Valjean kept on praying and preventing.

But there are some things you can't prevent, and he had left it to Valjean to break the news to Dennis. Dennis so much like Carpenter that the two of them turned heads in town, father and son, spirit and image. People seemed proud of them from afar as though their striking resemblance reflected credit on all mankind, affirming faith in the continuity of generations. He was like his mama, too, the best of both of them, and try as she might she couldn't find the words to tell him that his dog was dead, to send him off to school with a broken heart. The school bus came early, and in the last-minute flurry of gathering books and lunch money, his poster on medieval armor and his windbreaker, she chose to let the news wait.

She had the whole day then, after he was gone, to find the best words. Musing, she sat on the top step and began cleaning Carpenter's boots—not that he had left them for her to do; he had just left them. She scrubbed and gouged and sluiced away the sticky mud, dipping her rag in a rain puddle. After a moment's deliberation she rinsed the cloth in Lady's water dish. Lady would not mind now; she was beyond thirst. It was burying her that had got Carpenter's boots so muddy.

"Dead," Valjean murmured. For a moment she was overcome, disoriented as one is the instant after cataclysm, while there is yet room for disbelief, before the eyes admit the evidence into the heart. The rag dripped muddy water dark as blood onto the grass.

They had found Lady halfway between the toolshed and the back porch, as near home as she had been able to drag herself. The fine old collie lay dying in their torchlight, bewildered, astonished, trusting them to heal her, to cancel whatever evil this was that had befallen.

Carpenter knelt to investigate. "She's been shot." The meaning of the words and their reverberations brought Valjean to her knees. No way to laugh this off.

"It would have been an accident," she reasoned.

Carpenter gave the road a despairing glance. "If it could have stayed the way it was when we first bought out here . . . you don't keep a dog like this on a chain!"

It had been wonderful those early years, before the developers came with their transits and plat-books and plans for summer cottages in the uplands. The deer had lingered a year or so longer, then had fled across the lake with the moon on their backs. The fields of wild blueberries were fenced off now; what the roadscrapers missed, wildfire got. Lawn crept from acre to acre like a plague. What trees were spared sprouted POSTED and KEEP and TRESPASSERS WILL BE signs. Gone were the tangles of briar and drifted meadow beauty, seedbox and primrose. The ferns retreated yearly deeper into the ravines.

"Goddamn weekenders," Carpenter said. They had lodged official complaint the day three bikers roared through the back lot, scattering the hens, tearing down five lines of wash, and leaving a gap through the grape arbor. The Law came out and made bootless inquiry, stirring things up a little more. The next morning Valjean found their garbage cans overturned. Toilet tissue wrapped every tree in the orchard, a dead rat floated in the well, and their mailbox was battered to earth—that sort of mischief. Wild kids. "Let the Law handle it," Valjean suggested, white-lipped.

"They can do their job and I'll do mine," Carpenter told her. So that time Valjean prayed that the Law would be fast and Carpenter slow, and that was how it went. A deputy came out the next day with a carload of joyriders he had run to earth. "Now I think the worst thing that could happen," the deputy drawled, "is to call their folks, whattya say?" So it had been resolved that way, with reparations paid, and handshakes. That had been several years back; things had settled down some now. Of late there were only the litter and loudness associated with careless vacationers. No lingering hard feelings. In the market, when Valjean met a neighbor's wife, they found pleasant things to speak about; the awkwardness was past. In time they might be friends.

"An accident," Valjean had asserted, her voice odd to her own ears. As though she were surfacing from a deep dive. Around them night was closing in. She shivered. It took her entire will to keep from glancing over her shoulder into the tanglewood through which Lady had plunged, wounded, to reach home.

"Bleeding like this she must have laid a plain track." Carpenter paced the yard, probing at spots with the dimming light of the lantern. He tapped it against his thigh to encourage the weak batteries.

"She's been gone all afternoon," Valjean said. "She could have come miles."

"Not hurt this bad," Carpenter said.

"What are you saying? No. No!" She forced confidence into her voice. "No one around here would do something like this." Fear for him stung her hands and feet like frost. She stood for peace. She stood too suddenly; dizzy, she put out her hand to steady herself. He could feel her trembling.

"It could have been an accident, yeah, like you say." He spoke quietly for her sake. He had learned to do that.

"You see?" she said, her heart lifting a little.

"Yeah." Kneeling again, he shook his head over the dog's labored breathing. "Too bad, old girl; they've done for you."

When the amber light failed from Lady's eyes, Valjean said,

breathless, "She was probably trespassing," thinking of all those signs, neon-vivid, warning. He always teased her that she could make excuses for the devil.

"Dogs can't read," he pointed out. "She lived all her life here, eleven, twelve years . . . and she knew this place by heart, every rabbit run, toad hole, and squirrel knot. She was better at weather than the almanac, and there was never a thing she feared except losing us. She kept watch on Dennis like he was her own pup."

"I know . . ." She struggled to choke back the grief. It stuck like a pine cone in her throat. But she wouldn't let it be *her* tears that watered the ground and made the seed of vengeance sprout. For all their sakes she kept her nerve . . .

"And whoever shot her," Carpenter was saying, "can't tell the difference in broad day between ragweed and rainbow. Goddam weekenders!"

They wrapped the dog in Dennis' cradle quilt and set about making a grave. Twilight seeped away into night. The shovel struck fire from the rocks as Carpenter dug. Dennis was at Scout meeting; they wanted to be done before he got home. "There's nothing deader than a dead dog," Carpenter reasoned. "The boy doesn't need to remember her that way."

In their haste, in their weariness, Carpenter shed his boots on the back stoop and left the shovel leaning against the wall. The wind rose in the night and blew the shovel handle along the shingles with a dry-bones rattle. Waking, alarmed, Valjean put out her hand: Carpenter was there.

Now Valjean resumed work on the boots, concentrating on the task at hand. She cleaned carefully, as though diligence would perfect not only the leather but Carpenter also, cleaning away the mire, anything that might make him lose his balance. From habit, she set the shoes atop the well-house to dry, out of reach of the dog. Then she realized Lady was gone. All her held-back tears came now; she mourned as for a child.

She told Dennis that afternoon. He walked all around the grave, disbelieving. No tears, too old for that; silent, like his father. He gathered straw to lay on the raw earth to keep it from washing. Finally he buried his head in Valjean's shoulder and groaned, "Why?" Hearing that, Valjean thanked God, for hadn't Carpenter asked *Who?* and not *Why?*—as though he had some plan, eye for eye, and needed only to discover upon whom to visit it? Dennis must not learn those ways, Valjean prayed; let my son be in some ways like me . . .

At supper Carpenter waited till she brought dessert before he asked, "Did you tell him?"

Dennis laid down his fork to speak for himself. "I know."

Carpenter beheld his son. "She was shot twice. Once point-blank. Once as she tried to get away."

Valjean's cup wrecked against her saucer. He hadn't told her that! He had held that back, steeping the bitter truth from it all day to serve to the boy. There was no possible antidote. It sank in, like slow poison.

"It's going to be all right," she murmured automatically, her peace of mind spinning away like a chip in a strong current. Her eyes sightlessly explored the sampler on the opposite wall whose motto she had worked during the long winter when she sat at her mother's deathbed: Perfect Love Casts Out Fear.

"You mean Lady knew them? Trusted them? Then they shot her?" Dennis spoke eagerly, proud of his ability to draw manly conclusions. Valjean watched as the boy realized what he was saying. "It's someone we know," Dennis whispered, the color rising from his throat to his face, his hands slowly closing into tender fists. "What—What are we going to do about it?" He pushed back his chair, ready.

"No," Valjean said, drawing a firm line, then smudging it a little with a laugh and a headshake. "Not you." She gathered their plates and carried them into the kitchen. She could hear Carpenter telling Dennis, "Someone saw Gannett's boys on the logging road yesterday afternoon. I'll step on down that way and see what they know."

"But Carpenter—" She returned with sudsy hands to prevent.

He pulled Valjean to him, muting all outcry with his brandied breath. He pleased himself with a kiss, taking his time, winking a galvanized-gray eye at Dennis. "I'm just going to talk to them. About time they knew me better."

She looked so miserable standing there that he caught her to him again, boyish, lean; the years had rolled off of him, leaving him un-creased, and no scars that showed. He had always been lucky, folks said. Wild lucky.

"Listen here now," he warned. "Trust me?"

What answer would serve but yes? She spoke it after a moment, for his sake, with all her heart, like a charm to cast out fear. "Of course."

Dennis, wheeling his bike out to head down to Mrs. Cobb's for his music lesson, knelt to make some minor adjustment on the chain.

"I won't be long," Carpenter said. "Take care of yourselves."

"You too," Dennis called, and pedaled off.

Carpenter crouched and pulled on his stiff, cleaned boots, then hefted one foot gaily into a shaft of sunset, admiring the shine. "Good work, ma'am." He tipped an imaginary hat and strode off into the shadows of the tall pines.

A whippoorwill startled awake and shouted once, then sleepily subsided. Overhead the little brown bats tottered and strove through the first starlight, their high twittering falling like tiny blown kisses onto the wind-scoured woods. It was very peaceful there in the deep heart of the April evening, and it had to be a vagrant, unworthy, warning impulse that sent Valjean prowling to the cabinet in the den where they kept their tax records, warranties, brandy, and side arms. Trembling, she reached again and again, but couldn't find the pistol. Carpenter's pistol wasn't there.

Not there.

For a moment she would not believe it, just rested her head against the cool shelf; then she turned and ran, leaving lights on and doors open behind her, tables and rugs askew in her wake. She ran sock-footed toward trouble as straight as she could, praying *Carpenter! Carpenter!* with every step. And then, like answered prayer, he was there, sudden as something conjured up from the dark. He caught her by the shoulders and shook her into sense.

"What's happened? Babe? What is it?"

But she could not answer for laughing and crying both at once, to see him there safe, to meet him halfway. When she caught her breath she said, "I was afraid something awful—I thought—I didn't know if I'd ever—"

"I told you I was just going to talk with them," he chided, amused. She gave a skip to get in step beside him. He caught her hand up and pointed her own finger at her. "I thought you said you trusted me."

"But I didn't know you were taking the gun with you . . ."

Angry, he drew away. She felt the night chill raise the hair on the back of her neck.

"I didn't take the damn gun! What makes you say things like that? You think I'm some kind of nut?"

"But it's gone," she protested: "I looked."

And then a new specter rose between them, unspeakable, contagious. For a moment they neither moved nor spoke, then Carpenter started for home, fast, outdistancing her in a few strides. Over his shoulder he called back, edgy, unconvinced. "You missed it, that's all. It's there." He would make sure.

She ran but could not quite catch up. "Dennis has it," she accused Carpenter's back.

"Nah," he shouted. "Don't borrow trouble. It's home."

When he loped across the lawn and up the kitchen steps three at a time he was a full minute ahead of her. And when she got there Carpenter was standing in the doorway of the den empty-handed, with the rapt, calculating, baffled expression of a baby left holding a suddenly limp string when the balloon has burst and vanished. The phone was ringing, ringing.

"Answer it," he said into the dark, avoiding her eyes.

Finding the Chain

Ben wrapped a feed sack around the flat rock and hooked it onto the chains. There wasn't more than ten feet of sound hemp or baling wire on the whole farm and he'd used that to tie the dog out of trouble. Not that Shin would've run off; she wanted to run *in*, and she'd already fought a skunk and lost and come rushing back so fast nobody had the wit to grab her and drag her out before she ruined—"It's clean gone, you can just cut it up for stinking rags for all I care now," Cliffie raged—Grandma Gable's Storm at Sea quilt, which was still on the floor from where they had huddled to sleep the night before, cold, damp, and hungry.

By flashlight Ben had found the one can of tomato juice in the trunk of the car and had poured it over the dog, rubbing it into her coat, but there was no way, till he got the chimney swept of bats and birds' nests, to safely heat water to rinse her. She sat at rope's end, still reeking, grizzled pink with tomato and whining with embarrassment. She never had been restrained in her life—it had been honor system all the way, and mutual trust—and now this.

They had arrived late, well past dark, and the first thing Ben had tried to do for them, when they had finally got into the log cabin, was make a fire. It hadn't seemed worth it to pay a deposit to have an electric meter installed for just a weekend, so they came prepared to camp, to cook over the fireplace, and draw water up from the well. Ben laid a good enough fire to get things going and cheerful, only before he could turn his back the house had filled with smoke, all of it coming into the rooms, none of it going up the chimney. They had doused the fire with water and waved damp towels to get the air clear, deciding not to mess with the chimney till daylight.

First thing Ben did in the morning was run Mary J and Drew out to look around, to find something long enough to use to clean the flue. There were snow chains, eaten up with fertilizer, and trace chains, not long enough in themselves, but linked to the swing chains, they were about right. Ben reached up and unhooked the swing, hardly stretching. He left the swing on the porch, flat, and scaled the old ladder to the roof, telling himself, "Easy, easy." The mossy shingles were rain-slick. "No time to be airborne," he said.

He was whistling a little as he dropped the bundled rock down the chimney's crooked throat. Before he could even draw up, on the first sweep, here came Cliffie boiling out of the house like a hornet from a lit nest, yelling *whoa* and cussing like a Christian.

"Are you out of your mind?" she screamed. The echo bounced off the barn. Mary J prissed over to stand by her momma under the umbrella. All Ben could see was spattered shoes and neon anklets from that angle. Everything looked different. He almost laughed, till Cliffie shoved the umbrella back and he saw her face.

"Did soot get all over the house?" he wondered. It might have been an apology, but after all, it wasn't his fault. He had told the boy to run in and help his momma cover the hearth and seal it off with newspapers and duct tape. He'd even tossed the boy his car keys, so he could get the tape from the toolbox in the trunk. Ben reckoned Drew had just skipped off, and not accidentally either. Cliffie said the boy had some adjusting to do, that was all, and she never came down hard on his "pranks." Ben eased over onto his other hip and stretched his bum leg. Bad weather reminded every bone of where it had broken and healed.

"I told him to tell you," Ben said. "Where is he?"

"Don't start on him," Cliffie said. She'd been saying it for over two years, ever since Ben and Cliffie's first date, when Ben had offered Drew his hand and the boy pocketed his fists and turned away, sour as sorrel.

"I'm through *starting* on him," Ben said. Loud enough for the boy to hear, if he were skulking in the barn loft or on the back porch or stretched across the back seat of the car, reading his comics. He knew the boy wouldn't be sorry, early or late, for messing up. He didn't look for Drew to poke his hard head up over the edge of the roof and say, "Sir?"

"I've got news for that little pecker," Ben boomed. "The paperwork's come through. I'm his old man now."

Cliffie looked hurt. "I wanted to tell him!" She leaned on the ladder and stared up, but she wouldn't climb, wouldn't meet Ben halfway. She cocked her head like she heard nothing but bad news from an angel. Tears of rain ran down her face. Ben wasn't fooled. He knew it was rain. She'd laugh it off, or fight it out, or sue, Cliffie would, but never cry. "Not my Cliffie," he said.

She had been about to pull the ladder away and strand him up there, but when he spoke as cheerfully as that, and him wet enough to wring rainwater from his shirttail, she moderated. She and Mary J headed back to the house without another word. "You just cover the fireplace and save me a round trip," he called after them. If Cliffie heard it, she didn't say so. He posted himself by the chimney, listening. He could hear Cliffie comforting the baby, and warning Mary J not to run the batteries down on the transistor . . . Because of the crook in the chimney he couldn't see the light or if the fireplace had been covered, if they were ready. He called down to them—Cliffie had to hear it!— "Now?" and tried to sound like he was enjoying himself. "Say when," he hollered again.

Nothing

"If you can stand it, so can I," he decided, and having given her time enough, and warning—"It be on your head"—he let the bundle fall, giving the chains a good twist and scour, hoping, maybe, for the worst below. That's what it had come to after only twenty-four hours away from the Jim Walter home-on-stilts he had built for her in South End, with a view of the docks and marsh.

When Ben stamped back across the porch and into the house with an armload of wet kindling, he reminded her, "I'm no goddamn pioneer."

Cliffie had been so sick after the baby came she made Ben promise if anything happened—"Now, honey, please, just listen to me"—he'd take her back to her homeplace, have the funeral there, and bury her in the mountains with her family. "Mama's got the prettiest stone, marble,

and white as the winter moon. It says WILDROSE WOMAN / GOD
LOVED / SORROWS ENDED . . ."

Ben didn't want to hear that kind of talk. He said, "You're going to
get well and when you do, we'll all drive up there and see how the other
half lives." He promised.

"You mean it?"

Of course he did. But when she got well, he acted as though she
had taken advantage of him. It was two years before they finally got
away and headed due north. By then, the last of the Gables had died
out and Cliffie had been fretting all summer about what was happening
to "the things" left in the abandoned cabin. She couldn't locate a cousin
willing to go see, or find a tenant steady enough to keep the farm going.
Taxes kept coming due, and Cliffie was settling it in her heart that she
would have to sell. This would be the last trip. She would bring back
with her all that she could not bear to part with, and make her peace
about the rest. She wanted them to love the place as she did. She
wanted them to know everything, all the little stories. She wanted
everything to be perfect, and she was so excited the night before they
left that she kept getting up to write down something else on her lists.
Ben would turn over in bed, his back to the sudden light, and grumble
for her to settle down.

"You could sleep through a war," she told him.

"Not the one I went to," he said.

She had them out of bed and spooning cold cereal toward their
zombie faces by five o'clock the next morning. Even then, she was
telling them how great things were going to be.

Ben warned her again as they left the last traffic light in Glynn
County behind them, "It won't be like you remember it," as though he
expected her to reconsider, admit it was a mistake, and tell him to turn
around in the churchyard at Sterling and head back to the coast.

"I'm prepared," is what she said.

Ben had never been north of Lyons, where the sallow clay hills
begin, except for a class trip to Macon when he was a kid—to see the
circus—and his time in the army. He couldn't imagine what there was
about red mud for Cliffie to love and miss. He liked the rich flat black
sandy land, the rise and fall of the tides, the evergreen oaks . . .

He had to press the accelerator harder all the time now; every mile was uphill. Already his right knee felt stiff. The engine made a dry tapping sound, noisy as diesel, and he prayed the valves and lifters would behave themselves. He had packed extra quarts of oil and a can opener in his toolbox, but he wasn't like Cliffie, he couldn't plan ahead the way she did, for emergency and bad luck. He called it "borrowing trouble," but she'd had a lifetime to get good at it, no changing her ways now. The trunk of the car overflowed with things she had crammed in because they "just might need this up home." Besides the lunch she'd made for them, for the road, she had packed groceries, candles, matches, a hatchet, pillows, blankets, coal oil, and lanterns.

One suitcase contained the clothes they'd need if the weather stayed mild and another was stuffed with sweaters and warm hats and gloves in case it turned cold. "It can get mean in the mountains at Thanksgiving," Cliffie said.

She looked over the seat back to check on Mary J and Drew. They had set out perky enough, full of questions, jokes, quarrels, and fighting for place, but now had subsided into sleep, catching up on the dreams they'd lost in the early start. The dog, Shin, rode between them atop a pile of bedclothes that wouldn't fit in the trunk. She was a medium-sized dog, not young but alert, her hindquarters on the package tray, her front legs stretched out, her chin down, her ears up. She widened her grin into a sour yawn, but her eyes never left off for a moment searching the center line that came at them out of the dark.

"Dog is my copilot," Ben said, glancing in the rearview. Cliffie disapproved of dogs and blasphemy.

"We should've left her with Palma and them. They had room."

"They had room for Mary J and Drew too," Ben pointed out. He didn't want to leave the children behind, but he loved his dog. "She was my family, the same way Mary J and Drew were yours." He'd been wanting to say that for some time, waiting to see if she'd figure it out without having to be told.

The lights from the dashboard lit every hurt and hollow in her face with an eerie green. "We're all Stevensons now," he added, for once saying exactly the right thing whether she admitted it or not. "Little pitchers," she said, putting her long fingers over his mouth to hush him, adding, "Keep your eyes on the road." She sounded pleased.

It was false dawn. They were driving away from sunup. By the time it was true day, they had covered a hundred miles, had almost left the cypress lands behind. Jondi stirred and woke; Cliffie unharnessed him from his carseat and stood him on her lap to see out. "Look, baby boy, now we're getting somewhere."

When they stopped for a fill-up, Cliffie wrote down the mileage and the time and amount. She kept books on everything like that, had clipped coupons in case they had a chance to see some museums in Atlanta. "This isn't just another joy ride," she told them. When the kids wanted Cokes at the service station, she wouldn't let Ben shell out change for them. "We have our own cooler," she reminded them, "pretty soon we'll be stopping for lunch." All along the way she pointed out things she thought they might not notice, and explained history and geography, and what the fall line was and why so many pines grew and how to preserve the indigo snake from extinction. She was always teaching, whether she was in her classroom or not. She had even brought along a library book on the historical markers, so they wouldn't lose time stopping to read them.

"There's not an hour in the world for every little thing," Cliffie said, "but it's good to know what you're missing."

Mary J and Drew argued and begged to take turns reading the book, but they got carsick—"I told you so," Cliffie said—and had to walk it off on the roadside between endless cotton fields. Another good reason to travel U.S. 341, not the Interstate. Plenty of stopping room. "If you want to race, go to Daytona," Cliffie said. "All you smell on a four-lane is exhaust fumes . . . I'd know this was cotton with my eyes shut." She breathed in, in a testing way. "Everything done by machine now," she said. "No more chopping. No more laying by. No more protracted meetings, muddy baptizings, no more one pair of new shoes in November having to last all year." They gathered along the fence— Shin, too—looking. Ben and the kids stretched across to pick a boll or two. "The rains have about ruined it," Cliffie said, as they drove away. Jondi, who had never seen any kind of the real thing, just cotton batting and angel hair and aerosol flakes, kept pointing out the window at the dotted fields and calling, "Snow!"

"I never picked cotton," Ben said.

"I'd rather pick rags," Cliffie said, so bitterly he let up on the gas for a moment. She'd had it hard, so hard he wondered again why she'd want to go back and remind herself of what she'd left behind.

Cliffie had been so sure of the roads, the turns, the old landmarks, but in the rain her memory failed. It had never been but the dimmest daylight all day, and they had driven in rain from Macon on. Cliffie sat right up at the windshield, rubbing it with her hand, trying to see past the headlights. "This isn't where," she realized, looking scared. "Am I losing my mind?" Ben didn't complain; he backed them around in a wide place and they tried again. Finally they stopped at a dark store and Cliffie beat and beat at the door till an old woman dragged open a window in the house and yelled, "They're out of business. What?" Cliffie stepped around a pile of coal, to stand in a puddle and talk. As she came splashing back to the car, she was smiling. "We're just not there yet. Two more miles to Wildrose."

When they drove around the curve and the whitewashed church came into view, Cliffie said, "Of course," meaning *Here we are*, but Ben didn't understand, so he kept on driving, almost past, till Cliffie cried, "STOP!" He slammed on the brakes and they slid around in the mud. "I didn't say have a wreck," Cliffie said. "I didn't say break my nose." She had brought fresh-cut flowers from a florist. "Not artificial, not weeds. When will I ever have the chance again?" she explained, justifying those six red roses kept on ice in the cooler every mile of the way. The buds looked almost black now in the rain. That's how near nightfall it was.

Mary J got to steer the car when it slid off the road and stuck in the mud. Everybody but the dog and baby got out to push. Mary J liked the way her fingers curved around the wheel, and she was glad she still had polish on some of the nails and hadn't gnawed it all off. She had on so many coats of paint she could peel it off in one piece that tasted like banana oil. Kid stuff . . . She felt grown-up, driving, and she knew what she wanted for Christmas: a birthstone ring. "Aquamarine," she said, loving the sound of it, forgetting Jondi was listening. She wanted white gold, like her momma's. She could turn the stone under to her palm, and just let the gold show, like a wedding band. When she got married—didn't know yet *who*, but probably a fisherman, like Ben— she was going to live in a little house right on the marsh, and have a baby sweeter than Jondi, a little girl baby, and drive around in a boat the color of the sky. And if she didn't want to wash the supper dishes, she wouldn't. Her momma couldn't make her. And she wouldn't have to fold clothes or study books any more either. It might be another year or two, she didn't know just when she'd be a woman and could put her feet up and look at magazines and pin her curtains back with paper roses and have flowers everywhere, in a tire ring under the trees, and at the windows. "Window boxes, definitely," she said, sounding enough like her momma to make Jondi sit up and reach.

"Momma," she announced when everybody got back in the car and she slid over to let Ben drive again, "I'm not going to marry till I'm tall enough to see into the soup pot on the back eye. If a boy caint wait that long, he probably doesn't love me anyway. Right?"

Her momma felt her forehead. "I think this child has a fever," she decided. Jondi already had his ears filled with sweet oil and cotton, and coughed. "You next?" she asked. Mary J crawled over the seat back and lay in her corner and imagined what it would be like to be a nurse, like Aunt Palma. She would bring comfort and cheer to all her patients. She would wear a cape the color of midnight and walk quietly down the halls and carry a silver pen in her pocket to write important things on the chart . . .

As she brought luggage in from the car she imagined these were emergency Red Cross supplies. The next day as she carried Grandma Gable's red and gold candy jar from the hutch to set in the center of the table she imagined it was a bottle of blood. She held it to the light and said, "Plasma," and shivered. That wasn't why she dropped the jar. She didn't know why she dropped it. She couldn't believe she had dropped it. How could something that terrible happen? It didn't shatter, it broke in three shards, as if it had been meant to, and lay there empty as a shell. Her momma came running, picked up the perfect lid, kissed it.

"Not my bowl," she said. She knelt and picked up the pieces and tried fitting them together, like a puzzle. Ben came in and put his hand on Mary J's shoulder and said, "It's stopped raining. Why don't you and Drew take this grocery sack and hunt me some pine cones?" When she went out, he was telling her momma, "You going to have a funeral for it, or what? It ain't going to grow back. It ain't flesh and blood."

"You don't understand," her momma said. "I wouldn't expect you to."

Mary J handed Drew the bag. She went to the barn instead, and pulled the door shut behind her. It was so heavy.

Drew wasn't strong enough to drag the barn door open. He

didn't want to play with Mary J anyway. She was too bossy. He looked around, his first chance to explore the farm in daylight, in good weather. It was Thanksgiving day, after noon. They weren't going to have a turkey this time. There was no stove to cook on. They heated soup over the fire. The smoke smelled nice when wind blew it down the roof of the house and swirled it around in the yard. His momma told him to watch the weathervane. She said, "This is the fairing-off shower," and, sure enough, the arrow backed from east to northwest and the rains finally drizzled to a stop. The cold wind was rolling fog over the gray flanks of the Blue Ridge and Drew's momma said she didn't care what the man on the radio had to allow, *she* smelled snow. Drew couldn't smell anything but smoke and skunk-scent the dog had brought back. The ruined quilt hung on the slack line between the barn and the cherry tree. "Crazy place for a clothesline," his momma had said and Mary J and Ben laughed along. Drew couldn't understand. He never understood anything. They'd tell a joke and laugh and he wouldn't get it. At school they called him "Dumbo" partly because he was slow and partly because of his ears. He pulled his cap down over them. He liked winter best, when he could wear a cap all the time. When he was grown up he was always going to wear his hat, never take it off except when they played the national anthem; he'd take it off them, if the other soldiers did. He was going to be in the army. He'd grow. He'd be tall enough. He'd lead the way. "I'm not afraid," he said. He ran in the tunnel the quilt made hanging over the line; he held his breath. When he came out the other side, he took in a chestful of frosty air. It burned. It was getting colder. When he breathed out, he made steam clouds. He found a stick and broke it to length and pretended it was a cigarette, puffing on it, exhaling. It really looked like smoke. He wished Mary J was spying. She'd snitch and then he'd get her back for once . . .

Jondi had an earache and couldn't play outside. He wasn't even supposed to go on the sleeping porch. "Right back in here this minute or I'm coming after you!" his momma said when he went. He was watching Drew play with the chain. Drew had the chain around his shoulder. He dragged it then wrapped it around him again, at the waist, like a belt. He held it in both hands like a snake. He was going away with it. Jondi couldn't see where. Momma came and picked him up and carried him back into the house and set him by the fire. "Don't get in the fire," she said. "Be an angel," she said. When she had gone he crawled over to the shelves. There were no picture books. There was a basket. There was a jar. He liked the jar. It took both hands to carry it back. He sat on the floor and dumped it out. Buttons rolled everywhere. He laughed and chased them. His momma came back angry. "You put them up, look at this floor, I asked you to be an angel."

He reached into the jar and put a handful back. He gathered up another handful and put them back. It was taking a long time.

"Every last one of them," she said. She went away again.

Jondi thought of something fun. He dropped a button down the knothole in the floorboard. It disappeared. He had a savings bank. This was like that. He kept on putting buttons down the hole. He used both hands. Some of the buttons were metal, some were bone. He didn't have to force any; they all went.

"Gone," he said, reaching into the empty jar.

"What have you done with Grandma's button collection?" Momma shouted when she came back. Jondi cried.

Ben said, "I'll crawl up under there and get 'em for you, no use in hearts busting over something I can fix."

When he came back, he set the buttons on the porch. "Blow the dust off and they'll be fine," he told Cliffie. "Good as new." He went whistling off to the barn. He had an idea for a Christmas present for Cliffie, and he hoped there was a shovel around.

Cliffie felt like the whole trip so far had been one long erosion. They didn't appreciate this old place or the things in it. And why should they? "It's just somewhere else they'll probably forget they've ever been." She picked up the jar of buttons and was turning to go back into the house when she noticed the swing still sitting flat on the porch, its chains gone.

Before she could holler *Where?* Mary J came running out of the barn yelling, "Fire!"

Drew heard her. He was in the field, swinging the chain. Turning in a circle holding the chain. Whirling faster and faster till the chain stood flat out from him and pulled at his arms in their sockets. When he couldn't hold the chain any longer, or whirl any faster, he'd let go and tumble backward and the chain would fly out from him ad then drop in the sedge. He had invented the game on his own, and he liked it. His hands were stiff with cold. He didn't know where he had lost his gloves. He had let the chain pull him around in its circle all afternoon, and when he fell, he'd lie there and look up at the sky.

Clouds were coming fast. Low clouds, soft gray clouds. The sun struck through their gaps, casting golden shafts. Shadows raced. The mountains had vanished. Gusts of wind rattled the last soft downy seeds from the sedge and launched them across the pasture. When Mary J ran out of the barn and yelled, "Fire!" Drew was swinging the chain as hard as he could; he felt that this time he might be lifted from the earth and flung. He let go.

As soon as he scrambled to his feet he ran toward the barn. Shin stood at the end of her taut rope and barked. Momma came running down the steps, her hands over Jondi's ears to keep the wind off. "God help us, God help us," she was saying.

Ben had the shovel. He ran into the barn and Mary J and Momma were calling, "Come back! No! Don't"

Drew ran past them. He ran in after Ben. He didn't know why. Maybe he just wanted to *see*. He didn't think. He just ran. He wasn't afraid. He darted around the door and crashed into Ben, who came laughing out of the barn. "False alarm," he said. "That board looks like it's cherry red," he said. "I'd have thought the same thing. Its rosin's catching the sun . . . You did the right thing." Mary J beamed.

"I remember that board," Momma said. "I remember that board so well."

Everybody went back to the house, everybody but Ben and Drew. Ben said, "You come with me." They went back into the barn to put up the shovel.

"I gave you my keys this morning," he said. "Remember?"

"In the car," Drew said. "I left them on the—the—"

"Well, you go find them, and you open that trunk for me, and you get back here warp speed, you hear me? I got a chore for you."

Drew darted out.

"You owe me," Ben said. "If you're not back here in two minutes I'm coming to feed you to the hogs."

Drew said, "I ain't scared of nothing." Then he ran.

Ben was sitting on a crate when Drew came back. It was pretty dark in there. "You still here? Mister?"

It had been more than two years since Ben and Drew declared war. The boy never called him anything but *Mister.* "Here," Ben said.

"What you want me to do now?"

"Help me load this box in the car."

"Just old mud?"

"It's for your momma's Christmas," Ben told him. Maybe it was a crazy idea. "A surprise," he told Drew. "A little bit of here, for there."

"I hear you."

"I'm asking you to keep it a secret," Ben told him. "Man to man. You give your word and you keep it. You do that for me?"

"I'll do it for *Momma*," Drew specified.

"No, you'll by Jesus do it for me," Ben said, "or you won't do it at all."

The boy's chin came up and his lips narrowed. He didn't promise, Ben thought. Goddamn little peckerhead, he thought. Where's the payoff? He said, "Tell me something nice your daddy did for your momma. Just one nice thing."

Mary J asked Drew, "What do you mean 'crazy'?"

"He's giving her a box of dirt, the reddest dirt he can find, for Christmas."

Mary J wished she had thought of it. She decided right then to give her momma some rocks; she still had time before dark to find them, wrap them in a gunny sack, hide them, in the car under the seat. She'd find the prettiest stones, to outline the flower beds.

Cliffie said, "All I want is that other chain. They were both right here this morning and they got no business being anywhere else tonight." Drew just stood there, looking at her. "And don't stare at me like a refugee," she said. "I know it isn't all your fault. If Ben hadn't taken the swing down, you couldn't have lost the chain off it." She glanced across the yard at the field beyond. She could smell it so plain: snow. No use in telling them that again, getting their hopes up for nothing. But she wanted that chain, and if it snowed, they'd never find it. It would lie out there all winter, forever maybe, if whoever bought the farm left the field fallow. She could remember the day that porch swing got hung. They called it a "courting swing." She was finally old enough to keep company. She went with her daddy to the feed merchant—it was her sixteenth birthday—and watched as the bright links of chain reeled off the spool. He had bought a better grade than just getting by. "We want it to last," he had said. "A hundred years from now, my grandchirren's grandchirren'll be sitting out here in the breeze saying, 'Thank you, Charley Gable.'" He had died the next year.

Cliffie got up and paced. "I'm just going to look some more," she said. "I feel like a mama cat that's lost one of her kittens."

They could see her in the field, passing back and forth, looking down. She came to the far line and just stood there staring north where the Blue Ridge earned its name in fair weather. It was getting on toward sundown now, and the sky was still full of those tumbled clouds, plum-colored and ragged. Far off, crows laughed, fighting the wind.

Mary J eased off her chair and pulled on her jacket. She put her soup bowl in the dish bucket and skipped out.

"Mary J'll probably find it too," Drew said. "She likes being the hero."

Ben said, "I hope she *does* find it. . . . This has been some day." He folded a piece of bread in half and ate it. Two bites.

"What if she doesn't? What if nobody finds it?"

"Your momma wanted to take the swing home with us."

"We still can. They sell chain."

"Some things in this world there's just one of, even when you get something else just as good. Or better," Ben said. He and Drew studied each other, thinking it through.

"Work to do," Ben said, pushing back from the table. "You going to be here, you watch Jondi. Keep him out of the fire." He zipped his jacket and ducked out the door.

Drew said, "Easy when you tall." Meaning life in general. His daddy had been a featherweight Golden Gloves champ, five foot three. Everybody said Jondi was going to be big, big as Ben. "Look at those hands," they'd say. Drew pulled Jondi's hand away from the lantern and balanced the baby on his hip till he could get dressed for outdoors. He set the screen in front of the fire and slipped out the back way. He didn't want them to see him coming, as if he were tagging after.

Jondi jogged along in Drew's arms, asking *Why? Why? Why?* about everything he saw. Drew hoped Jondi wouldn't start crying when he saw their momma on the far side of the field. Drew just wanted to be by himself. He just wanted to find that chain.

But Jondi cried. He wouldn't toddle along, he wanted to be carried.When Drew set him down, Jondi grabbed to his leg like an anchor, and howled. Across the field their momma was calling instructions to him. Drew picked up Jondi and carried him to her.

Back of the house Shin was whining again. She ran as far as she could and then jerked over, held back by the rope.

Cliffie was saying, "Look!" She had found something. Not the chain. It was a little heap of trash, years old, in a ravine where they had brought the things they no longer wanted in the house or barn. A bedspring. A broken TV. Pickle jars. An old antenna. "Here's where they threw out," she said. "Look at this." She picked up the doorknob she had told them about. The white porcelain one that her great grandmother saved for the housewarming, from the other house, the one that burned. Cliffie had told them all about it. They had expected to see it on the front door instead of the deadbolt that had greeted them. They didn't have a key. They could see the key in the lock on the inside. They stood in the rain, locked out, and Ben went from window to window, trying each one. He managed to get the one in the kitchen open wide enough to slip Jondi through. Cliffie shined the flashlight from the porch toward him, calling him, and he had finally arrived at the front door and pulled the key from the lock inside and pushed it under the door so they could get in. All that because Cliffie didn't want to break a window . . .

The porcelain doorknob was chipped and the shaft wrung off. "I guess they knew what they were doing," Cliffie said. She turned her back, closed her eyes, and tossed it over her shoulder, refusing to look at where it fell. "The best way," she said. "I can't save every little thing."

Drew made sure no one was looking, especially not Mary J. He made it look as if he were just wasting time, prowling around in the weeds. Momma was saying, "Grandma always said a field that grows sedge is too sorry to plow." When they had gone on past, still hunting the chain, Drew stooped down and picked up that old white doorknob. It had rolled down the gully a little farther when his momma threw it.

He didn't even take time to rub it off. He couldn't force it into his pocket, so he hid it in his sleeve. His heart was pounding. He felt so proud, as though he had saved a life. He ran with his arm up, so the knob wouldn't slip out of his jacket sleeve. He slowed down when he got back in the field. He walked along kicking at the tufts of sedge, trying to remember where he had been the last time he swung the chain. He wanted above all to find that chain. If Mary J found it, it would be all right, but if he found it, it would be exactly right. She was searching along the crumbly edge of the brook, so he turned upland, his arm raised, his eyes down. He didn't see Shin chew through the last threads of her rope.

They were never going to find the chain. All they were doing was wandering around in the last light, hoping. Shin ran back and forth over the soggy ground, greeting each of them, forgiving them. They had been walking the terraces away from the house, Mary J here, Drew there, Jondi and Shin everywhere, and now that they had come to the far fence row, scattering its sparrows, there was nothing to do but turn back. They were by chance or grace almost in unison now, apart from each other, absorbed, looking down, but moving, pausing, and keeping pace.

It had begun to snow, the first flakes they'd ever seen; only Cliffie had been in snow before. They'd have stopped to enjoy it, to catch the white cool feathers on their hands and tongues, but Cliffie moaned, "That's gonna do it. Amen. Y'all go on."

Ben said, "I wish I had a big magnet."

"Or a giant rake," Mary J said. They closed ranks against the coming dark, against the soft, random flurries, against the idea of giving up. Not touching, still at arm's length, but now shoulder by shoulder, like a chorus line, they swept across the field. Shin barked them along, and raced ahead and then padded back. Finally she took her sober place beside Ben, on the right flank. Drew, on the far left, stumbled, fell, and pushed himself to his knees. The doorknob had flung out of his sleeve and he was so intent on getting it back, on keeping his secret, that he didn't notice the chain. That was what had gripped him. It lay in a loose curve, muddy, and till he touched it, got it in his hands and lifted it, he couldn't believe it. He had seen it in his mind's eye all afternoon; he didn't believe it. Then he jumped up and hollered, "Ben! Momma!

Over here!" and everyone swerved, everyone came clotting around him, reaching, touching. Holding on.

It was funny how they all held on. Even when they turned and headed for the house, its one window lit golden by the oil lamp, the smoke from the hearth fire beaten down flat from the chimney into the bare yard, the air between them and comfort filled with that confetti of feathers, they still held to the chain. It seemed so right. Ben wanted to say, "Don't nobody let go," but he didn't. Some things just have to happen.

Suggestions for Further Reading and Classroom Use

The stories collected here represent only a small sampling of recent fiction which deals in important ways with southern life and culture. For further reading or for use in the classroom many of these stories might be paired with other books in order to explore common themes and the necessities of different genres.

To set these stories in the context of work by southern women writers, a number of recent critical books are particularly helpful. These studies attempt to define a tradition—or traditions—of writing by southern women and suggest topics and texts for further reading. Especially useful are: Ann Goodwyn Jones, *Tomorrow is Another Day: The Woman Writer in the South, 1859–1936* (Louisiana State University Press, 1981); Louise Westling, *Sacred Groves and Ravaged Gardens: The Fiction of Eudora Welty, Carson McCullers, and Flannery O'Connor* (University of Georgia Press, 1985); Minrose Gwin, *Black and White Women of the Old South: The Peculiar Sisterhood in American Literature* (University of Tennessee Press, 1985).

An interesting perspective on the issues raised by these stories and by southern literary critics is Alice Walker's *In Search of Our Mothers' Gardens* (Harcourt, Brace, Jovanovich, 1983). Her essay "Beyond the Peacock," which appears in that collection, provides an important emphasis on home, on change, and on the relationship of African-American writers both to southern literature by whites and to cultural change. It would be interesting to pair the stories by Walker, Moore, and Spencer with stories by Flannery O'Connor, particularly "The Artificial Nigger" and "Everything That Rises Must Converge."

A historical dimension to the issues these stories raise can be found in several recent novels. A striking development in recent fiction is the number of books that have sought to work through the history of slavery, to bring a contemporary imagination to bear upon the most distinctive and the most horrible dimension of southern history. The parent text for all these novels is Margaret Walker's *Jubilee* (Houghton

Mifflin, 1966), a book which is still not so well known as it deserves to be. Outstanding recent novels by women that come to grips with the meaning of slavery include Toni Morrison's *Beloved* (Knopf, 1987) and Sherley Ann Williams's *Dessa Rose* (Berkley Publishers, 1987). These books, though they are not written by southerners, can, I believe, significantly reshape our sense of southern literary history and of southern history itself. They present powerful evocations of the spiritual and emotional meanings of slavery and show us how indelible, finally, the institution of slavery is in cultural memory. They provide a useful context in which to read stories like Spencer's "The Business Venture," Walker's "The Welcome Table," or Opal Moore's "A Pilgrim Notebook, Part I."

A number of very fine recent novels by African-American women who are not by birth southern can usefully be read in conjunction with this anthology. Particularly interesting in their treatment of the contemporary South are Paule Marshall, *Praisesong for the Widow* (Putnam, 1983); Gloria Naylor, *Mama Day* (Random House, 1988); Marita Golden, *Long Distance Life* (Doubleday, 1989); and Alice Childress, *A Short Walk* (Coward, McCann and Geoghegan, 1979).

Another context in which these stories might be taught, and an area they suggest for further reading, is context of language. Critics of southern literature often remark on its distinctive sense of language, and critics of southern culture sometimes wonder if the distinctiveness of southern language is being lost in the world of mass communication. The work of sociolinguists and others can tell us about the myths and realities of these trends, even as the writers of the stories collected here attempt to reflect the changing nuances of southern speech. Particularly interesting reading in this area are: Shirley Brice Heath, *Ways With Words: Language, Life and Work in Communities and Classrooms* (Cambridge University Press, 1983) and Crawford Feagin, *Variation and Change in Alabama English: A Sociolinguistic Study of the White Community* (Georgetown University Press, 1979).

Like language, culture is always shifting and changing, and these changes have been particularly marked in the South since the time of the Civil Rights movement. Recent work in southern social and cultural history has yielded several books about twentieth-century southern life which might be interestingly paired with stories in this collection. In particular it might be useful to group Margaret Jarman Hagood, *Mothers of the South: Portraiture of the White Tenant Farm Women* (originally published in 1939; rpt. Norton, 1977); Linda Flowers, *Throwed Away* (University of North Carolina Press, 1990), a study of rural culture in eastern North Carolina; Jacquelyn Dowd Hall, *Like a Family: The Making of a Southern Cotton Mill World* (Norton, 1987); the stories by Shirley Ann Grau, which show the changes in southern culture from a middle-class point of view; and Walker's stories and essays.

Attitudes toward sexuality and culture and writing by or about southern lesbians would be an interesting focus for further reading. It would be useful to compare Shange's, Tinsley's, and Spencer's treatment of relationships among women with the relationships in Shange's *For Colored Girls Who Have Considered Suicide When the Rainbow is Enuf* (Bantam, 1980), with Walker's *The Color Purple* (Harcourt, Brace, Jovanovich, 1982), with Mab Segrest's *My Mama's Dead Squirrel: Lesbian Essays on Southern Culture* (Ithaca: Firebrand Books, 1985), with Segrest's poems, and with Rita Mae Brown's novels.

Suggestions for further reading in contemporary fiction by southern women writers can be found in the bibliography appended to *New Stories by Southern Women*, edited by Mary Ellis Gibson (University of South Carolina Press, 1989).

Notes on Contributors

TONI CADE BAMBARA was born in New York City. She holds a B.A. from Queens College and an M.A. from City College of the City University of New York. She is well known as a civil rights activist and as a professor of English and African-American Studies. Her collections of short fiction include *The Black Woman* (1980), *Gorilla, My Love* (1972), and *The Sea Birds Are Still Alive* (1977). She has also edited two anthologies of black literature and written a novel published by Vintage Books, *The Salt Eaters* (1981). In the *New Yorker* Susan Lardner remarked of her stories that they "are notable for their purposefulness, a more or less explicit inspirational angle, and distinctive motion of prose that swings from colloquial narrative to precarious metaphorical heights and over to street talk, at which Bambara is unbeatable."

SHIRLEY ANN GRAU was born in New Orleans and currently divides her time between Metairie, Louisiana, and Martha's Vineyard. She holds a B.A. from Tulane and has published eight books of fiction. Her story collections include *Nine Women* (1985), *The Black Prince* (1955), and *The Wind Shifting West* (1973). In 1965 she received the Pulitzer Prize for Fiction for *Keepers of the House*. Her other novels include *The House on Coliseum Street* (1961), *The Condor Passes* (1971), and *Evidence of Love* (1977). Since her literary debut at the age of twenty-four, Grau has been acknowledged as a master of the short-story form. "As a short-story writer," Mary Rohrerger commented in *Women Writers of the Contemporary South*, "Grau's talent is immense though not revealed by a simple surface reading; for what is beneath the surfaces and interacting with them is what is characteristic of the short-story genre, and Grau has mastered the genre."

MARY HOOD is a native of coastal Georgia and currently lives and writes in Woodstock in the north Georgia foothills. Her short stories and essays have appeared in *Georgia Review*, *Harper's*, *Kenyon Review*, *Best American Short Stories 1984*, and *North American Review*. She has published two collections of short fiction, *How Far She Went* (1983) and *And Venus Is Blue* (1986), and she has recently completed a novel. She is the recipient of a Pushcart Prize, the 1983 Flannery O'Connor Award for Short Fiction, and the *Southern Review*/Louisiana State University Short Fiction Award. Writing in the *Kenyon Review*, David Baker commented that Hood's "is an unsentimental vision of the New South where front porches yield to shopping malls and Camaros outnumber cotton fields." Hood's South, he continued, "finds its families falling apart, its women stranded yet struggling individually to grow stronger, and its very past—the history and nostalgia so important to Southern tradition—vanishing or vanished."

OPAL MOORE was born in Chicago in 1953. She attended Illinois Wesleyan University and the University of Iowa, earning bachelor's and master's degrees in drawing and printmaking. As an art student, she also studied writing fiction and poetry. She completed the Iowa Writers' Workshop in 1982. Her fiction, poetry, and essays have appeared in *Callaloo; Obsidian II; Poet Lore; The Black American in Books for Children* (2nd ed); *Writers for Children: Critical Studies of the Major Authors Since the 17th Century; Black American Literature Forum;* and elsewhere. She is now living in Richmond, Virginia; she is working on a collection of stories and a critical study of the juvenile fiction writer Mildred D. Taylor. She teaches writing and literature at Radford University in Virginia.

NTOZAKE SHANGE was born in 1948 in Trenton, New Jersey, and now makes her home in Houston, Texas, where she is a member of the faculty at the University of Houston. She received her B.A. from Barnard College and her M.A. from the University of Southern California. Highly regarded as a poet, playwright, fiction writer, and screenwriter, she counts among her most recent works *Ridin' the Moon in Texas: Word Paintings* (responses to art in prose and poetry), 1987; *Three Views of Mr. Fuji* (play), 1987; *Besty Brown: A Novel*, 1985; and *From Okra to Greens: A Different Kinda Love Story; A Play with Music & Dance*, 1985. Commenting on the emotional intensity of her work, Shange told an interviewer that "our society allows people to be absolutely neurotic and totally out of touch with their feelings and everyone else's feelings, and yet be very respectable. This, to me, is a travesty. So I write to get at the part of people's emotional lives that they don't have control over, the part that can and will respond."

ELIZABETH SPENCER was born in 1921 in Carrollton, Mississippi. She received her B.A. from Belhaven College in Jackson and her M.A. from Vanderbilt University. She has published numerous novels and collections of stories, including *Fire in the Morning* (1948); *The Light in the Piazza* (1960); *Ship Island and Other Stories* (1969); *The Snare* (1972); *The Collected Stories* (1981); *Marilee* (1981); *The Salt Line* (1985); and *Jack of Diamonds* (1988). She lived for many years in Montreal, Canada, and has recently moved to North Carolina, where she teaches at the University of North Carolina at Chapel Hill. "Like all writers, I think, I write instinctively," Spencer says of her own creative process. "I write because I feel the urge to write and while I'm doing it, the hell with it, but the total pattern is something that recurs as a question: What am I really doing in a large sense? I think I never questioned this as long as I was writing Southern novels because in writing I was simply part of the Southern tradition."

MOLLY BEST TINSLEY grew up in an Air Force family and so comes from "no place in particular." Of her own sense of place and location she says, "Twenty-five years in various suburbs of Washington, D.C., haven't changed this sense of detachment. In my fiction I am trying to connect with the place underlying town, region, country, which I guess I would call *earth*." She is on the civilian faculty at the U.S. Naval Academy in Annapolis and has published stories in numerous magazines and quarterlies, including *Shenandoah, Greensboro Review,* and *Prairie Schooner.* Her first novel, *My Life with Darwin,* was published by Houghton Mifflin in the spring of 1991.

ALICE WALKER was born in 1944 in Eatonton, Georgia, and currently makes her home in San Francisco. She received her B.A. from Sarah Lawrence College and has published essays and fiction as well as poetry, including *In Search of Our Mothers' Gardens: Womanist Prose* (1983) and *Living By the Word: Selected Writings, 1973–1987* (1989); story collections *In Love and Trouble* (1973) and *You Can't Keep a Good Woman Down* (1981); and the novels *Meridian* (1976), *The Color Purple* (1982), and her most recent work, *The Temple of My Familiar* (1990). She has received an award from the American Academy and Institute of Arts and Letters, the Lillian Smith Award of the Southern Regional Council, and a Guggenheim Fellowship. *The Color Purple* was awarded the 1983 Pulitzer Prize for Fiction and the American Book Award for Fiction. Peter S. Prescott commented on this book in *Newsweek*, calling it "an American novel of permanent importance, that rare sort of book which (in Norman Mailer's felicitous phrase) amounts to 'a diversion in the fields of dread.'"

Motherhood
Interrupted

Motherhood
Interrupted

Stories of Healing and
Hope After Abortion

Jane Brennan

To order additional copies of this book, contact:
Xlibris Corporation
1-888-795-4274
www.Xlibris.com
Orders@Xlibris.com

39367

CONTENTS

ACKNOWLEDGEMENTS

Many people helped with this project and I thank them all! I would like to particularly thank Sarah Jennings, Loretta Oakes and especially Sharen Watson who helped with the editing of this book. Their expertise was invaluable to me as well as their friendship. I'd also like to thank all the women whose stories are in this book especially Laura Rohling and Joyce Zounis who have been extremely helpful. All these women are very brave and courageous and I feel blessed to know them. We've developed a special bond and I'm very thankful for them.

Lastly, I'd like to thank my husband Kyle Brennan without whom this book never would have come to be. His support and love is very precious to me. I love you, Kyle.

Sincerely,
Jane Brennan

Let there be hope . . . .

I would now like to say a special word to women who have had
an abortion. The [Catholic] Church is aware of the many factors
which may have influenced your decision, and she does not doubt
that in many cases it was a painful and even shattering decision.
The wound in your heart may not yet have healed. Certainly what
happened was and remains terribly wrong. But do not give in to
discouragement and do not lose hope. Try rather to understand
what happened and face it honestly. If you have not already done
so, give yourselves over with humility and trust to repentance. The
Father of mercies is ready to give you his forgiveness and his peace
in the Sacrament of Reconciliation. You will come to understand
that nothing is definitively lost and you will also be able to ask
forgiveness from your child, who is now living in the Lord. With
the friendly and expert help and advice of other people, and as
a result of your own painful experience, you can be among the
most eloquent defenders of everyone's right to life. Through
your commitment to life, whether by accepting the birth of other
children or by welcoming and caring for those most in need of
someone to be close to them, you will become promoters of a
new way of looking at human life. (John Paul II, *Evangelium Vitae:
The Gospel of Life*, 1997)

FOREWORD

I have been a Catholic priest for 25 years. In those years I have heard thousands of confessions and have conversed with untold-numbers of people. Rarely have I had encounters more powerful than with women and men confessing an abortion or complicity in one. In those moments I watch a range of emotions come over the one before me: fear, anxiety, confusion, humiliation, shame, sorrow, need, loneliness. But when they face and share these feelings, when they acknowledge and own the abortion, I watch as before me, miraculously, they experience something else, emotions they believed they could never experience again: forgiveness, liberty, joy, and peace. I am a privileged witness to a rebirth.

I was once talking with a woman who had undergone three abortions. She and her husband, the father of all three of the children they had aborted, had been married many years. They had given birth to other children now raised and on their own. They weren't particularly religious. They weren't Catholic nor, in fact, did they adhere to any religious tradition; they held a humanitarian ethic of secular values. She characterized their marriage as loving and stable. Yet it never seemed to her to be open or intimate. Approaching mid-life certain questions kept perplexing her. Why had they not been able to achieve honest openness and intimacy in their marriage? Why did it lack spontaneity and creativity? What prevented them from the deep happiness they expected and hoped for on their wedding day—that day they were so young, so in love, so open to one another and so attuned to the future.

Eventually she came to the conclusion that the answers to her questions were rooted in the three abortions. Although they occurred many years ago, they tainted everything that came thereafter. Her husband and she had agreed to abortion as birth control. Now she admitted that although they believed they were controlling birth, with each abortion they gave themselves over in fact to the control of death. The first, and then slowly but surely each subsequent abortion, snuffed out their joy in life, the sense of life is good together. In an insidious way the abortions of their babies caused the abortion of their own freedom and trust. She had come to this conclusion about the abortions themselves. "We bought the line they sold us. They told us that abortion terminates a pregnancy. To the contrary," she continued," I have been struggling to give birth to my babies for forty years."

In the natural created order, the womb is a sanctuary, a place where new life is protected, grows, and is born. Instead into this very sanctuary of life she invited death. She believed that by aborting her baby she was terminating her pregnancy; instead she conceived death itself. After many years, she understands that a mother's womb will not allow death to conquer life. She aborted the bodies of her babies but her heart still labored to protect their lives. For forty years she attempted to avoid the pain of those three abortions by living according to the dictates of an inadequate, secular moral code, one she believed justified her choices. Yet in her heart she was continually in labor; she was and is their mother.

I believe in the teachings of Jesus and of the Catholic Church. I believe in the principles of our tradition which touch upon life and forgiveness. A Christian believes that the death and resurrection of Christ—his victory of life over death, truth over deception, light over darkness—is for all people. Christian principles of life and forgiveness are valid for every woman or man who has procured or been complicit in an abortion. I believe that by Christ's grace all women and men of faith or no faith can come to know life, love, freedom, peace, even if they have known death. How?

God has so created the human heart that he has placed within it the desire to live and to give life. The human heart stands guard lest death enter its most sacred chamber, the chamber of life. But even if death should somehow strong-arm and defeat the guardian of that chamber and violate it through an abortion, the heart of a mother, of a father, still wants to give birth. The human heart is created in the very image of the heart of God himself. Since God is life and love, so too our hearts must love and give life. The woman with whom I met discovered that because God himself created her heart after his, her own heart would not permit death; so it labored to give birth. Since the heart of God cannot die, neither could the child of her womb.

As my encounter with the woman who had three abortions, the Christian scriptures speak of a similar encounter between Christ and a woman known to be a sinner. The story is told in St. Luke's Gospel, chapter 7:36-50. The woman discovered Jesus was nearby. She came to him, crashing the dinner party to which he had been invited. She couldn't verbalize her need for forgiveness, yet she was sorrowful and full of love. Concerned neither about the opinion of the Pharisee who hosted the party nor that of his guests, yet full of shame at her many sins she approached Jesus from behind. For his part, Jesus turned his back on his host and welcomed her warmly. The woman dared only to look upon Jesus' feet; he looked directly into her eyes. She washed his feet with her tears and dried them with her hair;

he dried her tears with his acceptance and forgiveness and washed her soul with his loving gaze. She was known to others simply as one who had sinned. Through his forgiveness of her sins Christ conceived and adopted her as his own daughter. The other guests judged her as sinful for all that she had done. Christ looked into her heart and saw who she was, that she loved much, and gave her back her life.

There are several identifiable things that every post-abortive woman or man must do to rise from the death of a child from an abortion. (These stages are not sequential or chronological; they take place simultaneously.) One must *accept and own* the choice of an abortion, that is, one must acknowledge that all excuses, external forces and internal fears were just that, excuses and explanations, not justification. In a real sense, ironically, one who has had or made an abortion possible must become truly "pro-choice," that is, they must claim their choice as their own and accept the consequences it has wrought. (Many "pro-choice" persons are dishonest. They insist upon the right to choose but deny responsibility for the consequences that there choices engender.) Along with owning their choice, a woman or man who has had or been responsible for an abortion must learn *to forgive those who were complicit in it*—partner-parents of the aborted baby; the deceased child's grandparents, who should have protected their own "little girl" from death but instead handed her over to it; friends who should have been expected to care for their friend but instead supported her choice of an abortion; society itself, even, which chooses death in the name of individual privacy when it should choose life in the name of community. Additionally one must *share one's story with another*, another who loves, accepts, brings to bear an understanding heart—another who can forgive. Catholics, for example, are blessed with the sacrament of Reconciliation and Penance. In the Sacrament of Reconciliation and Penance the penitent places herself/himself at the very feet of Jesus. As if from the Cross itself the Lord says, "Father, forgive them, for they know not what they are doing." How powerful are these words—they deliver life! What freedom it is to know that he who forgave his own executioners also forgives us for the ways we have brought death into the world, for whatever way we have given in to fear when we should instead have given ourselves over to love. Since a post-abortive heart still labors to give birth to the aborted child, one must *believe* her/his child is alive. Believing one's offspring to be alive makes it possible to know the child's own forgiveness of her/his parents for the abortion. Finally, healing from an abortion comes about with *self-forgiveness*, truly personalizing the love and acceptance of God and of others.

At some point every woman who has procured an abortion or anyone complicit in one acknowledges the truth that the burden of their abortion is too hard to bear, the sin too dark to be kept hidden any longer. Hopefully they will discover that truth and life, love and forgiveness are nearby. To all those who have had abortions, have been complicit in one, or know someone who has, I make this plea. Desire to be free of the birth pains you have suffered for so many years and give birth to new life, that of your baby and your own. Consider not the opinions and judgments of the crowd, of others. Come to truth and to life and be forgiven. As the sinful woman approached Christ from behind, even if you do not believe explicitly in the Son of Man let love gaze into your heart. Let forgiveness and liberation caress your cheeks as you would caress those of your newborn infant. As heavy as the weight of death you bear, especially the death of your own unborn baby, life itself is stronger. As dark as death is, forgiveness is lighter. As painful as your abortion is, forgiveness will bring you freedom and peace. If you love much, you can be forgiven much.

The stories compiled in this collection are stories from those who have in some way experienced the same journey of the woman known to be a sinner who sought out Christ and of the woman with whom I met. They have accepted their choices. They have shared their stories with God and with those whom they love and have been forgiven. They now share them with you so that you can know that you are not alone, that forgiveness and freedom, healing and peace are possible. In sharing their burden and their past these courageous persons prove to us that life and love can never really be snuffed out. God himself, who has conceived and created us in his own image and likeness, will be the midwife of our babies, our children, ourselves.

Msgr. Edward L. Buelt, Pastor
Our Lady of Loreto Parish
Foxfield, Colorado

INTRODUCTION

By

Jane Brennan

*H*ow *could she do that?*

I often hear this question asked by well-intentioned people while addressing the topic of abortion. Lacking personal experience, they do not understand how a woman could abort her own child.

Didn't she realize she was carrying a baby, cells that have already formed life? If we can just get women to realize that the cells growing inside them are in fact already a baby, then women would no longer have abortions.

These people mean well, however, in their zeal to protect the unborn child there is a tendency to overlook the plight of the woman who is often desperate, confused, frightened, or may be suffering from the wounds of her past.

I'd like to explain what I mean by telling you story, a true story, my story. It's not easy to tell but I feel compelled to share it so that people will understand and not judge women who made the horrible choice to abort, but instead reach out and help them.

*   *   *

The innocence and idyllic time of childhood can be wonderful, and many women celebrate memories of their younger years as magical and full of imagination. However, when innocence is shattered, repercussions follow.

I grew up on the East Coast in an average, middle-class family with a mom, dad, brother and sister. My mother was a stay-at-home mom, and my father was a bookkeeper. From the perspective of those around us, we were the typical American family. Nothing was further from the truth.

Like all families, we regularly visited my grandparents. When I was five years old, my grandfather started molesting me. I didn't understand what was going on, and was confused and frightened.

After several excuses of stomachaches, and conversations regarding my unwillingness to visit my grandparents, I finally told my mother why I didn't want to go. Somehow, she stopped the abuse but refused to talk to me about it, and my father simply pretended it never happened. My parents never comforted my hurting, little girl heart or told me that it wasn't my fault. Because I was alone in my turmoil, I wrongly believed I was somehow responsible for this terrible violation, and left to suffer the effects of my grandfather's abuse in silence. No one in our family was allowed to discuss our *secret.*

Two years passed, and when I was seven, a female relative started sexually abusing me. All the sick feelings I felt before returned once again. I felt so dirty and ashamed, and didn't know what to do. I couldn't talk to my parents. The door to communication regarding the subject of abuse had all but closed after the experience with my grandfather. I had no one to turn to, no one to help me. So I just kept silent and bore it all myself.

Eventually, I found a way to ease the pain and despair I felt from the abuse: alcohol. I got drunk for the first time when I was ten years old. I liked it. It felt good. For a few hours, I didn't feel like the dirty little girl I thought no one loved, so I continued drinking.

When I was twelve years old, I discovered marijuana. By the time I was in the ninth grade, I was drinking and getting high every weekend. The following year, it was practically every day. I always felt so different from everyone else, like I didn't fit in with the other kids. All I wanted was to feel normal, and I mistakenly believed that drugs and alcohol fulfilled this need.

I especially felt uncomfortable with boys. I didn't know how to talk with them, and when I was drunk or on drugs, I could laugh, talk and socialize easily with them. When I turned eighteen, I found something else to ease my pain: sex. I thought physical intimacy with boys meant they loved and desired me. I wanted to feel like I mattered to someone and the only way I could fill that yearning was to offer sex to boys who were interested in me. My life revolved solely around drugs, alcohol and promiscuity.

College and dorm life introduced me to new coping dependencies. Cocaine, speed, and hallucinogenic substances made me feel even better, more in control of life. But, in truth, my life was spiraling out of control.

During my junior year, the inevitable happened. I was pregnant and scared out of my mind. I had no idea what to do. But this was Boston, 1979, and there were no shortages of advertisements for abortions in the student newspaper. Abortion was publicized well around campus, socially acceptable and easily obtained.

I couldn't talk to my parents for fear of disappointing them. I had noone else to turn to. I was scared, alone with no money, no job and no support. Who would help me? I went to my boyfriend and the only thing he was concerned with was that *I* deal with it. So after speaking with several friends who agreed with me, I believed abortion was the perfect answer. My boyfriend gave me half the money I needed to take care of *my problem.*

When I arrived at the clinic, I had to see a staff counselor before anything else. She was very nice and seemed genuinely concerned about me. "The whole procedure will be very easy and then you can just go on with your life." She continued, telling me that I wasn't carrying a baby, just a "clump of cells." I didn't know anything about fetal development at that time, so I believed her and felt relieved that I had made a good decision, an acceptable one. Before I left her, she handed me a Valium and sent me to the examination room.

The doctor hardly acknowledged me and told me to lie back on the table. When he started the procedure, I nearly passed out. The pain was excruciating. After it was over, he sent me to the recovery room, which was essentially a room full of couches. I had one hour to rest and recover. "The next group of women will need a place to rest after you've recovered." They told me. A fleeting thought went through my mind at the comment. *This feels like an abortion assembly line.*

After lying on the couch for more than the allotted hour, the nurse behind the counter told me I had to leave. I didn't think I could get up, and when I did my legs were wobbly and weak. I was dizzy and didn't even know if I would be able to make it out of the clinic. Somehow, I did.

The dorm was a trolley ride away and during the ride, I felt nauseous and was afraid I was going to get sick in front of all the other passengers. I was also an emotional wreck with tears threatening to spill over at any moment.

When I arrived at my dorm room, I fell on my bed and let the tears come. A thought that I had done something wrong conflicted with what I believed was my right to take care of myself first. I was raised Catholic (although my parents were not very religious) and knew just enough of what the Catholic Church said about abortion. I pushed the thought away as quickly as it came. After all, the church was just a bunch of celibate, cranky old men who knew nothing about women. I made a choice to believe the counselor at the clinic rather than a faith I knew next to nothing about.

After the abortion, life seemed to get more difficult. I drank and used drugs more than I previously did, trying to fill the empty, numb and depressive emotions I was experiencing. They didn't help, and I couldn't see a way out of my pain. I had no idea how to help myself, or who I could turn to for support. I didn't know that God was a loving Father, so it never occurred to me to turn to Him. In my eyes, He seemed distant, punishing and uncaring, and held absolutely no meaning in my life. Once again, I turned to alcohol, drugs and sex.

I couldn't face my emotions and wanted to blot them out. I was very good at avoiding any vulnerability in my life by being the life of the party, drinking, laughing and flirting with all the guys, but when I was alone and sober, the pain returned. In those moments, I would reach for a drink, take a pill, or smoke some marijuana. It was a vicious cycle.

Around this time, I began to get involved with the feminist movement. The early 1980's was when radical feminism reached its peak. I was drawn to their message of claiming that women should have full control over their bodies. As a result of the abuse I suffered as a young girl, I never felt I had control over anything, least of all, my body. Feminism gave me a voice and for the first time, I felt empowered and confident. All the anger toward my grandfather, my female relative and my parents found an outlet in this movement, and the message these women conveyed about abortion being a woman's right justified my decision to *fix* my earlier problem. These women also hated the Catholic Church because of its staunch position on abortion, so I hated it right along with them.

I moved to New York City after graduation and found the fast-paced lifestyle of the city exciting and exhilarating. The men in the bars were easy prey, and drinking, along with casual sex was the norm for me, my right as a feminist. However, my *right* didn't do much to liberate me. The shame, guilt and disgust I felt when waking up in some man's bed overwhelmed me at times but I knew how to drown out these feelings with my old friends, alcohol and drugs.

Ironically, my first teaching position was in a Catholic school in Brooklyn. There weren't any openings in the public schools, so I took this job reluctantly. My employment in the Catholic environment did nothing to dissuade my feminist thinking. I still hated the church. I thought all the rituals and doctrines were fairytales and didn't apply to the modern woman.

I became a member and volunteer with NOW (National Organization of Women), and believed them when they said that religion was just another way to control women.

Eventually, the fast-paced lifestyle of the big city began to take its toll and my brother, who lived in Denver, CO, suggested that I move there. I knew I needed to slow down, and Denver was known to have a slower paced and relaxed lifestyle, which appealed to me.

Shortly, after arriving in Denver, I found a job working in a daycare center. It was there I met a man who was divorced and had custody of his two young daughters. We started dating and before long, I moved in with him. Both of us were heavy drinkers. Our lives were centered around alcohol, but I felt everything was normal. I was helping him raise his girls and living what I thought to be a respectable life. In truth, our makeshift family was barely surviving the craziness and chaos we had created.

About six months later, I became pregnant. I was afraid to tell this man at first because I thought he would be angry with me. I was using birth control, but it apparently had failed. I knew he didn't want anymore children, so when I finally told him I was having his baby, he shocked me by suggesting we get married.

I agreed to the marriage, however, I told him I was going to have an abortion first. *If I have the abortion, I can walk away from the marriage more easily if necessary.* I knew in my heart this marriage wasn't a good choice. I knew this man was controlling and abusive at times, but what I didn't understand was that I stayed as a result of not dealing with the trauma of my own past. I mistook his bullying for love.

He agreed to my suggestion, and seemed relieved at my decision to abort our baby. Though I didn't want to have another abortion, I didn't want to be tied to this man. I felt I had no other choice, and hung on to the words the counselor had shared with me during my first abortion experience, "It's not a baby, just a clump of cells." I also believed it was my right, so I set an appointment for another visit to the women's clinic.

When I walked into the examining room, I was very nervous. The memory of the last abortion flooded my mind. As the doctor examined me, I told him that I didn't know if I wanted to go through with this. "Do you want my nurse to hold your hand?" I could tell by his attitude that he was annoyed with me. The nurse, also annoyed, took my hand.

"Maybe I'll come back another day." Nearly panicked at that point, I was ready to leave that place immediately.

"No, let's just get this over with now." The nurse persuaded me to stay.

When it was over, they sent me home. The familiar sting of tears threatened to flow, and all I could think of was sleep, but my boyfriend expected me to continue as if nothing had happened. He was angry with me for wanting a nap. When I expected compassion, I received rage, the first indication of what was to come.

I thought once the abortion was behind us and we were married, things between us would settle down. Conversely, he became more controlling and began physically abusing me as well.

My parents came to visit in the spring, and stayed with my sister, who had recently moved to Denver. When my husband and I went to her home to have dinner with my family, my husband drank heavily, and by the time we got home he was quite drunk. He started pushing me around and I tried to leave, but he grabbed me and wouldn't let me go.

"Don't answer that!" My husband tried to take the phone from me, but it was too late. My sister already heard what was happening. She immediately hung up and called the police. As the officers were coming up our front walk, they saw my husband shove me onto the couch. They burst through the door and restrained him. My parents pulled up shortly after that. I packed a few things and left with them. My husband and I divorced four months later.

After the divorce, I experienced severe depression stemming from the very unhealthy notion that the divorce was solely my fault. My husband had always told me I deserved to get hit because I made him so mad. I didn't know any better, so I had believed him. As far as I was concerned, it was my fault he behaved the way he did.

Shortly after my divorce was final, I found an apartment, which I shared with another divorced woman. Over time, we became friends and went bar-hopping together.

This is not what I want for my life. This is the old me, not who I am now . . . I wanted to live differently. I was very tired of my lifestyle and dreamed of meeting a nice man, getting married and settling down.

One night, while on a date, I noticed my *date* was ignoring me and talking with another woman when my brother walked in with a friend. He introduced me to his friend, and through the course of conversation, I found out this man was in the midst of divorce, and he invited me to a party at his house in a couple of weeks.

"I'd love to come." He seemed nice, and he was a friend of my brother's, so why not?

One thing led to another, and we started dating. At first, I was hesitant with our relationship because of my abusive first marriage, but I soon began to trust him and feel safe. It wasn't long before we decided to marry.

My life was finally on course, and I was ready to start a family. I became pregnant shortly after we were married, and gave birth to our daughter. Two years later, we enlarged our family with twins. Having three children under the age of three was overwhelming to me, and in addition, I suffered from Postpartum Depression. Realizing I needed some help, I made an appointment with a therapist. Still having strong convictions about feminism, I was thrilled to find that my counselor held firmly to the same beliefs and convictions I did, but over time, her influence began causing problems between my husband and me.

I became more depressed and the therapist sent me to a psychiatrist who put me on three different types of medication. Nothing seemed to help, and I spent more time lying on the couch than caring for my family. My husband was frantic, and pleaded with me to stop seeing the therapist and get off the medications, but I wouldn't listen to him. Instead, I spewed anti-man rhetoric at him, and ranted about how men wanted to keep women down.

When I finally gained some energy, I began volunteering for Planned Parenthood, helping young girls and women procure both birth control and abortions. I joined NARAL (The National Abortion Rights Action League) and participated in marches, protests and conventions championing feminist causes.

During this time, my husband and I agreed that he would get a vasectomy. I was too unstable from frequent bouts of depression, and all of my ranting and raving about women's rights and feminist ideas frustrated him. Our marriage was in no condition to support another child, emotionally or ideally. Finally, my refusal to listen to him, coupled with all the chaos in our home, drove him to ask me for a divorce.

The idea of divorce was unthinkable to me because I still loved my husband. I quickly came to the realization that the therapist I had been seeing wasn't helping, but hindering my marriage. It took many months of heartache and apologies, but my husband and I finally reconciled.

My experience with the feminist counselor caused me to question my convictions, and over the course of time, I became disillusioned with them. I began looking for something in life that was true, something I could have complete faith in, so I started seeking for meaning in everything feminist convictions opposed. First on my list—church.

I visited several different congregations, and then decided to visit a Catholic Church. I knew my husband's background was in the Catholic faith, and if there was any possibility for us going to church together, I knew this would be the only church he would consider. I arrived at Mass a little late, with my oldest daughter, and was nervous about going in. My heart was pounding and my palms were sweating. I almost turned and walked away, but felt a strong urge to enter. Familiar words met my ears and tears filled my eyes, as a feeling of peace swept over me.

An usher led us to a pew and while I stood listening to the priest, I felt an overwhelming force, like an invisible beam streaming down from above, and it knocked me to my knees. Pain, shame, depression and despair left me in that moment and I knew there was a God who loved me. I also knew without a doubt that Jesus Christ was His Son, and He wanted to heal me. I started sobbing.

"Mommy, why are you crying?"

"Because, I'm so happy." After all the years of searching for peace and happiness, church was the last place I would have expected to find the thing my heart was missing—Jesus.

The next Sunday, our whole family attended Mass. Soon, we had our children baptized and our oldest daughter received her first Holy Communion. I learned how to pray and trust God, and His mercy and forgiveness invaded my being.

During this time, I felt an urgency to go to confession. The abortions, the drugs, the drunkenness and promiscuity, all the things I thought were my rights were actually sin. Through the compassion and forgiveness of

Jesus Christ, I realized that the children I aborted were indeed life, and not just a "clump of cells."

It had been 25 years since I had been to confession, and I was terrified the priest would throw me out of the confessional after he heard the entirety of my story. Instead of condemnation, I left that confessional with joy and freedom and in tears of awe at the wonder of forgiveness through Jesus Christ.

My husband and I decided to be married in the church, and he had his vasectomy reversed. A few years later, I gave birth to another daughter, and we named her Grace Mary, a living testament to God's grace.

I often look back and think about how life may have been different if I had been informed of choices *for* life and not against it. What path would my life have taken if I hadn't endured childhood abuse? Would my choices have been different? What if the counselor at the clinic had told me that I was carrying a baby, not just a "clump of cells"? I'd like to think that if I had encountered other options, I would have made different decisions. But there were no volunteer counselors on the sidewalk outside of the abortion clinics when I walked inside.

Today much progress has been made in this area. There are crisis pregnancy centers and sidewalk counselors to tell the truth. These ministries are necessary and they are helping to win the battle against abortion.

I share my story here because I want to help end the secret shame of women suffering from post-abortive trauma. I want everyone to understand that most women who have made the decision to abort their babies are not frivolous and uncaring. Often, they are women who are confused and terribly afraid of the responsibility of motherhood when their lives are already chaotic and full of pain. Many women regret believing the lie that the only solution to pregnancy was abortion, and the majority of post-abortive women deeply regret the choice they made, living with the pain everyday.

It is my hope that after reading my story and the stories of the other women in this book, that many women who have had abortions will not be afraid to tell their own secrets. We all need to let other women know that abortion is not just a clinical procedure or fundamental right, but tragedy. In and beyond this tragedy, there is forgiveness, but if we don't speak out, other women will have to endure the pain. I don't want my daughter, sister, girlfriends or any other woman to walk through the painful experience of abortion. In fact, I don't want abortion to happen at all. Yet, if they have walked this journey already, I want them to understand that there is forgiveness and compassion beyond abortion through Christ Jesus.

CHAPTER ONE

Beyond the Bandaide™

by

Joyce Zounis

"You like living in a wrinkleless world, don't you, Joyce?" a dear friend commented on a business trip once. I never really thought about it until then, but she was right. Anything that I could take control of, I did. I am a perfectionist at heart, but with a great reason. Too many experiences from my early childhood underscored the way I embrace life. Keenly sensitive to right and wrong, black and white, anything gray is always a problem for it is out of my control. I learned very early to iron out these areas.

It all started during summer vacation when I was six years old. With daddy being the youngest of twelve children, it was a given that we would load up old Betsy (the family station wagon), and head south to visit my cousins.

"C'mon, Joyce!" called my younger cousin from the cornfields. The corn stalks seemed to reach the sky. They were taller than anything momma had ever planted in our suburban backyard. I fought my way through the never-ending maze to catch up to my cousin as he yelled, "Slowpoke!" somewhere up ahead.

"I am **not** a slowpoke, you . . . you." I was so out of breath, I could barely speak. Deep in the field of corn it was getting a little spooky. "How do we get out of here?"

"We're ok. Come here, I want to show you something." What he did next has been forever etched in my mind. Even though he was younger, he touched me in unspeakable ways. I was so frightened and numb not knowing what was happening but sensed it was bad, very bad. I froze in shock, screaming from the depths of my little soul, but no sound escaped.

Every summer, for three years, the same thing would happen. I was so ashamed and believed this had caused God to stop loving me. And then the whispers began, *"Your daddy will never love you, you dirty little girl. No one will want you."*

I had promised myself all year long that I would not let him touch me that way again. But without my parents knowing what was going on they would pair me up with this cousin because we were in the same age group. Every time they did, it would happen again. Afraid to tell my parents, especially my daddy who had warned us to behave or else, I quickly learned to hide my secret behind the *bandaide* of my smile and obedience.

Daddy made the military his career. My younger sister Wanda and I would race to see who would get to unlace his boots and end up in his lap for a big hug when he came home. But no sooner did the boots hit the floor and the fun was over. His routine with the newspaper and quiet order helped to establish rigid rules and expectations, both defining my upbringing and later leading to teenage rebellion on my part. The demands of Dad's career were great, and Mom bore the heavy responsibility of parenting five busy children, not an easy task. I slipped into the role of a pleaser and tried not to bring attention to myself fearing my mom might find out my secret.

Some of my fondest childhood memories include attending church. Mom would polish us up and off to the neighborhood Southern Baptist church we would go. How I loved being there and learning about Jesus. I will never forget the courage and strength I felt as I walked down the aisle to proclaim Jesus as my Lord and Savior at the age of eight. Unfortunately my little secret began to confuse my growth as a Christian.

Without understanding, the shame I felt in the shadows of the cornfield deeply wounded my tender spirit, piercing the inner depths of my consciousness. *I can't tell anyone.* Sometimes Daddy would forget to take off his military uniform, at least in his mind. This Army sergeant, believed everything was to be in order. If it was right it was worthy of praise, if it was wrong, it was deserving of punishment according to deed. I knew great disappointment would be the verdict if he ever found out. And how could I ever tell God? I knew He would react just like daddy.

"If anyone ever finds out, no one will ever love you again." The whispers were getting louder. And the *bandaides* were getting bigger. I remember being in fourth grade, still going to church and thinking I had the power of a witch. As I carefully isolated myself from friends, while walking home alone from school I would chant horrible things trying to inflict the weight of my pain and rejection on to others.

These whispers became real for me while attending a church sleepover at the age of nine. The girl's leader read us a story and the moral was purity. Finally I had something to call it and now knew what I was not, pure. I panicked inside thinking everyone could see right through me. I emotionally disconnected with everyone there after realizing I was spoiled goods, just like the whispers had said. Not only was my home an unsafe place now I knew no one could ever know my secret at church as well. *Daddy wouldn't want me if he knew I was spoilt.* Early in my life the Enemy separated me from my father's love and in turn, my Heavenly Father arms.

Behind the mask of selected behavior I choose to protect myself from any outward affection. I denied and punished others, in particular my parents, for not protecting me. *"If they loved you they would have seen what was going on. They don't love you,"* the whispers taunted. When Mom and Dad would come into my room to kiss me goodnight, I would pretend to be sound asleep, curled up against the wall on the top bunk bed hoping they would turn away, softly closing the door behind them. And they did. If only they knew—if only I had known—how much I needed their hugs and kisses.

At thirteen I smoked pot for the first time and loved this new feeling of happiness. I desperately needed the high to escape the pain of feeling dead inside. I believed myself to be a Christian, just without a God who wanted me. *"How could He possibly love you after what you let him do to you,"* the whispers now shouted.

Not only did I discover pot, but my sexual violations now turned into invitations. One of my escapades, during the summer before my high-school sophomore year, landed me in a hotel room with an older guy that I had only recently met. The odor of pot and stench of alcohol greeted my mom and brother Chuckie, as they snatched me out of his arms and away from this dingy hotel. I was angry they had found me (and secretly humiliated), for my mother finally saw the real me.

I was great at changing the *bandaides* and masks in my life. Sometimes I would leave love notes under Mom's pillow. This proved to be the only way I could really share my heart with her. It was safe—no contact needed. Nothing prepared her for the note of 1977. I slowly penned the words that I was pregnant and that I had made an appointment to take care of the problem. Little did I know I had called an OBGYN office—a place I had yet to visit at fifteen. Without much dialogue between us, Mom stepped in and set the abortion appointment.

"Do not tell anyone about this, Joyce. We will never talk about this again." My mother was determined to keep this day a secret. Yes, another secret. As soon as we walked in to the waiting room, we spotted someone we knew. Mother was mortified, but kept her eyes from making contact. I knew she was simmering; now our secret was blown.

I was waiting for my name to be called just like any other appointment. I was so naïve, I wasn't thinking about what was going to happen, only about the lie I needed to tell my cheerleading coach since I would be late for practice. I was first taken to the fetal model counseling room to go over the abortion procedure. No one ever suggested anything other than the abortion. I was told by the counselor it would be real quick, I believed her. By the time I got through this session I had already mentally tuned out. I now put on a new *bandaide* over my emotions, and with my survival mask securely fastened I walked into the small impersonal room. The nurse instructed me to change into a gown and gave me a pill to take; a detached routine that seemed all too familiar to her.

It was a very warm September day, but all I remember feeling was cold, ice cold—physically, emotionally, and spiritually. I had also returned to that all too familiar place of being disconnected and the sterile feeling of the abortion facility certainly helped my fear to sink in. "*Let no one see.*"

My heart beat wildly in my chest as I was taken to the "procedure" room. The doctor came in, introduced himself and said the following. "If you ever see me in public, don't acknowledge me and for my part, if I ever see you in public I won't acknowledge you." At the time I thought he was trying to be the good guy, trying to help me with my embarrassment, but now I wonder if lack of acknowledgement leads to lack of responsibility.

Emotionally I completely died during my abortion. I looked at everything in the room but the equipment and then right before my eyes I saw the tube fill with blood and tissue. I fell into a trance as the vacuum finished removing my first child. I was now an empty shell of a mother. It wasn't until years later did I come to understand that you are a mommy whether your baby is a six day old embryo or a 60 year old person. Motherhood is interrupted when you deny that reality.

When I left the facility, not only was I emotionally detached from reality, but I was emotionally separated from my mom. That detachment did not help me change my life though. In my black and white world, my familiar *bandaide* stayed with me and I continued my life as if nothing ever happened. The gray was wiped out.

Other friends at school were doing it too. It wasn't just me. Abortion had become widely practiced among the high school sweethearts. My inner turmoil didn't seem to have a negative impact on my social standing either. I was a cheerleader, honor-roll student, Keywanette president, homecoming queen, and the high school's beauty queen. I'd even kept the same boyfriend throughout all three years of high school.

It was just a year later when I told this boyfriend the news that I was pregnant. After much fasting and praying on his part, I told him not to worry for I would take care of it. I knew the routine. Our years in school would not have to change. I had already done it once—I could never go back to being pure. What's another, right? And when I was told, "You're only getting rid of a piece of unwanted tissue," I thought it was the logical way to save the relationship. Though we dated for five years, our future marriage died the very day I laid down on that abortion table.

My actions and judgments about sexual intimacy and morality were completely out of control. After college I found myself married, not to my high school sweetheart, but to another young man. He intrigued me. His attention and lifestyle filled a void I had been longing for. Even though he was an agnostic I was his; hook, line and sinker. We held a secret wedding ceremony and our marriage was like no other that I knew. He was a grad student and I worked in marketing promotions. We actually never set up a home together. We were satisfied with our liberal arrangement as he lived at school and I traveled. I had two abortions with him prior to our marriage and then two during the marriage. I really believed this was unconditional love.

The power this obsessive relationship had over me stemmed from my belief that only he could make me complete and happy. Something I desired since my childhood. I was willing to do whatever it took to keep him in my life but an adulterous relationship on his behalf led to our divorcing.

Getting on the abortion table was like visiting the familiar emotional place from my childhood. I knew what I was doing was wrong but ignored the truth of the situation. The cornfields and the abortion table were the same place for me. I basically "flat-lined" inside to buy into the theory that what I was doing was right. My goal was to survive the situation; to ensure the future I wanted, the future I had to have.

Something else happened. While in the waiting room I began to comfort the other young women who were anxiously waiting their abortions. This made me feel a little better. I was the "pro" and I twisted the black and white with the gray to convince myself that everything was okay; it had to be.

On the heels of my broken marriage, I fell into a rebound relationship. About a year later I was pregnant. "I'm not going to have an abortion this time. I can't do it. I won't." My resolve to stay pregnant resulted in the birth of my first living child, a beautiful baby boy, who I called Trey. It was also the awakening, the birth of my dead emotions. Trey's father was nowhere to be found during his delivery, being in the arms of another woman.

When I was in recovery, God showed me that I no longer needed to be in bondage to this man and his abusive love. It took me three months to let go and on the very day I finally obeyed, I met Ted Zounis. It truly was love at first sight. Not only did he immediately love me, he fell in love with my baby boy too.

After three very traumatic separate incidents, we were married on a Friday evening by the justice of the peace, five and half weeks after we met. And on Monday Trey's biological father signed the adoption papers. Trey became Ted's son and to celebrate, we renamed him after his favorite Greek name, Costa. Finally, I had a real family.

My perspective toward life took on new meaning—life continued to be restored in my dead heart—as a mother. "Costa, honey, you are so precious. Do you know how much you changed your mama's life?"

Secretly my stomach churned at the thought of the babies I aborted as Costa wrapped his tiny fingers around mine. *What is wrong with me? Snap out of it, Joyce. Pull yourself together.* Without warning, hot tears often filled my eyes but would never fall, and overwhelming sadness wrapped itself around me. Unbeknownst to be me, grief followed closely with guilt and shame. This feeling that I had lost something precious, something I had never experienced before, caused me much discomfort, but I suppressed it, choosing to give it no expression. Fear kept me from laying bare the secrets of my heart—to anyone, not even my husband knew the real truth.

In the end, Ted ended up being an unwilling partner in my final abortion. His Greek father was very insistent that he would have nothing to do with me or my son—that I was an "KSeno"—a foreigner and "used goods". Two months into the marriage I started to buy into these ugly words that were now being screamed at me by the enemy when Ted was away serving in the military.

We were so excited to learn that I was pregnant and told everyone. However, my inner struggle with emotional abandonment, Ted's absences, and a diagnosis of torn ligaments that made the pregnancy difficult, enabled me to decide abortion was the only solution to this problem. Ted was completely against this idea, but did go with me, dismayed, to the abortion facility several weeks later.

My first and last abortion happened at the same facility. Eleven years had passed as I held back the gray world, kept it at bay until the sound of the vacuum turned on. Memories rushed over me like a raging river. *"Look at what you have done"* the whispers screamed. I started crying and the doctor became indignant and informed me that I was already a problem because he was missing his tee time. Splattered blood on his gown horrified me. *What have I done?*

Ted was equally distraught as we left that place, and ultimately, our child behind. When we arrived home, I went in, but not Ted. He headed across the street and found solace in drugs numbing the events of the day. For years Ted has felt the impact of that fateful day.

It wasn't long after that my job with Hilton Hotels moved our little family to South Florida. Money was tight. Ted was working odd jobs. While still living in the hotel, I thought I was pregnant. Knowing the routine all too well, I quickly pulled out the yellow pages while at work and called the local abortion facility for a free pregnancy test.

When I arrived for my appointment, I was shocked to learn that I had unknowingly called the TLC Pregnancy Center, a place that helps women and men with pregnancy related concerns, instead of an abortion clinic. I didn't even know that these places existed. The pregnancy test was inconclusive. They set another appointment for two weeks later.

The volunteers at TLC asked permission to hug me and celebrated with me when the test was positive. They offered to help both Ted and me as we faced the challenge of having a second child with little means of support. Their caring manner and assistance saved the life of our baby girl, Melina who is now 18 years old.

Ted and I were living a backslidden life. Even though we both knew the Lord since childhood, drugs were prevalent in our home and we never gave church a second thought. It was only through the gift of a church business card and little Costa mimicking our marijuana use that we finally decided we needed to make some changes in our life and marriage. We attended church together for the first time.

I can't remember a time I felt so enveloped by God's love. It was as if I had never left at all. The faith of the little girl I used to be, filled my heart once again. I always believed myself a Christian and did feel the Lord at different times, but it had been easier to turn my back on Him than to confront the reality of my ways. I knew He had seen all my attempts for man's attention, approval and love. What I did not realize was that my relationship problems continued because a man could not fulfill the love I so deeply desired.

Ted and I rededicated our lives that day, and laid down our drug habit. We continued attending church weekly, and both of us listened intently to Pastor Bob's messages. He soon began to share about an event called Life Chain from the pulpit. My secret past of *seven* abortions haunted me, yet I was compelled to participate in the Life Chain event. *But how could I possibly go to an event like that, much less participate in it?*

The enemy taunted me with his lies. *"How can you possibly support a cause like Life Chain? No matter how much you love God, you'll never go to be with Him. You killed your own babies."*

I was afraid, horribly confused by my emotions, but knew I had to participate in the Life Chain anyway. It was just one hour of prayer, but it proved to be one of the most difficult hours of my life. Even though I stood with thousands of Christians, I felt alone and isolated to the words on my sign, *Abortion Kills Children*. It felt like fire in my hands, and now in hindsight, I realize that was the beginning of God's purifying fire. The process of healing from my abortions truly started at that moment. I finally came face-to-face with the truth about what I had done to my children. I knew then that it was a sin.

Several weeks later, I turned on Christian radio for the first time. My husband had taken our three children out for a treat, so in a rare moment, I was alone in a quiet house. Carol Everett, a former abortion clinic operator, was the guest on a show. She shared how she had been indirectly involved with over 35,000 abortions including her own, yet she called herself an Ambassador of Christ, by His mercy and grace. She went on to tell her story of God's forgiveness and healing of her past. My big hang up was my number, seven. Right then God said to me, "Joyce if I can forgive her with 35,000 abortions, I can forgive you too."

Can God really love me? Can He really forgive me?

"Can you, Lord? Will you?" My voice trembled at the words, and tears I had hidden for years flowed freely as I revealed the hidden places of my heart. Just as He promised, Jesus forgave me. I felt as if a blanket of peace wrapped itself around my body, holding me tenderly. At last, honesty renewed my disjointed relationship with the Lord. All He wanted was for me to tell him and ask for forgiveness. He had always loved me—just for me—and He had never left.

Later that year, I visited TLC once more. I thought I was expecting again, but it turned out to be false pregnancy symptoms.

"Joyce, I would like to invite you to join us here at TLC as a volunteer. The changes in your life are clearly evident, and I believe you would have much to offer to other women with similar experiences."

"I-I don't know what to say." I swallowed hard. For lack of anything better to say, I told her I would pray about it, and drove home to do just that—pray.

While the phone rang, I tapped my nails on the splintered kitchen table.

"TLC." How may I assist you?"

Can I talk to E—, please?" The praise music played softy in my ear while I held for her. A click opened the line.

"This is E—. How can I help you?"

"Hi, this is Joyce. We spoke last week about the possibility of my volunteering for the center. Does the offer still stand?" Surely, the position was filled by now.

"Open and waiting just for you."

I agreed to meet with E—the following day, and she gave me a tour around the facility. Each time she opened another door, I found myself cringing with the anticipation of seeing the *machine*, but I never did.

"Okay, just a few details. Every lay counselor we bring in fills out the same application you did, Joyce." I watched her demeanor for signs of judgment, which I clearly deserved. "You've experienced abortion personally, is that correct?"

"Yes, that's correct." What I didn't tell her was that the number I put down was far lower than the actual number of my experiences. I looked away from her eyes, locking my vision on a beautiful portrait of an infant still surrounded by its mother's womb.

"Look at me, Joyce. It's okay. There is no judgment here, you know that." I turned and faced her again, my face damp with tears. "There is only one thing you need to participate in before you are able to counsel these women. It's called PACE, an acronym for Post Abortion Counseling and Education. It's a Recovery Bible study for women who have had abortions."

Through the power and grace of a stranger's prayers at this pregnancy center, several weeks later I agreed to participate. It was during this intimate and challenging time that I was able to embrace the grieving process from abortion. My experience with God's forgiveness and peace deepened, filling me with a beauty and joy I'd desperately needed since the past days of the cornfield.

Grieving fits into God's plan for reconciliation with his son, Jesus and I have been given the hope of being reunited with my babies in heaven . . . I'm now free of the horrific shame and burden of my abortions, yet my Redeemer is still healing me of the devastation of losing seven children through choice.

Motherhood was interrupted when I denied the existence of my children. But when I realized that I missed out on their laughter and loving them, I understand the pain that abortion causes. The choices I made and the actions of others have also impacted my five living children. Today they too grieve their seven siblings. As a Momma of twelve, I have found it is possible to move on, living beyond the bandaides, allowing myself to grieve and name my missing children, giving dignity to their existence and value to their desired lives.

I've also come to understand how my early sexual violations contributed to my promiscuity. Together, Jesus and I have resolved many issues including anger, denial, depression, fear, abandonment, loneliness, unhealthy sexuality issues, and the desire to punish myself. Because of what He has done for me, I have peace I can barely comprehend. He silenced the enemy's whispers and replaced them with His own, always telling me He loves me—past, present and always. Even with all my life's wrinkles.

Humbly, I serve as a bridge in which others, those who have suffered the consequences of the *American right* of abortion. These people cross over to find true healing and freedom through Jesus' love. The consequences of abortion can and do cripple the body, mind and soul, lasting a lifetime. Only God's sovereign judgment brings about His sovereign mercy, something I know I am to share in the midst of the battle to save His people not yet born. The abortionist said it would be over real quick but the consequences have lasted over 30 years.

I am only free because He set me free. His grace and tenderness have removed all my *bandaides* and I am living beyond my past. Nothing can change my past. The abuse, the promiscuity, the lies and the abortions, they are real. However, my worth and forgiveness, my joy and peace are all found in my everlasting relationship with Abba Father. I am forgiven, loved and set free!

Today Joyce has moved beyond the bandaide our culture placed on her private pain of child loss through choice. Her 21st century voice of truth has been featured on CBN's 700 Club, Daystar's Denver Celebration, Lasea Broadcasting, Sky Angel's FaithTV, Light On The Hill TV, Evangelische Vangelische International TV of The Netherlands, Focus On The Family *Citizen Magazine, Charisma Magazine*, Life Redeemed Radio, Point of View Radio, at the National Press Club, in Senate hearings, on retreats and many others places God allows.

Joyce's focus includes promoting and touring with the documentary, **"I was wrong."**, *which enriches experiences to engage the Church, our culture and the media by telling our abortion stories and of His grace & glory.* **"I was wrong."** is 30-minute documentary that captures the story of Norma McCorvey, 'Jane Roe' of *Roe v. Wade*, the gal of the 70's and the woman of God she is today. Since Norma had never had an abortion Joyce was asked to be the face and voice of the experience. In addition to telling her story of losing seven children through abortion, she takes you on a tour of a pregnancy care center in Texas & interviews a client while she is having an ultrasound performed. Please visit www.IwasWrong.info to view the trailer and order your copy of this life changing DVD.

CHAPTER TWO

Whatever Feels Good

By

Laura Rohling

In the 1960's in America a philosophy was born . . . . if it feels good, do it! Amongst the free love culture this philosophy was embraced by many and lived out in ways that were shocking to the traditional family values that characterized previous generations. As long as it felt good and you weren't hurting anyone else what did it matter? So everyone thought who followed this philosophy. The problem is that it did matter. Our actions do affect others. They are never isolated incidences and although they may seem not to harm anyone else, they in fact do . . . .

My mom left us when I was 12. After several years of physical abuse where my parents tried to beat each other to a pulp, she felt her options were better away from our family than with us. Truthfully, I had started suspecting she wasn't thrilled with the vocation of motherhood anyway, as I can't remember a single joyful holiday, let alone any happy, loving times between my parents.

After Mom left—the day after Christmas 1977, when I was 12 years old—Dad had to learn to juggle full-time career and single fatherhood. He made sure my sisters, brother and I were at Mass most Sundays and attending religious education once a week. If we were late for Mass, he would take us to the coffee shop for donuts and drive us to the highest hill in town, overlooking the ocean. I remember him saying, "Kids, on this hill, you're as close as you can get to God, so today, this is our church service." When Pope John Paul II came to town, he took the day off from work and drove all of us downtown to get a glimpse of him.

I saw my mother occasionally, but quickly realized she didn't want anything to do with the church or faith. Dad would cover for her by telling us she was Jewish. My siblings and I gave her Hanukah cards and tried to make Passover a joyous occasion for her for several years, until we figured out that she actually didn't adhere to any faith at all.

Dad had his hands full with a house full of young teens, and with supervision lacking, it was not unusual to find a few dozen friends at our house after school. Soon these gatherings became drug and alcohol fests. We smoked pot and snuck booze from the liquor cabinet. I was convinced that I was more mature than my years and surrounded myself with friends a few years ahead of me. I especially loved the attention from the older boys. I believed having someone interested in me, for whatever reason, made me lovable. This thinking is what drove me for a long time. So at 16 years of age, as a result of what I thought was a true love relationship I became pregnant. I had called an abortion clinic in a neighboring state because back then the state I lived in required parental consent, and the neighboring state did not. Luckily, at least in my mind at the time, I miscarried. I was so relieved.

My mindset at the time would have dictated abortion had I not lost the baby, and as I grew older, I believed the message of the day—"Anything goes as long as it feels good to you and doesn't harm anyone else." Along with feeling good, I also believed that the pro-choice vs. pro-life issue was a matter of personal choice for the pregnant woman, not the political arena.

My attitude toward my mom became admirable. I thought she was amazing, venturing out on her own with a big career. She was fun and adventurous. I put aside the fact that she had abandoned my siblings and me, and clung more tightly to her motto that had already become my own mantra. "Anything goes as long as it feels good to you and doesn't harm anyone else."

Several years passed, and slowly, each one of my siblings and I drifted from our Catholic roots. Reminders of our childhood faith only presented themselves at baptisms, weddings and funerals.

During this time, my dad found a wonderful woman and remarried. A caring stepmother, she loved us and guided us in the gentle ways only a mother can and we learned to be ladies and gentlemen by witnessing her social graces. She was a fabulous cook and her recipes soon became our own. What a precious time for our family. She was the mother we always dreamed of having and we loved her very much. We were so happy.

One year passed, and we received the news that my stepmother's previous breast cancer had returned and she passed away the following year. I was 23 years old. We were devastated and very worried about Dad. He mourned for two years before finally meeting a woman who helped him through his grief and they married several years later.

Around this time, I started going to clubs with friends and met the man who would become my first husband. I was convinced that my stepmother would have approved and that thought became my main reason for loving him. Violence on his part and immaturity on mine dominated our union, and we divorced a year and a half later.

Having learned the hard lessons of life early on, I took pride in my newfound independence and focused on developing a perfect world for myself. I was convinced that I was mature beyond my years, when in truth I was numb to most emotions. What I didn't realize was the impact this numbness would have on the two decades ahead.

I focused on my career and was largely successful. I was a female in a male dominated industry and that made me a desirable commodity in my field. However, I made a terrible choice and fell in love with the company's vice-president when I was 27 years old, 20 years his junior. He told me that he would eventually fall in love with me, but needed time. I was completely infatuated, and convinced he was the answer to my empty life. I wanted so desperately to be loved. Three years later, he took a job in Denver and I was devastated. I tried to move forward with my life by taking a position at a top marketing firm in Chicago, but couldn't forget this man. After three months, I found myself so lonely that I quit my job, followed him to Denver and worked for him again. I loved him desperately, but it was unrequited and I found myself alone, not knowing another soul in the entire region 3,000 miles from home.

I mourned that relationship but I needed to move on and vowed to get past the heartache. I worked hard to meet new friends and forced myself to mingle with new people. I also made the decision to venture out on my own with a new career as a marketing consultant. I grew a recognizable client list that was continuing to flourish. Things seemed to be going great and I was finally getting over "him".

It was then I met Robert. He was a wonderful person, but I had so much emotional shrapnel in my life all I wanted was fun and distraction. Before long, we both realized our relationship wasn't going anywhere, so we contemplated not seeing one another anymore. It was during this time I became pregnant.

How could I be so stupid! I'm certainly old enough to know better. I was terrified. I watched my desirable client list disintegrate before my mind's eyes, bringing financial ruin. I considered the fact that my family was far away, and I didn't consider my friends close enough to seek confidential advice. The idea that I would carry this pregnancy to term only entered my thoughts for a few moments and immediately, I went into crisis management without consulting Robert. I handled the problem just like any other project in my professional career. I had a checklist. I had a problem needing a solution, so I did the next logical thing and set an appointment with an abortion clinic. Plans firmly in place, I told Robert. He agreed to my decision and accompanied me to the clinic.

Saturday morning, on Labor Day weekend, I arrived at an OB/BYN office that doubled as an abortion clinic. I had no idea that two practices could exist in the same office. They called my name and I went immediately to the treatment room. Just as the procedure began, I started crying.

"Do you want to reconsider?" The doctor stopped what he was doing, wanting to be sure of my decision.

The next words out of my mouth sealed the fate of my baby. "No, please continue." I continued crying throughout the procedure. They hadn't warned me about the pain, and the noise of the suction and removal of the tissue-and my child-was excruciating. The procedure was over in a matter of minutes. I vaguely remember the doctor telling me I wasn't that far along; a gesture of consolation, I suppose.

When it was over, I met Robert in the waiting room and he drove me to my apartment. We had no idea what to say to each other, so we didn't say much at all.

"I have to go help a friend move. Are you going to be okay?" He handed me a bouquet of flowers, walked out of my apartment, and my life. It was the last time we saw each other. I remember spending my entire weekend filled with an empty sort of relief, sad, and lonely. I carried on for months in a numb stupor, good at going through the motions without regret or remorse.

Subtly at first, depression began taking a hold of my life, and as time passed, it overwhelmed me. I tried to snap out of it, but it was unshakable. Along with depression came insomnia, and my nights were filled with more wakeful hours than rest. At insomnia's peak, sleep eluded me for one, two sometimes three or four nights in a row. I needed help.

Counseling sessions became my lifeline, sleeping pills and antidepressants ruled my days and nights. At 32 years of age, I was finally facing the trauma of my childhood, but I never mentioned the abortion. It didn't occur to me that it was one of my most emotionally traumatic life experiences. I told the counselor about my childhood—my mother leaving our family, my stepmother's death and the little supervision I had when I was young. I shared the story of how I fell hopelessly in love with my boss, made a cross-country move to be with him and how my infatuation was unrequited. "None of this had been my fault. I'm just unlucky . . . . unlovable."

And still, the conversation of abortion never made it into any counseling sessions.

The sleeping pills helped me to sleep, and the antidepressants lifted me somewhat out of the depths of despair, but the counseling sessions didn't seem to be affecting any change in my life. I was still depressed. Weekends became my enemy, two days of sheer loneliness. I tinkered with my faith during this time, mostly to take up an hour or two on an otherwise lonely

Sunday, not knowing why, not really sensing anything during Mass, but it did consume time in an otherwise empty day.

I remember one evening, the usual occasion of joining some acquaintances for a Friday afternoon happy hour, but it was the same as before—lonely and monotonous. As I drove home, I considered three options: I could take the exit to my apartment and endure another lonely weekend, or I could simply drive into a barrier wall. The wall seemed a lesser option because I wasn't completely sure it would kill me. Another thought I had was that I could race over the side of a bridge. That would do it. Problem solved.

After living with the possibility of suicide for more than a year, I decided on a solution. I referred my clients to other marketing firms, packed up and moved home. I didn't have a job yet, but a good amount of cash after my successful consulting career, which enabled me to rent an east coast townhouse right on the beach. Interviews became a part of my everyday, and I received several job offers, but turned each one down. When my savings were depleted, I realized that I had moved home for the wrong reasons. My family was still unstable with no thought to making any healthy changes so I moved all my possessions into a storage unit, drove back to Colorado and ended up on a friend's sofa, jobless, broke and still depressed.

One Friday night when my friend was out of town, I spent the few dollars I had left on a bottle of wine. I sat down and wrote a letter to my friends and family. After that, I took 32 sleeping pills and washed them down with a 1.5 liter of Merlot. Nothing more to live for, I laid on the floor, praying to a picture of The Blessed Virgin Mary, crying for forgiveness and waiting to die.

What am I still doing here? Why aren't I dead? I woke up Sunday morning at 1:00am, not knowing if what I took was a lethal dose or not, but considered my awakening a true miracle. I started taking a closer look at God, and considered why I was still alive. I started visiting various churches, and found one that announced a pregnancy counseling and post-abortion information session for the following Sunday. I felt an urgency to be a part of that meeting although I was still in denial about abortion being harmful. My attitude hadn't changed. I still held fast to the belief of "anything goes as long as it feels good to you and doesn't harm anyone." Yet, the prompting to attend that meeting was too strong to ignore.

When I arrived at the church, I found a seat in the back and listened. The Priest stood up and explained the trauma of post-abortion syndrome. Everything he shared was exactly my experience from Labor Day weekend two years ago. He spoke of the hurt, shame and forbidden grief that women feel. He shared that many women, like me, have mistakenly believed the lie about how abortion is a simple procedure to remove unwanted tissue, nothing more. I truly believed that abortion was the only solution to my problems with no after effects, yet I realized that evening that I had been mourning the death of my child all this time, the death of a part of me, because I so easily believed in the lie of *choice*. This choice had killed my child and had almost killed me. What I decided to abort was not just tissue or a bunch of cells as I was led to believe but a soul, a human being. It could not have been anything else, for I mourned so deeply. I remember thinking, *what cancer survivor mourns the tumor she lost?* I had life in me-this is not a question.

After the sessions, I approached the Priest, pouring out my story along with the grief I had held in for so long, too long. It all came rushing out, the pain, the forbidden and ignored grief, and my denial of what happened. I understood the realization that I needed to take responsibility and seek forgiveness and healing. I had to admit choosing abortion was wrong, that it was a lie and ask for God's mercy. In an instant, I no longer believed that abortion was a woman's choice. The results of that choice have only been the loss of innocent lives growing securely in our wombs, along with deep emotional and spiritual pain in the wake of abortion.

I thought about the irony that all I wanted was to be loved and cherished as a child, and when I had the possibility of unconditional love and companionship of my own child, I extinguished it with very little thought.

The Priest showed me that God offered mercy and healing for the asking. At his prompting, I attended Rachel's Vineyard, a retreat for post-abortive women. The counselors helped me understand that my child was safely tucked away, nestled at home with Jesus. I learned of God's forgiveness and understood that if I couldn't forgive myself, I would be building a wall between God and me, as well as creating a barrier between myself and my child. The retreat was a healing place where I learned to accept what I had done, find forgiveness and grieve over the loss of my beloved baby.

A few years later, I met a good Catholic man and we began dating. One night, he asked me if I had ever had an abortion. He had no idea what prompted such a question, but I willingly shared my story. I was certain that this Mid-Western boy, raised in Catholic school would take off running from my sinful presence, but what happened next changed both of our lives. He saw me through the eyes of a faithful, forgiving Christ, and I saw him as a transparent, loving, faithful man of God. We married a year and a half later. The Priest who was instrumental in my journey to healing concelebrated the Mass.

It was a long road to healing, but I eventually learned to forgive myself. I realized that God is merciful and forgiving, and that my little one, who I named Patrick, is in the arms of our loving Lord.

Patrick, even though he never lived a day on this Earth, has blessed me in many ways. He helped me appreciate and love my mother for giving me life, and he was instrumental in bringing my husband and me together in marriage. Most importantly, Patrick ultimately brought me back to God, Who has become the focus of our family's life. He made me understand how precious family is, and that my children, all of them, are a gift from the Lord. I have hope that I will meet Patrick someday, along with two other children who were miscarried.

As Pope John Paul II said in the Gospel of Life, particularly to those with experience of abortion, "nothing is definitively lost." I believe that all is not lost, and in fact, know that all is well. God filled me with faith in Him, and I look forward to the time I will see my Patrick again. I wrote meaningful letters to all three of the children I never held in my arms. Here is the letter I wrote to Patrick . . . .

My Precious Baby, Patrick,

I can imagine how you have been waiting to hear from me, watching me struggle, torturing myself over what I did to you. I realize that by not forgiving myself I built a barrier that kept us apart, but have finally learned to forgive myself. No more walls. The reality of you, no longer denied, has made everything right after an act that was so very wrong. You are the reason I came home God, home to church again. You, my precious boy, are why I have faith in the love and forgiveness of God. You have made me believe in hope.

Patrick, by your very existence, you have bonded me to my wonderful husband-your new papa. He has spiritually adopted you now. You helped me to realize how incredible the gift of motherhood is and how precious your bothers and sisters are. I am humbled and awestruck at how something I was terrified of—the very existence of you—would be the primary reason that our family exists and grows today. I am constantly amazed by the fact that because of you I am happy, joyful and home.

My child, I look forward to the day when I can scoop you up in my arms, cover you with kisses and smother you with hugs. I can't wait until I can look into your eyes and see the forgiveness you have held in your heart for me. There will be so much to do when we're together. We'll have hundreds of stories to read, cookies to bake, snowmen to build, masterpieces to finger-paint and brain freezes to experience from eating ice-cream too quickly. I hope to roll all of the missed hugs, kisses and childhood experiences into Eternity.

I'm so sorry your mommy's fear and selfishness have made us wait to do all of these things, but I look with expectation to the time we will

have together. In the meantime, listen to your big sister and take care of
your baby brother. Share and be nice to each other. Mama and Papa love
you very much.

Today, I still live in Colorado with three incredible blessings, as of this writing, a five year old boy, three year old girl and a 19 month old boy. Life is busy and blessed, and every now and then, I see a smile or a certain look in one of my babies eyes that invites me to know that angels are watching over us all. I also work for the cause of life, sharing the realization that abortion hurts women, and is not just a simple procedure or an easy solution to a problem. I believe that along with myself, other women who have experienced the pain of *choice* will be the very ones who turn the tide of the culture of abortion in this country.

As far as that "anything goes as long as it feels good to you and doesn't harm anyone else," girl from back east, well, she's changed her ideas. And I'm always reminding myself, God is generous and full of grace, you lucky girl.

CHAPTER THREE

Filling Empty Places

By

Joan Samuels*

When our hearts are empty and we are desperately seeking to fill them up, what happens when we fill them up with the wrong things? A false comfort is not a true healing for the lonely heart. It is a temporary bandage and when that bandage no longer works where do we go? How do we find what our heart truly aches for . . . .

The oldest of four children, I was raised by loving parents in a middle-class suburb. While I was young, I attended a Catholic school, but due to family financial issues, I was unable to continue my education there beyond the 8th grade. My parents transferred me to the local neighborhood high school. Exposed to a very different learning environment and new people, I felt I needed to recreate myself. Eventually, I became known as *the* party girl, and this reputation afforded me the opportunity to date—a lot.

During my first year of high school, I met Sammy. Sammy came from a broken family and attached himself to mine. We spent all of our time together, and with time came the introduction of drugs and alcohol. Because of his addictions, Sammy eventually quit high school. His mother soon realized his substance abuse and forced him into a rehab center for several months.

After rehab, Sammy immediately joined the Armed Forces, and I missed him terribly. He felt the same and made every effort to come home to see me, even if it meant going AWOL during boot camp. However, his visits soon contained a devastating revelation. During our time apart, Sammy had been cheating on me.

By the time I was a junior in high school, Sammy was in the brig for his AWOL tendencies. Not only was I dealing with the effects of a heartbreaking relationship, but my family was also reeling from medical information about one of my little brothers. Robert was only 2 years old when doctors diagnosed him with a rare kidney disease. My parents were very frightened and consumed with his recovery. I was frightened too.

With Robert's medical treatment in process, my parents spent many days in hospitals with him, which left me with a lot of free time, and very little parental supervision. The pressure of caring for myself and worrying about my little brother took its toll, and the only way I found to escape was through the familiarity of something Sammy had introduced me too—drugs and alcohol.

As my family spent more and more time away from me, I grew closer to all the wrong people. The more I partied, the more I believed my friends liked me. Most of our conversations were raucous, lively and upbeat, but occasionally we delved into more serious and spiritual topics. Sometimes we talked about God. Everyone accepted everyone no matter where our conversations took us, and these friends soon became a poor substitute for family.

Pete eventually caught my attention. I loved the time we spent together, and he respected me. I told him about Sammy and how I hadn't officially broken up with him yet. I shared how my heart was broken over him.

"You know you're too good for him, don't you?" Pete moved closer to me. I sensed something different in his tone, and felt my face flush. "He has nothing over you anymore, you know that, right?"

"I thought I loved him." I felt a tear escape. Pete reached up and brushed it lightly away. "But maybe I actually didn't." Pete pulled me into his chest and every feeling I carried for Sammy disappeared in that moment.

Pete and I talked a lot on the phone and began to spend some time together, and I grew to love him. He respected me, which made me love him more. The official break-up with Sammy still hadn't occurred and I think Pete was waiting for me to do this before we committed to anything. Pete was one of the biggest "pot" dealers in town and had both a car and a Harley. I felt pretty special that he was interested in me. I began to dream we would have a life together.

Everyone I spent time with heard the same story of my undying love for Pete. I couldn't help myself. I was so happy to be with Pete and wanted the world to know. One evening I was out with a good friend, once again sharing the saga about how Pete and I met, and how I had fallen hard for him. "He's amazing. I can't even begin to tell you . . ." My friend, Don, just smiled and listened. "I mean it, Pete's incredible."

"I don't doubt it." He passed the joint to me and closed his eyes, tapping the steering wheel to the beat of the music blaring from his car stereo. It was a typical night for Don and me. We were close friends and frequently got high together and Don always made me feel special and desired, but this night ended very differently. One thing led to another and feeling good from the effects of the marijuana, we ended up having sex. At this time, I was confused about a lot of things going on in my life like what was happening with my brother, breaking up with Sammy and wondering if I'd ever be with Pete. I was also angry that Sammy had cheated on me and in some warped way, I thought I was getting back at him by having sex with Don. We continued our relationship throughout the month even though we both knew I was very much in love with Pete.

Another night, I faced the very same scenario, but with a different, close, male friend. In fact, Paul had been one of my best friends for quite some time. Paul made me feel confident that I could leave Sammy and have other guys interested in me. I told him how I felt about Pete, however as the night passed, we ended up having sex too.

Then one night, I was out with John, another male *friend*. John suggested going to Pete's house, but not until we finished the last of our cocaine. By the time we arrived at Pete's, it was very late. Pete seemed hesitant at first but when the opportunity presented itself, he snuck me into his room. Because of the effect of the drugs, I don't remember much, but I'm sure of one thing. We had sex.

From that night on, my relationship with Pete changed completely. He didn't talk to me much anymore. *Did I do something wrong?* I would ask my friends. My dreams of us spending our lives together began to unravel. I didn't think things could get any worse at this point. Until I found out I was pregnant.

I couldn't tell my parents. They were consumed with my little brother and were hardly ever home anyway. How could I possibly give them one more thing to worry about? The hardest part of the whole situation, the thing that I was most ashamed of, was the fact that I didn't know who the father of my baby was. Was it Paul, Don, or Pete?

My girlfriends rallied around me and helped raise money for an abortion. It was the only thing I could think of to do, and I needed to get it done quickly so Pete wouldn't find out. My girlfriends, who along with me were only 16 years old, didn't have quite enough cash to support an abortion, so with one of my friends, Becky, I approached Don and Paul. Even though I had been intimate with them, I considered them both close friends and knew they would support my decision. They helped collect the rest of the needed funds.

When I arrived at the clinic, the nurse told me not to worry about anything. "You're only 6 weeks along, so I want you to know we're talking about a clump of cells, not a baby."

Knowing that it wasn't really a baby I was carrying eased my mind tremendously, and I had no trouble agreeing to the procedure. I remember it being extremely painful, but it was over quickly. As I left the clinic, I was relieved, but at the same time, also felt very sad and empty.

Soon after my abortion, Don, without my permission, told Pete that I had recently had an abortion. He also shared something that immediately ended my relationship with Pete. "She didn't know who the baby's daddy was."

Pete never spoke to me again. My heart was broken.

I filled the following year with late-night partying and relationships with different men, desperately trying to ease my depression and fill the emptiness by hanging out in bars, fooling the management—and men—with my fake ID. Inside, I longed to be an adored wife with a faithful husband, but outwardly, I exploited my sexuality trying to find *the one*. I didn't know that the hollow feelings and depression I was experiencing were triggered by my abortion.

I was almost 18 when I met Tom, and he fell hard for me. He was 20 and he had a job, money, and most importantly, he lived on his own. The only drawback was that I wasn't particularly attracted to him. He was tough and protective, but lacked the passion, nurturing and emotional connection I desired from a man. Nonetheless, when my parents were tired of my late nights and lack of respect for the household, they strongly suggested I move out. I went straight to Tom's door.

After one month of dating, and an early graduation from high school, I felt that Tom was my ticket to marriage and living happily ever after. I was tired of my fast-paced party life and felt that living with Tom would accelerate my existence into the easy pace of marital bliss.

One month passed, and bored with soup and sandwiches, I decided to try my hand at making a homemade dinner—roast beef, mashed potatoes and gravy, vegetables and rolls. It was the middle of July and the air-conditioner protested by trying to catch up with the heat the oven was generating. However, it hardly mattered. I was making a meal fit for my man and feeling very proud of my efforts.

Tom, however, was not proud of me at all. "What were you thinking! Don't you know not to use the oven when it's 90 degrees outside! How can you be so stupid!" He yelled at me for hours, showing me a side of him I never saw before.

"I'm sorry. I promise it won't happen again." I felt as foolish as he said I was, and decided that from now on, I would never make him angry again. I knew he was right about the air-conditioning and the oven, and I wouldn't make the same mistake again.

As time passed, I realized the verbal abuse was the beginning of something much more volatile. He began to abuse me physically as well. One night, we argued about something and Tom slapped me in the face. I was so upset and needed someone to comfort me. After he left for work, I decided to meet up with some of my girlfriends. Little did I know, Tom had arrived at work intoxicated and was immediately terminated. Normally, he wouldn't have arrived home until 8:00 AM. He was home earlier, but unfortunately, I was not. When I did come home, Tom was waiting for me.

The next few hours were a blur. I remember walking through the door and Tom locking it behind me. He accused me of terrible things, and the more I denied any wrongdoing, the more he punched me. I tried to get to the phone, but he yanked me back by my hair. He continued beating me for hours and I thought I was going to die. As the sun came up, he began to calm down somewhat and wanted to have sex with me. I despised him for what he did, but knew this was my only chance to stop the beating.

The next day, I had bruises all over my body and called in sick from work. Tom, sorry for his actions, took me to the hospital. I believed the sincerity of his apologies and justified his behavior by the fact he was drunk and had just lost his job. He promised me he would never let it happen again. No one at the hospital questioned my injuries, and anyone else curious enough to talk to me about it heard the same lie. "I was drunk and landed in the middle of a bar fight."

Things between Tom and I were better for a time, but little by little, our arguments escalated in rage, and the abuse started again. The beatings were never as bad as the first time, so I justified that our relationship was getting better. When I discovered I was pregnant, I thought Tom would finally decide to marry me. I knew he wanted to marry and have a family someday because we had talked about it, and I was certain I didn't want to go through another abortion. Contrary to my expectations of a favorable reaction, Tom exploded in anger.

"Look, I don't want a baby, not yours or anyone else's, so you're going to have to take care of it." Tom slammed his fist on the wall, and I was sure the plaster would buckle beneath his angry outburst. Instead of compassion, I had received a bitter verbal lashing. Tom then reached into his pocket, drew out his wallet, and handed me a good amount of cash. "This should take care of it."

I hesitated, looking into the eyes of the man I thought was going to care for me and love me for the rest of my life. I saw nothing but a determined, icy stare. I looked back at his fist full of money thrusting toward mine.

"Take it, and take care of your problem! If you don't, I won't be here tomorrow." So there it was—the ultimatum. My hand trembled as I drew the bills from his grasp. I didn't know how I was going to find the strength to go through with another abortion. I considered calling my parents, but knew they were still in the midst of dealing with my brother and his health issues. With no other recourse, I walked into an abortion clinic once again.

I stayed with Tom, and later he decided to move us across country, promising to find work that would make a good living for the two of us. I was depressed, and felt I had no other choice but to follow this man. I didn't want to go back to my "party girl" ways and all the different guys with none of them ever leading into a meaningful relationship. I also felt ashamed and unworthy of a decent man and because I had two abortions, I felt guilty and undeserving of anything good. Over the next 15 years, Tom and I had two wonderful children together, and each of us found jobs that paid decently enough to raise our family.

Life with Tom was always challenging, and mood swings were common. I never knew what would set him off. The physical abuse lessened after the kids were born, but the verbal abuse continued. Just to be certain I always knew who was in control, Tom would occasionally punch the wall just beside my face, bringing to mind the horrific beating of the past.

With nowhere to go, and no one to turn to, I decided I would endure my loveless marriage long enough to get the kids through high school, and then leave Tom to venture out on my own. My dream of finding a man who genuinely loved me, one who communicated with compassion and concern for my well-being, gave me hope for a future. All I had to do was bide my time. My moment would come.

As they say, the best laid plans . . .

My course changed when Frank, a co-worker shared with me that his wife was seeking a divorce. He was distraught and thought that maybe I could help him somehow. I listened to him for months, empathizing with him over his plight. We lived in the same suburb, and he would often give me a ride to work and back, or we would ride the bus together. Prior to his divorce situation, we had simply been friends, work associates. There had been no discussion of personal issues, and we had respect for the fact that each of us was married.

Frank told me that his wife had been involved with two other men during their marriage and he was sure there were others he didn't know about. He told me that he tried desperately to encourage her to consider marriage counseling, but she refused, claiming she was bored with him and needed some excitement in her life.

As Frank transparently shared with me, I slowly began opening up with him about my own marriage. I told him that Tom had once cheated on me with my best friend and about how his marijuana and alcohol dependence strained our already rocky marriage. The more I shared with Frank, the more I wanted a divorce from Tom. During the course of time, vulnerable communication brought about something I didn't expect. I was in love with Frank.

Soon after I announced my intentions to divorce Tom, I became pregnant with Frank's baby. Frank and I were thrilled. Together, we told my parents, explaining to them that our lives were finally all we dreamed they would be. I knew my life with Tom was over and I was entering into a new relationship with a man who truly loved and cared for me.

Even though our love was growing, I decided I would live temporarily with my ex, Tom, just until our house sold. Frank decided he needed to finalize things on his end as well. We planned our future carefully, but with all of our efforts, the one thing we didn't anticipate was how our love for one another would affect our children. Frank had three kids from his marriage. I had two.

My 14-year-old daughter and 15-year-old son were furious with me for seeing Frank, and Tom escalated their anger by telling them that the divorce was entirely my fault. He lied to them by telling them if Frank hadn't come into our lives, we would still be married.

The stress of living with one man and loving another began taking its toll, and I knew I had to find a way to introduce my teenagers to Frank and his kids in a healthy way. Frank and I decided to take all of our kids on a camping trip.

That particular summer was extremely hot and humid, but Frank and I were determined to get the kids together so they could get to know one another. In spite of the weather, we finalized our camping plans. However, what was supposed to be an enjoyable time of bonding turned into disaster. All of our children struggled with confusion, anger and fear in the midst of our very adult decisions and circumstances.

Because of the outcome of our trip, Frank and I decided that it would be best to live apart for a year, each of us with our own children. After anguishing for days, we decided abortion would be the best way to handle our situation for the time being—my third abortion. Having a third abortion was the absolute last thing I wanted to do especially because of how happy Frank and I were but my children were not happy especially my daughter. She was hurt and felt abandoned. She was horrible to me calling me a "selfish whore" and with her dad's brainwashing was convinced I was out to ruin her life. I was pro-choice at this time in my life but with feeling so overwhelmed with my children's behavior (especially my daughters) and with my living situation being up in the air, I felt I had no choice but to end this pregnancy.

Years have passed since that time, and Frank and I, along with our children, eventually found our way into a healthy marriage and blended family. We also share a son. With his birth, our family dissolved all boundaries between each other and we truly became one.

Although our decision to abort our first child together is a huge regret, with help, Frank and I have learned to move beyond it. I sought counseling after my third abortion, and found a group of women who helped me in my journey to healing. I think I'll always be sad when I think about what I've done, but I have learned to move forward.

It has been a long, difficult road, learning how to forgive myself and believe that God could forgive me for taking the life of my unborn children. I've spent multiple hours finding support with other women in abortion recovery groups, and have attended week long retreats to help resolve the guilt, shame and pain of my past. I will always regret my decisions to end the lives of my babies, and often wonder what they would be like today. However, as much as I would like to, I can't redo, erasing what's been done. All I can do is share my experiences with others who may be in a similar situation, hopefully persuading them to choose life.

Through counseling, I found that my own lack of education concerning pregnancy and my Catholic faith was one of many links to my decisions toward abortion. Time with church support groups taught me about the reality of love, marriage and family. It was then I discovered the truth—even through my experiences, I had been pro-life all the time. Also as I became more knowledgeable about my faith and more involved in my healing, I realized how blessed I was. I had this husband from heaven, a beautiful son and a granddaughter, great kids and stepkids, an awesome job, a forgiving God and the list goes on and on. I decided to use these truths to help others. Today, I am active in the pro-life agenda, and once had the honor of speaking at the capital building representing women who regret their abortions.

Then, four years ago, I personally witnessed the irrational and desperate feelings of a pregnant, young woman. This young woman was my daughter. She was in her second year of college, full of dreams and plans for her future. Neither my daughter nor her boyfriend of six months was ready for a baby. They decided abortion was their answer.

My husband and I pleaded with them for hours, leading into days. "Please reconsider this decision." We shared our story and all of our regrets. We promised to support her through her pregnancy and beyond, assuring her that she could still finish college and get her degree. It seemed nothing could dissuade her or her boyfriend.

My past haunted me as I relived my own heartache through my daughter. My husband and I prayed that she wouldn't make the same mistake we did so many years ago. All we could do was pray, and it turned out praying was the very best thing we could have done.

Our daughter visited the doctor to consult with him about an abortion, yet the outcome was far different. This doctor explained to her that she was 11 weeks pregnant, and he only performed abortions on pregnancies 10 weeks or less. He then explained the baby's stage of development at 11 weeks. I believe that made all the difference. He told her that if she was determined to have an abortion, she should go to the downtown clinic where they performed abortions on pregnancies more than 10 weeks. Our daughter suddenly reconsidered, a direct answer to prayer.

Today, our granddaughter is a rambunctious three-year-old and our daughter graduated Magna Cum Laude from college. She is working in her career as an accountant and studying to earn her CPA license. Frank and I are proud of our daughter's decision, and prouder still of her own sweet little one.

I don't justify my abortions and still get sad when I think about them, but I've grown from my mistakes and continue to seek growth for my life. My prayer is that God will continue using me to communicate His message, one of hope and life.

* Not real name. Names have been changed

CHAPTER FOUR

Unexpected Tragedy, Undeserved Grace

By

Kathy Whaling

Sometimes in life we bury things so deep that it takes another tragedy to uncover them.

Everything was great! My self-managed life appeared to be going as planned. I thought I had my life and my family's life under control. It was April 20, 1999, my wedding anniversary. I anticipated spending the evening with my husband. We planned to go to our favorite restaurant for a romantic dinner, followed by a movie. After everyone was off to school, I headed out to the health club to meet my friend Sharon. As we sat there peddling our exercise bikes, I asked her if she wanted to go to the thrift shop afterwards. She couldn't go, so I went alone.

I picked out a few items to purchase and stood at the checkout counter. The phone rang and the clerk at my counter answered it. She put the phone down and spoke into the intercom, "Is there a Kathy Whaling in the store?"

"Yes, I'm Kathy Whaling," I replied. She handed me the phone. I wondered who could be calling me here. It was Sharon, who I had met at the health club earlier. She sounded so terrified I could hardly understand what she was saying. There was a crisis at the high school my three daughter's attended. Columbine High School was under attack.

Sharon lived directly behind the school. While she was showering, she heard gunshots being fired and bombs blowing up. She immediately got out of the shower and looked over her backyard fence. She saw screaming students running out of the school and trying to find somewhere to hide. She immediately thought about my children and called me.

Everything is going to be okay, I thought. *This can't be a big deal. Sharon was probably overreacting.*

I purchased my items and rushed to my car. Immediately, I turned on the radio. The radio announcer's voice was filled with terror. He attempted to explain the situation, but even he did not fully know what was happening. My heart raced, my shoulders tensed, and my tight grip on the steering wheel made my knuckles white. I raced toward home. As I got closer to home, I heard helicopters overhead.

Two of my three daughters, Stephanie and Chanelle, called on my cell phone, crying frantically. They were all right physically, but terrified beyond comprehension. I hadn't heard from my stepdaughter, Heather, yet. Heather had lunch at the time the shootings began, and for two boys with guns, it was killing time. I was extremely worried.

I pulled into the driveway and ran into the house. Immediately, I turned on the TV. The horrifying event unfolded before my eyes. I sat there in disbelief. There on the screen I saw my children's high school with terrified, crying students running out of it. Some fell as they ran. Other wounded students were lying on the ground. One father attempted to enter the school to save his children. A boy fell from a window with gunshot wounds. There was panic everywhere—complete mayhem! It felt like I was watching a movie. This couldn't be real. But the helicopters flying over my house, the neighbors coming over, and people calling reinforced the reality.

How could this be? This is Littleton—not the kind of place where something like this happens.

Three and half hours later my husband, Bob, pulled into the driveway. I ran outside. I saw Heather in the passenger seat. I breathed a sigh of relief. All three girls were safe at home.

Later that night, I walked into Chanelle's room. She was sitting on the floor in the corner with her head between her knees, sobbing uncontrollably. She looked up at me with swollen, bloodshot, blue eyes and asked, "Why, Mom? Why?"

With tears in my own eyes, I sat down on the floor with her and held her close to me. "I don't know, Baby. I don't know." I had no answer. Usually, when one of my children was hurt, I could give some kind of advice that helped alleviate the pain. But I couldn't make any sense out of this, so how could I help my children? I couldn't just kiss it, put on a Band-Aid, and tell them that everything would be all right. In that moment, I felt like a child that had accidentally let a balloon slip from her hand. Off it drifted into the sky, never to be seen again. In one instant, my self-managed, self-controlled life slipped away.

Who did this? Who was hurt? My biggest fear—was anyone killed? It was a nightmare.

Later that evening, I heard all three of my daughters screaming. Their loud, painful cries pierced not only my ears but also my heart. It was the most gut-wrenching sound a mother could possibly hear. The girls had just learned that some of their close friends had been killed. Cassie Bernall was dead. Cassie had given Chanelle a ride home from youth group the Sunday night before the shooting. Rachel Scott was dead. Stephanie and Rachel had been friends since 8th grade. I remembered how she had come over to our house and jumped on our trampoline. Stephanie still had a picture of them when they went to an 8th grade dance together. Isaiah Shoels was dead. Heather had sat next to him everyday on the bus to school. Heather loved riding the bus with Isaiah. She said he was always so happy and funny, and he brightened her day when she was feeling down. Isaiah had recently told Heather that he thought Chanelle was cute, and that he wanted to meet her.

My arms were the only safe place amongst the horror of it all, yet I felt completely helpless. There was nothing I could do to ease their pain. I was out of quick fixes. No kisses, candy-flavored pills, or cartoon Band-Aids could alleviate their heartbreak.

The next day, the headlines in the Denver Rocky Mountain News read, "On April 20, 1999, Columbine High School seniors Eric Harris and Dylan Klebold killed 12 fellow students, a teacher and then themselves." In the days that followed, my children attended four funerals in five days. These were the first funerals that they had ever attended. They had never experienced death before, not even with an elderly relative. It was unbearable to watch.

For the next couple of weeks, I found myself glued to the TV. I didn't want to go anywhere. I needed more information. I wanted to know everything. I wanted to know why. Finally, I realized that there were no more facts, and there would never be answers. I turned off the TV. What happened had happened, and that's just the way it was.

Slowly, as days passed by, the shock of the tragedy gradually wore off. Then I started to feel angry. I became critical and unmerciful, not so much at the boys who had done the shootings, but at their parents for allowing this tragedy to happen. I blamed them. The more I thought about it, the angrier I got. Every time I drove by the school (which was almost everyday); the flame of anger was once again fanned. My nice, middle-class, suburban community, had turned into a battlefield. My inward feelings of hostility and resentment started to affect my outward behavior. I lashed out at my husband. My family felt as if they were walking on eggshells around me.

Up until this point, I had lived with the illusion that I was in control. I had always been the one who had taken care of everyone in our home. I made sure that everyone was doing all right and had everything they needed. As far as I was concerned, there wasn't any crisis I couldn't handle. After all, I was "Super Mom!" Not anymore. I had lost control and I didn't know how to pickup the shattered pieces. I felt inadequate as the nurturer of my family. I was frightened and needed to be nurtured myself.

In this fragile state, I found myself seeking God in a new way. Before this I was one of those compromising Christians, who gave Christ-centered Christians a bad name. I went to church on Sunday, but lived by my righteousness the rest of the week. I didn't have much need for a full time, twenty-four hour Savior, since I thought that I could run my life on my own.

But now I began to pray. One morning as I was praying, I sensed that God wanted me to get the girls into counseling with a Christian counselor. I called the church where I attended and asked for a referral. They gave me the phone number for a woman named Dee Dee. I immediately called her and set up appointments. She was one of the nicest people I'd ever talked too. I told her a little bit about how I was feeling—the anger and all—and she suggested that I make an appointment for myself as well. However, I really didn't think that there was anything wrong with me. I thought what I was feeling was pretty normal and that eventually, I'd get over it.

Not right now. Let's take care of the girls first. Maybe we'll fix me later.

As weeks passed, I could see that God was doing some wonderful things with my girls. He was bringing their hope back and drawing them closer to Him. Their fears diminished while faith in God increased. It was overwhelming for me to see God at work in the lives of my children. For so long I had thought that it was my job to fix everyone. Now I realized that I didn't have to do it all by myself.

After a few weeks of seeing God's healing work in my girls, He softly spoke to my heart and said, "Now it's your turn".

Well, all right, God. I'll go see her just once, but there really isn't anything wrong with me now that my kids are doing better. I called Dee Dee and made an appointment for myself—just to please God. I drove to her office a few days later.

As I was sitting in her waiting room, I looked around nervously to make sure no one would recognize me. Then Dee Dee came out.

Oh no! Let's get this over with. I hope she doesn't think I'm crazy or anything. What is she going to talk to me about? Oh, dear Lord, what did I get myself into this time?

First, we chatted about the girls. The room seemed calm and peaceful, and I was surprisingly relaxed and comfortable—nothing like I had imagined. (In my mind, I had pictured her showing me inkblot pictures, and filling out a prescription for an anti-depressant by now.) Then the dreaded question, "So how do you feel about the Columbine incident?"

I told her that I was extremely angry, not so much at Eric and Dylan, but with their parents. "How could they not know what their kids were doing? If they had been planning this horrible event for more than a year, how could they not recognize the signs? How could they not know that their kids were making bombs in their garage and had guns in their bedroom? How could they not know about the web site? How could they not know that their kids were troubled? How could they allow their sons to put my daughters through this horrifying ordeal at such a young age? My girls didn't deserve this. How dare they!" The angry barrage of questions tumbled out of my mouth.

Dee Dee understood the reasons for my anger, but she also told me that I couldn't stay in that place. She gave me a choice of two responses. I could write a letter to the Harris and Klebold family, telling them how I felt. (I didn't have to mail it.) Or I could do what God wanted me to do—forgive them. She said it would be a gift I could give to God. In return, she said that God would bless me, and in reality, it would be a gift to myself.

You want me to forgive just like that? The letters seemed like an easier choice, but something compelled me to work toward forgiveness in obedience to God.

While my feelings of anger were justified, I knew that God wanted me to let go. Yet, I still felt reluctant.

The next morning I thought about what I needed to do and then said to God, "You will owe me big time for this one". (Looking back, I can't believe I said that!). Then I prayed, thanking Him for all that He had done for me and asking Him to bless those I loved. Then came the hard part: "Father, tell me why I should forgive these parents whose sons have put my children through such trauma? My children didn't deserve this. It has scarred them for life."

The Lord said to me in a soft whisper, "My dear child, it's because I have forgiven you for the same thing that Eric and Dylan did. Don't try to take the speck out of someone else's eye, when you have a log in your own."

God reminded me of what I had tried to forget and hidden for so long. My heart sank. I never thought of it that way. I had buried "my sins of the past." I had locked them away in the archives of my mind.

Then I responded, "Oh, my dear, sweet Lord Jesus—my Heavenly Father—how Sovereign you are". Then I asked God to forgive me for harboring such anger and bitterness. I forgave these parents I didn't even know. For the first time, I thought of what these poor parents must be going through. God helped me to see that my sin was no different than anybody else's sin.

Immediately, something wonderful had happened. God graciously replaced my feelings of anger with His wonderful peace. It first went through the top of my head and exited through my feet like a wave of cool air. I had never felt anything like this. I couldn't wait to tell Dee Dee the GREAT NEWS. I assumed that my troubles were over because God had "fixed" me, but I didn't realize that He was not nearly finished.

During my next visit with Dee Dee, I told her I had asked God why I should forgive Eric and Dylan's parents, and his response was that I needed to forgive them because He had forgiven me of my "sins of the past"—sins which were no different from what their sons had done. I had such shame and guilt for what I had done, but I knew that I could trust Dee Dee. With my head lowered, unable to look her in the eyes. I whispered the word, "Aaaabbboortions. I had an abortion 20 years ago, and then I had another one 10 years after that. Not just one abortion, but two!" There I said it! I waited for her reaction. Dee Dee was compassionate and empathetic, a far different response than what I had envisioned. And so I told her the whole story about the deaths of my babies and why I had felt at the time that there were no other options.

When I was 20 years old, I moved in with a man and soon got pregnant. I was terrified. I thought that if I told my parents they would disown me. I was fearful of my father. He was not a man given to too much mercy. In my mind, my only option was to terminate the pregnancy. So I had an abortion.

After the abortion, I got married to my baby's father but, I felt extremely guilty for what I did. Okay—I will try to live with this—somehow. I'll just tuck it away. But whenever I saw a baby, an anti-abortion ad, or the anniversary of my abortion came around, I felt even more guilt. There was no escaping it. I learned to live with this guilt. I coped, at least I tried.

When I was 23, a friend of mine asked me to go to a non-denominational church. I went and that's the first time I ever heard about letting Jesus come into your heart. He could "save" you if you confessed with your mouth Jesus as Lord and believed in your heart that God raised Him from the dead (Romans 10:9). God actually wanted to have a personal relationship with me. I wanted to know more about this Jesus who could "save" you, make you "born again", and fill you with the "Spirit."

I continued to go to church. Then one day I asked Jesus to come into my heart and into my life, to cleanse me from all my sins, and to make me whole again. I couldn't bear to live without Him.

My husband was a naval officer. At the time he was overseas, and I was left in the states with my baby daughter. Having Jesus in my life helped to take away my loneliness, and yet I still lived with guilt over the abortion even though I knew I was forgiven. I suffered in silence.

When my husband came back from overseas, he wasn't interested in Jesus and the things of God. So over time, I eventually drifted away. I already felt guilty, and it seemed too hard to live the Christian life in my own strength.

We moved from San Diego to Maryland where we had another daughter. Our marriage began to deteriorate. We eventually moved back to San Diego, and I ended up leaving my husband.

I got involved in another relationship, which only lasted a short time, because I began to feel extremely guilty for leaving my husband. I wanted to give my marriage another try, but now there was this big "problem" again! I was pregnant. It was with the other man's baby. What was I going to do about this one? My husband was already having a hard time dealing with the situation, so how would he handle it if he knew I was pregnant with someone else's baby?

What is everyone going to think of me? What will his parents think of me?

I never thought I would ever do something as horrifying as an abortion again, but once again I felt I had no other choice. So I had another abortion. Once again, I was heartbroken.

My marriage didn't last. I thought I didn't love my husband when in reality I didn't love myself anymore. I hated myself for what I had done. I felt tremendous shame. I never told my ex-husband about the abortion. It was my "secret."

Dee Dee sat there listening to my terrible past. When I had finished, she spoke to me about a God who never intended for me to live with this guilt that I had been feeling for twenty years—a God that doesn't condemn those who are forgiven in Christ. Now I realized how desperately I wanted to have my broken life "fixed."

Dee Dee told me that she could help me with the power of Jesus Christ. She felt anointed by God to help women with post-abortion counseling. In order to be released from this curse, I needed to write a letter to each of my babies. She said that God would give me their names. I was to write these letters before my next appointment, which was only four days away.

I felt numb when I left Dee Dee's office. I had no idea how I was going to do this difficult and painful task, but I was sure that this is what God wanted me to do.

Only four days to write my unborn babies a letter. Just the thought of it was terrifying. This was the most painful thing I had ever been asked to do—to open my hidden box of shame and guilt. I wrestled with myself and God over this formidable assignment." Yet, I KNEW I had to go through with it.

I spent the next three days thinking about what the names of my babies might be. I thought about a variety of names and wondered whether my babies were boys or girls. This went on all day Friday, Saturday, and Sunday. I still didn't have the names. Then around 11:00 p.m. Sunday night, as I was lying in bed about to fall asleep, God spoke to my heart and revealed their names. "Jeremiah, Joshua". That was all He said.

Then I wept, pouring out tears of deep grief and sorrow. My babies were boys! All the children that I had given birth to were girls. I would not have grieved any less if these babies were girls, but I had always wanted a son. And my girls missed out on having brothers. We had all missed out on so much.

I awoke the next day, knowing that I had to write the letters. I was scared. I tried to avoid it by making plans with one of my daughters to go to an amusement park. I convinced myself that I would write these letters from my lounge chair at the water park. We gathered our things together and headed outside to the car, but there was a big nail in the front tire of the car.

I called my husband and asked him if he would come home and fix the tire, and he said that he would. When he got home, he took the tire to the shop, and then he called me to say that the tire wouldn't be ready until later that evening. After I hung up the phone, God said to me, "Now. Do it now".

My daughter went to a friend's house, and I went to my bedroom. I sat down at a small table, pulled out a piece of paper, and picked up a pen. My hand began to shake. As I sat there for awhile with tears rolling off my face onto the paper, I heard that familiar soft voice say to my heart, "Kathy, don't be afraid. I come before you always. Come follow me my weary one, and I will give you rest" (Matthew 11:28).

I began to write the letters, one to each baby. I poured out my great grief and deep regret upon the page. I asked my babies to forgive me for the horrible choice I had made. I told them how I anticipated being reunited with them in heaven. Even though it was difficult to write the letters, I felt relieved and at peace afterwards. I felt comforted by my Lord Jesus (Matt. 5:4).

The next day was another appointment with Dee Dee. I didn't know what to expect. When I entered Dee Dee's office, she was somewhat surprised to see me. She was amazed that I hadn't canceled my appointment. Believe me; I had considered canceling my appointment!

As I sat there across from Dee Dee, she asked me if I had written the letters. I reached into my purse and pulled out two letters. I told her that I was tempted not to write them, but after living twenty years of guilt and shame, I was ready to give it to God. She asked to see the letters, and I handed them to her. She looked at the names and told me that after I left her office last Friday, God had told her that my babies were both boys.

Then she looked at me and said, "Are you ready to give your babies to God?"

"Oh, yes!" I replied.

Dee Dee and I sat face to face with our eyes closed, holding hands. She told me to envision myself in a very peaceful place. I closed my eyes and visualized myself sitting on a Colorado mountainside. The sky was blue with scattered white clouds. It was very quiet and extremely peaceful.

As Dee Dee and I sat there, we took turns praying. I told Jesus just how sorry I was for taking the lives of my babies. Tears streamed down my face and fell onto our hands. Then as I sat there on that mountainside, looking straight into the baby blue sky, something incredible happened. From the clouds, Jesus appeared with my babies, Joshua in one arm and Jeremiah in the other. They looked at each other with utter happiness and complete joy.

To be called before the Lord is reason enough to be ecstatic, but to see my babies as well—this was more that I could have asked for. Then my babies drifted off into Heaven, and as they did, I lowered my head and put my face into my hands. But Jesus lifted my head with his hand and with forgiveness in His eyes He said, "You no longer have to feel guilt and shame for your sins. I bore your sins on the cross and paid the debt in full with my blood. They have been made clean, as clean as fresh fallen snow, and are remembered no more. Go forth with your head raised high and tell about my good news." The bondage of guilt and shame was gone. I was truly set free.

Dee Dee and I looked at each other in awe. God had truly blessed me with the greatest gift a mother could ever receive. Writing those letters was the hardest thing that I had ever done, but the blessing in return was worth it. Even if I hadn't had the vision, I would have still felt blessed because of the inward cleansing of all the shame and guilt.

From that day on, Jesus has been by my side helping me each step of the way and leading me in ways everlasting. I have learned that the most important thing in living the Christian life is to trust God and put my full dependency upon Him. I now know that God is in control, not me. I've never felt so much peace, even through the storms.

April 20, 1999, if God had given me the choice to be part of the Columbine tragedy, I would have said, "Absolutely not!" Now, I would respond differently. Even though what happened at Columbine shattered many lives, God used this heart-wrenching situation to set me free. My God is capable of turning tragedy into triumph.

First Rights
© 2001 Kathy Whaling

CHAPTER FIVE

From Darkness into the Light

By

Angela Marie

Children should be seen and not heard. The story of my childhood communications. And I respected that boundary; after all, I had no choice. As a child, my self-worth was almost nonexistent. I really didn't feel I had any kind of identity at all.

My grandparents often took me to church, in fact, it was mandatory if I stayed at their home. Visiting my grandmother was a highlight in my life. She and Grandpa lived on a farm and gave me more attention than I ever received at home. Even though Grandpa died when I was 11, my farm visits continued.

Then, there was church. "If you're going to stay with me, you'll attend Sunday services, Angela. No ifs, ands or buts about it." My grandmother was adamant; so I went to church. I would have never forfeited my farm get-a-ways.

As I grew older, visits to Grandma's grew more infrequent, and as a result, I walked away from church at the age of 17—the same year I fell in love.

Scott and I started dating as high school seniors. Without him, high school would have been unbearable for me. I wasn't well liked in school and Scott faced the same jeers I often did. We were far from being a part of the popular crowd, but we didn't care. We only cared about us—together. We often spoke of what life would be like for us in the future, making plans to marry eventually. I was devastated when he decided to join the Navy.

"I love you, Angela. You know that, right?"

"Yes, I know. But you're leaving, and you'll be gone a long time. Why are you doing this?" I could feel my eyes brimming with hot tears. Scott handed me his handkerchief and pulled me close enough to hear his heart beat. He was my first love, and he assured me we would be married after he returned from boot camp. Knowing we would be together forever, I lost my virginity to him.

Only a few weeks later, I received the news that he had been killed in a car accident. I was numb with grief. I remembered God, at least the God of my childhood, but concluded that He was punishing me for my promiscuity. If I had walked away from Him before, I was running now.

I graduated in 1966, and started working right away. However, life was not all about work. I found plenty of time for play. Everyone did. My life revolved around work, drinking, and a promiscuous lifestyle. Already used, I felt I had nothing good to give. I felt dirty, cheap. Eventually, my ways caught up with me and I revealed my dilemma to one of my coworkers.

"I think I'm pregnant, Shelley." I couldn't bring myself to watch her reaction. I just hung my head in shame.

"I can help you with this, Ange. Don't worry, okay? Let's talk after work." Shelley walked back to her desk with such assurance, that I couldn't help feeling confident that all would be well. And I returned to my own stack of paperwork.

Shelley and I clocked out at the same time, and as soon as we were out of earshot of other coworkers, she explained to me that she had the phone number of a place that would help me. "It's illegal, but it's clean—a private home, but they have everything necessary. I know women who have gone there to take care of their little *problem*, and they're all fine. I'll call you later with the number, okay?"

"Okay. Thanks. You're a good friend." I slid into my car and gripped the steering wheel, steadying my breath. *I can't believe I just had that conversation.* On the way home, I felt as though I would be sick.

True to her word, Shelley called me that evening. "Don't worry about a thing, Angela. You can stay with me afterwards to recover, okay?"

My memory of the actual abortion isn't clear, but one thing I do recall. Even though the *back alley* facility was sterile and safe, all I felt was darkness closing in tightly around me. It was suffocating.

After the abortion, my promiscuity and drinking accelerated. Today, after much counsel, I know why. It's called *baby replacement.* I willed myself to change, to be responsible for my life, but I simply fell into my old ways—over and over again.

Whether unable or unwilling to change, within six months, I found myself with another unwanted pregnancy. Too embarrassed to talk to Shelley again, I did some research myself on how I could have a *legal* abortion. Somehow, it felt better to do the same thing, only legally. Some states had legalized abortion for life-threatening situations by then, but the state I lived in had not. That was my answer—I would go to the nearby state to help myself.

I found a psychiatrist who agreed that it would indeed be psychiatrically life threatening if I were to continue my pregnancy. With his support and the hospital's facilities, I was able to have my abortion without question. I walked into the hospital with the full assurance that I was doing what was best in my circumstances. Yet, the same darkness that enveloped me during my previous abortion nearly suffocated me again. I looked around the room, brightly lit, but all I felt was darkness.

Once again, my promiscuous behavior accelerated, until I met Gary, a man nine years older than me. I felt his age made him a worthy man—wiser in life. *He's an adult. He'll take care of me.* Or so my mind imagined. Instead of listening to their multiple warnings, I married Gary against my parent's wishes. They knew his temperament; something I had often overlooked.

I found myself married to an alcoholic, an abusive man. Estranged from my family, I had no one to turn to, so I stayed with Gary hoping he would change. The abuse grew more pronounced, but with each episode, he had an apology. I believed in his sincerity during those moments, thinking it would be the last time. But the violence continued to cycle.

When I was 19, I gave birth to our daughter, Hannah. She was beautiful. Gary loved her too; I could tell. Six months later, something was obviously very wrong with her. I immediately took her to the hospital where she was diagnosed with a head injury—a subdural hematoma. She was bleeding between layers of her brain. I remembered leaving Hannah in Gary's care a couple of days prior while I was working, and that was when she had started acting different. She was drowsy, sleeping more than usual. And when she was awake, she fussed constantly, pulling at what little hair she had. I started to suspect that my husband was not only a wife abuser, but that he also abused his little girl somehow. She may have been neglected and simply rolled off the couch; or because Gary was an alcoholic he may have carelessly dropped her. But the staff at the hospital didn't address any of this with me, and I remained silent.

Hannah was in the hospital for 10 days with no treatment other than observation and then released. Shortly after that, she was back in the hospital with the flu—a different hospital—and the doctor recognized the subdural hematoma, still an ongoing issue. They advised Gary and me to sign papers permitting surgery. Hannah needed a shunt. My husband refused to sign, and I panicked. He created such a commotion that security removed him from the hospital premises.

Shaken, I signed all the necessary paperwork immediately, but couldn't help but think that Hannah's situation was somehow related to my past. Was this my punishment for murdering my unborn children? Would Hannah survive this surgery?

Hannah did survive, but I realized that my marriage was in serious jeopardy. Only one thing complicated my ability to make a firm choice to leave—I was pregnant again. Confusion blinded my ability for healthy decision-making. My mom, though we were still estranged, recognized that now was the time to act on her daughter's behalf. She persuaded me to leave Gary, and since I was only 19 at the time (too young to file for divorce on my own), she filed on my behalf, and I moved in with my parents with Hannah and a baby on the way. Still, my behavior didn't change. And through it all, I gave birth to a baby boy, Eric.

I soon entered into a relationship with a married man, a safe relationship for me. My needs, emotional and physical, met without commitment. But commitment soon followed. Nick divorced his wife and shortly after that, he and I married.

Both of us knew that our pasts had the capability of damaging our future. We had both been riding the wave of self-destruction for a long time. We realized we needed to make some changes in our personal lives. That's when we decided to start attending church. We felt it would be good for our marriage to make a fresh start in every way, including having a church life. What we didn't know then was that we weren't just looking for a relationship with church, but with Jesus.

Many things started anew, but one thing I would never reveal—my abortions. Not even Nick knew. I felt it would be best to keep my abortion experiences secret. If no one in my life knew, I could truly make a new start. And no one knew, not for a long time.

Over the next nine years, I listened carefully to what the church's stance was on abortion. The more they talked (and judged) from the pulpit, the more sure I was that my secret would not be safe with the Christian community. Yet, my heart somehow still felt grace through the work of the Holy Spirit.

The next situation was completely unexpected. Hannah came to me with a crisis pregnancy of her own. I was face-to-face with my own past and unable to deny it any longer. Through her experience, I was introduced to the local pregnancy center through a grandparent's support group. This was the safe place I'd been looking for all along, and I knew the Lord was tenderly prompting me to share my own story. No more hiding; no more shame.

The first person that needed to know was my husband. When I told him my whole story, he exhibited the most gracious love and forgiveness I'd ever received from a person. He was truly an example of God's forgiveness on Earth. From that point on, I began to—slowly—test the *grace* waters of my church family by sharing my story with a few trusted friends. They responded with the same grace. Their reactions stirred a desire in me to offer others a safe haven to share their experiences without judgment too.

I began working with the pregnancy center, but was still in the midst of opening up about my own abortions. So, once again, I was testing the *grace* waters, only this time with people I wasn't acquainted with. This process took a few years, and no one pressed me to share anything I didn't want to reveal, but as I became increasingly confident in their support of others, my own confidence in them grew for myself.

I knew I was safe to reveal my secret, but hesitated still. I attended a retreat for post-abortive women, yet remained to myself for the most part. Shortly after that retreat, a volunteer from the pregnancy center—who had attended the same retreat, approached me.

"Do you remember who I am?" I looked at her, trying to remember where I might have met this woman.

"I'm sorry, I don't." Baffled, I waited for her to give me some clue as to who she was.

"Well, I'm not surprised." Her response took me off guard, and I felt like a wall had just gone up between us. "Do you remember the ABC Church retreat a while back?"

"Yes."

"Well, I was there, and I have to tell you, you acted like you were so above the rest of us. You were just snotty to everyone."

This news hit me hard, and I searched my vocabulary to find the right words to say. The only thing that came out of my mouth was, "I didn't at all mean to come across that way. Not at all. You don't understand." In that moment, I knew that I needed to come out with my story.

First, I needed to tell my children. They were grown now, and I had no idea what their reaction was going to be. They were both so gracious.

"Mom, I always felt as if I had an older brother or sister." Tears threatened to spill, and eventually did. There was no condemnation in her comment, just a knowing that someone was missing in our family. Now, she knew.

As we continued our conversation, I told them that I had been through a Bible study at the pregnancy center. They knew I was active as a volunteer there, but didn't know the whole story until now. "I went through a 12 week study called, Forgiven and Set Free. In one of the chapters, mothers are encouraged to name their aborted babies. I could never bring myself to do that. It was too much for me." I held my grown children's hands and asked if they would help me name the babies. "I think I'm ready now. Will you help me?"

My daughter, Hannah, named one of the babies. "Dillon Joseph."

My son, Eric, named the other. "Angela Marie."

Through my family, and all the others willing to listen to my story without judging me, and especially through the grace of God, I finally experienced complete freedom. No longer did I have to waste energy to keep my secret. I began speaking on Sanctity of Life Sunday at my home church and for other fellowships, representing the local pregnancy center. I counseled for years at the same center I had found my own healing.

Through all of my experience, I consider one-on-one counseling at the pregnancy center to have been most valuable in my healing journey. The education I received about pregnancy and the changes taking place in the unborn child's body made me wonder. If I had known the heart begins to beat at 21 days of gestation, would that information have persuaded me otherwise in the past?

More valuable in my own experience of counseling others is that I can give vital information to women considering abortion as a choice. Armed with the facts, I feel that young women have the ability to make a more informed decision. They also have the benefit of hearing a personal experience story from someone who's been there. Post-abortive pain is not something abortion clinics address, and I can speak first hand as to its reality.

My church family has also been vital to me. If I had known how supportive they were going to be, I would have shared my story sooner. Yes, they have days that support the right-to-life movement, such as Sanctity of Life Sunday, when the pulpit educates congregations about the horrors of abortion and the murder of babies. But I've found that grace is the umbrella that covers those who have experienced it themselves—even on those days.

Even more valuable has been the support of my family—Nick, Hannah and Eric. Without them, I don't think I could have completed my healing process.

Most valuable has been God's forgiveness and grace. Without Him, I could *not* have walked this healing journey. He is the source of all comfort. One Scripture I've based my own healing and counseling of others on is 2 Corinthians 1:3-4. His Word is the final Word.

Praise be to the God and Father of our Lord Jesus Christ, the Father of compassion and the God of all comfort, who comforts us in all our troubles, so that we can comfort those in any trouble with the comfort we ourselves have received from God.

CHAPTER SIX

A Journey to Rachel's Vineyard

By

Marie Reynolds*

A journey can merely be traveling from on place to another or it can be something else. Life's journey's can be fun, difficult, complicated or a host of other things. Yet, sometimes when we reach the destination after being on a winding path full of false starts, obstacles and detours we may find that a new journey has begun . . . .

Marie's Story

I have a son. His name is Christopher. He would be nearly 33 years old, if I hadn't made that fateful choice when I was 19.

I grew up in a loving, close-knit family, and enjoyed a healthy relationship with my parents. My teen years seldom saw conflict with my mom and dad, and because of their well-laid foundation, I prepared to leave for college as soon as I graduated high school. I had no idea what was ahead of me.

College brought on vaguely familiar challenges. One of those challenges was in the form of a young man named Brad who took an interest in me the first week of school. He asked me out on a date and then several more. I had not dated much in high school, and enjoyed his attention and companionship. We were inseparable and soon began an intimate relationship. Still, rather naïve, I seldom asked him to use protection. Diseases and pregnancy only happened to *bad* girls, not young women like me who were good students from a healthy upbringing.

The school year rushed by, and summer break held the promise of going home to visit my family. After a couple of weeks of enjoying my old room and chatting with my parents, I realized that I hadn't had my monthly cycle. I was late—and frantic.

I can't let anyone know about this. Mom and Dad will be so disappointed in me. What am I going to do?

I waited until my parents left the house for the grocery store, grabbed my mom's phone book and flipped through the pages until I found what I needed. Hesitantly, I dialed the number and waited for the nurse to pick up.

"Doctor Reed's office. How may I help you?"

"Umm, I need to make an appointment," I whispered, barely getting the words out. "I need a pregnancy test." *There, I said it.*

"When would you like to come in?" The receptionist's voice was light-hearted, unwittingly mocking my dire situation.

"Can I come in now?"

"I actually have an appointment that just opened up—a cancellation. Can you be here in 15 minutes?"

I can't believe I'm making this appointment at all. I wanted to hang up the phone and forget about my missed cycle, but knew that I needed to do the responsible thing. "I'll be there. Thank you."

After giving my name, I was humiliated. Except for me, the receptionist was the only other person that knew my predicament. "I'll pull your chart and have your information ready for the doctor when you get here." Her voice wavered, hesitating before she said good-bye.

Great. My reputation is already in shambles.

I left for the doctor's office before my parents returned home. I realized that the sooner I knew, the sooner I could take care of my *situation*. I will never forget the date—June 26, 1973. The test was positive.

The stigma of being pregnant was enormous for me, and I was beside myself. As far as I was concerned, there was only one solution. I scheduled an appointment for an abortion, and headed home to inform my parents. They were shocked, disappointed, confused and angry. Through the course of our conversation, I realized that they were also heartbroken at my decision, but I wouldn't be swayed. The *choice* was mine, and I was having an abortion with their approval or without it.

On July 2, 1973, I walked into the hospital pregnant, and walked out without an infant in my arms. I remember little about the procedure, as it took place under general anesthesia. Initially, the relief I experienced beyond the abortion was exhilarating. I could finally get on with my life without the pressure of an unwanted pregnancy.

Two weeks later, I went to the theater and ended up sitting behind a young mother and her infant. I can't remember the movie at all, my full attention riveted toward the smiling pair. Tears slid down my face. *My baby.* I was completely undone.

The grief and despair were overwhelming, and I couldn't turn to my parents. They were already devastated at my decision to end my pregnancy. *Why didn't I give them the opportunity to help me? They would have stepped in and supported me if I had given them the chance.* I realized that I hadn't considered any alternatives to abortion at all. Adoption never crossed my mind, nor did I ever once think about raising my child on my own. I was blind to any other solutions, except one—abortion.

The despair deepened and turned quickly to depression. I remember sitting in the bathroom during a break at my summer job, seriously considering suicide. *I could just take one of the box-cutters from the back room—end it all. Right here. Right now.* I was in the bathroom for nearly an hour, yet in the end, by God's grace, I chose to live.

Little did I know, I would soon meet the man I was destined to marry. During the same summer of my abortion, I met *Tom*. When we met, I was still reeling with spontaneous bouts of grief and trying to make sense of what I had done. He patiently listened to my story and supported me through my turmoil. We fell in love that summer, and if there was ever any doubts about his growing love for me because of my recent pregnancy, he never mentioned them.

At summer's end, I returned to college, broke up with Brad and carried on with college life. Even in the midst of getting on with my life, overwhelming sadness would occasionally sideswipe me at the thought of what I had done over that summer. Each time I encountered those emotions, I comforted myself with the knowledge that I would be obviously pregnant or be a single mother by now, and my college education would be on hold. I wanted to get through school and on with my career before I had children, and this simply wasn't the time to start a family.

Eventually, Tom and I got married. Neither of us shared any regrets over the knowledge of my abortion, and in fact, I became stridently pro-choice and worked in an abortion clinic for a time. I know now that I was doing this to cover and deny my own feelings about my abortion. I don't remember much about working in the abortion clinic other than it was a very sad place to work-they had counseling sessions weekly for the staff. Then I became pregnant.

All the guilt, grief and regret crept their way back into my life, and I was terrified that God would punish me by making me miscarry. I had dreams of stillbirth, or having a baby with serious birth defects. Yet, the months passed and I gave birth to a healthy baby girl—a miracle.

Nine years later, I felt compelled to confess to a priest about my abortion. I planned a meeting with my parish priest and told him what I had done. He listened with genuine compassion. I knew, in that moment after he had given me absolution that I was forgiven, but what I didn't realize was that this was only the first step in my healing process. The next step wasn't so easy. *How will I ever forgive myself?*

Guilt, shame and sadness lingered as the years passed, but a turning point arrived in the form of a woman who spoke about her experience during a women's retreat I attended. Her abortion left her with the same emotions I was feeling, and that day, I found out that I was not the only one.

When she was finished presenting her story, I sat down with a priest who counseled me. "You have been forgiven by God. Now, you must begin to forgive yourself."

Later that evening, I shared my abortion experience with a small group of women at the retreat, and committed myself to finding a way to heal. They encouraged me, even though it had been thirty years since my decision to abort. I was almost 49 years old at that time, yet all the emotions I had bottled up for so long were as fresh as they were when I was 19. At the prompting of these women, I joined an abortion support group at my parish with four other women and began the arduous process of healing.

During this time, my nineteen-year-old daughter became pregnant. My husband and I begged her not to choose abortion. I shared my story with her, and emphasized all the pain it had caused me over years and years. To our dismay, she chose to abort her baby anyway. It was then I understood the anguish my own parents must have felt at losing their first grandchild. My heart was broken, for the loss of a precious life, and for the future emotional turmoil I knew it would eventually cause our daughter.

I continued working through my own pain, compounded by our daughter's circumstances, and even though I was making progress, I could never quite fully grasp relief from my guilt, shame and grief.

Then, that summer, I received a diagnosis that would change my life— breast cancer. I had three children, the youngest only 13. I desperately wanted, needed to live. I prayed for the courage to go through whatever was ahead of me, as well as for the grace of acceptance. After a successful lumpectomy and a six-week radiation regimen, the doctors declared me cancer-free. However, experiencing breast cancer had a profound effect on me. Among other things, I vowed to completely resolve the rest of the issues concerning my abortion.

In October of that same year, I attended Rachel's Vineyard, a weekend retreat for post-abortive women. There were 20 of us, and we each began our journey by telling our stories. Every story was different, yet we all shared the common threads of pain, sorrow, guilt and shame. The sadness in the room was palpable. This was the first time many of the women had ever shared their experience. Slowly, gently, the leaders of the retreat helped lead us through the process of healing.

Prayer, readings, imagery, group work and symbolism all played vital roles in the process of reconciling our pasts. One experience that especially stands out as the most difficult thing I have ever done was the task of penning a letter the leader asked each of us to write—letters to the fathers of our aborted children.

The directions were simple. "Today, we will begin the work of communicating with the fathers of our aborted children. More than likely, many of you have possibly never told them you were pregnant in the first place. Some of you may have told them and they agreed with your decision to have an abortion. Others of you may have felt forced into aborting your children. You all have different stories, and the goal of this assignment is for you to speak your feelings into this letter. Say what needs to be said." Each of us took our notebooks and started the process of clearing out the too long stifled communications. For me, it was an epiphany.

My letter was full of anger, accusing questions and spiteful words. When I finished reading, everyone was silent.

"Perhaps this is an area you need to work on . . ." the leader began. She explained to me that I never forgave my old boyfriend for getting me into a situation as serious as teen pregnancy, and she went on to tell me that I had never even considered what this also may have done to him. Did he regret the past as much as I did?

After considering my emotional state, along with the direction of the counselor, I wrote him a second letter. The words were very different this time as I let go of my anger toward him. I formed my words carefully and succinctly.

My hope for you is that you have found peace in your life, and that you found true love with a devoted wife and a home filled with family and friends . . .

Releasing all my anger and replacing it with forgiveness removed a huge obstacle toward my healing process. A weight lifted off my shoulders, and I was ready to move forward.

One of the most profound experiences of the retreat for me was using imagery as a tool to *speak* with our aborted children. I closed my eyes and settled onto an image of my son, Christopher. I took his small hand in mine and looked into his eyes. "Christopher, my son, I am so sorry your daddy and I didn't let you live life with us on Earth. Will you please forgive us? Will you please forgive me?"

I realized then that our son had forgiven us long ago. The peace that had eluded me for so long found me, and I felt it wash over my spirit, allowing it to penetrate my being. By working through various stages of healing, my journey was nearly over.

Finally, the leader of the retreat directed each of us to write a letter to our children. After 30 years, I finally had the courage to put my thoughts and feeling on paper.

Dearest Christopher,

I want you to know how much I love you, how very much I have missed you. I'm so sorry I robbed us both of wonderful moments together. Do you know that you have brothers and a sister? I wish you could play with them, get to know them here, but I took that away from all of us. I'm so very sorry. Will you watch over them as they grow? One day, we will all be together and will be able to experience all the things we missed. I love you, Christopher.

Many Hugs and Kisses,
Mom

I took my letter to the final meeting of the retreat, a beautiful and emotional ceremony that celebrated the lives of our children. The sadness of the earlier part of the retreat was replaced by peace and joy—the quiet joy of Grace. We had come to the Rachel's Vineyard Retreat as women staggering under the weight of our grief and guilt, but were leaving as light-hearted women, able to laugh and share hugs with one another before driving away.

I often think about Christopher, as I keep a tangible reminder of my little boy next to the bed. I'm no longer wracked by sorrow, but smile when I glimpse the tiny angel on my wall.

Oh Christopher, I will hold you in my heart until the time we meet face-to-face before Jesus. I love you, precious one.

*   Not real name. Names have been changed.

CHAPTER SEVEN

Yes, there is Life after Death . . .

Jackie's Story
By Jackie Bullard

I had a wonderful childhood, growing up in Nashville Tennessee—the *Good Ole South*. Two loving parents raised me and my sweet sister, eleven years my senior. I must admit I was spoiled rotten. Mama told me she prayed to conceive me for a long time, and when I was finally born the whole family couldn't quit kissing on me. I was truly loved.

When it came to religion, our family believed in God but we did not attend church all the time. My parents taught me right from wrong but my spiritual foundation was somewhat weak. I got baptized as a young child, and I knew I loved Jesus, but I did not understand the true meaning of the Gospel.

My sister married when I was seven, and I was brokenhearted. But with her leaving to start a new life, all the attention turned to me, and I loved it. It was like being an only child. I thought I was a little princess and everything revolved around me. I had a tender heart and loved others but I was definitely spoiled. Still, Mom tried her best to bring me up with a sense of responsibility in spite of my somewhat indulgent life. Mom taught me how to cook, clean house and wash clothes. She worked, so I had a lot of chores, but it made me feel good when she came home to a clean house. I am thankful she taught me such valuable lessons.

When I became a teenager something happened to me—it was like my hormones took on lives of their own. I developed very early. I wore a bra as early as third grade and began my period at the tender age of ten. When I was thirteen, I met a boy behind my parent's back—he was sixteen. I had sex with him. This began a pattern of promiscuous behavior that would last for years. I had several boyfriends throughout my teenage years, and I had sex with all of them. Our family doctor put me on the pill because of painful periods. I thought I had found the gateway to paradise!

It didn't stop at sex. I started smoking pot and graduated to stronger drugs during this time. After all, it was *the 70's*. My parents were oblivious, and I perfected the art of lying to them.

When I was eighteen my best friend introduced me to a twenty-six year old man. We fell for each other, and I married him. The marriage lasted two years. He was a sweet guy, but I got antsy. I felt the need to spread my wings a little further, so I did.

After my divorce, I entered the restaurant business where I became a bartender. Then the partying really started. I added drinking to my repertoire of drugs and sex. Keeping up with work and other financial responsibilities were the only factors in my life that kept me from going completely wild—although occasionally Mom and Dad bailed me out if I needed help.

My life was full of endless parties and lonely nights. Looking back, I suppose I was trying to fill that God-shaped hole that sits empty in all of us.

When I was twenty-five I met another bartender who worked at the restaurant next door. We began to see each other and ended up in bed together one night. For some reason during that sexual encounter, I knew I became pregnant. Before I could confirm what my gut had already told me, he moved back to Texas.

There I was—single and pregnant. *What to do, what to do . . .*

Oh, I think I'll have an abortion. It must be okay if everyone is doing it, I thought.

I phoned the local Planned Parenthood. The person on the other end of the line displayed all the warmth of a McDonald's drive-through employee. She practically took my order and asked me if I "wanted fries with that." My best friend drove me to the clinic. Although she was not in full agreement with my decision, she supported me the best way she knew.

No Turning Back . . .

I remember feeling a cold, dark presence as I walked through the doorway of the Planned Parenthood facility. I immediately felt uncomfortable. Staff walked me into a room for their so-called "counseling" session. The counselor informed me that I was on the edge of my second trimester, but they were still going to be able to perform a basic abortion. I did not even know what they meant by the term "basic abortion," and I especially did not grasp the full meaning of a second trimester abortion.

I remember this question vividly: "You don't want to parent or give the child up for adoption do you? After all, it's just a clump of cells, not a baby."

I affirmed that no, I did not want to keep the baby or "clump of cells." Their response was a simple, "Oh well, in that case let's proceed."

From there, I remember staff ushering me into a room with other women lined up on tables. I watched as they continued herding other women in like cattle while I awaited my own procedure. When it was my turn in the line of the deceived, I begged them to stop as I heard the sound of the vacuum. I looked over and saw a glass container beside me filling up with the blood and tissue of my baby. Reality set in.

"Please stop, "I begged, "I am going to throw up."

The nurse grabbed my arm, offering no more comfort than, "SHHHHH, BE QUIET!" I knew then it was too late, and I would never be the same.

Oh God, what have I done?

I walked out of those doors that day empty and alone.

A few days later, after returning to work, I started bleeding and having severe cramps. I called Planned Parenthood, and the staff just blew me off. I ended up at another facility where I had to have a second procedure because they did not retrieve all the baby's parts in the first. I was devastated.

Fast forward six months. My lifestyle spiraled downward as I embraced even more tempestuous behavior than before. More drugs, more alcohol, and more sex. I started having panic attacks regularly. I did not know what was going on. I thought I was losing my mind. I began cutting on my arms. I remember sitting in a pool of blood, knowing I deserved to die.

One night I kept my promise to myself to put an end to it all, and ingested a bottle of pain pills. I slept for two days. After this close brush with death, I sought the help of a secular therapist. We did not even touch on the subject of the abortion during our counseling sessions. After all, it was legal and my right as a woman. How could it hurt me?

Time went on, and I became more introspective about my life. I decided I needed to change. I gave up the restaurant business and moved out to the country, closer to my parents. Life settled down a little. I could not anticipate the ride God was about to take me on!

When I was thirty, I married a wonderful man. Jeff was a sweet country boy, and I was still a city girl at heart, but we balanced each other. It was nice.

Married and far from the noise and pain of my former life, I began building my life one piece at a time. I started a catering business and hired a lady who invited me to attend church with her. I agreed to go with her one Sunday. I found myself sitting in the back row, squalling my head off. Talk about being convicted! My very first time at church with this woman put me in an uncomfortable position. I felt the Holy Spirit leading me back to the path of righteousness.

After that first visit, I chose not to attend church for awhile because my feelings were so intense. But it wasn't long before I gave my heart to Jesus and became a new creature. My husband followed soon after. He knew the Lord all his life, but had veered off the path in recent years. Now he was on the narrow path, and so was I.

But faith in the Lord does not erase hardship. We were about to reap the consequences of choices made years ago.

The Heartbreak of Infertility

When I was thirty-five, we started trying to get pregnant. It just wasn't happening. We prayed so hard for a baby and everyone we knew joined us in prayer. I just knew if I had enough faith, then God would surely give me the desire of my heart.

As time passed, and our arms remained empty, we both agreed God needed a little help. So, we sought out a fertility specialist. That first visit to the doctor began a journey of many uncomfortable procedures—everything from hanging upside down, to shots administered to me by my husband, to scheduling "meetings" for procreation. Feeling like we forfeited all our dignity, we decided to take one shot at in vitro fertilization. Then the news came. An intense examination by my doctor revealed that severe scar tissue damage from my abortion made it nearly impossible for me to conceive a child.

The very moment the words came out of his mouth, I felt myself falling into a pit of darkness. *What? . . . What? I can never have children? You mean, I killed the only child I would ever carry? No, this can't be happening. Is this a nightmare? Surely, he's wrong. No woman in my family has ever been sterile.*

This has got be a mistake, I thought.

But it wasn't.

My husband drove me home from the doctor's office in silence. Deep down, I felt I was being punished for the murder of my baby so many years ago.

As weeks passed, I sunk into the depths of despair. I repeatedly told myself I was the slug of the earth and God hated me. How could I have chosen to let my baby be ripped from my body? I did not deserve a baby or anyone's love—let alone God's love and forgiveness. I just deserved to die. My mom and my husband threatened to commit me to a mental hospital—they just couldn't bear to see me sinking deeper and deeper. I began faking happiness to avoid the lovely accommodations of the local sanitarium. I put a smile on my face and went about my daily duties, attending church, shopping at Wal-Mart . . .

Oh yes, Wal-Mart . . .

There's one shopping experience at Wal-Mart I will never forget. I had everything in my cart. I casually looked around me as I stood in line, waiting to check out. And there she was. A mother with a newborn baby stood directly in front of me. I turned the other way—only to see the pregnant woman standing next to me. On the other side of me sat a baby accompanying her mom. I couldn't take it. My eyes welled up with tears, and I felt a scream coming up in my throat. I abandoned my groceries as I ran out of the store, crying.

My struggles intensified so much, I could not attend baby showers or even hold babies. Adding insult to injury, my cousin announced she was pregnant—with triplets. Anger towards God welled up in me. I could not wrap my mind around the idea that unwanted babies were being thrown into dumpsters, and God would not allow me to have a child. I felt like I was really losing my mind and my salvation.

Light Shines in the Darkness

Jeff and I were living with my mom at the time all of this unfolded. My dad passed away March 21st of 1998. During his health crisis, he asked me to promise to care for my mother if something happened to him. My mother and father were married for 50 happy years, and their love was such a blessing to me. They were soul mates and loved each other dearly. It was tough to see Mom without Dad.

One afternoon, Mom came into my room and said she had been praying for me. She suggested we look into adoption. I cut her off before she could finish her thought and said if I couldn't have my own child, I didn't want any child. My mother responded, "Well if you feel that way, maybe you shouldn't be a mother."

Those words shook me to the bone. After my mother left the room, I threw myself on the bed and began to pray, not with words but with the groans of my spirit, seeking healing, mercy and deliverance from the Lord.

As the sun rose the next morning I awoke with the desire to attend church. I methodically dressed and put on my make-up with a little anticipation of what lay ahead. Near the end of the church service, our pastor gave an altar call. Usually my husband and I both go up to the altar and pray for a baby, but this time as I approached the altar I was alone. I began wailing at the foot of that altar and, there, God began releasing something from my spirit. Just then, I felt a sweet touch on my shoulder. When I turned around, there stood the pastor's granddaughter, 2-year-old Aubrey, wrapping her arms around me, telling me she loved me. She had toddled all the way to the front of the church from her pew. I knew at that moment I could love someone else's child as though she was my own. The following Monday we began adoption proceedings.

In Anticipation of New Life

We immediately knew we wanted a girl. My husband had a 16-year-old son, Corby, from a previous marriage, and we wanted to give him a little sister. We also knew we wanted to adopt outside our race. My niece, Tammi, birthed a beautiful bi-racial baby girl named Bethany when she was 19. For a while Tammi was unable to care for Bethany, and I helped raise her. I loved her dearly. Her bi-racial background changed many hearts in my family for good. She was truly a miracle sent by God, and her birth paved the way for another child in the family of a different race.

A year and a half went by. We maintained our excitement in anticipation of our daughter. We had no idea if she was even born yet. One weekend I attended a large Christian women's conference in Atlanta, Georgia. My mom and I traveled with several ladies in the church.

During the last night of the conference my mother and I were standing at the end of a row. The Holy Spirit fell in the coliseum, and something began happening to me. I started throwing up, but nothing was coming out. I began making noises that did not sound human. This went on for several minutes. My mother showed concern, but knew the Lord was up to something. I also knew this was God, but I did not know what was happening to me.

Suddenly, everything stopped. I felt different—light and free. Joy sprung up in my soul. I knew God had delivered me and purged me from all the guilt and shame of my abortion, and He was going to bless me with a baby. I'll never forget as I walked up to the front, a very tall gentleman tapped me on the shoulder and said, "Sister, you are about to get a blessing."

Two days after returning from our trip, we got a phone call. It was the agency telling us we had a baby girl. We were told she was 4 months old and a "difficult placement." Her birth mother had left her in the hospital. She chose Bethany Christian Adoption Agency to place her child, but then would never keep the appointments to review prospective parents. She had a drug problem and had no idea who or where the baby's father was. The baby was also born with cocaine in her system, but had no side effects.

The agency investigated their list of names and knew we would be the perfect parents for this child. They FedExed a picture to us—light mocha skin, blue-green eyes and soft, brown curls. She was beautiful.

We got very excited, and I began nesting for her arrival. One weekend prior to the placement, my husband and I drove to a lovely spot on Mont Eagle Mountain called Savage Gulf. We hiked up to a majestic sight overlooking a gorge. There, we found a giant rock that resembled an altar, and we got down on our knees and began to pray for our daughter and our life ahead. It was an extraordinary moment. We knew this was God's perfect plan all along.

Becoming a Mom Again

It wasn't long before we headed for Chattanooga to pick up our daughter. We arrived at the agency and waited with anticipation. A few minutes passed. We heard a knock at the door. A gorgeous baby girl was ushered in and placed in my arms. I cannot describe in words the joy I felt. This was my daughter, I was her mother, and nothing could ever separate us.

At that moment, I recalled Romans 8:39: "Neither height nor depth, nor anything else in all creation, will be able to separate us from the love of God that is in Christ Jesus our Lord."

As my husband and I looked into her eyes, we immediately fell in love. We named her Arabella Jayne; Arabella meaning "beautiful altar." The name was only appropriate after praying on the natural altar the Lord provided in Savage Gulf.

That day God showed me His infinite love for us, and His divine plan for us. All I could say was: *Thank you, Jesus, I love You, Jesus!*

When we arrived home, my mother was the first to greet us. Since the loss of my dad her life had been lonely and difficult. When she first laid eyes on Arabella a new joy came over her. This was her granddaughter, a gift from heaven, a new beginning for my mom. Throughout the day relatives came and went. I felt as if I was the queen of England bringing home her firstborn. We were blessed with so much love and support from our families.

We bonded immediately, and the blessings continued to flow. I knew the Lord was looking down on me, a mother for the first time at age 40, when Arabella began sleeping through the night right away. I stayed home with her, and she grew smarter and more beautiful every day.

As time went on, God started speaking to my heart about doing some kind of ministry work. I called the adoption agency, and they suggested I call a crisis pregnancy center to inquire about volunteering there. After talking to the director, I knew this was the direction I should take. I went through the training and started my counseling. Being post-abortive, I could share my testimony to help girls make the right decision.

But still God was speaking to me in another area. What about all the women who have already suffered the devastation of abortion? They need help, they need to be healed and set free from the guilt and shame just like I was. I discovered a program set up at the center for these women, and started helping out with the Bible study. Deep down, I knew I found the ministry God wanted for me. It was such a blessing to see women get healed and to go on to help other women.

I started sharing my testimony in churches and women's events. I joined an organization called Operation Outcry and had the opportunity to go to Washington, D.C. several times to speak during the March for Life. I have had the honor of speaking to congressman and senators from all over the country. I have participated in several radio and print interviews. I am so thankful God has used me in this capacity—all glory goes to Him.

God Works Through the Littlest Ones

On Christmas morning of 2002, just about the time we were about to open presents, my mother died of a heart attack. Arabella and I hit our knees and began to pray while my husband Jeff performed CPR on my mother. Even as we prayed, I knew she had already crossed over into the arms of Jesus to meet my dad. As we drove to the funeral home the next day, my daughter not yet three, ministered to me.

"Mama, don't be sad, Nana went to be with Jesus and we are going to see her again."

"That's right, Baby, you see it perfectly clear."

I knew then God would use her in a mighty way for His kingdom. A few months later we were sitting around the kitchen having dinner and laughing, when out of the blue she asked, "Mommy, your tummy was broken, right?"

"Yes, Baby."

"Another lady carried me in her tummy for you and Daddy, right?"

"Yes, Baby." (We had been telling her about the miracle of her adoption since she was two).

"Do you know her?"

"No, Baby."

"Do you love her?"

"Oh yes, Baby, we love her very much—she gave you to me and Daddy."

Then she said, "Mama, if you ever see her, will you hug her?"

Tears were streaming down our faces as I answered, "Oh yes. Yes, Baby, we will hug her."

At three years old, it was as if God was speaking straight through her to us. She truly understood.

Life Today

Arabella is seven now. She has long, golden, brown ringlets, beautiful eyes and skin. She loves school, and excels as an artist and dancer. But most importantly, her heart is pure and she loves Jesus. My husband and I have been happily married for seventeen years, and he gives me his full support in my ministry. He is a good father and a gentle, sweet man who loves me more than I deserve.

As parents we have always been truthful with Arabella about her past. We taught her about the miracle of adoption, but she still has questions. Recently I had an encounter with her that will change our relationship forever.

I've told her many times what I know about her birth mother and the events of her adoption, but this time was different. One night we were reading from our mother-daughter Bible. She wanted to read a particular story we have read many times. I argued with her, saying, "Let's read a story we haven't read before." But she insisted we read this one.

At the end of the story, there were questions for moms to ask their children. The book asked the parents to share a time when there was something we didn't like about ourselves, but we learned to accept it and be happy. So, I told her that when I was young I had very curly hair just like her, and everyone at school had long, straight "Marcia Brady" hair. I hated my hair. Then one day, I was in a dance recital, dancing a lovely, modern ballet. People approached me after the show and said my hair looked long and beautiful as I danced. After that day, I began accepting my hair—even liking it.

After sharing my story, I asked Arabella if she had an experience she would like to share with me. She did. She told me she used to feel sad sometimes about being adopted and bi-racial. She felt different from others. But one day, a new girl showed up at school. She was also bi-racial and adopted. Her presence made Arabella feel better about herself. She told me that she thought it was pretty cool now to be bi-racial and adopted.

I took this opportunity to tell her if she ever felt bad about being adopted again, please come and talk to me. In response she asked, "Who is my real, real, real, real, real mommy?"

I looked into her beautiful eyes, praying for God's words. "God chose me to be your real mommy, spiritually and in every other way except for giving birth to you. But I birthed you in my heart. I prayed and prayed for you, Sweetheart. I know I have told you this, but before God ever placed the stars in the sky, before the foundations of the earth, God chose you to be our daughter. He knew you before you were ever in the womb about to be born."

Then I asked her to look into my eyes and listen to what I was about to say.

"If I had a choice, and could go back in time and physically have a baby, I would choose you, Baby, I would choose you every time."

We both started crying and she grabbed me hard as she said, "Oh Mama, I love you so much."

I told her, "You are my daughter, my angel in every way, and nothing can ever separate our love for each other. I know that He will use your testimony someday to touch others just like Mama."

God spoke to me that day and said, *Not only do I want you to share your testimony about your abortion but I want you to let the world know about the miracle of adoption. How I gave you beauty for ashes and joy for mourning. How something so beautiful rose above something so evil. How just as we adopt children into our families, you are also adopted into Mine.*

God's love is so indescribable. If I had not experienced the inability to conceive a biological child, I would not be Arabella's mother. If Arabella's birth mother had chosen abortion like I did for my child, she would not exist on this earth. But she chose life for her and for that I will always be so thankful. We, His children, are all a part of His great tapestry. I have come to realize in God's amazing sovereignty, He sees the big picture, when we only see the snapshot.

I will go and proclaim:

> *He has sent me to bind up the brokenhearted,*
> *To proclaim freedom for the captives and release from*
> *darkness for the prisoners . . . to comfort all who mourn,*
> *and provide for those who grieve in Zion—to bestow*
> *on them a crown of beauty instead of ashes, the oil of*
> *gladness instead of mourning, and a garment of*
> *praise instead of a spirit of despair. Is.61:1-3*

Jackie and Arabella Bullard

The Poem

During my first post-abortion Bible study there was a memorial held for
our children. After my healing, I asked God to reveal the sex and name of
my child. He was a boy and his name would be Malachi. I grieved for my
child then and still do. During the service all the women came forward
and spoke about their children. When it was my turn, I shared a poem that
God had given me for my son.

Oh Child Of Mine

I never got to see your face with your smile so sweet
I never looked into your eyes or kissed your little feet
I never smelled your precious scent or cradled you to my chest
I never sang you a lullaby and put you down to rest
I never kissed your boo-boo gone and wiped away your tears
I never assured you of my love to calm your fears
I never pitched a ball to you and watched you hit it far
I never laid on a summer's night when you wished upon a star
I never got to see you grow unto a great young man
I never saw you stand before God to accept your wedding band
But someday when this earth is gone and Jesus splits the sky
We'll be together in love's embrace forever by and by

Dedicated to my precious son Malachi

The Vision

Arabella knows about my abortion and has traveled with me to DC and other pro-life events. The ministry is such a huge part of our lives that we couldn't hide it from her. We talk about Malachi often and hang an angel on the Christmas tree for him. We talk about one day seeing him in heaven and we wonder how old he will be. I want to share this vision that God gave me last year.

I was at a retreat for my ministry in San Antonio. During a prayer and worship time I began travailing for the babies who have been aborted. In the blink of an eye, God took me from wailing to laughter. I saw Jesus in a beautiful rolling meadow with the most vibrant colors I had ever seen. He was playing with Malachi who seemed to be a toddler, throwing him up in the air and catching him. Malachi was squealing with happiness. Jesus was so bright, with a beard and the whitest teeth. He was radiant. He told me, "Look, look as far as you can see." When I looked beyond my own child, I saw all of our children playing with the angels and each other. There was nothing but pure joy on their faces. He said to me, "Jackie, these are all the children, all the ones lost to abortion. They are waiting on all of you. They are not sad. They will run to you when you get to heaven, and I delight in them as I delight in you."

I am telling you about this vision to give you peace and hope. Your children will be waiting for you in heaven. Waiting for you to run to them and embrace them forever under the wings of our Savior.

Yes, there is life after death!

CHAPTER EIGHT

Set Free

By

Arlene Lehman

I was raised in a Christian home and accepted the Lord as my Savior around the age of ten. Growing up in a small rural community in the Midwest my environment was very safe and loving. I remain thankful for that. The youngest of five girls, my mom still refers to the year I was born as one of the happiest of my parent's married life. I was indeed a wanted child. Our family attended church every Sunday as well as the mid-week services on a regular basis.

Being raised in a generation where subjects such as child abuse, sexual abuse and pornography were not openly discussed, the word abortion was never mentioned in our home either. However, I am quite sure my parents were against it. In high school I remember one of my friends mentioning the word "abortion", and I wasn't sure what it was. A couple of years later in college I found a flier showing aborted fetuses. I couldn't believe it, and thought such pictures couldn't be real babies and that it was probably sensationalism or propaganda. Even though I was not educated on the topic, somewhere deep inside of me I knew abortion was wrong.

After graduating from high school I decided to pursue a career in accounting and attended a business college in a neighboring state. It was close enough that I could hop on the Greyhound and visit my friends, family, and boyfriend back home on weekends. Yet it was also far enough away that I was on my own. After a bad breakup with my boyfriend, I decided to move to Colorado.

I quickly found a job and an apartment and began my new life. About six months after I arrived I began a relationship with someone I met at work. Even then I knew Louis wasn't the man for me, but I was so lonely being away from my family that I found myself clinging to him. He became my whole life and I lost whatever bit of identity I had left.

My parents came to visit me a couple of years after I moved. During their visit I introduced Louis to them. I had to show them that I was doing fine, and I didn't want them to worry about me being so far from home.

A few months after their visit I found out I was pregnant. I couldn't believe it. I had been so careful. Louis said that he didn't want me to have to face the shame of telling my parents of my pregnancy. His words were that we should "get rid of it". I actually wasn't sure what he meant when he told me to have an abortion. I didn't know what it would involve. About all I knew was that I would not be pregnant anymore.

In his defense I believe he thought he was doing me a favor. This is one of the reasons I believe this book is important. My hope is to convey to others the devastation that abortion causes—especially when people do not understand the consequences of their actions. When Louis referred to the baby as "it", I sometimes think about the effectiveness pro-abortionists had before ultrasound machines. They were able to deny the human aspect of pre-born life and it swayed many women to their side. Not any more.

I found myself in a clinic and before the procedure I told the nurse that I wanted to see this "blob of tissue" that they were going to remove. Somewhere in the recesses of my mind I remembered that flier of aborted fetuses I had seen in college. Was it really a baby? The staff was quite hesitant to comply with my request and I was told that I would only be able to see some liquid and perhaps a little blood. But I insisted. I had to know.

I remember waking from the procedure feeling that something indescribably horrible had occurred. I was screaming for Louis and shook for what seemed like forever. It took a long time to recover. In spite of all that, I still wanted to see the remains. Little did I know that this was not the only "remains" of the quick and easy procedure

A nurse brought a small steel pan in so I could examine the contents. Sure enough, I saw only some liquid and a small amount of blood. It eased my mind that no little fingers or toes and no recognizable body parts were present. Maybe it was just a blob. (It wasn't until years later that I realized body parts had been removed. What woman could bear to see her baby brought in to her in shreds?)

Right there on that table I made a vow to God. I told Him that I knew I wasn't living as I should but if I ever were to conceive again I would carry that baby no matter what the circumstances. With that, my denial system kicked in and it was several years until the abortion was ever mentioned again. Whatever shred of self-identity and self esteem I had left had been destroyed along with the life of my child. I began a slow downward spiral over time that included depression, repression, withdrawal, and general unhappiness.

My relationship with Louis began to deteriorate as well. Although I still cared for him I didn't want to be with him. I had known all along that he wasn't the right man for me. I wasn't living the life-style I should have been, and I needed a grounded Christian atmosphere. Without a support system of friends or family, I was too weak to leave him. Louis compounded the problem by continually commenting, "I am always right and know what's best for you." I had become so fragmented and broken, I believed him. Over time, I regressed from a competent, strong-willed, stubborn person to someone completely dependent on another.

A typical scenario of Louis' abuse took place one Saturday when I decided to go into work to catch up on some paperwork as a bookkeeper. Louis would hear none of it. "You will do no such thing! You're staying home today."

Time dragged on and I felt trapped in the relationship, desperately trying to figure out how to get out of it. One week-end we had a big argument. I remember thinking that enough was enough and that I should leave. I began grabbing my belongings that I had at his house and throwing them into my car. Louis blew up and hit me. This was not the first time. Reluctantly, I unloaded the car and stayed. Later I learned that it is at this point in the cycle of violence that 6 out of 7 women are in danger of their lives.

Three years after my abortion I brought up the subject during dinner. "I wish I'd never had the abortion."

Louis slammed his fist on the table and exclaimed, "I wanted that baby!"

I became fearful as the conversation began to escalate, so I dropped the subject. To this day I can't reconcile the words he said during that dinner with the original solution that we should "get rid of it." I had the abortion because he told me he knew what was best.

Six years into our relationship, I found out I was pregnant again. I was angry at the news because Louis had insisted on sexual relations without taking any precautions. Deep in my heart, I knew I did not want a child growing up in domestic violence. But I had made that vow to the Lord and I was determined to fulfill it. Since Louis and I weren't married, my thoughts often drifted to the question, "Could I be a single mother?" A part of me wondered what would happen if I broke my vow to the Lord too. I didn't want to find out, I would keep that vow.

Early in the pregnancy I found out that the lump in my abdomen that I had been feeling was one of several fibroid tumors which were all attached to my uterus. The only way to remove the tumors was to have a hysterectomy, which ultimately meant terminating the pregnancy. A state of shock washed over me as I sat in that doctor's office.

A hysterectomy? What about my baby? What about my vow? I knew the implications of a hysterectomy would end any possibility of ever having children. I left that office determined to have my child. A second opinion yielded the same result. "In thirty years, I have only seen maybe two or three women worse off than you," that second doctor coldly pronounced.

Abortion was legal in Colorado at that time. However, I was told due to my medical condition that even if it were not legal I would qualify for an abortion because my life may be in danger. If I had only known that the original abortion may have caused the risks of complication in subsequent pregnancies, I may not have had it. I can not "prove" that this was the case, but neither can anyone else prove that it was not.

Complications soared as the pregnancy progressed. Chemical changes with my body caused the tumors to grow at an astronomical rate. My doctor kept telling me that there was no way I could carry the pregnancy to term. At best I would probably be bed-ridden for most of it. He reminded me that my body could not handle a growing baby along with five to eight tumors.

Louis tried to be supportive, but this time around I think he actually feared for my health. If the baby were to be premature and not fully developed or if the baby were to be mentally handicapped, Louis would not be able to afford it financially.

I cried out to the Lord like never before. After all, He could fix this, He could heal me, and He could perform a miracle. I was desperately trying to keep that vow I'd made six years earlier. I needed to trust that the Lord would deliver me, that He would make a way.

I began to attend a strong Christian church and learned the Word as never before. I was determined to stand on promises that I found in the Scriptures. Although Louis was somewhat emotionally supportive, I still had very little outside connections to anyone other than him. I was fighting this battle alone.

As the pregnancy progressed, my physical condition worsened. The blockage from the tumors close to my bladder and urinary tract was so extensive that twice I went to the ER to be catheterized to urinate. Still, I stood firm and was determined to carry the pregnancy. After the second catheterization, fear set in. I was too tired to fight anymore. I knew the longer I waited to have surgery, the harder it would be. I felt like a failure, but God wasn't coming through for me. I might as well listen to the doctors.

When the day of the surgery arrived, I was three months pregnant. The whole experience is still very vivid in my mind—just as vivid as the first abortion. I can still see myself, (now 20 years later at the time of this writing) lying on that cold, hard table. I was crying, with my hands on my stomach trying to comfort my baby that I already loved deeply. Unlike the first abortion I had at least fought for this baby. But that thought did not give a lot of comfort, I was still a failure.

I remember the intern removing my hands from my stomach. All the while I was praying that both the baby and God would forgive me, that somehow the baby would not feel pain, and that Jesus would put her back together again. At the time of the surgery I had seven to eight tumors, the largest weighing 2 ½ pounds. But for me, the loss of the baby outweighed the difficulty of the pregnancy.

This experience was by far the most difficult and traumatic part of my life. Even now when a difficult situation arises for me, I look back and tell myself that whatever I am facing can't be as bad as that fateful day.

Within two years of the surgery, my relationship with Louis ended. The already unhealthy situation could not take the stress of a second abortion and my deteriorating emotional state tipped the scales. By God's grace a path of escape—an end to the violence against me—was opened to me and I took it. Looking back, I can see the times the Lord protected me even though I wasn't living like I should have been. For me, this speaks profoundly of the love that the Lord has for each of us.

One day I found myself in a Christian bookstore. I happened to see a book (now out of print) titled, "Abortion's Second Victim." The subtitle included something about emotional healing for women who've had an abortion. I looked at it and thought, "I've had an abortion, but I'm Okay." Nonetheless, I bought it out of curiosity.

As I read the book I started to cry—and I was reading the introduction! The author seemed to know everything about me. She understood feelings I didn't even know I had (or was afraid to admit). Slowly, I began to feel better. The well-kept secrets of my life were exposed. My abortions hurt me. Tears were so dense I couldn't see. Then came the pain. The reality of what I had done and the damage that occurred sunk in. I had to stop reading.

Although I quit reading that day, I found the courage to pick up that book again. I made a point of reading it everyday. As painful as it was, I never stopped even if it meant reading just one page. The Christian author used Scripture and words of wisdom to reach my heart. Nothing heals like the Lord and His Word.

After I finished the book, I visited a church to listen to a guest speaker. Since it was a mid-week service there were no bulletins—except in the pew I chose. Waiting for the talk to begin, I curiously perused the paper. An announcement caught my eye. It advertised a group for post-abortive women who were in need of healing. I felt as though it was a personal invitation from God to me.

When I got home I called the number, joined the group and let the Lord do His work. Emotions ran the gambit from exhilaration at letting go of the secret that I had been carrying, to a frightened child wondering what the others would think of me. I soon found out that the other women there also felt the same way. We became a close knit group as we ventured through our healing process together, sharing secrets, feelings, and praying for each other. It was a safe place for me—the first in a long time.

Shortly after the group finished, I became a volunteer in a local crisis pregnancy center. I had the opportunity to share my story and testimony in schools and churches. I used this time to encourage other post-abortive women to find healing with the Lord.

In March of 1989, I took another step towards recovery when I received a telephone call from my sister.

"Dad's in the hospital. He's had a heart attack . . . and a stroke. They don't know if he's going to make it."

My heart sunk. "I'm coming home."

More than facing the possible death of my father was the overwhelming guilt of never telling my parents about my abortions. I never told them the story behind my surgery. Deep in my heart I knew it was important for them to know—especially my father—if indeed this was my last chance to talk to him. I had been active several hundred of miles away ministering and sharing my story, while the most important people in my life did not know the truth about me.

When I arrived at the hospital Dad was in ICU, unable to respond. Although he survived the surgery, he remained in ICU. I stayed for several days, waiting for him to be able to communicate. But I was torn. I desperately wanted to tell him before I had to leave, but I didn't want to drop any earth-shattering news on his delicate heart. Finally, I had an idea from the Lord.

The day before I had to leave I asked other family members if they would give me a few minutes alone with Dad. They agreed. My heart pounded as I knew this would probably be my only chance to share my secret or anything else with him. I prayed for wisdom. I started by telling him that we were all praying for him. I also said that if he didn't stay here on Earth with us that I had the assurance that he would be with the Lord. I talked about how wonderful heaven must be. Then I said that I believed God would have lots of "surprises" for us. By that, I meant my children. I believe that in Heaven he will meet my babies—the ones he didn't know anything about in this life.

I continued to tell him that I was involved in a church that actively reached out to help hurting people. I told him that I had started helping women who had abortions. Not knowing how much he understood I paused, and asked if he thought that was a good thing. He nodded his head yes, and with that I felt I had his blessing. Within a few moments we were interrupted by others entering the room. Although I was not descriptive about the abortions, I felt a huge weight off my chest. I was able to share information that provided healing in my life without jeopardizing his health.

Dad remained in ICU for several weeks before he went on to be with the Lord. Shortly after Dad's passing I began to wrestle with an internal struggle. My mentor at the crisis pregnancy center reminded me many post-abortive women take the death of a loved one very hard because they have never resolved the death that occurred during their abortion. Like a deer caught in the headlights, I realized I had never grieved my first abortion. Once I worked through the guilt, the shame, and the pain, the subsequent healing brought release and closure to this part of my life.

Through this healing I began to share my story everywhere I could. I talked with church groups, Bible study groups, schools and even on the radio. I developed a support group in my church for abortion recovery. I also led several studies for abortion recovery through a local crisis pregnancy center.

Shortly after these activities, I facilitated a group for battered women. Since domestic violence played such a large role in my abortions, I felt the need to help other women in this situation. I now understand that pregnancy increases the possibility of domestic violence by as much as fifty percent. This became apparent when I noticed that many women who joined the post-abortive support group also attended the battered women recovery group.

Leading these groups also facilitated my healing process too. I learned that whenever the Lord opened a door, I followed. As I continued to share, the Lord continued His healing in my life.

Several years ago I joined Operation Outcry, a group of mostly women who speak openly about the affect of abortion in their lives. Pro-abortionists have a difficult time disputing real stories. Real women sharing their genuinely difficult experiences, telling the truth of the devastation that followed cannot be swept under the rug.

In spite of all the healing and forgiveness the Lord continues to extend to me, the consequences of my "choices" remain. The effects of abortion are long-term, and twenty years after my fateful decision, I still struggle as indicated by the following example.

I am currently living with my niece and her family. She has four daughters, one of which just turned twenty. As I watched Alissa celebrate her birthday I couldn't help but think of the daughter I lost. My daughter should be here, celebrating with Alissa. She should be twenty too and have her whole life ahead of her. But the pain doesn't stop there. Because I aborted my children, I myself will never know the joy of ever experiencing life as a grandparent. There will be no second generation, nor will any other generation follow. How many babies were lost because of one "choice"?

The silence extends beyond me. For every aborted child there is one less soul mate for someone else. Abortion never affects just one person. The theory that abortion is a private choice is left in shambles.

If you are struggling with the pain or maybe the secret pain of an abortion in your life, please know that with God's help you can be healed. He can put the pieces of your life back together, just as He has done for me. All praise to the living God, because of His unlimited love, grace, and forgiveness, I can go on with my life. (Romans 8.28)

CHAPTER NINE

The Truth Will Set You Free

By

Shannon Phillips[*]

Before I start my story, I would like to share a little family background, as I believe it is pertinent to my life's journey, starting with my parents. Both my mother and dad grew up on South Dakota farms during the depression, so life was difficult from the beginning. My mom was the eldest of six Irish children, and each one heard the same thing from the time they were very young. They had limited choices for their future professions; upon graduation, they could either pursue teaching or become a nun. Two of Mom's sisters became nuns and the rest became teachers.

My mother, a country school teacher, was very unhappy with her career, but it never occurred to her to choose any differently. Her upbringing was harsh, and the choices her parents made for her left my mom with many regrets. Her parents also dominated choosing husbands for their daughters, and the most important requisite was that he must be Catholic. She once told me that she had fallen in love and become engaged to a man, but he wasn't Catholic. Her parents forbade the marriage, and my mother obeyed them, eventually marrying my dad, a devout Catholic.

My dad was a hardworking, strong, handsome, German man who joined the Navy at 17 years of age. He traveled the world as a young man, and later captured my mother's attention telling stories of his many adventures. During the course of their marriage, he did shift work at a power plant, later leaving that position to own and operate a gas station. When his business waned, he went back to work at the power plant, but not until my parents had lost everything. They went bankrupt, existing on food stamps and hand-me-downs for all the kids.

In the midst of financial struggle, my mother gave birth to 10 children. I was number 10. I didn't look anything like my siblings, nor did I act like them. They often referred to me as *the oddball*, and I felt like one, considering that I was everything opposite of them. In all, my parents had 10 children in the span of nine years. As I grew older, and questioned the size of our family, they told me that God never gives us more than we can handle. Hence, five more siblings were born after me.

One of my earliest childhood recollections was kneeling for prayer, every night. We rarely missed this tradition, starting when my oldest brother learned prayers for his First Communion. I remember the prayer today:

God Bless Daddy, Momma, Paul, Dale, Tracy, Teresa, Timothy, Terrence, Susan, Sharon, Shirley, Shannon, Maria, Elizabeth, Renee, Stephen and Samuel, all my aunts and uncles, cousins, and friends. Make me a good girl, sweet Jesus, come to me and stay. For I love you, dearest Jesus, more than I can say.

A strict Catholic upbringing sent all of us kids through 12 years of Catholic education. My parent's childrearing philosophy was mom raises the girls, and dad, the boys. Expectations were high. Proper appearance, honor roll grades and excelling in athletics were fully expected of all of us. Favoritism was shown the ones that excelled. They were granted special attention from mom and dad. From the age of 12, I bought or sewed all of my clothes and earned money to pay my tuition for school. I pretended to be a faithful, obedient child along with my siblings but unfortunately, we only feared God, and had no idea what it was like to have a loving relationship with Him.

On the surface, anyone who observed our family would have commented on how perfect we were. Perfect in our Catholic faith and successful in everything we did. Yet there were secrets that devastated the core of our relationships.

I learned at a very early age to keep family secrets well hidden. How could I let anyone know that each of us were cruelly punished for misdeeds? Appearances were everything, so we hid our cuts, bumps and bruises well. Discipline often took the form of harsh beatings with sticks, belts, switches, hairbrushes and wooden spoons. I cringe at the thought of one of my younger sisters being beaten severely for her inability to read. Elizabeth was learning disabled, and our mother refused to accept she was imperfect. I remember trying to wish my reading skills on my sister. I loved to read, and was proud of my school skills.

A Scripture comes to mind when I think of all the physical abuse, and wonder why the truth of it wasn't true in our household.

Can a mother forget the baby at her breast
and have no compassion on the child she has borne?
Though she may forget,
I will not forget you!
See, I have engraved you on the palms of my hands;
your walls are ever before me.
Isaiah 49:15-16 (NIV)

As a child, I took it upon myself to gather all the sticks hidden above doorways and other accessible places. I hid them, thinking I could stop or at least put off the beatings. I wasn't successful, but only made things worse for us when the implements of our discipline went missing.

Harsh punishment wasn't the only abuse we suffered. When I was about 5 years old, my oldest brother, Paul, began sexually molesting me. Five other sisters and one brother suffered at his hand as well. I was so confused and afraid. Communication with my parents was minimal at best, and I couldn't tell them something that would upset the balance of our *perfect* family appearance. Perfection, not only demanded in front of others outside of our home, but within the framework of our family, left us paralyzed. I remember trying to tell one of my sisters about our brother, but she told me to shut up. She became so upset with me that she once beat me in order to shut my mouth.

I lived in constant fear of my parents hitting me, my brother molesting me, and other siblings teasing and beating me. The only life I knew was filled with fear, shame, self-loathing, and deep-seeded anger. I dreamed of having a mother that protected me, and living with other families that seemed healthy and happy, but for appearance sake, I wore a mask hiding my pain and shame. The world never saw my hurt. I hid it well. Living in this atmosphere also taught me to be mean to others. I could give as good as I got.

My eighth grade year was a turning point for me. Mom was pregnant with her 15th child and because of complications; the doctor put her on constant bed rest. Responsibility for running our home fell on the girls. I remember helping to do 10 to 12 loads of laundry a day, cleaning a six-bedroom house, cooking and serving meals for the entire family and taking care of babies.

"I'll never get married and have kids," I remember saying. I thought it was insane.

"Shannon! Get in here!" By the time I got to her room, I found Mom struggling to put on medical support hose, and she was visibly upset. "Too much weight, too tired. I don't care if this baby lives. In fact, I hope I die too." As I helped her with her hose, I was frightened that Mom would really go off the deep end. I was too young to understand the medical and emotional issues of her experience.

The day my mom went to the hospital, I remember Dad calling us. "The baby's lungs aren't fully developed and the doctor is sending him to another hospital."

We heard the sirens of an ambulance speeding toward the hospital and knew it was for our baby brother. An awkward silence fell on my brothers and sisters, as we had no idea how to comfort one another.

"Hail Mary, full of grace . . ." one of my siblings began. However, we never finished our prayer, as each of my brothers and sisters drifted away. Left in the kitchen by myself, I begged God to let the baby live, but the Rosary hadn't helped, and our brother passed away. His death became another unspeakable topic, adding to our painful secrets.

From that point on, I wanted nothing to do with Catholicism or any kind of faith. I closed my mind to anything religious and learned very little as I attended catholic school. I went to Mass, but ignored the message. As I grew older participating in these activities was a farce. Any faith I once had was gone. In fact, I made fun of those who seriously practiced their religion. I was a hurting young woman, and although my experiences made me grow up quickly, I was stunted emotionally, and my behavior beyond college reflected my past. I was lonely, and made terrible life choices.

College graduation freed me from my family, and I moved to one of the most liberal, do-whatever-feels-good cities in the United States—Minneapolis. I jokingly refer to my time there as my "Mary Tyler Moore days," with no more parents to answer to, and no more church. It was two or three years before I went home to visit and I became the brunt of family gossip, but I didn't care.

Looking back, I can see my empty wandering through Scripture:

The man who walks in the dark does not know where he is going.
John 12:35 (NIV)

Looking for affection and acceptance, I began sleeping around with a couple of different guys and ended up pregnant. I knew from the experience of one of my sisters that having a child out of wedlock was one of the worst things you can do to a family. She married quickly, but my parents let her know how ashamed and embarrassed they were of her. I would not have been able to handle the shame of my parents, or their cruel and insensitive words. They would have only let me know how I made them look like failures as parents.

I also decided not to tell the potential fathers of my child about my pregnancy. It wouldn't have accomplished anything anyway. One of the men lived far away and the other was married, completely unavailable to me. I didn't want to get married anyway. My selfishness led me to what I thought was my only viable choice—abortion. I went to the clinic alone because I didn't want anyone to know or be burdened with *my problem.* After the painful procedure I left the clinic, an empty, numb woman.

Void of any spiritual nourishment, I chose to fill the emptiness inside with food. A few years after the abortion, I had gained nearly 125 pounds and didn't care if I lost them or not. I developed Type II Diabetes from becoming so heavy, but didn't care about myself enough to change. I would drop everything to help anyone else, yet ignored my own needs. I stopped dating altogether and developed a lingering depression.

Years later, I awoke one morning unable to walk, sit up or stand. For four weeks, I laid in bed, missing work. When I finally was able to visit the doctor, he diagnosed me with an enlarged liver, enlarged kidney and a growing cyst on my ovary. My blood sugars were out of control. One doctor wanted to go in and biopsy the cyst, but another refused, telling me that I was too heavy. I had to lose weight before they would do anything. I was too high risk, not only physically, but also mentally.

Because of the mess my life was in, I decided to seek counseling and found a therapist I felt I could trust. She invited me to examine my life through the eyes of an adult, not as a struggling child. As we worked on my childhood issues, I purposely kept my abortion secret. Through our early sessions, I had come to realize that she was not Catholic, and if I mentioned the abortion, she probably would have dismissed it as irrelevant anyway. I needed to be punished for what I did, deserving no less. I wanted forgiveness, but had no idea how to find it.

Until I went to Chicago . . .

While visiting Chicago, I watched my sister's children and took them to Sunday Mass. Family ties had inbred attendance for my nieces' sake, but the Church still held no interest to me. Perusing through the bulletin, I read about Rachel's Vineyard, a Catholic-endorsed retreat program to help post-abortive women. As soon as I arrived home, I searched online for more information. I found that there was going to be a retreat held near where I lived and registered to attend.

Before Rachel's Vineyard, I had never shared my abortion story with anyone. It was an extremely difficult thing to do, but I knew that this retreat offered me a safe opportunity to find what I was seeking—forgiveness. Not only was I looking for God's forgiveness, but I also needed to forgive myself. I had been self-destructing for too long without caring, and I knew this was my time to change.

The Rachel's Vineyard retreat offered me the opportunity to mourn the loss of my child. I named my precious baby and asked *her* to forgive me for never giving *her* the chance to live. I gave *her* a name—Sophie. Not only did I ask Sophie for her forgiveness, but I also sought God's forgiveness. This, I found was the missing piece of my life's struggle. I had held my secret so tightly until then that I had not allowed the Holy Spirit to do what needed doing in my life. I hadn't let him heal me.

The first steps were hard. Sharing my story was something I thought I would never do, but I was safe at that retreat, and after talking openly and listening to others, I found that I wasn't alone. At that retreat, I shed all my secrets, along with many tears and invited the Lord to do His work in me. I wanted His healing.

Blessed are those who mourn, for they will be comforted.
Matthew 5:4 (NIV)

I'll never forget that first night. "I can't remember what to say. I haven't been to confession in so long." I hesitated not knowing where to begin.

The priest told me that we had all night, and I could tell him anything. When he said that, I broke down and shared my story through a torrent of tears. When I finished, I fully expected him to be shocked at what I had done, but he wasn't. He stayed with me, explaining to me that my family may never change, and it was important for me to find forgiveness for both them and myself.

"It won't be easy," he said. "Give yourself time to talk with God. He will guide you."

"I don't really know how to pray though, and I don't like rote prayers." I wondered how far I could push this priest before he decided I wasn't worth God's effort. I wasn't trying to drive him away, I just wanted to be completely honest for once in my life.

The priest laughed. "You don't have to memorize a prayer or be eloquent with your words. All you have to do is tell God what you are feeling. Do you think He doesn't already know anyway?" I smiled and realized that yes, God knew all of me anyway, my thoughts, my speech, and all my actions, good and bad.

When I finished talking with the priest, I walked outside and found a place to sit quietly. Soaking in the beauty of the mountains, while looking down on the Gross Dam Reservoir, I cleared my mind of all the negative thoughts and anger, and prayed. This was the first time I had ever experienced peace in my life. A Scripture came to mind.

He said to the woman, "Your faith has saved you; go in peace."
Luke 7:50 (NIV)

As time goes by, I am continuing my healing journey, with the aide of one of my sisters, friends, professional counseling, the church and most importantly, God. Through the course of healing there have been difficult moments, including an emotional confrontation with the brother who molested me, and a conversation with my mother, who hasn't truly come to terms with the impact of Paul's actions.

Because of the truth coming out, our family has become estranged in many ways; but like me, they need to face the truth of our family's dysfunction in their own way. I have forgiven them, but I've learned it's also okay to remain distant. As my sister says, "We need to surround ourselves with people who love, respect and understand us." I agree.

I'm aware that there were multiple contributions leading to my decision of abortion—my own decision based on selfishness being first and foremost—but I also know that healing truly began when I trusted God with my pain, confusion and shame.

My life has seen many changes since starting my healing journey—physical, emotional, spiritual, and social. My doctor smiled as he gave me the good news. "You are officially no longer diabetic. Whatever you are doing, just keep doing it and I'll see you in six months."

Yes, my life has changed significantly—for the better. I pray for my family, as they still hide in a fog of secrets, but I choose to live in God's Truth.

His truth has set me free.

* Not real name. Names have been changed.

CHAPTER TEN

Nothing Less Than Perfect

By

Annie Moore

Being seen without fault or defect by the world, striving to be the best, the brightest not content with anything less than perfection does this satisfy our soul or is it just the appearance of perfectionism that satisfies us? What is it about the messiness, disorder, chaos and brokenness of life that scares us? Peace can come to us when we realize we don't have to be perfect . . . .

Growing up, my greatest fear was being a disappointment—to anyone. My only alternative was to be successful, and I was. I excelled in school, winning spelling bees and maintaining an A+ grade average. Nothing less than perfect was acceptable to me. I was active in my church youth group, and multiple school activities, all the while winning state and regional gymnastics competition. I also earned national recognition as a cheerleader, and was able to dance in Denmark and the former Soviet Union. Because I was outgoing and cheerful, I appeared to be happy, but in truth, I felt lost and empty.

I remember when I started taking gymnastics seriously at nine years of age. I used to leave school 30 minutes early to make it to practice by 3:00 PM. Each day was filled with activity and I reveled in it. I received a lot of attention and wanted to keep it that way.

One type of attention I learned to command at an early age was from boys. I don't remember a time I was without a boyfriend beyond the fourth grade. Although I wasn't allowed to *date* until high school, boys were allowed to come to my house. My mom worked at home, so she felt my friends (usually boys) and I would be *safer* there than anywhere else. To an extent, we were, but as I grew older, I visited other friend's homes and their parents were usually not home, bringing with it an invitation to seemingly innocent hand holding and stolen kisses. Dating was rather unimportant to me, because who needed a date when I could play games like, *Spin-the-Bottle* and *Seven Minutes in Heaven* without parental supervision?

Appearances were also very important to my family—and me. I remember being acutely aware of comments I received about my appearance at a very young age. "You are so cute!" "Look at you, you're so petite and pretty!" I relished in these complements and desired to keep them coming. The more I excelled in my activities, the more verbal accolades I received.

I was also extremely aware of negative comments and insinuations about my mom being overweight. These comments were meant to be hidden from her ears, but often fell on mine. I was embarrassed for her.

Success was also very important to our family, and bragging about achievements was emphasized. Unfortunately, our bragging was exaggerated with white lies, necessary for the keeping up of appearances.

By the time I reached middle-school age, I loved all the rough and tumble games of boys. I also loved their attention, and figured this was the easiest way to get it. I was right. My number one priority in relationships was that I needed more boys in my life than I did girls.

Over time, gymnastics became less important in my life, and that left me with much more time to socialize. My friends and I spent countless hours watching MTV. It was always on, whether we were watching or just listening. We dreamed of relationships with music icons and teen idols, making up stories about how we might meet them some day. The so-called lifestyle of teen media pulled at me, and I wanted to live that way, reckless and unreserved.

My answer to the *call of the wild* came in the form of sneaking out of the house on a regular basis. Usually, I met with other friends, especially boys who had also snuck out of their homes. Sometimes we went swimming at any pool we found accessible, but mostly we just hung out in yards and on the street. I can't remember exactly how old I was when I had my first drink of alcohol, but it was around 7th or 8th grade. Drinking quickly became a part of our routine which included: sneak out, have some wine coolers, flirt or more, and sneak back in.

High school life caught me by surprise and suddenly all those *innocent* behaviors I'd been practicing intensified. My friends and I, unknown to my brother would sneak out of the house, roll his car down the driveway and drive off to parties my parents had forbidden. The excitement of sneaking off to parties forbidden by Mom and Dad enhanced my ability to *date* dramatically. I became involved with several guys over the span of my high school years, making out and stopping just short of sexual intercourse.

When I was a junior in high school, I had mastered the educational system, manipulating it to my benefit. I regularly left school during off-campus lunches and met with my boyfriend, usually at his house. If I was late returning, it wasn't much of a concern for the school staff. I was the straight A, Honor Roll, advanced placement student, head cheerleader and an elected member of my school's student government. I learned how to forge notes from my mom and manipulated my teachers by telling them I didn't feel well and needed to go home. What difference did it make if I missed a class now and then as long as I kept up my grades and appearances of perfection?

When I was 15, I met a boy at my aunt and uncle's house. He was very sweet and unassuming. For some reason, my family felt it was okay to allow him to stay the night, and he slept on the couch in a room adjacent to mine. We started an intimate relationship and from that point on, I just assumed that sex was a normal part of every relationship with boys.

I had to keep up my image of perfection with my parents and everyone else, so I never asked about birth control and was naïve enough to think pregnancy could never happen to me. My luck ran out. The second boy I had sex with got me pregnant.

I had no other recourse but to tell my parents. I was humiliated to have to share something so disappointing with them, but had nowhere else to turn. When I told them, my dad explained that it wasn't feasible to actually have the baby, even if it meant giving it up for adoption.

"What about cheerleading and dance? How do you expect to maintain your GPA and graduate with honors from high school? What about college?" My dad hardly took a breath as he continued his tirade. "What about the embarrassment of being the pregnant, honor role cheerleader?"

All of his questions made sense to me. How would I accomplish all the things I wanted to do if I carried this baby to term. The battle of being *sensible* vs. being an embarrassment challenged my doubts, and I chose the abortion along with my dad. Mom tried to console herself, and me, with what my doctor promised her as fact: Before the second trimester, it's not even a baby, only tissue.

Regardless, I knew deep in my heart that I would regret having an abortion. As soon as the decision was made, even before they took my baby, a part of me died—the part of me that was allowed to feel. I became angry, sad, resentful and emotionally shut off. I kept up appearances for appearance sake, but knew that I had changed.

The day of my abortion, my parents and boyfriend drove me to the clinic, which was about an hour from home. The nurse at the clinic held my hand and told me there was no reason to worry. "This is a simple procedure, so don't worry about a thing, okay?"

The procedure was anything but simple. It has complicated my life in ways no one could have thought possible. Fear, pain, self-loathing and casting blame on everyone involved occupied my heart during the entire abortion itself. In the minutes after the doctor finished, I cried hysterically. The nurse brought me some crackers and juice to help me gain the strength to stand and walk out of the clinic. I was nauseous, grief-stricken and couldn't stop the flow of tears.

When I was finally able to walk out of the clinic, I found my boyfriend waiting in the car with a bouquet of flowers, a gesture meant to comfort me, but instead made me feel dirty and disgusting. I cried the entire ride home, and when I glanced toward my mother, I noticed she was doing the same.

"Why are you crying? I'm the one who lost a baby." I seethed.

Quietly, she replied, "So did I."

Indeed, my mother had just witnessed the death of the sweet, innocent and joyful girl she had known her daughter to be.

After the abortion, the cramping and bleeding were terrible, but the hemorrhage of my spirit was unbearable. I wanted it to stop, but wasn't willing to seek help. As far as I was concerned, those around me needed to know I was fine, still smiling. And although my parents adamantly deny that my abortion had anything to do with it, they divorced that same year.

During the latter part of high school, I covered my anguish with superficial Band-Aids using the tools of denial: drinking, promiscuity and perfectionism. On the outside, I maintained a respectable and successful school week, but on the weekends, I filled my emptiness with binge drinking and promiscuous relationships. As long as my life *appeared* to be fine, I could manage. However, the pain of what I had done was always there, just below the façade of smiles, and the sound of the spoken word, *abortion* would send shockwaves through my heart.

Faith in anything but my own success was nonexistent. I remember attending a few Young Life and Fellowship of Christian athletes meetings while in high school, but felt like the ultimate hypocrite. By that time, any relationship I had with God consisted of nothing more than occasional church attendance. The older I got, the more I questioned whether God had anything at all to say to me, *if* He even existed.

Soon after graduating high school, my most recent boyfriend proposed to me, and I accepted, but marriage would wait until after college. The only problem was I had no idea what direction my professional life should take. I went to college because all my friends did, and because I was good at it, I majored in dance. I pledged a sorority because it was expected of a successful young woman. Grades were never an issue, and I continued the trend of living an outgoing and respectable life to cover the emptiness just short of surfacing.

To further bury the pain, I vehemently defended a woman's "right to choose," although I could never bring myself to say the word, *abortion.* Society declared abortion legal and easy to obtain, so I felt that if I promoted this women's legal *right*, I would eventually overcome my own unjustified pain.

One semester passed, and my enthusiasm with dance waned. Living life one audition after another didn't hold the appeal I thought it might, so I transferred to the state college my fiancé attended. After taking one course in psychology, I changed my major. I had great hopes in a future of healing my own emotional state—because of my abortion—through the methodical and logical answers of psychological health. Unfortunately, healing of my psychological health was not the answer I received. Instead, I learned nothing under the viewpoint of liberal educators who held cynical opinions and couldn't agree on anything.

I was desperate for security and comfort, and tried to persuade my fiancé to marry during our sophomore year of college, but he refused. "There is no way we can marry now! What are you thinking? We don't have any money." His complete frustration with my suggestion of moving up our wedding date made me feel I was less than adequate for his lifelong plans, so I broke up with him, and transferred to another college.

The summer before my junior year, I met Ryan. We instantly connected and quickly became physically intimate. Ryan was 10 years older than I was, and owned and managed three restaurants in the Dallas area. He was supremely confident, driven with purpose and secure in his lifestyle—the very qualities I was looking for in a man. He was handsome, athletic and successful. Ryan loved the outdoors and a few months after we met, he took me to Colorado, where I hiked my first 14,000-foot mountain, learned to mountain bike and rollerblade, and began a love affair with the outdoors.

Certain we were right for each other, we wanted to get married quickly. Three weeks after my 21st birthday, just before I started my senior year of college, we were married.

What we didn't' know was that our emotional baggage would spill over eventually, and it did big time. Ryan's father had abused him, emotionally and physically, and my abortion and parents' divorce had left me with deep emotional and spiritual scars.

The way we dealt with conflict was completely opposite. In my family, I was taught to hide all emotion, told to always smile and say nice things regardless of any situation. Anger was to be avoided at all costs, and the expression of anger was usually met with a swift reprimand. My spouse on the other hand, was brutally honest, easily angered and very vocal with his displeasure.

Disagreements and serious discussions were painful for us, and we talked about the possibility of divorce several times a year. We put off having children until we could straighten out our marriage, knowing it wouldn't be wise to start a family with an uncertain future.

I finished college, graduating Magna Cum Laude with a BA in Psychology, and started a new job in a psychiatric hospital while working toward my master's degree. I soon realized that I wasn't ready to help others heal until my own healing was complete.

When I graduated college, not only did I have a degree in psychology, but I also had minored in English. With psychology no longer an option,

I picked up a few more courses and earned my teaching certificate. Surely I could help children through the education system, making a difference in not only learning literature, but through discussions of each story and the life lessons they contained.

I threw myself into teaching, getting up some days at 4:30 AM to prepare lesson plans. Along with teaching English, I coached cheerleading and sometimes stayed late into the evening for games and cheer events. Ryan and I shared little time together during the week, and on weekends, I usually had papers to grade and more lessons to plan. Again, I looked as if I had it all together with a perfect marriage and satisfying job, but the pain of my abortion still loomed just under the pretense of perfection.

Because I felt I was a good person, I also believed I was a Christian, but I struggled with the little faith I tried to lean on. How could God actually forgive me for what I'd done. I knew He forgave others, and hoped I was included but wondered how it could be. I couldn't even forgive myself. The more I thought about my past, the more angry I was at God for allowing what had happened to me in the first place. I couldn't speak with a pastor to help me through my issues; he would probably recognize that I wasn't really a Christian and send me away. I felt I had only one option—I continued suffering in silence.

Ironically, teaching English at a public school launched my journey to faith. As I taught my students to look for Truth in literature, I earnestly began looking for it myself. Ryan and I started going to church, although irregularly. I started watching the Christian teachers and students at my school, comparing their lives with those of my own along with some of the cheerleaders I coached. I noticed how unhappy and directionless the party girls—as I had been—were with their lives, and how full of joy the girls who professed and lived consistent lives of faith were. The Christian girls held fast to their faith and refused, quite easily, to go along with the crowd. I thought about my teenage years and wondered why I hadn't been able to do that.

After nearly seven years of marriage, Ryan and I finally felt secure enough to start our family. I was not at all surprised that late into my first trimester, I started bleeding. I'm not sure whether my ensuing grief was for my miscarried child or from the feeling I had caused it ten years earlier when I had willingly participated in killing my first baby. Maybe my abortion damaged me physically or left me infertile, or maybe God was punishing me for what I had done.

My doctor insisted that I have a procedure called a D & C (Dilation and Curettage) to remove the dead fetus from my womb. This procedure was similar to my abortion, the procedure I had been desperate to forget. I was further distressed when I received the papers from the insurance describing my miscarriage as a spontaneous abortion. When I mentioned it to my doctor, he brushed aside my concerns by explaining that it was only medical terminology for a miscarriage. I was not consoled.

Nothing positive ever comes from abortion, but when I called my parents, in tears, to tell them that I had recently miscarried, I blamed myself. "If I hadn't had an abortion, I wouldn't have lost this baby. I just know it's my fault," I cried. "God's punishing me."

Each of my parents told me the same thing, "You're miscarriage has nothing to do with your abortion." They each claimed their roles in what I had claimed for years to be *my* abortion alone. Their comforting words spoke volumes of love for me as their daughter. No longer *Miss Perfect Success*, I realized that I was just one person. Tiny fissures opened in the wall of my hardened heart, and I began forgiving myself.

I started talking to God and learning more about Him through His Word. I discovered something revolutionary to me; God sent His Son, Jesus Christ for people just like me. If He could love and forgive others, He could love and forgive me too. He used Noah (a drunkard), David (an adulterer), Rahab (a prostitute) and Saul (a murderer) for His glory. What made me any better—or worse? I finally learned what it was to be a Christian. Weak, flawed, and hurting, I found unconditional love and undeserved grace with God. No longer did I have only an academic knowledge of Jesus dying on the cross for my sins, securing my place in Heaven when I die, but I finally understood that God wanted me to draw near to Him in spite of my past. He still loved me and saw value in my life. Even more unbelievable to me, He desires to use me as an example of His love and grace *because of* my wretched past.

Not long after I came to know the Lord, I became pregnant again. Ryan and I very much wanted to have a baby, but I was still reeling from my previous miscarriage. How could I allow myself to love the precious life growing in my womb? I was so afraid of losing yet another baby. I didn't keep a journal, talk to the baby, or even glow like a pregnant woman should. In fact, I wouldn't even let Ryan tell anyone I was pregnant for nearly five months. I was scared that if I allowed myself to fall in love with our baby, I wouldn't be able to handle losing it.

With each day that passed, however, I did fall in love with my baby, and actually felt a twinge of excitement the day of our first sonogram. Ryan and I were the parents of a precious baby boy still in utero. When the doctor offered a prenatal test to find out if there were any abnormalities or health issues with our son, we refused them. I would not go through another abortion. This was our baby, and I would love him whether anything was wrong or not.

The sonogram also showed me something else. When I was 8 weeks pregnant, I was amazed to see the life I was carrying. I was able to see little fingers, his face and spine. His heart beat with life and I knew I had been lied to when I went for my abortion. The tissue, as they called it, was actually a tiny human being that God had designed and placed in my womb. I was overcome with grief that I had taken life, yet happy that this child would have a chance.

One night, I was lying in the bathtub, rubbing my swollen tummy. I was hoping to feel the first flutters of life, and broke into tears. I begged God to forgive me for taking the life of my first child, and asked Him to protect the one I was carrying. I promised that I would teach my son to serve Him. Carrying this life should have been one of the most joyful times of my life, but because of my past, I was miserable, constantly vacillating between joy, guilt and fear.

Finally, I went into labor, but when one of the nurses told me that the baby's heartbeat was irregular, I thought to myself, *I knew it.* I was hardly surprised when the baby got stuck and his irregular heartbeat slowed drastically. Immediately, my doctor decided to use a vacuum extractor, and after nearly 15 minutes of pushing, one of the most awesome, merciful blessings of my life was born. Caleb Jeremiah, not accidentally, shares his name with heroes of the Bible. Caleb means, "faithful to God." Jeremiah, his middle name reminds me of the prophet who assures us through the Word that God has a purpose for each of our lives.

I was stunned that God would allow me to have such a perfect, beautiful child. After he was born, I kept asking the doctor and nurses if Caleb was healthy. They continued reassuring me that yes, he was a thriving newborn. Ryan and I asked a visiting priest if he would pray over us with our new son to dedicate him to the Lord. He did.

Today, just shy of 37 years of age, and some 20 years after my abortion, I am blessed with a loving husband and two beautiful boys, Caleb and Grayson—gifts from a loving Father. While I believe the deaths of my first two babies were tragic and devastating for my family and me, they also changed my life. Without the healing from my experiences, I wouldn't have sought God to remove my pain, shame, guilt and regret. I could do nothing to take away my sins, but Christ could. I couldn't make myself whole again, but Christ could. He could and He did. I'm so thankful that He declared His Truth, replacing the lies I had mistakenly believed. The author of Hebrews declares what I now know to be true in my life:

Let us go right into the presence of God with sincere hearts fully trusting him.
Our guilty consciences have been sprinkled with Christ's blood to make us clean
and our bodies have been washed with pure water.
Hebrews 10:22 (The New Living Translation)

CHAPTER ELEVEN

A Revelation

By

Janet King[*]

Did I like kids? Did I want a family? You bet! As a young girl, I always played with dolls. I saw myself as a mother. But my home life was not a happy one, so I spent hours by myself playing house.

Neither my mother nor my father expressed physical affection to me or to my two sisters. They were influenced by some book in their generation that said if you hold or love on your kids, you'll spoil them—bad news for me and my sisters. My parents were against spoiling, so they followed the book's advice to the letter. As children we didn't receive any holding, cuddling, affection, tickling, rocking, big smiles, kisses, or cooing.

And we definitely didn't get any attention!

We also never received verbal support (like "I love you!"), affirmations (like "I'm so glad you're my daughter!") or praise. The three of us grew up starved for love.

The difficulties of a childhood void of physical love were compounded with my mother's drinking and what seems, in hindsight, like demonic mood swings. She drank some in the evenings and to excess on holidays or special occasions. Her drinking habits led to loud fights with my dad.

One such fight came on a night when I had a friend sleep over after a week at summer camp. She needed a place to stay before connecting with a ride the next day. After we settled into our beds, my mother walked in the front door, drunk and loud. She began arguing with my dad.

It was impossible to avoid hearing every word in our small house. She ranted and cussed, spewing ugly speech for what felt like a long time. Humiliation and grief overcame me. I remember burying my face in my pillow, weeping. I don't remember my friend's name, but I do remember her words.

"Oh, Janet, I'm so sorry. I'm so sorry!"

Did I confront my mother over this scene the next day? Not a chance! None of us ever confronted her for fear of getting lashed with more put-downs or cruel words. Scenes like the one above occurred from time to time.

My dad, however, was a kind and understanding man. Thank God one parent out of two was stable. But he was unable to express affection or support. His inability to visibly express his love left his children helpless, lost in our loneliness and despair. He often found ways to escape my mother and her moods by working long hours or going away on fishing and hunting trips.

It's no surprise that as a teenager, I had little self confidence. I struggled with insecurity and a sense of self consciousness. I desperately longed for love. Mom seemed indifferent to anything happening in my life. She took no interest in my clothes, hair, appearance or friendships. My father, however, did take an interest in our education and rewarded us for good report cards. He kept a close watch.

Mom was especially hurtful with her criticism, accompanied by mocking and ridicule. She liked to mock our intelligence:

"You can't spell that word? You're in the eighth grade and you can't spell that word!!"

Then she would point, laugh and mock some more with a malicious tone.

But in the midst of this cold and unloving atmosphere, God began to reach out to me with His love. I first heard about God's love at four years old when my grandmother took me to a Sunday school class at her Lutheran church. The following words sent my young mind into shock—a good and pleasant shock:

> "Jesus loves me! This I know—
> For the Bible tells me so!
> Little ones to Him belong
> They are weak, but He is strong!"

At the tender age of four, I remember thinking: *Somebody loves me! God loves me!* That revelation filled me with hope and planted a seed for the future.

Billy Graham's Message of God's Love

At age fourteen, that message of God's love appeared again through the influence of a ninth grade study hall teacher, Ms. Schmidt. She was a Christian, and on part-time staff with InterVarsity Christian Fellowship (a great Christian organization for college students). There were only six of us kids in the study hall, so the atmosphere was often casual. One day Ms. Schmidt wore a Billy Graham campaign button on her collar. Dr. Graham was holding a crusade at the Detroit Fair Grounds that very week.

My teacher's button intrigued me since the liberal minister at my parents' church despised Billy Graham and often preached against him and his crusades. When I told Ms. Schmidt about the minister's opinion, she said in a kind but direct way, "You're old enough to think for yourself. Why don't you go hear him and decide what you think?" She added, "If you'll find a way to get to the Fair Grounds, I'll give you a ride home." With a natural love for adventure, I jumped at the opportunity.

So two friends and I attended one of Graham's meetings. There, I heard Billy Graham emphasize God's great love for us. He quoted: "For God so loved the world that He gave His only begotten Son, that whosoever believeth in Him should not perish, but have everlasting life" (John 3:16, King James Version).

Billy's main singer, George Beverly Shea, sang,

"The love of God is greater far, than tongue or pen can ever tell . . . It goes beyond the highest hill and reaches to the lowest hell!"

The message of God's love to my heart was overwhelming! When Graham gave an invitation to receive Christ at the end of the service, I thought *What a great offer! To receive God's love, forgiveness and salvation. What a deal! And he backed it all up with Bible references! Anybody would be a fool not to accept an offer like this!*

I made my way down the sawdust trail to the front where a counselor prayed with me to receive Christ.

Ms. Schmidt started us right away in a weekly Bible study, and I began to grow in my Christian faith. She even had us lead the studies pretty soon after we accepted Christ. The group grew in number, and it became my oasis—my home away from home throughout my high school years and beyond.

After studying the Bible and seeing Christ work in Ms. Schmidt's life, I made a deeper commitment of my own life to Him at seventeen. My conversion, however, triggered the negative spirits in my mother. I became a target for her anger and venom, while my two sisters seemed to get off easy—at least for a while. She blasted me any time I said or did anything wrong.

"Oh, look at the Christian! What a hypocrite you are! You're supposed to be so spiritual!"

Then my mother would laugh and mock.

But college was in my future—my escape from an army of negative influences.

Through the help of Ms. Schmidt, I connected with InterVarsity at the University of Michigan. I loved the fellowship and interaction with other Christians. The academic and spiritual side of me grew, but underneath my joyful demeanor, invisible chains kept me bound. On the deepest level, I was full of fear, hurt, and negative expectations.

Semesters passed, and I watched several friends fall in love and marry. But I couldn't get to first base in a serious relationship.

Following graduation from the University of Michigan, I pressed on. I completed a Master's degree at Wheaton College—a prestigious Christian college. Again, I loved the fellowship with the other Christians I found there, but was unable to connect romantically. It took seven more years of inner struggle and soul searching before a marriage opportunity appeared. I longed for love, warmth and acceptance to soothe the rejection constantly throbbing in my heart.

Married Life Reopens My Childhood Wounds

I married at thirty. I didn't realize during our engagement that my husband had the same sadistic and cruel nature I experienced growing up with my mother. Nor did I realize my damaged state or how prone I was to choosing an abusive person for a mate.

Bob and I agreed at the start of our marriage to hold off on starting a family, and I was so glad we did. Two years later, at thirty-one, I found myself in a failing, unhappy marriage.

But one summer night Bob played a nasty trick on me. During an intimate moment—with no warning—he said he wasn't going to use a condom. That was all it took, and BAM I was pregnant.

I couldn't bear the thought of bringing a child into a marriage filled with hate and coldness. It was all I could do to cope with Bob on a daily basis. If we divorced, I could foresee an intense tug-of-war with his family over this child.

The therapist I was seeing at the time—supposedly a Christian—was all too eager to suggest abortion.

"It's only a little blob of cells," he said. "That's all! It's no bigger than your fingernail."

[By the way, the same therapist who encouraged the abortion also suggested I have several in-depth relationships (affairs) after my divorce and before remarriage. What ghastly advice!! Looking back, I marvel that I was so under the grip of his influence.]

The therapist's advise to seek an abortion sounded like the right solution. And since I opposed Bob's scheme (no warning, no protection), I felt no guilt in ending the pregnancy. Bob and I discussed the therapist's idea and agreed to seek an out-of-state abortion. (The State of Michigan had not yet legalized abortion in 1970)

My first experience with abortion seemed almost too simple. I remember being treated well by staff and medical personnel, but observed a greasy, dust-laden lamp hanging low over the operating table. My emotions were too much in turmoil to raise an objection over it, but I can still see that lamp.

No complications followed my abortion, but Bob was cold and distant on the trip home. In the months ahead, his mother clamored for his time and attention and won much of his loyalty. His abuse intensified toward me, and within the next year our marriage crumbled. At the end of year three, we filed for divorce, and I moved to Colorado.

In the first year away from Bob, I felt lonely—but dated little. At the time, I rejected the idea of sex outside of marriage and wanted to build a good relationship with a man. But a year later, I began attending dances and became immersed in the seventies' singles scene. Sexual involvement was common. I hated the idea of casual sex, but felt pressured at every turn. What gross and vile expectations compared to my earlier years of dating. Life now seemed out of control and all the old rules, the good treatment I received from men I dated in InterVarsity and at Wheaton, disappeared.

The Downward Spiral Continues

One night, I met a tall, good-looking Latino at a dance. We hit it off right away and began dating. In time we became intimate. Manny loved me and wanted to marry me, but he was possessive and jealous. Half of me loved him and longed to be with him, but the other half feared his possessiveness and wanted to get away.

I used a diaphragm for birth control during this time. In my second year with Manny, I had problems with the diaphragm and became pregnant. I now had no one else to blame but myself for an unwanted pregnancy. This time, with the influence of a different therapist, I chose abortion again.

Manny however, had a conscience regarding the unborn. He said that even if I didn't marry him, he would be willing to raise the child himself if I would see the pregnancy to completion. I thought seriously about his offer, but three thoughts kept me from accepting:

1. *I couldn't overcome the shame and embarrassment of being pregnant out-of-wedlock.* I especially couldn't bear facing my father. Sex was an unspoken word growing up, but somehow the message came through to us kids that getting pregnant outside marriage was the worst, most horrible thing we could ever do. When my older, unwed sister got pregnant at nineteen, I remember watching my dad break down and weep like it was the end of the world. He always possessed control of his emotions, so this scene was painful to observe. It planted a deep fear in me. Of our two parents, Dad was the stable one, and I loved him very much. It must have registered in my seventeen-year-old mind at that time that I would never do what my sister did.

2. *Again, I couldn't handle raising a child by myself.* I had no faith God could bring me and the child through these difficult circumstances.
3. *If I brought this child into the world, I knew I could never give him or her up.* I would bond with this baby and would want to keep the baby forever.

My biggest need during this intense decision-making time was for counsel about fear and shame, but I wasn't at a place where I could even be honest about those feelings or my need for help. So I went ahead with the abortion.

Once again, I had excellent medical care, no complications, and this time—no greasy lamp fixture.

Months later, the same problem occurred with the diaphragm, and I became pregnant for the third time. This time the therapist got upset with me and a woman in the support group lashed out at me, but not with any religious reasons or any moral or ethical arguments. This was the second instance of objection I ran into regarding abortion, but my conscience now was seared. My human reasoning said: *If abortion was okay one time, why would a second or third time be any different?* That first abortion in Michigan began the hardening of my heart.

I believe this therapist (secular) saw in me a desire and longing for a child with this third pregnancy. I remember him probing and trying to get me to find a way to complete the pregnancy. I'm sure my answers to him were filled with fear, fear, and more fear.

His gentle prodding was never enough to get over my wall of fear, and he would not violate his principles of therapeutic interaction. Later, through a post-abortion workshop, I discovered that a second or third abortion is common in women because of a desperate maternal longing to replace that which was lost the first time. These actions seems contradictory—and they are. It is this contradiction and conflict that creates enormous pain in a woman. The principle of maternal longing operated full force in me, and that therapist, no doubt, recognized it and understood.

After the abortion, I moved to Texas to get away from my possessive lover although we continued to see each other in spite of the move and in spite of pursuing other relationships.

My last abortion did not result from marriage or even a meaningful romance, but casual sex—a one night stand with a business man from Venezuela I met at a club. He acted aggressively and pushy, and I took a chance with no protection. I found myself pregnant—again. And once again, shame and fear ruled the day.

I went to an abortion clinic by myself. How far down the spiral I had come. Just like the previous three, there were no hitches, no problems with the procedure—only disgust with myself for my actions. I was the prodigal, and the pigpen I created stunk. I wanted out.

A New Start

I desperately wanted God to take the controls, and just at the time I hit bottom a friend invited me to a church that prayed for people's healing during the service.

They also held a class for older singles, many of whom were divorced. The leader of this group took a strong stand for sexual purity for divorced Christians. I'm sure he was praying that my life would come into line with God's Word.

It did. Within a short time, I recommitted my life to Christ. Repenting of my sexual involvements and abortions, I promised God I would walk in sexual purity. From that day until now, I have kept that promise.

After making this commitment, I noticed my prayers getting answered immediately—sometimes in bunches at a time. But they were prayers for my health or work or for others—not those of my deepest longings. I yearned for a mate and for children. I had always assumed I'd remarry and have kids the right way, but no wedding bells or kids appeared on the horizon. I believe my secrecy over my abortions hindered me spiritually: "He [She] that covereth his [her] sins shall not prosper." (Proverbs 28:13, King James Version)

Years clicked by, and still no changes. I kept quiet about my abortions, unaware that I also bore a ton of guilt along with my secret. The thought of exposing this part of my life—to Christians especially—struck terror in my heart. Prior to my marriage and divorce, I'd been a fairly self-righteous, judgmental, ivory-tower type Christian. Divorce brought a quick end to that Ms. Goody-Two-Shoes attitude, but I expected similar treatment from fellow believers. And worst of all, I now lived with my harshest critic—myself. Only two close friends knew my secrets, and I never breathed a word about abortion to anyone else. Reality, however, held a major shock in store for me.

Coming to Terms with What I'd Done

In December of 1986 my mother, still in Michigan, asked me to return to take care of her for a period of time. I spent three months with my mother in the winter of 1986 and 1987, attending a Pentecostal church near her home. One Sunday in January, before the message began, a woman acted out a drama as though she were a child in her mother's womb. Her words went something like this:

"It's now day _____ and I'm developing fingers and toes. Even though I'm very tiny, I want to get to know you, Mother. I'm so eager for the day I'll be born, so I can see what you look like. I can hardly wait for you to hold me and rock me."

The reader went on through eight or ten days like this, and then her voice said, "Oh, no! Something's happening! Ouch! Help! Help! Someone help me! Don't . . . Oh, please!"

Then the lights went out. Pitch blackness fell on the auditorium.

When the lights came back on, the pastor preached a message called "Abortion—The American Holocaust." This was pro-life Sunday! He quoted a lot of Scriptures, speaking of the sacredness of life and how we are all created in God's image. He told of the millions of abortions in the U.S. There I sat, frozen in my seat, heavily convicted and full of remorse. I wanted to bolt out of my seat and flee that auditorium, but couldn't. I knew that as soon as the service was over, I had to find some place to be alone.

I drove to a deserted parking lot, parked and sobbed. I sobbed and sobbed for a long time. For the first time I thought of those little ones I conceived as being like that child in the drama . . . and I realized how much I had lost!

I saw my own selfishness and my unbelief in my heavenly Father. Unbelief that He could and would have helped me with any pregnancy—even in spite of a messy divorce or later, in any of my other circumstances.

One other thought dominated my mind:

> *I never considered the viewpoint of the child! I never imagined a child could love me!*

My relationship with my own mother lacked bonding, trust, and closeness. She resembled Dr. Jekyll and Mr. Hyde with her drinking and mood swings. I learned to keep my distance to survive. I became addicted to distance and allergic to closeness and trust. As an adult, I couldn't imagine that a child could love me or that I could love a child. It's like that element was missing from my emotional DNA. It took so much to open my eyes, but that day in the parking lot was the beginning of my healing.

Today

Since January of 1987, I have participated in two post-abortion recovery groups. A fine group called Silent Voices led the first in San Diego during November of '94. Their approach was gentle and kind but truthful. They got to the very depth of my shame, guilt, and grief. We started on a Friday evening and ended at nine on Sunday evening. It is worth noting that my denial prior to the workshop was still great. I only attended through the constant urging of a close friend and her prayers. Even two days before the weekend, I wavered and wondered whether or not I needed to attend.

In February of 1996, I attended a second post-abortion recovery class at a large church in Denver, Colorado. This small group met one night a week for eight weeks and covered some of the same areas as the first workshop. It helped greatly with further cleansing, healing, and support. I still have occasional bouts with guilt or grief, but they seem minor and occur further and further apart. References like 1 John 1:9 ("He is faithful and just to forgive us our sins") and Romans 8:1 ("Therefore, there is now no condemnation for those who are in Christ Jesus") helped break the stronghold of guilt. I speak them over my life often to quiet the accusing voice of the enemy.

With deliverance from shame, guilt and grief, I have become a dedicated pro-lifer. As a college English instructor in the 90's, I arranged for debates in classes, promoting the pro-life position against tough pro-choice debaters. (We saw the pro-life side win nearly every time!)

In January of 2001, on pro-life Sunday, I told my story at Church in the City's morning services. Afterwards, a pregnant woman came to me, sobbing and distraught. She said she didn't want her child and had been telling her unborn baby she hated it and was planning to abort it. She said, "I know God wanted me to be here today to hear your testimony. I will not abort this child. Please pray for me!"

I saw her sometime later the next year—smiling, happy and pushing her baby in a stroller. What a joy to witness that change!

I continue to tell my story in public and currently lead prayer meetings for the U.S.A. We pray for pro-life legislation and that America will forsake abortion permanently.

Peace and blessings have returned to my life and the Body of Christ continues to be my family. I can see fulfillment multiplying in the areas where the Lord has me working. He is redeeming the destruction of my past and using all of it in ministering to other people. Thank God, He is the Redeemer!

He continues to heal and restore me in many ways. One of my major healings in the last five years involved exposing my rage and hostility toward my mother (now deceased). With the help of a Christian therapist, including journaling and some role plays, I've experienced much repentance, cleansing, and forgiveness.

I serve as a part-time hospital chaplain and substitute teach in the public schools. I believe according to Proverbs 28:13 that it pays to uncover and confess our sins. I am no longer silent. I tell students and teachers whenever possible that we need to protect the unborn. To every woman considering abortion, I say: Regardless of your circumstances, what you're thinking of terminating is sacred, and that child is created in the image of God!

* Not real name. All names have been changed.

Chapter Twelve

Rescue the Lame

By

Cynthia Carney

I grew up the oldest of six siblings in small town, Arkansas and finances were never easy. Dad worked long hours, but his paycheck never seemed to be quite enough to support our growing family. We seldom saw our dad, and when we did, we wished he were gone again. His job as a truck driver/ musician kept him on the road most days, a long way from home.

When he was around, Dad was a difficult man—abusive to our mother. My brothers, sisters and I made ourselves scarce when he was in town in order to avoid any wrath he might direct our way. My parents struggled to make their marriage work, and even though I didn't understand the circumstances behind all of their marriage issues, I do recall Mom saying something about Dad's girlfriends.

My mother was a lonely woman whether my dad was home or not, and the only place I felt she found solace was in church. I remember when Mom invited Jesus to be in her life. She seldom smiled before that day, but something really changed when she took a walk up the middle aisle at church. She began taking all of us kids to worship services three times a week—Sunday mornings, Sunday and Wednesday evenings. These were some of the happiest times of my life, especially after I asked Jesus to live in my life just like my mother did.

My favorite part of going to church was participating in anything musical. I loved singing and shared my talent by singing solos in front of the congregation. Performing came natural to me; it was part of my makeup. When we weren't in church, my siblings also joined me in theatrical action by putting on plays, with Mom as our willing audience.

Money, always sparse, left me unable to take piano or any other kind of fine arts lessons, even though I desperately desired to do so. I was so happy the day an older relative stepped in and offered to give me guitar lessons, free of charge—only those lessons cost more than I ever could have dreamed. He sexually abused me. Soon after he started abusing me, I became the target of another family member's abuse.

Childhood innocence no longer existed for me, and I started the first grade knowing I had a secret I could never tell. I knew something about me was very different from the rest of my classmates. A very sad little girl, I spent a lot of time outside, willing myself to learn to read under a huge tree in my grandparent's front yard, but looked more at the pictures than the words.

School was difficult for me. I struggled to keep up with the rest of the students my age. If it wasn't for my first grade teacher, I doubt I would have passed. However, under her direction—as both mentor and teacher—I managed to keep my grades up. I know her influence was vital to my elementary educational success. Academic achievement only followed me through the sixth grade though, as it was then my father decided to uproot our family from our home.

"What do you mean we're leaving?" I turned away from Dad so he wouldn't see my tears. "Why do we have to move now?"

"You're moving because I'm moving." He walked out of the room without so much as a backward glance; and my hidden tears fell without restraint. I was devastated.

It wasn't our last move. In fact, I received the same news at the beginning of my seventh grade year.

As I grew older, the stress between my parents became more obvious to me, and it didn't surprise me when they decided to divorce. Because of the divorce, our financial situation worsened. I did the only thing I knew to do. I lied about my actual age—14—and went to work as a supposed 16-year-old.

Growing up faster than I should have, I met a boy and started sneaking out at night to be with him. We became sexually active early in our relationship, and by the time I was 16, I was pregnant. But Dale and I loved each other, and I was certain everything would work out. There was only one difficulty. I didn't find out I was pregnant until after Dale left for boot camp.

Dear Dale,

I'm sorry to have to tell you this, especially in a letter. But since you left for boot camp, I received some news you need to know about. I'm just going to come right out and tell you. I'm pregnant. My mom took me to the doctor and he confirmed it. School is really hard for me, and I can't run track anymore. I'm tired all the time, and sick most mornings and evenings. I know this

isn't the way we planned things, but I need to know if you're going to marry
me. I'll understand if you say no, but I really hope you say yes . . .

Sincerely,
Cynthia

He did say yes. That same year, I married, gave birth to a beautiful baby boy and moved to Southern California to begin my new life as a Marine Corps wife and mom. I was amazed at the new sights and sounds of my new home. Fresh ocean air filled my senses; and sand tickled beneath my feet—from a real beach—for the first time in my life. *We're going to have a good life here, Richard.* Bundling my infant son a little tighter, I held him close. Life indeed was good, at least for the first couple of weeks.

Within a month of moving into our new home, my husband began physically abusing me. He insisted I go to work, "to earn your keep around here." He also decided my career. I was to be a secretary. Lacking any kind of experience in secretarial skills, he forced me to enroll in a business school.

"Either you go to school and get a job, or you go back home to your family. But if you decide to go home, be prepared to leave your son, because you are an unfit mother. There's not a judge in America who would grant you custody. You don't have a job or even a high school diploma." Without any sense of self-esteem, I believed every word he said, and vowed in my heart that I would keep my son no matter what. Richard meant the world to me.

My husband was anticipating my financial contribution to our marriage, and truth be told—even though I was repulsed by the way I was *persuaded* to go—so was I. I also found that I enjoyed some time away from home. While Richard grew older in the care of a babysitter; I was growing as an independent young woman.

A few months later, I noticed I wasn't feeling up to par. Over the next few days, I realized my symptoms were clearly not viral. The familiar feeling of morning sickness became more pronounced. I knew I was pregnant, but needed to take a test to confirm my suspicions.

On my way home from school, I saw a sign that read, *Free Pregnancy Tests.* So, I took advantage of their services, and they took advantage of my naiveté. While I was there, a *counselor* shared information I had never heard before. It seemed I had a choice as to whether or not to have this child. Only they didn't call it a child, they explained to me that what was growing inside of me was only tissue at that point, not a baby. They told me that my life could be "back to normal" in no time.

"Abortion is just like pulling a tooth." The counselor tenderly clasped my quaking hands. The power of suggestion, mixed with the affirming words of the clinic counselor played a major role in my decision, but I couldn't move forward until I spoke with Dale.

After telling my husband what I learned at the clinic, he advised me to have the abortion. "You know we can't afford another child right now, and you need to finish school." I agreed with him, and together we decided our baby's fate. I would have the abortion.

After a short time of deliberation, I gathered my courage and my husband drove me to the clinic. Scared of the unknown, I decided to talk to one of the other women in the waiting room.

"Have you ever had an abortion?" I watched the sullen woman carefully, as she replied.

"Today will be my fifth." I'll never forget the look in her eyes—the look of death. I wanted to hear more, sensing I was about to enter her world of misery; but the nurse called my name and quickly escorted me to one of the procedure rooms.

"How far along are you?" She asked while arranging the medical instruments. Everything in me wanted to stand and run, but I found my voice and answered her question. "A little further along than you thought originally, huh?"

She examined me and prepped me for the procedure. Lying there on the table, I recall hearing what sounded like a generator of some kind. I watched the doctor walk in, but never saw his face behind the surgical mask. What I do remember is what came next—the most excruciating pain I had ever felt in my life. So excruciating, I passed out.

When I woke, I was drenched in sweat. Trying to get my bearings, I held onto the edges of the padded table. The room was spinning and after a few minutes, I realized I was bleeding profusely. When the nurse noticed I was awake, she assured me that everything I was experiencing was perfectly normal and that I would feel much better in the morning. I rested as well as I could, falling in and out of consciousness. By the time my husband arrived to take me home, the sun was setting. I had no idea so much time had elapsed.

The following three days were horrible. Still bleeding heavily, I couldn't care for my son, and asked a neighbor if she would help me. The physical discomfort was difficult, but even worse was the emotional impact. I experienced a kind of shame I had never known before, and a part of me wished I had died on the abortion table, along with my baby.

I loathed my husband for agreeing to an abortion, but most of all, I loathed myself. *I'll just get pregnant again; I need to get pregnant again. It's the only way to heal my aching heart.* Two months after graduating from secretarial school, I gave birth to another son.

I was sure that as soon as the nurse placed him in my arms, my broken heart would heal immediately, but just the opposite occurred. A feeling of sadness I couldn't shake took hold and deepened as the next few years went by.

Physical abuse escalated as Dale continued threatening me with the loss of my little boys. Staying in my marriage was the only assurance I had of keeping my children.

The norm of military life usually consists of multiple cross-country moves, and our family was not immune. After a few years in California, we received orders to move to the Gulf Coast. *At least I'll be closer to my southern roots.*

Not long after settling into our new home, I gave birth to a third son.

Five months later, I was diagnosed with Type I Diabetes (Juvenile Diabetes). Mothering took on a new perspective as I fought to keep from going into diabetic comas daily. Even though my courage lacked when it came to needles, I learned to give myself three injections a day. I knew I was fighting for my own life, but also for those of my boys. I couldn't leave them with Dale. He would destroy them as young men; I knew that.

During that time, I listened to music for emotional comfort and often perused radio stations to hear a variety of songs. One day, a man's voice caught my attention. I tuned in. This show, called People to People, presented the Gospel in a way I hadn't heard. A vague familiarity of peace and comfort took me back to my childhood emotions of a sweet relationship with Jesus. The host of the program, Bob, shared the Bible *visually* through his unique approach of storytelling, helping me learn to pray once again. I rarely missed a program over the next three years. Every afternoon, I stopped what I was doing and tuned in. I hung on to every word with hope.

Dale continued abusing me and I was a broken woman. The beatings were far worse than they had ever been, and I feared for my life. God's Word was my only source of comfort. Every day, I picked up my Bible and started reading it for myself. I prayed and asked God to help me understand the words I was reading; He began to teach me, preparing me for what lay ahead.

Once again, our family received orders to move back to California from the Gulf. Typically, when our family received orders for transfer, Dale would move first and then I would follow with the boys. As far as I knew, that was how we would move again. However, once my husband arrived at the new base, he sent word that he wanted to separate. With no other options in sight, I took our three boys back to Arkansas, where we lived with my mother.

Devastation by my overwhelming circumstances soon turned to depression and suicidal tendencies. I was hospitalized in a Christian psychiatric program called, Rapha. My husband flew to Arkansas to be with our boys while I was in treatment, and in my weakened emotional state, appearances told me he had changed.

"I'm a different man. You showed me how to trust in God. I'm a Christian." I wanted to believe him so badly, but something in his tone didn't settle quite comfortably.

If he's really saved, he won't abuse me anymore. We can finally be a real family. He must see the longing in my eyes. "You got saved?" The question fairly stumbled over my tongue, as I hesitated. After all the years of abuse, how could I trust Him?

"Trust me."

I gave him the benefit of the doubt, and we loaded the boys into his car. We traveled to California once again.

Through a series of events, including my husband's court martial, I realized he could not be trusted. I took our boys and flew back to the South/ Gulf Coast. I knew I needed to pull myself together for my boys' sakes, as well as my own. My blood sugar was a mess again; I needed to see a doctor regularly. I also felt it was important to further my education to build a career to support my children. Armed with a plan, I moved forward accordingly.

We settled into a routine apart from the violence our family was accustomed to, trying to pull the shattered pieces of our lives together. I quickly established a routine for the boys, trying to work my own schedule around theirs. Between work, school and doctor visits, life was full.

A new friend entered my life. Eleanor quickly became not only my friend, but also a spiritual mentor. Her faith sustained me through some very difficult times, and little did I realize, she would be there for many more. However, in the meantime, life continued moving forward.

Sitting in the doctor's office with my youngest son was always an experience. Patience it seems is never in a young boy's genetic makeup. I tried everything to keep him calm and quiet. I was exhausted and barely able to keep from breaking into sobs; my sadness was so deep and desperate. Longing for silence, I handed my son, Kyle, a piece of paper and a pencil to keep him busy. "Draw a picture for Mommy, okay?" I picked up a magazine and placed it in front of my face. If the tears came, at least the other patients and my son wouldn't have to see them.

I didn't know my son would pull the magazine down and slip his drawing into its place. On that paper were four crosses—two lying on their sides, and two standing on either side. Just above the crosses were the words, *There's Hope.* Yellow sunshine rays surrounded the crosses in the drawing, and as I gazed on my son's artwork, I felt a surge of hope rising in me.

"How did you come up with this?" I continued studying the picture, amazed at the message it contained. A message that touched my life profoundly.

"I don't know, Mom. It just kind of came to me." I knew in that moment that God had used this little boy, my son, to speak peace to me. The sadness that had overwhelmed me earlier was gone. I knew there was significance in the number of crosses and the way they were placed in the drawing, but it wasn't completely clear. I carefully folded the paper, and tucked it into my purse for safe-keeping.

The following years were difficult as I struggled to make ends meet. My oldest son was living with his dad, while the two youngest stayed with me. Our broken family was evident to everyone around, and I continued struggling with my health.

Fighting a battle with drug addiction and other difficulties, my middle son seldom came home. I missed him and worried constantly about his well-being. A friend of mine called me one fateful morning and gave me news that turned my world upside down.

"Have you seen the news this morning, Cynthia?" Barely out of bed, I shuffled toward the television. My feet were horribly sore from the diabetes, and it took great effort to move any amount of distance. "No, I haven't. What's going on?" The words she spoke next took my breath away. I fell to the floor crying uncontrollably. My middle son had been killed—shot at point blank range. He was gone.

After Brandon's memorial service, the picture of the four crosses came to mind, and a close friend pointed out that they represented my children. He knew about my past abortion, and felt the two crosses lying on their sides were a representation of the two precious children I'd lost. One of them died during my abortion, the other in a murder of a very different kind.

My heart was completely broken, and faith in God was the only firm conviction left in my life. I could not trust in myself, but God only. During this time, I discovered one of my old college notebooks containing a poem I had written in the past.

Rescue the Lame
Where you were put to shame
I will renew your faith
And bring you to fame

There was a message of some kind hidden in the prose, but I couldn't figure it out. So I asked God. "Father, what shame are you talking about? I don't understand. Will you make it clear to me?" I had always felt ashamed of myself. The whole of my life had been so difficult. I was ashamed of many things, but I had a feeling the Lord wanted to clarify one particular area of shame.

Abortion. The word was clear. Abortion. I knew the depression I'd experienced in the past revolved around the time of year when I had the abortion. Another thought occurred to me too. The other time of the year I seemed to be at odds with was around the due date of my aborted child. My shame—abortion. I knew it then, as I had known it before, but wasn't able to directly identify it.

"I understand, Father. What do I do now? Your forgiveness has been great for me. I've always known that, but what do I do with this shame?"

You use it for my glory. My heart was captivated by this reply. I heard the words clearly, not from an audible voice, but from a comforting feeling inside of me.

"Whatever You want, Lord." Peace settled over me, transforming the shame of my whole life into a work of His doing—courage. Little by little, with my surrender, I felt courage begin trickling into my being. Confidence in who I was in Christ came slowly, but it came, nonetheless.

A few months later, I was watching John Hagee, an evangelist, on television, and he was interviewing a young woman about her abortion experience. This woman was from The Justice Foundation, which supports a project called Operation Outcry. She was inviting women to fill out an affidavit that would be presented to the U. S. Supreme Court regarding Roe vs. Wade, in hopes of overturning it.

I knew this was something God was calling me to and volunteered for this cause by writing and submitting my own affidavit. A couple of months later, after my youngest son left for school, the woman I had watched on John Hagee's show called my home.

"I want you to know, I read your affidavit. I'm calling after much prayer and deliberation. I believe you are God's choice to be your state's leader for Operation Outcry." On the receiving end of this conversation, I was stunned into silence. Several things went through my head. I didn't belong to a church at that particular time, and certainly did not feel qualified for such a position. However, after much prayer, God confirmed the calling with his word, and I accepted the position as a State Leader.

Speaking engagements were plentiful, and each time, I fought the fear of being in front of many people. God used these speaking invitations to take me through several places of healing. As I reached out to others, God took me deeper into my own healing journey. Mobilizing other women to come forward with their own stories infused me with the confidence I needed to become bolder each day in my own abilities. Something supernatural was taking place in my heart. God was moving.

My abortion healing was confirmed with a Scripture—Isaiah 28:18 (NIV).

Your covenant with death will be annulled;
your agreement with the grave will not stand.

The barriers of my past were removed. God made beauty of my life's ashes, and the tears I cry now are different from the tears I cried before. They are an outcry of deliverance for others, not tears of despair. I will never go back to that place of darkness. He has delivered me into the light, and it is impossible for me to go back.

God didn't use retreats or programs of any kind to heal me of my past, though I believe those are helpful and good. His journey for me looked different. He used a mentor named Eleanor, and the acceptance of a call, to bring me to a place of healing/deliverance, I never thought possible. Looking back at the journey, I did not have all the right credentials or even great faith, but then you don't need all that when you have a great God.

CHAPTER THIRTEEN

And The Walls Fell

By

Carrie Morgan[*]

Over the years, I carefully constructed a thick wall around my heart. Brick by brick, through each difficult moment of my life, I added more mortar and laid the bricks with great care.

I don't remember my father telling me he loved me as a child, at least not with words. I was too young to understand that his actions and hard work to provide for us were his way of showing love, so I didn't really feel it. Like most parents, he did what he thought was best to take care of his family. With regard to our spiritual formation, he supported our mother taking us to church, but only accompanied us for holidays. I believe his emotional distance may have been one of the first bricks, laying the foundation for many more to come.

I was raised Catholic and I remember my mother being active in church, but she didn't seem spiritually engaged. I admired her servitude toward others around her; her faith showed in her works, but her heart seemed distant. *God* was for Sundays. And I don't ever remember being made to feel special because I was a child of God.

There was a difference in both Mom and Dad's words versus their actions. Looking back, I didn't feel a deep emotional bond with either of them, though I didn't know it then. I would say I had a happy, stable, normal childhood but I can't help but wonder if subtle confusion about the intimacy level of my earliest relationships may have planted a seed for future conflict in my own spiritual walk. Perhaps the emotional void of my childhood laid the foundation for some of my life choices.

My spiritual life, learned and lived, was not fully *felt*. It was as if God was in the car with me, but I made Him sit in the back seat. This was the way with many of my early relationships. I didn't know how to fully engage.

Although I had many friends, and later, boyfriends, these relationships also seemed to lack the emotional closeness I craved. Alone in a crowd— that's how it felt. I wasn't completely aware of the building project going on around my heart, but was beginning to feel a tangible distancing between others and myself.

As the years went by, I grew to appreciate this wall, for it became the barrier keeping me from emotional harm. However, it also hindered my ability to receive and accept God's love, and the acceptance of emotions necessary to grow into the woman He desired me to become.

I spent many years on a quest looking for my own identity, often feeling as if I didn't belong, even though on the outside I appeared fine. During high school, I *learned* how to fit in mainly because I went to four different high schools in four years. Due to the lack of closeness and not feeling understood at home, friends became very important to me and I had lots of them. I never really stayed with one particular group of friends though. I can remember wanting people to like me. Sometimes, I was swept up by different influences depending on which group I was hanging around with at the time, such as drinking and drugs. Finally, in my senior year when we moved to another state, I felt at home and right where I belonged.

Not wanting to lose that feeling of finally being where I belonged, I was reluctant to go away to college but it was what everyone did, so I went to a college three hours from my home. My stay there was not very productive and I spent most of my time smoking pot and sleeping. Recognizing that I wasn't in a good way and needed the comfort of a familiar place, I left this college in the middle of my second semester and moved back home.

My parents weren't happy with my decision and they barely spoke to me. Determined to make it right, I got a job and things started to look up for me mainly because I wasn't depressed anymore and I was taking better care of myself. Yet, I still felt somewhat lost. I had let my parents down, all my friends were away at school and I felt apprehensive about my ability to make a decision for my future. It was during this time that I met a good-looking, rugged, cowboy with a wild reputation.

In the beginning, our relationship was wild and fun, and I fell hard for him—much too quickly. It was too late to walk away from our relationship when the abuse started. Adding even more difficulty, I realized he was an alcoholic with a drug habit. Yet this didn't stop me from furthering our relationship. I was naïve and in love and thought I could help him.

Our time together was turbulent. Verbal and physical abuse became commonplace; but each time he apologized I would take him back. The abuse progressively worsened. I was living a *Lifetime* TV movie.

At first, I was embarrassed and tried to hide it, but eventually I knew I needed help. Late one night, I turned to a trusted friend after being beaten and deserted on the side of the road with no way home. Another time I ran to a neighbor's in the middle of the night because my boyfriend wielded a loaded gun, threatening to kill me.

He lied continuously and cheated on me several times. Although I knew our relationship was unhealthy, he always managed to say the right words to draw me back into his arms. Why did I allow him to treat me this way, and why was I still hopeful he would change?

My parents found out and were distraught by the way Jeremy treated me. I had returned to college at this point, one close to home and they filed a restraining order. The school also filed one, in attempts to keep him away. However, this did little to keep us apart. Once after one incident that was particularly difficult to hide, I was convinced to press charges. *Finally, this will make me break ties with him.* But like so many battered women, I recanted and it didn't keep him from my life for long. We communicated by phone, or he would sneak notes to me. His charm always lured me back to secret meetings with him, and it was during one of these reconciling rendezvous' that I became pregnant.

When the nurse gave me the results of a pregnancy test, she handed me a pamphlet for a doctor who performed abortions as one of my "options". I thought this was strange because I had never even considered having an abortion. I wasn't sure what I was going to do, or how, but I was going to have a baby. I went to my parents to tell them my condition and prepare them for yet another way I've disappointed them.

My mother, knowing I was involved with an abusive man was desperately concerned for my safety and told me the only way she would help was if I broke up with him—for good. I agreed, but didn't know if I was strong enough to resist him. Our relationship was toxic—I knew that—but I didn't know if I could trust myself not to put myself or our baby in harm's way.

A few weeks later, I was again enticed by Jeremy to spend some time with him. "We won't be alone," he assured me; "We'll be with my family. I promise." Sounded safe enough. Late that night, I found myself huddled under a staircase with his sister-in-law. Jeremy and his brother were drunk and started to fight; and one of them had come through the front door with an ax.

"You can't bring a baby into this family," she pleaded. "I know how much you don't want to have an abortion, but don't you realize that if you have this child, you'll be forever tied to Jeremy? Trust me; you do not want that to happen, Carrie. Get out, and get out fast, while you still can!" Someone called the police, and when they told *me* to take Jeremy home, I knew what I had to do. There was only one way out.

Within a week, my mother took me to have the abortion. The doctor was a kind, older man, and the staff spoke tenderly to me. They were compassionate and *helpful.* This did not seem like one of the big *cold* clinics I had heard about. The nurse assured me I was making the right decision, and held my hand when tears slid down my face during the procedure. I knew I was ending the life of a precious child. *If I'm doing the right thing, why doesn't it feel like it?* I was only 19, supposedly an adult, but I felt like a scared little girl who just wanted someone to help me. The trusted adults around me all said this was the way. Then why did I feel so ashamed? Why were none of us able to look at each other in the recovery room? And why were no words ever spoken about it afterwards? Before and during, the messages I received were different from the silent shameful secret I was to hold later . . .

I later found out that while I was aborting his child, Jeremy was out with another woman. Our relationship was really over now—or so I thought. It wasn't a month later that I was back in the arms of the same abuser. Although I tried to hide the fact that we were back together, it wasn't long before a broken nose and black eye were hard to disguise. My friends and family were devastated. One by one they told me that if I didn't break ties with this man, they would all cut ties with me. And one by one, they did.

Trapped in the never-ending cycle of my battered existence, I no longer trusted myself to live a respectable life. How did I end up like this? I was at the end of my rope. Gathering all the medication I could find, I wondered if it would be enough. Alone again in my dorm, I contemplated ending it all. If I could just go to sleep and not wake up, the pain would stop.

As I lined up the pills and filled a glass of water, I felt an odd urgency to go to the basement of the dorm building. I was perplexed, but the feeling wouldn't relent, so I wandered the basement halls, where I happened to run into a counselor. She admitted me to a hospital; and I began the very slow process of emotional healing. I believe she was an angel.

I returned to school the following fall, a recovering *battered woman*. One particular class marked a major turning point in my life. My English professor not only taught me to properly write a paper, but also encouraged me personally. She helped me gain confidence in the young woman I could become. The topic for my term paper centered on domestic violence, and I received an *A*. It was the first time I could remember in a long while that I accomplished something good. The therapeutic impact of this paper far outweighed the grade; I felt hope.

Over the next several months, focusing on my personal growth was primary in my life. I experienced authentic independence for the first time, actually pulling my emotions and personal life together. Life was better than I could have imagined, and I couldn't believe I had been so willing to throw it away.

A few years later, I met the man I would marry—Daniel. Newly married and deeply in love, Daniel and I barely had time to establish our home when his younger sister came to stay with us, not once, but on several occasions. My new mother-in-law was a single mom, and when she had trouble coping with her daughter, she called us. The stress of an additional family member moving in and out of our home triggered a bout of depression. The additional drama hindered our bonding as man and wife—several bricks were added not to mention numerous disagreements regarding codependence. I had tried so hard to move beyond that.

The coming years, however, were not without joy. When our son was born, my heart overflowed. Was this that emotional bond of complete love I had been missing all my life? The dark cloud of depression finally lifted; and I cherished every moment of mothering my little boy. Yet something was still missing. Church; I desired a faith home for my family. I had strayed from my Catholic roots when I went off to college and beyond.

In time, Daniel and I settled on a Catholic parish not far from where we lived. I knew instantly, I had returned *home*. We settled into our new church with ease, both knowing the time was right for us to be faithful to God. Our growing family needed the foundation of faith to nurture our spiritual future and solidify our family values.

The next few years our church life grew along with our expanding family. I gave birth to another child—a girl—and then, a third, another boy.

After the birth of our third child, one of the priests from our parish came to visit me in the hospital.

"Congratulations to you, Mama Carrie." Father Anthony took my hand in his and squeezed lightly. My joy must have been evident, because his always gentle smile turned into a full-blown grin.

"Thank you so much; and thank you for coming to visit. Surely you have others to make an appearance to—others that need more than just congratulations."

"Actually, you're my last stop. Well, my last stop will be the nursery to see your newest addition, but I figure I should say hi to the mama before moving on to the baby."

Father Anthony was one of the main reasons my husband and I attended the parish we did. His consideration of both the major and not so major events in the lives of his congregation made us feel like we were members of a large, very tight-knit family.

"May I speak with you about something?" *Did I just say that aloud? And what do I need to talk to him about?*

Father Anthony pulled a chair next to my bed. "Of course, that's why I'm here. How can I help you?"

The abortion? Could that be it? Oh God, help me. I haven't thought about this in years. I never thought I would actually consider telling anyone about my abortion, especially now. Why would I at this point? But the urge was strong, so I took a deep breath and revealed my past. I couldn't even look at his face as the flood gates opened and I recounted my entire story. I felt such horrible shame, something I hadn't experienced in a long time.

"I'm so sorry—I don't know what else to say." I finally dared to glance his way, and when I did, I'll never forget Father Anthony's expression. I saw nothing but compassion and forgiveness in his eyes and incredible love. It was as if I was looking upon the face of Christ.

"God forgives every sin, Carrie, even abortion." His visit that day changed me somehow. I didn't just *confess;* he offered me *reconciliation* . . . The wall of shame I had so carefully constructed fell away, and the burden of guilt was lighter than before. When the nurse brought my newborn babe in for his feeding, I held him close and wept. The tears I shed were full of joy over my new son as well as a healthy grieving for the child I had aborted years ago.

Sometime later, I attended a retreat called CRHP (Christ Renews His Parish). It seemed as if the guilt resurfaced. Even though I knew in my head my past was forgiven, lingering sorrow and depression overshadowed the joys of my life, and I continued to make self-destructive decisions; often sabotaging things that were good because I felt I didn't deserve them. I listened to the women introduce themselves as a sense of foreboding and dread filled my senses. I had no idea what I was feeling—couldn't quite put my finger on it. "What is it, Lord?" I whispered during prayer. "What is this ache in my heart? Is it about my past again?" Hot tears spilled over as I received my answer. There was more healing to be done. That weekend, I felt cracked open like an egg, spilling all over the floor.

The retreat continued into the weekend and I listened intently to various women telling their stories of forgiveness and healing. Everyone's story/faith journey was different. Some of their lives looked nothing like mine, others were amazingly parallel, but God's forgiveness was always the same. These women had received His forgiveness and moved on with life. And then it dawned on me; I had not.

The realization that I had not allowed myself to invite the reality of God's forgiveness into my own life changed my perception of His grace. I saw/detected no shame or guilt or judgment—just love. *If God can, and did, forgive these women of their pasts and they have been able to move on in life, why would He not do the same for me?* I finally understood what I was missing. I knew God had forgiven me, but I hadn't been able to see myself through His eyes of grace. His death on the cross was for *me.* If it was for others, I could believe it for me too. The last portion of my wall was *knowing* that I was worthy of His forgiveness.

The wall I had so carefully constructed to protect my heart could finally come down. My heart was God's, and I knew it was safe. He would be tender with it. He promised in His Word. And He has been . . .

---

*   Not real name. All names have been changed.

CHAPTER FOURTEEN

A True Princess

By

Paula Talley

*You are not a pretend princess, my child. You are a real princess, and I am your
God, the King of all kings. I chose you before you were even born to be my princess.
You are very important in my kingdom . . . Remember, a crown and a palace do not
make you a true princess—it is your love for me and for others that will make you
special. Love, Your King and Father in Heaven.* *

I was only six years old when physical and sexual abuse entered my
life. The perpetrator was my own father. In time, my mother left him, and
we moved to Southeast Missouri to live with my grandmother. The abuse
stopped, but the damage remained. Covering my victimized existence, I
lived for perfection; and one way I gained any semblance of self-esteem
was through worldly beauty.

I entered many beauty pageants in search of that constant need to
be beautiful. During one competition when I was sixteen, a young man
named Larry Talley fell head over heels in love with me. I was young, and
not at all interested in becoming a wife. There was a big world out there
with plenty besides my small town living, and I intended to explore all my
options. At seventeen, I left home and headed for the big city—Memphis,
Tennessee.

Stars were in my eyes as I traveled to the city that Elvis made. But I lived
far from the lights of the stars. My home was the YWCA, and when a knock
came on my door, it was the same small town boy who had proposed to
me once before. Larry had followed me to the big city, staying for a year
before he decided to give up and go back home.

I was determined to meet the man I *really* loved—Elvis. One night I
convinced my new best friend to sneak in and meet the King of Rock.
"C'mon, Lily, we'll be fine. The fence isn't that high, and if we climb it
just so, we won't get a scratch on us. Barbed wire is a completely overrated
deterrent anyway. We can do this."

"Only you would think of a doing something like this—and only I would actually do it with you!" Lily was with me and with that I grabbed my new best friend's hand. We were going Elvis fence climbing.

As expected (but not desired), security nabbed us and took us toward the gate.

Lily had to be thinking the same thing, even though both of us were scared out of our minds. "Want to go to a party?" asked one of the security guards hauling us in. And with that, I became an acquaintance. Little did I know this would be the first of many evenings spent attending parties for Elvis. Also, about three weeks later I even went to Elvis' house. What an experience!

The first party I attended for Elvis was at the Fairgrounds. I have a picture of Elvis and me at this party. For six months after that, I attended many parties with Elvis' friends at a place called the Memphian. The time spent at the parties was enchanting, and it certainly helped perpetuate my understanding of worldly beauty. I was beginning to understand the power beauty held. What I failed to grasp was the power it could hold over me.

One afternoon another friend and I went driving downtown. Legionnaires were visiting Memphis for a conference and the media followed them. The Legionnaires pulled me out of my car and asked us to do the twist with them. We agreed. Little did I know the media would take my picture and it would end up on the front page of the newspaper. One of the executives of the bank where I was employed recognized my picture and called me the following week.

"Are you the Paula Kish who works in our bank and whose picture was in the paper?" he asked.

"It was really me," I answered, not knowing the implications of that response.

"I thought so." Soon afterwards, that same executive came down to the bank while I was working, took me to a back room and forced himself on me. It didn't stop there. He began showering me with roses and his attention. I knew he was a married man and I tried in my naïve way to stop his advances, but I was young and not able to completely comprehend how this would affect my life. His maturity made me an easy target and in his manipulative way he continued to pursue me. We had an affair.

He constantly told me how beautiful I was, which again propelled my sense of self-esteem to convince myself that the affair was okay. He was much older, but our age difference didn't deter anything about our relationship. There is no doubt that when I was with him, I felt like I was somebody special.

But his possessive behavior only escalated and he would call me ten times a day checking on me. Finally, on the verge of a nervous breakdown,

I took time off of work. He didn't stop. Friends helped me regain control of my life. In the end, the obsessive executive admitted, "I'm a dirty SOB for what I've done to you."

Hoping to regain control of my life I began to see single men. However, one night, during a date, I was raped once again. Reeling from all the events in my life, I ended up in the hospital. The man who assaulted me called and threatened me. The situation escalated to the point that the married executive threatened to go after the man who raped me. One night when the date rapist called me, the fear on my face was so startling that a friend grabbed the phone out of my trembling hands and told this man never to call again. He didn't. But the damage was done.

At this point, I convinced myself that I was okay and I could start over. Just three short months later, I met another man. We married not long after and had two beautiful daughters. But at the age of 33, I divorced him and became a single mom. Bitterness settled in my heart as far as men were concerned, and my callous (and careless) attitude set me on a path toward promiscuity.

I began looking for a new career and settled into the travel industry. However, since I had been at home with my two girls, I hadn't worked in eight years. Travel school took me to many different cities and one time in particular, I met a man at a hotel restaurant. One thing led to another, and we spent the night together. Weeks later, I called him to let him know I was pregnant. He immediately offered money for an abortion, and I readily received it.

So many fears rushed through my head. I had just started a new career! This pregnancy could only hurt my reputation as a professional in the business world. Worse, if my ex-husband or his family learned of my exploits, I thought I might lose my daughters. With all these fears, I decided abortion was my only option.

I told my supervisor my dilemma, and she offered to go with me to the abortion facility. Once we were actually there, I tried to leave, but she said I had no choice. I knew I had a choice—at the expense of my job—but a choice nonetheless. Unfortunately, I made the wrong decision.

Waiting in a cold room with several other women, I eventually got up the nerve to look at them. There they sat; sadness and fear etched deeply into their faces. What were their stories? The stories of my life played over and over in my head.

So many wrong turns, how did I end up here? It won't be long until each of us will have taken the lives of our babies.

The nurse called my name, and I followed her into the procedure room. While my baby was being sucked from my body, I felt nothing. Empty. Looking back, I believe I used a defense mechanism known as disassociation. The room was white, and against that backdrop, I could see the medical staff, but the vantage point seemed to be from a place beyond myself. After the abortion, I knew I had taken the life of my child, but I found it was easier to go into denial and tuck it away with the rest of my past.

Denial did nothing to lift the heaviness I felt, so in order to cope, I began drinking wine. There were plenty of opportunities. Being in the travel industry constantly allowed me the time to socialize with men, and more promiscuity followed. Most of my acquaintances thought I was a *jet-setter* living the *good life*, but in actuality, I was struggling financially and hated myself for the way I was living. But I tried to stay active, giving me less time to focus on the pain of my life.

Another drink of choice was something many don't consider. Nyquil. At first I began to take it when I had a cold, but then I began to drink it even when I wasn't sick. I was a functioning empty soul. I took care of my two daughters as best that I could and I remember my ex-husband always telling my girls that I was a good mother. We attended church too, but I didn't let God in really.

I maintained that façade, but deep inside my life continued in a downward spiral as the memories of my baby remained. I believed in my heart that I had aborted a boy, and I always missed my son, especially on the day that would have been his birthday.

Seven years of my life were wasted on promiscuous, out-of-control living. I reached such a low point that I almost made suicide an escape out of my misery. I remember driving to the riverfront in Downtown Memphis. I seriously considered driving over the river bluffs into its murky waters. No one would see any evidence of a car buried in a muddy grave. As seriously as I considered it, suicide just wasn't an option. I still had my girls to raise.

My mother became very ill that same year and I drove home to Southeast Missouri to visit with her. When she passed away, I had the responsibility of notifying friends and extended family members. One of her friends happened to be the father of Larry, the young man who pursued me across the state line many years ago.

During a phone conversation with Mr. Talley, he encouraged me, "Why don't you give Larry a call too, Paula. I think he'd want to hear the news about your mom from you, not his old dad."

My mind wandered to the past. *Where have the years gone?* Larry—the man who left our small town to follow me to Memphis—I wonder how he is doing. I thought about his perseverance and many marriage proposals. He had stayed a year in Memphis before he finally gave up and went back home. I'd often wondered where life took him, but hadn't considered getting in touch with him again.

"You really think I should call him—after all these years?"

The resounding affirmation in Mr. Talley's voice spoke volumes, and I couldn't disappoint a family friend. I scribbled Larry's information on a scrap piece of paper and promised to call.

I took a deep breath and dialed the number.

"Hello. This is Larry speaking." He sounded as if the years had no effect on his voice.

"Larry? This is Paula . . ."

"Paula? How are you? Where have you been all these years? Are you well?" Questions as to my well-being fired at me in rapid succession, and each time I opened my mouth to answer one, another came before I could say a word. "Are you in town? I would love to see you again."

Larry and I did get together. In fact, Larry once again followed me to Memphis. Only this time there was a wedding, and I followed him to St. Louis to live.

During our first year of marriage, I knew I needed to tell my husband about my past—all of it—so I opened my heart, telling him about the rapes and finally, my abortion. Larry reacted with a compassion I had never known before. His understanding went beyond my own as he tenderly comforted me. The only anger he expressed was for the men who had betrayed my naïveté. His expression of love mirrored the love of Christ—without judgment or condemnation.

Our marriage was unlike any relationship I had ever known; and for the next four years I embraced my new life. It seemed all was completely well until Larry suffered a heart attack. I rushed to my husband's side at the hospital, and as they examined him further, not only had Larry suffered a heart attack, but he was also diagnosed with lung cancer. Over the next three years, Larry underwent cancer treatment while still working full time. Five years after the initial diagnoses, Larry, the love of my life, died.

Grief was my constant companion for six years following my husband's death. Though I received many phone calls from concerned friends, one in particular stood out.

"Paula, God has a plan for you. You're going to begin a ministry from Larry's death." I pondered my friend's words and felt the need to begin putting my emotions down in words.

I love you, Lord. I truly do, but my heart is breaking. Please help me. These were the first words I had ever written regarding my personal experiences, and I have been journaling ever since. Getting my feelings down on paper not only created a safe place for me to express my emotions, but led me to a place of trusting a counselor with my pain.

I was not out of the woods yet. A series of events would catapult me further. Work at a large travel corporation became a source of great stress in my life. I got into a car accident that totaled my car which led to more stress. But the final blow came from a doctor's visit where I learned I had a heart murmur. Exhausted physically, mentally and spiritually, I went home after the doctor's appointment and crawled into bed.

Oddly enough the next day I felt refreshed in a different way. While I sat drinking coffee with my oldest daughter that morning, the Holy Spirit moved me to do something I'd never thought I could do. I told her about my abortion. In surprise, she said, "You what?"

That began the start of my healing. That night I told my youngest daughter. The next day a friend called who knew about the abortion to see how I was doing. "Paula, there's someone I want you to talk to . . ."

I connected with a woman who had a post-abortive ministry and I shared my story with her—another step in healing. At the end of our conversation, she encouraged me to talk again. "I want to connect you with another woman, Paula. Her name is Sally, and she shares the same past with you."

Sharing with this prayer warrior was difficult enough, how was I going to share my story with someone I didn't even know. But I did.

The next day, this precious lady called me, and as we shared our stories, the floodgates opened. I cried for what seemed hours. That phone call sealed my decision to attend the abortion recovery Bible study, *Forgiven and Set Free*. If the compassion of the women who led this study was half as genuine as this woman on my phone, then I knew I would be in safe hands.

My first meeting proved to me that I wasn't alone in my pain. Many other women were hurting just as I was. I learned that as a result of my past, including my abortion, that I was harboring deep-seeded anger. This anger had damaged my relationships with so many others in my life. During the course of this study, I was able to recognize and move through the emotions I was feeling. And I knew I was forgiven, once and for all. I had been set free. We each received a crown that day, a symbol reminding us that we were daughters of the King.

I'll never forget one of the last things we participated in. *Forgiven and Set Free* concluded with a memorial service for all the babies we had aborted. It was an incredibly emotional experience, but much needed to bring closure to the death of my son, whom I named, Jeremiah. My beloved, Jeremiah.

When I got home and unpacked, it occurred to me that I still had an old crown from a beauty pageant so long ago. I dug it out and set the two down together. Now I understood. This old tarnished crown represented worldly outside beauty—beauty that humans perceive. But my new crown represented who I am in Jesus' heart—a beauty that can never fade.

Today I minister to many others including widows, post-abortive women and single mothers. But it is only through my confessed sin of abortion that God has healed me enough to allow me to minister to others. *Thank you, Lord. You have blessed me indeed.*

There are times when I see a young man and wonder what my son would have looked like if he was here—his smile, his eyes, his personality. I often think of Jeremiah 29:11, "For I know well the plans I have in mind for you, says the Lord, plans for your welfare, not for woe! plans to give you a future full of hope." To help my healing and to bond with my son, I wrote this poem.

"To My Son Jeremiah"
Forgive me, oh Lord, for what I have done.
I know my child would have been a son.
I've named him Jeremiah, for the weeping prophet who shed many tears.
You knew him in his mother's womb, and you knew my son as well
I've learned after many years.
I've lived with guilt, anger and shame for so long,
that I was exhausted and totally enraged.
I needed my daughters to know they had a brother, Jeremiah,
so I shared my story with your sisters, Jill and Paige.
At times I think I've caught a glimpse of you,
As I gazed in a young man's face.
Would you have looked like him?
Wait! Is that you passing by?
What a wonderful way that young man grinned.
Then I think how many others are feeling this way.
Precious friends, I know the pain you are going through.
I now begin to heal and experience God's amazing grace.
I now realize that if God would give his Son Jesus to die for me.
Then I can share your message and run the good race.
I'll see you in heaven some day, Jeremiah. Forgive me for what I have done.
I'll share my story in hopes that others will know
not to take the lives of their little ones.
"For I know well the plans I have in mind for you, say the Lord, plans for your welfare, not for woe! Plans to give you a future full of hope."
Jeremiah 29:11

* **(by Sheri Rose Shepherd, in His Little Princess: Treasured Letters from Your King, published by Multnomah Publishers, 2006.)**

CHAPTER FIFTEEN

His Thankful Disciple

By

Elizabeth O'Neil*

It is finished, I told her. My best friend, mentor, and sister of the heart, Candace, finally knows my secret, my shame. I have known her for twenty-six years, and only now had I been able to tell her. And now I am here telling anybody willing to listen to my story.

My name is Elizabeth O'Neil. I had a wonderful childhood. My parents worked very hard to make sure we had a safe, fun childhood, filled with love and laughter. It was everything they wished theirs had been.

My dad worked for the government. Any time he could get a promotion by moving to a new assignment, we moved. I attended 11 schools in 13 years. I spent five years of my childhood living in West Germany. Most people measure their childhood memories by their age or who their friends were. I remember how old I was by where we were living.

Growing up in Germany during the late sixties and early seventies was great. I spent most of grade school in Germany, so in some ways it was very easy to believe the fairy tales I loved to read. After all, we had a castle within walking distance of our home! Our schools believed in the value of field trips and taught the current interpretation of evolutionary theory. I remember learning how humans go through the stages of evolution in the womb: from embryo, to the amphibious stage (our tailbone was supposed to be the remnant of our tail), up to the point we became fully human just before birth. I thought that was a pretty cool concept, and when we were visiting the Museum of Natural Science in Frankfurt, I didn't understand why the teacher and the parents shooed us out of the room when we happened upon a wall covered in jars. The teacher told us they were real examples of before a baby was born, and we didn't need to see them. I wanted to see the tail!

My mother taught us girls two things. First, we could be or do anything we wanted to be (even if we were female) and second, if you want to learn more about something, there's a book written about it somewhere.

The Fairy Tale Crumbles

After graduating from high school in Texas, life went into fast forward. Within an 18 month period, I started college, took ROTC, got engaged, went to Planned Parenthood, lost my virginity, found out I couldn't join the Air Force because of a knee injury, suffered from a major undiagnosed depression, and flunked out of college. My dad then got orders for Ohio, so my parents packed me up and moved me with the family (against my wishes). My boyfriend started dating someone else, and we broke up.

Somewhere in all the flurry of events, my dad informed me that he had gotten a girl pregnant when he was a junior in high school and married her. I had an older sister by 4 years I previously knew nothing about. Her mother wrote my father a "Dear John" letter when he was in the Navy, divorcing him. He allowed the new husband to adopt his daughter because divorce wasn't common and he didn't want her to have any unnecessary difficulties. The only drawback—he had to agree not to contact her until she turned eighteen.

In Ohio, I worked as a typist at the local Air Force Base while attending night school at a nearby university. I was so lonely. My sister Ashley attended the same university, and when she told me they offered Army ROTC at night school, I signed up again. There, I met a young man—a veteran and a member of ROTC. We dated for about 8 months before getting engaged. I was 19. After spending the summer at ROTC summer camp at Fort Riley, we married. I earned the primary income for the two of us. Mere weeks into the marriage, I knew it was nothing like my parents'.

I was receiving steroid treatments for my knees when my new husband told me he had genital warts. Then, I discovered I had conceived during our first two weeks of married life. I panicked. Due to my steroid treatments and my husband's STD, my doctor informed me that my child had an 85% chance of being born with severe defects. I couldn't handle everything.

My mother drove me to the clinic and stayed in the waiting room. I remember the protestors outside. They were very vocal. They also broke into the clinic and were forcibly removed while I was having the procedure done. Later that evening, I collapsed on the bathroom floor from pain. I was rushed to the hospital emergency room. After a brief exam, they just left me to myself once they found out I had had an abortion that day. Three days later, after what I now know were labor-type pains, I passed something the size of my hand the doctor missed while distracted by the protestors.

Life, work and college went on and my marriage got worse.

In June 1980, I received my commission as a 2nd Lt in the Army Reserve. Between Christmas and New Year's my husband of 16 months moved out. He came back unexpectedly one weekend the following February. I thought he was back for good. Monday morning, while I was at work, he left for the final time, taking with him everything we owned. I filed for an uncontested divorce. My divorce was final in March—it only took 6 weeks.

He did leave me with one thing, though. Within a couple of weeks, I was experiencing morning sickness.

Once you have been down the slippery slope, it is much easier for Satan to deceive you again. I didn't want to go to the same clinic, and didn't I want my mom to know because I thought she would worry, so that April I went to a clinic in Cincinnati where I had my second abortion.

I reported to Ft Lee, VA the first week in May for training with the intention of putting Ohio (and all that it represented) behind me.

Starting Over

My very first day at Ft. Lee, I crossed paths with the woman I would be friends with for the next 26 years. Not a bad start. I met Candace, a small 2nd Lt., when her huge bags were dumped on the sidewalk, and I offered to help her carry them.

It didn't take long before I realized the guys in our course outnumbered the girls about 4 to 1 at Ft. Lee. I noticed several cute guys, and decided I would have fun but not get serious about anyone. I knew where that led you . . . .

As Memorial Day weekend approached, one of the Lt's found out I was from Ohio and offered me a ride home. I needed to pick up some of my stuff, so I agreed. But he got very sick, so I ended up driving. Then, I got too tired to drive just as we were ready to enter Ohio, so he took over. When I woke up we were somewhere in the middle of Kentucky! By the time we finally arrived at his parents' house at the end of a long gravel road, I wondered where he was taking me!

A week later, we had our first date. He took me to Mass and then to play tennis. I told him I wasn't Catholic, and I didn't know how to play tennis. I loved the Mass and was impressed by the fact that he knew all the responses and when to sit and stand. I realized then that faith held an important place in my life even if I didn't go to church myself.

After Mass, he quickly realized I was telling the truth when I said I didn't know how to play tennis. We sat and talked instead. I remember telling him that he didn't want to date me because he was a good Catholic, and I was divorced. And for some reason, I told him about the abortions, too. I think I was trying to scare him away.

We dated a little in June. I went out with a few other guys. By July, I knew I was getting serious about him. Our training days started at 5am and ended after evening study sessions and I saw him seven days a week. In August,

I found out I had been accepted on active duty. I finished the course at Ft. Lee, and visited with my parents on the way to my new assignment in Texas. I thought Don and I could at least call each other, and see if we were really serious about each other. I still wasn't sure I was ready to open myself up to being hurt again.

In less than a week, Don called and proposed over the phone. His sister was getting married that December, and he already had leave scheduled. So, he suggested we get married right before Christmas and then put in the paperwork to get stationed together. I agreed.

We married a week before Christmas in Ohio during one of the coldest blizzards in memory. We took a couple a days off for a honeymoon, visited with our families on Christmas, and then I went back to Texas and he went back to Virginia. Five months later, the Army sent him to Texas.

The Joys of Family Life

As soon as I got back to Texas, I started the paperwork to get my first marriage declared null by the Catholic Church. It was approved 18 months later. In September 1983 I received the Sacraments of Baptism, Reconciliation, Confirmation, and we convalidated our Marriage. I also received my First Communion as part of the wedding Mass. We had two witnesses, and I was 7 months pregnant with my first daughter. She arrived exactly 4 weeks late at the military hospital. It was a 28 hour labor and the doctor told me not to have any more big babies—Caitlyn weighed 9 lbs., 1 oz.

I loved my three years in the military in Texas. But, after Caitlyn's birth, I really wanted to stay home with her. So, at the end of my three years, I left active duty and returned to the Army Reserves. By this time, Don had orders for Ft. Lee again for his Officer Advanced Course. Candace was still stationed there and would be in his class. We attended Mass every week, but we were only nominally religious. While at Ft. Lee, I had a first trimester miscarriage.

At the end of the 6 months, the orders said "Germany." I was excited to return to the fairy tale land I loved as a child. To add to our joy, Candace and her new husband, Kevin, were headed to Germany as well. My sister Ashley was also stationed not far from our assignment.

Our time in Germany was fun and stressful. After a near miss with a terrorist bombing in Frankfurt, we began attending Mass behind security gates. Security searches became a way a life as the threats became more real.

In May 1986, just three weeks after Chernobyl, my son Michael was born. We were told not to go outside for weeks because of the fear of the fallout. My labor was just 6 hours and ironically, my 12.5 lb son was my easiest delivery. Near the end of September, Candace and Kevin invited us to go to Venice with them for a weekend unit trip. By the time we arrived, I knew that it wasn't car sickness I was experiencing. It took until December before I was able to convince the military doctors my pregnancy wasn't just in my head.

During this pregnancy, Don and I became military foster parents. Our love for children perplexed many in the community, but we loved being a part of these kids' lives. Finally, my daughter Erin was born.

After Erin's birth, my husband, unhappy with his job, made the decision to leave the Army. We decided to move to Florida, near my parents. Don was tired of snow, and my Dad was trying to start his own consulting firm there.

The Struggles of Civilian Life

We arrived in Florida with little money, no real job prospects, and three children. It took eight months of us doing any job we could find before Don was hired with a Defense Contractor at much less than he had earned as a Captain. Life got hectic. Don was trying to finish his Master's degree, and I would work all night at a temp job only to come home and rewrite his papers for class the next day.

Caitlyn was enrolled at the local Catholic School in their K4 program. Her education ended up being my education too as I learned all the traditional Catholic prayers I never knew, thanks to her teacher, Anne Bradshaw.

In the spring of 1989, I found out I was pregnant again. Caitlyn was 5. We moved into a house 2 blocks from the parish and the school. It had a pool. We had many fun swimming parties with my family members when they were in town.

During my fourth pregnancy, I started receiving dirty looks. Strangers would comment on the number of kids I had, and even my mom advised me not to have any more kids. She had almost died having my youngest sister. Finally, even my OB doctor talked to me about not having any more. I had a history of big babies, I had to be tested monthly for gestational diabetes—the list went on and on. Don and I discussed it and decided that life in the civilian world was too uncertain and expensive to be having more babies, so he agreed to have a vasectomy.

Our daughter Bethany was born the end of January, 1990. Five days later, Don left for reserve duty. Beth spent a lot of time in a backpack while I volunteered at the school. Everyone at the school knew her and spoiled her.

A year later, Don had his bags packed waiting for orders for the Gulf War. Three times the bag sat at the door and each time the military changed their minds and sent someone else. Then, Don had orders for three weeks in Panama beginning the first part of September '91. School had started in August for the children. Caitlyn was a second grader, Michael was in kindergarten, and Erin had just started Anne Bradshaw's K4 class. While their Dad was gone, I suffered from a kidney infection and bronchitis. My parents were out of town, and I struggled to care for our four children. Beth would sit and play quietly near me while I lay in bed, too sick to get up.

I had been trying for months to get Beth in the swimming classes at the YMCA but they kept cancelling them because not enough people signed up. Her first class finally came—the 1st of October. I was also beginning a class that night at the local Jr. College—I wanted to go back to school and finish my degree. The day was sunny and beautiful, and I was finally well again. I left for class happy as I waved goodbye to Don and Beth in the doorway.

About 30 minutes into the class, the police officer came. He told me one of my children had been hurt, and he would take me to the hospital. I told him I could drive myself the 12 miles. I asked him which child—he told me my youngest. I knew Don panicked at the sight of blood, and I figured the worst that could have happened was a fall off the bunk bed. It wasn't until after I got to the hospital and they ushered me into the private room with my husband that I found out that Bethany had opened the back door and gone swimming like I taught her to do that morning. She was too young at 20 months to know she couldn't really swim—that Mom had been holding her up in the water. The medical staff could never revive her heart. My baby was dead.

My parents were called, and they brought our other children with them. All Don could do was cry. I told him to pray. I figured, he was the one raised Catholic, he must know something that would bring her back. I didn't know how to pray other than the prayers I learned with Caitlyn. I asked for Father Martin. He came and gave Beth her last Sacrament and helped explain what had happened to the children. My Dad drove us home.

I experienced all of the normal stages of grief, some more than once. What no one else could ever begin to understand was that I had finally realized just how precious a baby's life is. The full enormity of what I had done years ago in Ohio hit me. I grieved for the loss of three of my children, not just one. Many days I would just sit and cry or I would yell at God for taking my baby from me. Finally, my prayers were filled with pleas for forgiveness.

A Time of Spiritual Growth

Anne Bradshaw was a godsend to me in the weeks that followed. I had never been home alone during the day before. When I couldn't stand the quiet at home, I would walk down to the school and she would put me to work in her classroom. A year later, I decided to go back to school full time beginning in January. One of my classes was a comparative religion class The first week of February the Instructor told us about a Lutheran guy that was coming to talk about the Blessed Virgin Mary and some place called Medugorje. I was curious and it was being held at my parish so I went after class. I was a little bit late so I sat at the back right in front of an entire pew of priests. Wayne Weible (the "Lutheran guy") spoke and at the end of his talk he told us to raise our hands and receive Mary's blessing from Medugorje. I felt silly with so many priests right behind me but I did it anyway. When he gave us the blessing, I felt a tingle and then a peace come over me. That instant, the pain of all of my loss and grief finally left me. Afterwards, I followed the crowd into the gym not knowing what to do or say about this thing I had just experienced. I remembered my mother's advice and bought the book. I read about Mary's apparitions and then I went and found the Catholic bookstore and found another book and then another. The more I read, the more Mary was bringing me to her son, Jesus.

From 1991 through 1995, after Beth's death, our family experienced an incredible leap in spiritual growth. We started praying the rosary every night as a family. At first, we prayed one decade a night, and sometimes the kids fell asleep during that! The children joined the Junior Legion of Mary, and I read more about the Church and the Bible. One year during Advent, after the children were in bed at night, Don and I prayed and studied St. Louis de Montfort's Total Consecration to Mary. Consecrating ourselves and our family to Mary remains one of my happiest memories.

In early July of '95, my mother was diagnosed with stage 4 lung cancer that had spread to her brain. My sister, Melanie, had just set her wedding date for the end of November. The doctors told her to move it up to September or my mother wouldn't be there. A couple of hurricanes, (including Opal), lots of prayers, chemo, and nine months later after my sister's wedding, my mother went into remission.

Thankful for my mother's survival, family life continued to click along. During the summer of 1996, we moved to Pensacola for a great job offer Don received. We were very active in our Catholic Home school group there. We had about 40 families in our group. These were some of the most devoted, knowledgeable Catholics I have ever met. I learned so much from these couples about our faith.

The pro-life group at our parish asked everyone to take a little "10 week unborn" baby and pray for the baby and its mother for 9 and half months. We were asked to pray that the mother would choose life. I told my son to name the baby so we would know who we were praying for. He wanted to know how he was to choose the name, and I told him to go back into the chapel and talk to his guardian angel, then he would know. He came back and told us the baby's name was Jacob. We didn't know any Jacob's but I said ok. So, for 9 and half months we prayed for baby Jacob and his mother.

But our spiritual renewal began to wane. Don spent a lot of time on the road with his new job. The rosary at home took a back seat to "activities." Don coached the kids on some of their teams, and I was the driver. Some days I spent 6-8 hrs driving to my Dad's and then back and forth across town getting everyone to their activities. I began to feel like "the schedule" dictated our lives.

In October of '98 my parents took the children and me with them to visit relatives in Oklahoma. I met my older sister Theresa for my 40th birthday. She is now an active part of our family.

In May 1999, I traveled to Virginia to be with my sister Melanie for the birth of her daughter. She had helped me with two of my children and my Mom, although still living, could not travel. While I was gone, Don began to play on the parish co-ed softball team.

Then, Caitlyn was accepted at the summer program of the Cincinnati Ballet that summer. I spent a month in Ohio with her, and while I became closer to my in-laws that month, I felt lonely because Don never called me. While I was gone, Don signed Mike and Erin on to the Home school swim team. A friend of mine, Louise, invited Erin to spend a lot of time at her house that summer. Erin, 11, loved having an adult confidante. Adding to the fun, Louise's daughter Sarah played on Erin's soccer team and their two dads coached the team together. They were also members of our parish, the parish softball team, and home school group. Our two families saw each other at least 3-5 times a week.

A Time of Great Suffering

As summer faded to autumn, my pleas to lighten the activity schedule fell on deaf ears. Our home schooling schedule suffered because the kids were exhausted. We never had family time at home anymore.

Autumn chilled into winter. In January 2000, Don became a 4th degree in the Knights of Columbus. After the 4th degree ceremony there was a formal banquet. I spent the entire evening watching my husband and

Louise flirt with each other. Her husband and I were too shocked to do anything but just sit and watch!

Between January and April, our family experienced one crisis after another. Mike fell off his bike and broke his right collar bone and left wrist. Erin fell at soccer and needed a walking cast. I had a minor car accident, requiring me to use a small rental car instead of my usual large van. We arrived to visit my parents in the rental cal and Dad insisted that I drive him the 90 miles back to Pensacola to go to the hospital there. My Dad had suffered a heart attack the night before and he was afraid my Mother would be left home alone if he left in an ambulance. After triple by-pass surgery and weeks of complications my dad recovered. I finally returned home from caring for my parents at their home.

Now, I would be able to address this problem in my marriage. Instead, three days after I returned, Don told me he wanted a divorce.

I wanted reconciliation, but he wasn't interested. He refused to attend any type of marriage counseling with me. That August, Don and I had to tell the kids that he wanted a divorce. The kids all reacted differently. Michael became very withdrawn. Erin even attempted suicide by overdosing on pills.

A week after the suicide attempt, Caitlyn came forward to tearfully tell me that at 16 she was pregnant. I sat on the floor with her, and we cried together. She—for all of the reasons and fears pent up inside of her. I—because I knew her childhood had just been stolen from her. I also knew I had to tell her about my abortions and let her know that she had a choice. She could choose to keep her baby, and I would help her for as long as she needed and wanted my help. She didn't have to have an abortion or give her child up for adoption.

Facing my daughter and telling her of my past was one of the most difficult things I have ever done.

As the separation progressed, pain from my past continued to rise to the surface. I could no longer keep my abortions in the dark. After moving out in January of '01, Donald tried to convince the children to live with him instead of me. My children were old enough to legally choose for themselves. Don even went so far as to tell them about my abortions to convince them I was a terrible person.

My son didn't believe him, but confronted me with his new knowledge. When I admitted to him what I had done before I became a practicing Christian, my son told me I must have thought my reasons were right, and that I wasn't that person anymore. The children all chose to stay with me. With spiritual and legal counsel, I filed for divorce because there was nothing I could do to legally stop him from divorcing me.

Life after Death

Life became intolerable for the kids and me in Pensacola, so we decided to move. We chose a suburb of Atlanta, and I am sure our choice was the Holy Spirit's prompting. Kevin and Candace had moved to the town several years before, and we had visited them several times in their new home and attended Mass together. I knew my children would find a spiritual home in their parish. The priest was a quiet, gentle Irish man who had a sense of peace and holiness about him. The bright light in all of this was that my grandson, Jacob was born during June 2001.

I came to a Job Fair in Georgia in July, hoping to find a job and a place to live. I was offered a job and we moved two weeks later. The divorce proceedings continued to be ugly. Don swore under oath that he never had an affair. Nine days after the divorce was final, Don married Louise in a ceremony with her kids in attendance. His relationship with our kids has never been the same.

My first two jobs in Georgia did not work out well, and the repercussions of 9/11 made times even harder, but God took care of us. I can't begin to describe the many outpourings of support we received during those times of uncertainty. Every time I had trouble paying the bills, the funds showed up somehow. Even strangers provided us with a gift basket worth $350 one Christmas when I could not afford gifts. I was finally offered a solid job at an ethical company—an answer to prayer.

Then, one weekend, our Parish sponsored a retreat for women, and my friend Candace insisted I attend. I left the kids with Caitlyn, now 18 and a mother. The women presenting the weekend, including Candace, made sure it was filled with love and understanding. The Holy Spirit was very active there. The weekend was followed by six months of formation, and then my group of women gave the retreat for the next group. I was designated as a speaker. My witness to God's Love in my Life was the first time I ever told anyone (except my ex-husband and children) about my abortions. I am not a public speaker so this terrified me, but ultimately it freed me from the feelings of shame I carried over the years. These women now knew my darkest secret, and they still accepted me and loved me.

Several years have passed since that retreat weekend. My dad sold his home in Florida and moved to Georgia to live with the kids and me. He needed help caring for my mom and his help was a Godsend for us. I am still very close friends with my women's group.

My daughters attended college and have married. My son is still in college. I took a year off from work, and 30 years after I started, I finished my bachelor's degree, cum laude. My mother passed away from long term side effects of the radiation to her brain. Her cancer never returned.

Me? God placed a wonderful man in my life. He is a gentle, faith-filled man. When I told him about my "secret," his response was the same as my church sisters. We married a little over a year ago. I have learned that it is not by my strength but on God's that I must rely. He has a plan for me. His love endures forever, and I am his Thankful Disciple.

*   Not real name.

Healing the Post Abortive Woman

By

Jane Brennan and Loretta Oakes

It is clear that the face of abortion can more clearly be expressed by those who've had an abortion and these women should be an integral part of a post-abortive ministry. The post abortive woman gives testimony to the child lost and is a living witness to this tragic decision. They speak to the spiritual, physical and emotional consequences for making the legal choice that our society offers.

Post-abortive women are crying out for reconciliation, a deep forgiveness that can only come from God. Some people question why the Christian perspective is needed. Many women that come to the Church seeking healing have already been through therapy for topics such as depression, relationships, commitment, and addiction. But time after time therapists don't see the abortion as an issue in their patient's lives. Therefore they do not examine or address the problem in therapy.

Those in need of healing are told their decision was simply seen as a choice, not a life. What is evident, however, is that these women are grieving the loss of a child. Secular therapy discounts the seriousness of the decision and even the life of the child lost in that decision. When these issues are not addressed, healing cannot take place.

These people are mothers to their missing children and these children need to take their rightful place in their mother's lives. Intellectually, the reality is that we are mothers to our children for all eternity.

And that is what should be addressed. Anyone attending a post abortive ministry is taught that they are a mother forever to this aborted child. All the energy that has typically been spent on healing and reconciliation must be put into perspective with the personal loss these people have encountered. Post abortive mothers must deal with their decision to abort and with the question of what's happened to their child.

This is where the impact of spiritual guidance comes in. Mothers come to understand that their child has not been abandoned by God. No, the exact opposite! At the moment of the abortion, God claimed that child immediately and lovingly holds that child forever, bringing him or her to the communion of saints to live for eternity. The child has always been in God's loving care.

This understanding is fundamental for a mother facing the lost child and being a mother to that child. In fact, the aborted child is a life-line and it is through the love of that child that the mother is even in search of healing.

The objective of a post-abortive program is to move away from what happened that awful day of the abortion and realize there's more to embrace. God wants that mother to understand and embrace motherhood for that child.

We understand that someone has made the decision to end the life of their child. Although the pain may be masked for many years, later loss in life eventually triggers the original trauma of the loss of their child. Abortion is a trauma.

But there is healing and all the stories in this book provide the reader with that understanding. Healing is a process that takes many shapes, but finding a strong post abortive program is key to finding peace.

The Healing Process

A woman seeking help with the tragedy and pain of a past abortion should look for a post abortive program that will first listen to her abortion experience and what that story continues to be. The conversation begins with the woman's story.

Revealing details are an important aspect of putting that story in perspective. Experiences help define who we are. A caring listener is able to provide a safe place for the post-abortive woman to unearth these details and ultimately provide the path to the next level of healing.

Moving on to the next level of healing usually involves the post abortive person addressing feelings and emotions that have been denied since the abortion. These emotions may include anger, guilt, grief, sadness and ongoing pain.

During this stage of healing the person begins to see how they've been expressing these negative emotions in their own lives. This revealing experience helps the post abortive woman see that her difficulty in relationships truly lies with her inability to establish true intimacy with another person. She may begin to see that alcohol, drugs or sex has been her self medication for her heartfelt pain and loss.

What may be more difficult for the post-abortive women to express is the anger they feel toward a parent or spouse or friend who was instrumental in their abortion decision. Deep seeded resentment and a sense of betrayal becomes evident in an adult child if they were taken to the abortion clinic by a parent who they trusted to care for them.

As these emotions and feelings of loss and betrayal are examined, the beginning of acceptance of God's mercy and love become part of the healing process. Openness to God's forgiveness and mercy is always possible for the woman in pain after an abortion.

What a post abortive mother learns is that her aborted child is their lifeline in healing. They begin to understand that they will one day be reunited with their child. They begin to see that they are truly a mother for all eternity for this child. No matter how many children they have here on earth, their aborted child is as much a part of their family life as the others. Bonding with their missing child can be done in a variety of ways including naming their child, letters to that child and simple conversations or prayer.

Is there truly hope for me?

Yes! Hope is the object of this healing process. Every aborted child waits in heaven to be reunited with their mother. Every aborted child wishes them love and forgiveness.

Guilt, remorse, anger and hopelessness are all addressed in post abortive work. No matter what led to the abortion decision, God is there with outstretched arms to provide the hope and constant love.

Seeking a supportive and spiritual post abortive program is key. No one can do it alone. Everyone is a child of God and as such is entitled to God's infinite love and mercy. The first step is the hardest, but as seen through all the stories in the book, that step leads to an everlasting healing that can change a person's life.

Post-Abortive Resources

www.Silentnomoreawareness.org

Rachel's Vineyards Retreats—1-877-467-3463 (Hope-4-me)

Project Rachel—HopeAfterAbortion.com

Word of Hope 1-888-217-8679
www.lutheransforlife.org

Forgiven and Set Free
By Linda Cochrane
A Bible Study for Post-Abortive Women
Baker Books PO Box 6287, Grand Rapids, MI 49516

Real Choices
Listening To Women; Looking for Alternatives to Abortion
Frederica Mathewes-Green

A Season to Heal
Help and hope for those working through Post-Abortion Stress
Luci Freed & Penny Yvonne Salazar

Forbidden Grief
The Unspoken Pain of Abortion
Theresa Burke with David C. Reardon

Making Abortion Rare
A healing Strategy for a Divided Nation
David C. Reardon

The Cost of "Choice"
Women Evaluate the Impact of Abortion
Edited by Erika Bachiochi

Rachel, Weep No More
How Divine Mercy Heals the Effects of Abortion
Bryan Thatcher, MD, & Fr. Frank Pavone
To obtain copies of this booklet: Please call
1-800-462-7426

Hurting from Abortion?
The National Helpline for Abortion Recovery is just a call away
866-482-LIFE—24/7 Free, Confidential
Documentary—"I was Wrong"
www.IwasWrong.info

DVD—Beyond Regret: Entering into Healing and Wholeness after an Abortion
By: Paraclete Video Productions
http://www.paracletepress.com/index.html
Toll Free—(800) 451-5006

Real Abortion Stories:The Hurting and The Healing
Edited By Barbara Horak
www.realabortionstories.com

Giving Sorrow Words: Women's Stories of grief after abortion
Melinda Tankard Reist
Acorn Books, Springfield, IL

A Time to Speak: A Healing Journal for Post-Abortive Women
Yvonee Florczak-Seeman

Post-Abortion Trauma
The Silent Side of Trauma
Co-Authored by Mark Kretschmar and Julie Woodley

Documentary
"I was Wrong." Captures the changed hearts of two women forever altered by abortion and brings a deeper understanding of how abortion strikes at the heart and soul of America. Meet Norma McCorvey, "Jane Roe" of Roe v. Wade and Joyce Zounis. To view trailer and order DVD
www.IWasWrong.info

Jane Brennan, MS
Post-Abortive Counseling
Providing hope and healing for the Journey.
Jane@motherhoodinterrupted.com

LaVergne, TN USA
25 July 2010
190852LV00004B/32/P

8 KEY  STRESS MANAGEMENT

8 Keys to Mental Health Series

Babette Rothschild, Series Editor

The 8 Keys series of books provides consumers with brief, inexpensive, and high-quality self-help books on a variety of topics in mental health. Each volume is written by an expert in the field, someone who is capable of presenting evidence-based information in a concise and clear way. These books stand out by offering consumers cutting-edge, relevant theory in easily digestible portions, written in an accessible style. The tone is respectful of the reader and the messages are immediately applicable. Filled with exercises and practical strategies, these books empower readers to help themselves.

8 KEYS TO STRESS MANAGEMENT

SIMPLE AND EFFECTIVE STRATEGIES TO TRANSFORM YOUR EXPERIENCE OF STRESS

ELIZABETH ANNE SCOTT

FOREWORD BY BABETTE ROTHSCHILD

W. W. Norton & Company

New York · London

For information about permission to reproduce selections
from this book, write to Permissions, W. W. Norton & Company, Inc.,
500 Fifth Avenue, New York, NY 10110

For information about special discounts for bulk purchases, please contact
W. W. Norton Special Sales at specialsales@wwnorton.com or 800-233-4830

Manufacturing by Quad Graphics Fairfield
Production manager: Leeann Graham

Library of Congress Cataloging-in-Publication Data

Scott, Elizabeth Anne.
8 keys to stress management : simple and effective strategies
to transform your experience of stress / Elizabeth Anne Scott ;
foreword by Babette Rothschild. — First edition.
pages cm. — (8 keys to mental health series)
"A Norton Professional Book."
Includes bibliographical references and index.
ISBN 978-0-393-70809-7 (pbk.)
1. Stress management.
I. Title. II. Title: Eight keys to stress management.
RA785.S394 2013
155.9'042—dc23
2012045877

W. W. Norton & Company, Inc.
500 Fifth Avenue, New York, N.Y. 10110
www.wwnorton.com

W. W. Norton & Company Ltd.
Castle House, 75/76 Wells Street, London W1T 3QT

1 2 3 4 5 6 7 8 9 0

This book is dedicated to my wonderful husband, Jamey, and my beloved sons, Jake and Cameron James. They keep my life exciting, meaningful, and filled with love.

And to my grandparents, James and Phyllis Kudrna, and Leo and Charlene Schuetz. They have been a source of inspiration to me and have shown by example how to manage stress and live a long, happy, and healthy life.

Finally, this book is dedicated to everyone who encounters stress and would like to manage it in the healthiest way possible. We may all experience stress in unique ways, but I believe we all share the desire to be our best, for the benefit of our loved ones, for ourselves, and for the world around us.

Contents

Acknowledgments

I feel so fortunate to have this book published, as I believe that stress is one of the most relevant and timely topics in most people's lives. It is my sincere desire to help others learn strategies that can enable them to improve their lives and experience greater fulfillment day to day. This book would not be in your hands without those who have offered me support, encouragement, and resources along the way, so I would like to offer my sincere gratitude to my friends, family, and colleagues. While all of them deserve my thanks, certain specific people deserve special mention.

First and foremost, I would like to offer my heartfelt gratitude to my series editor, Babette Rothshild, for creating this wonderful series and inviting me to be part of it; for providing wise and gentle guidance; and above all, for offering her support, which made the process of writing this book infinitely easier than it could have been. I would also like to extend my sincere appreciation to my editor, Deborah Malmud, for offering me the opportunity to publish this book. Her expert guidance and support was greatly appreciated, and I feel very fortunate to have worked with her. I would like to heartily thank everyone at W. W. Norton for working with me on this book; the whole process has been wonderful.

I can't express enough appreciation for my husband, Jamey, and our sons, Jake and Cameron James, who make my life so rich and whose patience and encouragement were extremely important.

I would also like to thank my dear friend Elmarie Hyman, and my parents, Scotty and Jeanne Schuetz, for offering themselves as proofreaders. Having that extra bit of support really helped. I owe special thanks to Tom Head and Rod Brouhard for their advice, which helped me to move forward with writing this book. I really appreciated the support of my friends Kris Doyle and Laura Dolson, who, with Elmarie, acted as cheerleaders, motivators, and sounding boards during the process. My family, particularly Dann Schuetz, Heidi Atienza, and Cindy McCormmick, as well as my colleagues, cohorts, professors, and classmates, have aided me with their ideas, insights, thought-provoking questions, and encouragement throughout the years. I would like to thank all of my professors and mentors, particularly Dr. Emery Cummins, one of my earliest and most influential mentors. I owe quite a bit to Dr. Martin Seligman and the other passionate researchers in the field of positive psychology for their groundbreaking work. All of these people, plus several not mentioned by name (I trust you know who you are), have opened up new avenues of personal and professional growth for me, and this book would not have been written without them.

Foreword

Babette Rothschild, Series Editor

Hans Selye first studied, identified, and named the condition we call *stress* in the 1950s, publishing his findings in his classic book, *The Stress of Life*. In his quest to understand stress, he observed problematic changes in body systems and organs as a result of persistently high levels of adrenaline and other hormones, now recognized as "stress hormones."

Stress is commonly associated with disagreeable states and experiences, but objectively is neither positive nor negative. In fact, stress is simply a response to physical and emotional demands, what Selye called *stressors*. It is important to note that stress is not always bad or even undesirable. You might be surprised to learn that many things you experience as pleasant are actually the results of stress, such as the pleasure of sexual climax; the invigoration of a challenging bike ride; the love, warmth, and "high" of a wedding day; and the nourishment and satisfaction many experience while working in their gardens. Stress can also be a lifesaver, as when a person encounters a life-threatening situation and is able to achieve the superhuman speed or strength necessary to flee from or fight off the danger. Nevertheless, when we talk about stress we are usually referring to unpleasant stress, set in motion by adverse events or circumstances or exacerbated through our perceptions and thoughts.

Every being experiences stress more and less on a daily basis. It is inevitable, not something we can avoid, so it might be a good idea to learn how to better handle it. Recently I suggested to my colleague, Dr. Christiane Wolf, a certified teacher and trainer in Jon Kabat-Zinn's program of mindfulness-based stress reduction, that it would be more accurate to call that program "mindfulness-based stress *management*." Bottom line: Because we cannot evade stress, just about everyone (myself included) could learn to better manage it and to reduce the unfavorable impact it can have on the body and mind.

When first conceiving of the 8 Keys to Mental Health Series, I put the idea of a book that would help readers with stress at the top of my list of central topics. I wanted to find an author who had a natural flare for speaking directly to the reader, so that the eventual volume would be more of a personal tutorial than a text or a tome. One day Christiane, my aforementioned colleague, introduced me to Elizabeth Anne Scott's Web site. An expert on stress management herself, Christiane had found the information there to be particularly intelligent and unusually helpful. She recommended that I take a look. When I opened the link, I was immediately intrigued and impressed. Scott, I thought, really has her finger on the pulse of people with stress and knows how to help them. From her site I could see that she had an extremely accessible and smart writing style—and *lots* to say.

One might think that Scott, a young mother of two who married her freshman-year sweetheart, could not personally know much about stress. Nothing could be further from the truth. At 15 she survived a devastating car accident, emerging with her neck, pelvis, and arm broken. It took her many, many months to recover emotionally as well as physically and to catch up academically and socially with her classmates. During that ordeal she both learned and taught herself plenty about managing stress. What she gained during that trying time further helped her to survive the pressures of college and young motherhood. Now she juggles caring for her family with writing her PhD dissertation, while also meeting the demands of authorship. Stress management is definitely high on Scott's personal agenda.

8 Keys to Stress Management contains the best and most useful information and techniques that Scott has amassed following her accident, as a student and a professional. You will see from her writing that she is a natural-born teacher and you will be comforted by her encouraging tone. The book is well organized in a logical progression and is full of instructive as well as illustrative exercises that will help you from the first chapter to begin lowering your own stress. Scott's volume is a terrific addition to the 8 Keys to Mental Health Series.

Preface

How would it feel to be able to go through your day feeling less stressed about problems that arise, without needing to prevent the unpreventable? To see opportunities that others might miss and to open doors that lead to new paths of happiness? To better savor the good times and to let the bad times roll off your back more easily? With a little practice, this can be your new norm.

This book has been written to help you shift your whole experience of stress in your life, so that you have a whole new range of possibilities. You will learn techniques that will help you to better manage the stress you face, strategies for structuring your lifestyle that will enhance your internal and external coping resources, and habits that can increase your resilience to stressors you will inevitably encounter as you move through life.

I know from experience—both personal and professional—that these techniques work. I have received feedback from clients and readers that the strategies in these pages have helped people live healthier, happier lives. I have also practiced virtually all the techniques discussed in these pages at least once and can attest that they do work. This collection of stress management tools has helped me to effectively cope with everything from mundane life hassles to serious crises and major life challenges, and it can help you as well.

You cannot eliminate stress from your life, and you may even face stress that momentarily throws you off balance. However, these techniques—used either alone or in different combinations—can enable you to quickly get back to a place of feeling centered, sometimes even before you realize you needed centering. In fact, several of these strategies can help you to learn and grow from the stress you face, coming out stronger in the process. Rather than merely surviving the stress in your life, you can thrive through the process of learning to cope. This book will show you how.

8 KEYS TO
STRESS MANAGEMENT

Introduction

Potential stressors are everywhere. The experience of stress is so unavoidable that attempts to eliminate all stress would simply create *more* stress. However, some types of stress are benign or even helpful, and all stress can be minimized and managed. Even small steps toward stress relief can bring great payoffs, as they lead to a chain reaction of positive change. Therefore, efforts made toward stress management, particularly well-planned efforts, really *can* transform your life. By gaining a deeper understanding of what constitutes stress, where it comes from, and how it affects us, we can know what steps to take to better manage the stress in our lives. First, let's deepen our understanding of stress.

What We Mean When We Talk About *Stress*

The term *stress* is used to express many things and can be used as a noun, verb, or adjective. "I'm dealing with too much stress in my life." "I'm stressing about how to get all this work done." "This is so stressful, I have a stress headache and stress cravings for chocolate!" While we generally know what we mean when we use the word, there are a few nuances to be aware of.

When we talk about the stress in our lives, we are generally talking about *stressors*. A stressor is a situation that causes us to need to act and that can trigger our body's stress response. Such triggers can be positive or negative, but they all have in common that they require a response. Basically, stressors are the things in our lives that cause us stress.

When we say that we are *stressing*, we usually mean that we are coming from a place of feeling the effects of stressors in our lives. Our stress response is triggered, and we are not functioning as our usual, relaxed selves. You will hear more about the effects of stress and how the stress response alters your regular patterns of functioning, and the main thing to remember is that there are many ways, both obvious and subtle, in which we change when we are facing an overabundance of stressors or are not handling them in an optimal way. We are more likely to snap at people we care about, make mistakes that we wouldn't normally make, eat foods that we know aren't good for us, and do things that can actually create more stress in our lives. This book is designed to help you get out of that stressed state and function from a place of being centered.

When things feel *stressful* to us, this usually means that the demands of the situation exceed our available resources for coping. These resources can be psychological or physical—if you do not have the money to pay your mortgage, do not have the extra time to complete a massive collaborative project at work, or do not have the patience to handle 20 screaming toddlers for the afternoon, your situation will feel stressful to you. Sometimes we have resources available that we do not know how to obtain, and other times, we need to find a new way to handle the situation, but much of stress management is about maintaining the internal and external resources to help manage the stressors that come in life. I will be discussing that throughout this book as well.

Now that we have a clearer understanding of what we mean when we talk about *stress*, let's explore the different types of stress. Some kinds of stress can be good for us, other kinds can be detrimental, and they need to be handled differently. Because of this, it is important to understand what you are facing and to know what your goals are with stress management and what they should be.

Not All Stress Is the Same

When we read about stress in the media, most of what we read is negative. And when we talk about the stress in our lives, rarely are we extolling the virtues of this stress. Studies on the effects of stress generally document its detrimental effects. However, not all stress affects us the same way, and not all kinds of stress are bad for us! Most of us experience a mix of the following types of stress in our lives.

Eustress

This type of stress is actually beneficial to have in our lives. Eustress, which is Greek for "good stress," is the type of stress that keeps our lives exciting. This form of stress gets our blood pumping and puts us on the alert, as do other types of stress, but the feelings we experience from eustress are feelings of excitement. Eustress comes when we are being challenged in a beneficial way (not too much and not too little), or when we experience something we find to be stimulating. This can happen when we work toward a goal that is important to us, when we enjoy a lively party, or when we ride a roller coaster (for those of us who experience thrill rides as enjoyable rather than terrifying). Eustress is important for us to experience. Without the types of engaging, invigorating experiences that bring eustress, life would be less enjoyable and less meaningful, and we would be more prone to feelings of depression.

Not all news about eustress is good, however. The body does not discern between eustress and other, less enjoyable forms of stress (*dis*tress). As a result, eustress can cause wear and tear on the body and contribute to the cumulative total of stress that we experience. In this way, eustress can still have a negative impact. However, because eustress makes us feel vital and alive, it's best simply to be aware of the potential positive *and* negative effects of eustress and plan accordingly. For example, you may want to limit your thrill-seeking experiences if you are already under high levels of stress. Or you might balance the number of challenging projects you take on, no matter how much you would enjoy them individually, in order to keep eustress levels from becoming overwhelming. The key is to find a balance.

Acute Stress

Eustress is a subtype of acute stress, which, whether in the form of eustress or distress, is short-lived. It comes in the form of an event that demands a response—a challenging test, a mild fender-bender to deal with, a party to throw. Episodes of acute stress don't generally exact a heavy physical toll (unless they occur constantly) because they are over relatively quickly. Our bodies have a chance to recover, and we move on with our lives.

Nevertheless, it is a good idea to learn to manage the effects of acute stress by learning some quick stress relief techniques (see **Key** 2) if you find that you are not automatically returning to a state of relaxation once the acute stressor has passed. However, this is not the type of stress that typically requires a full stress management plan.

Episodic Stress

This type of stress comes when our acute stressors pile up. We begin to see a toll with this type of stress, simply because the body doesn't have a chance to return to normal levels of functioning as easily; the stress response remains triggered to a greater degree and for a longer period of time than it was designed for. This type of stress—as well as chronic stress—is the culprit that we are usually talking about when we discuss the negative effects of stress in all their multifaceted splendor. This type of stress seemingly does not let up. We experience it on a regular basis, with varying levels of intensity, so that we never quite have a chance to recover. We can generally feel this type of stress as "stressful," and we know when we are experiencing too much of it. Creating a stress management plan can be quite helpful for episodic stress, because not only can we then tackle and eliminate some of the situations that are causing these episodes of stress, but we can also develop ways to alter our reactions and coping style so we can experience less of the damage typical of too much stress.

Chronic Stress

This is the type of stress we feel when we are in an unpredictable and demanding job situation, a highly conflict-laden relationship, or living with a hectic schedule of difficult activities that allow for very little downtime. One key difference between episodic stress and chronic stress is that situations that bring chronic stress tend to feel overwhelming, and people experiencing chronic stress do not always see an immediate way out. When we experience chronic stress, we are at greater risk of losing all hope of finding solutions, and we may give up on trying. This type of stress feels so pervasive that when we are experiencing it, we may not even be aware of the extent of the stress and of the changes we experience because of it.

Chronic stress goes beyond what the human body was designed to handle. The stress response is carefully calibrated to handle threats to our well-being by motivating us to make changes and providing the burst of energy required to move us on our way. This response is designed to help us ward off dangerous predators and pull ourselves together to overcome obstacles that put our lifestyle in jeopardy. We were not designed to be in this state-of-emergency mode long-term, however. Remaining in this state for too long, or experiencing it with too much intensity, can cause damage to the body and can even create lasting changes in the mind. Those experiencing chronic stress are more likely to need therapeutic support in creating a plan to manage the stress, but the key pieces of information in this book can help. Beyond finding support from a therapist, which may or may not be part of the stress management plan for those experiencing chronic stress, there are other important actions to take as well, which will be discussed in this book.

The Sources of Stress

Stressors lurk in many places: at our jobs, in our relationships, among the tasks that make up our daily responsibilities and obligations. One definition of what leads to stress is "any situation that requires a response, adjustment, or change" from us in order for us to maintain balance, which includes a great many situations. That said, the situations that are experienced as most stressful hinge on our evaluation of them—that they require resources that we simply do not possess. This evaluation—the assessment that a given challenge demands more from us than we are able to give—may or may not be correct in the absolute sense of the word. In fact, part of what we experience as stressful comes from what we see, and part comes from how we look at things. To adequately manage stress, we must address both these issues—change the circumstances we can reasonably alter and adjust our ways of looking at and responding to the challenges that are left. There are many ways to accomplish these two goals, and this book shares the most effective among them and helps you to learn how to implement these strategies in your life.

The Effects of Stress

Stress affects us in many ways. It would be difficult to find a list that would name all the ways in which stress affects you, personally. There are two reasons for this difficulty: First, there are myriad ways in which an individual can be affected by stress; second, we are all unique in our responses. That said, there are several signs and symptoms that are commonly experienced by people under stress. The following may not be the only effects of stress you may face, but they are commonly experienced consequences of excessive stress.

* **Digestive issues.** Because the stress response is connected to the digestive system, stress can cause constipation, acid reflux, and

other digestive issues and can contribute to irritable bowel syndrome and Crohn's disease. Stress can also be related to obesity, which is linked to a host of other health issues.

* **Heart issues.** Short-term stress is related to a quicker pulse and to heart irregularities; long-term stress can lead to heart disease, higher cholesterol, arrhythmias, high blood pressure, increased risk of stroke, and other serious issues. Considering that heart disease is a top killer of both men and women, stress can present a serious threat to health.

* **Psychological issues.** Those facing heavy levels of stress are more likely to experience anxiety and depression, as well as other conditions. Stress can also affect our relationships, because we react differently when our stress response is triggered. These issues can affect quality of life, which, in turn, affects health.

* **Lowered immunity.** Studies show that people exposed to a brief stressor—a difficult math test, for example—were more likely to catch a cold when they were exposed to a cold virus a few minutes later. Other research has shown that those under heavier levels of stress experience slower rates of wound healing. As you can imagine, the effects of long-term stress are more pronounced, and the toll on immunity is heavier. This means that when under stress, you are more susceptible to virtually all environmental threats to your health.

Signs of Too Much Stress

Because stress affects us each in individual ways, there is no single clear way to tell when stress levels are too great. There are many signs, however, ranging from subtle to severe, that can paint a picture of our stress levels. One person may experience headaches or lethargy, while another person may find that excessive sweat is the first signal that stress levels have got out of hand. When subtle signs of stress are ignored, it is likely that symptoms will become more severe. First and foremost, if you *feel* that you are under too much stress, you *are*. Generally, it is much more common to fail to recognize how much stress one is experiencing than to believe stress levels are a problem when they are not. Aside from emotional feelings of stress, here are some other common signs and symptoms that point to high levels of stress:

* Excessive sweating
* Cold hands and feet
* Digestion issues (upset stomach, "butterflies," diarrhea)
* Emotional eating or loss of appetite
* Muscle tension, twitches, or shakes
* Quickened pulse or heart palpitations
* Nervous tics, nail-biting, hair-pulling
* Impatience, frustration, hostility
* Frequent headaches
* Feelings of depression
* Feelings of anxiety, panic, or being overwhelmed
* Lowered libido
* Difficulty with concentration or memory
* Feelings of exhaustion or lethargy
* Sleep issues

These are a few common signs of too much stress, although they are not the only ones. If you are experiencing any of these, or several at once, this book will be especially helpful.

Changes Can Make a Difference

This book is specifically about understanding stress, looking within, and making healthy changes. All three of these activities are important. If you do not have a foundation of understanding about stress and stress management, you may lack a sense of direction—knowing what changes can bring about stress relief—as well as a sense of motivation to change the status quo. If you do not look within yourself, you may not have an adequate understanding of which changes would work best for your particular situation, and you may not be able to adequately troubleshoot when you encounter roadblocks in your path toward change. And without making actual changes in your life—whether they are changes in your attitude, behaviors, or lifestyle structure—you will see no results. Here are some of the various types of changes you can make in your life and how they can affect your stress levels.

* **Change your level of stress.** You may not be able to eliminate all the stressors you face (nor would you want to), but you can lower the level of stress you have in your life. With stress relief techniques that help you to reverse or minimize your stress response (discussed in **Key 2**), as well as strategies for cutting down on some of the unnecessary stress in your life (addressed in **Key 5**), you can take your stress levels down a few notches, from *overwhelming* to *challenging* or from *frustrating* to *exciting*. For example, simply knowing how to take a mental break with a mini-meditation during your lunch break can help you to feel less stressed at work for hours afterward. This one change, with or without other stress management activities, can make a significant difference in how you feel on a day-to-day basis.

* **Change your attitude and perceptions.** Some stressors cannot be changed. However, we can change the way we think and feel about them and, in doing so, can alter the affect that these currently stressful situations have on us. For example, you may face many tasks at work that add up to a feeling of being overwhelmed. If you learn to face each one as its own *challenge* rather than seeing the entire situation as a *threat*, you can feel more empowered and less stressed when you go through your to-do list. In **Key 4**, we'll examine which thought patterns have the largest effect on our perceptions of stress and explore ways to alter these mental habits.

* **Increase your resources.** We feel stressed when we do not have the resources to handle a specific challenge. Learning how to increase your available resources—whether by enhancing your social circle (see how in **Key 6**), getting your body into a more

optimal level of fitness (discussed in **Key 3**), or even simply planning ahead with stress management (the **final chapter** of this book has a plan for this)—can help you to feel prepared. When you feel more prepared and empowered, the stressors you face have less of an effect on you.

* **Alter your level of resilience.** Even though some of what goes into our resilience to stress is just part of our personal makeup, there are many things we can do to raise our level of resilience. Taking on these changes can mean that whatever we face in life, we experience it as less stressful. **Key 8** covers three habits in particular that can help you to build a greater level of resilience to stress.

The Challenge of Change

An important thing to remember about stress management techniques is that they are effective only if you actually practice them (rather than just thinking about them or reading and then forgetting descriptions of them). Managing stress necessarily means making changes. Whether this change comes in the form of adding a new habit that can reduce your stress levels, working to eliminate a source of chronic stress in your life, actively altering your perspective and thought patterns, taking on a new routine that will build your resilience to stress, or practicing other stress management techniques that are covered in this book, you will be required to do something differently. This may present the biggest challenge.

Understanding or even learning these techniques will probably come more easily to most readers than will the act of practicing them on a long-term basis. This is because taking on new habits and changing behavior over a prolonged period can be difficult. Our minds tend to maintain the status quo. As we repeat behaviors, experiences, and even thought patterns, connections become strengthened in our neural pathways; behaviors become automatic, and we practice them without having to think.

An often-cited example of this type of automatic, unconscious way of thinking and behaving is in a drive to work. When you work in a new place, it takes an effort to find the address, and you may think about every turn you make. After you have made the drive a few times, you no longer have to check the directions; your path is familiar. After a few weeks or months, you may realize that you are not even thinking of where to turn; it's as if your mind is on autopilot, as you go where you need to go and attend to other things. (One day you may even find yourself driving to work without thinking, intending to go somewhere nearby. It actually requires thought to stop the automatic procession to your familiar destination.)

This is how the mind works with many things. If you are a habitually negative thinker, it may require some effort to think in a different way, but after a while, the new, positive thought patterns become habit. If you tend to say yes to too many obligations that put you in a state of episodic or chronic stress, it may take an effort to draw boundaries, until one day this becomes automatic. Every change you decide to make in the interest of stress management can become easier with practice. The trick is to create the new habit. This is when change presents a challenge.

The Stages of Change

Often when we try to make changes in our lives, we see ourselves as failing after a few weeks or months. The first few days or weeks are full of promise as we determinedly maintain the new habits, but after the initial excitement and burst of motivation wanes, life gets in the way and we face challenges that we may not overcome. This is where many of us slip up and call it quits. In fact, one study showed that 88% of people who make New Year's resolutions fail to follow them through. A high proportion of those who attempt to take on a new habit find themselves going back to old habits and giving up after a relatively short time, often within the first days or weeks of the attempt.

This may not come as surprising news—change is challenging, and if we all set out to do what we hoped to do, we would all be ultrafit, meticulously self-disciplined, and fabulously unfettered by stress. The more interesting point, however, is that these "failures" that cause many of us to give up are not actually failures at all. The only failure is that we have stopped trying. Backsliding on goals is part of the process of change, and it can even be a beneficial part of it, if you know how to use these slips to your advantage.

A New Model of Change

While most people think of the process of change as a two- or three-stage process (decide on a goal, go after the goal, achieve the goal), many therapists and wellness coaches follow a different model, which incorporates all of six stages! This model is known as the Transtheoretical Model of Change, named by its originator, Dr. James Prochaska, because it takes into account the processes of change observed across many different psychological theories and approaches, including psychoanalytic, humanistic, gestalt, cognitive, and behavioral. This approach is not "new" by most standards, as it dates back to 1994, but it is often experienced as a new concept by those seeking to enact a change. The stages are as follows:

1. **Precontemplation.** During this stage, you do not even realize you need to make a change. You may think you're just fine running yourself ragged and becoming sick once every few weeks as a result. You may think that the physical symptoms that come from too much stress are simply a part of living. At this stage, you're not looking to make any changes. New information is generally what it takes to raise your awareness and move you to the next stage.

2. **Contemplation.** In this stage, you are considering that you may have a problem and begin thinking seriously about solving it. You would like to get unstuck, and you may have a loose plan in your

head that you would like to follow in the next 6 months or so. You may think that perhaps you should consider exercising more, when things calm down in your life. You may want to get more sleep when you can find the time or may want to cut out some of the unnecessary stressors you face, when you have a chance to really think about it. At this stage, you recognize the value in making a change, but you are not ready to make a real change yet. You may stay in this stage indefinitely, as the motivation to change needs to be strong enough to propel you into action, which can be difficult when you are already feeling overwhelmed. The time when you need to focus on stress management may be the exact same time that you feel too stressed to take on something new. What moves you to the next state of readiness is a focus on the solution rather than the problem, and a focus on the future rather than the past. (And the baby steps you will find in this book can ease you into it!)

3. **Preparation.** Here, you are planning to take action in the next month, and you are making the final tweaks to your plan. You may still need to convince yourself that taking action is really what is best for you before you dive into the next stage. You may make a few small changes in this stage, in preparation for a big leap. For example, you may start cutting out caffeine after 2:00 P.M. as you start preparing to get more sleep and take better care of yourself. You may learn a few breathing exercises as you start to think about how some bigger changes might bring even greater stress management benefits. Once you really understand that you need to make changes for the sake of your health, happiness, and future, you may feel pressed to make many changes, effective immediately. Do not rush yourself out of this stage before you are ready; focus on creating a plan that you feel will really work, and you will have greater chances of success.

4. **Action.** Now you are actively making the change! This is the most obvious stage of change, and it feels great. You may be exercising or meditating on a daily basis, may be clearing your schedule to allow for some downtime, or may be taking on other daily

habits to help with stress relief. This is an exciting phase of change! However, the danger here occurs when people feel that they have completed their transformation once they have maintained new habits for a few days. At this phase, if you experience any fluctuations in your success, you may perceive them as failure and then lose motivation. Do not forget: In the action phase, you are not at the end of the road—yet.

5. **Maintenance.** This phase, according to Dr. Prochaska, can be short, lasting perhaps several months, but can also persist throughout one's life. This stage involves the critically important process of coming back from relapse and adjusting plans. Temptations show up, willpower runs thin; this is to be expected and accounted for in the maintenance stage. You may get so busy at work that you skip a few workout sessions and lose your momentum. You may succumb to sleepiness at night and miss your journaling practice, or you may just forget to practice breathing exercises before you get to a place where you feel overwhelmed. You may start to feel that your new plans worked for a while, but your stress is just too great; in other words, you may take these setbacks to mean that your plans aren't working. Rather than being disappointed and discouraged if you see this happening, you can expect it, and move back to your target goal with your head held high.

6. **Termination.** This is the goal of change. The termination phase occurs when you no longer feel any temptation to go back to your prechange habits, and maintaining the change is truly effortless. This means that you automatically work out each day, just as you eat regular meals. You instinctively calm yourself with breathing exercises or visualizations. You don't go to sleep at night without writing in your gratitude journal. At this stage of the change process, you no longer need to work at it, or the level of work required is not something that requires specific focus—it just happens naturally. (Note: some experts believe that this phase never comes, especially for certain habits such as smoking. However, many others experience this stage and see it in others, so this is the ultimate goal.)

Why You Have Never *Really* Failed

If you notice the fifth stage—maintenance, which involves coming back after a relapse—you'll see that what we normally deem as "failure" is really just part of the process. Think about it—when babies learn to walk, there are *many* falls on the way to success. We don't expect perfection on the first try from a baby, and we shouldn't expect it from ourselves, either. Sometimes those "falls" can be quite helpful—they can show us what we may need to change about our plans. A good coach or therapist uses these commonly occurring experiences to glean information that can be used in the continuing process of change for clients. Such experiences let us know where our obstacles lie and, in doing so, can help us to make contingency plans for our next efforts. They let us know how we are progressing, by seeing if we progressed farther this time before we slipped, for example. They can let us know if we are setting the right plans in motion or if we need to meet our ultimate goals in a different way. The only way they spell failure is if we decide to quit because these slips have happened. And the reasoning behind quitting when you face a setback comes from not realizing that the setbacks are part of the path to success.

How to Use This Book

Ideally, you would be coming to this book with plenty of time and energy to read it thoroughly, fully explore all the resources that it includes, put together a plan, and carefully follow through on it. However, life doesn't always allow for that. You may have just a few minutes here and there, or you may need to start feeling relief from your stress more quickly (like *today*), or you may have other challenges that prevent you from being able to take this optimally thorough approach.

This is okay!

This book is set up to be effective and enjoyable when used in

a variety of different ways. You can choose from any of the following options.

Read Through from Beginning to End

This book has been laid out specifically so that you will find information in the order that it is most effective. I start off with a foundation—a solid understanding of stress and how it can affect
you—and then explore different layers of stress management techniques that can build on each other. If you read this book in the
order in which it is written, answering questions and trying techniques as you go, you will be walked through a program that works,
in an order that is easy to process.

Skip Around and Read What You Feel You Need

You may have picked up this book with a specific issue in mind. If
you flipped to the table of contents to see how to manage relationship issues, for example, you will find that that chapter can stand
alone. Each section can be helpful to you if that is the only section
you read. (If I refer to concepts discussed in other chapters, I will
generally let you know the important parts of the concept and
point you to where to go to find out more.) So if you like to skip,
don't feel bad about it.

If you are a skipper, however, I would encourage you to read
all of the chapters that call out to you and take a look at the ones
that you think may not apply. The chapter on positive psychology,
for example, might not be the reason you picked up the book (as
you may not have known about this branch of psychology before),
but you may find that the study of happiness has a lot to show you
about stress management that you never realized you needed to
know. You may be looking at quick ways to relieve stress immediately, but later realize that long-term, resilience-forming habits
can help you to manage your stress even more effectively. So if
you have the urge to skip through, by all means go to the chapters
that carry the most appeal first; but don't discount the other chap-

ters. You never know what information might be more helpful than you would ever expect.

Skip to the "How to Manage" and "Activities to Try" Sections

This book provides a considerable amount of information on stress, the factors that contribute to it, and the ways in which we can manage it. You will find that developing an understanding of all three of these points is most effective in developing a comprehensive stress management plan. However, if you are short on time and feeling eager to have a place to start quickly, you can skip to the "How to Manage" sections and find ideas on how to make changes in your life right now. These sections focus on changes that can be made, rather than reasons why changes are needed, or other information about these potential changes. For specific step-by-step instructions on new techniques, skip to the "Activities to Try." They are most effective when read in context, but these activities can be effective à la carte as well. If you are looking for new ways to manage stress, these are the key places in this book where you will find them.

Put Exploration Questions into Action

With each of these keys, I have included information on the topic itself and how to enact changes, but I have personalized the concepts by including "exploration questions" that allow you to look inward and see how these concepts apply to your life. These questions allow you to personalize the information and start putting what you have learned into practice. You may choose to explore the questions one at a time or all in one sitting. I strongly recommend that you actually answer them on paper (or in a file on your computer) so that you can not only fully explore the answers that come from within but also have a record of what your answers were. However, if this does not feel comfortable for you, it can still be helpful to mentally answer the questions. The important point is that you are thinking about how these concepts apply to your own life and identifying ways in which you can transform the realizations into action to create positive changes in your life. The answers can help you to remember the key concepts that have resonated most deeply with you. They can also help you to maintain your motivation to make changes in your life and help you gauge how far you have come as you journey forward.

Take On One or Two Changes at a Time

There is a lot of information presented here, and it can be tempting to try to make many changes immediately. This can be overwhelming. Taking on too much at once can put you in danger of feeling burned out on change and wanting to give up.

That is why it is important to pace yourself. In the final chapter of the book, I explore ways to create a cohesive stress management plan and to move forward with it in a way that can ensure the greatest level of success. For now, though, there are a few simple concepts to keep in mind about moving forward. One of them is to consider limiting yourself to one or two major changes at a time. This is not to say that if you are reading about breathing exercises and find that they come naturally, you should put the book away and practice only breathing for a while. However, if you are tackling a significant change such as altering your thought patterns or systematically eliminating stressors from your life, you may consider focusing mainly on that, at least until it feels comfortable to continue. If you pile on a new exercise regimen, alterations in your diet, and daily meditation classes, you may find it all to be too much.

Use the Final Chapter Resources Anytime

As you read through this book, make a note of which techniques seem to beckon you. Which ones might fit best with your personality? Which might make the biggest impact in your life? Which could be most beneficial? You can make notes in the back of this book so you don't forget. There is also information on worksheets in the final chapter that can help you to organize your thoughts. You can use those worksheets as you read the book, or you can read everything and then reflect on everything at once. Either way, you have resources in the end to help you to identify and target the change or changes that will work best for you, at the pace that will be most beneficial. Stress management should not be stressful; it can require some effort in the beginning, but by maintaining balance, you can experience the process as a comfortable one.

KEY 1

BECOME AWARE OF YOUR STRESSORS

Worry often gives a small thing a big shadow.　　　—SWEDISH PROVERB

It's never too late to be what you might have been.　　　—GEORGE ELIOT

Stress is a regular—even healthy—part of life. Although it can be beneficial in many situations, it is detrimental in others. Understanding the subtleties of stress, and having a clear understanding of its causes and effects, can greatly help you to use this book. This chapter will provide you with a quick overview of different types of stress and of the main effects of stress on your body, mind, and overall health. You will also learn the most effective ways to use the book and to put what you learn here into practice for maximum benefit in your life.

When we're faced with a looming deadline, a difficult social situation, or an immediate challenge, the source of our stress is clear. But more often, we experience stress from multiple sources and experience it with such frequency that we are less aware of where the stress is coming from and of how we are being affected by it. This chapter will cover the signs and symptoms of stress in detail. It will examine common sources, such as jobs, relationships, and hectic schedules. The chapter will empower you to better recognize the sources of your stress and its impact and will list questions you can ask yourself to assess your stress levels, so you can gain a clearer idea of how to combat it.

Frustration Coming from All Sides

Madeline felt frustrated. Little things were upsetting her. Events that normally would barely even register as stressful or annoying—someone cutting in line at the grocery store, a series of phone calls interrupting her workflow—were enough to create strong frustration and anger. In response to these relatively minor triggers, she would snap at people around her and stay in a bad mood for quite some time. This would leave her feeling more frustrated and angry, because she had fewer positive experiences with friends and co-workers throughout the day during these times, and this would contribute to her general feelings of stress. For Madeline, life started to feel more and more difficult, as if everything she experienced was simply becoming more stressful. Frustration seemed to be coming from all sides.

Upon further exploration, the reasons behind this became more clear to Madeline. At first, she thought her agitation was merely a response to the stressors at hand—the difficult people who seemed to surround her. However, as we discussed her experience and explored what she was feeling, it became apparent that there was more going on under the surface. Madeline was reacting to a series of bigger challenges she had faced earlier in the month: She had learned that her son was struggling in school, and because of financial difficulties that had just gone from bad to worse she was dodging calls from bill collectors. She had not forgotten about these stressful events, but had not realized the toll that they were taking on her ability to cope with minor stressors. Once she realized that the challenges she faced were putting her into a more or less constant state of stress, Madeline was able to find more patience as she focused her energy on brainstorming solutions to her challenges and practicing coping techniques for the added stress they brought. While these issues did not have easy answers, once she understood the extent of the stress that they brought, she had a greater ability to manage it.

Why Awareness Is Necessary

As someone reading a book on stress management, you are likely aware that stress may be an issue in your life. So why have I included a whole chapter on becoming aware of stress? Because we have to understand where our stress comes from, as well as how it is affecting us, in order to know what to do to manage this stress. And understanding the source of our stress is sometimes less clear than it would seem. In fact, recognizing the extent of one's stress can be surprisingly difficult.

When our lives are relatively stress free, a stressful event stands out. (Remember those acute stressors mentioned in the Introduction?) In a relatively low-stress lifestyle, a new stressor presents a contrast with what we are used to, so it becomes relatively easy to feel the stress that it presents and to know where this stress came from. However, as we face an increasing number of stressors (moving from acute to episodic stress), we tend to be triggered much more often.

It becomes more difficult to recognize where our stress comes from as stress becomes increasingly abundant in our lives, for a few reasons. First, with several sources of stress, we may just feel "triggered." We may be able to name a few sources of our stress — perhaps the most pressing and obvious sources — but we may miss some of the other, more subtle areas of life that are stressing us.

In addition, once we are operating from a place of feeling stressed, we tend to react to things differently, in ways that exacerbate what we are already feeling, and create additional problems. (I cover this in more detail later in this book.) That means that stress that originated in one area of life can easily move to a different area. You may not notice the stress that you are feeling until it gains momentum in other areas of your life, so you may miss some of the initial stress triggers that created the cycle in the first place.

Finally, once we reach a state of chronic stress, we may actually become less aware of individual sources of stress. In what psychologists call *learned helplessness*, we may have learned that our attempts to escape the stressful situation we face are futile, may have accepted this state of constant stress as normal, and may not be attempting to change it anymore. We may be less aware of when we are stressed and when we aren't, because we generally feel low-grade stress almost constantly. We may not be aware of specific sources because the stress seems to come from everyone, and it affects most of the main areas of our lives at this stage. (For example, stress from work affects our relationships if we are short-tempered from a difficult day, poor relationships can affect our health, and health concerns create more stress and can cause obstacles at work.) It becomes a self-perpetuating cycle. In what follows, I discuss in more detail a few of the ways in which stress builds upon itself.

Becoming more aware of where the stress is coming from can help us to better manage it, particularly when we experience higher and more constant levels of stress. Examining the most common sources of stress can help—when you read about the types of stressors that many people face, your biggest stressors will likely become evident as what you read resonates with your experience. You may wish to take notes as you read about these stressors and realize which ones are affecting your life, or you may decide to read first and examine your stressors all together afterward. Either strategy works, so try what works for you.

Common Sources of Stress in Our Lives

Stress can come from many sources and affect people in different ways. The end of a relationship can be a freeing experience for one person and a crushing one for another. Even the experience of sitting at a desk and working while the sounds of birds and lawnmowers come in through an open window can feel soothing to one person and frustrating to another. Because of this variation, we cannot say for certain which experiences are inherently stressful to everyone, and to what degree.

That said, surveys have shown that certain experiences tend to feel particularly stressful for many people and that certain situations are more commonly experienced as stressful. The following are some of the top sources of stress that people commonly experience. This is not an exhaustive list, but when you are looking at where the stress may be coming from in your life, here are some popular culprits.

Work

Many people cite work as one of their biggest stressors, and there are many reasons for this. Given that most of us spend a large proportion of our time at work, jobs are often closely tied to our personal identities, our finances, and our lifestyles as a whole. This makes our work lives quite influential on our overall well-being. People with jobs that have certain characteristics are at risk for higher levels of stress, as well as an increased risk of burnout, anxiety, and depression. Here are some of the most serious on-the-job stressors.

Unclear Requirements

When workers aren't clear on the extent of their responsibilities, it becomes difficult for them to fulfill these obligations. This is obvious, but there are many work situations with unclear requirements, where workers know that they have missed something only when it becomes a problem. When people are not clear on what their jobs entail, they can be asked to do things that are not their responsibility, and they may be unsure if they can refuse. They can work hard all day and never know if they have done enough. They can find themselves feeling insecure or resentful and not know what to do about it. Particularly when those in charge are not clear communicators, this can present a stressful dynamic.

During difficult economic times, when companies are downsizing and workers who remain are given job responsibilities that were formerly handled by others, this can become even more of an issue. People may find themselves expected to do more than they were originally hired to do, or they may feel that their jobs will be in jeopardy if they do not offer to take on extra tasks. This can inject additional pressure into an already stressful work situation.

How to Manage

If you find yourself in a job where requirements are unclear, you may not even realize that this is a significant source of stress—you may simply be aware that you feel stressed at work, and aren't sure how to meet all the demands. If an unclear job description is part of the problem, be sure to talk to whoever is in charge and see if you can get (in writing) clarification on these issues. If you are self-employed, be sure to take the reins in communication and clarify with your clients what their expectations are, letting them know what they can expect from you. (Read more about communication and boundary setting in **Key 6**.)

Unattainable Demands

In other job situations, the demands are clear but impossible to meet. Workers may be expected to get more work done than time permits or to do work that requires resources they do not have. This type of situation becomes disheartening, because workers feel overwhelmed and eventually consider giving up. Situations like these can pose a threat to self-esteem, to feelings of job security, and to hope for any sense of accomplishment.

Again, this is a situation where self-awareness becomes very important. People in jobs in which there are unrealistic demands can feel very stressed if they do not realize that the demands are unattainable, and do something about it. They may feel that the work is draining and difficult, but realizing that it is unrealistic to be able to complete it can actually be a relief.

How to Manage

It is helpful if you can look at your situation objectively and see that the expectations placed on you are unrealistic. Perhaps the worst thing we can do is to hold ourselves to unrealistic demands and judge ourselves for not measuring up, rather than recognizing when something is simply not possible. If you find yourself in a job situation where you believe that the demands are unrealistic, it is important to talk to your boss about this and see if you can objectively show what it is about the job that might be unreasonable. If you are a freelance worker, you may have to have a talk with yourself and adjust your own expectations. Communication with clients and boundary setting are also crucial. (Again, see **Key 6**.) Because attempting to meet impossible demands can be so disheartening and can induce burnout and depression, this is a situation that should be addressed in whatever way is feasible.

Low Recognition

Job situations that offer low compensation, that are considered menial, or that in other ways fail to provide a payoff for the required efforts can be disheartening and stress inducing. When things happen at work that cause people to feel that they are not respected for the work they do, this can damage self-esteem, motivation, and drive, making a job feel more challenging and draining. It is not necessarily about ego gratification as much as it is about feelings of being valued. Feeling a sense of unfairness about being passed over for promotions; feeling belittled by a manager, co-worker, or clients; and feeling taken advantage of are all stressful feelings that can contribute to feelings of chronic stress and a lack of satisfaction with a job.

How to Manage

If you feel a lack of recognition in your job, there may be ways to create recognition in your life without having to change jobs in order to get it. If talking to your manager, boss, or company's human resources department doesn't work, you can create a supportive network of friends and co-workers, and you can congratulate one another on your accomplishments. Consider having a regular lunch meeting where you all share what you are most proud of (and take turns figuratively patting each other on the back) or get other support with your challenges—it may sound unnecessary, but therapists and coaches commonly have supportive groups like this, because they can be very beneficial. You may also simply have a supportive friend or two with whom you can exchange celebratory phone calls. Another option would be to have a hobby outside of work that provides this positive feedback that we all need, even if it is not directed toward your accomplishments at your job. The point to remember is that lack of appreciation can be a stressor in any job, and steps can be taken to manage that stress.

Another option that can be quite effective for alleviating stress in a situation like this is to find deeper meaning in your job. If you can recognize ways in which your job benefits others, for example, the job becomes more important than just the tasks involved, and doing the work takes on greater significance, even if the tasks themselves are not intrinsically enjoyable.

High Penalties for Mistakes

In fields like medicine or transportation, there is necessarily a narrow margin for error—if mistakes are made, people can die. These are not the only fields in which there are highly negative consequences that accompany mistakes; some companies will fire people for small errors, certain managers will berate employees when mistakes are made, and in other situations, the consequences are simply part of the job that cannot be changed. Freelancers and business owners may lose customers when small errors are made, and those unhappy customers may be vocal in their dissatisfaction.

Whether the penalties are the decision of the company or simply part of the job, work situations that allow for few mistakes can be unnerving. They can keep us in a constant state of vigilance and bring feelings of self-doubt and insecurity. After a while, the pressure can take a toll.

How to Manage

There is not a lot that can be done to manage situations like those described above, other than to take care of ourselves so that we are functioning at our best (see **Key 5** for more on this) and manage our stress as effectively as possible so we can handle a little extra stress from such jobs.

Lack of Challenge

It would seem that an unchallenging job would bring relief from stress, but certain types of jobs that lack challenge can actually be *more* stressful than jobs that present a greater level of challenge. This is because we naturally crave growth, and it can feel good to do work that uses our unique strengths. (See more about this in **Key** 7 in the section on gratifications.) People actually tend to feel less stress when performing tasks that present just the right level of challenge—not so much that the work is stressful, but not so little that it becomes painfully boring and meaningless. Those who work at jobs that are repetitive and unchallenging may find them-selves dreading going to work. This is not as heavy a stressor as some of the others discussed here, but it can certainly take a toll.

How to Manage

If you find yourself at a job that does not use your strengths or chal-lenge you, there may be a simple fix. Putting time into hobbies that do challenge you when you are not working may provide you with the stimulation you need to feel more balanced in your life as a whole. In this case, more of a challenge means less of a feeling of stress.

Relationships

Relationships can bring us the best of times and the worst of times. While often beneficial to our health and happiness, our relation-ships can also present obstacles that are frequently cited as main stressors in people's lives. While we discuss the interplay between our relationships and stress in further detail in **Key 6**, there are a few relevant points to remember here when it comes to relation-ships as a stressor. The following are types of relationships that can be stressful.

Toxic Relationships

It can be highly stressful to be in relationships in which we are not respected. When we are subject to frequent criticism, gossip, unrealistic demands, contempt, mocking, and other negative experiences—when we do not feel safe being ourselves—we may not realize the toll it takes on us. Likewise, in relationships in which we find ourselves not being our best, it can be bad not only for us but also for other people in our lives. We may become used to the situation, may fail to recognize the damage that is done, and may neglect to do anything to change the circumstances we are in. Relationships that habitually make us feel bad about ourselves can be constant sources of stress, because they can lead to negative rumination, feelings of low self-esteem, conflicts to constantly resolve, and other threats to our happiness and self-worth.

Caregiver Situations

People who are in constant charge of the welfare of loved ones are exposed to a particularly intense level of stress, the severity of which varies according to the level of needs that the caregivers must meet. Regardless of how much caretakers may love their relatives, the responsibilities can be draining, and the feelings associated with them can exacerbate the stress experienced from the workload.

When children are small, they require a nearly constant level of care and involvement. Studies show that marital satisfaction declines in those early years of parenthood as parents work to meet these demands. While young children ideally share a close bond with their parents or caretakers, the feeding, changing, chasing, tantrums, and other demands that are part and parcel of caring for small children can take a toll and create stress.

Those who are caring for sick, disabled, or elderly relatives often experience similarly high levels of stress. In fact, this type of stress can be much more taxing. First, it can be emotionally difficult to contend with the reality that a loved one is in need of constant support; caregivers feel for their loved ones and would prefer to see them healthy and able-bodied for their own sake.

Needing care can be difficult on these loved ones as well, and caregivers often feel this, perhaps feeling guilt over their own feelings of stress in the situation. The workload can be even more difficult than that of caring for small children, because it can be unexpected, emotionally draining, and more physically demanding to deal with an adult who needs help with basic self-care, medical procedures, and other challenges.

Caregivers may feel even more stress if they experience guilt for their feelings of exhaustion and being overwhelmed. However, even the most loving caregivers are human, and sometimes the demands of meeting another person's needs can take a toll on our ability to meet our own.

How to Manage

Getting support—both emotional and practical—and carving out time for self-care are vital for stress management at this stage. Ideally, the responsibility of caregiving should be shared among several people so that no one person becomes burned out. Involving siblings in the care of an elderly parent or dividing responsibility among spouses and perhaps using outside resources in caring for a child with special needs can ensure that each caregiver has the opportunity to adequately care for his or her own needs. However, there are not always others who are willing or able to help. Fortunately, there are support groups for parents and caregivers in the community, and getting acquainted with these resources can make quite a difference. If you are feeling overwhelmed as a caregiver, I encourage you to take action now by researching resources (others you can trust and support groups in your community) that can help.

Hectic Schedules

Overwhelmed seems to be the new normal for many people. We, as a society, have begun to expect much more from ourselves in recent years than was the case for previous generations. Many people find themselves working longer hours than ever before, and often working more than one job. We fail to take vacations when they are offered. One recent survey found that only 45% of respondents planned to take a vacation over the summer—the lowest percentage in the survey's 11-year history—and of those, only 35% planned to take longer trips; most were expecting to take only the weekend for their vacation.

We fill our spare time with more responsibilities, and then we wonder why we are exhausted (or perhaps we have stopped wondering or even recognizing it).

How to Manage

Becoming aware of the hectic pace of our lives can be a first step toward carving out a more reasonable lifestyle, but sometimes it takes looking seriously at our schedules to realize that we have had too much, and to know which activities to cut out. One way to take an honest look and begin the process of optimizing your schedule is to create a thorough schedule for yourself, if you haven't already. Rather than merely listing your major commitments, find a calendar application that you can use on your computer (I like iCal and Google Calendar), and list *all* the things that make up your schedule. Block out and label how much time it takes you to get ready in the morning, how much time you spend driving, and even your relaxation time, and see where your time is committed. For an even more accurate picture of where your time currently goes, you can check in with the calendar throughout the day and see if you are actually doing what you are projecting you do each day. Plotting out a detailed schedule like this can allow you to really see where your time goes and to more clearly see where time may be wasted or discern which activities are not really serving your goals and life satisfaction. (We cover time management more thoroughly in **Key 5**, but becoming aware of when we are overcommitted is a first step.)

Health

Stress and health are closely linked. Stress can affect our health, as I mentioned earlier in this chapter, and health issues can bring considerable stress. In fact, dealing with health issues represents one of the bigger stressors that people face. With longer life expectancies and greater medical advances, we tend to experience more chronic illnesses (such as heart disease and cancer) than infections and viral diseases, which claimed more lives a century ago (and, interestingly, virtually all these chronic illnesses have direct or indirect links to stress, among other risk factors). The stress of living with chronic conditions and serious health threats can touch not only those who experience the stress but also their friends and family. And conditions that are less serious can take a toll as well.

How to Manage

The knowledge that we need to take care of our health can weigh heavily on our minds when we are stressed and too overwhelmed to make the best choices. The reality of dealing with a serious health condition brings much more stress. The best thing we can do is to carve out time to be proactive about remaining healthy, find support where possible, and practice stress management techniques to support our overall health and wellness. Picking up this book (and reading it) is a very important first step that you have already taken. Following the advice in **Key 3** on taking care of your body, and the tips in **Key 8** for maintaining resilience-promoting habits can be your best bet for enhancing overall health and wellness.

Life Adjustments

As I discussed in the Introduction, one of the most often cited characterizations of stress is that it results from any situation that requires a response from us. This means that events in our lives that are both positive and negative can bring stress—it simply comes from having to formulate a response. Different life events take a heavier or lighter toll, but each event can cause stress. One of the more popular ways to measure stress in a person's life is by using the Holmes and Rahe Stress Scale (named after the psychologists who created it), which names 43 stressful life events and weighs each according to the amount of stress that it creates and its likelihood of leading to associated illness. The scale is scored by tallying the "value" of each of the events that have occurred in the past year. While this scale may not present a perfect measure of stress experienced (for example, a divorce or a death in the family may have a heavier impact on one person than on another, depending on the relationships involved), it does provide a reliable general measure and a clear basic picture. It also demonstrates the point that each event in our lives can take a toll on our overall stress levels. The list includes events as obviously stressful as "death of a spouse," "divorce," and "incarceration"; midlevel stressors like "change in frequency of arguments" and "change to a different line of work" and relatively benign events like "change in eating habits" and "vacation." While the scale helps to provide a clearer picture of how much stress has been encountered in the past year, simply looking at your life and assessing the events that have brought the most stress can help you to get more in touch with where your stress is coming from. This can be effective because you may have a clear understanding of exactly what impact each event has had on you, based on personal factors and other issues that are going on in your life. Looking at the stressful events in the past year or so also helps you to get into the frame of mind that can allow you to become more aware of your stressors and become more proactive in handling them. Which types of stressful events have you faced in the past year, and what toll do you think they have had?

Attitudes and Perspectives

We don't always realize it, but the way in which we perceive and process our lives can actually be a source of stress in itself. When we look more closely at the negatives than at the positives of a situation, we can experience it as more threatening and, therefore, more stressful. When we dwell on negative events in our lives, we exacerbate the stress we are feeling. When we approach various situations in our lives as competitions for perfection, feeling a need to best those around us and beating ourselves up for anything short of an impossible ideal, we can cause unnecessary stress in ourselves and in those around us. I explore this in greater detail in **Key 4**; the important thing to note here is that becoming aware of these thought patterns is vital. If we don't realize that our patterns of thinking can have an effect on our stress levels, we are trapped in a dynamic that follows us wherever we go and magnifies the stress that we experience in our lives. Here are three main thinking patterns to be aware of:

* **Rumination.** This involves dwelling on the negative, particularly when there is nothing you can do about it. It is natural to want to fix problems as they arise, but rumination is a negative and unproductive form of dwelling on things in our lives that are already causing us stress. Rumination can eat up hours of what could have been a more pleasant day.

* **Negative thinking.** Focusing on the negative in a situation, expecting things to go wrong, explaining away the positive things that happen in life—these are all patterns of negative thinking. If you find yourself zeroing in on the pessimistic side of things, you can save yourself a lot of stress if you stop. Noticing this pattern is the first step.

* **Cognitive distortions.** There are several types of cognitive distortions (again, discussed in detail in **Key 4**). The link between them is that they ignore a vital piece of reality, and they cause stress. These patterns of distorted thinking are automatic and designed by the psyche to protect people from stressful realities; unfortunately, they tend to cause more stress in the long run than they eliminate in the present. Notice if you begin to discount certain realities, convince yourself that you are "right" in situations without objective proof, or otherwise distort in your mind

what is objectively happening around you. Facing things the way they actually are is ultimately less stressful.

Activity to Try: Become More Aware of Your Sources of Stress

After reading about the main sources of stress that people experience, and what about them makes them most stressful, you may already have a clearer picture of where the stress in your life is coming from, and you may have some ideas about where to start in managing your stress. The following exercises can help you move further along in the process of unearthing the origins of your stress and of creating a list of which major areas to address when answering the question, Where do I begin?

Activity to Try: Maintain a Stress Journal

It can be quite helpful to maintain a running list of the stressors in your life, as a way to track where your main stressors and energy drains lie and to enable you to create a plan for managing them. When maintaining a stress journal, you may simply reflect on your day each evening and record what seemed to be the biggest stressors you encountered. Over the course of a few days, you will notice patterns that point to the chronic stressors in your life, as well as the most taxing situations you face. As you record what you face with regularity, you will likely notice more of what is taking a toll and can be motivated to make changes that can stop the stress.

Schedule Periodic Check-Ins

Maintaining a stress journal can be a very useful tool for identifying sources of stress. However, we sometimes tend to put more emphasis on some types of events when we look back over the day, and we fail to remember other stressors that played a role. For example, if you have a stressful commute to work because you are engaging in rumination about the day before, you may set yourself up for a more stressful day at the office, perhaps even making mistakes that you wouldn't have made if you were in a more relaxed state. Looking back over your day, you may not remember that the ride in was stressful because of what you were thinking about, or may not even remember the ride as being stressful at all. However, the effects are there, and this is a situation that should be addressed.

In cases like this, it can be helpful to periodically check in with yourself throughout the day and notice what is causing you stress from hour to hour. This is a practice sometimes used in studies on stress, and it can be effective for short-term use as you examine the areas of your life that are bringing the greatest levels of stress. Simple, periodic check-ins can take a few minutes here and there, and this system can accomplish two goals: It can help you to become more aware of what is stressing you, so that you can begin to make changes that will help the most, and it can help you to immediately change what you are doing in cases where that is possible. (For example, in the scenario we just discussed, you may have been immediately less likely to continue in rumination if you were reminded that you were doing so.)

Check-ins can be simple. You can set an alarm to go off every hour or half hour or at whatever interval you choose, and simply gauge how you are feeling and why as the alarm goes off. Recording what you are experiencing in your stress journal can work well here, although you can still gain some insight by simply stopping and assessing.

A typical stress check-in log might look like this:

9:00 A.M. Drove to work, and found myself ruminating about what Angelina said yesterday.
10:00 A.M. Found myself cleaning up a mess that Jenkins made with a client last week.
11:00 A.M. Just caught myself daydreaming instead of working. I'm more exhausted than I realized.

Another way to do this is to notice how you feel and why at various natural stopping points throughout your day: when you arrive at work (or school, or back home from driving your kids), when you take a midmorning break, when you have lunch, and so on. By becoming more aware of how you feel and when, you can spot stressors that you may have simply accepted, and you can see if you are able to eliminate them from your life.

Try Lifestyle Scan Meditation

Helpful in providing more immediate answers on what is stressing you, this exercise takes about 5 minutes. While journaling about stress in real time or over the course of a few weeks may yield a more accurate picture of your situation, this can work more quickly and supply you with some answers as well.

1. Take a minute to relax. Find a quiet room, get comfortable, and close your eyes.
2. Vividly imagine going through your day. In your mind's eye, see yourself getting up in the morning and getting ready, then going through the activities you would normally perform in the course of a day. Imagine getting dressed, driving to work or school, or whatever you do in your day.
3. With each imagined activity, note how you feel about what you are thinking about. Do you feel a touch of anxiety when thinking about the drive to work? Do you find yourself tempted to ruminate about the difficult co-worker at the office? Do you feel a touch of anxiety when you think about helping your child with homework or meeting up with your significant other? The feelings you have during this visualization exercise will not be as intense as they would be in real life, so you need to be sensitive to what comes up for you—notice which areas of life feel stressful when you think about them.
4. Write this down. You may want to explore your feelings on paper after the visualization portion of this exercise, or you may simply want to make a note of the areas of your life that feel stressful and

move on from there. This list will come in handy as you go through the next keys and start formulating a plan to manage the stress.

Ask a Friend

Even if you are not sure what is causing you the greatest amounts of stress in your life, there are people who can likely tell you: your friends and family. Think of the people you talk to the most, and the most candidly. What would they say brings you the most stress? Bluntly put, what do they hear you complain about the most? Think about what they might say—and if you're not sure, you may want to ask them!

Rate the Main Areas of Your Life for Stress

Imagine each of the following areas of your life and rate the stress that they cause on a scale of 1 to 10, with 1 meaning that they bring no stress, and 10 meaning that they bring unbearable stress. On the lines below each main topic or on a separate sheet of paper, add what parts of this aspect of your life may bring the most stress. (For example, under "job stress" you may list "lack of recognition," or "impossible workload"; under "relationship stress," you may list the name of the person who seems to cause the greatest level of stress.)

1. Job stress ____
    a. _____
    b. _____
    c. _____
2. Relationship stress ____
    a. _____
    b. _____
    c. _____
3. Stress in my weekly schedule ____
    a. _____
    b. _____

    c. _____

4. Stress and my health ____

    a. _____

    b. _____

    c. _____

5. Stressful events of the past year ____

    a. _____

    b. _____

    c. _____

6. Stress and my thought patterns ____

    a. _____

    b. _____

    c. _____

Questions to Ask Yourself

* What aspects of my job trigger stress?
* What areas of my relationships feel stressful?
* Which friends and loved ones tend to contribute to conflict in my life?
* Do I feel that I am too busy?
* What commitments in my life tend to bring stress? And in what way?
* What aspects of my health might be causing stress?
* Am I taking care of my body well enough?
* What events in my life have caused the most stress during the past year?
* Is my attitude helping or hurting me?
* Are there any ways that I might be creating more stress for myself with the way I think about things?

Evaluate Your Answers

As you look over your answers to these questions, you will likely see a pattern. You may find that the same issues are coming up multiple times. If you are going through a divorce or a change in employment, this may show up in your answers; if the situation is stressful enough, you may find that most of your answers have something to do with this situation. Or perhaps some of the questions bring answers that have a strong emotional component for you, and other questions feel benign. These questions are meant to bring your awareness to the issues that are affecting you the most, so if you find that certain topics are really resonating with you, these are the issues to focus the most attention on, when possible. For example, if you read the question "Do I feel I am too busy?" and have a lukewarm response, time management may not be an issue for you; if you feel like screaming yes! at the page as you read the words, you may want to put special attention into time management, which is covered in **Key 5.**

KEY 2

LEARN TO QUICKLY REVERSE YOUR STRESS RESPONSE

Tension is who you think you should be. Relaxation is who you are.
—CHINESE PROVERB

When we experience stress, the body's fight-or-flight response is triggered. With increasing stress, this response remains triggered long term and affects functioning in ways that exacerbate stress levels and put our health at risk. This chapter explains the stress response and provides simple and effective strategies to stimulate the body's relaxation response, which returns the body to prestress functioning. By the end of this chapter, you will have tools to bring yourself to a more relaxed state in minutes.

Why Is My Heart Pounding?

Jonathan found himself feeling overwhelmed. After a long day of putting out fires at work, and with further responsibilities waiting for him at home, he found himself in a veritable parking lot on the freeway, turning what would have been a 20-minute drive into at least an hour-long mess. As he thought about how much he just wanted to go home and relax, how many cars surrounded him, how slowly things were moving, and how little he could do about it, he discovered that his shirt was sweaty, his neck was aching, and his heart was pounding in his chest. He was going through a full stress response, even though the grueling challenges that he had faced at work were behind him and the only discernable stressors he had to contend with were the ones in his head.

This was not uncommon for John. He had a habit of becoming more stressed during his commute home if traffic was congested. We had talked about this before, and now he was prepared. In the past, he would have become angrier and angrier, tailgating, cutting people off, and using his horn often as his body responded to the stress in an equally aggressive manner. This time, he simply sat there and took a deep breath. He let it out slowly, then took another. By breathing deeply and focusing on the current moment, he was able to calm his body and his mind. Once he did this, he was able to enjoy listening to music. He was able to appreciate that, although sitting and listening to music was not his first choice of activity at that moment, he would enjoy himself much more if he were calm. And once he was, he found that he did enjoy his commute much more. He came to see it as a time to relax, rather than a time to feel trapped. Once he was able to calm his stress response, he could think more clearly and choose to shift his perspective. And this altered his experience of stress.

Fight or Flight: When It Was Useful and How It's Outdated

One of the beautiful things about the human body is its capacity to heal and adapt. We have different physiological systems that all work together to keep us healthy, safe, and able to face whatever comes our way (or at least attempt to). The body's stress response is integrated with several other bodily systems, so that once in motion, the stress response compels us to fight off attackers, or at least outrun them.

This stress response, also known as the *fight-or-flight response*, is triggered by the mere perception that we may face a threat to our physical or psychological well-being. Once activated, the response stimulates a jolt of energy, as adrenaline, cortisol, and other hormones are released to allow us to move quickly; we also experience a burst of strength, so we're able to fight for our lives. This response is designed to slow bodily functions that aren't essential for the fight (or would hinder it) and give us the ability to function physically beyond our regular capabilities. The body's stress response doesn't endow us with superpowers, but it does help us to perform at our best when it comes to moving quickly, fighting, and taking needed action.

The body is also equipped with a relaxation response, which returns the body to its normal, pre-crisis mode of functioning once the threat has passed. The heart rate slows, breathing becomes more deep and regular, and the body becomes relaxed again. If the fight-or-flight response is like flexing a muscle, the relaxation response is like letting that muscle loosen.

For centuries, this was an effective means for survival. Our world, however, has changed, and the challenges we face have evolved to become more psychological than physical. Nevertheless, the body's stress response has remained largely the same. This means that, in some ways, we are overprepared to face what comes our way—we don't need to physically attack co-workers who are trying to compete with us for promotions. In other ways, our stress response leaves us underprepared for our daily stressors; we may need a burst of clarity and level-headedness in the middle of a crisis, when instead, we are often left struggling to think while in a muddled place of panic.

The Role of Perception

It complicates things that the stress response may become triggered at the wrong time: The fight-or-flight response is triggered not only by an actual threat to safety and well-being, but also by the *perception* of threat. This means that if we believe that something is about to harm us, the body is mobilized to defend itself, whether or not we are in actual danger. And, as mentioned earlier, because most of today's "threats" are psychological (the threat to your status in a relationship, to your security in a job, to your ability to move through traffic and make it to a meeting on time), the stress response is often triggered unnecessarily, even when there is a real threat.

In addition, the stress response can become triggered when no threat exists—when a mate is *not* cheating, when a job is *not* at stake, or when we are otherwise mistakenly concerned that we're at risk of something negative happening in our lives. This leaves us feeling stressed more times than are necessary. It can lead to a cycle whereby we are stressed more often than not and therefore frequently results in the states of episodic stress and chronic stress that I discussed in the Introduction. Under such conditions, the stress response is activated for a prolonged period of time, without the body's returning to its relaxed state.

This is when stress becomes a problem.

The Effects of Chronic Stress

While the stress response is vital to human survival because it helps us to become motivated to act when necessary, it was not designed to be constantly triggered. We were never meant to function from this place permanently or even for prolonged amounts of time. When the body gets to a state of chronic stress, the negative health effects we discussed in **Key 1** can occur and take a lasting toll on us both physically and mentally. Basically, the body moves into a state of imbalance, and we suffer negative effects both physically and psychologically as a result.

How to Manage

Although we can't always change what we face in life, and we can't change our body's natural, automatic response to the perception of stress, what we can effectively do is to work around the body's stress response, to minimize our experience of chronic stress. This means taking an approach that covers several bases at once. We can work at minimizing how often our stress response is triggered by altering the thought patterns and habits of perception that may trigger our stress response too frequently. This could mean increasing our degree of optimism, reframing our situation, or focusing on resources, all of which is covered in **Key 4**.

We can also work on creating lifestyle habits that decrease our body's reaction to stress. Habits such as meditation, for example, alter the brain and change the way it responds when stressed. If such habits are successfully practiced, when the stress response is triggered, the response is less intense and the body returns to its relaxed state more easily, something we discuss in **Key 8**. We can also take better care of ourselves physically so that we aren't overly sensitive to the stress response (**Key 3**), rally our resources so we're better able to handle challenges that arise and not perceive them as stressful (**Keys 6 and 7**), and cut out stressors whenever possible so the stress response is triggered by fewer events (**Key 5**).

Perhaps one of the most important ways we can minimize the negative effects of chronic stress is to develop effective ways to reverse our stress response once we realize it's been triggered. Because chronic stress results when the body remains in a state of constant stress, if we can learn to return the body to its resting state—a state of stability, or *homeostasis*—between challenging events, we can create a greater amount of time the body feels relaxed and unaffected by stress. Better still, by practicing techniques that bring us to a relaxed state, we can train our bodies to become quickly relaxed with little effort, and this can become increasingly automatic.

By learning relaxation techniques and cutting down on the chronic stress we experience, we can feel more relaxed in the present moment, and we can also allow ourselves to avoid the negative effects of chronic stress that we would otherwise be experiencing. By practicing relaxation techniques regularly, we can minimize the body's experience of stress without changing anything else. Combined with other effective stress management techniques, relaxation techniques become all the more powerful.

Activity to Try: Relaxation Exercises

With this in mind, let's explore some of the simplest and most effective relaxation techniques. Activities that physically relax the body can work well for stress management because they not only enable you to calm your body's stress response, but also can help you to separate physical reactions from emotional stress so that, in time, you may be less physically reactive to the stress you face. Each of the following relaxation techniques can work quickly on its own and can bring even greater benefits if practiced repeatedly or with other stress relief techniques. As you read, think of the situations in which you usually find yourself feeling stressed and make mental notes of which techniques may be the best fit for those times.

Activity to Try: Breathing Exercises

Relaxation breathing is one of my favorite techniques to recommend and is something I use quite frequently in my own life. Breathing exercises are simple in that they can be learned in minutes and practiced by virtually anyone, including children and those with physical challenges. These exercises are versatile and convenient in that they can be practiced almost anywhere at any time (even *during* a stressful event) and can be modified to fit individual tastes. With practice, relaxation breathing can become automatic, so that relaxation becomes a mode to slip into, rather than something to be achieved only with the help of someone or something else, or under the right conditions. Simply, conveniently, and easily, breathing exercises *work*.

How Breathing Exercises Work

What differentiates stress relaxation breathing from the type of breathing we do every day is subtle but significant. When everything is running smoothly and the body is relaxed, we naturally breathe from the diaphragm, with the belly extending and contracting with each breath while the shoulders remain relaxed and loose. We breathe in deeply, filling our lungs, and breathe out with ease.

When we face stress and the stress response has been triggered, we tend to breathe less efficiently. We engage in a more shallow form of breathing, where our shoulders remain tight and rise and fall with our breath, while our abdominal muscles may remain constricted. We breathe more quickly because we are not getting as much air as we should. This is all in keeping with the changes that prepare us to fight or run, to act quickly, but it is not healthy for us. Sadly, some people find themselves breathing this way virtually all the time that they are awake.

The act of consciously releasing the tension in the body and forcing our breathing to mimic the more relaxed breathing that our body enacts at a resting state can help to reverse the body's triggered stress response and thus help us to physically relax. It can also help us to relax emotionally, because the body no longer reacts from a position of feeling stressed.

How Breathing Exercises Can Work for You

Relaxed breathing is an integral part of yoga, so if you are interested in learning this type of breathing directly from a teacher, taking a yoga class or two can be a great idea. A teacher can talk you through the process and let you know if changes need to be made to your technique.

For most people, however, reading instructions on stress relief breathing is sufficient and an easy and effective way to learn the process. The following instructions provide a quick and simple method for breathing your way into a more relaxed state:

1. Find a quiet place to relax, and get comfortable.
2. Focus on your breathing. Relax your shoulders, and let them hang down, away from your head. Quickly notice where there is tension in the rest of your body, and let that relax as well.
3. Notice your breathing. Is it shallow? Are your shoulders rising and falling with each breath? If so, relax even further until your

breathing is slow, steady, and deep and your belly expands and contracts with each breath, even if you have to loosen clothing to allow this to occur comfortably. This is called *diaphragmic breathing* (because it comes from your diaphragm), and it is the way we naturally breathe when we are sleeping, or when we are relaxed.

4. To further regulate your breathing, you may want to count with each breath—count slowly to five on the inhale, and count slowly to eight with each exhale—to keep it at a relaxed pace.

5. Once you feel that you are breathing in a fully relaxed manner, you can stop counting and stop focusing on altering your breathing. Rather than changing your breathing patterns at this point, simply notice your breath as it moves into and out of your body. You should feel more relaxed within minutes. You should also have a clear memory of what this more relaxed form of breathing feels like, so you can move into it more easily in the future when you need to quickly relax.

Visualizations

Research shows that visualizations affect the body as well as the mind. When we vividly picture ourselves engaging in an activity, the brain can't tell the difference between what we are imagining and what we are actually experiencing. The mind believes that it is experiencing what we are visualizing. Our pulse may quicken or slow down based on what we believe we are experiencing, and other responses can occur as well, including those that aid relaxation.

While it is somewhat surprising that the mind is fully engaged in visualizations and "believes" that these experiences are true, what is more remarkable is that the muscles involved in visualizations are actually, in reality, engaged as well. This works quite well for athletes and for people preparing for public speaking and other challenges that require practice and confidence for mastery, but it can be quite helpful for relaxation purposes as well.

Stress management visualizations can work in several ways.

First, the mere act of imagining circumstances that are less stressful than the ones you currently face can shift your attention and can help you to replace thoughts that will trigger your stress response with thoughts that can allow your relaxation response to engage naturally, or at least will stop the stress. This can be helpful if you tend to ruminate about things that have upset you in the past or worry about things you must face in the future.

Second, the visualizations themselves can get you into a more relaxed state of mind, not just with the absence of stressful thoughts, but also with the presence of more relaxing, happiness-inducing thoughts. If you close your eyes and imagine yourself on a soft cloud, floating above the noise in your life (instead of being in the midst of a stressful office environment) or imagine being in a place where you always feel at ease (such as your favorite chair at home), you can encourage your body to feel the way it would normally feel in that environment. Visualizing positive things happening in your life can help you to feel more confident about facing challenges and can help you to break thought habits that are negative.

Another benefit of visualizations is that you can visualize your body into a more relaxed state by imagining it so. If your heart is racing, you can visualize images that suggest a slow pace, such as a gentle ride down a stream in a canoe; you can also directly imagine that your pulse is slowing down. If you feel tension in your shoulders, you can visualize the tension leaving your body by conjuring up an image of the tension seeping out of your body through your pores, or a feeling of relaxation flowing from your head to your toes as though a cup of water were being poured on you and washing down your body. You get the idea.

Visualizations can work fairly quickly in helping to relieve stress. The technique generally requires some privacy or quiet time for focus, but with practice, you can shorten the length of time it takes to work and strengthen the response you feel. (For example, with practice you can create a "happy place" for yourself—a mental image you create that relaxes you and helps you to stay at peace. Over time, you can get into the habit of relaxing at the mere thought of your happy place.) You can experiment with what types of images to use; later in this chapter, I offer examples to give you ideas. You can also download recordings from the website of this book that can help you to relieve stress through visualization. (For more information, go to 8KeysTo StressManagement.com or ElizabethScott.info.)

Progressive Muscle Relaxation

Progressive muscle relaxation (PMR) is a technique that focuses mainly on the muscles themselves. While it takes some time to master, even short sessions of PMR can bring about a more relaxed state. The idea behind PMR is to tense and relax all the major muscle groups in a systematic way, draining the muscles of residual tension in the process. With practice, it becomes much easier to relax the entire body this way, often in seconds rather than in minutes, a technique known as deep muscle relaxation (DMR). Learning PMR and DMR is relatively easy, but it takes practice. It is most effective to learn this practice from a professional, although you can learn from recordings and videos as well. Here is a simplified version of PMR you can try right now:

1. Set aside a few minutes, find a private place away from distractions, and sit or lie down in a relaxed position.
2. Tense the muscles in your scalp. Hold these muscles tensed for at least 30 seconds, lifting your ears (if you are able) and clenching whatever you can. Then relax. Allow all the tension to drain from the muscles in your head, and simply "be."
3. Repeat this with the muscles in your face. Keep the muscles in your cheeks, jaw, and the rest of your face as tense as you can, and hold this for about a minute. Then relax, and let all the tension drain from your muscles.
4. Repeat this with your neck. Then move to your shoulders, upper arms, lower arms and fists, back, abdomen, glutes, thighs, calves, and feet.

5. Over time, you will be able to more quickly tense and relax each area, and the process of relaxing will begin to feel automatic.

Self-Hypnosis

When the idea of hypnosis comes up, many people still think of hypnotists who appear on the stage—entertainers who will hypnotize volunteers from the audience and get them to act like a chicken when they hear the word *marshmallow* or perform unnatural feats of strength. Most techniques used in hypnosis, particularly self-hypnosis, are much less embarrassing, and much more useful in helping participants change behaviors they *want* to change. Self-hypnosis works in a way that is similar to visualizations, except that the state of relaxation is deeper and the mind's engagement is more immersive.

We can self-hypnotize for many purposes, such as stopping smoking and getting rid of anxieties and phobias. But self-hypnotization is an especially potent tool for stress management. You can tap into your subconscious mind and plant suggestions that allow you to relax, let things roll off your back, and maintain habits that relieve stress. Hypnosis generally requires a few sessions for maximum effect, but it can begin working quickly. A session lasting a few minutes and aimed at relaxation can work well.

There are several different ways you can use hypnosis and self-hypnosis for stress relief. You can find many self-hypnosis resources online (an audio file is available from 8KeysToStress Management.com), and you can create your own script and recording.

Mini-meditation

Meditation is a very powerful tool for stress management. It works best when practiced for at least 15 or 20 minutes per session, because it takes a while for the mind to quiet itself and it is the practice of *keeping* the mind quiet and still that delivers many of the most noted benefits of meditation. (You can read more about meditation in **Key** 8, which discusses long-term habits that build resilience to stress.)

Mini-meditations—meditation sessions that last 3 to 5 minutes—can also be helpful in reducing stress in that they can minimize your stress reaction and help you to quickly calm your mind. Taking a few minutes to focus inwardly can help you to stop focusing on the stressful situations around you, which can help you to get out of a mindset of feeling threatened and allow you to reverse your stress response. (**Keys 4 and** 8 contain a set of simple instructions for meditation; for a mini-meditation session, simply set a timer for 3–5 minutes, follow the instructions, and stop when the timer goes off.)

Autogenic Training

Autogenic training can be quite useful for quickly calming the body and reversing the stress response. It involves training the mind to alter physiological responses that are generally automatic. Autogenic training has been used for increasing circulation by, for example, focusing on warming the hands or feet through thought.

Autogenic training can be used for minimizing or reversing the stress response and can be quite effective. However, it works best when learned from a professional, and it takes some time and effort—it's not easily learned in minutes, unlike breathing exercises. Autogenic training requires extra front-end effort, but it promotes the ability to quickly and easily destress your body using only your mind. You can learn to control other bodily systems as well, if you wish.

Find Support

Having a supportive friend to lean on during times of stress can bring relief. In fact, during such times a "tend-and-befriend" response often occurs, especially in women, that causes us to seek out and offer support, which can be beneficial in surviving stressors more easily, for us as individuals and as members of a group.

Long, conversational sessions with a good friend or therapist can be extremely useful in destressing (more information on building a supportive network of friends can be found in **Key 6**). However, getting a quick pep talk from a close friend can be an even simpler way to get to a place of feeling more relaxed and grounded and can be considered its own stress relief technique. Studies show that getting this type of support can reduce levels of the stress hormone cortisol in the bloodstream—a standard marker of stress—and can make people feel less distressed.

The important thing to remember is to give back as much as you take from any relationship. Be sure you are well matched with the friends you lean on, so you are not asking from them more than they are comfortable providing. And be sure to be there for them when they need some support. It is important to have effective ways to calm down quickly, but keeping an eye on the long-term development of relationships is important, too.

Questions to Ask Yourself

* Do I need techniques to help me relax in the middle of a tense situation, or would it be sufficient to have a relaxation strategy to use during lunch or at the end of the day? (Breathing exercises can work at any time; mini-meditations and progressive muscle relaxation may require a small break and a place in which to relax. Finding support may require more time.)

* Do I have any limitations that might make certain relaxation techniques more difficult? (Physical pain, for example, might be too distracting for progressive muscle relaxation.)

* Which techniques sound most enjoyable and intriguing? (Some people find meditation more challenging if their mind races when they are stressed. Others may find visualizations to be especially enjoyable because they like to use their imagination.)

* Can I see myself doing any of these long term? Which ones

seem the easiest to habitually practice? (These questions can help you to weed out any that might feel boring or complicated.)
* Given the times when I need to destress the most, which of these techniques would be most convenient or effective to use during those situations?

Evaluate Your Answers

Because there are several different options for relaxation techniques (and this has not been an exhaustive list), we have several activities to choose from. The answers to the questions listed above should provide you with some clues for where to begin when you look for strategies to help reverse your stress response. These strategies will be your first line of defense against stress, so it is important that you have at least one or two that you can consistently use to calm yourself inside, and face your stress in a more proactive way. Looking at the situations in which you would need to use your techniques can help you to avoid methods that would not be a good fit with your life. Examining the characteristics of your personality can help you to avoid stress relievers that might naturally feel more challenging. Look at your needs and keep them in mind as you realistically evaluate the quick stress relief strategies in this chapter and others, and make a short list of potential stress relievers that appeal to you the most. Then put them to work for you!

Tips to Get You Started Now

While there is an entire section at the end of this book that can help you to form a cohesive plan to approach stress management, if you are looking for a quick way to get started, I recommend that you start here. Finding relaxation techniques that work for you can provide you with a quick route to reversing your stress response and approaching stress management from a more empowered place. Also, these techniques work quickly—in a matter of minutes—and require little practice before they provide at least some measure of effective stress relief. If you are able to quickly minimize your feelings of stress and gain more motivation by using these methods, you may find more success with the techniques you read about later in this book.

Here are some simple ways to get started right now with the relaxation techniques noted earlier in this chapter:

* **Try a different technique each day.** You may find that you'd like to try each technique as you read about it. While this is definitely a possibility, you may not have the time to try out each of them right now. If you sample a different technique each day for the next week or so, you may find this to be a more comfortable pace. You'll also get a chance to see how each one helps you to relieve stress in real situations in which you would use them. (Practicing breathing exercises while you are already relaxed and reading a book may feel different from using the exercises when you are in the middle of working on a deadline at the office.) Using different techniques in the same situations over the course of a week can allow you to get a real sense of what works best for you in these situations; this is a simple way to compare and contrast them as you go.

* **Try each one for a week.** Sticking with the same technique for a week can help you to get better at it, making each technique feel more natural and easier to use. This strategy also gives you a better chance to see how well these techniques work over time. Immersing yourself in a single burgeoning habit (rather than trying a series of different techniques in a short amount of time) allows you to gain an association with that habit—to get in the habit of feeling relaxed more quickly and automatically when you begin to practice it. Switching to a different habit after a week will allow you to try several before you become so tied to any of them that you won't want to try anything else, but still lets you get a real feel for how each technique works to help you relieve stress if used regularly.

* **Maintain a journal to see what works best.** One of the most effective ways to forge a new habit is to maintain a journal around

it. To make an analogy, people who are attempting to spend less money can find greater success by first recording what they are currently spending and on what, and then finding ways to cut down on the things that they buy, based on carefully assessing where their money is going and looking at where it is being wasted. Journaling can continue to be useful as spending is recorded moving forward—writing down everything you spend can be a good motivating factor in helping you want to spend less, if only to avoid having to admit to it in black and white.

Journaling can help with stress relief in a similar way. You can record the times of day that you feel stressed, which can help you to remember when to use your techniques. You can record how each of the techniques seem to work for you, making it easier to compare and contrast them. Finally, you can write down the frequency with which you use them, which can remind you to do so and reinforce the habit as well. The journaling route takes some effort, but can bring a high payoff in terms of helping you to better evaluate when you need to relieve stress and how to best do so.

TAKE CARE OF YOUR BODY

A good laugh and a long sleep are the best cures in the doctor's book.
—IRISH PROVERB

When we aren't taking care of ourselves physically, we tend to feel more stressed. Poor nutrition, inadequate sleep, and a sedentary lifestyle can exacerbate reactivity to stressors. This chapter will provide you with research supporting the importance of proper nutrition, adequate and consistent sleep, and regular physical activity, as well as easy techniques that promote the maintenance of self-care and a healthy lifestyle. Here is how you can feel better emotionally by working on staying healthier physically!

A Downward Spiral of Stress and Self-Neglect

Janice found herself working harder than she had been before. When her company downsized, she found herself feeling so lucky to still have a job that she gladly accepted the extra responsibilities left by the co-workers who had been let go. As she struggled to find a new equilibrium, she found that she was too busy for the healthy meals she had previously made herself after work, and she often just picked something up on her way home. (And the most convenient stops on the way from work to home were fast food restaurants.) She also found that her sleep schedule suffered as she spent more time at work—she had less time for everything else, and that extra time had to come from somewhere. She also stopped going to the gym: When deciding whether to sleep or work out, she discovered that sleep would win out every time.

Over the next few weeks, she found herself more and more stressed. She had trouble concentrating, she was short-tempered, and she felt less and less able to cope. At first, she thought the stress was coming from the fear of losing her job, or even from the challenge of taking on new responsibilities. However, when we looked at the different factors that went into her rising stress levels, Janice was surprised to observe how her self-care was plummeting, and she realized that it was contributing to her stress. She understood that it went beyond the stressors at work. She was no longer taking care of herself, and the results were surprising. The combination of sleep deprivation, poor nutrition, and lack of exercise seemed to feed off itself.

When she recognized what was going on, she took a hard look at her schedule, cut out some activities, and worked at restoring self-care in her schedule. Within a matter of days, she felt happier, more energetic, mentally sharper, more patient, and better able to take on the stresses of her new job responsibilities. She was amazed at what a difference a little sleep, food, and movement could make!

Stress and the Importance of Self-Care

When we find ourselves working hard to meet heavy deadlines, dealing with difficult people, and facing more than we feel we can handle, we tend to let a few things go. Operating from what feels like crisis mode, we may try to handle the most pressing concerns first and let other things slip—we may get a little less sleep, may skip a few workouts, and may grab the closest thing there is to eat, in an effort to save time and give 110% to the demands we face. Unfortunately, such short-term sacrifice can hinder our ability to face demands long term. Just as a perpetually triggered stress response can create an escalating pattern of stress, operating from a place of being overwhelmed can tempt us to make choices that will only make things more difficult for ourselves over time.

If you face a short-term challenge that requires you to put in your all for a few hours, or even a few days, you may find yourself cutting corners on how you take care of yourself physically. As days stretch into weeks, however, you risk putting yourself into a much more stressful, unhealthy situation that can affect you for much longer. And, perhaps worse, you may not realize that your self-neglect is fueling your stress, or you may not know how to get out from under its effects. It is important to know the risks of short-term and long-term neglect of self-care and see what you can do to continue to take care of yourself, even (especially!) when you are under heavy levels of stress.

Optimal Functioning

It's no secret that we function at our best when we're feeling at our healthiest and happiest. And we naturally feel the urge to do what's healthy because it just feels right. In this way, we set ourselves up for success by doing what feels good naturally—eating well, sleeping when we're tired, getting together with friends when we're lonely, and doing things that we enjoy in order to maintain balance. We're designed to intrinsically sense when something is out of balance and feel compelled to correct it.

This system hits a roadblock when our environment throws us too many curveballs or when we don't listen to our inner voice that tells us we're headed in the wrong direction. When we feel overly stressed, we tend to crave things that may give us a temporary lift but that don't support our long-term health and functioning. There are several reasons why this happens and there are steps we can take to counteract the effects, but if we don't stop the negative progression of things, we could be headed for trouble.

Downward Stress Spiral

When we are under stress, a number of things happen. We may be too busy to heed our body's signals. We may find ourselves staying up all night to work on a pressing project rather than going to sleep when we're tired, or grabbing a quick (and less-than-healthy) meal because we can't take the time to cook more nutritious food. These trade-offs may seem to be small shifts and can be tolerated in small doses. However, they set us on a self-perpetuating path that can cause us to feel more stressed, and this stress can actually make it more difficult to pull ourselves back into our naturally healthy behaviors.

This is because we behave differently when we are coming from a place of chronic stress. Just as we think differently (see **Key 4**) and react differently (see **Key 2**) when experiencing life's stressors, we tend to handle self-care differently when we are operating from a place of already feeling stressed. We may crave different foods, may have a more challenging time getting to sleep and staying asleep, and may even have a harder time relating to others. This can put us into a place of being more stressed, because we may be coming from a nutritionally deprived, sleep deprived state and have less social support to help us through it. Of course, this can lead to greater stress, more cravings for the wrong things, more conflict, and a continued downward spiral.

Health and Wellness

Ultimately, stress management is not just about feeling at ease (though this is important); stress management is important because it leads to greater overall health and longevity. Managing stress isn't just a luxury; it's a necessity for proper functioning. Taking care of ourselves physically, a practice known as *self-care*, is important for two reasons. It is important for our health not only because of the direct positive effects we gain from a healthy diet, adequate exercise, and supportive relationships, but also because having these things in place can help us to avoid the additional stress (and resulting threats to our health) that can come from unhealthy habits and poor self-care. Moreover, when you are less stressed and living a healthier life, those around you benefit as well, so in making these types of changes, you can have an impact on those people while making improvements in your own life. The following sections delve deeper into what specific changes bring the greatest benefits and are the most necessary to make.

Important Aspects of Self-Care

There are many behaviors that can fall under the umbrella of self-care, such as brushing teeth, getting monthly massages, and practicing stress management in general. Because certain habits bring the greatest benefits, we'll focus on those. The following three main areas of self-care have been included because focusing on them can significantly alter your experience of stress. Sleep deprivation and poor nutrition can exacerbate stress and lead to poor health consequences, and shifting from a sedentary lifestyle to an active one can promote long-term resilience to stress. Let's look more in depth at each of these, how they affect us, and the shifts that can help the most with the management of stress.

Proper Nutrition

Providing your body with the right kind of fuel is perhaps more important than we realize. Of course, we have all heard the motto "You are what you eat" and similar truisms, and the reality is that what we put into our bodies has an immediate impact not only on how we feel physically days from now, but also on how we feel emotionally minutes from now. A diet that contains too much sugar can make us more reactive to stress, as well as making us more vulnerable to disease and premature aging. A solid balance of protein and carbohydrates, found in a mix of healthy food that does not contain an abundance of sugar, starch, fats, or artificial ingredients can set you up to function at your best, with less stress.

Effects of a Poor Diet

Diets that contain empty calories can leave us without the mental and physical energy we need to face the challenges in our lives.

(Remember that when we feel that the demands of a situation exceed our resources for coping, we feel stressed.) Foods that contain excess amounts of sugar and caffeine can give us a jolt of energy and a quick boost to our mood, but this is followed by a "crash," which can leave us feeling lethargic, depressed, and craving more. And because these stimulants are addictive, we tend to continue the cycle of poor eating habits and increased stress.

Long-term effects of an unhealthy diet include such health risks as obesity and diabetes. Obesity increases your risk of many other health conditions, among them high blood pressure, sleep apnea, heart conditions, and diabetes. These are serious health conditions that can be highly stressful and even life threatening. Altering your diet is not easy during times of stress, but it is necessary for your health.

Diet Saboteurs

When we are in a stressed state, we often find it more difficult to maintain a healthy diet. There are a few reasons for this, some of which are related to our reactions to stress and some of which originate in the reasons we are stressed in the first place. Here are the main stumbling blocks to watch and some corresponding tips that can help with each one:

* **Busy schedules.** When we are especially busy, we tend to grab whatever food is quick to obtain. Unfortunately, the most convenient foods are often the least healthy. Grabbing junk food on the run can keep you from getting too hungry if you have a few busy hours, but it comes at a cost to your overall health and emotional state. If you keep a few healthy options close by and opt for them instead, you can avoid the fast food trap.
* **Bad influences.** Studies show that weight gain is contagious—if you spend a lot of time with people who are overweight and have unhealthy eating habits, there is a likelihood that you yourself will adopt such eating habits. If co-workers bring in sweets to share, friends routinely want to meet and eat at restaurants that serve unhealthy fare, or you live in a house that is filled with junk

food that others buy, you probably already know the pull that this type of peer pressure can exert. It is important to have a plan to avoid these temptations, and stick with it.

* **Cortisol cravings.** When our bodies have elevated levels of the stress hormone, cortisol, we tend to crave sweets more strongly. This may have been a healthy adaptation at some point, but now it tempts us to reach for the ice cream in times of stress. (And if we have an abundance of ice cream available, this can become a recipe for overindulgence!) Using some of the quick stress relievers I discussed in **Key 2** can help to calm the body's stress response so it becomes less challenging to reach for carrots or celery instead.

* **Emotional eating.** Often when we feel stressed, we tend to crave comfort food, which is generally not the healthiest food, but it reminds us of our childhood, or of happier times. Other times, when we are emotionally stressed, we eat to fill a void or to feel that we are doing something nice for ourselves. We eat for an emotional pick-me-up, but we may wind up with the opposite. When you find yourself eating when you are not actually hungry or choosing foods that will not sustain you in a healthy way, try to do something that will make you feel better emotionally that does not involve food, such as seeking support from a friend, writing in a gratitude journal, or doing things that generally make you smile.

* **Habit.** When we are facing stress, we may find it more difficult to take on new changes. If you are used to eating an unhealthy diet, the very time you would do best to change this might be the time during which it would be most challenging—times of stress. It is wise to maintain healthy habits when you are not already overwhelmed. When you do so, maintaining these habits when it is both most important and most challenging will be easier to do.

How to Manage: Improving Your Eating Habits

In addition to the tips mentioned above, the following proactive steps can help you to avoid letting your stress push you into a downward spiral of unhealthy eating habits and ensuing spikes in stress levels:

* **Stock your kitchen.** If you find yourself reaching for the quickest thing available, it's best to be surrounded by convenient, healthy options. Plan ahead by stocking your kitchen with healthy fruit- and vegetable-based snacks, such as apples and celery that can be enjoyed with peanut butter, carrots and broccoli that can be eaten raw with a favorite dip, hummus with bruschetta and pita, or even just a ripe banana. Cook extra portions of some meals that can be easily reheated, such as vegetable-heavy chili, oven-baked chicken, or hearty soups. And don't buy foods that you know you would be better off not eating. If your environment supports the habits you want to maintain, you will not have to rely on willpower as heavily, and this can relieve stress.

* **Know where to find healthier fare.** If you find yourself eating out quite a bit, you can still avoid the traps of unhealthy eating if you plan ahead. Know where the healthiest restaurants in your area are located, and be aware of the healthiest meals on the menu.

* **Become aware of your obstacles.** If you tend to binge on a specific food when you're stressed, try to switch to a healthier option. If you find you eat the wrong things at a certain time of day, be sure that you are surrounded by better options during that time frame. If you find that you forget to eat when you are stressed, you may want to set an alarm on your phone or computer to remind yourself to eat. If certain people send you into a stress binge, see if you can minimize contact. Think about what your triggers are, and find a plan to work around them.

* **Start new habits.** One simple way of cutting out negative habits is to take on new habits in your life that are incompatible with the unhealthy ones. Start journaling to manage emotional stress, and you may find your stress cravings diminish. Start exercising more often, and sweets may hold less sway. Add healthy foods to

each meal, and you won't have as much room in your stomach for the less healthy options. See what new habits you can take on!

* **Enlist support.** Your friends may have the capacity to be negative influences, but they can also be wonderful allies. Announce to others your intentions to stay on track with healthy eating, and they will be less likely to offer you unhealthy options and more likely to gently remind you when you are going off track, even if they do not plan to make these changes themselves. You may also want to enlist the support of a group like Weight Watchers, where you can find support and information and be congratulated on your success in sticking to your healthy eating goals.

* **Try mindful eating.** Sometimes when we feel we *can't* have something, our cravings for it only grow stronger. If you experience increased cravings when you try to cut certain things out of your diet completely, you may want to try simply cutting back and really enjoying what you do allow yourself to have. Mindful eating can be an effective tool to use here. By intensifying your focus on your food as you eat it, you can expand your enjoyment of the things you crave and minimize the amount of it you need to eat in order to feel satisfied. Focus on every sensation you feel as you eat; if you do so, one bite of ice cream can be more satisfying than an entire bowl. Give it a try, and see how much less you can eat and how much more you can enjoy it.

Exercise

During times of stress and of feeling overwhelmed, few of us naturally feel like taking a brisk jog or sweating at the gym for an hour, unless we are already in the practice of doing these things. In fact, many people find themselves skipping workouts during times of stress either because their schedules keep them feeling too busy to work out or because they feel exhausted from the demands they face. However, maintaining regular exercise is important, for several reasons.

Benefits of Exercise

We all know that exercise is important, but we may underestimate its true value. Regular physical activity decreases your risk of experiencing the most serious medical conditions, including heart disease, cancer, and stroke, as well as diabetes, high blood pressure, and high cholesterol. Should you suffer from such conditions, exercise improves your functioning level. It is also a fantastic tool for stress relief! Proved to lower cortisol levels in the blood after only 3 minutes, physical activity helps to balance out your hormonal levels, reverse the stress response, release tension, boost your confidence, and clear your mind when you are stressed. Regular exercise supports overall wellness in countless ways and is linked to increased longevity. If you can take on only one healthy habit, exercise might be the most beneficial one you can choose.

Problems That Arise from Lack of Exercise

As with healthy eating, the time to ensure that we get enough exercise is when we may feel we have the least time and energy for it—when we are stressed. Here are some problems that may creep in when we skip a few too many workouts:

* **Lethargy.** Paradoxically, when we expend energy through exercise, we tend to feel more energetic overall. Likewise, when we remain sedentary, we generally lack energy overall, and this lethargy can affect our ability to face other challenges in our lives. Just as giving love can bring us more love in our lives, expending energy through exercise can bring us greater levels of energy in general.
* **Unmanaged stress.** Because exercise is such an effective stress relief tool (see **Keys 2 and 8** for more on this), we deprive ourselves of stress management help when we fail to remain active. Just as exercise can eliminate stress in the body and mind, less physical activity tends to mean more stress. Adding exercise sessions to your schedule can keep stress levels lower in general.
* **Health issues.** As mentioned earlier, lack of physical activity is

correlated with higher incidences of health issues. Dealing with these issues can be quite stressful in itself. In this way, failing to prioritize physical activity creates greater stress in the future, not only because of the missed stress management opportunities but also because of the health issues that can occur. Regular exercise is proactive stress management.

Exercise Saboteurs

In addition to feeling too busy or too tired for a good workout, there are a few other obstacles you may face that can get between you and your exercise goals:

* **Past failure.** If you have tried to start an exercise habit and have failed in the past, you may be reluctant to try again. You may feel that your lifestyle just can't accommodate it, or that you don't have what it takes to maintain a regular schedule of physical activity. We touch on this more in **Key 8**, but it is important to know that you can achieve different results with a different plan. There are forms of exercise that can contribute to your overall health and take only 10 minutes. There are types of exercise that can appeal to just about anyone. Don't let your past dictate your future.

* **Physical injury.** If you have been injured in the past, it is important to consult a doctor before you begin a new exercise regimen. This is easily done, and it can increase your confidence and allow you to know which exercises to practice and which to stay away from. You may also wish to hire a trainer to learn proper form and reduce risk of injury in the future. Make an appointment today, and don't let past injury (or fear of future injury) stand in your way.

* **Habit.** You may simply be in the habit of remaining sedentary. That's okay; you can form a new habit. It just takes a little time. Whatever stage of change you are in, you can move yourself into a new exercise habit relatively easily, with a little preparation and motivation.

How to Manage: Start and Maintain
Regular Exercise Habits

There are many ways to ease into an exercise program, and even more varieties of exercise are available to try. While we explore this further in **Keys 7 and 8** and touch on it in **Key 2**, here are some simple ways to make exercise a part of your life and some ideas to remember to make this a smooth process:

* **Join a gym.** Making the commitment to join a gym can actually stimulate motivation, strengthening your decision to get more exercise. After all, if you invested money in this habit, you will want to get your money's worth. Gyms also offer many supportive options that can help you along the way, including different types of classes, access to personal trainers, and various types of equipment that you can experiment on; some even have saunas, hot tubs, and showers, which can make the experience both relaxing and convenient.

* **Get a buddy.** Workout buddies can do two things. They can motivate you to do your best with a little friendly competition or support when your motivation wanes. They can also keep you on track—you may be much less likely to cancel a workout if you know you will be letting a friend down. Workouts with friends can be more enjoyable and feel less like work, so this can be an added bonus.

* **Find the right exercise for you.** If your workouts feel grueling and joyless, you probably aren't doing the best types of exercises for your lifestyle and personality. There are many different types of workouts you can try. The intention is to pick one that fits your goals and personal style. Exercise truly can be fun, whether you enjoy team sports, solitary sports, dancing, yoga, swimming, cycling, or various types of classes. If you don't like the choice you made, choose again!

* **Set realistic goals.** Often people push themselves too hard in the beginning and then give up. By setting more realistic goals, you are not only more likely to avoid injury, you are also more

likely to succeed, because you will be less likely to become discouraged and burn out. Start slowly, reward yourself for small
milestones, and keep trying. If you find yourself skipping workouts, don't quit—you may need to adjust your plan, but you can
find a way to make exercise work in your life. It can and should
be enjoyable!

Sleep

Sleep is more vital to our wellness and overall functioning than we
might realize. It is also closely linked with our stress levels. Safe-
guarding your sleep is important for many reasons.

Effects of Missed Sleep

We may not notice the effects of missed sleep in their entirety,
because they can be subtle. However, they are also pervasive. Sleep
deprivation has been used as a method of torture because it can be
distressing and damaging, even in the smaller doses that we typically experience as part of a hectic lifestyle. When we do not get
the full 7–8 hours of sleep that our bodies need, we experience
cognitive impairments and slower reflexes, as well as a greater
emotional reactivity to virtually everything that we face. This not
only can exacerbate the stress that we may already feel, but also
can cause us to create situations that will bring more stress. For
example, if we become irritable because we are very tired, we may
get into arguments with loved ones, which can produce more conflict than usual in our lives and sap us of emotional support. When
we are not thinking as clearly as we would have been had we been
better rested, we can make simple mistakes that lead to stressful
consequences, such as missing questions on a test that we otherwise would have been able to answer or making errors at work and
weakening our chances at job security. When we lack sleep we can
also make mistakes that result in consequences that are extremely
negative. For example, people operating on less than 6 hours of
sleep are significantly more likely to be involved in an automobile
accident than those who have had a full 8 hours. Over time, sleep

loss can affect overall health. Lack of sleep weakens immunity, leaving us more susceptible to virtually all diseases and conditions. (This, of course, can also contribute to stress levels.) There are many reasons to strive to get enough sleep, and stress management is one of the most compelling ones.

Sleep Saboteurs

As with many other aspects of self-care, sleep is important for stress relief. When get inadequate sleep, particularly on a regular basis or for several days in a row, this can feed into a cycle of more stress and more missed sleep. Here are some of the main culprits for missed sleep:

* **Busy schedules.** As with exercise and proper nutrition, busy schedules can cause us to shave hours off our time in bed. Some people get to the point where having adequate sleep is seen as a luxury. However, when we look at all the negative effects of missed sleep, it becomes easier to identify activities that can be cut out or at least time slots where power naps can be added.

* **Outside influences.** If your friends, family, or roommates tend to skimp on sleep, you may find yourself doing the same. It becomes difficult to be the first one to go to sleep, particularly when there is still fun to be had. In such circumstances, you may need to accept that you are going against the grain in favor of meeting your most important needs.

* **Stress.** People often find that stress itself makes sleep more difficult. Whether we are staying up later because our stress responses are triggered and our bodies can't relax or we're busy thinking about our problems and their potential solutions, stress can make it more difficult to fall asleep. Other times, we may wake up during the night and find that stress-filled thoughts about the next day make it difficult to fall back asleep. Even finding the kind of high-quality, restful sleep we need can be affected by the stress we face. Managing stress can bring better sleep, just as better sleep can help us to more effectively manage stress.

* **Habits.** We may not realize when our habits are getting in the way of sleep, but this can definitely be a factor, too. Consuming

caffeine too late in the day can have a significant impact on sleep, because caffeine stays in the body for many hours and can make it difficult for us to drift off to sleep. Exercise right before bed can affect us as well, as our physiology is keyed up and not ready for the deep relaxation of sleep just yet. Similarly, the use of visual electronics late at night can shift melatonin levels and fool the body into thinking it is earlier than it is; when this happens, sleep is affected. By avoiding late-afternoon and nighttime caffeine and avoiding electronics and exercise for at least an hour before it is time to sleep, you can make it easier for your body to fall asleep and stay asleep.

*   **Underlying health issues.** Certain health issues can affect sleep, as can various medications. If you have tried the techniques recommended in this book and are still having difficulty sleeping, or if you suspect that the problem is more serious than can be addressed here, consult with your doctor. It is important to get to the root of the problem, and there are many things that can be done to bring on sleep more easily.

How to Manage: Improving Your Sleep

Aside from the tips mentioned above, there are several strategies that are effective when you are working on altering your sleep patterns. The following are some important things to keep in mind:

*   **Plan ahead.** Many of us wait until we are tired or have completed everything on our to-do lists before we fall into bed. The problem with this is that we may not realize how tired we are *until* we fall into bed, and that to-do list may be too long. Plan ahead in the following ways, and you can ensure better chances of the right quality and quantity of sleep.
    *   Be sure sleep is in your schedule. Set a bedtime, and stick with it as closely as possible.
    *   Cut out activities where possible, in order to create more time for sleep. (**Key 5** has some effective strategies for this.)
    *   Let others know when you need to go to bed. Set boundaries, and stick with them.

○ Cut down on late-afternoon caffeine, as well as late-night exercise and electronics, or at least allow a 1-hour buffer between those activities and the time you would like to fall asleep.

* **Adopt relaxing rituals.** There are several things you can do to get your body and mind into a more relaxed state, which can facilitate sleep. The following activities can become part of your nighttime routine and can help to relieve stress as well as more easily usher in sleep.

○ **Take a bath.** Nighttime baths can provide a wonderful way to relax. Adding lavender bath oil can be one way to use aromatherapy to your advantage—studies show that lavender scents not only can promote falling sleep, but also can improve quality of sleep. The warm water can relax your muscles, and if you wash your hair at night, you can save yourself time in the morning.

○ **Create a sleep-friendly environment.** Be sure that you cover the basics. Have a cool, comfortable place to sleep; soft, clean sheets help. If you are having trouble with sleep on a regular basis, try to use your bed for sleep *only*—if you need to read, work, watch television, or perform other tasks, try to do this in another spot so that your subconscious mind connects your bed with sleep and nothing else. If environmental noise bothers you and you cannot avoid it, consider investing in a sound machine that can soothe you to sleep and block out distracting background noise. Let your surroundings support your sleep.

○ **Exercise (but not too late).** I have been warning you against before-bed exercise, but all nighttime exercise isn't bad! In fact, engaging in physical activity during the day and in the evening and even later—before it gets *too* late—can actually bring greater relaxation and sleep readiness when it's time for bed. Again, just be sure you are done at least an hour before you need to fall asleep.

○ **Journaling.** As you will read in greater detail in **Key 8**, journaling can be a highly effective stress relief tool and can take several different forms. Particularly if you find the thoughts in your head swimming around as you try to relax, letting them out on paper can be an effective way to prepare for sleep. If you are concerned about a problem you face, you might want to take a few minutes to brainstorm solutions on paper before you head off to sleep. And if you are feeling slightly melancholy before bed, a gratitude journal can help. This flexible practice can bring you a high degree of inner peace so you can relax and sleep.

○ **Meditation.** Meditation is another strategy that can facilitate sleep and that you also can learn more about in **Key 8.** Getting your mind and body into a more relaxed state naturally makes sleep come more easily, and meditation accomplishes both goals beautifully. Especially if you are stressed and busy and have trouble with meditation because you feel there is not enough time, meditation practiced before bedtime may work perfectly.

* **See a doctor if difficulties persist.** It bears repeating that there are sometimes underlying medical issues that can impede sleep. Be sure to talk to your doctor if you face persistent sleep problems and these techniques do not help. There may be other issues at play.

Key Points about Healthy Habits

Healthy habits are important, but do not always come easily, especially when we are stressed. The following are central pieces of information to remember as you work on maintaining and ingraining healthy habits into your lifestyle. Keep these in mind, and you can keep yourself on the right track for a healthier body and a less stressed mind.

Healthy Habits Take Time to Develop

Practicing healthy habits can feel good the first time we try them, but they take time to become automatic. As I discussed in the Introduction, neural pathways form slowly and over time—just as we strengthen mental habits with repetition, we can strengthen our tendency to participate in lifestyle habits through repetition. Just as traveling to a new job can demand focus and planning the first few times but becomes automatic once we learn the route, lifestyle habits may feel strange at first and require some initial effort, but become virtually second nature if we work them into our routines and practice them continually.

Conventional wisdom has it that it takes roughly 3 weeks to develop a new habit, but the amount of time can vary among individuals, based on how much time and effort is put into preparation and execution, the difficulty of the habit, and several other factors. Change can generally come after a few weeks of regular practice. Whatever the time frame, with practice, we eventually do not have to think about maintaining the new habit; it just feels automatic. This is not to say that the habit will require no effort at all—just as traveling to work still takes *some* effort—but it will feel like less of an option that you have to push yourself into taking and more like something you just do, a natural part of your life that would be missed if discontinued.

So remember: Get through the first few weeks or months, and the road becomes much easier. This is an important point to keep in mind, because the first few weeks of a new habit are often the most difficult. Knowing that the road becomes smoother after that initial push past inertia can sometimes make the difference between losing momentum and persevering into long-term success. (Read more about maintaining long-term habits in the last chapter of this book, "Creating an Action Plan.")

Healthy Habits Feed off Each Other

We have discussed how unhealthy habits tend to feed on themselves when we are stressed. (Chronically stressed individuals not only are less likely to maintain healthy habits because they may lack the energy to make the effort, but they also generally find unhealthy habits more tempting simply because the stress that they are under causes them to crave the wrong things.) Fortunately, things work the other way as well—healthy habits tend to make us want to maintain more healthy habits! This is because a change in one area—such as a new exercise program for a previously sedentary individual—can lift the stress that is blocking the way to healthier living in other areas. So if you start exercising more, you may find yourself craving fewer sweets and carbs. And you might find that your mind is clearer than it had been, so that you sleep better at night and get better-quality sleep. You may find that you are more relaxed, more patient, and more forgiving, which can help in your relationships. So keep this in mind: **One change makes all the other changes come more easily.** What a great incentive to make that first change!

Small Changes Can Make a Big Difference

When we are stressed and living a less-than-healthy existence, it is easy to feel overwhelmed. People often find that they are less motivated to make changes in the areas of health and self-care because there is *so much* that needs to change that they find themselves getting discouraged and wanting to give up on the effort before they even try. Why try, they reason, when the ultimate outcome will probably be failure?

It is important to realize that baby steps work. Not only does the accumulation of individual steps ultimately lead to a destination, each little step might make the next one easier, especially in the realm of self-care. This is how it works: When we are feeling stressed and overwhelmed, we have less energy to change our habits, and we may be more likely to crave unhealthy activities, as discussed. Just as healthy habits feed into other healthy habits, healthy changes tend to self-perpetuate—taking a brisk walk to reduce stress can lessen the incidence of stress, which in turn can help us to feel less overwhelmed, less physically drained, and more energetic. Then exercise like walking becomes easier and more attractive. Taking a short walk can lead to longer walks, and the habit can build upon itself. (The same is true with healthy eating, getting more and better sleep, and other self-care activities.) So bear in mind: **Just getting started with a healthy new habit will make it easier to maintain that habit.** Now, don't you feel more motivated already?

Make One Change at a Time

Learning about the benefits of healthy lifestyle habits can be inspiring. Thinking about all you can gain from changing the way you live can switch from feeling exciting to feeling overwhelming pretty quickly, however, if you try to make too many changes at once. If you try to do this, it can become intimidating to know where to begin. Focus on one area of your lifestyle at a time, for example, getting more sleep, or even one new habit at a time, such as avoiding caffeine after 2:00 P.M. Then you can add new changes from there, letting the momentum of the previous changes work in your favor.

Don't Give Up!

If you find yourself slipping back into your previous habits, **do not give up**. Remember from the Introduction that this is part of the process of change (see Stage 5 of the Transtheoretical Model of Change). In fact, you can actually use the experience of backsliding to propel yourself forward toward your goals. Again, the last chapter in this book, "Creating an Action Plan," is focused primarily on the process of implementing these changes and can help you to put together a complete plan, but this is an important tip that can go a long way in helping you to get to the planning stages.

Questions to Ask Yourself

* When I am stressed, which areas of self-care do I tend to neglect?

* How might inadequate sleep, improper nutrition, or lack of exercise be affecting my stress levels?
* What are the simplest ways in which I can ensure better self-care? What are the most effective?
* Of the techniques discussed in this chapter, which ones seemed to resonate the most with me?
* If I could choose only one area of self-care to work on first, which would I choose because it would make the biggest impact?

Evaluate Your Answers

The answers to the questions above can help you to zero in on the areas of your health that you may be neglecting the most, and the new habits you choose to adopt that will set you on a healthier path. Where you begin with your self-care plans will depend on your answers, and on your goals. What poor habits are impacting you the most? Would you like to begin with action plans that are best for your health, or the ones that are easiest for you to adopt?

Activity to Try: Make an Action List

After answering the questions above, read back through the lists of action steps in this chapter and choose a few that you would like to put into effect in your life, either now or in the near future. Then, based on which ones appeal most to your needs and priorities, choose one or two to focus on first. For more help in maintaining new habits, create your list and see the final chapter of this book, "Creating an Action Plan," for next steps.

Activity to Try: Make an Exercise List

One of the best ways to ensure that you will begin exercising in the near future is to make a list of exercises you think could be fun. If you are having a difficult time coming up with some, go online and research gyms in your area. Look at the schedules of their exercise classes, and see which classes appeal to you. If you find a gym that appeals enough, consider joining! If classes at the gym aren't your thing, research adult sports leagues in your area, talk to friends about what they do for exercise, and put your feelers out for more ideas. Don't stop until you have a list of at least two activities you would enjoy doing for exercise. Then get moving!

KEY 4

GET INTO THE RIGHT
FRAME OF MIND

Not what we have, but what we enjoy, constitutes our abundance.

—EPICURUS

We may not always be able to control our circumstances, but we have significant control over *our responses* to our circumstances. Because our experience of stress is heavily dependent on the way we choose to think about our stressors, we can considerably reduce feelings of stress by cultivating attitudes that support serenity, that focus on the positive, and that help us use our resources. This chapter will focus on strategies for understanding and maintaining such attitudes; such strategies include journaling, practicing optimism, and cultivating gratitude.

One Grade, Two Perspectives

Taylor took a challenging test and received a C–. This was the first test in his first semester of college, yet he made several projections about the future based on this grade. "I'm in over my head here. I didn't study enough, and obviously I'm not cut out for this class. In fact, I'm probably going to do poorly in most of my classes here! I wonder if I'm even college material. Maybe I should just give up now."

Francis took the same test and received the same grade. He was a freshman taking his first test, and he, too, made a few projections. "Wow, this is a lower grade than I had expected. I didn't study enough, and obviously I'll have to work harder. This is just one test, though, and I'll do better on the next ones, and I can pull my grade up easily. I'll do better in my other classes, too. I'm sure everyone bombs a test or two during their first semester. I'm sure this is just a fluke, but I'll study harder on future tests, just in case."

The differences in their reactions fall along the lines of typical optimists and pessimists. The way they interpreted the same event differed enormously, and their motivation and resulting behavior were quite different as well. The way optimists minimize their failures and maximize their successes—and the way pessimists do the opposite—has an impact on their stress levels and the degree of success they find in life.

The Importance of Frame of Mind

When many people think about stress management, they think about how to cut down or control the stressors they face in their lives. While there are ways to minimize or reduce the number of stressors (as we will discuss in **Key 7**), it is not always possible to eliminate all stressors, nor is it desirable (as we learned in **Key 1**). Often we may find ourselves in situations where we cannot change our circumstances, or at least not right away.

This is why our frame of mind is so important—we can control our responses to our circumstances, even when we cannot control our circumstances. In exerting such control, we can lessen the negative elements of experiencing stress. This one crucial strategy that is available to everyone could be a stress relief plan in itself, and it has been for many people who have had to accept lifestyle factors that are stressful and beyond their control. Let's look at why.

How Mental Factors Affect
Our Experience of Stress

Potential stressors surround us constantly. Some of these stressors affect us more than others, and some of them affect *some people* more than they affect others. There is a pivotal factor that determines which stressors affect which people and to what degree: perception. The body's stress response is triggered by *perceived* threats to our health and safety, and each of us may perceive things somewhat differently. It has long been observed that two people can experience the same situation and react completely differently: One driver may react to a traffic jam with stress and rage, while the driver in the next car may accept the possibility of being late and choose to relax and listen to the radio. Two people may face the same challenge and deadline at work; by the end one may feel overwhelmed and burned out, while the other is invigorated and excited at the project's completion. It is important to understand how these differences arise and to see how this understanding can be put to good use in keeping us relaxed in the face of potential stressors. It is vital to know, first, that one factor that we all share can make the difference between triggering our stress response and allowing us to remain in a relaxed state. In the following section I describe and elaborate on this factor.

One Pivotal Perception

As we noted in the Introduction, when we face a situation whose demands we believe we cannot meet, we feel stress. This means that in a given situation, if there are requirements that are taxing but we are able to meet them with a moderate amount of effort, we may feel challenged or invigorated. If a situation demands resources or abilities we do not possess, we generally feel stressed, especially if there are heavy consequences from failing to meet these demands. If we are able to meet a challenge we face, we experience it as just that—a challenge. We may feel excited, but we generally do not feel stressed. If we calculate that a challenge we face is beyond what we are able to manage, we may experience that challenge as threatening—to our physical safety, our standing in a community, our ability to meet our financial or relationship needs, or even our very sense of self. This is the main factor that determines whether we experience something as stressful or not: our perception of a situation as a *threat* or as a *challenge*. Several personal factors may influence whether a given situation is perceived as threatening or challenging, but when the mind perceives a threat, the body responds with a stress response. The following factors influence whether something is experienced as threatening or challenging.

Inborn Traits

As personality psychology—and virtually any parent of more than one child—can tell you, certain personality characteristics are innate. Psychologists refer to the "Big Five" personality factors as the key features that can be measured practically from birth: openness to new experiences, agreeableness, conscientiousness, extroversion, and neuroticism. Where we stand with these five basic factors can affect how we react to what we experience in a multitude of ways. Someone who is an introvert may feel threatened by giving a presentation, even to a small group of people, when a similar challenge would be experienced as fun by an extrovert. Someone high in conscientiousness may feel stressed by a large and important assignment at work because this individual may gauge that he or she cannot satisfactorily complete the job in the allotted time, whereas someone who is less committed to doing an above-average job may feel less stress. Conversely, the same conscientious person may feel less stress in the long run because he or she has produced better work—this may lead to greater success in life and the resources that come with this, and lead away from the negative consequences that can come from a shoddy job. These factors affect how we behave, and they also affect how we feel and what we perceive; the traits are part of who we are and part of how stressed we feel.

While these five traits are inborn, we do have some control over how strongly we experience them, and to what degree they express themselves in our personality. While someone with a high level of introversion may never become the life of the party, as will someone who has a strong predisposition toward extroversion, psychologists estimate that we can alter our set point for happiness by about 40–50%, and this may be an accurate estimate for these traits as well. With practice, we can shape our natural tendencies to such a point that we will tend to see and react to things differently. We can shape the traits that we were born with.

Available Resources

Because our perception of stress pivots on our estimated ability to meet the demands we face, our beliefs about our resources can greatly influence our experience of stress. I use the words *our beliefs about our resources* because we often have greater internal and external resources than we believe we possess. These resources— from physical resources such as tools and possessions; to social resources such as friends who are able to lend support; to internal resources such as energy, intelligence, or personal resilience—can help us in many ways, but we need to be aware of them before we can use them. If we have a greater ability to meet a challenge than we believe we do, we will still experience stress, because it is our estimation that we cannot meet this particular challenge. (If we overestimate our resources, this can lead to stress as well, as we may realize too late that we are in over our heads.) Being aware of the personal resources you do and do not possess can help you to accurately appraise your situation and to experience stress only when it is warranted. Strengthening your resources can diminish stress as well. Because we all have our own unique set of resources, we may respond in unique ways to the same potential stressor.

Past Experiences

Early in life, we started learning from our experiences, and these lessons shaped how we think about ourselves and the world around us. The assumptions we made about the world then continue to affect what we think and experience into the present. Those who experience early trauma may be sensitive to certain experiences now, so that related experiences in the present can cause stress that may not be felt by most other people in the same situation. (Conversely, the same person may have developed particular strengths in response to facing the trauma and recovering from it, and these strengths may add an extra dimension of resilience and diminish feelings of stress.) We may have encountered certain challenges in the past that we could not meet, and as a result we may have developed a sense of helplessness that takes over in similar situations we face now. By contrast, we may have developed a sense of self-confidence from early successes that translates into feelings of resourcefulness now. The experiences we have had and, more important, what we have come to believe from these experiences, affect how stressed we feel today.

Habitual Attitudes

As we build on our experiences, we get used to certain thought patterns, and they come to define us. Just as we may find ourselves at home after an end-of-day commute without remembering the specific turns we took because the route has become automatic, we may automatically respond with familiar thought patterns out of habit.

If, for example, we have had early experiences of rejection after an argument with a loved one and decide from this that conflict leads to loss, we may become much more stressed by conflicts than someone who has found that resolving conflict tends to lead to a healthier relationship in the future. A belief that conflict leads to rejection may translate into habitual thought patterns of anger, avoidance, or at least negative reactions when conflict threatens to arise—and all these can bring stress. Seeking out conflict is not necessarily a good idea in many situations, but accepting and working through conflict in a respectful way can be beneficial for relationships, and those who have developed habitual thought patterns that support this may experience not only a greater number of healthy relationships, but also less stress within those relationships.

Examining your habitual thought patterns and challenging them can enable you to *choose* your responses to the potential stressors you face. While it takes time to change habits—and habits of thought are no different from other lifestyle habits—it is very possible and well worth the effort to do so.

What Thought Patterns Contribute to Stress?

Understanding how thoughts may contribute to stress is an important step, and realizing that it is possible to change these thoughts is another valuable one. However, before we are able to change our thought patterns to better support stress relief, it is crucial to be able to identify the thought patterns that are commonly the most damaging—and the most empowering—so we can make changes that really count. The following thought patterns can have the greatest impact on stress levels.

Pessimism and Optimism

People often think that pessimism is characterized by seeing the glass as half empty and optimism by seeing it as half full, meaning that pessimists will more often notice the negatives in a situation while optimists focus on the positive, sometimes to a fault. This is partially true, but the defining features of optimism and pessimism are a little more complex than that. Your tendency toward pessimism or optimism is linked to your explanatory style, or the way you explain to yourself what you experience. When it comes to explanatory style, optimists and pessimists are opposites. When positive events occur, optimists tend to process these situations within the framework of three main assumptions:

* Optimists credit themselves with everything that goes right in their lives.
* Optimists take one success as evidence that more success is imminent.
* Optimists assume that the effects of their successes will be lasting.

Pessimists tend to be ruled by the opposite:

* Pessimists attribute positive events to chance or other factors outside themselves.
* Pessimists believe that successes in their lives are isolated incidents.
* Pessimists believe that their successes will be short lived.

When it comes to negative events, optimists and pessimists switch places and tend to process these events in opposite ways, with optimists believing them to be short lived, isolated, and caused by factors outside of themselves, while pessimists believe that negative events will have lasting effects, are indicative of more negative events to come, and are somehow the pessimist's fault.

These very different patterns of perception lie at the root of an optimist's propensity to see the positive in a situation and a pessimist's tendency to point out the negative. Optimists believe that they will succeed, so they tend to celebrate their successes, see opportunities everywhere, and trust in their own abilities—all things that lead to a greater belief in personal resources and a reduced experience of stress. Pessimists may sometimes find themselves more prepared (because, seeing potential problems, they are more likely to create backup plans), but they also see fewer opportunities, believe in themselves less, and expect the worst. Pessimists are more stressed for good reason.

While people (especially those prone to pessimism) may guess that optimists are seeing only what they want to see, research backs up the reality that optimists really do have it better. And more interestingly, it's been found that optimists aren't happier because *they have better lives*; rather, they see these benefits because of *their optimistic way of seeing the world*. Specifically, optimists tend to enjoy better emotional health, increased longevity, greater success in life, and, of course, less stress. One study examined the impact of optimism, as well as positive affect (being in a good mood) and social support, and were able to discern that these factors had an impact on physical health measured at 17% and an impact on psychological health of 33%! This further underscores the importance of positive thinking, happiness, and having supportive people in your life.

Pessimists, on the other hand, not only miss out on the happiness that optimists enjoy, but also experience poorer health, according to several studies. Pessimists tend to have a higher incidence of contracting infectious diseases and have poorer overall health and earlier mortality. They also enjoy less success in life than do their more optimistic counterparts. Pessimistic thinking patterns can be subtle, but it is worth identifying and eliminating them, because this can lead to a much more positive experience in life.

Cognitive Distortions

Because of all of the factors that go into our perceptions of stress—habitual thoughts patterns, past experiences, inborn traits, and more—maintaining true objectivity is extremely difficult, if not impossible. There are specific ways in which people tend to distort what they see around them; these are our brain's way of protecting our ego, but they can cause stress. Psychologist Aaron T. Beck identified this phenomenon and coined the term *cognitive distortions*. These distortions can help us momentarily avoid the emotional pain of viewing ourselves as responsible for less-than-perfect circumstances or of noticing disappointing events that are happening to us, but the distortions leave us feeling hopeless, victimized, angry, and stressed. Most of us have a tendency toward a few of these, and becoming more aware of them can help us recognize them when we are using them, and start to make changes in how we think. The following are common cognitive distortions and examples of each:

* **All-or-nothing thinking.** Using extremes in thought, with no gray area. "It's not just a bad day, it's *the worst day ever.*"
* **Overgeneralization.** Taking isolated events and assuming that all future events will be the same. "It's not just one frustrating day, *this always happens.*"
* **Mental filter.** Glossing over the positive. "It's not a few negative things happening, *it's a whole day of nothing but bad experiences.*"
* **Disqualifying the positive.** Treating positive events as flukes and giving more weight to the negative. "There is no 'bright side' because *nothing good could come out of this.*"
* **Jumping to conclusions.** Deciding what to believe and then looking for evidence to support assumptions, rather than letting the evidence lead to a logical conclusion. "Because a few things went wrong, *everything else will go wrong, too, and somebody must have wanted this to happen on purpose.*"
* **Magnification and minimization.** Blowing things out of proportion or failing to assign events the significance they deserve. "This is *the end of the world,*" or "*It's nothing.*"
* **Emotional reasoning.** Taking emotions as facts. "I'm *feeling angry with you,* therefore *you must be wrong.*"
* ***Should* statements.** Living by a rigid set of rules and believing that others need to live by these inflexible rules as well. "*They should know* what I want without my having to ask."
* **Labeling and mislabeling.** Placing negative, often inaccurate labels on oneself and others. "*You're just a whiner.*"
* **Personalization.** Blaming oneself or others for events that are outside one's control. "*You ruined my day.*"

Cognitive distortions can lead to greater stress in several ways: They promote conflict in relationships, keep us feeling bad (notice how many of the examples above are associated with a pessimistic explanatory style), and keep us focused on what we cannot control instead of what we can. Becoming more aware of cognitive distortions that creep into your life can help you loosen their hold, feel more empowered, and experience less stress.

Rumination

Have you ever been upset about something and just could not get it out of your head? What begins as an attempt to find a solution to a problem can slide into rumination, whereby people obsess over stressful, negative situations, playing and replaying them in their heads, but without finding solutions. Rumination is actually a combination of reflection and brooding; reflection on a problem can lead to a solution, but brooding is associated with greater levels of stress and a more negative mood. This kind of thinking can be quite stressful, as it exacerbates feelings of helplessness, frustration, and hurt. Aside from being associated with a more negative and stressed frame of mind, fruitless rumination is linked to less proactive behavior (being stuck in a negative situation), self-sabotaging behaviors (such as binge eating), and even health issues such as hypertension. If you find yourself trapped in a state of rumination, it is most certainly affecting your stress levels and quite possibly your health.

An Important Caveat

It would be stating a fallacy to claim that all stress is entirely a matter of perception. Certain experiences are perceived as stressful when they demand from us more than we are able to give. Situations that are uncontrollable, that require abilities we do not possess, or that keep us overloaded for long periods of time tend to take a physical and psychological toll regardless of our perceptions. This has been documented by research and is important to point out because often people who understand the role of mindset may feel that they are failing in their positive-thinking strategies or related methods if they find themselves feeling any effects of stress at all. It is critical to remember that practicing these techniques and getting into the right frame of mind for stress relief can have a significant impact on our experience of stress, but the effects of stress may not be entirely eliminated through this one key strategy alone. If you feel a reduction in stress but your experience of stress is not entirely eliminated right away, continue to celebrate your progress and do not give up. When we use strategies to change our mindset, we generally feel less stressed, and this reduction in stress can free up energy to enact other changes that you will read about in this book. While this strategy alone may not erase all stress, it still presents a powerful way to relieve stress, and, alone or with other stress relievers, it can make the difference between healthy and unhealthy levels of stress.

Key Points to Remember

To sum up the important factors to remember when it comes to thinking styles and their impact on stress, the following are critical points to keep in mind:

*   We can control our responses to circumstances, even when the circumstances themselves are beyond our control. In doing so, we can greatly lessen our negative experience of stress.
*   Whether or not our stress response is triggered depends on whether we perceive a situation as a potential *threat* to our physical, emotional, or psychological safety.
*   Not everyone experiences potential stressors the same way; we do not all find the same things universally stressful.
*   Our perception of stress can be unique depending on inborn traits, available resources, past experiences, and habitual thought patterns, each of which can influence how we react and how stressed we feel in different situations.
*   Certain thought patterns, particularly pessimism, cognitive dis-

tortions, and rumination, can be damaging to your peace of mind, and even your health.

* Some situations, even when not perceived as "stressful," take a toll. While changing your thought patterns does not eliminate all stress (and no strategy can do this entirely), it can produce significant positive changes in your outlook and experience, which can lead to other positive changes.

Activities to Try

Because it is possible (and advisable) to examine our own thought processes and change the habitual thinking patterns that create stress in our lives, there is plenty of reason for optimism. Simply becoming aware of how such factors as pessimism, rumination, cognitive distortions, and other thinking patterns affect your life is the first step toward loosening their negative effects on you. Once you become aware of how these ways of thinking can color your experience, you may begin to automatically notice and challenge them. However, if you take your awareness to the next level through action, you reduce the likelihood that you will gradually forget what you have learned and remain in the same patterns of thought and behavior. The thought-changing exercises below can cement your learning, translate into lasting changes, and have a strong impact on your stress levels.

Thought Stopping

Now that you may be aware of a few thought patterns that you want to change, it is important to remember that it *is* possible to alter these patterns of thinking that may feel automatic. It will, however, take time and some effort. As we think in a similar way repeatedly, the brain becomes accustomed to following this familiar path, just as we may drive home from work every day without giving much thought to which turns to take—it feels automatic. An important step in changing your undesirable habitual thought patterns is to learn to catch yourself and stop when you find that you are traveling down this well-worn path. Thought-stopping exercises can help you to become more aware of what you are thinking and stop yourself from continuing with these thoughts. The following thought-stopping exercises can help you to substitute pessimistic thinking patterns for optimistic ones, shift ruminative thinking to more present-focused thoughts, or disrupt other ingrained thinking patterns that you would like to stop.

Rubber Band Snap

The rubber-band-snap technique is an old technique designed to pair a negative stimulus—the minor pain you feel when you are stung by a rubber band snapping against your skin—with your unwanted thoughts, so that in time, those thoughts carry a negative association and you are motivated to avoid them. The strategy is simple:

1. Wear a rubber band on your wrist.
2. When you find yourself indulging in a thought pattern that you would like to avoid, pull the rubber band away from your skin and let it snap back and sting you.
3. Repeat as necessary.

The rubber-band-snap technique allows you to control the intensity of the negative feeling you feel and acts as both a reminder (seeing the rubber band on your wrist can remind you of your goals), and a deterrent (constant band snaps will becoming annoying at best and may even cause minor pain). This technique has helped many people give up a multitude of negative habits over the years. After a short time, you likely won't need this technique anymore.

"Stop" Thinking

If you are more visually oriented, are opposed to discomfort, or simply don't want to be seen wearing a rubber band on your wrist, this similar technique may be more appropriate for you. Visualize a stop sign in your mind—the more detailed, the better. You may use a standard traffic sign, or you may imagine a sign of your own with bright words, a red hand, or anything else that means *stop* for you. As you find yourself engaging in one of the thought patterns you are hoping to eliminate, envision this image as soon as you catch yourself, and change your focus. This technique is more powerful than merely catching yourself and switching your focus, because you are creating a stronger and more memorable stimulus to connect with the habit you are trying to drop. This may more effectively help you to shift your focus as well, as it will no doubt be a quite different thought from the one you were thinking.

Take a Deep Breath

A few generations ago, it became popular for people to count to 10 when they felt overwhelmed or angry, as a way to collect themselves and shift their focus. This strategy was popular then and is still useful today because it works. However, taking deep breaths for a count of 10 can have the same effect and elicit the positive benefits of relaxation breathing, without the attention-provoking behavior of counting aloud. Deep breathing can relax the body and oxygenate the blood, clear the mind, and even reverse the body's stress response. Here are some tips to remember:

* As you breathe, relax your shoulders and breathe from your diaphragm. Your shoulders should stay where they are—not moving up and down with each breath—and your belly should expand and contract as you breathe.
* To regulate the speed of your breathing, mentally count to 3 on the inhale, and 5 on the exhale. This lengthens your breaths naturally and shifts your focus inward.
* When you feel your mind clearing after a few seconds, choose a thinking pattern that you would prefer to make habitual.
* Pair these mini-breathing sessions with longer meditation and breathing sessions, and you will gain more robust benefits, as your body will remember the relaxed state you experience in

those longer sessions and return to this state more quickly and easily.

That's it. It is as easy as it sounds; you just have to remember to do it.

Journaling

Writing in a journal (or typing your thoughts on your keyboard) can bring some fantastic benefits. Journaling has been associated with decreased symptoms of asthma, arthritis, and several other health conditions. It has also been linked with improved cognitive functioning, decreased depressive symptoms, increased immunity, and reduced levels of stress. Journaling has been recommended by therapists, health practitioners, and coaches as a route to stress relief and inner change. The following journaling techniques can be quite helpful for getting into the right frame of mind, as well as for general stress relief.

Emotional-Processing Journal

Journals that are meant for the processing of emotions can supply an outlet for venting negative feelings and can be a forum for processing emotions and brainstorming solutions. The exploration questions in this chapter could be successfully processed through this type of journaling. The following are some tips for maintaining an emotional-processing journal:

* Don't feel obligated to write every day, but do so if it works easily for you. If you set journaling goals for yourself that you can't maintain, it becomes tempting to give up the practice.
* Write about your positive *and* negative feelings, but be sure to also spend time focused on finding solutions. Studies show that this is the most beneficial strategy for this type of journaling, and it can help you to avoid falling into a pattern of rumination.
* Write about what you feel and why you feel it. If this starts to bring up experiences that are more intense than you believe you

can deal with alone, you may want to explore these emotions with the support of a therapist.

Gratitude Journal

While gratitude journals have always been around, they have become much more popular in the past 2 decades and have even been the focus of research in the fields of positive psychology and health psychology. Studies show not only that gratitude journals can increase levels of happiness, but also that this type of journaling can even lift the symptoms of depression. The benefits are found to be greatest when you do the following:

* Write about three things each day. Write about what they are and why you appreciate them. They could be events that happened, actions you took, or people in your life.
* Write about your feelings surrounding these things.
* Write at the end of the day, if possible, reflecting on what has happened on that particular day. This works well because it encourages you to think throughout the day about what you are grateful for and can include in your journal, and it helps you to get into a good frame of mind before you fall asleep.

Mindfulness

Meditation has long been popular in the Eastern world, and it is now gaining traction worldwide as an effective route to stress relief. Now that the field of health psychology is yielding solid research that prove the effectiveness of meditation and mindfulness practices, therapists, coaches, and doctors are recommending these activities for patients and clients who need to learn to relieve stress. Aside from the purely physical benefits of slowed breathing and a relaxed body, the psychological benefits delivered by a peaceful, present-focused mind have been proved many times over. The following mindfulness exercises can help you to learn to clear your mind of negative, ruminative thoughts. With practice, obtaining a clear mind becomes automatic.

Mini-meditation

Mini-meditation works in much the same way as the breathing exercise mentioned earlier in this section and for similar reasons. While meditation has been shown to produce the greatest benefit when performed in sessions of 20 minutes or longer, 5-minute and even shorter meditations can clear the mind and can allow practitioners who meditate fairly frequently to quickly get back into a familiar place of inner peace. Mini-meditation can be practiced in a few simple steps:

1. Breathe deeply and slowly, relaxing your shoulders and expanding and contracting your belly with each breath. (For more detailed instructions on this, see the earlier section on breathing exercises.)
2. Clear your mind of all thoughts as you focus on your breathing.
3. As thoughts drift into your mind, gently redirect your focus back to your breathing.

One important point to remember, especially if you have a tendency for perfectionism, is that it is natural for thoughts to drift into your mind; this happens even with those who have been practicing for many years. When this happens, it does not mean you have failed in your practice. The idea is to gently redirect your attention as it happens. If you find yourself feeling bad, try to instead congratulate yourself for noticing that your mind has wandered, as you shift your focus back to your breathing.

Thought-Stopping Exercise

This meditation practice is similar to mini-meditation and, like mini-meditation, may be practiced for a few minutes, or it can be practiced for an hour or more. The main difference with this meditation is that there is slightly more engagement with the thoughts that may drift into your mind. Many people who find it difficult to let go of their thoughts enjoy this exercise, because the thoughts are briefly addressed before being set aside. This exercise also provides practice in detaching from thinking patterns and experiencing them more as an observer might, rather than becoming immersed in them or even fully engaged. This skill can help you to detach from negative thought patterns throughout your daily life. Here is how it works:

1. Go to a quiet place, get into a comfortable position, and fall into a deep, relaxed breathing pattern.
2. Focus on your breathing and remain in the present moment.
3. As thoughts drift into your mind, briefly label them—*judgment, worry, question,* or whatever type of thought it is. You may even stay with the singular label *thinking.*
4. Repeat, and continue your meditation for as long as you wish or until the alarm goes off, if you have set one.

This practice can help you to feel less invested in your thoughts and to become more aware that your thoughts can be controlled by you.

Chocolate Meditation

This popular practice is often taught in 8-week Mindfulness-Based Stress Reduction (MBSR) courses, which are proved to lessen the severity of stress and a multitude of other health-related issues, including anxiety disorders, depression, relationship issues, sleep problems, eating disorders, and more. The chocolate meditation is also popular because it is delicious. (Don't worry, the benefits of a small amount of dark chocolate outweigh the detriments for most people.) The following are some quick tips on how to practice chocolate meditation:

1. Hold a small piece of dark chocolate between your thumb and forefinger.
2. Take it in with all your senses. Smell it. Experience how it feels pressed against your fingers: Is it soft, cool, starting to melt? Study the color and texture, and really notice how it looks and how your

hand looks holding it. Spend as much time as possible noticing the details.

3. As you raise the chocolate to your mouth, experience how your arm feels as it bends, how your clothing feels rubbing against your skin (if you are wearing sleeves) or how your skin feels (if you are not) as you bend your arm. Experience the feel of the chocolate as it touches your mouth.

4. As you begin to eat the chocolate, take a tiny bite first, and let the chocolate melt in your mouth.

5. Continue to experience this slowly, with this level of focus on the present, until the small piece of chocolate is gone.

This is a brief exercise designed to help you to experience the benefits and practice of a novel type of mindfulness meditation, derived from MBSR. In an MBSR class, the event of enjoying chocolate meditation may be more thorough and effective, but practicing it yourself can be useful in relieving stress. Practice this type of meditation daily, and you will find it easier to clear your mind of negative thoughts and focus on the present moment.

Questions to Ask Yourself

* Think of the last success you had in your life, or one that stands out particularly clearly in your mind. On a piece of paper, describe what you said to yourself to explain how you achieved this success. What factors contributed to your success, and how did this success influence your expectations for the future? When you are finished, read over the description and pay close attention to how you attribute your success to the relevant factors, referencing what you know now about explanatory style.
  ° Do you lean toward optimism or pessimism?
  ° If you lean toward pessimism, what are some realistic ways in which you might change your focus to make it more optimistic?

◦   What is one important idea to remember when you meet your next success?

*   Complete the preceding exercise, but instead of writing about a success, write about a time when you experienced disappointment with something you attempted.

   ◦   According to the guidelines of explanatory style, would you classify your reaction as optimistic or pessimistic?

   ◦   If you lean toward pessimism, how might you realistically change your self-talk to ease up on yourself and take a more optimistic view?

   ◦   What one salient point would help you to remain more optimistic in the face of future setbacks?

*   When you find yourself falling short of your goals, or encountering a frustration or disappointment in life, do you tend to take what you can and learn from the experience, and then move forward? Or do you find yourself reacting with one of the following responses (or another, similar response): putting the experience out of your mind without really thinking about it and moving forward as though it didn't happen, beating yourself up over the "failure" and backing away from future challenges, blaming others and getting angry? Think of specific times in your life that you have encountered situations like these, and reflect on how you handled these experiences.

   ◦   Has your response changed over the years? If so, how?

   ◦   Would you like your response to change? If so, in what way?

   ◦   What key idea can you keep in mind to encourage yourself to handle these disappointments in the healthiest way possible for you?

Evaluate Your Answers

Simply asking yourself these questions and exploring your answers can help you make progress toward changing your thought patterns, through raising your own awareness of where you are now and where you would like to go. Think carefully about each question, and ponder what your answers are telling you about yourself. Which areas of thinking would you like to change? When you identify where you are in your process and where you would like to go, see if you can identify the most pressing thought habit that you would like to change, based on how you would like to be thinking in the future. Then practice one or two of the activities listed in this chapter, and work your way to a more positive, less stressed frame of mind. In time, these new thought habits will become automatic.

CUT DOWN ON STRESSORS WHEN POSSIBLE

Beware the barrenness of a busy life. —SOCRATES

We can't remove all stress from our lives (and, frankly, we wouldn't want to), but we can remove a significant amount of it by identifying our chronic stressors and eliminating them wherever possible. While other chapters have covered strategies for coping with stressors that cannot be eliminated, this chapter will help you to identify areas of your life where you can eliminate or reduce chronic stress triggers and create action plans for enacting these changes in a realistic way.

Pecked to Death by Ducks!

Danielle liked that she was everyone's go-to person. She ran a successful business, had children, and held positions of leadership in several groups in her spare time. If people needed to get something done, they could go to Danielle, because she was efficient and loved taking on projects. She also felt overwhelmed at times, when all her commitments needed her attention at once. Sometimes she felt invigorated by her many activities, as when, for example, she was working on completing a project she really enjoyed. Other times, she thought of herself as "being pecked to death by ducks"—

when she had many different people needing "just one small thing" from her at once or when she noticed a few too many things in her life that needed a minor amount of attention. All these small responsibilities had a way of adding up to a heavy load. Everyone has a limit; when Danielle started experiencing heart palpitations, she didn't recognize the chance that she was approaching hers. When she had her first panic attack, she had to reexamine her lifestyle.

After talking to her doctor and learning that stress was a factor in her case, she started taking a closer look at her life and her choices. In the process of examining her life, she realized that she pushed herself harder than was necessary or healthy. As part of finding a healthier balance, Danielle learned to examine her body's signs that she was getting in over her head, and she learned to make changes before she felt overwhelmed and experienced physical sensations that led to panic attacks. She also discovered that she had many responsibilities that were not beneficial to her and only drained her energy. Armed with a new understanding of where her "ducks" were hiding, she took the initiative to cull the clutter of her life and put a stop to the unnecessary "pecks." This took some energy at first, but she found that she was much less stressed once she did some cleanup. Now Danielle still has a full, busy life, but her schedule is filled to a manageable level, and she enjoys it without the undue stress.

Why It's Important to Cut Down on All Stressors

Volumes have been written on the importance of remaining un-stressed regardless of circumstances, on the concept that a great deal of stress lies in our perceptions, and on the fact that we always have choices to make and options to take. (I explored this truth in **Key 4**.) However, these elements are only part of the equation. While internal shifts are powerful and can go far in helping us to relieve stress, it is important to remember that cutting out stressors whenever possible is also a valid and important stress management strategy.

When we think about cutting out the things that cause us stress, we often focus on the biggies: the job that causes us endless frustration, the marriage that makes us feel trapped, or the financial straits that keep us up at night. These things are important to tackle, but they often don't come with easy answers or quick solutions; often we need to work toward amenable solutions with such challenges and move forward in specific steps and phases. Quitting a job may be done in an e-mail that takes 5 minutes to write, or a marriage can end with the words "I don't—anymore," but the fallout from such choices (fallout such as the often difficult search for a new job or the process of divorce and emotional healing) means that stress relief doesn't come in the same short time frame.

Stop Sweating the Small Stuff

Another way to relieve stress—one that is considered less often but can bring more immediate results—is to cut out the small stressors that add up to feelings of chronic stress. These are those little things that we are able to endure but that take a toll on our peace of mind: the annoying friend who can't take a hint, the messy desk that seems to swallow up important papers, the weekly commitment we always seem to dread.

Life coaches call these things *tolerations* because, as the name suggests, we simply tolerate them. We may not even pay attention to their presence in our lives, but we *feel* it. A common focus in coaching is to identify and eliminate tolerations and to work toward keeping them from creeping in and taking over. We all have tolerations in our lives, and they do take a toll.

The Toll of Tolerations

Tolerations aren't overwhelming in themselves, but they can push us over the edge, taking us from feeling serene to irritated or from stressed to overwhelmed. And as I described in previous chapters, when we are operating from a place of feeling more stressed, things tend to snowball.

Eliminating these small stressors doesn't always seem worth it when we think about how much more stress we could eliminate by cutting out our larger sources of stress. This is why most of us just let the small stressors continue on as unquestioned parts of our lives. However, they are not as harmless as we may think or as forgettable as we would hope, and they are worthy of the relatively small effort it takes to eliminate them, given the overall toll they can take when they add up. Here are a few specific ways in which we sabotage ourselves by letting these nagging little energy drains remain in our lives.

We Have a Finite Amount of Energy

Just as we have only so many hours in a day, we have a limited amount of energy to spend during those hours. When we allow ourselves to focus on small things that aren't vital to our lives—especially when those things are experienced as physically or emotionally draining—we are making choices. We may not realize that our expending what seems a minor amount of time and energy in one area of life means that we have that much less time and energy for something else that may be more important. (We may even reason that we'll make time for or push ourselves to do both things, but this may be at the expense of our peace of mind or precious downtime, which also should be considered important.)

If Crisis Strikes, You Need a Margin of Error

You may need extra time and energy for life's unexpected hiccups—a surprise trip to the dentist, an unexpected empty tank of gas—as well as for major crises such as serious illnesses and car accidents. If you are working to maximum capacity with a high number of obligations that each carry a low level of importance, you will have a harder time rising to the occasion.

You Want to Operate from Your Least Stressed Place

Because we respond differently when we are operating from a place of stress, these little things can add up to a big difference in our behavior and reactions. Are they worth the state of episodic or chronic stress they can push us into? What about the mistakes we make when we're not at our best? The relationships we strain when we snap at our loved ones? The enjoyment of life we miss because we are feeling stressed instead of excited by new challenges? This is something to seriously consider.

Even with Healthy Mental Coping, Stress Takes a Toll

We have covered strategies for altering our thoughts and perceptions so that we do not feel unnecessarily stressed. This doesn't mean, however, that we should not do whatever we can to cut down on the stressors we face. There is evidence that even with the best mental coping strategies, situations that require action from us—situations that are generally regarded as stressful—can still exact a physical toll, even if we do not perceive them as distressing. There is no need to take a risk with the negative effects of stress. If you are not getting a strong payoff from the things in your life that keep you busy and drain your energy, those things should be eliminated. Period.

How to Manage: Cutting Out Stressors

You may already be very clear about the sources of your stress from the activities discussed in **Key 1**. If you have a list of identified stressors to address, you are ahead of the game! Here are some strategies that can address many of the common, low- to medium-grade stressors we face. Some of the more stressful situations we face in life may require particular responses that are best addressed by resources specifically geared to them (financial planning resources help with pressing money issues; books on health issues assist in dealing with the stress that comes with a serious medical condition), but most of the midlevel stressors that leave us feeling "pecked to death by ducks" can be addressed by using the advice below.

Set Boundaries with Co-workers and Friends

Do you have co-workers who take up your time with conversations that don't interest you, and do they seem to read body language poorly? Do they push their work off onto you or eat the food you keep in the office refrigerator, or are they generally difficult to be around? Setting boundaries at work is key. In setting boundaries, you simply are clear about what you are willing to do and not do (I touch on boundaries in greater detail in **Key 6**). Rather than relying on body language to communicate that you would rather not be engaged in conversation, why not politely excuse yourself? Let your co-workers know when they have crossed the line with you. Don't allow yourself to be sucked in. You can be polite, and still simply avoid them as much as possible, and cut out the stress they bring as a result. This may not be an issue for everyone, but for those of us who are stressed by situations like these, giving ourselves permission to just say no can be quite liberating.

Engage in Stress Management at Lunch

If you feel stressed at work, why not give yourself a midday boost with a regular stress management ritual? Take a brisk walk, meditate, drink tea, and reflect on the things in your life for which you are grateful. If boredom, lethargy, or low-grade stressors plague you at work, giving yourself a pick-me-up can be just the thing to combat them.

Maintain an Orderly Environment

One of the most common tolerations coaches hear about is the messy office desk. Whether you work in a cubicle, a home office, or a corner suite, a disorganized desk can make your job more difficult and sap your time and energy. Taking an hour or 2 to create a system that works well can give you an energy boost and make your job run more smoothly. Decorating and organizing the rest of your office can help as well, since clutter can be a low-grade stressor.

Learn Time Management

Create a system that works. A to-do list can be written in a computer program, stored on a phone, tweeted to yourself, or scrawled on a piece of paper the old-fashioned way. Maintaining a running list, as well as keeping things on a calendar, are important tasks to begin, if you are not already doing so. It is also a good idea to plan ahead, allow yourself more time than you think you need to complete tasks, leave your house earlier than you think you need to, and otherwise organize your time so that you are not dealing with the stress of constantly rushing. This is easier said than done for those of us who are not naturally organized with our time, but it is a skill that can be learned, and it can bring far-reaching stress relief benefits as you find yourself no longer stressing over the clock.

Ask for What You Need

At work, and in all relationships, it helps to be up front and clear about your needs. If you have found yourself becoming upset in the past when someone has not met your needs, think back to how you asked for your needs to be met. *Did* you ask? Were you clear? Some of us tend to let our own needs come last, feeling that we do not want to inconvenience others, and we end up feeling the effects of too much stress as a result. Others often *want* to help, but they don't know how if we do not tell them. So whether you need a quiet space in which to work or you need to feel more heard in your relationships, actually asking for those needs to be met is one of the surest ways to make it happen.

Have a Simple System

In virtually all areas of life, it helps to plan ahead. And these plans need not be complicated. In fact, finding the simplest route from A to B can help to cut out all types of stress. For example, when you are running errands, you tend to hit the places you need to visit in a logical order based on location, right? This principle can be applied to many other areas of life, from meal planning (one night's roasted chicken can become the next night's chicken soup) to seeing friends (why not save time and plan a get-together rather than meeting everyone individually?) to planning a stress management routine (exercise can meet fitness goals as well as stress management goals!) and you can save time and energy in the process. While not all of these streamlined approaches will appeal, this type of thinking can yield new ideas that can cut out unnecessary stress more often than not.

Be Proactive

If something in your environment is causing you stress, you may be in the habit of trying to ignore it and just get through the day. You may find yourself reacting mostly to things that scream the loudest and demand your attention the most. Consider taking a little time each week to address one or two things *before* they demand attention, before they cause so much stress that you can no longer ignore them. In the long run, you will save energy, and you will be able to take the time when it is convenient for you, not when you are facing a small crisis and you have no choice.

Activity to Try: Don't Say Yes When You Want to Say No

It can be difficult to say no to requests around the office and in other areas of life. We want to be helpful, and we might be concerned about letting others down. Letting ourselves become overly stressed because we have overcommitted ourselves, however, causes everyone stress in the long run, as we may be less than enthusiastic and wind up doing a halfhearted job. Becoming adept at saying no is an important skill for stress management. The following hints will help you learn to say no.

* The first step to saying no, as with drawing boundaries in other ways, is to become clear with yourself that it is okay to do this, and that you really want to say no to this particular obligation. (If you are not sure, vividly imagine yourself at your most stressed, and ask yourself if it is worth the risk of returning to this state.)
* If you really want to say no, just do it. You do not owe the other person an explanation—although in some instances it is a good idea to offer one. (An explanation softens the blow, but with someone who is pushy, it can also represent an opportunity for argument.)
* If you are dealing with someone who does not respect boundaries, no explanation is necessary, and it is preferable not to give one.
* Release yourself from guilt by reminding yourself what you are saying yes to with this no.

Questions to Ask Yourself

* What areas of my life are causing the most stress?
* If I could wave a wand and eliminate three daily stressors, what would I choose to cut out?
* How many stressors could I eliminate in an afternoon?
* Which stressors do I deal with on a daily basis that are unnecessary?

Evaluate Your Answers

The questions above can help you get started in the process of cutting stressors out of your life. First, noticing the most taxing stressors you face can provide you with an area of focus and a jumping-off point. Imagining them as simply *gone*, without focusing on the obstacles that stand in the way of making that happen, can often be enough to help you move into the frame of mind to find new possibilities. Use the answers to these questions to guide yourself through the process of identifying stressors to eliminate. Then use the following process to move through the next steps, and cut stressors from your life.

Activity to Try: Cut Out Tolerations

1. Make a list of all your tolerations. Identify the ones that cause the most stress, the ones that would be easiest to fix, and the ones that would bring the biggest long-term payoff. Then choose one to tackle, according to whether you want the biggest payoff or the quickest results, for example.
2. Mark your calendar—plan one stressor to eliminate each week.
3. Create a more organized space for yourself. First, cull the clutter. (You can do this in a series of evenings or in one sweeping effort over a weekend.) Then organize what you have left. Finally, reward yourself with a fresh coat of paint, some scented candles, or other inexpensive and appealing decorations.
4. Choose one obligation in your life right now that you are ready to give up.
5. Plan what enjoyable activity you would like to put in its place.
6. If you find yourself thinking that you don't have time to replace the obligation you just eliminated with something fun—you have too many other obligations to deal with—take this as a signal that you need to cut out at least one more obligation, if at all possible. Keep working at it until you have created space for at least one activity that is relaxing and enjoyable.

KEY 6

CULTIVATE HEALTHY
RELATIONSHIPS

Shared joy is double joy; shared sorrow is half a sorrow.

—SWEDISH PROVERB

From the first gentle caresses from a loving mother to the last warm hand that ideally encases ours before we take our last breath, the ways in which others touch our lives can have a wonderful, soothing impact. Supportive relationships have been found to promote not only stress relief, but also physical health and longevity. This chapter will focus on the benefits of healthy relationships and the toll of conflict and will provide tools for fostering a healthy social life. It can help you to improve the relationships that mean the most to you and to let go of the ones that are bringing you down.

People We Know

Most of us know at least one person who takes the wind out of our sails. While we all have our own idea of what is annoying, people who are critical, unfriendly, judgmental, and prone to complaining tend to fit most people's definition of *toxic*. They are the people who will be the first to criticize your ideas and the last to offer praise. They have a certain tone of voice or look in their eye that lets you know in an instant that you are somehow failing to measure up to an imagined standard of adequacy. You know in your gut who these people are in your life: Are you looking forward to seeing them? Does any part of you dread the thought of encountering them? Are you so used to them that you are fine seeing them, but you know what their reactions to you will be, and they make you uncomfortable? People like this can drain your energy over time and can introduce subtle, steady amounts of stress into your life.

Most of us also know at least one person who shines brightly in our lives (if we're lucky). This type of person is there for you when you need a pep talk, celebrates with you when you want a high five, and is someone around whom you can completely be yourself. If you were facing a crisis, he or she is someone you know you could count on, and someone you would always want to be there for, as well. Such people are good for our health and our happiness and are perhaps some of the best stress relievers of all.

Why Relationships Matter

We may find ourselves pushed to achieve at work and school and spend whatever leftover time and energy we have on our relationships, but with the benefits that healthy relationships bring, they should be highly prioritized in our lives. Michael Frisch, a researcher who studies happiness and emotional well-being, has called healthy relationships the "holy grail of happiness," and for good reason. They add support, enjoyment, and meaning to our lives, as well as other benefits, as described below.

Healthy Relationships Are Associated with Better Health

Numerous studies have provided solid evidence that healthy relationships are good for us, not only emotionally, but also physically. People in happy relationships experience a host of advantages, including enhanced immune functioning, lower emotional reactivity, a decreased incidence of emotional health issues, and increased longevity. Those who have rich social lives tend to live longer, stay healthier, stress less, and enjoy life more.

The central point here is that relationships need to be *healthy*, or at least reasonably so. Relationships that are emotionally toxic, or that bring more negatives than positives, can be more detrimental to us than most other types of stressors. Therefore, it's important to be proactive in managing our social lives and maintaining balance. The contrast is stark: Healthy relationships deliver enhanced health, increased longevity, greater levels of happiness and well-being, and reduced levels of stress, while toxic relationships engender stress and can negatively affect our health.

How Toxic Relationships Bring Greater Stress Than Other Stressors

Certain stressors affect us more than others. The perception of threats to your safety, such as from the sound of someone attempting to break into your house, can trigger your stress response and produce a stronger response than can a mere buildup of annoyances during a long day at work. Relationship difficulties tend to hit us harder than many other problems because in many ways we need other people for our own safety. We may be able to physically survive with relatively few connections these days, but remember that our stress response was designed for a distant time when physical threats loomed everywhere and being excluded from the group meant you didn't have the safety of the pack to protect you. Your body responds to the type of threats that might leave you out in the cold. In fact, we need human connection to survive and thrive. Just as babies who are not cuddled and cared for adequately can suffer from failure to thrive, we are less physically healthy as adults when we have fewer supportive relationships. And when relationships tear away at our self-esteem, the effects of this can absolutely be sensed and can be experienced as toxic. Such relationships tend to activate the stress response more often, and the consequences of this affect the body and the mind.

Developing Relationship Skills

Before we kick out of our lives all imperfect friends and loved ones (and wouldn't that include just about everyone?), we would be well advised to recognize that it is more effective to focus on making our existing relationships healthier. While we can't change other people, we can alter how we behave in our relationships, and often that's enough to make a profound difference in the entire dynamic. Changing our part in what family therapists call the "dance"— the interplay of expected roles and reactions—creates room for new ways of being with each other. Rather than withdrawing from relationships, manipulating others, or engaging in less healthy self-protective behaviors that ultimately cause more stress than they relieve, focusing on developing relationship skills can help you to refurbish the relationships you have that need a little fixing up.

Here are some simple changes you can make to reshape relationship dynamics in a positive way. Whether you are in a relationship that drains and stresses you and are wondering if you can save it, or whether your relationship is good and you just want it to achieve its greatest potential, the following skills can benefit you. These skills can help you to create relationship dynamics that are more supportive and respectful of both parties, and they can benefit you as well as those you love.

Setting Boundaries

When we hear about setting boundaries, we usually think of ways to keep people at arm's length. This is an effective function of boundary setting: If we feel that our rights are being infringed on, rather than cutting the offending parties out of our lives, we can simply set boundaries, so these individuals can take a certain amount of liberty with us but no more. In setting personal boundaries, we decide how close we'd like others to get to us—how much sharing we would like, how much we are willing to give, how much we would like to take—and communicate that to the other person in a respectful way. This often involves enforcing a desired amount of space and respect in our relationships.

Boundary setting, however, can also foster closeness. It's not all about pushing people away. When we set boundaries with others, we actually allow them to become closer to us than we may have otherwise allowed, because we know that there is a line—that they can get close to us without going too far. Without healthy boundaries, people tend to either let others get too close, and then push them way back, or cut people off entirely. (Ironically, a cut-off relationship is not considered one with healthy boundaries, because there is no closeness to begin with; boundaries suggest that people can get close, but not too close, not that they cannot get close at all.)

What constitutes healthy boundaries? Different people have different comfort levels when it comes to boundaries, so boundary setting necessarily requires participation from all people in the relationship. Some people are more comfortable with closeness than others, and as long as this works for them, this is healthy. If people set boundaries that continually cause them stress because the boundaries are too lax or rigid (they either allow too much contact or keep people at too far a distance), the boundary-setting patterns may be an issue. But a friend who likes to have close boundaries and has healthy, fulfilling relationships with others who have close boundaries can be considered to have "healthy boundaries." Likewise, someone who prefers more distance can also have boundaries that are considered healthy as long as they let people close enough that their relationships are strong and survive.

Activity to Try: How to Set Boundaries

The process of setting boundaries can help strengthen your relationships and relieve some of the stress within them. Here are some tips that can help you with this process:

* **Know where your boundaries lie.** There are a few different ways to set boundaries with people, and the important first step with each of them is the same: Become clear with yourself about

where your boundaries lie. If you do not know where you stand, you cannot effectively communicate this to others, no matter what techniques you use. This aspect can be challenging in itself because you may not know where you want to draw the line (and others may sense that, which may be why they are overstepping your boundaries in the first place). Examine how you feel, and what you would like to allow, and decide where your boundaries lie.

* **Communicate this clearly and firmly.** Now that you know what to say, the *how* becomes easier. That said, it is important to be up front and clear when you let people know. State what you need and expect with kindness, but also with confidence. Your statement should not sound like an accusation, a question, or a dirty secret. You are entitled to your boundaries, and it helps others to know what they are, so you are being a good friend by communicating.

* **Back yourself up.** If your boundaries are not being respected, take action. This does not need to be angry, punitive action; you simply need to get yourself out of a situation in which you are putting up with something you said you would not be willing to do. For example, if you are scheduled to meet a friend for lunch and you have agreed on a time, that is establishing a boundary— you will be there at a specific time. If you friend does not show up and does not call after a respectable waiting period, it is okay to call and say that you will not wait indefinitely, or you can even leave after a certain amount of time if your friend cannot be reached. You can reschedule, and make it clear that you can wait only a certain amount of time the next time as well. This frees you from waiting indefinitely, without your having to take more drastic measures such as cutting off the relationship or never agreeing to meet this friend again.

How to Manage: Work on Communication Skills

Healthy communication involves effective listening, as well as ways of speaking that make it easy for the other person to clearly understand what you are both thinking and feeling. Effective communication involves both parties, but by learning communication skills that you can use, you lessen the burden on the other person. With these techniques, you can make it easy for the person if he or she *wants* to hear you and understand, and avoid unintentionally contributing to any conflict that may already exist. The following are some communication strategies to keep in mind as you navigate discussions that could potentially turn to conflict.

Using Messages
It becomes easy to sound as though you are making accusations against someone when you are both upset. "You really made me angry"; "You were so inconsiderate." Statements tend to want to escape our lips starting with "You, you, you!" This is a simple shift, but resolving *not* to begin sentences with *you*, and instead starting with *I*, can soften your statements and take out the sting. Better still, following up with the word *feel* can really help you express yourself without blaming the other person for your experience. This moves the point of the conversation from accusations, which can automatically bring out defensiveness in the other person, to an explanation of your personal experience, which is more likely to invite understanding. Taking things a step further, the following structure can make things even more clear, while keeping communication from becoming combative: "When you [whatever behavior you observed], I feel [whatever emotions you are feeling]." This lets the person know exactly what it was that upset you and exactly how you felt as a result. This helps you avoid other communication pitfalls such as interpreting the person's motives and applying negative labels and allows you to focus simply on the behavior and the feelings, which lets a more emotionally neutral discussion ensue.

Listen, Then Speak
It may feel unfair that you have to be the one to listen first, but what is often the case in typical arguments is that both parties are simply seeking to be heard. Both of you may be merely mentally

crafting what you are going to say next, rather than truly listening to one another. You may both be simply waiting for a chance to speak, and forgetting to listen. By listening first, and asking for clarification until you are sure you understand, you are showing the other person respect and demonstrating how the person may show you the same courtesy. Even more important, you are gathering important information that can alter what you say next. (Conflicts can be resolved so much more easily when both sides understand one another!) By seeking first to understand, then to be understood, you are increasing the likelihood that you will both be heard.

Cool Down If Necessary

As you may remember from **Key 2**, when the body's stress response is triggered, it becomes more difficult to think calmly, rationally, and clearly. This can make it difficult to communicate in a healthy way. If you are a little upset, talking things out and coming to a place of mutual understanding will likely help you both to feel better. However, at a certain point, it becomes counterproductive to attempt to resolve a conflict if you, or both of you, are so "triggered" that coming to a place of understanding is just not feasible. At this point, it helps to take a break and cool off. Rather than storming off, try to calmly affirm that this is an important issue to discuss, and you would like to go over it when you can both be more calm. Then decide on a time when you will come together and talk again. In the meantime, try your best stress relief techniques, so you can come back to the discussion from a more centered place.

Let Go of the Need to "Win"

Some people pride themselves on never losing an argument. If this is a goal of yours, it's time to reevaluate. Rather than thinking of communication in terms of winning and losing, bear in mind that the real goal is for mutual understanding to occur. New solutions can be explored, and compromises can be reached. But if you are bent on winning the argument, the relationship loses.

Be Respectful

Perhaps the most important point to remember is that the other person should be given respect. This means avoiding sarcasm, mocking comments, personal attacks, stonewalling (refusing to respond), or other manipulative tactics designed to increase personal power or make the other person uncomfortable. Remember that you care about this person and you want both of you to be happy. Then try to come to a place of mutual understanding. If you have that intention in mind, many of the other details become just that—details.

Activity to Try: Cultivate Empathy

Sometimes the key to letting go of anger when you face conflict, and the key to understanding the other person, is empathy. When you can more easily grasp what the other person is feeling, it becomes easier to understand that person's actions. And it becomes more difficult to remain angry. Cultivating empathy is easier than it may seem. Empathy eases the path to forgiveness and can enhance altruism. Because forgiveness and altruism are linked to enhanced wellness and reduced stress, deepening your capacity for empathy brings added benefits.

Your capacity for empathy is partially inborn and is partially shaped by your experiences and habitual thought patterns, but you can work to deepen your capacity for this important skill in the following ways:

* Actively seek to understand what others are feeling and why, not simply what they are saying. Then work toward being able to guess more accurately.
* Think of a time when you felt what the other person is feeling now. Vividly remember what it was like, and think of how you would have liked others to respond to you.
* Think of all that this person brings to you, and how much you would miss the person if he or she were not in your life.

＊   Practice loving kindness meditation (mentioned in **Key** 8). This can deepen your capacity for compassion and kindness toward others.

How to Manage: Cutting Out Toxic Relationships

One of my favorite quotations—from an unknown author—is this: "At some point, you have to realize that some people can stay in your heart, but not in your life." (This quotation has also resonated with many of my readers and has garnered quite a bit of positive feedback when I have shared it online.) I believe that it strikes a chord because it gives us permission to let go of relationships that are toxic, even if love is still present. While we can continue to love and respect others, they are not always a good fit for what we are trying to maintain in our lives. Simply put, certain relationships cannot be saved by even the greatest efforts at improvement, particularly if only one party puts in the effort. (Even if both parties are making an effort, sometimes we simply want different things, and these things conflict with one another's pursuit of peace.)

When to Let Go

How can you tell when a relationship is worth saving and when it is better left in the past? There are no hard-and-fast rules. However, if you find that a particular relationship seems to add more negatives than positives to your life, and you can't see a clear or viable solution, you may want to consider letting go. Obviously, if a relationship is abusive, it is best if you let go and move on. But what about relationships that make us feel bad more often than they make us feel good, but the thought of losing them creates stress? The following types of relationships can be toxic, but the decision to either hang on or cut ties can be a difficult one:

＊   The relative who constantly makes belittling comments, but who is not around except on certain holidays.
＊   The gossipy friend whose brand of friendship chips away at our self-esteem, but who can be fun.

* The boyfriend or girlfriend who is volatile or critical, but who can also be supportive and committed.

The relationships with each of these individuals bring something negative to the table, but aren't an easy fix for various reasons. Cutting a family member out of your life can create consequences in your other relationships, and severing ties with a relative you barely see isn't always worth the upheaval it may cause. Friends who aren't overtly toxic and bring positive experiences to your life may be missed. Having someone who loves you and offers support may seem to be something to invest in, particularly if you are someone who has not had positive experiences with previous romantic relationships. We need to look at the big picture and the balance of positives and negatives that someone offers before we decide to unilaterally sever ties.

A good first line of defense is boundary setting. Healthy communication can also breathe new life into a less-than-thriving relationship. If other measures are taken and a particular relationship makes you feel bad more often than it makes you feel good, you may want to look at the cost of cutting ties. If it seems worth the fallout, this may be one of those instances where letting go is necessary. Particularly if you believe that you are dealing with someone who is resistant to change and inflexible, even after the person is made aware that some of his or her behaviors are hurtful to you, the relationship may be worth reexamining. Relationships with narcissists and sociopaths, for example, tend to cause much more heartache than the relationships are worth, and usually the best way of managing these relationships is to let them go.

How to Let Go

Letting go gracefully can be difficult, particularly if you have mixed feelings about whether it is a good idea to sever ties. Having a respectful conversation about why the relationship is not working may be wise, if you are dealing with someone with whom you can have a respectful conversation. If the relationship is a friendship rather than a romantic association, it may be more feasible and practical to simply become "too busy" to get together as much as before, and let the relationship peter out. Another option, one that would be effective with a closer relationship, is to explain what it is about the relationship that is not working for you and (without coming from a place of being punitive) let the person know what changes would need to occur before you could pick up the relationship again in the future. The ideal with letting go is to do so with minimal drama, as the point of letting go of toxic relationships is to relieve stress. Creating an even more toxic situation, with a new enemy, is something to avoid.

How to Manage: Focus on Healthy, Supportive Relationships

Focusing your time and attention on healthy existing relationships, and creating new ones as well, can be a healthy new focus for your emotional well-being. Whether you are doing so as part of an emotional recovery from a toxic relationship or simply because it is a good idea, renewing your focus on those who make you feel good inside, and returning those good feelings as best you can, is worth your time and energy. Here are some things to keep in mind when building a healthier social circle.

Meet New People
Do not shy away from adding to your social circle. The next person you meet could potentially be an important person in your life. Do not overlook new opportunities. You may seek out new friends.

Be Equitable
Be sure to give back as much as you take from your relationships. You may not have the exact same attributes to offer, but be sure that you are not doing a disproportionate amount of giving or taking, or resentments can grow and sap the relationship of its positive energy.

Stay Positive

In finding the balance between positive and negative in our relationships, an equal amount of each is, in fact, not the best we can hope for. An equal number of positive and negative interactions is actually detrimental—for our relationships to be considered positive, supportive, and beneficial overall, we need a much higher number of positive experiences than negative ones.

A few experts on relationships have come up with their own recommended ratios of positive to negative interactions, but probably the most popularly cited ratio comes from relationship researcher John Gottman, who has studied couples and their interactions and can predict (with more than 90% accuracy) which couples will stay married and which will divorce in the near future, based on observing a few key aspects of their communication styles. (I will explore that in a minute.) This important researcher has discovered quite a bit about what makes a relationship healthy or unhealthy, and one of his findings is that a relationship requires no fewer than five positive interactions for every single negative one, in order to feel pleasing to both parties. This means that for every time you ask your partner to *please* stop doing something annoying, you need to point out five things about that person that you appreciate. For every fight, you need to have at least five times where you enjoy (not merely tolerate) each other's company. For every time you make each other feel unhappy, you need at least five times where you have made each other feel fantastic, in order to maintain a positive balance. (Although this research was conducted on couples, I would apply this rule to friendships as well.) For some relationships, this comes quite easily; for others it can be a struggle.

Face Issues When They Arise

Knowing the importance of positive interactions (and the damaging effects of negative ones), it can be tempting to brush problems into the back corners of your awareness and avoid confrontation when things are bothering you. Perhaps paradoxically, this is not a great idea, either. When we attempt to avoid conflict by avoiding discussions, we risk actually perpetuating the conflict by failing to resolve the underlying issues that are leading to conflict in the first place. Keeping in mind the communication strategies I discussed earlier in this chapter, here are a few more techniques for navigating relationships in general.

Don't Force Your Agenda

We all want to be heard, and mutual understanding is vital for a healthy relationship. It is also natural to want to get what you want out of the relationship. However, if you find yourself pushing hard to get what you want at the expense of the other person's needs, this can weaken your relationships. This seems an obvious point, but we can sometimes do this without fully realizing it. We may tell ourselves that it's for the other person's own good, that if the person understood the situation better, he or she would want what we want, that if the person did ultimately agree, he or she obviously didn't object to the pressure *that* much.

The problem with pushing your agenda is that if you do it too often, and at the expense of the other person, the relationship eventually suffers. Have you had feedback in your relationships suggesting that you could stand to listen more? That you seem to need to control things a little too much or that people don't always feel heard when they are with you? If you hear this once or twice or from just one person, it may be a fluke. If you hear it somewhat regularly, it is something to explore. (When you are being completely honest with yourself, what does your gut tell you?) Try to aim for win-win situations and compromise whenever possible. When that isn't possible, see if you can take turns in who gets to have the first choice in outcomes. This can help to keep things equitable and keep everyone feeling respected.

Avoid Contempt Like the Relationship Killer It Is

One of the most telling findings that John Gottman found in his studies on relationships (remember the psychologist who studied the patterns of couples' arguments and could predict which unions were destined to dissolve?) is that contempt is a strong sign of impending doom. Contempt is evident when one or both partners show clear disdain for the other person—there is not just disagreement with the partner's ideas, but disapproval of the partner as a person. It goes deeper than a mere argument and cuts at the core of who the other person is. If you find yourself treating with contempt people with whom you disagree, this has to stop.

Organize Girls' Nights, Game Nights, and Date Nights

One of the best ways to enhance the social support you have in your life is to work on maintaining the relationships you already have with friends and family. We may think of them often or stay in contact via social media, but seeing them in person and creating new memories is important as well. Getting together with others is something we should all be doing on a regular basis. We may do this when we are younger and have fewer responsibilities, but it is a healthy idea to continue the practice throughout our lives. In fact, it is during those times when we have greater responsibilities and greater stressors that we need our relationships for increased support. Organizing a monthly or weekly night to get together with friends creates the perfect venue for relaxation, bonding, and blowing off steam from the stresses of the week. Having a regular date night with your significant other can add another layer of strength to your relationship and can stave off stress that may result if your bond weakens because of a lack of time spent together merely having fun. And maintaining this regular habit ensures that it will actually happen on a regular basis—it can get you past the inertia of not wanting to plan anything or of having busy schedules. This may all be easier than you think. Here are a few simple ways to make it happen:

* Have a standing invitation for friends to come over for games and drinks—or whatever you find to be fun. If you ask people to bring food, drinks, games, or whatever you will be sharing, all you need to do is make your house somewhat clean.
* Have a standing weekly or monthly night when you all get to-

gether, and have everyone take turns planning what you'll do. This ensures that the work of planning is evenly distributed, and everyone gets to have his or her first choice of activity at least once every few times.

* Arrange for a sitter at regular intervals, and allow yourselves as a couple to be spontaneous in what you plan for the night.

Get Involved in Groups

Maintaining our current relationships is important, and so is the act of making new friends. The obvious benefit to joining an established group is that you can meet many new people who share at least one of your interests or beliefs. Studies show, for example, that people who are involved in a religious community enjoy superior health and longevity and at least some of these benefits accrue from their involvement in the group: They gain social support, involvement in activities, and a sense of belonging. Membership in other groups can also bring feelings of belonging, introduce you to potential new friends or romantic partners, and provide you with social opportunities that you may enjoy. An added bonus: You may be involved in planning, but you will probably be able to join already planned events rather than having the responsibility of planning your own. By reaching out to new people, and maintaining healthy ties with those already in your life, you can create a truly supportive social circle that involves less stress.

Questions to Ask Yourself

* Which relationships in my life give me the most comfort? The most stress?
* What changes can I make that could reduce some of the stress in my social life?
* What are my best habits in communicating? What are my worst?
* Do I give about as much as I take in my relationships?
* What one person causes me the most stress, and what is it about him or her that is stressful?

* What one person brings me the most happiness, and what is it about him or her that I appreciate?
* If I could change three things about my social life, what would they be?
* Am I generally happy in my relationships?

Evaluate Your Answers

After your reading about relationship skills and dynamics, the answers that come from these questions may take on new significance. Noticing the habits that contribute to your relationships in a positive and negative way can help you to identify new ways of relating that can serve you. Identifying people who cause you the most stress and bring you the greatest comfort can help you to decide if you need to change where you place your attention. Look at your level of happiness in your relationships. If it is not what you'd like it to be, you now have more tools to make changes that will enhance your relationships and life satisfaction, and reduce stress. Identify at least one change you would like to make, and see where that takes you.

KEY 7

PUT POSITIVE PSYCHOLOGY INTO ACTION

One joy scatters a hundred griefs.   —CHINESE PROVERB

It's difficult to feel stress and joy at the same time. One strategy for minimizing stress is to maximize feelings of happiness and meaning in life. The field of positive psychology moves beyond mere positive thinking and has identified research-backed strategies for creating a more enjoyable lifestyle as well as maintaining a happier and more relaxed frame of mind. This chapter will explain some of the main concepts and techniques that have been identified as delivering the greatest benefits in this area. You'll learn how to experience *flow*, enjoy *pleasures*, and engage in *gratifications* throughout the week and discover how to create a life that is not conducive to stress.

The Hunt for Happiness

Sophie wanted to feel happier, so she worked hard to attain things that she thought would bring happiness: She threw herself into a career that gave her a nice income, and she met each goal she set for herself professionally. However, she always seemed to slip back into feeling dissatisfied with life a few weeks after she reached her goals; she discovered that they didn't bring lasting happiness. She also found that when she bought herself nice things, she was happier for a short while, but then the happiness went away, and she couldn't understand why. She felt that something was missing in her personal life, so she turned to online dating to find love, but as she came home disappointed from date after date, unable to find someone who wanted the same things she wanted, she wondered what, ultimately, would bring the happiness she sought. One night, she realized that most of her journal entries were complaints about things that weren't going well in life or were about disappointments she was facing, and she knew she needed a change. She wasn't sure what she could do differently to feel more joy from day to day and to make her happiness last, but the hunt for happiness was bringing considerable stress!

When we talked about research in positive psychology, she found some answers. We discussed why certain things bring fleeting happiness and other things create happiness that is longer lasting and why both types of life ingredients are valuable. We focused on activities that would cause a more positive overall mood so that Sophie didn't have to rely primarily on events outside of herself in order to be happy. Understanding what would bring more lasting happiness, as well as different types of positive feelings, helped her to feel that she had a road map in life and could know which direction would lead her to the type of life satisfaction she craved. After only a few days of focusing on different things suggested by positive psychology research, Sophie felt much happier, and her new levels of happiness remained in the weeks and months that followed.

Positive Psychology: Why It Matters

Positive psychology is a branch of psychology that studies what makes us resilient, or as Martin Seligman, the originator of positive psychology, put it, it is "the study of what makes life worth living." As president of the American Psychological Association in the year 2000, he set out to forge a new focus to illuminate solutions from the perspective of what contributes to wellness, resiliency, and happiness. In doing so, he provided us with a wealth of new answers for important questions on happiness and life satisfaction. He created a new paradigm from which we can approach our lives.

This relatively new field centers on studying what makes us healthy and happy, rather than looking at factors that contribute to pathology and disease. This is an important distinction that provides a unique and valuable perspective on how to live and what our goals should be. Traditional psychological models have focused on factors that create stress or lead to a stressful experience, so we know what to try to avoid in our lives. Positive psychology, on the other hand, focuses on what factors are common among people who are thriving, and it gives us insight into which traits and lifestyle features we may want to adopt in order to thrive even more and which specific behaviors will get us to that healthier place.

Is Positive Psychology Just About Looking on the Bright Side?

While positive psychology involves techniques for developing a greater sense of optimism, such as focusing on the areas of life for which we are grateful and concentrating on our strengths and increasingly using them in the course of our lives, there is more to this field and its techniques than a mere shift in perspective. Positive psychology shows us what activities and lifestyle features are more likely to bring happiness and meaning into our lives and in this way work to drive out unnecessary stress. The activities recommended by practitioners in the field of positive psychology tend to operate on an internal level as well as an external one. Positive psychology practices include specific changes that involve adding certain features to one's lifestyle—gratifications and pleasures, for example—and eliminating elements that impede happiness on a consistent basis. So positive psychology can bring a greater feeling of optimism, but this comes from more than just a shift in perspective. These techniques can work well not only by cutting down feelings of stress but also by adding positive feelings, which can make us more resilient to stress in our lives.

How to Manage: Popular Positive Psychology Interventions

The field of positive psychology has yielded several promising strategies that have been proved to promote our experience of happiness. These activities can be used by just about anyone and can help relieve stress, enhance meaning in life, and deepen our positive experiences. They tend to be enjoyable to practice as well, so adding one or several of these experiences to your life can be enjoyable and effective.

Pleasures

Pleasures are exactly what they sound like—things that bring us pleasure. They can be things we buy, things we eat, or things we do. Here is a list of common pleasures:

* Things to buy
    ° Clothes
    ° Books
    ° Games
    ° Toys (yes, adults can still play with toys!)
    ° Collectibles
* Things to do
    ° Movies
    ° Walks outside
    ° Parties
    ° Vacations
    ° Nights out
* Food
    ° Favorite meals
    ° Desserts

- ° Chocolate
- ° Drinks
- ° Snacks
- * Experiences
  - ° A warm bath
  - ° A massage
  - ° A day off
  - ° A thrill ride
  - ° A concert or favorite playlist
- * The absence of something we don't enjoy
  - ° A day off
  - ° Hiring a housekeeper
  - ° Eating out (instead of cooking)

Activity to Try: List of Pleasures

What are some of your favorite pleasures? Take a moment to think about what you enjoy the most. Then make a list of as many of them as you can think of. This list may include some of the ideas above, as well as some of the things you have enjoyed at different times in your life. Include as many as you can think of, and you'll be able to draw from this list when you need a pick-me-up.

The Benefits of Pleasures

These enjoyable experiences bring a temporary lift to your mood and can bring additional benefits because of this. Psychologist Barbara Frederickson initiated a significant body of research that studies the effects of positive emotions (which can come from the experience of pleasures), and discovered that there are many benefits. Her work centers around what is known as broaden-and-build theory, which maintains that positive emotions have a beneficial function for the survival of our species as a whole. This acclaimed theory holds that positive emotions broaden our existing intellectual, physical, and social resources, building up reserves we can use for coping with threats we may face in life. Indeed, when we are in a positive mood, our relationships do run more smoothly, which is quite beneficial for coping. Here are a few of the benefits that have been discovered:

* **Improved cognitive functioning.** Those who are in the throes of positive emotions have been found to have a broader attention span, greater working memory, increased verbal fluency, and a greater openness to information. All these advantages can improve performance on the job and in relationships, which can bring yet further benefits.

* **Quicker recovery from anxiety.** One study demonstrated that those who got an emotional lift (from watching a short, happy film of a puppy playing with a flower or waves crashing on the beach) tended to recover from an episode of anxiety more quickly. (Specifically, their heart rates returned to normal levels sooner than those of people who saw films that produced feelings of sadness.)

* **Greater physical health.** Those who tend to be happier also tend to be healthier. Many studies have shown a correlation between happiness or overall life satisfaction and health measures such as absence of disease and increased longevity. Even maintaining a lower reactivity to stress (which seems to be linked to positive emotion) is associated with greater levels of wellness. Because positive emotions are an easy route to happiness, pleasures are worth including in your life.

How Pleasures Work—and Stop Working

Pleasures work by giving us a quick emotional lift. They work quickly and can pertain to our senses—they bring a pleasing taste, sound, or feel—or can appeal to our emotions and memories. They work quickly to bring a little joy to our lives, but their benefits also fade quickly. And they fade in two different ways.

The first way in which pleasures are fleeting is that they may bring a quick mood boost, but they generally do not create lasting happiness. The positive feelings that they bring can be prolonged (and we will discuss how to do this in a minute), but they generally bring some quick positive feelings. For deeper, more lasting happiness, they work better in combination with other strategies.

The second way pleasures have fading effects is that the same pleasure loses its strength rather quickly upon repetition. The fifth time you ride a roller coaster, the experience will not be as intensely exciting as it was the first time. A day at the beach isn't as amazing if you've gone the previous day. The third bite of chocolate will not be as deeply delicious as the first, no matter how good the chocolate. This means that you can't use the same few pleasures over and over again and expect the same effects, and you should be careful not to "overdose" on them in a single session, either. You do not need a full chocolate bar or a week at the beach to get a good dose of pleasure from the experience.

How to Manage: Prolong the Effectiveness of Pleasures

There are a few tricks to getting the most out of our pleasures. While the joy they bring may be fleeting, there are a few ways to stretch out those good feelings. Consider the following:

* **Use the power of anticipation to your advantage.** When we look forward to exciting things in our future, we get to enjoy them before they happen. Have you ever found that your whole morning was more fun because you knew you would get to take the second half of the day off? Or do you find that your excitement begins on the first few days *before* a vacation? You can find this type of anticipation with pleasures, too. To maximize the benefits of anticipation, try to plan some of your pleasures in advance, rather than finding them spontaneously every time, and you will maximize your enjoyment. Knowing that you have a treat waiting for you in the afternoon, for example, can make your lunch hour more fun.

* **Savor the experience while you are enjoying it.** You can turn virtually any experience of pleasure into a practice of mindfulness (see **Key 4** for more on how to do this), and in doing so,

maximize your enjoyment of it. Positive psychology has found that the act of savoring experiences is an important, effective way to increase our joy in life. Particularly for those who are prone to rumination, savoring experiences by noticing every detail as they unfold, remaining in the present moment, and capturing a vivid memory of the experience can be ways not only to enjoy life more, but also to teach ourselves how to more effectively let go of the negative and hold on to the positive.

* **Remember these good times.** Whether formally cataloging your positive experiences in a gratitude journal (a highly recommended practice—see **Key 8** for more on this) or simply looking back on them as you go through your day, actively enjoying our memories is another way to get the most out of our pleasures in life. In fact, one study found that recounting happy memories brings not only prolonged feelings of happiness, but also decreased sensations of pain. Specifically, researchers asked participants to recall their happiest day and relive it in their memory for 8 minutes, 3 days in a row. At the end of the session, and when measured again 4 weeks later, those who relived happy memories scored higher on measures of well-being. Specifically, it was found, these participants showed increased long-term positive affect (they had lasting positive emotions) and decreased pain. What's more, they scored higher on measures of personal growth and overall wellness than did subjects who wrote analytically about their experiences. If you find yourself dwelling on things that make you unhappy, or if you find yourself engulfed in stress, you can take a quick mental break from negative feelings by recounting your happy memories of the pleasures in life.

Activity to Try: Work More Pleasures into Your Life

The key to using pleasures to boost your mood is variety. Because their effectiveness diminishes over time, the same pleasures will not carry the same benefits if you experience them repeatedly, as mentioned earlier. (At least these pleasures will not bring the same *type* of benefits—rituals are something else, which we will discuss more in a minute.) There are many ways to add pleasures to your life without sapping them of their effectiveness, however, and there are many ways to introduce these little treats into your daily life. The following are some effective ways to work pleasures into your week:

* If you are new to the concept of pleasures, and it feels like work to come up with a collection of them to add to your day, start with just one. Enjoy one new food, one new activity, one new experience, or one small treat for yourself. This one pleasure you allow yourself can brighten your whole day as you anticipate it, savor it, and remember it.

* Some people really like the idea of adding pleasures to each day, but have trouble coming up with variety. (I could think of only different types of chocolate to have each day at first; this is great if your goal is to add pleasures *and* pounds to your lifestyle, but not as helpful if you want to stay physically fit.) If this sounds like you, you can add at least one *type* of pleasure to each day—a new kind of food, a new activity, a new small purchase, a new experience, and so on. This makes it easier to create variety.

* Enjoy your pleasures on a "rotation," whereby you change them regularly, but cycle through a collection of them. This way, you can maintain a sense of novelty, but you do not have to constantly come up with new ideas. This is a nice strategy for those who enjoy routine.

* Swap ideas with friends. Ask others what their favorite treats to themselves are. This can also become a bonding experience, as it can help you to feel more connected to another person when you enjoy what he or she enjoys, and it gives you something to talk about later.

* Look at your schedule and think about the times when you generally feel a little more tired, frustrated, or stressed. Then see what type of pleasure might fit into that space. For example, if

you find that midafternoon your enthusiasm for life wears a little thin, remind yourself to take a quiet tea break or walk outside. Or if you find yourself running errands at that time, you may want to create a playlist of songs that always make you feel good or buy an audiobook you know you'll enjoy and let yourself get a little more enjoyment while on the run.

* Plan ahead and create a list of pleasures you can choose from when you feel you need a pick-me-up. (There is a worksheet coming up for you to use, or you can create a list on your computer or mobile device, so you can always have your list with you.)

* Create rituals. One exception I have found to the pleasures-lose-their-strength-over-time rule is the use of pleasure-based rituals. Enjoying the same type of tea each day as I write is an example. I may not appreciate each daily sip of Vanilla Rooibos tea as much as I loved it the first time I tried it, but I enjoy it each day, more than I would if I didn't have it as part of my routine, and about as much as I enjoyed it the day before. Having a special place to sit and enjoy my work is another example. When I climb into my familiar chair, the fond memories of other productive days mixes with my experience of this one, and I find that I enjoy it more than I would enjoy working in any other spot. That pleasures do not bring the same intensity of experience time after time is true; however, they can still bring joy when incorporated into a ritual or routine. Just don't forget to also cycle in new pleasures, to keep things fresh.

Gratifications

Gratifications are another gift from positive psychology that can help us to relieve stress and enhance our enjoyment of life. When incorporated with care, gratifications can add extra meaning to our lives, help mitigate the stress we may feel from a boring job or a grueling schedule, and provide the type of fun that makes time fly.

Gratifications and Flow

Gratifications are activities that employ our special skills and talents. They provide the type of eustress that can make life more exhilarating and enhance our self-esteem. When we engage in gratifications, we experience a state of "flow" in which we lose our sense of time and become less self-conscious. The concept of flow was first popularized by psychologist Mihaly Csikszentmihalyi, who discovered that certain activities that challenge us in just the right ways can bring a feeling of total absorption. We slip into this near-meditative state when we engage in activities that include just the right level of challenge—activities that are not necessarily easy, but are engaging and enjoyable. When we experience this state of flow, we lose track of time and self-consciousness, and we feel less stressed when we are finished.

Gratifications are activities that incorporate flow. Many people organize their lives specifically to include these activities, and those who do not would be wise to try it. Gratifications can help with stress relief in a few ways:

* When we engage in gratifications, we can experience that sense of flow that leads to total absorption in what is going on around us. This can lead us to feel less stressed about what we are experiencing in life. Losing awareness of our stressors can help with issues such as anxiety and rumination and can help interrupt a cycle of stress that can result from too many stressors occurring with no breaks in between. Gratifications can provide the downtime that we need, to afford us a break from the stressors in our lives.

* Gratifications can build our self-confidence and an awareness of our own strengths. Because stress can result when we feel that we are not up to the challenges we face, this boost of can-do can extend beyond the activities we are engaging in and remind us that we may be more capable and powerful than we realize. Simply put, persistent stress can erode confidence in our own abilities; gratifications can help to bring that confidence back.

* Gratifications can give us a boost of positive emotion that can help move us through the day. They can give us reasons to be excited about getting out of bed in the morning. This can counteract feelings of exhaustion we may experience when we are under too much stress.

Key Differences between Gratifications and Pleasures

While both gratifications and pleasures can bring feelings of happiness, make life more enjoyable, and help to relieve stress, there are some key differences. Gratifications and pleasures are not interchangeable, and they both can be used for different purposes. Ideally, because they can both enhance our lives, we can incorporate a mix of them into our lifestyles. Here are some important differences between gratifications and pleasures:

* Gratifications require more effort, and bring a higher payoff. While it is easy to buy an ice cream cone to give yourself an emotional lift, it takes more effort to complete a karate class to develop skills and get an aerobic "high." However, the positive feelings and other benefits of the karate class (or other gratifications) will generally last longer than the emotional boost that comes with pleasures like dessert.
* The benefits of gratifications increase over time, while pleasures lose their strength over time. This is one of the most important benefits of gratifications, so it bears emphasis: gratifications can become *more* enjoyable as we continue to enjoy them! For example, you might get as much (or more!) enjoyment from the final stroke of a painting as you would when you put that first streak of color on the canvas; the final kick in a kickboxing class may come with a wave of positive feelings that may not have been present when you first dragged yourself to class and started moving.
* The benefits of gratifications increase with repetition. As you develop the skills that are involved in gratifications, you tend to enjoy these activities more, rather than getting less excited with

them over time. This means that a longstanding meditation habit does not lose its luster; your fondness for the habit will likely deepen with each month of practice. The same is true for hobbies like knitting or wood carving; as you get better at them, you can grow to enjoy them more than you did when you were a novice. Jobs that require skills can bring the same joys; this is why some people love what they do and don't want to retire at a specific age. Gratifications can bring meaning to our lives because they come to be increasingly important to us, and they become more tied to our identities and self-esteem.

What Are Common Gratifications?

Gratifications can take many forms. Perhaps even more than pleasures, they are highly personalized in the appeal that they hold; one person's gratification may be another person's tedious task, depending on natural talents, skills, and tastes. The following are a list of common gratifications that appeal to many people. They can provide you with inspiration and the right frame of mind to come up with your own list of gratifications that are targeted to your own personal make-up. See what appeals here:

* Gardening
* Crafting
* Woodworking
* Learning a new language
* Playing music
* Completing crossword or Sudoku puzzles
* Writing (short stories, books, poetry, or even personal letters)
* Martial arts
* Cooking and baking
* Computer programming
* Drawing, painting, and other art endeavors
* Games of strategy
* Meditation
* Hobbies not listed here
* Jobs that play to our strengths

How to Manage: Work More Gratifications into Your Life

Creating a lifestyle that includes a mix of several gratifications is ideal for stress relief. However, even adding one regularly practiced gratification can help quite a bit. The following are different areas of life that can include gratifications, and some potential ways to introduce these activities into your existing lifestyle:

* **At work.** Ideally, we should all work in careers that require our own unique mix of talents and that challenge us in just the right way to feel inspired and vital, but not so much that we feel overwhelmed. If you do not have such a job, gratifications can help in a few different ways.
  ○ **On the job.** If there are any ways to work in new responsibilities at work that use your special skills, it would be worth doing what you can do to make that happen. Interestingly, even if it increases your overall workload, adding some tasks that engage and challenge you in a way that you enjoy can feel less stressful than having slightly fewer tasks that all feel mundane or overly taxing. If you can trade some tasks that feel overly difficult for a few that you would experience as gratifications, the way you feel at work could shift in a significantly more positive way.
  ○ **Off the job.** If you cannot alter the types of responsibilities you have at work, you can still gain from engaging in gratifications outside of work. Engaging in stimulating activities outside of work hours can alter the way you feel overall, and these benefits can seep into your job performance. This can potentially alter for the better your confidence level at work and perhaps even provide you with extra enjoyment of the challenges you face there; instead of seeing certain tasks as difficult enough to feel threatening, you may be able to approach them in a more relaxed way and see them as challenges. (See **Key 4** for more on how this helps with stress.)
* **At home.** During your off hours, you have more time and freedom to play with gratifications in your life. You can add hobbies

to the mix, even if you need to cut out other activities in order to make time for them. Given all the benefits of gratifications, you can see why such a move would be worth the effort.

* **Gratifications with friends.** There are many gratifications that can be satisfying as group activities, whether we enjoy them internally or as part of being among others. Games that require interaction—whether in the form of physical sports or intellectual strategy games—can move a group of people into a state of flow. Knitting in a group can be an enjoyable way to engage in this gratification. Making gratifications a group activity brings a few benefits:

  ° Sharing an enjoyable activity creates a social bond.
  ° If you engage in gratifications as part of a group, you may be more likely to continue with it, as seeing friends may pull you into making this activity more of a priority.
  ° The idea of not wanting to cancel on friends and let the group down by your absence might also push you to continue. Remember, many of the benefits of gratifications strengthen over time, so it can be helpful to have these outside factors to encourage you to persist with the habit.

Gratitude

Cultivating feelings of gratitude has been shown to have a very positive impact on health and happiness. Studies find that cultivating a sense of gratitude can help you to maintain a more positive mood in your daily life. Increasing your levels of gratitude is one of the simpler ways to increase emotional well-being and resilience to stress and can also bring higher overall satisfaction in life and a greater sense of happiness. This can contribute to enhanced emotional well-being and can also improve your relationships. Those with greater levels of gratitude tend to have stronger relationships, because they appreciate their loved ones more. That appreciation is felt, and the people in their lives tend to do more to earn this gratitude. In addition, those who feel gratitude tend to sleep better and enjoy improved health.

Activities to Try: Cultivate Gratitude

You can enhance the feelings of gratitude you experience in simple ways. The following techniques have been shown to create a tangible shift in the amount of gratitude you experience. See what works best for you:

* **Gratitude journal.** Maintaining a gratitude journal can be so enjoyable that many people find themselves looking forward all day to their journaling time, and this inspires them to notice more and more things in their lives for which they are grateful. There are a few different ways that a gratitude journal can be maintained:
  - It can be a long list of items that are appreciated each day.
  - It can be a declaration of one or two things that are appreciated, announced via social media.
  - It can be one thing written about in great detail in your journal.
  - As mentioned in **Key 4**, the gratitude journaling technique that has been found to be most helpful is writing about exactly three items at the end of each day. It is a manageable number, and it provides just enough space for really experiencing gratitude without feeling overwhelmed by the amount of writing involved.
* **Gratitude letter.** A favorite gratitude-enhancing technique from the field of positive psychology is the gratitude letter. This exercise involves honoring someone in a slightly grander gesture. It works as follows:
  1. Choose one person from your past who has done something for you that you really appreciated.
  2. Write a detailed letter to this person, outlining what it was that they did for you and, more important, the impact that their actions had on your life, and how you felt about it. Let them know that you appreciate them, and why.
  3. Read the letter aloud to the individual in person.
* **Everyday gratitude.** It's easy to express gratitude to people in

your life on a daily basis: Just say it. If you're not in the habit of letting people know how much they mean to you or how much you appreciate the small gestures they do for you, this may take some getting used to. If you are already in the habit of doing this, try branching out and letting more people know—people you encounter at work, in a class you take, or when you go out to eat. This is the simplest way to share feelings of gratitude, and it brings an immediate payoff.

Questions to Ask Yourself

* Are there areas of my life where I could be happier?
* What pleasures might I enjoy the most?
* How many pleasures can I comfortably add to my week, and what should they be?
* Am I experiencing enough flow in my life?
* What one gratification would I like to experience more often?
* What would be my preferred way to increase my feelings of gratitude for what I have and for the people in my life?

Evaluate Your Answers

As you read over your answers, notice which ones seem to jump out at you. Do you get excited at the thought of adding pleasures to your life? Do you look at the areas of your life where you could be happier and long to make changes there? Let your interests guide you. If you have a special feeling that you need more flow in your life or need to focus on gratitude, for example, go with that. Use the activities in this chapter to create a happier life.

KEY 8

PRACTICE LONG-TERM
RESILIENCE-FORMING HABITS

The bamboo that bends is stronger than the oak that resists.
—JAPANESE PROVERB

Certain stress relief techniques, when practiced repeatedly, can actually build long-term resilience toward stress. This chapter shows you the research behind some of the most beneficial of these activities and provides clear strategies for adopting these habits long term. Choose from meditation, exercise, or journaling, or incorporate all three.

Libby's Stress Solution

Libby found that after the birth of her second child, she felt overwhelmed. She spent most of her days changing diapers, planning play dates, and meeting the many needs of her two small children, which was wonderful in many ways, but consuming as well. She had just moved to a new area and had no family nearby, so she was also working on creating a group of friends. Her body had not returned to its pre-baby state, and her lifestyle had been considerably altered. She felt isolated and stressed and became short-tempered, which made it harder to care for her baby and toddler, as well as for herself.

She realized that she needed an outlet. We examined her needs and options, and she decided to try a martial arts class with her husband. They attended a rigorous 2-hour class twice a week, and things began to change. Her responsibilities remained the same, but her ability to cope improved with every kick. She found that the vigorous aerobic activity created an outlet for frustration, the exercise strengthened her body, the martial arts moves instilled in her a sense of confidence, and the social outlet of the class gave her a chance to make new friends and to connect with her husband through topics other than work and children. Even better, she found that she became less stressed about the frustrations she faced in her life. She always left the class feeling better than she had when she arrived, and the activities she did there gave her a sense of calm that lasted, at least partially, throughout the week. This one habit met many needs for her, and this shifted how she felt in her life. As she felt more energized and encouraged, she was able to add even more stress relief techniques to her repertoire.

Why Long-Term Habits Differ from Repeated Short-Term Habits

The benefit of adopting a full stress management plan, rather than one or two favorite stress relievers, is that you can create a strategy filled with different activities that manage stress in different ways. We have looked at ways to recognize when and where stress is an issue in your life (**Key 1**). We've gone over short-term stress relievers that quickly reverse the stress response (**Key 2**), and have seen plenty of quick ways to cut down on feelings of stress. We have also looked at ways to take care of your body (**Key 3**) and mind (**Key 4**) so that you are functioning at your best and are not unwittingly creating stress for yourself. We've looked at different lifestyle ingredients that can create a buffer from stress and offer more tools to manage it (**Keys 6 and 7**). A final—and very helpful—key to an effective stress management plan is having at least one long-term habit that builds your resilience to stress by decreasing your reactivity to it. This can be an invaluable asset.

The approaches covered in this chapter have been proved to work in two important ways. First, they can cut down on stress each time you practice them. (They have been touched on in previous chapters because they do so.) Each of them have been shown to cut down on stress within minutes of their being put into practice, so they can be effective stress relievers the first time you try them.

Perhaps more important, however, these techniques have been shown to change the way people react physically and psychologically to stress over time! As with gratifications, these stress relief strategies only bring greater benefits with practice. After a few weeks of practice, you will feel stress relief come on more quickly. After a few months, you will find that you feel less stressed, even when you are not practicing these techniques, and that you naturally react to stress with less intensity. With greater practice, you will find that it is progressively easier to relieve stress with these strategies. Because their benefits are cumulative, they not only help you to relieve the stress you are experiencing now, but also can help you better manage the stress that you haven't even encountered yet.

This can be a great help with episodic and chronic stress. As mentioned in **Key 1**, because stress can build upon itself, and because we can create more stress for ourselves when we are functioning from a state of being overwhelmed, we need strategies that disrupt the buildup of stress and the momentum that can come from a chain reaction of stressors—stressors feeding into more stressors. However, rather than relying on only disrupting the cycle of stress and on cutting out major stressors, you can lower your stress levels over time with these resilience-promoting habits. These habits decrease the intensity of our reactions to all stressors and ensure that each stressor makes less of a contribution to our overall stress load. They can act as a safeguard against stress, particularly in situations where we face a high degree of stress in our lives and may not always be able to take time out to practice stress relief techniques when we start to feel overwhelmed.

Habits That Work

Not all stress relief strategies bring equal levels of resilience. This chapter includes three of the most effective techniques to reduce stress. They each can be learned independently, bring benefits in minutes, and bring cumulative benefits over time. They can also be practiced by virtually anyone. I encourage you to try each one and to consider making one, two, or all three a regular part of your lifestyle.

Meditation

As you may recall from **Key 2**, this powerful technique has gained popularity in recent years as researchers have discovered its considerable benefits for stress relief. Besides the basic short-term benefits of meditation as a quick-fix stress reliever, some of which I discussed earlier, additional strengths are imparted by this technique when it is practiced long term. The following are some of the benefits you can gain from meditation if you practice regularly for more than a few weeks.

Types of Meditation

There are many different types of meditation that can be practiced, and all of them can bring benefits for stress relief. Each variation may appeal to different people based on personal tastes and personality characteristics; some forms of meditation are simply easier or more comfortable for a given person than others, and some forms may appeal at different points in one's development. Generally, meditation techniques are broken into two main types: concentrative and non-concentrative.

Concentrative meditative techniques center around a focal point; the attention is directed at an object, sensation, or idea.

This feature allows copious variations of concentrative meditation; a focal point can be a candle, a mantra, a piece of chocolate, or the sound of one's own breath.

Non-concentrative meditation, also known as mindfulness meditation, has a more detached approach. Rather than a close focus on an object, an awareness of all things is the central concept of this form of meditation—it can be said that the present moment is the focus. Concentrative approaches tend to be easier for beginners to learn, but both types are effective for stress management, and both types can be easily practiced once learned.

Benefits of Meditation

Both concentrative and non-concentrative meditation deliver enormous benefits, which we are learning more about all the time. Meditation works quickly and subtly, and perhaps the best thing about it is that its benefits increase over time. While even those who have been practicing meditation for years can find it to be challenging, the practice deepens over time. Those who meditate regularly are able to get into a deeper state of relaxation more quickly, so that not only are long meditative sessions more beneficial with practice, but mini-sessions carry greater benefits for this group as well.

Meditation has been shown to produce benefits with as little as 3 minutes of practice. However, longer sessions, and cumulative numbers of sessions, bring greater benefits. Dr. Jon Kabat-Zinn, a researcher from the University of Massachusetts, has spearheaded many studies on meditation and has popularized a type of meditation training that involves eight weekly training sessions with daily homework assignments throughout. These classes have been studied, and many benefits have been demonstrated after these 8 weeks of practice. Some of these benefits include the following:

* Increased feelings of well-being
* Enhanced ability to focus
* Reduced feelings of anxiety
* Lower blood pressure

* Increased capacity for empathy
* Improved health across a wide array of measures (including allergies, sleep disorders, depression, and binge eating)
* Lower reactivity to stress

Activity to Try: Breathing Meditation

One of the most popular forms of meditation, especially for beginners, is breath-focused meditation. Because our breathing is constant, rhythmic, and effortless, the sound and feel of our own breath provides a wonderfully convenient and efficient focus for meditative practice. In addition, because meditation works best with a more physically relaxed form of breathing, learning this type of breathing and learning meditation tend to go hand in hand. When the body is stressed, our breathing shifts to a more shallow, quick pattern, and returning the breath to a more relaxed pattern can help to reverse the stress response, so the relaxed breathing that comes with meditation is useful for stress relief in its own right. Here are some easy steps for a simple breathing meditation:

1. Find a quiet place to relax, and get comfortable.
2. Set an alarm for the length of time you would like to practice. (This will allow you to fully relax and know that you will not miss anything important that you have to do after the session, worry that you will fall asleep, or otherwise have your mind cluttered with thoughts.)
3. To further regulate your breathing, you may want to count with each breath as with the breathing exercise in **Key 2** — count slowly to 5 on the inhale, and count slowly to 8 with each exhale — and keep your breathing at a relaxed pace. This counting can also provide you with a focus for a few minutes, which may help you to more easily move into a meditative state, especially if you are a beginner.
4. You can stop counting and stop focusing on altering your breathing once you feel that you are breathing in a fully relaxed man-

ner. Rather than changing your breathing patterns at this point, simply notice your breath as it moves into and out of your body. As your mind wanders (and it inevitably will) to thoughts of anything other than your breath, gently direct your attention back to the sound and feel of your breathing. Don't think about it; just do it. This is the important part of the practice.

5. You can continue until your alarm goes off or until you naturally feel your session is complete.

Other Variations of Meditation

This breathing meditation is a simple one to teach and to learn, which makes it a popular meditation for beginners. As mentioned, however, it is one of numerous forms of meditation that might appeal to you. The following are a few more popular types of meditation, with a brief description of each:

* **Mantra meditation.** This is a highly effective form of meditation and may be easier than other forms for some people to practice. It involves focusing on a specific mantra, which can be anything you choose. (Many people like to choose sounds like *om* and *one*, which are simple and nondistracting to repeat; others like to choose a word or words that have meaning, such as *hope* or *peace*. Whatever mantra you choose is obviously up to you, and you can choose based on what resonates with you.) Mantra meditation follows the same basic pattern as that of breathing meditation, except you repeat your mantra, either aloud or inside your head. As you slowly repeat it, you focus on the sound of the word and the sensations you feel when you repeat that word (if you are repeating it aloud). As your mind wanders to other thoughts, gently redirect it back to the mantra.

* **Music meditation.** This type of meditation has the considerable benefits of listening to music, combined with those of meditation. Choose music that is soothing and enjoyable to you, and simply focus on the sound of it. Let the feelings flow through your body, and focus on the sensations. Be careful to keep your mind clear, however, and simply focus on sensation.

* **Loving kindness meditation.** This meditation, also known as *metta*, brings positive thoughts and feelings to you and can help you to let go of any anger and animosity you may be feeling toward others. Rather than focusing on a mantra, this meditation involves focusing on feelings of love and appreciation. First, you surround yourself with these positive feelings—visualize yourself surrounded with love and light, and see if you can feel this in your body. Next, think of each person you love and envision them surrounded with love as well. Really feel it in your heart and in your body. Then move on to acquaintances and those you don't know as well, to those toward whom you may feel mild distaste, and eventually to those with whom you may be angry or resentful. Allow yourself to let go of the negative feelings you may have had, as you allow the positive, loving feelings to fill your awareness and surround your vision of that person. You can direct loving kindness meditation toward whole groups of people and even other countries. Benefits include reductions in anger, negative mood, stress, and anxiety and increases in positive social feelings and in hope.

* **Additional meditations.** If you are reading these keys out of order, you can find additional meditation techniques in **Key 4**.

Exercise

Exercise is a highly recommended stress reliever for several reasons. As I discussed in previous chapters, physical activity brings many benefits other than stress relief, and these benefits alone—increased wellness, longevity, and happiness—make exercise a habit that is well worth the effort; and as a stress management technique, it is more effective than most. The combined benefits of these two facts make physical exercise a lifestyle feature worth pursuing.

Benefits of Exercise

I touched on exercise in previous keys, dealing with it in depth in **Key 3**, so I will just offer a quick refresher here. Exercise can reduce feelings of stress in as little as 3 minutes, and the long-term benefits of regular physical activity are numerous and impressive. Regular physical activity brings increased longevity and enhanced physical health across a wide array of measures. Regular practice even alters the body's reactivity to stress and quiets the mind, so stressors in your environment have less of an impact. Exercise promotes emotional and physical health like no other activity and should be a part of any healthy lifestyle.

Caveats

As with virtually all stress relievers, there are some drawbacks to exercise, especially if used as the only stress relief technique in one's arsenal. For those who can take the time and have the physical capacity, exercise is wonderfully effective in beating back blues, increasing overall health, and relieving stress in many ways. However, there are a few caveats to watch out for and reasons why exercise should not be one's only source of stress relief. Keep the following in mind when building a stress management plan that includes physical activity as a main staple.

Start Slowly and Stay Safe

You may be tempted to go from no exercise to a high level right away, to get into shape as quickly as possible and relieve as much stress as you can. Don't. You could injure yourself or simply burn out. You could end up overly sore and decide that exercise is not for you. It's much better to start slowly and work your way into more intense exercise sessions that you enjoy, rather than push too hard and end up giving up.

Don't Give Up

Every January, the gyms are packed, and it is difficult to find a parking space. Cut to March, and you see long stretches of empty pavement in front of the gym. Many people who start exercise programs predictably drop out after a few weeks of committed work.

(Remember that 88% statistic on New Year's resolutions we talked about in the Preface?) What often happens is that people find themselves missing workouts a few days in a row and eventually decide they don't have what it takes to maintain the habit. Do not let yourself be fooled into believing this—you can maintain a regular workout habit if you would like to do so. You may need to alter your approach, but there are several potential paths to success for you. None of them, however, involves giving up when you face a setback.

Life coaches generally see their clients having trouble with maintaining new habits between the 3rd and 7th week of adopting them. This is the window in which the momentum that comes from excitement over the new change begins to wane and the sense of accomplishment from maintaining the habit for a few months has not yet occurred. During this more challenging time, it is important to steel your resolve, adjust your approach if necessary, and give yourself the tools you need to keep going with the habit. (See the next chapter, "Creating an Action Plan," for specific tips on how to do this.)

Don't Make Exercise Your Only Choice

Some stress management techniques work so well that it's tempting to use them as our only method of stress relief. Exercise is a highly effective stress reliever, but it should be one of at least a few other tools for stress relief, for a few reasons. First, it cannot be used in every instance. There may be times, for example, when you need to calm down quickly and leave the situation you are facing in order to take a brisk walk. You need a few stress relievers that work quickly and can be practiced virtually anywhere. In other instances, addressing the source of your stress is important; obviously, using proactive, solution-focused coping techniques such as boundary setting or eliminating tolerations can work here.

Also, there may be times when you do not have access to exercise, because of physical injury or other circumstances. The body can actually go through a feeling of withdrawal if you are used to a certain level of activity and this stops abruptly. If exercise is your only tool for stress management, the stress of this will be compounded, and other stressors will be even more challenging to manage. It is a good idea to have exercise as an important part of your life, but maintaining a few other stress relief habits for balance is an even better idea.

Try Different Forms of Exercise

For stress relief, virtually any activity that brings aerobic exercise is a good option to consider. Within 3 minutes of commencing aerobic activity, cortisol levels fall, and the benefits just grow from there.

Three Types of Exercise

The following types of exercise are highly recommended for stress relief, as they have particularly effective stress-reducing properties for short-term and long-term stress management:

* **Yoga.** The gentle stretching and balance of yoga may be what people first think of when the practice comes to mind, but there are several other aspects of yoga that contribute to stress relief and healthy living. Yoga involves the same type of diaphragmic breathing that is used with meditation (see **Key 2**); in fact, some styles of yoga involve meditation as part of their practice (indeed, most forms of yoga can move you into a meditative state to some degree.) Yoga also involves balance, coordination, stretching, and, in some styles, strength training—all of which support wellness and stress relief. Yoga can be practiced in many different ways. Some styles of yoga feel like a gentle massage from the inside, while others will have you sweating and leave you sore the next day, so there is a school of yoga that can appeal to most people, even those with certain physical limitations.
* **Walking.** Walking is one of the most easily available stress relievers, which is wonderful because of the benefits that this technique brings. The human body was designed to be able to walk

long distances, and this activity generally does not cause the same degree of wear and tear on the body as does running such distances. Walking is a workout that you can easily individualize through the speed you use, the weights you carry, the music you listen to, and the location and company you choose. This type of workout can also be easily broken up into 10-minute sessions and no classes are necessary and no special gear is required beyond a suitable pair of shoes. (This is an advantage, because studies have shown that three 10-minute workouts bring roughly the same benefits as one 30-minute session—great news for those who have to find their exercise in smaller chunks because of a busy schedule!)

* **Martial arts.** There are many forms of martial arts, and while each may have a slightly different focus, ideology, or set of techniques, they all deliver benefits for stress relief. These practices tend to pack a punch, offering both aerobic exercise and strength training, as well as the confidence that comes from fitness and capabilities in self-defense. Generally practiced in groups, martial arts can also offer some social support benefits, as classmates encourage one another and maintain a sense of group engagement. Many martial arts styles bring philosophical perspectives that promote stress management and peaceful living, which you can choose to adopt or not. Certain styles, especially those with high levels of physical combat, have a higher risk of injury, however, so martial arts practice is not for everyone, or at least not all styles work for all people. If you sample a few different martial arts programs and talk to your doctor before settling on a style to pursue, you will have a higher chance of finding a new habit that can keep you more fit and resilient for decades to come.

Other Types of Exercise

These three examples are not the only types of exercise; they simply bring some standout benefits and can be practiced by most people. There are many other forms of exercise that can also be highly effective, such as Pilates, running, weight training, swimming, dancing, and organized sports. They all bring their own stress management benefits to the table, so explore and practice the form of exercise that appeals to you the most.

How to Manage: Choosing an Exercise Plan

As you look at various kinds of exercise and try to decide which type of workout would be the best fit for your lifestyle, there are a few points to consider. Each form of exercise carries unique benefits and appeals to specific types of people. The key is to find the right habits to fit your personality and lifestyle. After all, exercise is one of the more difficult habits to maintain, and choosing a style that is not the best fit for you can make it more difficult to maintain this as a long-term habit. Here are some points to consider when choosing a new practice to take on:

* **Look for fun.** First and foremost, exercise should be enjoyable, or you will not have the motivation to continue in it for any significant length of time. Workouts are easier to get through on an individual basis and easier to repeat collectively if they feel more like fun than work. One person may find that a walk on a treadmill in front of the television makes time fly by, while this could feel grueling for someone who prefers to walk outside in nature; the same exercise can feel very different based on such details. Therefore, try to think of what is fun for you. Explore ideas like sports, classes, and various types of activity, and see what resonates with you.

* **Get others involved.** It is easier to stay on track with virtually any habit if you have others involved with you. Research shows that exercise is no exception to this rule. If your workouts are part of a larger social structure, such as a series of classes that involve the same people over time, or a buddy system approach where you meet up with a friend on a regular basis, it becomes both easier to keep up with workouts and harder to give up. Having the fun of seeing friends or classmates waiting for you can be a positive motivational tool to help you keep up with your workout schedule; knowing there will be people there to enjoy can some-

times give you that extra push you need to keep things going. In addition, reluctance to let others down can compel you to pursue your activity; you may feel an extra pull to attend class or keep your workout date because you don't want to disappoint others. This may also remind you that you do not want to disappoint the part of you that really wants to maintain this healthy habit.

* **Build it into your schedule and lifestyle.** It becomes much easier to maintain any habit if it becomes part of your schedule, and because of the investment of time and energy, this is particularly true for exercise. Think about what time of day you could most easily exercise and when the type of exercise you would like to do would best fit, and schedule it in! Gwyneth Paltrow, who has become a busy working mom and advocate of healthy living in recent years, advises morning visits to the gym; this allows her to get her daily exercise out of the way and provides a boost of energy for the rest of the day, she explains. Morning workouts are opportune for those who would like to manage their weight as well as their stress levels, because workouts boost the metabolism for hours afterward, as well as leaving you feeling more relaxed. However, lunchtime or evening workouts may be more convenient, depending on the flow of your day. And weekend-only workouts are better than no workouts. (My best time to work out is at night—my husband and I like to discuss the events of the day while walking; it allows us to exercise and connect at the same time, and it works best for our busy schedules. We are just careful to be done at least an hour before bedtime so exercise doesn't interfere with sleep.) Think about what works best for your specific needs, and don't be afraid to experiment. If one time of day doesn't work well for you, another time will.

* **Don't give up or set too-high goals.** People often overdo it when they begin a workout habit and either injure themselves or burn out on the habit before it becomes a permanent part of their routine. For the sake of safety, and to maintain the habit long

term, be sure you start slowly, pace yourself, and work out safely, even hiring a trainer in the beginning if necessary. Remember, you are in this for the long haul; slow and steady wins the race.

* **Change things up if necessary.** If you find that it becomes increasingly difficult to maintain your workout habit, or if you dread going back to the workouts you did at a previous point in your life, don't be afraid to change things! Even for exercise regimens that are working, altering your routine can build new muscles and produce more effective workouts. (The body has a tendency to plateau and experience diminishing returns when the same muscles are exercised in the same way for a long period, so changing the type of exercise can have a beneficial impact.) Periodically changing your workout can keep things interesting and allow you to make adjustments if your resolve is starting to wane.

* **Consult a doctor before you begin.** With any physical activity there is the risk of injury. Before starting an exercise regimen, it is best to talk with your doctor.

Journaling

The previous two strategies have numerous benefits for stress management and overall health. While journaling clearly does not offer the same physical benefits as exercise or the same level of relaxation as meditation, it does have significant positive consequences for body and mind, effects that grow over time. It is also a flexible and accessible practice, so it merits inclusion here.

Journaling can bring about specific emotional shifts (based on the intentions you have with your practice), which can result in enormous stress relief. It can be practiced in a few different ways and can take 5 minutes or an hour, depending on the time and the goals you have. If you feel you don't have time to commit yourself to a full meditation or exercise habit right now, journaling is definitely a practice to consider.

Benefits of Journaling

As a stress relief technique, journaling brings a wider variety of benefits than one might expect. It reduces the symptoms of a variety of health conditions, among them asthma, arthritis, and chronic pain. It improves cognitive functioning. It strengthens the immune system, preventing a host of other health issues. It can aid in the process of forgiveness. Gratitude journaling has actually been shown to lift depression in as little as 3 weeks. And journaling in general relieves stress.

Types of Journaling

Based on your needs, your journaling practice can take on whatever form you wish. You can maintain a long document on your computer that includes entries for each day, write in a beautifully bound book in a rainbow of entries using a color-coded pen, scrawl your thoughts on a collection of papers, write them on the steam in your bathroom mirror, or find one of a host of options in between. (My journaling has taken all of these forms over the years, and more.)

Certain writing techniques, however, are particularly effective for meeting specific ends. The following are a few different methods of journaling that seem to have the most positive effects for stress relief. Regardless of how you record your thoughts (digitally, in multicolored ink, or traced in steam), these areas of focus can serve you well.

Activity to Try: Emotion-Focused Journaling

We all have our issues that cause us stress. Exploring the emotions behind our stress, and exploring the events behind our emotions, can enable us to get beyond our feelings of agitation and into a place of inner peace. If you find yourself fixating on a stressor in your life, journaling about your feelings surrounding the issue and exploring the connections of why you may feel this way can enable you to gain some insight, as well as some closure. We may not always have the perfect experiences in life to bring about the type of closure we would prefer, but we can give ourselves a sense of closure and a point from which to move on if we can explore our feelings and make peace with them. With emotion-focused journaling, a few different ingredients can go a long way toward the relief of letting go:

* **Examine.** If you give yourself space to explore what you feel and why, it can become easier to let go of these feelings. Start with the feelings, and work backward, looking within. How do you feel? Describe it in detail, in whatever imagery feels right for you. (It can be in a series of adjectives, metaphors, or whatever seems to fit.) Then work on tracing back why. If your feelings come from a certain event, what needs of yours were not being met when that happened? What do you feel you need now? Exploring your feelings, needs, and experiences can help you to make sense of the stress you are experiencing and help you to move beyond it.

* **Acknowledge.** Sometimes we just need to give ourselves permission to feel a certain way, and then we can move on. Seeing the words in black and white can help you to realize when your feelings are valid, and you can acknowledge that fact. (If your feelings seem a little misplaced, you may further explore the real root of where these feelings are coming from, or you may find it easier to let go and move on.) If you feel you need to talk to a close friend or a therapist to gain more support, journaling in this way can help you to organize your thoughts before you take them to someone else.

* **Explore.** As you look at what is upsetting you and what felt wrong about the experience, it can also help to look at the benefits you may have gleaned from such situations. Finding benefits in your negative experiences is not the same as saying that you are glad that they happened or that you would have preferred these events over other possibilities. (Sometimes when people experience

very difficult, even tragic, circumstances, they feel that the act of finding the benefits of these experiences fails to acknowledge the pain that they brought; in actuality, finding the hidden benefits of our hardships is a way of maintaining some of our power in the situation and of refusing to "waste" the pain that was endured. (See **Key 4**.) One way to do this is to list, or explore in detail, the positive things that have come from experiences that have caused us pain or frustration. For example, a painful breakup may have taught us a few things about what we want and don't want in a relationship or about our own personal strength. Surviving a serious injury or loss may yield the benefit of enabling us to have a deeper appreciation for all the things that we still have in life. Again, if this type of journaling feels too emotionally intense, do not be afraid to enlist the help of a therapist, and use the journaling practice as a tool to maximize the benefits you can gain through therapy. That said, many people find that this type of journaling practice provides some of the self-exploration benefits of therapy, but as a solitary practice.

Activity to Try: Solution-Focused Journaling

Journaling techniques that explore feelings can cause an emotional release and uncover the deeper roots to our experiences. Techniques that involve exploring solutions for our stressors can be particularly effective in facilitating the process of letting go of stressful feelings. This works particularly well with feelings of anxiety or rumination, where perhaps steps can be taken to move beyond this state. This type of solution-focused journaling can work in two parts, as follows:

> * **Explore your stressors.** As with emotion-focused journaling, solution-focused writing can begin with an exploration of the feelings that underlie the stress you are feeling and with a tracing back to what events are causing these emotions.

※ **Brainstorm solutions.** Rather than stopping at the feelings-exploration stage, or even at the benefit-finding stage (which is optional here), actively searching for solutions can provide a strong sense of empowerment and can move you from a stuck, stressed place to a point of feeling that you have options. (In terms we explored in **Key 4**, this can move you from having an external locus of control to a more internal one.)

Activity to Try: Gratitude Journaling

Gratitude journaling has been mentioned in other keys, but it brings so many benefits that it bears repeating here. Gratitude journaling can have a positive impact on emotional well-being to such an extent that it can even lift depression. While there are several different ways to practice gratitude journaling, there is one method that researchers prefer:

1. At the end of each day, choose three things for which you are grateful.
2. Write about each one in detail, focusing on what you appreciate the most.
3. Be sure that they are things that happened that day and that you write about them at the end of the day. For some reason, this formula has been shown to bring the greatest benefit.

Additional Types of Journaling

While the three forms of journaling above have been found to carry the greatest benefits, there are many forms of journaling that can bring about stress relief. Here are two more.

Goal-Oriented Journaling

This type of journaling helps you to clarify where you are in life and where you would like to be. You can identify goals and break them down into smaller steps. Then you can track your progress. This allows you to more easily move through the stages of change, providing a venue in which to congratulate yourself when you achieve successes, and enables you to track where you may have gone wrong in your plans or where you might want to change them. This is a fun and validating way to journal, and it does not require daily writing.

Dream Journaling

Because dreams can provide insights into our subconscious minds, it can be interesting and useful to maintain a dream journal. These journals allow you to better remember your dreams and to keep track of ongoing themes. Write in your journal every morning after waking up, and you will likely find that you remember your dreams more vividly and more often. Dream journals can allow you to get in touch with your deeper goals so you can meet them and with your sources of stress and anxiety so you can better manage them.

How to Manage: Getting Started with Journaling

The habit of journaling is a simple one to maintain, although, as with any new habit, there are a few things to keep in mind. The habit doesn't work if you do not actually practice it, so, particularly with gratitude journaling, shorter entries on a more regular basis can be more beneficial than longer entries that seem like so much work that they are rarely written. Also, remember that you can practice journaling at any time, so if you haven't written in your journal for weeks, you can always pick it right back up and keep writing. Here are some things to keep in mind as you get started:

* **Choose your venue.** As mentioned earlier, there are many convenient ways to maintain a journal. Some people like the ease and convenience of typing their thoughts on the computer, while others enjoy the old-fashioned feel of pen and paper. Sometimes having a beautiful journal can inspire you to write more, while

for others, a plainer book brings less pressure to create entries that are more "profound" than authentic. Think about what will work best for you and your tastes. And don't forget to take steps to ensure your own privacy, if this is important to you. Journaling is generally most effective when you do not need to self-censor.

* **Choose your style.** While reading the preceding descriptions of methods of journaling—emotion focused, solution focused, and gratitude focused, you may have found that a particular style resonated with you. Or you may find that different styles of journaling work best for different situations—emotion focused when you are feeling a cacophony of emotions and are having difficulty managing them, solution focused when you are feeling anxiety about a particular situation, and gratitude focused when you are feeling sad or unsettled and would like to refocus on the positive aspects of your life. Keep in mind your goals for journaling—how you would like to feel—and the style of journaling will be easier to choose.

* **Be flexible.** If you skip a few days, don't give up. If your writing is messy (or your typing contains errors), that's okay. If you are aiming to write about three things for which you are grateful, and you can think of only two, that's still two positive things in your life! You want to draw pictures with your words? Do it. Let yourself relax, and be flexible with your practice. This will make the habit easier to maintain, and more enjoyable as well.

Questions to Ask Yourself

* What are my goals with stress management? Do I need to relieve physical tension, lessen anxiety, alleviate mild feelings of depression, practice letting go of stressful thoughts?
* Which of these strategies would be easiest to maintain in my life?
* What benefits might I gain by each of these habits?
* How would these long-term habits fit into my lifestyle?
* Who can help me stay on track with these?

* What other support do I need in my life?
* (If you have tried any of these in the past and not continued with the habit) What stood in my way the last time I tried to maintain this habit, and might things be different this time?
* What would I need to do to make things different?

Evaluate Your Answers

Getting into a long-term habit requires commitment. It helps to know exactly what you want to do and why. Looking at your answers can help you to understand a few things that will assist you along the journey and get you back on track if you should find yourself losing your drive.

Knowing what goal you are most hoping to reach can help you to decide on the right habit for you. For example, if you want to clear your mind of stressful thoughts, a daily journaling habit can help you to process what's on your mind. An exercise session can help you to clear your head and shift your focus and can help you to be less reactive toward stress over time. A meditation habit can accomplish the same goal, but in a different way, so knowing your needs and keeping in mind what parameters you have can help.

When you look at your answers, you will see what you need to keep in mind to remain motivated. You'll see what you need to put into place to keep yourself on track and what to do if you find yourself straying from your goal. In the next chapter, you will find more ways to put these answers into action in your life.

CREATING AN ACTION PLAN

Fall seven times. Stand up eight.   —JAPANESE PROVERB

Often you can gain a valuable understanding from books such as this one but find yourself unsure of where to start in putting the ideas to action. Other times, you may not know which ideas to try, or you may attempt too many changes at once and end up dropping the endeavor entirely. Or you may simply be good at *planning* change, but have trouble taking your plans to the level of real action. This chapter will provide you with clear steps for creating a short-term and long-term plan for stress management, a time line for putting the plans into play in your life, and contingency strategies for times when you may find yourself facing setbacks.

This book has covered many strategies for reducing the stressors in your life and effectively coping with the stressors that remain. It may be difficult to know where to begin in putting these changes into action. It may be tempting to try several major changes at once, or hold on to your ideas of what you might want to change, and never take the next step by putting those ideas into action. As you may remember from the stages of change mentioned in the Introduction, it isn't always easy to make lasting changes, and having a plan in addition to information and ideas definitely helps. By the end of this chapter, you will know of several ways to make changes that will last, without overwhelming yourself in the process. You will also have a plan on paper, ready to be put into action.

Why and How to Create a Plan

Managing stress becomes much easier if you have a plan. Your plan can be as simple as "When I feel frustrated, I will take three deep breaths"; or it can involve a combination of different stress management techniques to be used in various situations. I recommend stress management plans that are multifaceted enough to cover a variety of challenges but simple enough to actually be put into practice. In other words, merely relying on breathing exercises alone might not be enough of a plan for someone who has more variety and intensity in the types of stressors they face than can be handled effectively by mere breathing exercises, even if they are practiced often. Likewise, a stress management plan that involves a wide variety of proven techniques may not be effective if the techniques are so numerous and challenging that they are not properly learned and regularly used. You need a plan that fits the types of stressors that you face *and* the level of time and energy you have available to learn and practice the techniques.

Putting Together Your Plan: Finding the Right Mix

We all naturally find our own ways of coping with stress, but some strategies are more effective than others. (Calling a friend for support, and being available for this friend when the favor needs to be returned, can be a more healthy way of managing stress than binging on chocolate cake, though both activities might be instinctively appealing.) The key to finding an optimal stress management plan is balance.

All activities bring a mix of pros and cons, and finding the best balance of both is part of the adventure of planning your coping strategy. (For example, exercise or meditation regimens bring many benefits, but they require time and energy; visualizations can take less time and energy, but bring a different level of payoff.) Part of creating a stress management plan is finding the balance between the benefits you are seeking and the level of time and effort you are able to put in.

Planning ahead is also important. If you wait until you are feeling stressed, you may revert to less helpful reactions to stress (chocolate cake, anyone?), rather than using proven, proactive approaches that can help you to most effectively manage your stress. However, if you have already created a plan—one that takes into account your personality, lifestyle, and specific needs—you will find it easier to handle stress in the way you hope to. Let's take the next step and put together that plan.

An Ideal Plan

Everyone's ideal stress management plan will be unique. Based on what you already enjoy doing, the type of stress you need to manage, and a host of other factors, you may come up with something that's entirely different from what your best friend would create or from what you might create 10 years from now. This is okay; we have many techniques to choose from, and the plan can evolve as you do.

As we get started with creating a plan, you can ask yourself the following questions to explore what needs you have to meet and what mix of techniques might work for you:

* How quickly do I need relief from stress? (This can help you decide between focusing more heavily on fast-acting stress relievers or investing time into techniques that can lower your stress levels more gradually but permanently over time.)
* How much time do I have to invest in learning new techniques?
* How much stress do I have to manage?
* Is this short-term stress I am feeling, or do I generally experience this level of stress?
* Which areas of my life are causing me stress?
* Would I prefer to invest effort into eliminating stressors from my life where possible or focusing on developing resilience toward stressors that may come my way?

After answering those questions, reading previous chapters, and examining your life, you should have a few ideas of where to begin. Here are a few more thoughts to keep in mind as you piece together the ultimate plan you have for addressing your stress. As you make a list of new habits to ultimately adopt, or as you review the list you may have already made, you may want the plan to fit the following criteria:

* **A mix of short-term and long-term techniques.** Ideally, if you have a few techniques that can address both the short-term needs of quickly reversing your stress response and the long-term needs of increasing your resilience toward stress in general, you will be able to more effectively manage stress than if you were only addressing one of those needs. (Notice that certain stress relievers can be used for both purposes. This is very useful and may be where you want to begin when you start putting your plan into action.)

* **A plan that fits your specific needs.** If you are the type to gravitate toward a collection of techniques you can use in various situations, creating a multilayered approach can work quite well. If you feel you have time to learn only two or three new techniques in the near future, be honest with yourself and just plan for that. Be realistic with what you are willing and able to do, and you will be more likely to follow the plan. (That said, keep in mind that it is useful to have at least two strategies to fall back on, in case one does not work for all situations.)

* **Address the areas where you need help the most.** Don't shy away from addressing areas that are stressful, simply because facing the stress is intimidating. You may not be ready to weed out some toxic relationships or start a long-term exercise habit right now, but if those are strategies that would address some of your biggest areas of stress, I encourage you to make a note of them as things to try in the future and perhaps build up to it.

* **Create a flexible plan.** Allow yourself permission to take a little extra time preparing yourself to move through each stage if you need it. For example, if you need to gather more information

before you feel ready to move into action, do it. If you find yourself slipping back into old habits, remind yourself that this may happen and that recommitting yourself is part of the process. Don't demand perfection from yourself, but expect to stick with your goals. Remember that you are in this for the long haul.

Questions to Ask Yourself

Such questions often are found near the end of the chapter, but in this case, because you have likely decided on a few changes you might want to make, it will help to do some self-exploration before moving on to the next step. Here are some questions to ponder:

* Which areas of your life would benefit the most from change at this point?
* Which changes might be easiest to make?
* Which changes might bring the greatest benefit?
* Which changes would work best if I started as soon as possible?
* Do I feel ready to make a change in the next few days, the next few weeks, or the next few months?
* Do I need more information before I decide on a course of action? If so, which questions need to be answered?
* (If a goal is identified) Have I tried to make this change in the past and relapsed or given up? If so, what did I learn from the process?
* What resources can help me to change?

Make a List

These questions can help you to determine the stage of change you may be working from and help you to look at what you may need to do to move forward. At any stage of change (or at least a stage that would include reading a book on stress management), you can make a list of areas of life you would like to alter—potential changes you may want to make in the future. I suggest you begin by making this list now. You do not need to make any of the changes right away, but it would help to examine which areas of your life you would like to turn your focus toward, and perhaps what specific changes you are considering. Once you make this list, you can go about prioritizing which change to focus on first.

Determine Areas to Focus on First

Often when people are looking to create a stress management plan, they balk at the idea when they think of the long list of changes they feel they should be making. After reading the eight keys addressed in this book, you no doubt have a list of new habits you may want to adopt, old habits you may want to phase out, and desired outcomes attached to each. (Even if you have already made some of the changes suggested, the fact that you are reading this chapter suggests that you have more changes on your list.) Addressing so many issues at once is, of course, impossible. And choosing which one to tackle first can be challenging; each change brings benefits, and has its own level of effort attached. Fortunately, there is no wrong answer when it comes to deciding which stress management shifts to make; all the recommendations can help.

A first step must be taken, however, and your decision may hinge on a few different factors. Whatever seems to make sense to you is fine; virtually *any* step toward stress management can leave you with added energy to take the next step—and the next! However, taking a few moments to weigh the pros and cons of your next step here can be helpful when you are working to maintain motivation to continue in your efforts. If your decision is not already clear, here is some food for thought.

As you now know, not all stress relief techniques bring the same benefits. Some deliver quick relief and can be practiced in minutes. Others take longer to work, but can alter the ways in which you react to stress. And other changes can minimize the amount of stress you encounter in your life, thus making it easier to handle those stressors that are harder to eliminate.

Perhaps as you picked up this book on stress management, you had a certain technique in mind or a specific problem you wanted to tackle, and perhaps the decision of which strategy to put into action first is an easy one for you. Sometimes as you read, the clear choice jumps out at you. However, this isn't always the case for everyone, and the choice of where to begin is often more challenging. The following are a few different ideas that may help you to decide. See what resonates with you. If they all seem good ideas, simply pick one and get started. Remember: Eliminating any stress you choose from your life will leave you with extra energy and peace.

Merits of Making the Most Beneficial Changes First

If you want the most bang for your buck, it might make sense to find the stress management technique that would bring the greatest benefit and enact that one first. This would make sense because, if you took on only one new habit (or dropped one stress-inducing one), it would be best for that one habit to be the one that would transform your life in the most positive ways. And if you are committed to making several of the changes discussed in this book, choosing the one that is most beneficial for you as your first change can be a good idea because it can provide a base of stress management upon which any future changes can be made. For example, if you decide to make the change of altering your habitual self-talk patterns to reflect a more optimistic outlook (**Key 4**), you can more easily change your attitudes in other ways as well. If you cut the most pressing identifiable stressor out of your life, you may find it easier to cut out more. Working an exercise habit into your lifestyle might get you into the habit of structuring your stress relief activities, so working in a quick daily meditation session could come more easily as well. Lowering your stress levels in one way can pave the way for additional changes.

Merits of Making the Quickest-Acting Changes First

Quick relief strategies make nice first steps for two reasons. First, the fact that they bring rapid relief can help you to feel more motivated to make additional changes. You may find yourself thinking,

"That one change has really altered how I feel! I wonder how much better I can feel after making more changes." As the saying goes, nothing breeds success like success!

Another benefit you may note from adopting a fast-acting stress reliever first is that you will have a simple tool to quickly lower your stress levels. Not only can you use this type of stress reliever immediately and often, but you also may find that other changes are easier to make once you initially lower your stress levels. Remember from previous chapters that we react differently to stressors if we are already feeling overwhelmed? (For example, if we are exhausted, we may have less motivation to go to the gym, even though exercise is a powerful tool for stress management.) Getting yourself to a point where you are not on the verge of feeling overwhelmed can help you to tackle future changes from a place of empowerment and enthusiasm. Given this, taking on the quick and simple stress relievers first may be the easiest way to approach creating a stress management plan.

Merits of Making the Slowest-Acting Changes First

Some of the most effective stress management practices can take some time before they confer their most powerful benefits. And because their benefits may be a little slow to arrive, these techniques could be the best ones to begin working on first. This is because the sooner you begin a habit, the sooner you will see its long-term benefits. If you begin now with habits such as exercise, meditation, and altering thought patterns, you will experience some immediate stress relief. However, these techniques can bring increased benefits over time, so planting the seeds today can yield you greater, quicker results weeks and months down the road. And as you experience increasing benefits from these practices, you can add other stress relievers to your life.

Merits of Making the Easiest or Most Enjoyable Changes First

As you read this book, certain techniques have undoubtedly stood out as easier or more enjoyable, based on your personality and life situation. Perhaps you are already athletic, and resuming an exercise program is intriguing to you. Or maybe you are a thinker and are inspired by the many ways in which altering your thought patterns can change your life. If one of these stress relief strategies appears easier to take on or more enjoyable to learn, this might be the natural place to start. Finding some easy success can boost your confidence and motivate you to keep going with your plans. And the stress relief strategies that naturally appeal to you the most may just be the most effective for your particular situation. People sometimes think that the easiest path can't be the most effective; however, when it comes to stress relief, the easiest path could be exactly what you need!

Time to Begin

Now that you have reviewed your needs and goals and have a plan on paper, it's time to move toward action. As you move from planning your change into taking action, there are a few things that can help you in the process. You may have a list of several goals you would like to accomplish; here is how to take action in making them happen.

Choose One Major Goal

Creating a new habit in your life or making a major change can take focus. It may take a few days, weeks, or months for a new way of combating stress to become automatic (or at least become a habit that is established enough to come easily in times of stress), but the process will require some focused energy. If you direct your attention to one goal at a time, the process will be easier. Once you master one habit, you can easily move on to the next.

Get a Vision of Success in Your Head

When creating a new habit there will be times when you need to stay motivated. It helps to have a clear vision of something that represents the goal you are shooting for and the reason why you want it. It can be something inspiring, such as an image of yourself feeling relaxed, or it can be something negative that will motivate you to want to work harder, such as an image of something that represents excessive stress for you. (This is a trick used by therapists and coaches, as well as groups like Weight Watchers, and is known as *anchoring*, in that you are anchoring yourself to an image that motivates you.)

Create Specific Steps

Remember that change takes time and happens in a series of stages. One of my favorite analogies for change is the idea of the 1,000-pound burger. The argument follows that just as we would not feed a baby a 1,000-pound burger and expect it to grow into an adult overnight, we should not expect to throw ourselves into a new habit and be immediately transformed.

We need to break our progress down into a series of smaller steps and reward ourselves for each of them. Try a smaller aspect of the larger goal you seek and maintain that for a constant period of time. (For example, if you would like to begin a meditation practice, commit yourself to meditating for 5 or 10 minutes a day, and see if you can maintain that for a week or two.) Then, celebrate your success and add a little more to your goal. Eventually, you will find yourself being able to easily meditate every day for 30 minutes (if this is your goal), whereas you may have given up after a few days or weeks if you had tried to maintain this from the beginning, without building up to it.

Follow this process with each new change on your list. Before you begin the process of adopting a new change, map out the smaller steps you can take to forge a path to your end goal and celebrate each step. Remember, just as a tiny baby can transform into a strong, capable adult, you can grow into the person you strive to be. Just keep going, one baby step at a time.

Choose a Start Date

You may find yourself reading this book and becoming inspired to make changes, but finding that you can't put your best efforts into the changes until next week—or next month. But if you wait until next week (or month) to start making changes, you may not feel as much motivation or urgency and may forget much of what you had planned. Choosing a date to start your change, preparing for it, and throwing yourself into it is a good process with which to enact a change. In this way, you can be in a stage of contemplation and still be moving toward planning, or you can be planning, and this gives you a way to move into action with increased momentum. Even if the date is months in advance, getting a general range of when you aim to be ready to make changes, and doing what you need to do to get ready for that time to come, can help you to succeed.

Create Contingency Plans

We will inevitably face roadblocks in our quest for change. Even when we plan well, we may face unexpected obstacles in our path. That's why it is important to create backup plans. For example, you may plan to meditate when you feel frustrated, but what about when you are pressed for time or can't find a quiet place? Then sticking to this plan (or feeling you "should" be sticking to it but have failed) could actually create more stress. (Taking a few deep breaths and then meditating when you have more time or privacy is a reasonable alternate plan.) Rather than being caught off guard by what life throws at you, having a Plan B and a Plan C can help you to get around what might otherwise leave you derailed.

Don't Give Up

Oftentimes when people find themselves going off track, they get discouraged and give up. This can be tempting, but knowing in advance that giving up might become attractive, and knowing *when* giving up might become attractive, can help you to combat these feelings instead of succumbing to them. If you feel like giving up, you may simply need to change your plan. Here are a few questions to ask yourself:

* What is it about this situation that makes me want to give up?
* What would make this easier?
* What is my biggest obstacle here? (This can help you to identify what you may need to change or work around.)

* If I abandoned my goals, what would I lose? (This can help you to maintain motivation to find another way.)

Change Your Tactics or Your Goal

If you find yourself slipping up in your quest to create new habits, this is normal—don't beat yourself up over it. But don't ignore this information either—it can provide you with clues about what you can change in the future. Here are some questions to ask:

* Looking at what it was that presented the greatest obstacle for you, what might you look out for in the future?
* Thinking back, what might have helped you to resist the urge to give up on your goal?
* Is there anything you can change in order to make it easier the next time?

If you find yourself failing to meet your goals in a consistent manner, this should tell you something, too. Perhaps the goals need to change, or maybe you can gather some more resources to make things easier. If you look at each slipup as a potential clue, and as part of the process of perfecting your new system, it will be easier to stay on track with your goals and even gather further momentum, rather than becoming discouraged and deciding to quit.

Tools to Help You Along

Taking on any new lifestyle change can be difficult. Inertia causes us to naturally resist change—even changes that will be really good for us—so do not worry if making changes doesn't seem to come naturally. While your mind might seem predisposed to maintaining the status quo, you can change things in your life and your way of thinking that can help you along on your path and make changes come more easily to you. The following structures can help you to put into action the ideas presented in this book and help you to keep your motivation when times get tough.

Get a Buddy

It is helpful to have a support person, or "goal buddy," to help you along with your goals. This is beneficial for a few reasons. First, and most obvious, having a goal buddy can be helpful because of the moral support the person may give you. If your motivation wanes, someone who is going through a similar struggle may know just the thing to tell you in order to reenergize you. If you find success, you know that someone who is facing the same challenges can really appreciate that hard-won success and can help you celebrate your victories. Success tips, pep talks, and small celebrations are easier to come by when you have a partner in the journey.

Second, goal buddies can be helpful because they represent the part of you that wants to meet this goal—but they are *not* you. If you find yourself making excuses to yourself, you may let it slide; however, another person might not let you out of your responsibilities so easily. You may also be less comfortable telling another person you would just rather watch reruns or play games on the Internet than work toward your goals; sometimes our excuses sound ridiculous when said aloud to another person whom we respect.

Finally, perhaps the main benefit of having a goal buddy can be summed up in one word: *synergy*. The successes of your partner can bolster your motivation (through either inspiration or friendly competition) and vice versa. Your buddy's successes can motivate your own, and you may find that helping your buddy to avoid letting go of his or her goal has the effect of strengthening your resolve to stay with your own goals. Having a buddy to go through this situation with can be helpful in many ways. And shouldn't stress relief be as stressless as possible?

Announce to Others

Studies show you will be less likely to give up on a goal if you announce it to even one other person. There are several reasons for this. For one thing, the simple act of announcing your intentions to at least one other person can make your goal seem more real—you necessarily define your goal before or during your announcement because you need to be specific to put it into words. Also, the act of putting it out there helps the goal to take on a life of its own, as it will be something that may be brought up in future conversations and may come into your mind as something you've committed yourself to, rather than remaining a fleeting wish for the future.

Another reason that announcing your intentions can give them weight is that you may be far more likely to stick with a goal when dropping the goal could lead to having to admit that you gave up. Those who love you and make you feel accepted may want to know why you abandoned your goal, and they may have words of encouragement and support to keep you going. Those who would like to see you fail might be rather pleased to know that you've dropped your goal, and knowing that this could be their reaction just might keep you more motivated to stay the course.

The more you talk about your goals, the more you may want to avoid dropping them, for the simple fact that in your subconscious you would be uncomfortable knowing that you gave up. When you discuss something and focus on it, you become more invested in it and more excited about the possibilities of having it. You can gain motivation by wanting to make your focused-on goals a reality, just as you can gain motivation in wanting to avoid explaining why you gave up. Whether you want to save face, get support, or gain motivation, announcing your goals is something you should do only if you are sure you want to go after them; it is something that can keep you moving forward when you might have otherwise given up.

Hire a Coach

Life coaches—particularly those who specialize in wellness coaching—focus heavily on helping clients make changes like these. If you are not familiar with the term *life coach*, this is a relatively new profession (coaching was founded in the late 1980s but really started to gain traction in the 1990s and 2000s), which is focused on helping people make positive changes in their lives and stick with these changes. There is some overlap between coaching and therapy, but coaching tends to focus on the present and the future, with very little attention on the past. It also centers on actions more than on psychological issues, though both therapists and coaches can concentrate on both, and this is a fairly large generalization.

People hire coaches for different reasons; making healthy changes is one of the most popular. A good coach can help you to understand and overcome obstacles that keep you from easily making the changes you have been wanting to enact in your life. They can also help you to get your motivation and confidence back after you have hit roadblocks, and they can help you to identify tools and resources to keep you on track. If you try making these changes on your own and find that it is simply too challenging—or if you would merely like to have an ally who is committed to your success, you may consider hiring a coach.

If you decide on this route, you can search online for a wellness coach or life coach or contact Wellcoaches or the International Coaching Federation for recommendations. Then talk to a few coaches and get a sense of who seems a good fit.

Find a Therapist If You Need One

Sometimes we have more serious, deep-seated issues that cause us stress. It may be a deeply rooted family conflict, an unusually heavy situation we face, or even an imbalance that may call for a more therapeutic approach or the help of antidepressants. If you find that these suggestions aren't enough to help you get your stress levels to a manageable place, or you just suspect you need more help than a book can provide, do not be afraid to talk to a professional.

Therapists can help with deeper issues that may be causing us stress, such as stress-inducing attitudes that provoke us to react to the challenges we face in a less healthy way, persistent self-sabotaging behavior with roots we don't understand, or other issues that are challenging enough that we don't feel we can tackle them alone. A therapist can also help us to know if we are dealing with a condition such as an anxiety disorder or depression and can help us to find resources to manage these conditions. Therapists can help us to work through issues that elude our understanding or just seem too heavy to bear. And therapists can work in conjunction with coaches, and with books like this one.

Set New Goals!

Once you have successfully created a new habit (or abandoned an old one), you will likely feel excited and empowered. You can use this motivation to set and reach your next goals. The confidence, pride, and stress relief you have attained can push you along a new path filled with many healthy new habits and goals met along the way. Once you get the ball rolling, it gets easier for success to build upon success.

Key Points to Remember

* When deciding what changes to make first, there are many places to start, and all of them can work, depending on your needs and personality. You can start with the quickest and easiest, the most beneficial, or the most enjoyable changes, for example, and find different forms of success with each approach.
* Each stress relief plan will be unique to the person creating it. Ideally, your plan should include a mix of fast-acting stress relievers, long-term resilience-promoting habits, and strategies to manage the specific stressors in your life. However, depending on how much or how little energy you have to devote to your plan, as well as several other factors, you may add a smaller or larger number of strategies to the mix.
* Whether you are ready to make your change this week or next month (or in the next six months), there are steps you can take to

prepare for the change you plan to make and to ensure a greater chance of success.

* If you are not ready to change yet, gathering more information can help you gain momentum and motivation. If you feel that you will be ready soon, putting together plans and backup strategies can provide you with the extra structure and support that can help you achieve success.

* And if you have already thrown yourself into the new change, only to see yourself slip up or feel like giving up, you can gain valuable information from the experience that can help you to get closer to success in the future.

As You Continue on Your Stress Management Journey . . .

As I mentioned at the beginning of this book, the goal here is to enable you to shift your experience of stress in your life, and just a few changes can create a new balance. Just as chronic stress can cause a downward spiral that leads to burnout or worse, a few simple stress management techniques can build on each other and form an upward spiral of healthy thought and behavior, which can be surprisingly powerful. These techniques don't work if you don't put them into action, but the mere act of reading about stress, evaluating its impact on your life, and making plans to create change *is* part of putting them into action. Taking concrete steps that others can see is another part of action, and so is recommitting yourself to your goals if you find yourself backsliding. Be gentle with yourself and trust the process, and you will be able to make life-altering changes with relative ease.

As you finish this book, I would like to congratulate you on taking some important steps toward managing stress in your life. (Even if you have skipped around considerably, you no doubt have also found at least a few concepts that can shift how you think about stress or ideas that you can put into action now.) Also,

I would like to remind you that this book can be used as a resource again and again. Different chapters may speak to you at different times in your life, and certain techniques may appeal at various times in your life as well. If you find that you are no longer making progress toward stress management, you can remotivate and recommit yourself by picking up this book and finding new strategies that you are now ready to try. For more resources, go to 8KeysToStressManagement.com.

Resources

You will find additional resources on the website 8KeysToStress Management.com. Among them are the following:

* Downloadable worksheets for further exploration and organization
* Audio files to aid in relaxation
* Videos that can further your understanding of certain techniques
* Meditations to try
* Information about workshops that can help you put each key into action in a personal and interactive way.

In addition to those resources, I recommend the following books and websites for further information on some of the concepts discussed in this book. These are all resources that provide deeper explorations of some of the most important concepts that can help with stress management.

Key 2: Learn to Quickly Reverse Your Stress Response

About.com Stress Management, at Stress.about.com

You will find hundreds of articles here (written by yours truly) that can help you to reverse your stress response and manage stress in your life. You will find techniques discussed in this book, as well as several others, if you would like more ideas.

Key 3: Take Care of Your Body

YOU: *The Owner's Manual,* by Dr. Mehmet Oz
This book provides additional information on how to maintain a healthy body, as well as further research on how the body functions, in engaging, easy-to-digest language.

Brain Rules, by Dr. John Medina
While this book focuses on the brain and its functioning, there is quite a bit of information on how the body and brain interact. The book provides more detailed information on how to care for your body and mind for optimal functioning and stress relief, from a molecular biologist's perspective.

Key 4: Get into the Right Frame of Mind

Learned Optimism, by Martin Seligman
This book, written by one of the leading psychologists in the areas of optimism and positive psychology, defines the extent to which we can alter our tendency toward optimism, provides a wealth of information on optimism, and walks you through the process of cultivating optimism.

Buddha's Brain, by Drs. Rick Hanson and Richard Mendius
This book offers a more thorough explanation of the neuroscience behind stress and stress management, if you want a more thorough picture of what is going on inside your brain when you are stressed.

Key 5: Cut Down on Stressors When Possible

Getting Things Done, by David Allen
This is a classic time management book that describes a complex but effective system for organizing and prioritizing your life's activities. If you find yourself juggling many different activities in your life, but certain things fall through the cracks, this book could be a lifesaver. This system is very popular, but it isn't for

everyone. It takes some time to learn and implement the strategy, so if you are looking for a simple system you can start using quickly, you may want to look elsewhere.

Take Time for Your Life, by Cheryl Richardson
This book is a new classic that helps you to use life coach–tested techniques to cull the clutter of your lifestyle and streamline your activities so you're doing more of what you want to do in your life.

Key 6: Cultivate Healthy Relationships

Ten Lessons to Transform Your Marriage, by John Gottman, Julie Schwartz Gottman, and Joan Declaire
This book discusses the most salient findings from Gottman's relationship lab and also covers a gamut of oft-experienced relationship challenges. The book is geared toward marriage, but most of the tips are applicable to dating relationships and even friendships.

Key 7: Put Positive Psychology into Action

The How of Happiness, by Sonja Lyubomirsky
This book, written by a researcher in positive psychology, explores much of the recent research on happiness that explains how much of our experience of happiness can be changed and how we can go about doing so.

Finding Flow, by Mihaly Csikszentmihalyi
This groundbreaking book on the phenomenon of flow explains the concept further, and shows you in detail how to incorporate flow into your life. It is written by the lead researcher in the area and is an engaging read.

Authentic Happiness, at www.authentichappiness.sas.upenn.edu/
Default.aspx
This website, from top positive psychology researchers at the

University of Pennsylvania, offers several resources that can help you to put the principles of positive psychology into action in your life. One of the most popular and applicable is the VIA Signature Strengths Survey, which I highly recommend.

Key 8: Practice Long-Term Resilience-Forming Habits

Mindfulness-Based Stress Reduction Workbook, by Drs. Bob Stahl and Elisha Goldstein

This workbook provides a simple and applicable collection of activities and meditations that can help you to create a regular mindfulness and meditation practice. If you don't have time to take a mindfulness-based meditation course, this book is a great alternative.

Changing for Good, by James Prochaska

This book discusses the stages of change in detail and walks you through the process in a thorough manner. If you were intrigued by the process of change that you read about in this book, you will find that *Changing for Good* provides some sound additional details that can help you to enact the changes that will improve your life the most.

References

Carrington, P. (2007). Modern forms of mantra meditation. In P. Lehrer, R. Woolfolk, & W. Sime (Eds.), *Principles and practice of stress management* (pp. 363–392). New York: Guilford Press.

Chafin, S., & Gerin, W. (2008). Improving cardiovascular recovery from stress with brief poststress exercise. *Health Psychology, 27*(Suppl. 1), S64–S72.

Cohn, M. A., Fredrickson, B. L., Brown, S. L., Mikels, J. A., & Conway, A. M. (2009). Happiness unpacked: Positive emotions increase life satisfaction by building resilience. *Emotion, 9*(3), 361–368.

Dainese, S. M., Allemand, M., Ribeiro, N., Bayram, S., Martin, M., & Ehlert, U. (2011, March). Protective factors in midlife: How do people stay healthy? *GeroPsych: The Journal of Gerontopsychology and Geriatric Psychiatry, 24*(1), 19-29.

Emmons, R. A., & McCullough, M. E. (2003). Counting blessings versus burdens: An experimental investigation of gratitude and subjective well-being in daily life. *Journal of Personality and Social Psychology, 84*(2), 377–389.

Friedberg, J. P., Suchday, S., & Srinivas, V. S. (2009). Relationship between forgiveness and psychological and physiological indices in cardiac patients. *International Journal of Behavioral Medicine, 16*, 205–211.

Forcier, K. (2006). Links between physical fitness and cardiovascular reactivity and recovery to psychological stressors: A meta-analysis. *Health Psychology, 25*(6), 723–739.

Froh, J. J., Sefick, W. J., & Emmons, R. A. (2008, April). Counting blessings in early adolescents: An experimental study of gratitude and subjective well-being. *Journal of School Psychology, 46*, 213–233.

Grossman, P., Niemann, L., Schmidt, S., & Walach, H. (2004). Mindfulness-based stress reduction and health benefits: A meta-analysis. *Journal of Psychosomatic Research, 57*(1), 35–43.

Kristeller, J. (2007). Mindfulness meditation. In P. Lehrer, R. Woolfolk, & W. Sime (Eds.), *Principles and practice of stress management* (pp. 393–427). New York: Guilford Press.

Kuppens, P., Realo A., & Diener, E. (2008). The role of positive and negative emotions in life satisfaction judgment across nations. *Journal of Personality and Social Psychology, 95*(1), 66–75.

Lyubomirsky, S., Sousa, L., & Dickerhoof, R. (2006, April). The costs and benefits of writing, talking, and thinking about life's triumphs and defeats. *Journal of Personality and Social Psychology, 90*(4), 692–708.

Maruta, T., Colligan, R. C., Malinchoc, M., & Offord, K. P. (2000, February). Optimists vs pessimists: Survival rate among medical patients over a 30-year period. *Mayo Clinic Proceedings, 75,* 140–143.

Moskowitz, J. T., Epel, E. S., & Acree, M. (2008). Positive affect uniquely predicts lower risk of mortality in people with diabetes. *Health Psychology, 27*(1, Suppl), S73–S82.

Ostir, G. V., Markides, K. S., Black, S. A., & Goodwin, J. S. (2000). Emotional well-being predicts subsequent functional independence and survival. *Journal of the American Geriatric Society, 48*(5), 473–8.

Peterson, C. (2000). The future of optimism. *American Psychologist, 55*(1), 44–45.

Peterson, C. (2006). *A primer in positive psychology.* New York: Oxford University Press.

Seligman, M. E. P. (2002). *Authentic happiness: Using the new positive psychology to realize your potential for lasting fulfillment.* New York: Free Press.

Shapiro, S. L., Brown, K. W., & Biegel, G. M. (2007). Teaching self-care to caregivers: Effects of mindfulness-based stress reduction on the mental health in therapists in training. *Training and Education in Professional Psychology, 1*(2), 105-115.

Sime, W. (2007). Exercise therapy for stress management. In P. Lehrer, R. Woolfolk, & W. Sime (Eds.), *Principles and practice of stress management* (pp. 333–353). New York: Guilford Press.

Taylor, S. E. (2011). *Health Psychology* (8th ed.). Boston: McGraw-Hill Higher Education.

Wood, A. M., Joseph, S., Lloyd, J., & Atkins, S. (2009). Gratitude influences sleep through the mechanism of pre-sleep cognitions. *Journal of Psychosomatic Research, 66*(1), 43–48.

Index